THE CHRONICLES of DRAGON

BOXED SET 1
SERIES 1, BOOKS 1-5

CRAIG HALLORAN

The Chronicles of Dragon (Boxed Set 1)
Series 1, Books 1-5
By Craig Halloran

TWO-TEN BOOK PRESS
P.O. Box 4215, Charleston, WV 25364

ISBN eBook: 978-1-941208-79-3
ISBN Paperback: 978-1-941208-80-9

http://www.thedarkslayer.net

Illustrations by David Schmelling and Joe Shawcross
Map by Gillis Bjork
Edited by Cherise Kelley

Publisher's Note

To my son, Nathaniel Conan. Words can never express how much you mean to me, but I wrote you a book anyway.

NALZAMBOR
Key Location Guide

TABLE OF CONTENTS

The Hero, The Sword, and The Dragons

-BOOK 1-

CRAIG HALLORAN

CHAPTER 1

I WAS RUNNING HARD, PUSHING MYSELF past human limits, to the only place I knew could help. Home. I already could tell that my wound was fatal, and with every step the loss of blood made me more woozy. Orcs were hot on my trail, at least a dozen, howling for my head. I was certain they would not stop; they were stubborn and stupid, slow as well, but I was smart and fast. I was a dragon, after all… in a very man-like sort of way. By appearance, I was a man: big, long haired, and rangy—more than capable of whipping a few lousy dragon-poaching orcs, until they got the drop on me. So now I was running for my life, my dragon heart pounding in my chest like a galloping horse, mile after mile, until I had no choice but to come to a stop. I looked down at the crossbow bolts protruding from my side, through my back.

"Egad!" I exclaimed, checking the wounds. The blood had already stained a patch in my armor, and I knew it was still worse than it looked. Every breath I took was painful and biting. I knew I was bleeding inside, and I had to stop it or die. I pulled the lid from my canteen and drank, which did little to quench my thirst, but it brought some relief. I reached inside my satchel, my little bag of tricks, and fumbled for a vial.

Over the years, I've picked up a few useful things, like potions. Magic potions. They can do many things. Turn you invisible. Make you bigger. Smarter. Faster. Stronger. And even heal. In this particular case, it was a healing potion in a vial as big as my index finger, which was pretty big, but it only looked to have about one drop left as I shook it before my eyes.

"Ugh," I moaned, the pain not getting any better, "I don't think this will do it." I looked down at my wounds and tried to decide: should I take out the wooden shafts first or afterward? I'd been hurt before, plenty of times, but this festering wound was a tricky one.

"Just do what you always do, Dragon."

That's what I call myself, and I talk to myself a lot. My real name is much longer, difficult to pronounce and spell, but part of it is Nath. So, if a commoner ever asks, Nath Dragon is my name; saving dragons (and other things) is my game.

I tore a piece of bark from a tree, pinched it between my teeth, and bit down. Beads of sweat erupted from my forehead as I began pulling the first bolt through my skin. The good thing about them being crossbow bolts was they weren't as big as arrows, but they sure did pack a punch. I groaned, certain I was going to die as I ripped the rest of the shaft free.

I felt sick. My skin turned clammy, and the sound of the woodland crickets became loud and irritating. In the woods there are many dangers, and I wasn't anywhere close to being out of harm's way. Anything could pick up the trail of the wounded: overbearing bugbears, wily wood elves, pesky witches, dog-faced gnolls, transforming wolves, tricky sprites, were-shadows, or even worse … dragons. Yes, there are bad dragons, too, but it wasn't likely I'd run into two dragons in one day or that a dragon would want to fool with me, for that matter. But they did on occasion; I'd seen it for myself. The most beautiful and dangerous creatures in the world. The noblest and greediest, too.

"Do it, Dragon!" I was gritting my teeth on the tasteless bark once more. The pain was excruciating, each bloody inch I tugged free twice as painful as the last. *Don't black out.* A wave of wooziness assailed me as I got the last bolt free and slipped to my hands and knees, trembling like a leaf. I put the healing vial to my lips and watched that last pink drop slide down the tube and land on my tongue. Elation. Exasperation. It coursed through me, head to toe, mending every fiber, sealing every unnatural pore. The relief was astounding but the healing incomplete. As quickly as it had started, it stopped, but at least I wouldn't be dripping blood anymore. Spitting it, perhaps.

Clatch-Zip!

Clatch-Zip!

Two bolts ripped past my face and quivered in a nearby tree.

"Stupid bloody orcs!"

I pushed myself to my feet with a groan and began sprinting through the woods, each step feeling like a punch in my stomach. I had to get home, find my father, and explain to him how I had gotten whipped by orcs, which never would have happened if I'd been allowed to kill them in the first place.

Zip! Zip! Zip!

My legs churned harder and harder as I began to outdistance my pursuers, cutting across the grassy plain, and the barrage of bolts began to subside. So on I ran, the sounds of the angry orcs fading away, leaving only the wind in my ears and the sharp throbbing pangs in my stomach. I just hoped I had enough strength left to return home.

Of course, my father probably wouldn't be too pleased by my return, either. I had his sword that I named Fang, a beautiful glimmering object of steel and magic woven together like its own living thing. Well, it hadn't been given to me; I'd sort of borrowed it, and by then I was pretty sure my father would know it was missing. He wasn't the most understanding when it came to such things, either.

So I ran, through the shallow waters, over grassy gnolls, by shining cities whose towers almost reached the clouds, each long stride a hair shorter than the last, until I made it to just within my keen eye's shot of the Mountain of Doom and collapsed.

CHAPTER 2

A S THE SUN ROSE, WARMING the chin hairs on my haggard face, the last thing I remembered was the blackness of the coming night. For all I knew, I'd been asleep for a day. I don't think a screaming ogre could have woken me. At the moment, everything felt fine. Then I moved.

"Ugh," I said. I wiped the morning drool from my mouth and spat out the tangy taste of my blood. I still had miles to go, and I wasn't so certain I could make it. Upright as I could be, I staggered forward. My stiff legs were no longer capable of churning after days of running off and on, but I knew I had to keep going, seek help, and not die.

Ahead was the Mountain of Doom, which isn't its real name but a shorter name I'd given it because I never cared to take the time to say things properly. I swear, long names are given to things just so others will have something to talk about or just to give some little wretch yearning for knowledge something significant to do. I can spell it, backward as well as forward, but I'm not going to. Learning it once was more than enough already, and I see no need to repeat myself. It's just a word. But the Mountain of Doom, my home, is beyond words. It's something you just have to see for yourself, and if you ever do, and you're wise, you'll gape in wide-eyed wonder, turn, and run away.

The base of the mountain is miles wide, maybe a league or two. I used to have to run around its base as a boy, every crevice treacherous, loosely footed of shale and streams of lava hot enough to burn your leg to the bone in an instant. That area is called the marsh of sulfur. The peak's nose reaches into the blue, snow caps blending into that cloudy sky (such as it was that day) before disappearing. Steam. Smoke. Those gases billowing from cave mouths, some small, others large and even enormous, seemed to illustrate that the mountain was more than a clump of rock and clay, a living and breathing part of the world itself.

I wiped the sweat from my brow and fought for secure footing over the shale as I made it two miles deeper into the rising heat. The heat didn't bother me; I was used to that, but it wrought damage on my glorious mane of recently mangled hair.

I stood straddling the crest of a ravine, where a small stream of lava was flowing below. The face on the mountain, a frightful grimace it seemed, some said was a coincidence or a design of arcane wizards that once took shelter there. Or it was a massive scarecrow created by dwarves that wanted to be left alone. It was, without question in my mind, the face of a dragon. A massive cave filled with rows of teeth could be seen, smoke rolling from its mouth. The eyes shimmered with fire, and the nostrils dripped lava. It would be hard to argue that it didn't look like a dragon, that it was just happenstance, an illusion, something the feebleminded shared to encourage fear to be spread by other feeble minds.

I sighed. It was pretty much the reason no one came here very often and lived. Mile after mile I trudged along in agony, deeper into the valley of living lava, until I had nowhere else to go but up. I looked back, the green grasses and tall trees no longer within sight, the rising mist now hiding my view of the gentler, softer world.

The base of the mountain was sheer, black rock, no smoke or stairs or solid footholds. Not smooth but rough and spanning hundreds of feet high. This was the part that kept the adventurers at bay: the curious, the daring, the foolish, and the greedy that wanted the dragon's hoard, rumored to be large enough to fill every household in an entire kingdom or more. It was impossible to get in, but to get out, with loads of treasure, would take at least a thousand of the stoutest men. Unless of course you knew a secret way, which it so happens I did.

A natural archway greeted me like an old friend as I fell onto my knees before it. No runes, no nothing, just a familiarity that I had from long ago. I began to speak to it, my raspy voice struggling to be clear, as my tongue was thick and swollen with fever. Word after word, minute after minute I chanted in a language more ancient than man, more difficult than women, more lengthy than a river. It took thirty minutes before I finished, and nothing happened.

"Open," I tried to shout, slamming my fists into the rock. My voice was gone now, withered away like the ashes of a burning log, my efforts spent in failure. *Noooooooooo!* I collapsed, holding my belly, the taste of blood filling my mouth, my last flavor before dying.

The archway shook and quaked, angry. From the corner of my watery eye, I saw a sheet of rock lifting. *Thank goodness.* I lay there in pain, misery, and suffering, eyeing the portal open to safety but unable to move. How long, I did not know. The archway shuddered and buckled, and the doorway began to sink, a mouth closing, lips soon to seal shut. *Move!* But I could not. It seemed my death was likely to come first.

CHAPTER 3

SOMETHING POWERFUL GRABBED MY ARM and started dragging me though
the portal as the doorway closed shut like a clap of thunder. Gruff hands rolled
me over and pushed on the bloody patch on my armor.

I screamed so loud my voice began to crack.

"See, yer alive," a strong voice said, "...for the moment. Now let's get you
patched up, restored to full health, so your father can be guilt free before he kills ya."

"Thanks, Brenwar," I groaned, "you always know what to say to make me feel
better."

"Har!" He reached down and grabbed both my hands. "Up you go!" He almost
jerked my arms from the sockets as he ripped me up from the floor. I looked down at
Brenwar with a frown as big as his, glowering in pain. My dwarven friend was as big
and stout as a sand-filled barrel, raven bearded, and armored in heavy metals from
his chin to his toes. You'd think he'd sound like a wagonload of scrap metal when
he walked, but all I heard as I followed was the sound of well-oiled leather rubbing
together. I followed him up a cavernous stairwell designed for monsters, not men,
spiraling upward without end. I knew where I was but wasn't certain where Brenwar
was going.

"In here," he said, stopping at an opening I swore hadn't been there a moment
ago and shoving me inside. "Wait." His booted feet stomped up the stairs, echoing
then fading away.

I was in an alcove where a lone torch hung, its orange light offering warm
illumination to the scenes of many dragon murals painted across all the walls. I gasped
as one of the images of a painting came to life. A female dragon, tall as me, slender and
batting her eyes, walked over, her tail tickling my chin. I knew she was a female because
her belly scales were lighter than the others. Male dragons tend to be darker. But if you
truly know dragons, as I do, the eyes were a dead giveaway. The females have lashes on
their lids, nothing too pronounced but noticeable all the same.

Her scales, copperish and pink, reflected the most beautiful colors, and her comely face offered a smile. In her hands was a vial, the same as the one I had drunk from days before, which she tilted to my lips. I gulped it down, fell onto a pillow big enough for a cow, and let the magical mending begin.

I burned, inside and out, with satisfaction. My weary bones were revitalized. My innards—dormant, agonized, and bleeding—now regenerated. My vitality was back. My aching feet were no longer sore. I felt as strong as a horse as I tore off my armor, stretched out my mighty frame on the pillow, and shouted at the top of my lungs with glee.

I swear the lady dragon giggled before she pecked me on my head.

"Thank you," I said, combing my hair from my eyes. The dragoness was beautiful, her features soft behind her armor and razor-sharp claws. After all, beautiful things have to defend themselves. I waved as I watched her disappear back into the mural among her kind, a queen defending in a glorious battle of dragons charging across the sun-glazed sky.

"Ah!" I elated.

I fell back on the pillow, wanting to sleep, as my mind told me I needed rest, but my body was ready to go.

"A bath perhaps," I said to myself, getting up, grabbing my gear and sword.

A gruff voice disagreed. "You can have your bath later, Nat—"

I glared at Brenwar.

"Er, I mean, Dragon. Your father waits." The husky dwarf walked over and took Fang from my hands. "I'll take that."

I held my head in my hand. I could leave now if I wanted. I was healed and all the better for it. My father, he wouldn't come after me. He never did. He threatened to chase me down but usually just sent Brenwar instead, who was slow. A team of galloping horses wouldn't make him fast.

"So be it," I said in resignation. Up through the Mountain of Doom I followed, one heavy step at a time, the revitalized feeling in my organs replaced with a queasy feeling. My energy, endless one moment ago, was now gone. Oh, I was fine, my health fully operational, but that didn't do much good in the presence of an angry father who I had been reluctant to listen to for quite some time. When we stopped in front of a massive set of doors that stood almost five stories tall, Brenwar looked up at me with a hard look in his eyes and said, "I told him you needed bathed, but he insisted that you come now." He reached up and patted me on my lower back. "I'll see to it you're bathed before the funeral. It's been an honor knowing you, Dragon." With that, Brenwar, my only true friend in the entire mountain, pushed the door open far enough for me to squeeze through, and like a fat rat out of a metal can, he scurried away.

And there I stood, at the threshold of all thresholds, looking back over my shoulder for escape but finding none. If I had had some dragon scales by now, things would probably be all right, but I didn't. With great hesitation and a trembling heart, I stepped inside.

CHAPTER 4

IMAGINE THE THRONE ROOMS OF the greatest kings in the world combined and all their wealth lying at their feet. That's nothing compared to my father's throne room, and those kings are nothing compared to my father. There he sat on his golden throne, treasure covering the floor as far as eye could see, glimmering and twinkling in the light of the lanterns. Like a man he sat, more than three stories tall, monstrous wings folded behind his back, dragon head resting in the palm of his clawed hand, eyes closed. There had never been a king that big.

I pushed the door closed with a loud *wump*, stirring the golden coins that slipped from their pile toward the floor. To my relief, my father, a heavy sleeper, did not stir, yet my heart pounded in my chest. I supposed that it should be pounding in my chest, but I had figured that feeling, that nervous feeling you get as you tread into the unknown, would fade away with age. It hadn't. I pushed the hair back from my eyes and proceeded forward.

My father, the largest living thing in the world so far as I knew, was scaled in red mostly, a brick red, with trims of gold along his armored belly, wings, and claws. His taloned toe alone was almost as big as me, and I was big, for a man anyway.

"Come closer," he said from the side of his mouth. The power of his voice sent tremors through the room, upsetting more piles of precious metals and jewels.

I kept going, taking my time, having no desire to begin the conversation but very eager to end it. I stopped a good fifty feet away, craning my neck upward, trying to find the first word to say. My tongue was thick in my mouth, and I thought of all the brave deeds I had done, but it all seemed so minute before my father.

He snorted the air, opened his dragon's maw, and said, "You smell dirty. Like an orc."

That bothered me. He always had to say something that bothered me.

"It's good to see you too, Father," I shouted back, my words barely a gerbil's compared to his. And I was loud, loud as an ogre when I wanted to be.

One eye popped open, brown like a man's but flecked in gold and glaring. The other eye opened as well, the same as the first, its intent no less hostile. My father leaned back on his throne, long, powerful neck stretching between the massive marble pillars behind him, which held the ceiling. He was glorious and powerful; his mere presence began to charge my blood. I was proud to have a father like that, but I hadn't told him so in a long time.

"Ah ... the fear in your sweat is gone already, I see, and replaced by your spiteful tongue," he said, moving very little, poised rather, pleasant, as if he was being served dinner. "Still, it is good to see you, Son, as always."

That part got to me a little, but only because I knew he meant it. The way he said it was the truth. Everything he said was true, I knew, whether I wanted to agree to it or not. My father, which is what I called him, because his real name would take the better part of the day to say, had a voice of a most peculiar quality. Powerful and beautiful like a crashing waterfall. Wise and deep with all the wisdom in the world combined. Soothing and uplifting. But my proud ears had gotten accustomed to it over the years.

"Yes, well, Father, it's good to see you, too. There's nothing quite like taking a long journey home. Scraping and clawing for your life, bleeding out your last drop," I laid it on thick, "gasping for your last breath, only to be saved at the last moment of life, healed, only to be jostled and dragged here without a moment's rest." I began pacing back and forth, hands on hips, throwing my neck back. "And you complain, of all things, that I have not had a bath."

Ever seen a dragon smile, one with a mouthful of teeth as long as you? That's what I was seeing now, and it bothered me.

"Well, you know how I feel about those foul creatures, and I was excited to see you, smelling like orc's blood or not, and it's been so long, several weeks at least," my father said.

Now my father was being ridiculous. Dragons are never in a hurry to do anything. It takes them a minute just to blink. They aren't slow by any means or measure, no matter how big they are, but they take their good time doing anything. Hours are minutes to them, if even that long.

I plopped down on a huge stack of gemstones, inspecting a few before tossing them away.

"Father, it's been almost a decade," I said, agitated. "Have you even moved since the last time I was here?"

"Certainly, Son, I've moved quite a bit since you've been here."

"I see." He never moved except when it was time to feed, which wasn't very often. He hadn't moved since I was a boy, either. "Father, what would you know of me?" I had to push things, be impolite; it was the only way to make this conversation go quicker.

"I see things as well, Nath ..."

"No, don't!" I yelled, but it was too late. He began pronouncing my full name, which is as long as a river, syllable after syllable, ancient, poetic, and powerful. I listened, minute after minute, mesmerized, my aggravation beginning to subside. My name was a beautiful thing: prosperous and invigorating.

"… nan," he finished, over an hour later. "Have you gained any scales?"

There it was. The dreaded question about my scales. Here I was, a son of the greatest dragon but without a single scale. Despite all the right I had done, it seemed I'd done my own fair share of wrong as well.

"No!"

My father snorted. I saw a look of disappointment in his eyes, and I felt disappointed as well. I'd failed. Despite all my great deeds in the lands of Nalzambor, I was not living up to expectations.

He sighed, and it seemed such a terrible thing.

"How long, Son?"

I kicked at the piles of treasure.

"Two hundred years."

Like a man, my father reached up and grabbed his skull with his four-fingered hands. I knew what was coming next.

"Son, the first hundred years of your life were the most wonderful of mine. You did everything I said. You listened. You learned. You grew. And when you became old enough, I let you choose. Stay in the mountain and continue to grow or risk losing everything you are just to see the rest of the world." He shook his head. "I never should have given you that choice."

"I wanted to see things for myself. It was my right. You told me I needed to understand the world of men," I argued.

"Yes, I did. But I told you not to get too close. Don't get caught up in their ways. You are not one of them. You are one of us."

"How can I be sure? I still look like a man. I talk like a man."

He stopped me, head leering over at me, his eyes showing a glimmer of the infernos within.

"True, Son, but I warned you not to *act* like a man. I showed you what dragons do, how they act, how they respond."

I rose to my feet and resumed my pacing through the hoard, coins jingling beneath my feet.

"Maybe I don't want to devour herds of sheep and goats like a beast. I like my food cooked and making use of knives and forks. It's civilized. Unlike the dragons that pillage the flocks."

Father said, "The herds are for feeding, man and dragon alike. Forgive me for forgetting to use my knife." He waggled a talon at me. "If you had your scales, you'd understand, Son. You are meant to be a good dragon, the same as me."

I wanted to please my father. I really did. But, as the years passed and the hairs on my skin became more coarse, I had an aching doubt that I was ever going to become a dragon. There were many things that I could do that men could not. Living long was one of them, but I never felt sure.

"Father, how can I know that I am a dragon? If I was a dragon, certainly I'd have scales by now. The others do."

"Son, you are not like the others. You are like me. As I've explained, there are dragons like the rest, and there are dragons like us. I am the keeper of this world, a protector of men as well as the dragons. But I won't live forever, and who will protect them when I'm gone? It has to be you."

Me. Yes, I knew it was supposed to be me. Deep down in my heart, I knew it was true. But one would think I'd have a sister or brother to share the responsibility. I continued to pout.

"What about my mother? Will you ever reveal her to me?"

"Oh, stop. You were hatched from an egg."

"I was not hatched from an egg like a goose!" I yelled. It infuriated me, him saying that. I knew I had a mother, and I suspected she was mortal, but my father, truthful and wise, had been holding something back all along. And it infuriated me that I did not know.

"More like a little crocodile," he said, joking. "You had scales when you were born, we… er, I was so proud. But after a few years, they fell away." His voice saddened. "And that's when I knew."

He had slipped! There was indeed a mother; I was certain of it. But I could not remember her face or anything of her at all. Was she a dragon or a mortal?

"Knew what?" I asked, even though I had already heard the answer before.

His voice was heavy as he said, "That you would be the child that replaced me. That the responsibility was yours, whether you liked it or not. As I did not have a choice, Son, neither have you. There is only one great dragon in the world, and if it isn't me, it must be you. Without us, the world is doomed."

That was it: the ship's anchor strapped onto my back. The burden of an impossible responsibility that weighed me down to my knees. *I didn't ask for this.*

CHAPTER 5

T HE MORE HE KEPT TALKING, the smaller I felt. It was a big part of the reason that I didn't come home to visit too much. He told me about the Dragon Wars, where one brood of dragons battled another for the sake of mankind. Every race—man, elf, dwarf, gnolls, orcs, and ogres—had been in danger those days, but the dragons, the good ones like my father, won out. It had all happened long before I came, and it was impossible to believe that there had been such devastation. Mankind, all of the races that is, had been on the border of extinction. My father had sacrificed everything to prevent that, and he had the scars and missing scales to prove it. Still, it was all hard to believe, that life on Nalzambor had been so cold and hopeless.

I stretched on a sofa, as soft and exquisite as one could be, and listened again. There must have been something I was missing. Why didn't I have my scales? And yet again, he told me why he thought I didn't.

"For every life you take, you must save another or more. It does not matter if they are good or evil; who can really tell? There is good in everything, evil as well ...."

I knew better: orcs were evil. Gnolls, orcs, and bugbears, too. And renegade dragons, remnants of the Dragon Wars, were, too. It never made any sense to me to let them live.

He knew what I was thinking. "It's not just the orcs, Son. Men and elves can be just as bad. Have you not seen how they treat people? Would you treat your people like that? Outrageous."

It made sense. I'd spent so much time among them that I rarely noticed anymore. Some of their kind, men liked, and some they didn't like. They would feud and war with one another. Brag and boast about their riches, their kingdoms and princesses. I just laughed at them. They hadn't seen anything like I had, so their commentary was quite meaningless to me, but the company was very entertaining.

"My father was the same as me and you. He made this throne, but this treasure was here long before he came, even his father before him. And like us, they were born dragons that turned to men. You are not like your brothers and sisters, nor was I. They care little for the world of mankind, but it's important that we do. Men and dragons need one another. It's how life is."

I never really understood why dragons needed men except to make treasure, which was still one of those things I enjoyed searching for in my journeys. I met many great men, elves, and dwarves, but I never saw any reason we needed them. They tended sheep and cattle. Made objects that I assumed dragons were too big to craft. That was another thing. I never saw a dragon build anything.

"When I was your age, I was a bigger man, stronger, faster than the others. Our dragon hearts account for that. Like a horse's times two. I was cocky, too, for a while. I befriended the dwarves and learned about blacksmithing and forged the sword you've become so fond of over the years."

I jumped to my feet.

"You made Fang?"

"Indeed."

"But, if you weren't supposed to kill anybody, then why did you make the sword?"

"Because it's a symbol of truth, hope, and strength. The men respected a man that swung a blade. And I never said you couldn't kill, just that it's only a last resort. But again, take a life, safe a life or more."

"How many did you kill?"

"Enough to remember each and every one. Seeing life diminishing in a dying creature's eyes is a sad thing indeed. We are here to save lives, not take them."

I thought about that.

"But don't we save lives when we take the lives of those endangering others?"

"How can you know for sure? At what cost, Son? Men will always fight and feud, whether we help them or not. They'll listen for a while, then wage war with one another. In all of your heroics, how much have you really changed?"

It was true. Battles were won and lost. Good men died, and bad ones lived. Evil withered in the dirt only to rise again into a strong and mighty tower. There was nothing that held it back for long. Not war. Not power. Not peace. This was the part that gave me a headache. Holding back against evil, the despicable beast.

"Save the ones you can, Son. Expect no rewards nor thank-yous, and move on, which I don't think you are very eager to do."

I liked being with people, but they aged quickly, and sooner or later I would always have to move on. It was hard to watch them fight so hard for a life that wasn't long lasting. And maybe that was what I liked most about men. Every day mattered to them. Each one was new, never the same, filled with new adventures over every horizon. Men, good and bad, knew how to live.

I let out a long sigh. I still had no idea how to get my scales.

"I can see in your eyes that you are frustrated, Nath—"

"NO! Don't say it again!" I held my hands up.

"Sorry, Son. You should stay among your brothers and sisters awhile. I'd enjoy your company. Maybe my guidance will sink in."

He was talking another hundred years at least.

"No," I stammered, a good bit angry at myself, "I want to earn my scales. I want to be a dragon!"

My father leaned back, dragon claws clasping his knees, and said, "Take the sword. The one you borrowed. It was going to be a gift anyway, but you slipped out of here like a halfling rogue before I could gift it to you. Take Brenwar," my father's tone darkened, and so did his smoldering eyes, "and do not return this time without your scales."

"What? I can't come back?"

An impatient tone took over his voice like a dam about to break.

"NO! Take with you that which you need. You've earned that much at least, but do not return without your scales."

I shouted back. "Earned it for what?"

"Saving our kin. The dragons. Like I've told you to. Focus on the dragons. The little green one, Ezabel, was quite grateful for your intrusion. She sends her best. And she's not the only one."

"Really?" I said, surprised.

"Son, have I ever lied?"

"No," I said.

"Or been wrong?"

I remained silent. I wasn't ready yet to admit that, so I shrugged.

My father shook his neck, a column of red armor over pure muscle. Then he said, "I don't just sit here as you think and leave every once in a while to gorge myself on cattle. I do many things you aren't aware of. I see things that you cannot."

That was new, but I wasn't so sure I believed it. If he ever did pop out of the mountain, I was certain the entire world would know; each and every being would be screaming like the world was on fire. I know that I would be if I wasn't his son. Then I realized he'd gotten me off track.

"Am I really banished as you say?" I asked, unable to disguise my worry.

"Yes," he said, his voice stern. "It's time you decided. Do you want to be a dragon or a man? Which is more important to you, Son?"

It was a hard question to answer, and it shouldn't have been. Among the dragons, I wasn't so special, but among the people, I stood out. The women, smelling like blossoming rosebuds, running their delicate fingers in my hair, whispering words in my ear that would make a bugbear blush. I liked it.

And the elves, when you came across them, were so pure and delicate in beauty. Their mannerisms were quaint, direct, their cores as strong as deep tree roots. A bit arrogant, though, and I'd be lying if I said I didn't enjoy humbling them from time to time.

The dwarves, brash and bold, like my dearest friend Brenwar, were the fiercest fighters and stubbornest competitors of all. They were hardy, grim, and a little mirthful, and I found nothing but comfort among their kind.

"Ahem." My father interrupted my thoughts. "Do you really have to think about it so much? By now the choice should be clear!"

I waved my hands up in front of me, saying, "Oh, no-no-no, Father. It's dragons. I want to be with the dragons. It's just that I find myself feeling so sorry for the others." I lied to some small degree. I also wasn't so sure I wanted to sit where he sat forever, even with all the treasures of the world at my feet. There had to be more to what he did.

Father lowered his head all the way to the floor, his face a dozen feet from mine, hitting me with a snort of hot air. I felt like an insect when he said, "I've been in your shoes and walked the same path, and I know what you are thinking. You think like a man. It's time to grow up and think like a dragon. Now, with all my heart and wisdom, it is time for me to go. Take care, Son."

He reared up, went around the throne, and melded into an enormous mural of himself that was painted brilliantly on the wall. All of a sudden I felt alone. His presence, for the first time in my life, seemed gone. It was clear that he was serious about my scales, and I'd better be getting serious as well.

I spent the next few hours shuffling through the piles, loading a sack with anything I thought might help me, knowing full well it was up to me, no matter how many tricks I had in my pack. I departed, taking one last long look back at the mural of my father and wishing that I was on the other side of the grand painting as well. Brenwar awaited me, leaning against a wall, arms folded over his barrel chest, bushy black brows raised with alarm.

"You live!" he said, more in a grumble, but a surprised one.

"Ha! You didn't really think he'd kill me, did you?"

"I would've."

"For what?" I demanded.

Brenwar slammed my scabbarded sword into my chest.

"For stealing."

"Borrowing," I said, correcting him. "Besides, it was mine to take anyway."

"I know."

"You did?" I said, surprised. "But how di—"

"Just keep walking, chatterbox. I'm ready to go. I feel so blasted small in this place. And there's no ale or dwarves…"

Brenwar kept going on, but I couldn't listen. My mind was too busy wondering if this would be my last time at home or not. My scales! I had my doubts I could do it, but determined I was, and a good bit deflated, too. How could I ever be a great dragon like my father? I didn't even have one scale.

CHAPTER 6

BRENWAR'S STOUT LEGS WERE TOO slow to keep up with my long-legged pace, so we rode on horseback. Otherwise he'd complain the entire way. I wasn't usually in such a hurry, so I normally preferred to walk, but I felt a degree of haste these days. Northward we went, toward the five great cities.

The Human city of Quintuklen was filled with magnificent castles and shining towers that overlooked vast rich and reaching farmlands.

The dwarven city of Morgdon was a mass of stone blocks and metalworks, like a dwarven-made mountain, grim and impenetrable.

The elven city, Elomelorrahahn, which I just called Elome, the most majestic of all, was hidden in the fog and forests.

The Free City, Narnum, hosted all the races, at least all those not so monstrous, damaging, or tormented. It was a trade city where all the merchants from all the races came to do business, and I found it the most exciting of them all.

The most dreaded, not so vast or appealing, was Thraagramoor, or just Thraag, grim as a mudslide, crumb poor, and run by the orcs, ogres, and goblin sorts.

"Well," Brenwar said, "which way will it be?"

The Mountain of Doom lay in the south, leagues and days from the others. The cities were each two weeks' ride from each other. They formed a rough circle, with Narnum, the Free City, hosting the middle. Everything in between was unprotected and dangerous land.

"Free City, as if you didn't know," I said, hoisting my canteen to my lips.

"I thought we were to be rescuing dragons and such? There'll be no dragons in that city."

"Ah, but is there not talk of dragons wherever we go?" I was grinning.

"I say we go to Morgdon first, then. My kin will be happy to see you again." He stroked his beard. "Not so much as me, but they'll be glad."

Visiting with dwarves was almost as bad as visiting with dragons, except the dwarves were always working, drinking, smoking, or frowning. Their voices were gruff, their conversations short, but they also took time to host their guests. They liked to talk about the things they built and the battles they fought in—with vivid detail. But if you'd heard one dwarf story, you'd heard them all. I was polite when I said, "How about on the way back then, Brenwar?"

He grunted, kicked his short little legs into the ribs of his horse, and charged forward. "To Narnum it is then, Nath! But by my beard, they'd better not have run out of dwarven ale, else I'll drag you back to Morgdon by your ears!"

I couldn't help but smile as he spurred his mount, the hot air of the sun billowing in my recently chopped hair thanks to those dreaded orcs. It would grow back before we made it to Narnum City, where I could find an elven barber to refine it with a dash of magic here and there.

We traveled dusk to dawn, over the plains, through the woodlands, over some mountains, through some small lake towns, and well past the ruins. All the way we chatted with caravans and merchant trains. It was spring, and farmers, miners, and merchants were moving along the dusty and cobblestoned roads, taking their wares to every city in the north.

As usual, I heard the same rumors of war, for there were battles and skirmishes everywhere. There were soldiers from many races, all eager to lay down their lives to make money for their families. Brave men we met, and I admired them all. Of course, there were others, too, up to no good. Some spoiled and bold and others as crooked as a busted dog's tail. But I didn't chat too long. I had heard it all before. I'd fought in wars myself.

Nearing the end of the tenth day, my hips were sore from all the hard riding, and words couldn't describe my elation when I saw the tiniest tip of a spire in the middle of Narnum City.

"Brenwar! We're almost there. Two hours' ride at most, wouldn't you say?"

"Aye, I can't see it, but I know the road as well as you. I knew when we were five hours away three hours ago." He snorted. "I knew we were a day away a day ago. I see no reason for celebration. It's not like we haven't been here before."

"Ah, it's just better to actually see it. Having the goal in sight. Can't you ever get excited about anything?"

"I'll be excited when I have a barrel of ale under my bones and a full tankard as big as my head. It looks the same as it always has: not dwarven."

Well, I was happy. The past few months I'd been outside the cities, tracking down dragon poachers and hunters. Life wasn't all fun and games for me despite all my advantages, but when I went to the city, I made the most of it. And anyway, a place like Narnum, a mix of everything in the world, was where I went to find the ones who tried to hunt dragons.

This city in particular was different from the rest. A mix of everyone tried to thrive here, and for the most part it worked out. All of the races, good and bad, had a say in Narnum, which for lack of a better word was nothing more than a giant marketplace ruled by many dukes and earls that feuded with one another most of the time, paying little attention to the troubles of the people if they were not their own. There was never enough for most of them, and what they gained, they quickly lost. At least that's how I'd seen it over the past two hundred years.

A tower rose more than three hundred feet tall, like an ivory tusk had burst from the ground. It was a beautiful thing. Massive windows adorned its circular walls where an outward staircase spiraled upward like a green vine. I could see tiny bodies moving and peering through the bay windows. I dreamed about the day I'd be able to fly around that tower, wings spread wide, soaring through the air. But for now I was a ground pounder, same as the dwarves and men.

The closer we got, the more people we saw, dozens becoming hundreds, hundreds becoming thousands as we approached the only great city that had no walls. A river flowed through the city from east to west. I could see the tall buildings, some reaching more than a dozen stories tall, but most were not so tall at all. There were guardsmen and garrisons all along the way. The protection of the city was well paid for. The citizens, hard workers, liked it that way, and I didn't fault them. I'd want my efforts protected as well.

The roads were paved with cobblestones and brick. The markets thrived with activity as we trotted deeper into the city. A half-elven auctioneer worked the stage in the marketplace, selling pieces of jewelry to a crowd of excited onlookers. He was dashing, not as dashing as me, but his lips were as fast as a hummingbird's wings. Banners marking the neighborhoods fluttered in the air. Children played in the fountains, and some begged for coins. Women aplenty hung from the windows, whistling at me, to Brenwar's chagrin.

"Quit ta' flirting, will you! Let's find a tavern, eat, drink, and make grumpy!" He was hollering at me.

One buxom gal was yelling my way, "Handsome warrior, will you come and stay with me tonight? I've the softest lips in all of Narnum."

"I can see that," I said, momentarily mesmerized.

The women kept calling to me, one compliment following the other.

One shoved the other, saying, "No, my lips are softer."

"You are so gorgeous, and look at those broad shoulders! I will massage them all night."

"Your handsome eyes, are they your mother's or father's? I've never seen gold in a man's eyes, not even an elf's. So splendid and superb," a comely gal with long lashes noted, posturing from her window.

I stood and gaped at all of the wonderful things coming from their painted lips. I couldn't help myself.

Smack!

Brenwar jostled me hard in my side.

"Come on, Nath Dragon!"

I didn't budge ... spellbound. Flattery was a weakness of mine, something my father had warned me about, but it didn't seem to ever sink in. I didn't want to fight what they were saying and saw no reason to, either.

"In a minute," I shrugged. "As you were saying, ladies."

They all laughed and giggled as Brenwar took my horse by the reins and dragged me away.

"Fool!" he grumbled. "You'll never learn, will you?"

"I hope not," I said, waving at the ladies, whose attentions faded from me and coated the next traveler with their wares and pleasantries. I frowned.

"Whatcha frowning fer? You'd think you'd learn by now." He thumped his bearded chest with his fist. "Next time, I'll lead us in. You always go the same way. You're as drawn to those sirens as an orc is to stink."

"Am not!"

Through the city I went, my passions subdued, the sun dipping over the horizon. I led us into a less-traveled part of the town, through some alleys and well off the commoners' path.

"Let's try this one," I said, pointing at a tavern, dark and dangerous, three stories tall, constructed of timber, and roofed in red clay tile. It gave me a shivering feeling. "There's plenty of trouble to find in there." So in I went, oblivious to the stranger's eyes that followed me from the road.

CHAPTER 7

THERE WAS MUSIC, HOLLERING, AND tale telling inside, and I liked that. Mostly men of questionable pedigrees, long gazes, and hard faces. The smell of roasted pheasant filled the air, and I was ready to eat. Brenwar pushed his way past me and saddled up to the bar.

"Ye got dwarven ale?" he asked a tall, bald man wearing a black apron.

I took a seat alongside him, paying no attention to the stares glaring on my back. This city was used to travelers of all sorts coming and going all times of the night, but this place was one of those that kept close to its own.

"The same for me and two full pheasants, not charred, either." The two coins that I plunked on the table widened the barkeep's restless eyes. "And your undivided attention when I ask."

The barkeep slipped away, a small woman appearing moments later with two tankards of frothing ale as big as her head. Brenwar gulped his down in several large swallows, let out a tremendous belch, and looked at me.

"You can have mine," I said, turning my attention away from the bar and toward all the people inside.

Two men, one a bald giant, another part orc, each laden in muscle, arm wrestled over the wiles of a dainty girl with a look of trouble in her eye. A coarse group of men and women sat at a long table near the stone fireplace in the back, the adventuring sort, somewhat like me, some of them casting nervous glances over their shoulders.

An elven man wearing light-purple garb and long, pale-green hair sulked in the corner and played a black lute of many strings for a small group of swooning women. His music was wonderful and strong. All in all, the tavern, a roomy little hole, was nothing compared to so many other taverns that tended to be much larger and more occupied. Still, it offered what I'd been looking for: trouble.

Three orcs sat in the back, beady eyes glancing my way and back. Another man, long and gaunt, sat huddled in the corner fingering a blade, his tongue licking his lips as he gazed at me like some kind of meal.

At one end of the bar was a fair-haired woman, a long sword strapped on her full hips, her tongue as coarse as that of the hulking man she accompanied, the one who had sneered at me earlier. I wasn't so sure they presented the kind of trouble I was looking for, but they were trouble. The kind that conspire and thieve. Rob graveyards, fight fiends and ghouls for gold. Kidnap women, sell children, and don't look back on their deeds with regret. Of course, my father would tell me not to be so judgmental, but I could detect evil, and it hung as heavy as a wet blanket in here. But did they trifle with dragons? That was what I was here to find out.

Brenwar's elbow rocked me in the ribs.

"Time to eat," he said.

Two steaming pheasants greeted my senses with a delightful aroma. One thing you could say about these rundown taverns of disreputable ilk: they tended to have tasty food. My stomach rumbled, and my mouth watered. I hadn't realized how hungry I was until I started eating, tearing off big hunks at a time. Brenwar grunted and almost smiled, trying to keep the juicy bird meat out of his beard.

"Say," I said to the barkeep, shoving a gold coin his way, "I'm in need of some *dragon* accessories."

The man glared at me and said, "I don't know a thing about that, and it's best you take such business elsewhere." He shoved the coin back

I shoved it back saying, "Beg your pardon, sir. Then a bottle of wine will do."

He hesitated, took the coin, and pulled a bottle down from the top shelf, setting it down and pointing to the door. "Once it's gone—you're gone." His eyes grazed the pommel of my sword on my back. "No dragon talk in my place." He turned and left.

"Cripes!" Brenwar said, wiping his mouth on his sleeve. "Why don't you just scare off every dragon poacher in town? Why don't you go ask for some orc accessories as well?" He glared at the orcs, still huddled in the corner, grunting with dissatisfaction over something.

I slapped him on the shoulder and said, "You eat and drink; I'll do the rest."

As we sat and gorged ourselves on bird meat and wine, I felt the tone in the room shifting. The patrons that sat near us began to fade away elsewhere. Many of the patrons seemed to stiffen, some leaving and more notorious sorts arriving. The men began to bristle and brag, their comments about their exploits designed to catch my ear. Like most bad people, it seemed they didn't like me. Despite my rugged armor and attempt to blend in, I looked more than formidable. So far as I could tell, I was the tallest man in the room, my shoulders, arms, and chest as knotted and broad as the rest. What they hadn't noticed about me before, they had noticed now. But I didn't come here looking for a fight. Or did I?

I tapped the big brute at the end of the bar on the shoulder.

"Do that again, and I'll cut off your hand," he warned.

"No doubt you would try," I said, smiling over at the fair-haired woman with the curious and inviting eyes. "I'm in need of dragon accessories."

"Get out of here!" He shoved me away.

Dragon accessories were a profitable business. A single scale was almost worth a piece of gold. Dragon teeth, scales, skin, claws, and horns, whether they contained magic or not, were highly prized possessions that adorned many wealthy citizens. It was a practice that made me sick, seeing my kind displayed for fashion. Dragons were the same as the other races but treated like something different. Of course, not all dragons were good, but most people viewed them all as bad.

I shoved him back.

"You touch me again, you'll be the one to lose your hands." No one shoves me around.

The fair-haired woman forced her way between us, pushing her angry friend back with both hands, saying, "No blood here tonight." Then she whirled on me, poking her finger in my chest. "Go and sit down. I don't know what game you're playing, but I'll not stand for any talk of dragons. We fight for gold, not poach."

"I can see that now. But I pay well. Pardon me," I said with a slight bow, retaking my seat. *That ought to get them going,* I thought.

The man and woman warriors grumbled with each another, then departed, but she gave me one long look over her shoulder as they went. Now Brenwar and I sat and waited. The barkeep continued to glower at me, but he didn't throw me out as long as we kept paying, and Brenwar was still eating and drinking. So I sat, noted all the scowls, and waited and waited and waited. I was a dragon, so waiting wasn't such a bad thing for me. But words travel faster than the wind sometimes. That's when two lizard men wandered in, both taller than me, crocodile green, dressed like men, and armored like soldiers. Their yellow eyes attached themselves to me first as they ripped their daggers out and charged.

CHAPTER 8

L IZARD MEN. BIG, STRONG, AND fast like me, except not nearly as smart, but that didn't really matter when all they wanted to do was kill you.

I slung my barstool into one, cracking it into timbers over its head.

"Blasted reptile! Ye spilled my drink," Brenwar bellowed, clubbing another on its head with his tankard.

Slowed but not stunned, the lizard sprang on top of me, driving me hard to the floor. I locked my fingers on its wrists as it tried to drive its dagger into my throat. Its red lizard tongue licked out as it hissed, angry and fateful. The lizard men weren't many in the world, usually pawns to greater evil but effective pawns nonetheless. I drove my knee up into its stomach with little effect as its blade strained inches above my neck.

"Dieeeesss, dragonsssss!" it said with a heave.

It felt like the veins were going to burst in my arms when I shoved back with all my strength. Over the sound of the blood rushing behind my ears, I could hear a rising clamor and more hissing voices. Not good. Yet Brenwar's bellows were clear.

"NO!" I yelled back. In a blink, I freed one hand and punched its long nose, rocking back its head.

Whap! Whap! Whap!

The lizard man jerked away from my stinging blows, but my hands felt like they were punching a wall. Still, lizard men hate getting hit in the nose; so do most lizards, for that matter. My blood was running hot now, the warrior in me suddenly alive as I jumped on its back and smashed its face into the floor. The dagger clattered from its grasp, and I snatched it up and rolled back to my feet.

Brenwar had the other one on the ground in a choke hold.

Crack!

And now it was dead, but the first two weren't the last. Three more were charging my way, not with daggers but with heavy broadswords this time. I can't imagine what I had said to draw so much attention.

Shing!

There was an audible gasp in the room as I whipped Fang's glowing blade through the air. Every eye was wide and wary, and I had to remember I had no friends here except Brenwar. The lizard men stopped for a moment, but they were well-trained soldiers ordered to move forward.

The first lizard man charged past Brenwar, sword arcing downward and clashing hard into mine, juttering my arms.

Bap!

I punched its nose, rammed my knee in its gut, and jammed my sword into the thigh of the one behind it, drawing a pain-filled hiss from its lizard lips. Two more were down, and the third had an angry dwarven man latched on its back. I raised my sword to deliver a lethal blow. I know, I know. My father warned me that killing is only a last resort, but I don't care what anyone says: lizard men and orcs don't count.

"Stop!" The barkeep screamed. "STOP!"

No one moved, not even the lizard men.

Crack!

Well, that was one lizard man that wasn't going to move again for sure as Brenwar rode its dead body down to the floor.

"YOU, with the magic sword, get out of my TAVERN!"

"Me? But they attacked me!"

My longsword Fang hummed in my hand, its blade glimmering with a radiant light like the first crack of dawn. I brought the tip of its edge toward the barkeep's nose. I wasn't in any mood to be accused of something I didn't do.

He held his hands up but tipped his chin up toward the folks behind me. I had a bad feeling as I turned to look. The two arm wrestlers stood now, each with a short sword in hand, eyes narrowed and ready to jump. The orcs, once three and now six, had drifted closer. The adventurers at the long table now stood. A staff glowed in one's hand, and a sword glimmered in another. One warrior, grim faced and wearing chain mail, had a crossbow pointed at my chest. One woman, small and slender, stood poised on a chair, a handful of throwing knives bared. There were more, too, each focused on me, ready to fight or kill if need be.

"You can all try to take me if you want, but you won't all survive. Is your life worth the risk or not?" I glared back at the barkeep. "Your patrons can't pay if they're dead."

It was a bluff. I wouldn't have killed any of them except the orcs. I swear they don't count. Neither do the lizard men, three of which had begun crawling back out the way they came. Lizard men didn't get along with me. We went way back. Well, I didn't mention it before, but I've been around awhile, and when you live a long time and do what I do, you tend to make enemies. I had plenty to go around. Chances were that one of my enemies knew I was here and had sent in a squadron of goons to kill me.

"Just go," the bartender pleaded, his eyes nervous now.

I looked at the two dead lizard men on the floor and asked, "What about them?"

"I'll take care of them. The lizards don't hold any worth with the authorities."

Brenwar had resumed his eating, his blocky, mailed shoulder hunched back over his pheasant. I was still itching for a fight. The tension in the air had not slackened. My legs were still ready to spring. That's when the man in the corner stood up and walked toward the center of the room. Long and gaunt, hooded in a dark cloak, he seemed more of a ghost than a man. All eyes now fell on the man that held a hefty sack in one hand and dropped it on the table to the sound of clinking coins.

Slowly, he pulled his hood back, revealing a shaven head that was tattooed with symbols and signs I knew all too well. He was a Cleric of Barnabus, a cult of men obsessed with the dragons. Meddlers in a dark and ancient magic. I hadn't expected to come across one so soon. His voice was loud and raspy as he pointed at me and said:

"This bag of gold to the one that brings me his head!"

Clatch-Zip!

A crossbow bolt darted toward my ducking head and caught the barkeep full in the shoulder.

"What!" Brenwar roared, readying his dwarven war hammer, sharp at one end, like an anvil on the other.

"Don't let that cleric escape, Brenwar!" I said, smacking the muscled goons' blades with Fang. I clipped one in the leg and took a rock-hard shot in the jaw from the other. He gloated. I retaliated, cracking him upside his skull with the flat of my blade.

"Agh!" I cried out in pain. A row of small knives was imbedded in my arm, courtesy of the little rogue woman. I'd have to deal with her later. I had to get the cleric, who was scurrying away toward the door. Brenwar was a barricade at the door, a host of orcs swarming at him.

"Let's dance, you smelly beasts!" he yelled, hitting one so hard it toppled the others.

He could handle himself, and I had bigger problems: the party of adventurers had surrounded me. Well, mercenaries seemed to be more likely the term for them. I leapt back as the lanky fighter with the brilliant sword tried to cut me in half. He was a young man, confident in his skills.

Clang! Clang! Clatter!

He lacked my power or speed as I tore his sword free from his grasp.

Slice!

I clipped muscle from his sword arm and sent him spinning to the floor.

Then everything went wrong.

The little woman jammed a dagger in my back. The wizard fired a handful of missiles into my chest, and the crossbowman, now wielding a hammer, slung it into my chest. That's why I wear armor, forged by the dwarves at that. My breastplate had saved me from dying more than a dozen times, but I'd gotten careless. I should have negotiated with this hardy brood, but I wanted to fight instead. I was mad. I was Nath Dragon, the greatest hero in the land, as far as I was concerned. It was time they saw that.

I banged the tip of my sword on the hard oaken floor. The metal hummed and vibrated with power.

THAAAAROOOOONG!!!

Glass shattered. Men and women fell to the floor, covering their ears, all except me and Brenwar, who stood on top of a pile of what looked to be dead orcs. I could see him yelling at me, but I could not hear. His lips mouthed the words, "Shut that sword off."

I sheathed my singing blade, and the sound stopped immediately. The entire tavern looked like it had been turned upside down. Everyone living was moaning or wailing. The loudest among them? The Cleric of Barnabus. Huddled up in a fetal position, shivering like a leaf.

Fang's power was pretty helpful when it came to ending a fight with no one dying, but it didn't work on every race, or most of the time, for that matter. Fang only did what it wanted to do. My father said the sword had a mind of its own, and I was pretty sure that was true. I grabbed the cleric by the collar of his robe and dragged him over the bar. Brenwar had the cleric's bag of gold in his hand when he came off and plopped it on the bar. The barkeep, grimacing in pain from the crossbow bolt in his shoulder that had been meant for me, smiled as the dwarf filled his hands with the gold and spilled coins on the bar. "Fer the damages. The rest I'll be keeping."

"So long," I said, tying and gagging the cleric and hoisting him over my shoulder. "And thanks. This man will have just what I'm looking for."

The remaining patrons, still dazed and confused, holding their heads and stomachs, paid no mind at all as I left. They should have learned a lesson today: never pick a fight with an opponent you don't know anything about; it just might be a dragon.

CHAPTER
9

N̄O ONE OUTSIDE SEEMED TO mind as we pushed our way through the bewildered crowd of the neighborhood, loaded our prisoner onto my horse, and galloped toward a part of town I knew better. The authorities weren't likely to give much chase, if they even bothered at all. Some parts of the city were void of the common rules of order.

"Here," I said to Brenwar, turning my steed inside a large barn full of stables.

A stablehand, a sandaled young man with straw colored hair, greeted us with an eerie glance at my wriggling captive.

"No questions," I said, handing him a few coins.

"No problem," he said with a smile as broad as an ogre's back.

Stables and barns are good places to do business, or interrogations, for that matter. No echoes, and the smell of manure tends to offend most people, keeps them away. I shoved the cleric from my saddle, and Brenwar dragged him inside the stables over the straw and stood watch outside.

As I said, the Clerics of Barnabus are an evil lot, and we go way back. The fact that one had already come after me was a stroke of luck, both good and bad. Bad because they almost got me killed. Good because this man would lead me to their next nefarious plot. Normally, some desperate person would tell me something or find someone that would when I asked after dragon articles. I'd follow their information, and sometimes that led to a dead end, but ofttimes it led me to where I was going. The Clerics of Barnabus, it seemed, had become privy to my ways. And when it came to dragons, they had eyes and ears everywhere. From then on, I would have to be more careful how I went about gathering information.

Now the hard part: interrogation. Taking information from an unwilling mind by force. It wasn't a very dragon-like way of doing things, but it didn't always have to be brutal.

I pinned the man up against the wall by the neck and jerked the rag from his mouth. His impulse to scream was cut short as my fingers squeezed around his throat.

"Urk!"

"That's a good little evil cleric. Keep quiet, and I'll let you breathe." I squeezed a little harder, forcing his eyes open wider. "I talk. You answer, quietly. Understand?"

He blinked.

That was pretty much all he could do, and I took it as a definitive yes. I could tell by the tattoos on his head that this acolyte was only a few notches above a lackey of the cult. He had some magic, but nothing I couldn't handle.

"See my dwarven friend over there?" I said.

Brenwar peered inside, holding a manure shovel in his hand.

"Look at what he does to people that don't cooperate."

He took the shovel, blacksmith hands holding both ends of the wooden handle, and grunted.

Snap!

The skin on the cleric's already gaunt face paled. His eyes blinked rapidly.

"Now, I'd say that shovel's thicker than your skinny bones. So I suggest you answer my questions in detail, or you'll be going home in a wheelbarrow."

The man's chin quivered. I couldn't ask for a better result.

"Y-You're, you're N-Nath Dragon. Aren't you?"

"You didn't know that already?"

"I was told it was you, but I did not believe until I saw for myself. Someone mentioned you'd come into town. I followed you in. Fully ready to see you dead. There is such a high bounty on your head. But you move so fast. Impossible. Unnatural. I knew I'd lost as soon as it started, but I had no choice but to try," he said, grinning sheepishly.

I slapped him in the face.

"Please, no flattery if you want to walk again."

Evil ones always try to beguile and convince a person their distorted intentions are only for the best or out of necessity. It's tough to sell me if you're a man, but an attractive woman is a different story, and I knew right there and then I had best be more careful.

"We hate you, Nath Dragon! We'll have your head by dawn!"

"My, it seems you've forgotten what happened to my dear friend and the shovel. Brenwar!"

"No!" The evil cleric pleaded. "No. I can't have my arms and legs splintered. I'd rather die. Make a deal with me."

"No."

"Hear me out. I know where many dragons are kept, near this city. Small ones."

He had my attention. The little ones, some as small as hawks, others bigger than dogs, weren't easy to catch but were easy to keep. The thought of them being caged infuriated me. I pushed harder on his throat.

"You tell me now, and not a single bone of yours will be broken."

He nodded. I eased the pressure.

"Take the trail to Orcen Hold."

Finnius the Cleric of Barnabus lived, and Nath Dragon and his dwarven companion, Brenwar, were long gone. But still he struggled in his bindings, and his knee throbbed like an angry heart where the dwarf had whacked him with the busted shovel.

"Let me help you with that," a woman said. Her dark-grey robes matched his, but she had short raven-colored hair and thin lips of a pale purple.

She pulled the gag from his mouth and helped him to his feet.

"Have you done well, acolyte Finnius?" she asked, cutting the bonds from his wrists.

"I did exactly as you ordered, High Priestess." He rubbed his reddened wrists. "They are halfway to Orcen Hold by now. Your plan, Priestess, I'm certain will be successful. In a few more hours, Nath Dragon will be ours."

She rubbed her hand over his bald head and smiled.

"You'll be needing more tattoos after this, Finnius. I had my doubts you would pull this off, but it seems you did quite well. Assuming, of course, they arrive as expected."

"Oh they will, Priestess. Nath's eyes were as fierce as a dragon's when I said it. He'll not be stopped."

She walked away and said, "That's what I'm counting on. This day, the Clerics of Barnabus will forever change the life of Nath Dragon."

Finnius limped along behind her toward the front of the stables, where the stablehand greeted her from a distance. A long serpent's tail slipped out from underneath her robes. Striking like a snake, it knocked the boy clear from his feet, smacking him hard into the wall. Finnius swallowed hard and hurried along.

CHAPTER 10

ORCEN HOLD. NOT NEARLY AS bad as it sounds but still bad, miles northeast from Narnum toward the orcen city of Thraagramoor. It's a stronghold filled with brigands and mercenaries, all swords and daggers for hire that sometimes form an army, and you never know whose side they are on.

It isn't just orcs, either, or even mostly orcs for that matter, but men and some of the other races as well. The name most likely kept unwanted do-gooders like me away. I'd never been there before, but the world was vast, and even in my centuries of life, I still couldn't have been everywhere. That would still take some time.

Brenwar and I rode our mounts up a steep road that wound up a hillside rather than around it, which would have been wholly more adequate. On the crest of the hill, no more than a mile high, I could see there was a massive fort of wood posts and blocks jutting into the darkening sky. Pigeons scattered in the air, wings flapping, before settling back along the edges of the walls. Pigeons are crumb-snatching carrion, never a good sign, rather a bad one, as the black-and-white–speckled birds are drawn to filth. Of course, what would one expect from a place named Orcen Hold?

I pulled my hood over my head as the drizzling rain became a heavy downpour, soaking me to the bone in less than a minute. I hated being wet, drenched, saturated in any kind of water that I hadn't planned on. You'd think a tough man like me would be used to it by now, but I saw no reason to like it. I like the sun, the heat on my face, the sweat glistening on my skin.

As the horses clopped through the mud, we made our way around the last bend, stopped, and looked up. Orcen Hold was a good bit bigger than it had looked from below. A veritable city that could host thousands, where I assumed at most were just a few hundred. Well fortified. There were watchtowers along the walls with soldiers spread out, crossbows ready to cut down any unwanted intruders. Ahead, the main gate, two twenty-foot-high doors, stood open behind a small moat. I couldn't shed the foreboding feeling that overcame me any more easily than I could the water soaking my back. It didn't seem like the kind of place where two men entered and got to leave... alive, anyway.

Still, we trotted over the drawbridge, through the doors, and underneath the portcullis that hung over us like a massive set of iron jaws.

"Yer sure ye want to do this?" Brenwar's beard was dripping with rain.

"I'd do just about anything to get us out of this rain."

Behind the walls over Orcen Hold lay a small city, not refined but functional. The roads, normally covered with the brick and stone customary to most cities, were dirt now turned to mud. The buildings, ramshackle and ruddy, were tucked neatly behind plank-wood walkways. People were milling about, dashing through puddles and across the streets from one porch to the other. Some shouted back and forth in arguments of some sort. The children, possibly the most mottled ones I'd ever seen, played in the mud, their faces, grimy, poor, and hungry. And the smell. I could only assume it would have been worse without the rain, so for a moment I was thankful for the deluge.

The Troll's Toe. That was the place we were looking for. The Cleric of Barnabus, Finnius was his name, had proven to be a very unwilling participant after he let loose the location called Orcen Hold. His tongue had frozen in his clenched jaws. A well-placed spade to the knee, courtesy of Brenwar, and he'd told me what I was certain I needed to know.

The light was dim as the sinking sun continued to dip behind the clouds and disappear, turning an otherwise hot day cold. The wind began to bang the wooden signs that hung from chains in front of the buildings, making the dreary trek from an unknown city worse.

The firelight that gleamed from behind the dingy windows was a welcoming sight despite the coarse faces that glared at us with more remorse than curiosity. Blasted orcs. If it weren't for them, I swear that life on Nalzambor would be an excellent party.

"There," Brenwar said, pointing his stubby finger in the rain. "Seems we've found what yer looking for. But Nath, it's not too late to turn back. I'd say we're outnumbered here, uh, about a thousand to one."

"I thought you liked those kinds of odds," I said, trying to wipe the rain from my face.

"Er ... well, I do. But, this place reeks. If I'm to die, I'd like it to be somewhere a little closer to my home."

"Die?"

Brenwar looked a little bit ashamed when he said, "I just want to make sure I get a proper funeral. I'll not have a bunch of orcs burying me in the sewer. Or you, either, for that matter."

Brenwar was a bit obsessive about his funeral. It's a special thing for a dwarf. If they had their way, they'd die in battle, but they just wanted to be remembered for it. Brenwar, an older man by dwarven standards, had lived longer than even me and more than likely had a couple hundred years to go. He'd been with me so long, it didn't seem that he could ever die. But I'd seen other dwarves as great as him perish before.

The wind picked up, banging the sign to the Troll's Toe hard against the rickety building frame as we hitched our horses and went inside. Warm air and the smell of bread dough and stale ale greeted us as we sat down at a small table away from the firelight. The crowded room was momentarily quiet, more on account of Brenwar's presence than mine. It wasn't often you saw a dwarf in Orcen Hold, but Brenwar's bushy-bearded face wasn't the only one. Still, I couldn't shake the feeling we were all on our own.

CHAPTER 11

IT WAS A ROUGH BUNCH, as bad as I'd ever seen: tattooed, scarred, ornery, peg legged, eye patched, and hook handed. It looked like the perfect place to get in trouble. The men were as coarse and rude as the orcs and half-orcs that snorted and blustered around the bar. The women were as crass as the men, singing and dancing on a small stage, their voices as soothing as a glass of boiling water.

"Now what?" Brenwar asked, looking back over his shoulder.

"We wait," I said, waving over a waitress with hips as big as an ogre's.

"What will it be, weary travelers?" She had a gap-toothed smile.

"Two of whatever tastes best with your ale," Brenwar spouted. "Human food, not the orcen mishmash that tastes like mud and worms."

She tried to make a pretty smile, but it was quite frightening when she said, "As you wish, dwarven sire."

"I think she likes you," I said.

"I certainly don't see why she wouldn't," he said, watching her prance away.

I sat there, sulking and soaking, damp hood still covering my face. It wasn't as if anyone would recognize me, but I'd still stick out like a sore thumb. There was something about my eyes and looks that drew stares, and for the most part, I like that kind of attention, but here, it was the kind of attention I didn't want. I just needed to lie low and wait until the opportunity presented itself. In a pain-filled voice, Finnius had assured us that I would know.

My appetite was barren, but the food wasn't half bad as I sat there and picked at it. Something about the greasy meat and cheeses they served in the worst of places always made me want to come back for more. It was getting late, though, less than an hour from the middle of the night, and my wet clothes finally began to dry. The rain no longer splattered on the window panes, and I could again see the moon's hazy glow. I craned my neck at the chatter about dragons that lingered in the air, but it was hard to make anything out over all the singing voices and carousing.

Brenwar nudged me, pointing over toward a mousy man with hunched shoulders whispering among the tables. I watched him, his lips flapping in a feverish and convincing fashion. Some shoved him away, while others minded his words with keen interest. He had my interest as well. *Dragons.* I could see the word on his lips as plain as the nose on his face. I wasn't a lip reader or mind reader, but when it came to anything about dragons, I could just tell.

Like a busy rodent, he darted from one table to the next, collecting coins and scowls while directing the people toward the back of the room, where I watched them disappear behind the fireplace mantel. *Don't ask for it. Wait for it.* That's what the cleric Finnius had said. It made sense, too. Asking would only rouse suspicion.

"You think he'll make it our way or not?" Brenwar combed some food from his beard.

The little man's head popped up our way as if he'd heard Brenwar's question. He scurried toward us, his ferret face nervous, eyes prying into the shadows beneath my hood. Brenwar shoved him back a step.

"Some privacy, man."

The small man hissed a little then spoke fast.

"Dragon fights. Five gold. Dragon fights. Five gold. Last chance. One. Two. Three ..." his fingers were collapsing on his hand. "Four. Fi—"

"Sure," I said, sliding the coins over the table.

He frowned.

"Five for you!" he said, offended, scowling at Brenwar. "Seven for the dwarf!"

"Why you little—" Brenwar made a fist.

"Six," I insisted. You have to barter with dealers like these or else they won't respect you, and that can lead to trouble.

"Fine," he said, snatching the additional coins I pushed his way. He left two tokens, each wooden with a dragon face carved into it. "Under thirty minutes. Be late and no see."

I looked over at Brenwar as the little wispy-haired man left and said, "I suppose we should go, then."

Brenwar finished off the last of his ale and wiped his mouth.

"I suppose," he said, casting an odd look over at the large stone fireplace. "It's underground, it is. I feel the draft and the shifting of the stones. We're over a cave or something carved from the mountain. Bad work. Not dwarven." He got up and patted his belly. "Probably collapse on us, it will. They probably let the orcs build the tunnel."

"You'll dig us out if it does, won't you?" I followed him behind the mantel. He didn't say a word.

One thing about Nalzambor, there were always new places to go. It was impossible to ever see what was behind every door in every city, and for the most part it was exciting. The chill from the damp clothes and biting air had worn off now, and the hearth of the stone fireplace was like a warm summer day. I put my hand on the rock, nice and toasty, which made me think of when I used to lie alongside my father's belly when I was a boy. He'd tell the most excellent stories, and even though they usually lasted more than a week, I never got bored of them.

We followed a man and woman of questionable character down a narrow, winding stairwell.

"Bah. Orcen engineers. There should be no such thing," Brenwar complained, his heavy feet thundering down the steps.

At the bottom, two half-orcen men waited, armored in chain mail from head to toe, and two more stood behind them, spears at the ready. The tips of my fingers tingled. I realized I still had my sword and Brenwar his war axe, but the pair before us, with steel swinging on their hips, paid their tokens and moved on down a tunnel to where many loud voices were shouting. The half-orcen man snatched my token from my hand and sneered.

"Take down your hood."

Brenwar stiffened at my side, hands clutching his weapon with white knuckles.

I looked down into the half-orcen eyes and growled, "I paid my share. No one said hoods weren't allowed. You have something against hoods?"

His lip curled back, but he couldn't tear his eyes away. I wouldn't let him. I looked deeper into him. I could see his hate and fear. There was little good in him but enough man left for him to step aside.

"Go ahead," he said, blinking hard and moving on to the next people.

Making our way down the tunnel cut through the rock, I could feel the cool draft nipping at my sweating neck. The sound of voices was getting louder now. A mix of races I could hear. Men mostly, but orcs, too, and a few dwarves as well. We emerged into a cavernous room, part cave, part auditorium, with seats carved from stone that formed a crude arena. The excited voices were shouting at a shimmering black curtain that covered an object in the center about twenty feet high and thirty feet wide. The hair on my neck stiffened as I pushed my way through the crowd that circled and pressed around the wall that surrounded it.

"Kill the dragon!" someone cried, jostling my senses.

An outcry of agreement followed along with a series of cheers. I could feel more bodies pressing against mine, a frenzied and gambling horde. From above, a powerful voice, amplified beyond the powers of nature, shouted out.

"SILENCE!"

I'd never seen so many loud and obnoxious people fall silent at once, yet they did, looking upward at the sound of the voice. A man as tall as he was wide stood in robes laced in arcane symbols, glittering different colors in the light. A dragon's claw, a big one, jostled around his fat neck as he ran his pudgy fingers through a mop of brown hair. He seemed tired, expressionless, and bored. He yawned, his mouth opening three times bigger than it looked.

Brenwar nudged me, saying, "That ain't no man."

Whatever he was, he kept on speaking.

"SILENCE!"

He said it once again, long and drawn out. At this rate, I'd never see what was underneath the curtain.

"LET ... THE ... DRAGON ... GAMES ... BEEEEEEEE ... GIIIIIN!"

There was a clap of thunder and a flash of light, followed by a series of gasps.

I gawped at what I saw next: a cage. A series of ironworks constructed into a see-through dome of metal. But that wasn't what got me. I'd seen plenty of cages before. Instead, it was who was perched inside on a swing. It was a dragon no taller than a dwarf, glimmering with orange and yellow scales, clawed wings covering his face and body. He shone like a diamond inside a room full of coal. My nerves turned to sheets of ice when the big fat man said, "SEND ... IN ... THE ... TROLLS!"

CHAPTER 12

I T SEEMED SO OUT OF place to imagine such things as trolls fighting a dragon, albeit a small one, to the death. My inner self was recoiling, uncertain what to do, when the cage doors opened on a tunnel to a rousing chorus of cheers. A troll—ten kinds of ugly all wrapped up into a ruddy piece of brawny flesh towering ten feet tall—stood there pounding its fist into its hand. The smacking was so loud it popped my ears. I tore my eyes away from the troll that lumbered, arms swinging into the walls, shaking the cage on its way into the chamber. The dragon was as still as a crane on his perch, unmoving. *Good boy,* I thought. I could tell he was a boy by the scales on his belly, a little darker than the orange and yellow scales on his body, unlike the girls, who were usually lighter than the rest.

The troll, naked except for a burlap loincloth, narrowed its small eyes on the dragon and let out a terrible yell, loud and getting louder. A battle cry of sorts. A chorus of bestial fury. The dragon remained at peace on his perch, not showing the slightest degree of motion.

The crowd quieted, all eyes as full as the moon and fixated on the dragon. My own heart was pounding in my chest like a team of galloping horses. The troll, every bit as dangerous as it was dumb, lumbered around the dragon like a predator sizing up its prey. Despite their lack of intelligence, trolls aren't impulsive, but once they make a decision, which usually involves something other than them dying, they stick to it.

"What's going on?" Brenwar muttered.

"I'm not sure."

"KILL THE DRAGON!" someone cried.

That's when the chants began, a rising crescendo of fury, and like a frenzied ape, the troll beat its chest, charging the unmoving dragon, massive fists raised and ready to deal a lethal blow.

The dragon's wings popped open, his serpentine neck striking out as he began breathing a stream of white lava.

The troll screamed in agony, thrashing under the weight of the dragon's breath that coated it from head to toe with brilliant-white, burning oil. The troll's flesh charred and smoked, its efforts to escape diminishing. From where I stood, the heat was like sticking your face too close to a campfire. The crowd roared so loud I couldn't hear myself think. I slapped Brenwar on the back, unable to hide my elation as the little dragon finished, leaving nothing left of the troll but the smoldering bones and an uncanny stink.

Brenwar looked up at me, eyes as big as stones, and said, "Did you see that? I've never seen a dragon with breath like that!"

Dragons. There were all kinds. Different makes and families, and each kind had a special weapon or two of its own. The orange dragons, called blazed ruffies, were among of the noblest and deadliest of them all. I had to get this one out, and soon. He was still young, and it would be at least a day before his breath returned.

"That should do it," I said. "Let's stick around and see what we can do to sneak this dragon out of here."

There was a lot of murmuring, most good, some bad. It seemed most of the people that liked to take chances had been smart enough to bet on the dragon. I was expecting everyone to leave, but most of them were sticking around and talking. Of course, how often do you get to see a live dragon fight? Their fascination sickened me.

I looked above as the fat man whose mouth was too large for his face spoke again.

SEND ... IN ... MORE ... TROLLS!

My heart sank down into my toes. "What?" I couldn't hide my exclamation. Wooden double doors opened on the other side of the cage into the tunnel again. Two trolls, this time carrying shields and clubs and wearing helmets, charged the orange dragon on the perch. The crowd screamed. I screamed. The dragon didn't stand a chance. He'd last another minute or two at most.

"We've got to get him out of there, Brenwar!" I yelled.

The dragon zoomed from his perch, dashing between the legs of one troll, who swung, missed, and bashed the other. Dragons are fast no matter how big they are. But no dragon with spent breath and little room to fly could last for long in that cage.

"Find a way in, Brenwar!"

As soon as I pushed one person away, two more appeared. The crowd was in a frenzy, trying to get a closer look. The cage, so far as I could see, didn't have a door or opening except into the tunnel on the other side. I heard a sound like a rattlesnake's rattle. The ruffie clawed his way up one troll's back, tearing its flesh up like dirt, drawing an inhuman howl. He perched on one troll's head and taunted the other with the rattlesnake sound made by tiny fins that buzzed by his ears.

WANG!

One troll struck the other on its metal helmet just as the dragon darted away. It looked like two clumsy dogs trying to catch a mouse. One troll would swing, miss, and hit the other. That wouldn't last forever. Dragons, for all their speed and skill, tire quickly after their dragon breath is spent. They are magic, and magic needs time to recharge. Trolls, however, tire about as easily as a wall of stone. Those two wouldn't stop or slow until they were dead.

"Brenwar!"

I couldn't see him, but I could see people falling like stones, a path of people parting within the throng before closing up again.

The voice from above came again.

"STOP ... THEM!"

I saw him, the fat mage, like a toad on a stool, pointing straight at me. The crowd, dazzled by the spectacular fight, gave the man little notice, but the guards, the ones armed to the teeth, were ready and coming after me. If they got me, I'd never get to the dragon in time, and I still hadn't figured out a way inside the cage.

"MOVE!" I shouted, but the people paid me no mind.

That's when I heard it, an awful sound, the sound of a dragon crying out, his shrieking so loud it hurt my ears. A troll had ahold of his wing. The dragon fought and fluttered, talons tearing into the troll's flesh, but its grip held firm. That's when something snapped inside me. A geyser of power erupted within my bones. Fang, my sword, was glowing white hot in my hands. I was surrounded, but my mind was no longer my own. The guards and men were falling under the wrath of my blade. I ignored the fear-filled screams and howls of fury. I could not tell one man from another. All I wanted to do was save the dragon, and nothing was going to stop me.

There was blood and fury in my eyes as I swung Fang into the iron cage. Fang cut into the iron as I chopped like a lumberjack gone mad. *Hack! Hack! Hack!* I was through, a troll's massive back awaiting me. I sent Fang through its spine and caught a glimmer of the dragon slithering away. Brenwar was yelling. I turned in time to see the other troll's club coming for me. I dove. *Whump!* The club missed my head. I rolled. *Whump!* It almost broke my back as I scrambled away. *Crack!* The troll fell over dead, thanks to the help of Brenwar's war hammer catching it in the skull.

"Come on!" He pulled me to my feet. Ahead, the large wooden double doors, at least ten inches thick, barred our escape from the coming wrath of who knows what.

Brenwar charged, war hammer raised over his head, bellowing, "BARTFAAAAST!"

There was a clap of thunder, the splintering of wood, and a giant hole in the doors that had momentarily barred our path. The dragon was gone like a bolt of orange lightning.

"Follow that dragon," I yelled, following Brenwar down the tunnel.

The dwarven fighter's short legs churned like a billy goat's as he charged down one tunnel and through another. My instincts fired at the sound of armored soldiers coming after us down the tunnel.

"Do you know where you're going, Brenwar?" I cried from behind him.

Brenwar snorted, "I'm a dwarf, aren't I? Not a tunnel made that can lose me."

We found ourselves running down a long corridor, where a wooden door had been busted open that led outside into the once again pouring rain. The pounding of armored bootsteps was coming our way, as were voices barking orders and calling for our heads. It was time to make a stand.

A group of heavily armed soldiers rounded the corner, armored in chain mail from head to toe, the silver tips of their spears glinting in the torch light.

"Get him," one ordered from behind, thrusting his sword in the air.

I whipped Fang's keen edge around my body and yelled back.

"The first one that comes within ten feet of me is dead!"

The soldiers stopped, looking with uncertainty toward one another. That's when I noticed the blood dripping from my sword. Their eyes were on it as well, and a hollow feeling crept over me. How many had I killed? Everything was a blur. Perhaps it was troll's blood, but it didn't seem dark enough.

"Skewer that man!" The commander's face was red. "If you don't follow orders, then you're dead men anyway. We've got strength in numbers. Attack!"

The first two spearmen lowered their weapons at my belly and advanced. All I wanted to do was buy time. Just a few seconds more. I leaped in, batting one spear away with my sword and yanking the spear away from the next man. The soldiers shuffled back. Now I faced them with a sword in one hand and a spear hoisted over my shoulder.

"The next soldier to advance will catch this in his belly," I said, motioning with the spear.

"Cowards! Charge him! Charge him now!"

The unarmed spearman stepped back as another took his place.

I launched my spear into his leg. The man let out a cry of pain as he tumbled to the ground.

I ducked as a spear whizzed past my face.

"Charge!"

I hoisted Fang over my head and said, "Stop! I surrender!"

No one moved, every eye intent on me.

The commander shouted from the back, "Drop your sword, then!"

Slowly, I lowered my arms. But I had another plan. I'd use Fang's magic to blast back my enemies as I'd done in the tavern.

"What are you smiling for?" The commander moved forward.

"I'm just glad to put an end to the violence, is all. Oh, and you might want to hold your ears."

"What for?"

I banged the tip of Fang's blade on the stone corridor's floor.

Ting.

Nothing happened. I tried it again.

Ting.

Drat!

"Fang, what are you doing?" I shook my sword.

The commander was not amused. "You going to drop that sword or not?"

I was flat footed now with nowhere to go but out. I grasped my sword in both my hands and pulled it in front of my face.

"I've changed my mind. I'm going to fight you all. To the death!" I let out a battle cry and charged forward. All of the soldiers hunkered down. In stride, I pivoted on my right foot, twisted the other way, and dashed through the busted doorway into the rain.

I was drenched the moment I made it out into the river of mud that was supposed to be a street. I heard a horse nicker nearby and dashed that way. Brenwar, my horse in tow, was galloping down the road, hooves splashing in the water.

"Run, Dragon!"

The heavy boots were trampling behind me as I sprinted alongside Brenwar, grabbed ahold of the saddle on my horse, and pulled myself up.

"Great timing," I yelled up toward Brenwar as we began our gallop away. "I couldn't have done better myself—*ulp!*"

Something that burned like fire slammed into my back. Another spear sailed past my head, followed by another. The pain was excruciating as I galloped onward with a spear in my back, holding on for dear life.

It was dawn before we stopped riding. I could barely keep my head up, and I swore I'd black out any second. We didn't slow, not once, taking trails little known to most. I'd been that certain our pursuers were many. I was restless when we stopped along a silvery stream and gave the horses a moment to drink.

"Finally stopping, are we? Think we lost them?" Brenwar said.

I slid from my saddle, grimacing.

"What's the matter with you, Nath? You look like ... Egad! Is that a spear in your back?"

He hurried over and inspected my wound.

"Ouch! I don't need speared again, Brenwar!"

"Why didn't you say something, you fool? You could've bled to death."

"It's not that bad," I gasped. "Only a javelin, right?"

"Sure, and I'm a fairy's uncle. Still, it's a small one. Not barbed for hunting. It's wedged between your armor and your back. Hold this." Brenwar put my reins in my mouth.

"What for?" I tried to ask.

"Just bite down. I've got to pull the spear out."

I shook my head.

Brenwar yanked out the spear. I screamed. It felt like my entire back was pulled out, and I fell to my knees.

"I'm going to need to stitch that up. And quick. Are you sure you are feeling sound? That's a dangerous wound. Another inch it'd be inside a lung."

It hurt, but I'd been stitched up by Brenwar before. Besides, I had some salve that would accelerate the healing.

"All done," he grumbled as he poked his finger in my face, "and next time, tell me something."

"Thanks, Brenwar." I rolled my shoulder, and my back still burned like fire. At least the rain had passed.

"You sure you're feeling well? You don't look well."

"I've been recently skewered. I'd assume that's it."

"Pah ... Yer fine, I guess," he said, walking away.

The sun, warm on my face, a feeling that normally gave me comfort, gave me none. Brenwar, usually full of boasts after a battle, was quiet. I picked up a stone and skipped it from my side of the stream to the other.

"Another dragon saved," I said. "A fairly powerful ruffie, at that."

"Aye," Brenwar said, refilling his canteen. "Some fight, too. Works up the ol' appetite, it does." He thumped his armored belly with his fist. "How about I snare a rabbit or two?"

"I've got my bow."

"Are ye daft? Ye didn't bring yer bow," he argued, his busy face widening with worry.

"What?" I said, "You look like you just swallowed a halfling. Brenwar ..."

The world wobbled beneath me. Bright spots burst in my eyes: pink, green, and yellow. Brenwar's arms stretched and stretched and stretched toward me, beyond me. His face spun like a pinwheel and was gone. Silence. Blackness. I fell, I think.

Finnius stood alongside the High Priestess of the Clerics of Barnabus with a nervous look in his rodent eyes. He'd seen men dead before, but not so many, not like this. He couldn't imagine how Nath Dragon had done all this, but the witnesses, the ones that had survived the horror, assured him he had. The arena beneath the Troll's Toe in Orcen Hold looked like a battlefield. A battle that they had clearly lost, not to mention losing a dragon as well. The High Priestess, however, didn't seem worried. Arms folded over her chest, a dark twinkle in her eyes, a smile cropping up from the corner of her mouth, she said, "It won't be long, Finnius. Nath Dragon will be mine."

CHAPTER 13

I T WAS DARK. I SMELLED burning wood. Meat roasting over a fire. My eyes opened to a brilliant, starlit sky, and I felt whole again. I rolled over to where a campfire blazed and Brenwar kneeled, turning rabbit meat on a spit.

"Dinnertime already?" I got up and walked over.

Brenwar looked at me like I'd come back from the dead.

"What? Has it been a day or more? You look like I've been sleeping for a week." I stretched my arms out and yawned. "I must admit, though, it feels like I've slept for a week, maybe longer. I guess saving dragons is bound to catch up with you."

"Or turning into one," he said. At least, I thought that was what he said.

"Brenwar, is that some kind of joke?"

I looked at him, the sky, and the moon before turning back toward the stream that was no longer there. A very bad feeling overcame me, like a part of my life was missing.

"Say, how'd I get here? Where's the water? Brenwar, how long have I been out?"

He mumbled something.

"Louder," I insisted.

"Three months! Three months, Nath Dragon! And I've been out here counting daisies and trapping furry little animals." He rose to his feet and poked me in the chest. "Now, three months isn't long for a dwarf, but it's not short by any measure, either."

"Why didn't you wake me, then?"

He jumped to his feet and yelled, "Don't you think I tried? I could've set you on fire, and you wouldn't have moved! I should have let the harpies carry you off."

"Harpies?"

"Pah," he said, waving me off.

I raked my fingers through my hair and checked the beard that had grown on my face. I scratched it with nails that were unusually long, on my right hand anyway.

I held my hand out and stared. Brenwar's downcast face stayed down, kicking at the dirt as I looked at the black scales on the fingers of my dragon-like hand.

"Gagh!" I said, jumping away from myself.

I looked at my other hand, the left, and it was fine, but my right—with black, glimmering scales and thick yellow claws like my father's—was a thing of beauty. A rush of energy and excitement went through me as I jumped high in the air and screamed with delight. I felt like a child again.

"I can go home again, Brenwar! I've gotten my scales! Or some scales."

I ran my new and old fingers over my face.

"Brenwar, is my face unchanged?"

He nodded.

I was relieved, but I wasn't certain whether I should have been or not. I shed the blanket from my shoulder, and everything but my right arm was fine, or human at least, and I still wasn't sure if that was a good thing or not. I checked behind me.

"Do I have a tail?'

"No!"

"Why so glum, then, Brenwar? I've gotten scales!" I said, marveling at my arm.

He shrugged and said, "Don't know."

He was being stubborn, naturally, but something bothered me.

"What?"

"I ain't seen no man become a dragon before," he said, taking the rabbit from the spit. "Hungry?"

I gazed at my arm, its diamond-like scales shimmering in the twilight, like broken pieces of coal. I could feel power, true power, like I'd never felt before. I swore my right arm was twice as strong as my left, and my left was already stronger than most men's.

"Come, then, Brenwar! I can't wait a moment longer. It's time to go see my father!"

"So be it then, Nath."

The trek through the Sulfur Marsh at the bottom of the Mountain of Doom had never gone quicker as Brenwar and I made our way through the secret passageway. Most of the time when I came home, I was either half dead, as had been the case the last time, or filled with dread because I had not gained any scales. Despite my father's and my disagreements over the past two centuries, I never wanted to disappoint him. This time, however, I had the upper hand. I had my scales, and my days as a man were numbered.

I took a moment to pause in reflection as I stood outside my father's chamber doors. The detail in the doors and the rest of the caves and tunnels appeared to have a greater meaning to me now. The brass framework interwoven in ornate patterns on the wooden doors said something to me. The symbols carried power.

"So," Brenwar's gruff voice interrupted my thoughts, "are you going inside, or are you going to stand there and gawk? It's a dwarven door, you know. You'd think you'd never seen it before." His thick fingers were playing with his beard. He seemed nervous, if that was at all possible.

"It's fine work. I just never noticed before. Do you think I should knock?"

"There's a first time for everything."

True—in all my years, I hadn't bothered to knock before. I wasn't certain why it was different this time, but it was. This time of all times, the little things seemed to matter.

I looked down at Brenwar's face, then at the door, and lifted my fist to knock. Both doors swung open on their own.

"ENTER, SON, AND MY FRIEND THE DWARF."

I led, my chin held high, like the time I'd saved my first dragon. I felt like a boy again, new and refreshed, a spring in my step because the hard feelings at failed efforts were gone.

My father, the grandest dragon of them all, sat on his throne, his eyes burning like fire. I'd never seen such an expression on him before. Fearsome. Deadly. Secrets as ancient as the world itself protected beneath the impenetrable scales and horns on his skull. His voice was like a volcano about to erupt, turning my swaggering gate into a shuffle.

"COME CLOSER."

The gold pieces piled up were slipping like shale, and the entire cavern seemed to shake. I was thirty yards from the foot of his throne when I opened my mouth to speak; my day of glory had come.

"STOP!"

I froze. Something was wrong. Brenwar dropped to a knee beside me, head down.

My father sat there, monstrous claws clasped in his lap, a side of his razor-sharp teeth bare.

"REMOVE YOUR ARMOR."

"With great joy, Father," I said, unstrapping the buckles on my chestplate. Certainly he had to have noticed my dragon's hand at least, yet he said nothing. Perhaps there was to be more of a ceremony with the full showing. I tossed my armor and garments aside, standing with my naked chest out, my incredible black-scaled arm up high.

My father sucked his breath through his teeth, his face smoldering with fury, and roared so loud I thought the mountain had exploded.

I fell to the ground, holding my ears, crying out and pleading for mercy. I couldn't think or focus; I just screamed as I felt like the entire world was going to end. A sharp cracking sound exploded nearby as one of the marble columns fell. The room filled with heat so hot I could barely breathe. My whole world had gone wrong. I'd never been so terrified.

Somehow I rose to my feet despite all the feeling in my legs being gone. My hands were still clamped over my ears as I watched my father continue his angry bellow. Brenwar was almost covered in treasure, his face devoid of expression, eyes watering like he'd seen a horrible ghost.

I yelled out, "What is wrong, Father?"

His roar stopped, but my ears kept on ringing.

His voice was lower now.

"What have you done?"

I stood, shaking, stupefied, and gawping.

"What have you done?" My father asked again, the rage in his voice gone but the molten steel tone remaining. "Have you ever seen a black-scaled dragon?"

I looked at my arm, shook my head, and said, "No."

Then I realized something must be horribly wrong.

"The ruffie you saved has been here and told me what you have done. I hoped that it was not true, though I knew that it was. Did you even realize that you killed so many?"

The truth was, I didn't have any idea how many I had killed at all. I hadn't even thought about it.

My father looked down, and I felt like it was the last time I'd ever see him again. My heart began to sputter in my chest as I fell to my knees, tears streaming down my cheeks, and begged, "No, father, I'm so sorry. Let me fix this."

"It's too late for that. You have cursed yourself. You are no longer welcome in Dragon Home. You'll take no swords, no gold, no magic … not anything. You are on your own. If there is any hope left, you'll have to find it on your own. I've told you all I can. Now go, to never return unless those scales are a different color."

My father gave me one long, lasting look with nothing but sadness and disappointment in his eyes. I'd failed him, I knew it, for the last time. I felt smaller than the tiniest coin in the room as he turned, walked away, and disappeared back into the mural.

Alone, I wept my way through my father's throne room, never looking back, through Dragon Home, through the Sulfur Marsh, until I wept no more.

Bearded and lonely, I sat inside a cave at least a hundred leagues from my father as another season passed while I contemplated my failure in self-pity. No men killed. No dragons saved. My cursed black scales remained.

If there is any hope left, you'll have to find it on your own, my father had said.

He'd said many things, and it was time I put them together. I rose from the crag where I had stooped and bellowed the fiercest bellow I could muster. It was time to figure out what I must do to become a dragon, and a very good one at that. Like my father.

From out of nowhere, Brenwar showed up and tossed a beautiful sword at my feet. It was Fang.

"Brenwar! How did you get this?" I asked in alarm and jubilation.

"Yer father only said *you* couldn't take anything from his cavern. He didn't say anything about me." He winked and added, "And that isn't all I got, either."

Thus begins the Chronicles of Dragon.

THE CHRONICLES of DRAGON

Dragon Bones and Tombstones

-BOOK 2-

CRAIG HALLORAN

PROLOGUE

STARLIGHT. THE LAND OF NALZAMBOR was filled with stars, more than could be counted, more than could be seen. The biggest one, the most brilliant, lingered behind the moon like the twinkling eye of a dragon. But now was not the time to pay attention to such beautiful things. Not the shimmering waters, the soft grasses, the gentle breeze, or the trees filled with fruit aplenty. No, such things didn't matter now in the mystic land of Nalzambor, at least not when death, despite all the beauty, still whispered in the air.

CHAPTER 1

I SAT HIGH IN THE BRANCHES, spying the orcen camp below. Brenwar and I had spent weeks trying locate it. Brenwar wasn't with me. He didn't climb trees, not unless he really had to.

Below, the gruff voices bellowed and drank, celebrating their prized catch: an evergreen dragon. I could see her well from my perch. She was a rare flower, a thing of beauty among the decay of mankind. Small and young, the creature was no bigger than a man. Her tail, slender and serpentine, curled around her body as she lay still. Green, a brilliant green like emeralds, was the color of her scales. Her underbelly was not fully developed, yet it was armored in citrine yellow. Long necked, with a small nose and snout, she had two leathery wings folded over her back. Her chest was rising and falling as if she was out of breath. I could sense her fear as she lay alone and helpless. I had to free her; after all, that's what I did. Or at least, what I was supposed to be doing.

I watched and waited. Certainly Brenwar's signal would come at any moment. The waiting wasn't so bad. And the watching part was another matter. Watching orcs—all of which were brawny, fatty, and boar-like in the face with little tusks jutting from the bottom of the mouths—was offensive. They were crude.

One sat on a log by the fire, picked his nose, poured a nasty stew in his mouth, and belched. Another was plucking the lice from his beard while a different one picked lice from his hair and tossed them into the iron pot of stew. Their purpose in my world was a mystery, because I'd yet to see anything good from a single one of them, ever.

Where are you, Brenwar?

The moon rose to a full zenith, a full, bright yellow, and it wasn't long before the party of orcs began to drift into sleep.

Two orcen guards stood watch alongside a wagon that housed the metal cage that contained the dragon. Both were alert, chests out and spears ready. I knew from experience that the slightest abnormality in the camp would make them sound the alarm. Sneaking up on them wasn't a very good idea. I could get one shot off with my bow, killing one, but getting the second shot off before the alarm sounded would be difficult. And I had to remember that I was not supposed to kill.

My back was beginning to ache, and my legs were becoming numb. I needed to move. Brenwar, on the other hand, well, he could stand like a statue for days. I've seen him do it. He could beat a stone in a standing-still contest. But me, no. I was a man of action, and I had things to do. A dragon was suffering, endangered, helpless. It made me feel miserable, too. With or without Brenwar, I was going to free the dragon. I didn't rustle a single leaf as I climbed down. A stiff breeze blew my hair into my eyes. It was good, being downwind from the camp. The orcs had snouts almost as good as those of hounds, and I had to be careful they didn't catch wind of me. Of course, on the flip side, I got plenty a noseful of their foul dander.

Wretched things.

I never ate bacon because of them, and I love meat, in all its forms and flavors.

I hunched down behind the tree I'd been sitting in and watched as one of the orcs poked at the dragon with the butt of his spear. It lit a fire in me as I watched the little dragon's tail tighten around her body. The orcs' mocking laughter stirred the warrior within me. My impulses took over. My anger rose.

Control, Nath. Keep it under control.

I reached for my bow, Akron. Compact in size, forged by magic, it hung from the armor on my back. I snapped it into place.

Snap. Clatch. Snap.

The bowstring coiled into place like a living thing. Akron, a wonderful weapon made in the forges of the elves, was a gift from long ago. I spit on the tip of my arrow and rubbed it in. The black arrowhead began to glow with a yellow fire as I nocked it. My dragon arm was steady, solid as a red oak. My aim was true as I listened to the stretching sound of the bowstring. The orcs' throats were as clear as the nose on my face.

Save the dragon. Kill them all if you have to.

Oh, how much I wanted to. But killing, no matter how evil the opponents, wasn't the best way to earn my scales. I hated that part. It was so hard to understand.

Small breath. Release.

Twang!

A streak of yellow light whizzed through the night, soaring past the orcs' heads and into the lock on the dragon's cage. The orcs jumped as if their feet were on fire, gawping at the arrow juttering inside the metal lock.

The dragon remained still.

One orc grabbed his head, bewildered, studying the arrow in the lock.

Wait for it.

I nocked the next arrow.

Boom!

The arrow exploded. The orcs fell to the ground. The sound wasn't so loud, except it came in the dead of night, and in all likelihood I had woken up everything sleeping for a quarter mile. As I watched the pieces of the large metal lock scatter everywhere, the green dragon came to life, her small winged arms clawing at the cage. The dazed orcs scrambled back to their feet, fighting to secure the cage door, one putting his body into it, the other trying to lock it with something else.

Twang!

The orc screamed as the arrow imbedded itself in its ankle.

Twang!

I sent the other howling to the ground as I caught it in its hip.

Two down, none dead, but the dragon was still trapped inside.

Drat!

The camp was a flurry of activity now. Orcs rose from under their blankets, ripped their swords from their belts, and began barking orders. The dragon thrashed inside her cage. The latch, lock or no lock, was still holding. I moved. Bounding across the camp, ducking under a chopping axe, I lowered my shoulder, bowling the next orc over. In a single bound, I made it to the wagon and pulled the cage door free.

A thunderous cry of alarm went up as the dragon's long neck jutted out. She stepped from the cage, spreading her magnificent wings in the moonlight. With a single whoosh, she darted into the sky and disappeared from sight. They're fast. So am I, but the problem is—I can't fly!

"You're welcome!" I yelled, for all the good it did. Of all the dragons I saved, none ever thanked me. Not that they could talk. Well, some could. Most couldn't, and I only knew a few that did. But one would think, for all the times I helped them, they'd at least come back and help me, but they never came.

"Kill him!" the orcs yelled, surrounding me.

I leapt into the wagon and pulled out Fang, its blade glimmering like wildfire. Still, none fled. The orcs were stubborn like that, always letting their greedy intentions get the better of them. The orcs were not cowardly, just stupid. They closed in, weapons brandished, their faces eager for my blood. An orc with a face like cottage cheese let out an angry cry, and they charged.

I leapt on top of the cage as a battle axe whacked a chunk out of the wagon where I had been standing. One by one, they jumped into the wagon, heavy swings nipping at my toes as I danced and batted their steel away, careful not to let my feet slip between the bars. It was chaos as one fought over top of another, trying to tear my legs from underneath me and cut me down in a tide of my own blood.

The dragon I had freed, as with all dragons, was worth a lot. Worth enough for these thugs and rogues to gorge themselves on ale and food for months, maybe even a year. If you ever want to make somebody really mad, just take their money.

The nearest orc bellowed as I sank my blade, Fang, into its shoulder. Fang is short for its real name that is as hard to pronounce as it is to spell, at least for me.

Impossibly long. What else should I expect of a sword made by my father? *Chop! Chop! Clang!*

Their blows rattled the cage, tearing more wood from the wagon. I wobbled on my legs as two more of the beastly orcs heaved the wagon in an attempt to shake me to the ground. It was getting hot now, my breath heavy as my sword arm became heavy from deflecting all their blows. My muscles were being put to the test as I struck quickly, clipping an ear, before dancing away from another's broad stroke. I slipped. My foot went down between the cage bars, catching my knee on the metal, filling my head with an explosion of pain. I cried out.

"We've got him! Kill him!"

Three orcs surrounded me, trying to pin my arms down. I cracked one in the nose with the sword's pommel and punched another in the jaw. Its head rocked back, but my fist stung from the blow. The orc wrapped its meaty arms around my throat, arcing my spine like a bow, bending me backward over the cage.

I was suffocating. The sweaty thing had me, and I could smell its breath, as foul as garbage. I heaved. It heaved back as I cried out in agony. My leg, still pinned between the cage bars, was ready to snap. My sword, Fang, was useless. I let it slip through my fingers, hanging onto the pommel, revealing a small dagger within that I called Dragon Claw.

Slice!

I stabbed the orc's belly. It recoiled and teetered from the wagon. Bloody dagger in hand, I jabbed it into the second orc's arm. It had power, determination. It was me or him. I had the feeling that before I poked another dozen holes in its arm, my leg would break. The pressure was building, and I felt the tendons in my knee stretching. I swung at him with my dagger, but I could not reach him.

"Let go! Beast! Let go!" My lungs were bursting inside my chest as I cleared my leg from the cage and dodged another blow. I hopped to the ground, rolled over Fang, and reinserted Dragon Claw in the pommel.

Now ten orcs still lived, each snorting in open hostility, not a one willing to yield, though the one I had stabbed in the belly might have been dying, based off the pain-filled groans I could hear. Unfortunate, but it happens. I fought for my breath. It was time to speak.

"This has gone far enough, orcs. I've scratched you, maimed you, but I can do much, much worse," I said, pulling back my shoulders and standing taller than their tallest—and orcs are big, bigger than men on average. My voice was as big as me, but that didn't really matter if the orcs were too stupid to recognize Common. I could always speak in orcen if I wished, but why lower my standards? They might take that as a compliment.

"So, what will it be, little piggies?" I said, twirling Fang's glowing blade through the air. "Limp home and live," I shrugged. "Or die." Which was a bluff, because I'm not supposed to kill them, remember? If anything, they'd figure I was as bad a shot with a bow as I was at swinging my sword.

Dripping blood from their injuries, lathered in sweat—orcs sweated more than anything else I knew—they gathered closer. I'd played the game too long. It was time to get serious.

Dragon saved. Disappear? Disarm? Oh, what to do? Where in Nalzambor is Brenwar?! Fang glimmered in the grip of my fingers, a bright piece of steel that shimmered with radiant, living light. It felt alive in my hand. It was hefty, its flat blade wide, its hilt big enough for two hands, but in my grasp it was as light as a stick, perfect in weight and balance.

Shing!

I struck the belt buckle of the nearest orc, dropping his pants over his ankles. The rest jumped back. But as far as they were concerned, it was another miss.

Oh, great, they're going to attack.

They came at me like a sweaty swarm of hornets, steel stingers in their grasp, ready to skewer me alive.

I was big, an easy target, but I was fast, too.

"Kill him!" the orc said, kneeling down and trying to pick his pants up from the ground. I think "kill" is a very common word for orcs, meaning the same in their language as in mine. I ducked just in time as a sword whistled over my head. I rolled under the wagon to the other side. My blood, still pumping from the moment this all had started, was just warming up. The warrior in me had lost patience when I popped up on the other side and began swinging.

Crack!

I clipped one under the chin with the butt of my sword.

Glitch!

I stabbed another in the thigh, bringing a forthcoming howl and limp.

Slice!

Another orc clutched its bleeding arm where I cut clean through the triceps. I meant to do that.

Parry!

Clang!

A battle axe clattered into the back of the wagon, drawing astonished grunts. I shifted behind the next attacker that was poised to poke a hole in my back with a spear.

Chop!

I sliced though the shaft of the spear, drove my sword into the beast's shoulder, and spun away from another two-handed blow.

Parry.

Clang!

Fang tore a blade from its wielder's grasp.

Glitch!

I stabbed the orc in the chest and watched it, beady eyes now wide, fall over and die.

Oops!

Yes, I'm not supposed to kill other people in order to earn my scales, but I don't consider orcs people. And no one can really say whether or not killing something evil prevents me from getting my scales. And my father said I could kill if my life was in danger. I was pretty sure it was.

I punched an orc in the face with my dragon fist, my right hand. Stabbed Fang into the shoulder with my left arm. It was like having a weapon in each hand, but my dragon arm and Fang had issues, and I'll talk about that later.

I kept the pressure up, my lungs burning, sweat dripping from my hair into my face as I watched all the remaining orcs try to scramble away from my wrath. Like most people, they were hard headed until faced with the possibility of an inevitable death. Then and only then they became reasonable.

The orcs cried out. Bleeding from wounds, some ran; others began to grovel and pray. I ignored them. They could live … for now. Though I was certain it was a mistake. I fought for my breath and thirsted.

"Thanks for the help, Fang," I said to my sword. I swear it could hear me.

Fang responded with the hyper-low hum of a tuning fork. That was the magic within. Ancient. Mysterious and wonderful.

I ran my battle-numbed fingers over the two dragon faces on the brass-fit pommel, their gemstone eyes red and green. I took a deep breath and slipped it back into the scabbard that hung at my side.

I looked back at the orcs, their expressions defeated yet evil. I could have told them, "Let the dragons alone or I'll be back," but what good would that do? Now it was time to depart and find Brenwar. I felt good as I dashed into the woods and disappeared into the night. One more dragon in the land saved from the clutches of evil, and sometimes from the clutches of the self-proclaimed good as well.

You see, dragons are hard to find, but not so hard to catch. They, like most people, like shiny things: gems, pearls, gold, diamonds, silver, and did I mention gold? Dragons love gold as much as I hate orcs. If you can find them and leave a pile of gold near their nests, caves, nooks, or holes, chances are, like a trout and a silvery lure, they'll try to snatch it. Drop a net over them, and they're yours, but beware. With claws as sharp as swords, teeth as cutting as knives, and breath as dangerous as anything you ever saw, they aren't so easy to take alive. That evergreen dragon was a little one, but there are others twenty times her size.

My good deed was done, and I turned to walk away.

Clatch-Zip!

Something exploded in my leg.

"Argh!"

Fool! I stumbled to the ground. My chest and stomach were burning like fire. It felt like my entire core was being torn apart as I rose to my feet and ran. I looked down to see a crossbow bolt sticking through my thigh. It hurt. It was a good shot. I dashed into the woods, one foot stumbling past the other, branches slapping my face. *Orcs!* That's the problem with leaving them alive: if you do, they don't usually stop until you're dead.

CHAPTER 2

ANOTHER BOLT WHIZZED PAST MY head. I half crawled, half limped, and somehow dove behind the cover of a red oak tree.

Thunk! Thunk!

I made it!

"Drat!" I said, reaching down and yanking the bolt from the back of my leg. "Stupid orcs! How'd they catch up on me so fast?"

I stood up, groaning, my back against the tree, one bolt sailing past, followed by another. I listened. It sounded like there were only two of them, but there might have been three rustling in the bushes and half grunting, half whispering their plans to one another. It seemed they had me right where they wanted me: trapped, with nowhere to run, not that I could. Well, certainly I could outsmart a few orcs.

Whop!

Bam!

Boom!

I stiffened. What was that? What was that, indeed. The sounds of battle didn't come from me but from beyond the tree. I stood with Fang in my grip and peeked around the bend in the tree.

"Come out from behind there, Nath Dragon!"

I let out a sigh. It was Brenwar, standing tall, for a dwarf at least, three orcs crumpled at his feet.

"Hah!" I said, limping forward, using Fang as a crutch. "It's about time you showed up, Brenwar!"

He eyed me, and I knew what was next: a lecture. Brenwar liked to lecture me on the things I did wrong, but this time it would be different. This time he was wrong and I was right.

Brenwar hefted his war axe over the plate armor on his shoulder.

His voice was gruff when he said, "I told you to wait for my signal, Dragon."

One of the orcs started to move.

Brenwar whacked it in the head with his hammer. "But you couldn't wait, could you? Just a few more minutes was all I needed. But once again, you rushed headlong into danger without thinking about the consequences." He eyed the blood dripping from my leg.

I slid Fang back into its sheath and folded my arms across my chest. "My leg will be fine. It's not that bad." I tried not to grimace, but I did. "And none of this would have happened if you would have been there in the first place."

Brenwar was scowling now.

I threw my arms up. This wasn't my fault. It was his. "I couldn't wait forever. You know how I feel about that. Seeing a dragon caged infuriates me."

An angry growl rose in his throat.

I could feel the heat coming off of him, hot like a furnace.

"I'm not talking about your leg, NATH!"

He stepped over a fallen long and punched me so hard in my chest I could feel it through my armor.

"You killed two orcs, fool!" He hit me again, same spot, but harder.

I fell to the ground.

"You killed—AGAIN!"

So I did. But it was in self-defense, and Father said that was all right, if you had to. Now my own anger was beginning to rise. No one pushes me around. No dwarf. No man. No orc and no dragon. I started to rise, but a jabbing pain throbbed in my leg. So I pointed at him instead.

"Don't do that again, Brenwar! What I did was in self-defense. It's as much the orcs' fault as it is mine."

Brenwar slammed the blade of his war axe into the log.

I winced. He was angry, much more so than I.

He sat on the log and looked me square in the eye.

"Patience, Nath. I was on my way. If you would have just waited, you wouldn't have had to kill any of them. I'd have distracted them while you freed the dragon. Just like we've been doing for months now." He shook his head as he tugged at his beard with his iron fingers. "Now look at you."

"What?" I said, checking over myself. I didn't see anything wrong other than the hole in my leg. "Is it my face?" I patted it over. "Do you have my mirror? Brenwar, where's the mirror?"

Brenwar just stared at me, pupils blank, eyes expressionless.

"There's something wrong, all right," he said.

I was mortified. Was it possible I'd gained black dragon eyes or a black dragon's snout? Everything felt the same, but I could not help but wonder. "Brenwar, tell me! What is it?"

He muttered something.

"What?!"

Brenwar did something he rarely does unless he's finished a few tankards of ale. He smiled. Or at least I thought he did. It was hard to tell underneath his black beard that looked like wool from a lamb.

"Are you jesting with me?" I asked, standing back up, ignoring the pain. As my anger rose, I looked down on him. "Brenwar, why would you do such a thing? It's not something to be joking about. Not at all."

He let out a short chuckle, pointed at me, and said, "You'll think better of it next time, before you start carving into orcs or any other kind. Ha! You should have seen your eyes! You should be worried. And you should be thanking me, too. Your father told me to keep you in line. And you're out of line right now."

I stormed away. The pain in my leg wasn't so bothersome when I was angry, but it still hurt. But something else ached worse: my heart. I ripped a hunk of a tree out with my dragon-clawed hand, took a seat behind it, and wiped the dampness from my eyes. I missed my father and my home in the Mountain of Doom. And even though I'd been away years longer, it already seemed like I'd been gone forever. There was no worse feeling than knowing I could never go home again.

I sat there and sulked for the next few hours. My heart was heavy, and my angry thoughts turned sad as the moon dipped from view with the sun. Brenwar was right, of course; he always was. You would think that after two hundred years of life I'd know much better by now, but I had such a hard time controlling myself. I hated dragon poachers and all their kind, and I'd be lying if I didn't admit to loving the lust for battle. I had to be better, be wiser, if I was going to solve the riddle that had become my arm and hand. I had to turn my scales any color other than black.

"You ready?" Brenwar said, stepping into view.

I nodded.

"Brenwar, how many dragons must I free to get things back to normal? We've freed so many dragons recently, at least seven that I count. Father said that for every life you take, a life you must save, or something like that. I've saved more lives than I've taken. In all of these months, only those two orcs have I killed, and only because I was trying to save myself from death."

He shook his head and grunted.

"Well thanks, Brenwar," I said, shaking my head. I knew it wasn't up to him to solve my problems. I gazed at my right arm, the dragon arm. It seemed a great way to compensate a man that was left handed. If anything, it did things that my left could not do. It was stronger, faster, and though I shouldn't admit it, it was a magnificent thing.

Whop!

I ducked down. Brenwar slammed his axe into the tree, inches above my head.

"Have you gone mad, Brenwar? You almost took my head off!"

He ripped his war hammer out of the tree and yelled at me.

"I should be taking your arm off, Nath! It's your problem!"

"I know that!" I shouted back. I wasn't an idiot. Why would he say such a thing?

"No, you fool! That's not what I mean. If you could just see yourself looking at it. You like it! You crave it! Your eyes are like a dwarf's in a gold rush: hungry as a bear for honey. Thirsty as a fish out of water." He waggled his dwarven hammer in my face. "You have a dangerous look in those eyes of yours. The kind men get when they have enough power and want more."

I laughed him off as he walked away. "You're being ridiculous, Brenwar." I carved my initials in a rock with my dragon claw. It was another one of those awesome things I liked to do. I smiled as I followed him, saying, "I don't like it." *I love it!*

CHAPTER 3

TRAVEL WAS SLOW GOING FOR the next couple of days, and Brenwar had barely said a word, which wasn't odd for a dwarf, but I could still tell he held a grudge.

I stopped, pulled off my boots, and dumped some gravel from them. We were in the Shale Hills, a network of ravines and green forests with hilltops and valleys covered in a blue-grey shale.

"Hold up, Brenwar," I said, stuffing my boot back on.

The journey would have been more pleasant on horseback, but we'd given them up two rescues ago. Brenwar said they made too much noise. I agreed, much to my regret now. My wounded leg was still in agony. I'd used up the last healing vial on the last adventure. But I wasn't letting it slow us down. I poured out the shale from my second boot, stuffed it back on, and began my tracking of Brenwar.

His tracks, faint but discernible to my eye, led me to a stream that gently flowed over a bed of smooth shale. It was a nice place, lots of ferns, red and green, both sides lined by pines. On the other side of the stream sat Brenwar, refilling his canteen, taking a drink, then refilling it again. He eyed me, shook his head, and turned away. I was starting to get sick of this now.

"Brenwar, are you done pouting at me? Not communicating isn't going to solve my problem. A little advice, such as where we are going, wouldn't be so bad right now." I skipped a stone across the stream. "Of course, I could always rescue dragons all by myself."

"Is that so?"

Well, it was so, but I wasn't going to say that. Brenwar taught me everything I know about tracking, but I fared pretty well on my own now. The fact that I was part dragon gave me an edge even he didn't have, but his centuries of experience provided him with an edge that I had not yet developed. Besides, I needed Brenwar to keep me under control. I needed that, but I wouldn't admit it to him.

I sloshed across the water and stuck my nose down in his face. He still hadn't answered a question of mine. And I was beginning to suspect maybe it wasn't me but rather the questions he didn't want to answer. "Brenwar, why did you take so long to arrive back at the orcen camp?"

He started to turn away, but I stopped him.

"Let go, Dragon. It wasn't so long," he huffed. "It hardly makes a difference how long it was now, anyway." He started to pull away.

I exclaimed, "I waited up in the tree for hours!"

He huffed. "So?"

"No, no, no, no, Brenwar. Not a couple of hours—several hours. You've never left me hanging around that long before."

I got in his face.

He tried to look away.

I could see it in his eyes: he was hiding something. There was certainly something he didn't want to tell me. I wanted to know what that was. It was driving me crazy now.

"Tell me, Brenwar, or I'll ask you every minute of the journey. I'll talk like a chatterboxing gnome if I must. You know how good I am at it."

"All right then!" He shoved himself back and shook his head. "I had to go."

I gave him a funny look. It didn't make any sense to me what he meant.

"Go where?" I said.

He grunted, gestured with his hands, looked around and whispered, "I—had—to—go." He nodded toward the ground.

"Huh?"

He made another gesture I didn't comprehend. Then another.

"Oh!" I didn't know what to think at first, but like a sock in the belly, it hit me. I started laughing so hard that I fell over. My voice echoed from one end of the ravine to the other.

"Will you quit laughing, you idiot! You'll bring the entire hills upon us!" He tried to stop me. "Quit that!"

It didn't do any good. I couldn't get rid of the thought of Brenwar being late because he had to go to the bathroom!

"Did you pile or pee?" I asked, only to erupt in laughter once more. "BRAWAH-AH-AH-HA!"

"Pah! Both, if you must know!"

I was still laughing when I said, "Well, it's nothing to be embarrassed about." I was being sincere.

"Ho! It's not like that happens often at all... er," he was twisting his beard and rubbing the back of his head, "...it happens. Now just leave me alone."

He walked away, leaving me alone with my laughter. Great dragons! I hadn't laughed like that in ages. There was nothing quite like a bellyful of joy to take away the aches and pains of the soul. I caught my breath, giggled a little more, and sat up on the stream bank.

It took a while before Brenwar sauntered back.

"Let's go, Laughing Dragon."

I held my finger up.

"Certainly, but my question remains unanswered. You only told me part of the answer. You told me the circumstance, but I still don't understand why having to relieve yourself took so long. Hours, at least?"

He grumbled and kicked at the ground.

"Did you have to go really far away? Were your bowels bound up? Was there—"

"No! No! And No!" he said, looking as if he wanted to hit me again. "I'm a dwarf! We don't go all the time. We can hold our water weeks at a time if we want to! And when we go, it takes some time, concentration, and privacy. Happy are we now, Nosey Dragon?"

"Ah!" I held my finger up once more, not my dragon finger, mind you. "One more question, though."

He folded his arms across his chest and sighed.

"What is it?"

I reached out, and he helped me to my feet.

"Is that why you're always so grumpy?"

Up the stream we went, hour after hour, from dusk until dawn. Brenwar was speaking more—well, maybe a few words per hour. When he's onto something, he's all business about it, and according to him, he had heard long ago that many dragons were held captive deep in the Shale Hills.

"How many?" I asked him.

He shrugged and said, "How should I know?"

Well, I hoped it wasn't too many. In most cases, we only rescued one dragon at a time, but I'd rescued as many as three on one occasion. Little ones: one bronze, one green, one red, their scales like shiny mineral stones.

But dragons weren't all just one color. They had different abilities as well. Some could fly. Others could swim, and some could even cast spells. That's right, and you shouldn't be surprised, because they are magical creatures, after all. Even I had magic like that, but I didn't have the hang of it yet.

I stopped in the stream, the waters rushing over my boots. Some loose shale was sliding down a hill. Brenwar was looking at me and I at him. Something was coming down the hill. Something big. I made my way into the reeds along the bank. Brenwar did the same. I readied my bow, Akron, and waited.

Whatever had caused the disturbance on the hillside wasn't moving now, but in my bones I could feel that something was coming. It was dusk, and many creatures in the forest came out at that time to hunt. I filled my nostrils and exhaled in relief. It wasn't one of the giant races, but I wasn't comfortable that I couldn't smell anything, either. That left me uncertain. Curious, too.

I shifted around in the reeds and water, trying to get a better look up the hill. It was dim, the time of day that the dipping sunlight casts the darkest shadows. There is no moon or sun to adjust your sight. That's when your other senses come in. You can't always trust your eyes, but your nose and ears can serve you just as well if you let them. I stepped farther out of the reeds. The wind rustled the leaves in the trees. The waters gurgled at my feet, but I heard the faintest sound. A heavy step. Two heavy steps. I thought what was coming was big, certainly bigger than me, which doesn't mean much.

"Dragon," a voice said in a hushed whisper, "get back here."

It was Brenwar, but I wasn't going to listen. I had my bow, and I was fast, so if something was going to try and eat me, it would have to catch me first. Up and down stream I noticed the last glimmers of sunlight. I was more than halfway across when something emerged from the woods. A dark mass on two legs with arms as long as its feet crept through and huddled by the waters. Its head was large, more shoulders than neck, almost the size of a horse's but more like a man. It looked right through me then scooped a handful of water into its mouth. The icy look in its eyes froze me, and how it did not see me, I didn't know. It just wasn't one of those things I recall ever seeing before.

I held my arm out behind me and made a sign of caution. I was sure Brenwar's keen eyes would pick it out. The creature's head turned my way again, tilted, and paused. Now my heart was racing. I saw the white of its teeth. A set of fangs in particular. Its body stiffened, and something fluttered at its side. It looked as if the ape-like creature had—*wings!* It came closer, wading into the stream, big fists splashing in the water.

I didn't move. I didn't dare move. The last thing you should do when you are facing the unknown is panic. Or move, until you figure out what that move is going to be. My bow was ready. It was just another extension of my body after years of practice and training. If the winged ape made any sudden moves, I would shoot a pointed feather into it. But this thing was big, much bigger than me, and I wasn't going to start a fight with it if I didn't have to. It's not as if it was an orc or a lizard man. If that were the case, I'd have shot ten times already.

It growled, spread its wings, pounded its chest, and charged.

CHAPTER 4

MY FIRST SHOT ZINGED OVER the ape's head. Not because my aim was off, but because it wasn't. That thing was fast. Really fast, almost as fast as me, I hated to admit. My second shot hit the pack of muscles in its shoulder and bounced off like a toothpick hitting a wall of stone. You see, there's a difference among the three types of arrows I use: non-magic arrows for hunting, moorite ones that can shoot through almost anything, and enchanted ones with special abilities. I didn't need a magic one ninety-nine times out of a hundred, but I needed one right now.

Drat!

And the third shot, a magic arrow from my quiver, well that wasn't going to happen. The ape was too close, too quick, and just a few yards from rushing into me. I hooked Akron over my shoulders. The dwarven armor Brenwar had made me had a design for that. I braced myself for impact, reaching down to wrap my hand around the hilt of Fang.

Too late, Dragon!

Brenwar jumped from the reeds and slammed his war hammer into the ape's chest, drawing forth a howl of anger. Brenwar was a couple hundred pounds of solid brawn facing eight hundred pounds of raw muscle.

The ape snatched Brenwar from the waters of the stream, hoisted him over its head, and hurled him like a log. He disappeared into the woods.

Brenwar would never live that down if we lived to tell about it, and I wasn't ready to die without recounting it one last time.

I ripped Fang from its scabbard and thrust at the ape's belly.

It jumped over top of me, landed in the stream, and kicked me in the back.

I slammed into a boulder, and Fang almost slipped from my grip. I held on as I fought to regain the wind that had been knocked out of me. Whatever that thing was, it was strong, fast—a real monster. Not as big as many I've faced but still bigger than me.

It came at me again, face full of fury, its black eyes intelligent and cunning. A real killer.

I chopped.

It twisted.

I stabbed.

It jumped.

I cut.

It ducked.

I pressed the attack.

It howled as I clipped its arm. It shuffled backward, spread its wings, and flew away, disappearing into the night.

Eyes skyward, I stood, alone, basking in the light of my sword's glow. Where did that thing go? I whirled around as Brenwar burst from the brush, brandishing his hammer.

"Where is that thing? Nobody! Not nothing, not anything throws a dwarf without permission! Especially when yer not a dwarf!"

"I think I scared it away," I said, sheathing my sword. My leg was aching more now than ever and had started to bleed again. "What was that, Brenwar? Any idea at all?"

The once-quiet forest was alive and well now. The night owls hooted, and the pixies were singing. Of course, the pixies often disguised themselves as crickets and such. It was really hard to tell the difference.

"I don't know what that was," Brenwar said. "It's not any part of the lore that I know, and the dwarves are well schooled on all the creatures and monsters of this world." He stormed up the stream. "But whatever it is, I'm going to see that it doesn't throw a dwarf anymore. Not ever! I'll have its head, I will!"

I unhooked Akron and loaded a magic arrow. I wasn't going to take any chances. Whatever that thing was, well, I'm certain it would have torn me apart without Fang's help. And don't get me wrong: I've been in plenty of fights without my sword. This thing was different. And its eyes had left an uncomfortable impression on me. And that was dangerous. That worried me.

Ahead, Brenwar had started a new path out of the water and along the tree line. It seemed he didn't want to take any more chances being out in the open. As for me, I remained in the middle of the water, bow with arrow, scanning the skyline behind and below. If that thing was up there, I still wanted it to see me. The fight in me wasn't finished just yet, as my senses and instincts were challenged. It was one of those things that my father had instructed me to work on. He said I needed self-control, and I'm sure he was right, but I needed to test myself, too. I wanted to be ready for anything, and I always felt like I was, until recently.

The moon had risen over the treetops now and shone over the water. The heavy spots of clouds spotted the sky like dull grey orbs that absorbed the moonlight. My magic arrow tip twinkled like a sliver of mercy, so bright and shiny it was. The magic arrows could penetrate just about anything, as the tips were of a dwarven made metal called moorite. Brenwar had made the arrows for me himself, and his people had blessed them with accuracy and strength. No winged ape was going to dodge one of these. No, it better not come back, but I hoped it would. I wanted to know what that thing was.

"Brenwar," I said, "do you want to camp? It's getting late."

I suppose," he replied, "but I'm not making a fire. I'll not have that black fiend sneak up on me at night."

I couldn't agree more. There was no need for a fire on such a warm night, and for the most part we made fire to roast the critters that we hunted. We had other things of the dwarven sort packed up to eat: strips of dried beef and a round disk of blessed bread that would fill your belly for hours. It didn't make for the tastiest of meals, and you had to wash it down with a lot of water, but it would get you through the day. I wasn't hungry at the moment anyway. Besides, there was nothing like fishing in the morning and the smell of fish roasting over an open fire. And this stream was full of trout bigger than my feet. I could feel them swimming by as I waded in the waters.

"You should rest that wounded leg," Brenwar suggested.

I nodded and gave in.

The next morning, I woke up after a restless sleep that left me feeling empty and edgy. I have to admit that we dragons like our sleep, even though dragons don't require it. I did, however, because I was still more man than dragon. But that night my dreams were filled with darkness. The winged ape was there, a shadow in the background. There was a graveyard as well and dragons, many dragons, some living and many dead.

"Ye were restless," Brenwar said, as he roasted a large trout I'd caught earlier.

Brenwar didn't sleep much. He slept and guarded at once somehow, a dwarven art I never had much interest in. It was one of the advantages to having him around like this. And it probably was another good explanation as to why dwarves could be so cranky—sleep deprivation. But they did sleep, just not for very long, or unless it was after one of their harvest festivals when they'd eat, drink, and be merry for weeks on end and sleep for days, even weeks after that.

"No, I didn't sleep well at all," I said, tightening the bandage on my leg, "but the rest isn't bothering me, that black creature is. I want to know what that thing was, Brenwar. It was dangerous."

He tossed me a hunk of cooked fish and said, "We're rescuing dragons, not hunting monsters. I don't think that creature is a threat to us. I just think we surprised it, is all. It's someone else's problem now. Eat. I'm ready to go."

"Ah, you just don't want it to toss you around again."

"That's enough, Dragon! I'm in no mood for your humor, and you better not be telling anyone about that," Brenwar warned. "I've got plenty of tales I could tell about you, but I don't."

I smiled. "Fair enough, friend. Consider the incident stricken from my lips forever, but not forgotten."

We filled our bellies with fish and broke camp. My irritation subsided, and my stiff leg began to loosen as the bright sun of the new day warmed my face. It seemed to lift that cloud of darkness within.

"So, where do you think these dragons are that we're going after? What have you heard?"

"There's always poachers in the hills, hiding something or another. I just figured we'd go and poke our noses around. It's well known that these hills hide many things, both good and evil."

Brenwar's answer was pretty vague, but the dwarves didn't often get into the details unless you were talking about building, mining, or blacksmithing. Then they became a waterfall of information, and I must admit, I didn't really want a lengthy explanation either, but I needed some kind of guidance.

After an hour more of hiking, we'd abandoned the stream and resumed our climb up the loose foothills. Tiny bits of shale had found their way into my boots and were digging into my toes, but I trudged along behind Brenwar. He was surefooted and steady, not likely to be slowed by anything. Still, it bothered me that he hadn't said much about where we were going.

In the dragon business, I came across information in the cities and villages. People talked. People talked a lot, and even the best-kept secrets were never really secrets, just something spoken of less rather than more. But at the mere mention of dragons, if someone knew something, in most cases their eyes lit up. Sometimes it took patience, other times charm, bribes, or a stern convincing, but it often gave me another direction to go on. Once I found the right path, I could figure out the rest of the clues from there.

We crested another hilltop, miles now above the stream, the hundred-foot-high evergreen trees swaying in the wind. I tied my mane of red-brown hair behind my head and took a drink from my canteen. So far as I could tell, we were in the middle of nowhere. Just some forest leagues away from civilization, and I had a feeling Brenwar wanted it that way. I was certain he was keeping me out of trouble by keeping me from the cities. It hurt to think about it, actually.

I missed the cities, but my dragon arm caused me to stick out like a sore thumb. I had a way to cover it up if I had to, but what would all of those fawning women think? A man with a dragon arm. As much as I loved it, I was insecure about it. I didn't want people to think it was a cursed thing.

Brenwar headed down the hilltop and started toward another. This forest, unlike most, didn't have all the signs of life of the others. Other than the trees, the rocky ground didn't support roots for the small plants that fed the critters and bucks. That made the hunting more scarce and made the hills seem more dangerous. It was a natural place, but it was grim and foreboding with the black ground against the green.

I woke up from the dullness of the journey when I heard the sound of an axe chopping into wood. I couldn't imagine why anyone would be cutting down trees this deep in the forest. But stranger things happened in Nalzambor, I figured, as Brenwar and I trod down the hill to investigate.

I couldn't see a person, but the chopping sounds remained steady. On silent feet, I closed in, only to discover the echoes had drifted farther down the hill. I motioned for Brenwar. I was going to lead this time.

The chopping stopped. I didn't hear, smell, or see anything out of the ordinary. But as the wind drifted into my nose, I smelled something out of the ordinary in the forest. Brenwar had a look of concern on his face as I began to back out of the clearing.

Snap! Snap!

Too late! A net rose beneath our feet, jerking us off our feet and binding us like fish more than a dozen feet over the ground. We were trapped.

CHAPTER
5

"**Y**OU SHOULD HAVE LET ME lead!" Brenwar fussed and struggled in the net as we hung there like a giant's lunch.

I fully expected a small army of orcs or lizard men to surround us as I fought to get my knife. I couldn't reach it.

"Grab my knife, Dragon," ordered Brenwar.

"I can't reach it. You try and grab mine," I ordered back.

"I can't even see it. Cripes, I think you're on top of me. Get off me! I'm not a stool."

We thrashed at our bonds, but all the wiggling did was ensnare us deeper in the heavy cords. The net was made for bigger prey than us, perhaps an animal, but it could be cut.

"Of all the Halls in Morgdon, I'll not be trapped like some kind of morsel!" Brenwar exclaimed. "Get me out of here, Dragon! I'm not going to die in such a helpless predicament as this."

"You get us out of here."

"You sprang the trap, not me!"

Our packs were full of plenty of gear that would help—if I could get to them. I could feel Brenwar's pack beneath my seat. That wasn't going to work. My left arm was pinned at my side, but my dragon arm was free enough to reach behind my back. The long claws on my dragon fingers caught my attention. I had an idea. I began sawing at the net's cords with my claws.

"What are you doing up there?" Brenwar asked.

"I'm trying to free us. That's what you want, isn't it?"

"With what are you freeing us?"

I didn't reply. Brenwar admonished me about using my black dragon arm for anything, no matter what it was. But I didn't see the harm in it. It was a part of me. It wasn't as if it was evil or had a mind of its own. Not like Fang, anyway.

"Ah, Brenwar, what choice do I have? It's the only way to get us free right now."

"No, it isn't."

"Then what is?"

I continued to saw in silence. That's when they showed up. Two figures in dark cloaks approached, bows aimed at our bellies. At least, I thought it was two. As the net continued a slow rotation over the ground, I'd see one, then the other. Hoods were pulled over the tops of their heads, and their cloaks dangled over their toes. I wasn't certain what to say, trying to figure out if silence was the best answer, uncertain if they'd speak first or not. But my nose told me this: it wasn't orcs or lizard men, either, so that was a plus.

"Um … could I trouble you, stranger, to let us down? It seems we've accidentally triggered a wildebeest trap."

I heard the tension on the stretching bowstrings and bit my tongue. The pair weren't playing around, and perhaps we were trespassing, and I wasn't so certain my clever tongue could get us out of here. I cleared my throat when I noticed the pudgy fingers wrapped around the bow.

"That's a very nice elven-made bow you have, sir. Some of the finest craftsmanship I've ever seen." I was trying to be complimentary. The bow was elven but hardly worth commentary. "And those shoes, are they elven made as well?" That's when I noticed one nod at the other. Both of them were beefy and similar in dress: elven clothes, ornate, blending, and fanciful. It seemed these two brigands had either robbed or bartered for their clothing and were hiding from something up here.

"Cut him down," one said to the other in Elvish.

"Dragon," Brenwar said in a whisper. "They speak Elvish. But they can't be elves. You ever seen a fat elf before?"

"No—Eeeee-yah!" I cried out, falling to the ground. I landed on Brenwar. I think it would have been softer if I had landed on a bench of stone. "A little warning first would be nice!"

The two characters stood over us, bows ready, as I picked my way out of the net and assisted Brenwar. The two of them were speaking in Elvish, and quite naturally I could understand every word they said. I knew all of the languages, mostly. So in Elvish I spoke back.

"Thank you for letting us down," I said with a small bow. It always helps to be polite and sincere when arrows are pointing at you. "And I apologize for springing your trap. What were you trying to catch? If indeed this is your trap."

They backed away and spread out a little farther from us and one another. The pair were almost as tall as men, each heavyset. They moved their girth with grace and ease, and I could see the clothes underneath their cloaks were woodsman-like but splendid in design. I just couldn't figure what men were doing in elven clothes and speaking Elvish, at that. My, if any elves saw this, they would frown upon it. The elves—wonderful, sophisticated, proper, beautiful, and in most cases arrogant— would possibly kill a man for this.

They didn't say a word, so I continued in Elvish.

"If it's all the same to you, we'll be getting out of your way."

"Hold your position," a voice said, a mixture of polish and salt in his tone. He sounded elven. "I'd be curious to know what you're doing in these hills."

"These hills don't belong to you," Brenwar fired back. Dwarves and elves don't get along so well. "I'd be just as curious to know what you are doing here."

Both of the men flipped back their hoods.

I blinked my eyes.

"Brenwar, are you seeing what I'm seeing?"

He nodded.

Both men had long brown hair, almost as gorgeous as mine but not quite. Their features were without a blemish or mark, their eyebrows perched in neat lines, and not a single crease in their foreheads. High cheekbones and strong chins, all distinctions of the elves—except one thing.

"You're the fattest elves I've ever seen!" I said. The words just came out. I couldn't help it.

Brenwar's belly rumbled with laughter.

"I knew they weren't perfect! I knew it!"

Both of the elves folded their arms across their chests and gave us disappointed looks. I felt like a child for a moment, realizing how rude I was. There were all kinds of big people in the world, but fat elves? No. They were all so lean and graceful. I'd never seen an ounce of girth on one of them, and I'd seen plenty of elves in my day.

Fat Elf One walked over and looked down on Brenwar.

"Be silent, dwarf. Else I'll seal that big mouth hole shut."

Brenwar's laughter stopped.

"I'd like to see you try," he warned. "No elf can best me, not fat or skinny. Ye better mind your choice of words if you want to see your next meal, you puffy face!"

"You bearded hog!"

"Ye've got a fanny like an orcen woman!" Brenwar stuck his fingers out. "Two of them!"

As much as I hated to, I stepped in the middle. It was pretty clear these elves, as odd as they seemed, weren't our enemies. And they didn't seem like the type we wanted to make enemies of, either. They were formidable underneath their girth. Seasoned and deadly.

"Let's start over again, shall we?" I said. "I'm Nath Dragon, and this is Brenwar Bolderguild."

Fat Elf One stepped away, while Fat Elf Two came up by his side and said in Common, "I am Shum." He bowed. "This is my brother Hoven." His brother nodded.

The big-hipped and rangy pair just looked at us, and I wasn't certain whether I should speak or wait for them. But I did have a one predominant question on my mind.

"Oh," Shum broke the silence, "I'm guessing you want to know why we're so ... eh ... large for elves."

I scratched my head. I didn't want to admit to things. After all, it would be rude, but seeing an elf in such shape was unique. "Well, forgive me, but I've seen many elves and—"

He held out his hand.

"Not all elves are as vain as you know them. In our case, we are thicker thewed and bigger boned, a gift to some, a curse to others."

"Are there more of you?" I asked.

"Oh certainly. We have families: young, old, big, and small like the rest. But we move much and befriend little. A tiny conclave that comes and goes. We prefer the vast lands and all their riches. We are the Wilder Elves. And we are also part of the Elven Roaming Rangers of Nalzambor."

I couldn't believe my ears.

CHAPTER
6

BRENWAR LOOKED AT ME, AND I looked at him. The Roaming Rangers of Nalzambor were a band of the most elusive people in the world. A heralded group of do-gooders whose deeds were whispered in all corners of the world. It was no wonder we were snared in their net. They were said to be the renowned hunters and trappers in the land. And now we stood facing two of them, neither of whom was very intimidating. Perhaps they were lying.

"You can't be serious."

"Indeed I am," Shum said, his face calm and resolute. "I imagine you'd expect someone different, but I tell you we are who we say we are."

"Well, your brother Hoven hasn't said anything," Brenwar said, adjusting the buckles on his armor.

"He's discreet, Brenwar Bolderguild."

"And I've never heard of Wilder Elves, either," I said.

"Nor should you have. Of course, I'm certain you aren't aware of all the dragon kind either, are you, Nath Dragon?"

I smiled. I couldn't help it when I found out that someone had heard of me. It made my heart swell. I extended my dragon arm. "Is it that obvious?"

Both elves drew close to me, eyeing my arm in fascination. Hoven reached out, touched it, shook his head, and backed away.

"Forgive my brother, but he gets excited at times."

"You call that excited?" Brenwar said.

"For him it is," Shum said. "Come with me. I've some food prepared, if you'd like to eat.

The food was good and the cave setting quaint, tucked back in the hills. The elves certainly knew how to cook their venison.

Shum passed over a small bowl filled with nuts and berries. Brenwar scoffed at it.

"The whispers serve you well, Nath Dragon. Your hair, eyes, build, all as the rumors describe, yet there's been no mention of your arm as of yet."

"Nor should there be," I said, eyeing him. "So, are you going to tell us what you were trying to trap out there? That was a pretty big net. A winged ape, perhaps?"

Shum and Hoven's eyes widened like moons. They both leaned in.

"You've seen him!"

"Aye, fought him off, we did."

"Where? Where did you see him?"

I had their full attention now. Both of the elves were hungry for every last detail. But I wasn't going to tell them anything if they didn't tell me what I wanted to know first.

"What is it, and why are you after it?" I asked.

Shum shifted in his spot, his double chin dipping, eyes narrowing a little.

"I cannot say. Dragon, tell me, did you wound him? Did he wound you?"

I leaned forward.

"An arrow shattered on its hide. My sword licked at its skin, grazing it a few times, but I did get one good lick in. It grabbed Brenwar and—"

"Dragon!" Brenwar warned.

I held my tongue a moment and then finished.

"And it was gone. Shot into the moonlight and disappeared. In all truth, Shum, the beast, monster, or whatever it was… well, it was glorious and dangerous."

The tension in the air evaporated. Their faces looked relieved. I couldn't tell if it was a good or a bad thing. Something wasn't right. Awkward, I'd say.

"So, what do you call this beast?" I asked.

"It doesn't have a name. It is a new threat, you might say, and Hoven and I are charged with its capture. I don't think anyone that faces it in combat would live. And I must say, Nath Dragon, the fact that you're still standing after facing off with it is inspiring. All the others who've encountered it are dead."

Shum was sincere. Both the elves feared it. It seemed their charge was a life-or-death matter.

"How long have you been tracking it? Perhaps we can help," I said.

Shum shook his head and said, "Years. We haven't seen it in years, either. We just follow the signs and the stories. It seems the creature does have an affinity for these hills, however. It dwells here at times. Of that much, we are certain. But its terrors are reported all over the lands."

"There are many terrors," Brenwar said.

"And that makes him all the more difficult to track." Shum rose to his feet. "I'm grateful for the information, and perhaps I can be of some assistance to you as well."

"You sure you don't want our help?" I said, rising.

"It's our problem. I see no need for you to endanger yourselves. But we do share much in common as trackers. You want dragons, and I want that monster. I honor what you do, Nath Dragon, rescuing the great lizards."

I didn't like the name "lizard," but he meant it in a reverent way, so I let him continue.

"We've seen dragons in the Shale, but not many. Still, where the rivers meet and beyond the horizon over the mountain lies a graveyard. They say many bones can be found there, of all the races and all the monsters, even dragons. Treasure hunters and adventurers traverse from time to time, but the risk is high." He stood up and stretched his long arms. "Poachers lie in these hills as well. They have hidden outposts and make many traps for dragons. The dragons like the seclusion here but not that the poachers have invaded. Their lives are in danger. Of course, we've come across many dead poachers, as well... many scorched to the bone."

"And what of the winged ape, Shum? What happens if we come across its path again?"

Shum and Hoven's piercing eyes locked on mine, and they both shook their heads.

"Run. Hide. Don't cross with it again if you want to live, Nath Dragon. The creature is dangerous. Much more so than it appears. Consider yourself fortunate."

Brenwar bristled at the remark and said, "And we're supposed to believe two potbellied elves can take it and we can't? Hah! Now that's a laugh."

"Watch your boast, dwarf," Shum warned. "Roaming Rangers are some of the best fighters in all of Nalzambor. I suggest you save your energy for the trials you face ahead. We are not your enemy, and you should be glad of that."

Shum donned his cloak and extended his hand. Elves were tall in some cases, even taller than me. Shum and his brother Hoven were half a head shorter but just as heavy if not heavier. We braced arms, and I could feel the power in his grip.

I said, "Thanks for the warning, brothers. And thanks for the information."

Without another word, they departed, two ghosts disappearing into the dimness of the forest. I wondered if I'd ever see them again. The Wilder Elves. The Roaming Rangers. One thing was certain: they were hiding something. I was pretty good at detecting that. But what it was, I wasn't sure.

"Let's go, Brenwar. And I'll lead this time. We've got some dragons to save."

CHAPTER 7

IT TOOK A DAY AND a half before we made it to where the two rivers merged. They weren't big rivers but small ones, the kind you could throw a stone across, or skip one if you were really good. Which I was.

Brenwar sat on top of a tree stump as I shook the last bit of shale from my boots. Lucky for me, the terrain changed where the rivers met. The travel would be on softer ground—dirt and moss, ferns and flowers—once we crossed the river and headed up the mountain. I was still bothered by the encounter with the Roaming Rangers, though.

"Brenwar, what did you make of those two?"

"They looked a pair of pretty ogres."

"No, that's not what I meant. Don't you find it odd that they don't want us to fight that winged ape? Wouldn't you think that if it was so dangerous, they would want us to help them kill it?"

He hopped from his stump.

"An insult, it was. Thinking the two of us couldn't take that thing. We've faced greater dangers than that. I've faced greater dangers on my own, and I still have my arms, legs, and head to show for it."

"Agreed."

I squatted over the river's edge and doused my face with water. It was an insult to think they didn't need our help or that we were overmatched. After all, I had chased the creature off. Of course, that was with Fang in my hand. If I hadn't had it, I wondered if things would have turned out differently.

"Do you think we'll ever see them or it again?"

"Doesn't matter, Dragon. You focus on the dragons. You don't need to meddle in other ones' matters."

Brenwar was right. There was nothing I'd rather than do than toil in the affairs of the other races. I loved coming to their rescue. I loved to hear the stories they told about me. It was an addicting elixir, the sounds of my accolades like honey on my tongue. I couldn't help but want to assist them. However, my father had told me time and time again that men, elves, dwarves, and all kinds have to help themselves at times.

"Well, I still would like to see them again. My, big hips and bellies on elves. I never would have imagined it in my lifetime."

"Me neither, but I couldn't care less if I never saw them again," Brenwar said, refilling his canteen.

"Why?"

He gave me a dirty look and said, "'Cause they're elves."

I laughed then took a forlorn look back over my shoulder. If we came back this way, and I would do everything in my power to see to it that we did, I was going to check on them. After all, the Roaming Rangers were renowned trackers, but Nath Dragon was a tracker of his own renown as well. And if they couldn't find that winged ape, then my bet was that I could.

With the Wilder Elves miles behind us, it was time to focus on finding dragons now. They were family, and it was my charge to rescue them from their own greedy and self-destructive habits. That's right, I wasn't the only dragon with issues; there were plenty of others as well. For example, some dragons became so greedy and obsessed with precious items that they'd kill for them. And thanks to them, most dragons had bad reputations with the peoples of Nalzambor.

As a matter of fact, you might be wondering why most dragons didn't reside in Dragon Home, or rather the Mountain of Doom. That's because, like me, they were curious and often sought a hoard, a life, or treasure of their own. Face it, dragons didn't like to share. Still, plenty maintained a peaceful existence beyond the halls in Dragon Home. Of course, that's probably because they slept so much.

Up we walked, down we walked, around the mountain we went when a glimmer of steel caught my eye.

"See this?" I said, kneeling down and picking up the handle of a broken sword.

"Aye," Brenwar added, "a battle was near."

Farther up the base of the mountain we went, which was more like a slanted forest on a hill. I found some blood on the leaves and on the ground. I readied my bow and listened. The wind whispered in my ears, and the scent of death was near.

"Do you smell that?" I asked.

"All too well." Brenwar brandished his war hammer. "Let's go."

On cat's feet, I wove in and out of the trees, my senses on high alert, my bow ready with a magic arrow. I wasn't taking any chance of that winged ape getting a jump on me again. But my blood was charged for a fight. I could still smell the hair and breath of the beast. It was strong in my memory.

I stopped. There was breathing ahead, somewhere in the trees. An unseen enemy beyond.

Brenwar gave me a signal and moved farther up in the woods out of sight.

I pushed a branch and leaves from my face. Ahead in the forest lay a clearing where a battle had indeed been fought. There was a charred body and another one broken and dead. The breath I'd heard moments earlier was gone. So far as I could tell, the danger was long gone.

I stepped into the clearing to continue my investigation. The bodies, charred and still smoking, were goblins. I hated goblins, too, and I bet that doesn't surprise you. They were some of the most notorious dragon poachers of all. I ran my fingers over an impression in the ground. *Dragon tracks!* My heart thumped harder in my chest. Looking at all the signs, broken branches and stirred-up dirt, I'd say at least twenty goblins had trapped one dragon and dragged him down. But what kind of dragon was it?

The body smoking on the ground was my best clue. The goblin's leather armor was dry and brittle. Its sword was fused to its hand, and all its hairs were singed from its body as if it had been hit by a lightning bolt. A blue razor. That was the type of dragon I thought had done this. Fast, fast as lightning, and its breath a jolt from the heavens. I hadn't seen one in decades.

"Brenwar," I said. No response. He must have been onto something, but I wasn't worried. There was never a reason to worry about Brenwar, and if he thought you did, he'd be insulted. There was a glint of light in the dirt at my feet like a piece of shining metal. A dragon scale. I picked it up, as big as two of my fingers, a metallic blue. It had been a blue razor, all right, a dragon more known for its speed than its strength. Blue razors didn't grow to be very big, no bigger than a horse, and judging by the tracks, this one wasn't much bigger than a pony. Now, you would think that a dragon would be really hard for something as stupid as a goblin to catch, but goblins aren't stupid, just ugly. Orcs are stupid. That's why they're dangerous. Don't forget that.

The goblins, or in this case, dragon poachers, had been hunting dragons for centuries, and they'd developed tools and weapons to use. They used netting and slings to trap the dragon's wings, and all the rest they did by force. The goblin charred to a crisp on the ground was given the honor, as his goblin leaders would have convinced him, to absorb the dragon's breath. Volunteering his own death to capture a dragon would bring the fallen goblin's family great honor.

I could see the entire scuffle between dragon and goblin playing out in my head. The blue razor sniffing out a small hoard of treasure and gathering it with his small hands into a pouch under his wings. I bet you didn't know that, did you? Dragons have pouches and other secrets as well. The goblins shooting a net over the dragon, pinning his wings so he couldn't fly to escape. Next, the first goblin charges at him only to be scorched alive. Another goblin attacks and is downed under the power of the striking dragon's claws. His breath exhausted on the first goblin, the sheer number of goblins overwhelms him. I was sad thinking about the dragon's capture. If Brenwar and I had come sooner, maybe we could have prevented it.

There was dragon blood in the dirt as well. Not much, but enough to know the dragon was injured and in jeopardy. On a positive note, dragons are worth much more alive than dead. At least ten times more, and it made perfect sense that the goblins would be searching for buyers.

Brenwar emerged from the woods, scratching his black beard as he said, "I found wagon tracks and a large path up ahead. They've been moving half a day, if that."

I slipped my magic arrow back into my quiver and hooked Akron.

"Let's get moving, then," I said.

I stepped, stopped, and turned. I could feel eyes on me. The hair on my neck rose. The breathing that had come and gone was back, but it was heavier and louder than before.

"Don't move," a coarse voice warned from somewhere behind my back.

CHAPTER
8

I FROZE. IT WASN'T MY INCLINATION to freeze; that wasn't natural. Not when someone had a bowstring stretched and an arrow pointed at my back. At least, I supposed my aggressor did. No, I wanted to move and move fast, but Brenwar's eyes suggested otherwise. Whoever was behind me needed serious consideration.

"Arms up, I suppose?" I said. I'd been in this situation before. They always wanted your arms and hands where they could see them.

"Just turn around and keep your hands where I can see them," it demanded.

See, I told you they'd want to see my hands. So I spread my arms out to my sides as far as I could reach them and turned.

It was a goblin. And it was one a little higher up on the frightful scale. Goblins come in a variety of shapes. Some are taller than dwarves, others as tall as a man. Some heavy, some thin. Not much different than men, except they never bathe, and they have an affection for mud and dirt. They abhor crossing a river and will languish and brag to one another of their grimy coats. If you ever want to make a goblin mad, really mad, give him a bath. It's torture. They hate water.

This goblin stood tall, his muscles thick, hands meaty, greasy brown hair hanging over his shoulders. He wore leather armor and a necklace of small bones tied around his neck. One of his long, pointed ears was cut off, and the other displayed a painful-looking earring chained to his nose. Even goblins have their own sense of fashion, I suppose. But the worst thing about this goblin was that he had the drop on me.

"A dragon poacher," I said, "except it seems that you are missing a dragon."

I got the feeling he didn't care for where my conversation was headed. The aim of the goblin's arrow rose from my chest to my face. He wasn't going to miss.

"Drop all your gear—both you and the dwarf—and toss it over, quickly."

Brenwar was rumbling behind me.

"There's only one. Take him."

I objected.

"You aren't the one with an arrow pointed at you."

The goblin's eyes narrowed, and he let out an awful hiss.

"Foolish dwarf, more are coming, don't you know. I'm the scout. Now leave your gear, and I'll let you go. Tut-tut!"

Goblins aren't patient or kind or merciful. If they say they won't hurt you, they're probably lying. If they say they have more support coming, they are lying. Goblins are liars. They'll say anything to get what they want and then cut your throat, but they'd rather cut your throat first.

This goblin, judging by his size, figured he'd shoot me down and then battle Brenwar. I didn't want to get shot, not from this close. Besides, I'd already been shot just a couple days ago.

"Dragon," Brenwar said, "I'm not yielding to any goblin."

You see, this is one of the problems you have traveling with dwarves: they aren't going to bargain with anyone, especially with those evil races. Brenwar would rather that he or I died first.

The goblin spat a big glob on the ground and smiled wide. I swear I could see bugs crawling around his teeth.

"The dwarf is foolish," the goblin said as he pulled back the bowstring, "and you get to die."

Twang!

I plucked the arrow from the air, inches from my nose. The look on the goblin's face said it all as I held the arrow in my dragon arm.

"Impossible!" I gaped in my own incredulity. I hadn't even had time to think; I'd just reacted, or at least my arm had, anyway.

Brenwar pounced on the goblin, his stone-hard fists raining down blows, knocking the goblin unconscious. He kicked the goblin in the ribs once more for good measure and dusted off his hands.

"Did you see that?" I said, marveling at the arrow.

"I saw it, all right. Luck is all, Dragon. All you had to do was duck."

I tried to recall the last thing I'd been thinking. *Duck! Dodge! Dive! Evade!* Any of those things I was committed to, but catching an arrow? Well, that never entered my mind. I squeezed the arrow in my grip and snapped the shaft with my dragon thumb. What else could my amazing arm do?

"Quit playing with it, will you?" Brenwar tied up the goblin with some rope and stuffed a gag in its mouth. "We've got to find dragons now. This one stayed behind for some reason or was tracking back. Methinks they're worried they might be followed."

"Other poachers, you think?"

"It wouldn't be the first time." Brenwar slung the goblin over his shoulder. "You know that. Now carry my sack. Daylight's burning."

"What are you going to do with the goblin, Brenwar?" I held my nose. "It stinks."

"Evil stinks. You should be used to it by now." He started hoofing it up the mountain. "When it comes to, I'll beat what we need out of it, but there ain't no sense in waiting for that when the poachers have a lead on us."

I slung Brenwar's pack over my shoulder along with mine. His pack was twice as heavy. Of course, most of the stuff was mine anyway, so I shouldn't complain. But it didn't do my ailing leg much good. So I tried to block out my discomfort, opting to marvel at my incredible arm all I could. It was fast! Insanely so, and I liked it.

"Quit looking at it," Brenwar growled, forcing us deep up the mountain and into the woods.

CHAPTER 9

AFTER THE FIRST FEW MILES, my wounded leg was in agony, and I'd forgotten all about my dragon arm. I just wanted to stop. I had no idea how Brenwar carried so much, no problem, no complaint, no issue at all. I wiped the sweat from my eyes and groaned. I could see the trail of the goblins. Moving a dragon over the faint and rugged pathways wouldn't be easy, but they had their ways. Judging by the tracks, there were many to carry the load, too, so at least I had a good idea about the sizable force we'd run into. They were careful to cover their tracks, but it wasn't enough.

Ahead, Brenwar stopped. The goblin had awoken and now was wriggling in its bonds, eyeballing us with hatred. Brenwar's shoulders heaved up, and the goblin fell to the ground with a *wump*.

"Interrogation time," Brenwar said, a row of white teeth showing over his beard.

Now, you might be thinking that interrogations could be cruel and painful. And that they might conflict with the higher standards that I'd set in life. And you're right; they can and they will sometimes. Of course, that's what Brenwar's for.

I dropped the two packs on the ground and started rubbing my aching shoulders. "Finally."

Brenwar jerked the rag from the goblin's mouth and drew back to wallop it in the nose.

"Easy, Brenwar," I said, "let's give it a chance to speak first."

Brenwar stayed close, eyes intent on the goblin's mouth. Goblins have many tricks, and they only need a few seconds to send a warning.

"Nah, I don't trust him." Brenwar wrapped his fingers around its throat. "Just ask yer questions and make it quick."

The first question was the obvious choice.

"How many in your troop?"

"Heh ... heh ... I'll not tell—*urk!*"

Its eyes widened as Brenwar squeezed. I could see its grimy coat of skin begin to turn red in the cheeks.

I checked the dirt under my dragon-claw nails. My, my black claws were so shiny.

"Oh, goblin," I wagged my finger in his face, "I don't think you want to toy with us again. Now, when I ask you a question, I suggest that you answer, with all the forthcoming integrity I've come to expect from your race."

Brenwar's fingers slacked.

"I don't have integrity," the goblin said. "Goblins don't know what that is."

"Ah, an honest goblin, that is a good thing. Perhaps we can compromise on the information I require, then."

It cocked its ugly head. It seemed as if it wanted to scratch its head and consider what I had suggested. Goblins were always open to bargaining, especially when it concerned their lives.

"C-Compromise," it said, eyes sliding over toward Brenwar then back to me. "What kind?"

Now that was good. The goblin was open to negotiation, but I think it had more to do with its own self-preservation than anything else.

"You tell me where they are taking the dragon and what to expect, and I'll add a few coins to your purse."

"What!" Brenwar objected. "You'll not be giving the rotten life such a thing. I'll not pay for answers I can get for myself.

"No! No! NO!" the goblin cried. "Take the coins I will. I like the coins. Fair deal. Fair deal. I like my life. I'll give you all the information you require, just don't let the dwarf hurt me."

Even the biggest of goblins could turn out to be the biggest of whiners and babies. One thing was for certain: every creature valued its own life in Nalzambor. The problem was that they didn't all value the lives of others.

I tossed the first gold coin at its feet.

It licked its lips.

"Tell me where they are going and how many."

Sure, a single coin didn't seem like much of a sacrifice in comparison for a dragon, but this goblin wouldn't see any of the profits anyway. He'd be lucky to get so much as a few coppers or a silver for his efforts. Poor goblins. And whatever they'd sell the dragon for, they could have gotten a hundred times more.

"Around the mountain where the sun sets, there's a city in the cliffs that overlooks the valley. Small city, cut from stone, ancient and abandoned long ago. Our hideout is there."

It seemed simple enough, assuming there was such a place. But I needed to know more about what they intended for the dragon. I tossed another gold coin at his feet.

"Nath …" Brenwar growled at me. "That's quite enough!"

I held my hand out.

"Are other dragons kept there?"

It was a good question. For all I knew, they might have a dozen up there.

It shook its head.

"How many dragons have you sold?"

I didn't want to ask them how many they'd killed. I didn't want to know.

"Three."

I couldn't hide my sneer. My guilt was also beginning to overwhelm me. If only I had gotten here sooner.

I kneeled in front of the ugly creature and held the biggest gold coin it had ever seen in front of its face. Its beady eyes blinked repeatedly in the reflecting gold light, and a drop of drool fell from its lips onto its chest.

"Who have you been selling the dragon to?"

It didn't answer.

I didn't like that. I enclosed the gold coin in my hand.

"Do you want this coin or not?"

It nodded. "Yes. Yes. Yes."

"Who are you selling the dragons to?" I shook my dragon fist in its face.

It closed its eyes and turned its chin away. Whoever they were doing business with, the goblin had greater fear of them than of me or Brenwar.

I caught the light with the gold coin and reflected it into the goblin's eyes.

Its eyes popped open. Its breathing became loud and heavy as it made a raspy sigh.

"With this coin, you can start another life far, far away. We won't say a thing."

It was in turmoil now. Its eyes shifted among me, Brenwar, and the coin. But something was holding it back, something dark and powerful. I could see the fear in its eyes, and goblins didn't scare easily.

"Tie him to the tree, then, Brenwar. It seems he would rather suffer than enjoy a fistful of gold," I said, picking up the other coins and dropping them into my pouch.

"I'd be happy to. But I don't think that's a very nice thing to do to a tree." He looked around. "I'll see if I can find a fallen log instead, or maybe a rock."

I shrugged. "Whatever you think is best. I just want to get going."

The goblin's face was contorted with emotion.

"I'll tell! I'll tell! Please, show me my coins again."

"A change of heart, I see." I set all the coins in my hand, the biggest one in the middle. "Well?"

"The Clerics of Barnabus."

My heart stopped in my chest.

CHAPTER
10

"**F**INNIUS!" SHE SCREAMED.

Finnius's heart jumped as he emerged from a side room in the great hall, rubbing the ornate tattoos on his shaved head then wringing his hands. He was medium in build with a slight hitch in his step. His large eyes probing and evil, he approached with caution.

"Yes, High Priestess," he said, bowing.

She sat on her throne, shoulders back, chin up, shifting on the tangerine-colored cushion and tapping her perfectly white teeth, an impatient look on her face. On either side of her, two bald men sat cross legged, muttering incantations under their breath. Finnius felt his heart flutter.

She was different. Radiant. Exotic. Evil incarnate. She was the High Priestess of Barnabus, Selene. The acolytes of Barnabus—loyal, dutiful, and deadly—would do anything she asked, anything she asked at all. But at the moment, their task had escaped them. Finnius knew her wrath would not be contained much longer.

She smoothed her dark robes over her chest as she rose from her chair and walked down the steps. Six lizard men with barbed spears stood tall, heads bowed as she passed. Her black dragon tail spilled out from under the hem of her robe and cracked one lizard man across the face, spinning him to the floor.

"Walk with me," she said.

Finnius shuffled a half step behind, watching her tail disappear under her robes.

She led him into the depths of the temple, down a stone staircase, and into a torch-lit room. The lizard men and acolytes knelt. Two eight-foot-tall lizard men stood guard at a tall, heavy iron door. He had little desire to go in there, but he had no choice in the matter. On the bright side, it wasn't a torture chamber, but what lay within was far deadlier.

"Open it," she ordered.

Her voice was commanding and persuasive, a rushing river with the power of a waterfall. He'd seen her speak and crack stone walls. He loved it and feared it, but he wanted such power for himself as well. Of course, he wanted her just as much. After all, she was the High Priestess, as pretty and evil as they came.

He unhitched the ring of keys from his belt and unlocked the door. One lizard man slid the bar from the door while the other pushed it open before stepping out of the way. Selene took the lead, the cool draft billowing the dark hair along her face. Finnius fell in step behind her as the door was closed after them. Selene snapped her fingers, and a row of smokeless torches flared to life. They had an orange hue and only lit one side of the tunnel, which seemed too long to be underground.

"Finnius," she said, slowing her pace, "how many dragons have we captured this season?"

His mouth became dry as an empty well. *She knows this already, but I must squirm anyway.*

She always asked questions. Probing for failure. Searching for a reason to pounce. He cleared his throat.

"Eleven."

"Ah, I see, and how many did we acquire last season?"

"Ahem … eh … Twenty."

He felt himself shrink when she stopped, turned, and looked down into his eyes. He scratched a dry patch of skin on his hand and swallowed hard.

She folded her elegant arms across her chest. "Hmmm … so we have caught fewer dragons this season than the last, yet we have more resources at our disposal than ever before." Her voice rose to a higher volume. Her pleasant expression faded. "How could that be, Finnius?"

Finnius could hear his heart thumping in his ears now. He knew why. She knew why, so why did she have to ask? Even worse, why did he have to answer? He remembered the last acolyte who'd failed to answer a similar question. He'd been brought into this tunnel with the priestess and never emerged. Finnius was that cleric's replacement.

I don't know. I don't know. I don't know.

He wanted to say that. The truth was he couldn't actually say for sure, but that is what the last cleric had said. He looked her in the eye.

"Nath Dragon."

Selene's perfect lips curled, and her nostrils flared. She was getting taller now; he was certain of it as he watched her face contort in the orange light. It was dragon-like. Mysterious. Then gone.

"Nath Dragon, indeed," she said, putting her arm over his shoulder and leading him down the corridor to where another large door waited. "Come."

This lone door was as tall as the last, a black slab of stone, no keyholes, locks, or bars, just a smooth surface. Butterflies fluttered in his stomach, and sweat beaded his forehead. *Always something different and dangerous every time.* He drew little reassurance from her arm around his shoulder despite how thrilling it was to have her touch him. *She can't be killing me. She just can't be. She needs me. Doesn't she?*

She stepped in front of him, raised her arms, and loudly proclaimed a series of mystic words. It was in a language even he didn't comprehend, and all his attempts to pronounce it himself met with failure.

The black door shimmered and wavered. Selene reached out for his hand, smiling. He was trembling when he took it and she pushed him in.

CHAPTER 11

I LET THE GOBLIN GO. WELL, abandoned him to his bonds, actually. But that gave Brenwar and me enough time to distance ourselves from him.

The journey around the mountain was long, the brush heavy, the bugs becoming more irritating the deeper we ventured. I'd already spit three bugs from my mouth. But my leg wasn't so bad now, not with Brenwar carrying most of the burden again, and it was getting better. After all, I healed pretty fast.

"What are ye thinking, Dragon?" Brenwar asked, pushing past some vines.

The Clerics of Barnabus. That's what I was thinking. Fiends of all kinds. My enemy of enemies. The mere mention of them left a foul taste on my tongue. It was like swallowing hot vinegar every time I heard them mentioned. I clenched my teeth and balled up my hands. I hated them.

"The Clerics, Brenwar. We need to put a stop to them. We need to crush them all."

"I know."

It seemed every poacher in Nalzambor was paid by the clerics now. Kings of the dragon trade. The Clerics enslaved the dragons. They killed the dragons. They tortured them as well. They wanted the dragons' magic. It was the remnants of dragons that they sold: bones, talons, teeth, scales, and even parts from the flesh within. The power within dragons allowed them to cast many spells. The thought of it all lit a fire in my belly.

I continued.

"Everywhere we go, they turn up. We need to track them down one day, Brenwar. We need to save the dragons from their clutches, once and for all."

Brenwar stopped me with a disapproving look and sniffed the air. I could smell it, too. We were closing in. The goblins were close, just a few miles ahead now, I'd say.

I gritted my teeth and took the lead.

"Time to free the dragon."

The travel around the mountain's base was long. From where I stood, I couldn't see the peak for all the trees, but the mountain wasn't so big, not as big as Dragon Home, the Mountain of Doom. I had to admit, I missed that grisly exterior more now than ever. I even wondered what my father was doing. Was he worried? Mad? Or had he given up on me entirely? It all tugged at my heart.

I climbed up onto a crag above the trail we'd followed the goblins on. Below was a wonderful view of the valley the goblin poacher had told us about. It was miles away, but I could still see the birds darting in and out of the tree tops, and I could smell the water that ran down the mountain to form a lake or swamp down there. Most likely a swamp. Goblins have a penchant for stagnant water, but for the most part they drink a homemade concoction called swill. A cup of dirt would taste better, judging by the smell.

"We need to see its face," I said as Brenwar crawled up the rocks beside me. Dwarves didn't like to climb. They'd rather just carve a tunnel through a mountain than go above or around it. They swore it would save time in the long run, which it might, but we couldn't take years to dig a tunnel.

"Sun's setting." Dark clouds had formed about. "Storm's coming. Best we get moving. The face will be black as coal in the dark, assuming there is one."

In less than an hour, we made it to the bottom of the mountain and saw the goblin hideout for the first time. The rain was a heavy drizzle now. I shielded my eyes from the drops.

The mountain was flat on this side. A cliff face. A network of ledges and doorways. So far as I could tell, the mountain hideout could harbor hundreds if not thousands of goblins. Finding a dragon in there would not be easy. But at the moment ,there was a greater concern.

"How are we going to get in there?" I asked. "There are no stairs or footholds that I can see." I held my hand over my eyes. "But I don't see any guards, either. Do you?"

"No. But I bet I can find a way in," Brenwar said. "If there's a secret door in the stone, I'll find it. There could be another entrance they use, too. We'll just have to go back and follow the trail."

Just like in the Mountain of Doom, there could be a well-concealed entrance. But walking right up to it wasn't the best idea. I was certain there would be guards or a guardian. Probably not anything we couldn't handle, but alerting them to our presence would be the problem.

"I have an idea. Follow me."

We pushed our way through the forest until we came across the stream that came from the mountain and formed a waterfall that plunged into the valley. The water was clear below, a small lake surrounded by a lush and beautiful forest. It was unlikely goblins ventured into the valley, not near such crystal-clear water. It was a break.

I looked at Brenwar, who said, "I know what you're thinking, Dragon. I like it. Let's go."

It took a little bit of time before we made it to where the valley bottomed out and the waterfall formed the lake. It was dark now, the warmth of the sun gone, replaced by a chill in the air. The sound of the waterfall was loud, steady, and soothing. Not a bad place to sit and fish for a while. I'd have to remember to come back here one day when all the goblins were gone.

I climbed over the rocks, Brenwar at my back, and we plunged underneath the water of the falls. I shivered. The water was cold coming from the mountaintop, and being cold wasn't one of my favorite things. Behind the waterfall, it was pitch black. I pushed my wet hair from my face and drew Fang from its sheath. A soft illumination reflected off the damp stones behind the falls. I squinted into the dimness.

"I don't see anything."

Brenwar huffed. "It's because you don't know what to look for." He ran his hands over the stones, feeling, pushing, and probing nooks and crevices. Anything below the ground or leading into, it the dwarves are experts on. If there was a way under the mountain, the water would lead us there, but it was dangerous if you didn't know what you were doing. Plenty of adventurers drowned this way. I really hoped we wouldn't have to swim to get into this cave, assuming I was right and there was one.

"Here it is," Brenwar said. One second he was standing in the light, the next he was gone.

"Where'd you go?" I asked.

"Come on, will you!" his voice echoed from behind the dripping rocks.

"Huh," I muttered, squeezing through a dark crevice I'd overlooked. I'm a dragon. I'm not very keen on dull rocks and such things.

It was muddy and damp by the time I traversed the crevice and made my way inside. The cave was small, just a little taller than me, with passageways in several directions. Brenwar drew a deep breath in through his nose, moving from one passage to the other. He tipped his chin and led, boots splashing.

Now, of all places, I was stuck in a series of caves beneath the mountain with a glowing sword in my hand, fighting for foot- and handholds, unable to tell if we were going up or down. I had to trust Brenwar with that. But I'd be lying if I said the dark caves didn't worry me. I wanted to get back outside already. I'll take the rain over darkness any day.

"I hope it doesn't flood," Brenwar said.

I could see the waters rising at my feet.

"What do you mean?"

Brenwar looked down at the water and said, "The rains must be getting heavy now." He shrugged. "Nothing to worry about now, we're flooded in."

My breath grew thin.

"What?"

CHAPTER 12

TWIST. TURN. CRAWL. CLIMB. SCRAPE and sweat. It was like that every agonized step of the way. I wiped the mud from my face and accidentally rubbed it into a scrape I'd gotten on my cheek. I could only imagine what a mess my hair was now. I should have tied a few knots in it. I felt like I was suffocating down here, too.

"Are we there yet?" I asked. It might have been the hundredth time for all I knew. I'd lost count after thirty.

Brenwar didn't slow, climbing up over a ledge, plodding through a shallow lake, whistling a cheerful tune. He couldn't be more happy underground. He was like a pig in mud. Me, I couldn't get out of there fast enough. I'd rather fight a hundred goblins. Something about being in these caves with no sense of direction got the better of me. I wasn't in control, and without Brenwar, I might get lost—probably would, actually.

Now, you're probably thinking that dragons live in caves, and that's true, many do, and it's not so bad when you have a lot of room and you know your way through. But this? No thanks. I liked having the open air to look at and everything beyond.

"Here," Brenwar said, standing in a spring of water burbling at his feet, pointing upward.

I could see a faint light, a brown hole you might say, among the all-encompassing black. It flickered. My heart leapt in my chest. A torch or lantern was near.

"You think we're at the top?"

"Think? I know it. Just twenty yards below that hideout." He thumped his chest. "I told you so."

I sheathed Fang and allowed my eyes to readjust to the darkness. I could see the ceiling better now. A circle of dim light. It illuminated the both of us now.

"What do you think that is?"

Brenwar pointed.

"A well. See all these stones?"

There was part of a formation that had crumbled at the base. It was possible that the people who had built the hideout had abandoned the place once the source of water dried up or was destroyed. Most ruins had thrived at one time or another, but time, war, famine, and the elements destroyed the greatest cities in the world. It happens as sure as the sun and moon set in the sky every single day.

"So," I said in the dark, "how do we get up there?"

"I brought us here. It's up to you to do the rest."

"You don't think there's another entrance farther along?"

"No. There's no other entrance at all. This is the one. Trust me. I know."

I rubbed my chin and gave some serious thought to this one. I couldn't jump twenty feet in the air, and I couldn't fly, either.

Brenwar growled, fumbled through his pack, and pulled something out. A rope. A grappling hook was attached to it.

"You could have mentioned that you had that among your assets before. It would have spared me troublesome thoughts."

"Do I have to think of everything, Dragon? What would you do without me?"

"I guess I would have just gone through the front door."

"This was your idea," he huffed.

Brenwar whirled the hook on the rope and slung it upward toward the hole. *Clank.*

I slapped him on the back.

"Great shot!"

I tugged the rope and nodded.

"You go first," he said. "I've done more than enough already."

Up I went, hand over hand, foot after foot, until I could clearly see the outline of the well that once stood. I hung in midair and listened. I always gave it sixty seconds or so. You had to make sure the coast was clear. No sounds, no rustles, no footsteps or voices. It seemed we'd found as good a place to enter as any. I climbed over the lip of the well and shook the rope. I could hear Brenwar coming, but it would take him awhile. Dwarves aren't the fastest climbers—or the fastest anything, for that matter. But I couldn't complain. So far, so good.

That's when I heard voices. My hand dropped to my hilt. Goblins. Two of them, chatting back and forth, coming my way.

"Guards!" I whispered into the well. Brenwar only had about ten more feet to go. "Drop if you have to."

"I'm not going to drop—"

"Sssssh!"

The room I was in was big, at one time a common area of sorts, long abandoned with very few places to hide. I glided toward the wall farthest from the well and squatted in the shadows. Yes indeed, the goblins were a patrol, making their rounds. I had suspected it, but my wishful thinking had gotten the better of me. I couldn't let them see the grappling hook or Brenwar. I had to stop them or the alarm would be sounded and the entire hideout would swarm with goblins.

Here they came, side by side, both big, the size of men, wearing helmets and armed with spears. They didn't look my way, but one was carrying a torch, and the other's yellow eyes were fixed on the well.

I reached for my bow, then thought better of it. I could hit one, but I couldn't kill it fast enough. Its screams would send a warning. *Drat!* That left me with Fang. Oh, if I could just sneak up and chop them down, it would be so easy. That wouldn't be such a good idea, either. Too risky. That left me with my wits. My brain. Oh … and my dragon arm. What wonders would it allow me to get away with? Could I get away with it in time?

"Huh. You smell something, brother?" one goblin said to the other.

It sniffed the air.

This was it. They'd be onto us any second. I had to spring.

Then the speaking goblin farted and said, "I bet you do now. Heh-heh."

The other took a deep snort and said, "I can do better than that," and let one rip.

I didn't know whether to laugh or be sick as the foul odor wafted to my nostrils. *Yech!*

They both let out some rugged chuckles and took seats on the well's stony rim, the grappling hook right between them, and farted again.

I don't think Brenwar's going to like that.

"Ah! Ah! Ah! Ooh!" the goblin laughed and patted his belly. "I'm hungry." He reached inside a pouch, stuffed some bugs in his mouth, and crunched them up. "Mmmmm. Take some."

I needed to kill them now. I wanted to kill them now. And the foul smell started to make my eyes water and my stomach churn. What I really wanted to do was run. I had to escape the stink.

"What is this, brother?"

Oh no! The goblin had discovered the grappling hook.

"Eh … hmmm, that looks like a—*urk!*"

It looked like one of the goblins was sucked down the well. The other opened its mouth to scream. I flew across the room and cracked it across the jaw before the first syllable came out. Its yellow eyes rolled up in its head just before Brenwar jerked it down inside the well and climbed out.

"Great goblin farts!" Brenwar exclaimed, holding his nose, stamping his boots.

"Quiet," I warned, holding my nose as well. "I wouldn't call them great."

"Well, what would you call them?"

My stomach wrenched in my belly, and I spit up into the well.

"The words evade me; now let's get out of this stink hole."

As I stepped away, Brenwar jerked me back.

"Let's lighten the load," he said, slipping off his pack and setting it over in the shadows.

I tossed him mine. Brenwar set them side by side, unfolded a cloth that got bigger and bigger, and covered the packs up. He muttered some words, and our covered packs blended in with the stone. It was another one of those delights he'd brought from my father's throne room: a Cloth of Concealment, and it was helpful all the time.

He lumbered over, swinging his arms, war hammer ready.

"Better get going; it won't be long before they miss those two."

I looked back at the well. I'd say we had an hour at most.

"Let's go."

The hideout was a network of rooms and tunnels, some lit, some not, carved from stone. From room to room, corridor to corridor, there were sparse furnishings, few decorations, and here and there, runes were written on the walls. Nothing extraordinary. It seemed many races had used this place as a hideout over time, though. We moved in the shadows, darting from alcove to alcove, avoiding the light and the sounds of anything coming. Other than the two guards we'd encountered, there was nothing. No chatter, no shuffling of feet, not even the crick of a cricket or the scurry of a rodent.

I stopped a moment and gathered my thoughts. The goblins must have felt safe in their hideout, and maybe only a couple of guards were needed to make the rounds. Still, it was weird. It wasn't usually this easy sneaking into any place, and even though we had put some thought into it and come through the utmost back door, something was eating at me.

Brenwar jostled me with his elbow and sniffed the air.

"Smell that," he said.

Ah, indeed I did. It was goblin brew. The making of swill. The mix of sweat. We were getting close to the goblins, but where was the dragon? "Follow me."

Now, when it comes to saving dragons, there is only one thing you need to concern yourself with: getting them free of the net, shackles, or cage they're in. If you pull that off, any dragon is smart enough and fast enough to do the rest on his or her own. In a flash, they'll be gone, which probably explains why they never thanked me or stuck around to help. Which always bothered me. After all, I was putting my life on the line, and I had the scars to show for it.

"TUMBA—TUMBA—TUMBA—TUMBA ..."

It seemed the goblins were singing, or celebrating, perhaps. I was guessing that dragon, a rare blue razor, would be very valuable. But they weren't going to collect a single coin. I would see to that. I swore it!

We squatted down behind a balcony that overlooked a great hall. Peeking over the ledge, I could see boiling vats of goblin gruel and swill bubbling on beds of red-hot coals. There was a throne at the end of the hall on which a massive humanoid sat, covered from head to toe in deep-purple robes. The goblins ate, drank, sang, and wrestled with one another... at least thirty of them that I could see. It was a celebration.

"That's a lot of goblins," I said.

"Aye."

I felt a knife in my heart when I noticed the dragon curled up inside a heavy iron cage. A girl, at that. My keen eyes picked up the lighter belly and long, dark eyelashes. That made me sad and mad at the same time.

"Let's move," I said, unfolding my bow, Akron. Its workings snapped to, the bowstring coiling around the wood and into place. I was ready. I was ready to take them all on.

Brenwar grabbed my elbow and pulled me back. I jerked away.

"Easy, Dragon. Give them more time to celebrate. They'll by drunk soon enough. Easier to strike them."

Well, soon enough wouldn't be soon enough for me, but I conceded.

"And what happens when the patrol doesn't return?"

"Well, let's hope they don't remember."

I kept my eyes on the robed figure on the simple stone throne. Mysterious and powerful he or she seemed, yet unmoving. The figure felt evil, though. I felt compelled to launch a magic arrow into that hooded skull. Take down the leader and they all fall down. Darn that need not to kill! I resisted, slipped my arrow back into my quiver, and, against all my compulsions, I waited.

CHAPTER 13

DRAGONS. CAGED. QUIET. UNHAPPY. FINNIUS had never seen so many of them before. The door he'd been shoved through, the one he swore he'd taken before, had led him elsewhere. Where had Selene taken him? He dabbed his handkerchief on his head. *Mercy! It's hot in here.* He tugged and rapidly jerked at the neck of his sweat-soaked robes.

"What do you think?" Selene said, reaching out and stroking the whiskers of a cat-faced dragon.

Finnius stayed back.

It was as big as a horse, feline in its features, with a dark red belly and red scales. Two tails whipped back and forth, banging against the walls and the iron on the cage, its eyes penetrating and evil.

"Care to pet it?"

Finnius kept his arms folded in his sleeves. There was no way he would pet that thing. He was close enough already. But how did he answer without sounding too fearful?

"I'm just fine, High Priestess. But, if you insist." He shuffled forward.

A wry smile came across Selene's lips as she said, "Your caution is warranted. Come any closer… and he'll kill you."

Finnius backed away, his face recoiling.

"You should have seen what happened to the last one who got too close." Selene patted the dragon on the nose, drawing a part purr, part roaring sound. "The poor man sizzled and fried. Skin bubbled right off of him."

Catching the dragon's eye, he gulped. Its eyes glowed with a sinister yellow light.

"Er … how exactly did that happen, if I may ask?"

"Some other time. Now walk with me."

The room was more or less an underground stable, but instead of being filled with horses, it was filled with dragons, all of which were restrained in one way or another. A chain was cuffed to each neck. A muzzle on all of their snouts except for the catlike red one. It was different than the rest. A creature of its own free will.

She flipped her hair over her shoulders as she made her way to a smaller stall. A green dragon the size of a large dog was curled up in a ball. Shackled and muzzled the same as the rest.

"How well do you know your dragons, Finnius?" Selene said.

A question. Any answer could be wrong or right. It all depended on the mood Selene was in, which seemed to be pretty good at this time. But he'd seen her put a fellow acolyte to sleep before, permanently, for saying "Yes," which was the correct response, but she'd wanted to hear "No." He cleared his throat.

"Just what I have read, which, I am sorry to say, is little."

"And what have you read about what we have here?"

"A green lily?"

"Good, keep going."

"Well, unlike most dragons, it feeds off plants, not animals. Can be snared with honey or gold. Flies less and walks more, with a preference to hide in the heights of the trees."

"Ah ... well done, Finnius."

He smiled a little.

"And can you tell me the most important part about this dragon?"

Finnius pulled his shoulders back a little and lifted his chin.

"The breath weapon. A stream of yellow powder. Like pollen. It paralyzes."

"Not bad, Acolyte. Not bad at all. But that's not all it can do." She pointed at the back of the dragon. A row of yellow scales flared up and down its back. "Those humps. Poisonous. Rare and pure. Assassins will pay a very high price for that."

"How do you extract it?" he asked.

"There is only one way to do that. You have to kill it."

A little something tugged at Finnius's heart just then.

"Is there something wrong?"

What was that, sympathy? It couldn't be.

"Pardon, High Priestess. Eh ... I was of the impression you were keeping them alive. Just some confusion on my part."

She shook her head, saying, "Come."

He followed. He'd probably follow her anywhere. Drawn like a frog to a lily pad. He could not help it.

She took a seat along a bench in the back of the stables and patted a spot for him.

"Dragons are much like people. Well, they're better than people in most regards. They can be guided down the paths of good or evil. Some are born of evil dragons, but most are born of good dragons. Do you recall the Great Dragon War?"

Who didn't remember the legends about those wars when people and dragons battled side by side for the preservation of good-natured Nalzambor? The entire mission of the Clerics of Barnabus was to begin that war again and triumph this time. But in order to do so, they would need more dragons. Whoever controlled the dragons controlled the entire world. Free dragons, free world. Enslave the dragons … destroy the world.

Finnius dabbed his head again before stuffing his handkerchief under his robes. His sweating slowed from drops to a fine trickle. Finally, he felt comfortable. "Yes, High Priestess."

Selene's face darkened, and her eyes were like burning coals.

"We lost then, our numbers decimated because we were careless." She poked him in the shoulder. "One, we didn't have enough dragons." She poked him again. "Two, we didn't kill enough before we started."

He could see the regret in her eyes, the anger, a fire deep in her mind, as if the battle was still going on. In a sense, it still was. Most of the world didn't know that, though. The strange thing was that she spoke as if she had been there. But the Great Dragon War had taken place hundreds of years ago. Selene looked much too young to have lived that long.

She continued.

"As for the green lily dragon, well, if he doesn't submit to my will, turn from his better nature, then what is left of him will fetch a fine price on the markets. Those yellow humps, just a couple of them garner enough gold to fund a war."

There was that feeling in his gut again. *Sympathy? It can't be.*

"No chance he'd be sold as a pet?"

"The poison is worth more than all the rest of him."

Dragon hide. Claws. Scales. Teeth. Wings. Every bit of it was a high-priced commodity.

"And the blood?" he asked.

She didn't answer at first. She just sat and sat and sat, making part of him wish he were elsewhere, anywhere but there.

After several minutes passed, Finnius cleared his throat.

"Ah," she said, "I keep all of that." She stretched out her arms as she got up and said, "Keep up the effort, Finnius, and I'll show you things you never could have dreamed of. But for now, I'm going to reveal a little more. I'm going to show you what is next in store for Nath Dragon."

CHAPTER 14

The reveling of the goblins didn't show any signs of slowing, and I was tired of waiting. And their chants were getting annoying.

"TUMBA—TUMBA—TUMBA—TUMBA ..."

I wanted to shoot them all. Stupid sing-songy goblins. Brenwar might disagree with me, but he pretty much disagreed with me most of the time. The longer the goblins sang, drank, ate, and fought one another, the worse I felt for the dragon.

As she lay curled up in her cage, the goblins danced around the bars and taunted her. And why not? After all, they had captured her. But the swill they drank gave them a little too much courage. Now, if I'd seen a lock on the cage, I could have shot it with an arrow and shattered it. But this cage was solid steel bars bolted down into the stone. No lock or door in sight. The truth was, I didn't have any idea how we'd get the dragon out until we got down there. I punched Brenwar in the arm.

His popped open his eye and asked, "What are ye thinking, Dragon?"

"How are we going to get the dragon out? She's sealed in that cage."

"Well, we might just have to kill them all first and figure it out later. Or we can interrogate one after another until we figure it out."

"You think you can take thirty goblins and whatever or whoever that thing on the throne is?"

He peeked over the wall.

"Certainly."

Now it was my turn to grunt. The throned man, humanoid, or whatever it was, bothered me. It had barely moved an inch the entire time I'd been here. It just sat in its robes, hands and feet covered, moving its head in slow nods and shakes when the goblins spoke to it. It was big, too, bigger than me, not that it bothered me. I wondered if it was the winged ape.

"Do you think it's a mage or a cleric? A sage or druid?"

Brenwar rested his war hammer on his chest, leaned back along the wall, and shrugged.

"It doesn't matter what it is." He licked his thumb and ran it along his blade. "It will be dead soon enough."

Being around Brenwar didn't make controlling my urges to fight any easier. He was a bad influence. I just didn't understand why I was held to a higher standard. Brenwar was good and noble, but he could kill in battle without regret or consequence, it seemed. But as Father had told me, "To each kind their own purposes. Your purpose is different than theirs."

My eyes went back and forth between the dragon and the man on the throne. The thing on the throne bothered me. Mages, wizards, warlocks, and witches were all a cunning bunch. They loved traps and wards and little creatures called familiars. The familiars really kept a close eye on things and could be most anything, in most cases small: cats, birds, lizards, snakes, monkeys, or even mice. That's just a few samples, and they can be much odder things. So I'm always careful around any animals that look at me too long, but so far, in this hideout I'd hardly seen a thing. Everything had been going well—too well.

"Something's wrong," I said.

Brenwar eyed me. He'd been around me long enough to know my instincts are often right.

The commotion in the grand hall came to a stop.

I felt my spine tighten from my waist to my neck. The hairs on my neck stood on end when I saw two goblins dragging another goblin in. And it wasn't just any goblin, either. It was the one we'd throttled and bribed in the woods. The goblins shoved the broken prisoner onto his knees before the throne. Its body shook as it fought against its bonds and cried out for mercy. I got the feeling that it would have been better off if we'd killed it ourselves. We could have been merciful, at least.

"Brenwar, I think our time is up."

The figure on the stone chair leaned forward. The goblin cried out, only to be silenced with a sharp blow to the back of its head from a goblin soldier.

One of the guards set the coins I'd given it down on the steps. I could see the big one sitting in the middle, twinkling in the torchlight like a tiny sun.

The goblin spilled his guts. I could hear the conversation, and the goblin told all that he knew, which wasn't so bad. For all he knew or they knew, we weren't within miles of the place. How would we get in, anyway? The figure in the robes sat upright at the mention of my dragon arm, however. The figure stood up taller than I had even figured. Seven feet high at least. Then another pair of goblins, from another direction, rushed in. One was holding a grappling hook.

"Uh oh," Brenwar said, checking the straps on his armor.

I slid two arrows from my quiver. I nocked one and bit down on the other.

I knew things had been too easy.

CHAPTER 15

I GOT MY FIRST GOOD LOOK at the figure in the robes. Its hands and fingers were large, clawed, and hairy, like a bugbear or gnoll. The figure reached down, grabbed the prisoner by the neck, and hoisted him high in the air. Every other goblin slunk back. Some froze, and the hot air seemed too cool, with icy intensity. The goblin's feet twitched in the air as the figure carried him down the steps for all to see. Then, in a loud male voice, the figure spoke words of power... ancient and mystic.

A sliver of ice went down my spine. *A magic user! Always unpredictable.*

His hands burst into flame, and the goblin's face caught fire as it screamed, twitched, and died. A pungent smell wafted my way: burnt goblin skin and hair. The figure dropped the goblin to the floor, where it fell apart like pieces of a charred tree. The magic user held his arm up for all to see. It was radiant with red, yellow, and blue flames that danced from one hand to the other. He was a formidable one, to control magic like that. Still, what he was, I wasn't so sure.

The magic user clapped his hands together. The fires extinguished as he spoke in a thick voice.

"Find them."

At least it was a man, but what kind of man I wasn't certain.

"I'm shooting him," I said.

"No, wait," Brenwar warned. "There'll be less of them to shoot in a moment. They'll be searching these endless tunnels for hours trying to find us, if we're careful. Shoot now and they all swarm us."

Point taken, but I didn't like it. I wanted to move. I needed to get down there and see if Fang could hew through that dragon cage. Below, the goblins, most of them half drunk or worse, fumbled through their gear and stumbled into the surrounding tunnels. One moment footsteps echoed everywhere, the next moment they faded away. Three goblins remained, surrounding the dragon's cage, armed with battle axes, swords, and spears. I noticed the throne of the magic user was vacant. The magic user was nowhere in sight. The gold coins on the steps were still there, however. *Excellent!*

"I've got a plan."

Brenwar eyed me and said, "You do?"

Remember those gold coins I gave that goblin? Well, they aren't coins. They're something else, an item from Father's treasure trove I learned to use long ago. I muttered some words of magic of my own. My human fingertips tingled as I twirled them around. One by one, each coin rose on its edge and began to roll.

Brenwar huffed under his beard, "Magic." Then he moved on. He had some idea what I was thinking. He usually did.

Tink. Tink. Tink.

Down the steps they came, rolling over the stone floor toward the dragon cage. The goblins eyed the coins, one looking at the other, curiosity filling their blurry yellow eyes.

"Just keep watching," I muttered under my breath.

The coins circled the cage once then stopped upright, and each fell before a different goblin. They wanted to grab those coins, each of them; I could feel it. One scratched his head. The other bent forward. The third kept an eye on the throne before stooping closer.

Poof. Poof. Poof.

Each coin burst into a cloud of gold dust that coated a goblin from head to toe. They coughed, hacked, and clutched at their necks before falling over. Not dead, mind you. Just sleeping.

Those coins, well, as I said, they came in handy. I'd figured if that goblin we met ever came back to the hideout and ratted us out, we'd need all the help we could get. So I planted my own surprise just in case. I hopped off the balcony, landing like a cat on the main floor as the gold dust settled.

One of the goblins started snoring.

The dragon, well, she was sitting up in her cage, tail swaying back and forth. She was so beautiful, her scales like shiny blue shields with jagged streaks of black. Her long lashes batted as she stared at me. She was fine.

"It won't be long," I said. "I'll have you out of here soon."

I tugged at the metal on the bars. It was thicker than I could bend. There was no cage door, either, just where the iron was bolted to the stone. Perhaps Brenwar's hammer could bust it up, or perhaps my sword could cut through it.

"Stand back," I said, drawing Fang.

The dragon reared back and struck at me with an angry hiss. Her razor-sharp teeth snapped at me.

"What?" I said. "You have to trust me." I drew Fang back again.

She hissed, louder this time. Opened her mouth to release her breath. I lowered Fang and backed away.

Brenwar appeared at my side, pushed me back, and said, "It's magic."

"What do you mean?"

"See the markings on the floor?"

Oh, now I saw them. Arcane symbols and designs were beneath the dragon's feet. The cage was woven with similar designs as well. It left me cold. These dragon poachers were more than what they appeared to be. That was when the unsettling feeling crept back in between my neck and shoulders.

"Heh-heh-heh … go ahead," a disturbing voice said. "Go ahead, cut into the cage and see what happens."

It was the voice of the magic user, who now stood on the balcony where Brenwar and I had stood earlier.

"The only person who can open that cage is me. And if anyone else tries to open it by any other means, it will be very, very painful for the dragon. Deathly so."

The figure flicked a lance of energy from his fingers. It sailed over my ducking head, striking the cage bars. The blue razor roared and fluttered her wings, curling back up on the floor in a tight knot.

"Drop your weapons unless you want to see the dragon start to smoke," the magic user warned.

Over the years, I'd faced, fought, dropped, kicked, and punched my share of wizards, shamans, and illusionists. And like I said, they were a crafty bunch. And sometimes, when they got the drop on you, it was best to do as you were told. I looked around. All the goblins that had been gone had returned now, and then some.

"I'm not surrendering to any goblin, Dragon," Brenwar growled under his beard.

I set Fang on the ground and held my hands up.

"I don't think there's much choice."

CHAPTER 16

WITH THE ESSENCE OF THE dragon's life linked to her cage, there wasn't much choice other than to give up. The pair of goblin soldiers took my sword and bow along with Brenwar's hammer while the others surrounded us. Above, the magic user jumped from the balcony and descended slowly, robes softly touching the floor.

The goblins held our arms while two others started to bind them.

"Leave them be," the magic user proclaimed, "and bring them to my throne."

The magic user took his seat as we were shoved onto the steps.

"Don't do that again, goblin!" Brenwar warned, rising back to his feet, only to be shoved down again.

"That's it!"

Brenwar stuffed his heel in one's belly and shattered the knee of the next, making it let out a cry of pain.

"Enough!" The magic user said. "Let the prisoner be."

Finally, the man pulled back his hood.

"I am Corzan the Necromancer. Lord of the Burrow Goblins."

Lord of the Burrow Goblins? Hah! I wanted to laugh but could not. I could laugh at a goblin, yes, but him, no. He worried me. My eyes met his. What I saw was unsettling.

Corzan had the devilish features of a goblin but was still a man. His face was ill tempered and scarred. A sorcerer of many battles won and lost. His eyes were dark, intelligent, and probing. But he didn't look like a necromancer. No, too rough around the edges, very atypical of his ilk. His hair was long, thin, and black as coal, and his sideburns came down to form a beard that hung inches below his chin. His ears were clipped in metal points at the top and bottom. I'd never seen that style before, but it looked uncomfortable. His strange hands were coarse haired and rough, with dark metal armbands wrapped around his wrists. He sighed as he folded his fingers and set them down in his lap, showing the humanity that he must have possessed at some time before. His serene gesture gave me no additional comfort at all. He was trouble.

"So, I can only assume you have come to steal my dragon?"

"It's not *your* dragon, Corzan. Dragons are free creatures. Such is the way on Nalzambor. Dragon poaching is a crime, well known in all the world."

"Hah!" He slapped the stone arm of his throne. "Dragon poaching has been around all my life and always will be. The people of this world capture, hunt, and eat the other creatures to decorate their tables. Cows, sheep, horses, goats—and no one complains. I don't see how dragons are any different."

That last phrase really got me going. My nerves inflamed as I stepped forward.

"Dragons aren't animals! They are the oldest race on Nalzambor. Vastly superior to the likes of you—poachers."

Corzan motioned with his arm and said, "And yet one sits in my cage. Hah, I hardly consider them superior. Quite easy to catch, skin, and eat, like any other rodent."

Red faced, I stepped forward again, only to have four goblins lower their spears at my belly. I had Brenwar to think about, too. And getting myself killed wasn't going to do the dragon any good. I had to settle down. Think things out. I let my anger subside.

"So, you are Nath Dragon, I see. Every bit as ill tempered as the troubadours sing. It's nice to see it for myself, but something is different." His eyes shimmered with light as he waved his hand.

My dragon arm shot up in the air. I fought to pull it down but could not. I'd lost control.

"What are you doing, Corzan? Let me go!"

"Fascinating!" Corzan said, eyeing my arm like a splendid robe of wizards. "Hah, it seems maybe my comments about the dragon might be wrong. Either that, or you are part animal. Of course, I'm sure you consider yourself part dragon." He returned to his seat. "There you go."

I gasped as my arm was freed. I didn't know what had happened, but this necromancer wasn't one to fool with. No one had ever taken control of my body before.

"How did you do that?" I said, rubbing my dragon arm.

"Like I said, I'm a necromancer, and I know things about dragons." Corzan pulled out his necklace of bronze dragon scales and claws. "Certainly you of all people understand the mystic powers of these things."

He was right. Dragon parts could be used against the dragons to control them and make them do one's will. Many dragons had been used to commit evil acts against their will, while some dragons didn't mind doing evil. Just like the Necromancer bound the blue dragon to her cell, he'd done something similar to me. I wasn't sure how, but I did realize that with my dragon arm, I might be more vulnerable than I had previously understood.

"Impressive, Corzan, but I'm still here, and I can only assume you want something from me." I might as well be nice about it. "Care to share?"

"Very well, Nath Dragon… your enemies are close."

I looked around.

"I can see that."

"No, we are not your enemy. Just your captors. The Clerics of Barnabus, now they are your enemies."

My stomach churned at the mention of their name.

"And you would be selling this dragon to my enemies, which would make you my enemy. All the dragon poachers are my enemies. So please, don't try to use clever words to imply that you are not my enemy, Corzan."

"As you wish." He shrugged. "If it makes you feel better to be my sworn enemy, then I guess I can live with that. But the Clerics of Barnabus are not my allies, either. I have my own ambitions, Dragon. My own wants, needs, and desires. Lord of the Burrow Goblins? Do you think I was born for that?" He slammed his fist down on his throne. "No! I am cursed by it!" He clutched his hairy fingers. "Look at these hands. Have you ever seen a man with such hands before?"

"Have you ever seen one with a dragon arm before?"

Corzan brightened. A glimmer of humanity returned in his eyes.

"Huh… touché. But, honestly, a dragon arm or goblin hands, which would you take?"

I smiled and said, "I think you know the answer to that. Now, can you back up and tell me about this issue with the Clerics?"

"They pay well for the dragons but for information on you as well. They want you dead, but I need you alive."

"Pardon?" I should have been elated by the statement, but I wasn't. *Alive for what?* "First things first." I pointed at the blue razor.

"I trapped the dragon to trap you. And my plan worked out all so well, thanks to your friend the dwarf."

"Me!" Brenwar objected. "I had nothing to do with that. He lies."

"Oh, don't be so hard on yourself, Brenwar Bolderguild. My familiar made the suggestion to you when you were miles away."

"What familiar?" I asked.

Corzan held out his hands.

"Come, come to me, little creature," Corzan beckoned.

I followed Corzan's eyes to Brenwar's black beard.

"What's every one looking at?" Brenwar said, bunching up.

That's when I saw it. A tiny face popped out of his beard. A pixie! As it crawled out, its mosquito-like wings came to life. Brenwar gawped, swung, and missed as it darted over to Corzan and landed on his shoulder. I could hear the faintest whisper on its tiny black lips now. "Dragons beyond the shale."

"Would it kill you to comb that thing every once in a while?" I said.

Brenwar pointed at the pixie, saying, "Nothing lives in a dwarf's beard without permission. You'll be paying for that, you little pixie—you will." He slapped his hands together.

The pixie squeaked and dove into Corzan's hood.

You see, I told you about those familiars. It just proved Corzan knew we were here all along, but what did he need me for?

"So, let me understand this. The Clerics put a bounty on me. And you wanted to catch me to turn in to the Clerics? Or did you have something more zany in mind?"

"The price on your head is high, but I don't value gold. I value magic, and they cannot offer me any more than I can get for myself. No, what I need is something else entirely. And the Clerics, well, they gave me an idea of how I could obtain what I do not have."

I folded my arms across my chest and said, "And what might that be?"

"There is an object of power, an artifact that I cannot acquire." He licked his lips. "I want you to get it for me."

"And what makes you think I can get it if you can't?"

"I think my evil nature denies me access to such things."

"So you've tried?"

"And failed, so to speak."

"So," I said, "what and where is it?"

"At the top of this mountain is an ancient graveyard. Inside a tomb is an object of power. A Thunderstone. Bring it back to me."

The recesses of my mind sparked with memory. A Thunderstone. My father had mentioned those before. There were many of them scattered in the world, each with different powers of its own. This was something worth looking into—not so much for Corzan but for myself.

"So, just walk in there, get it, and bring it back. What's up there that I need to know about?"

"A guardian is all."

"What kind of guardian?"

Corazon formed a smile that could crack stone as he tapped his fingertips together.

"A troublesome one."

"Pretty vague. So, am I to venture to the graveyard and battle this troublesome guardian unarmed?"

Corzan rubbed his chin with his hairy hand.

"No. You can have your weapons and gear. You can take your friend. Just bring me the Thunderstone, and I'll let you and the dragon go."

Let us go. I didn't think so. Magic users were notorious for going back on their word, both good and evil. They always had some stipulation that they failed to mention. So Corzan's words were no good. But I didn't have much choice in the matter, either.

"How much time do I have?"

"Not much. The Clerics of Barnabus will be here in two days, if not sooner. The climb up the steep mountain is long and treacherous. Still, you have plenty of time."

"And what happens if I'm not back before then?"

"I would suggest you return before they come if you want this dragon freed. They won't want any delays, and I've no desire to agitate them."

"And what will you do when they arrive and the dragon is gone?"

Corzan laughed, a wicked sound that suggested I'd been duped.

"If I have the stone, that won't be an issue. Just bring it to me, and all things will fall in order. Do we have an agreement?"

Never make deals with wizards, magic users, sorcerers, and especially necromancers. Never... ever!

Everyone said that, but they still made them.

A wizard's word is never good.

That's another one I heard all the time. The best thing you could do when dealing with a magic user was to not put it in writing and watch your behind.

"We have one," I said.

"Get your gear and go, Nath Dragon. And be wary of the scales."

CHAPTER 17

Still in the rain, we made our way up the mountain like two ants on a giant's belly, the top too far to see. The climb wasn't so difficult, not for me anyway, but Brenwar struggled to keep up.

"Slow down, I don't have long legs like yours," Brenwar huffed from behind me.

Like I said, dwarves would rather dig than climb. Digging just wasn't prudent at this time. And I'd already spent an hour convincing Brenwar that climbing was better than trying to find another secret tunnel. Of course, he seemed to inspect every rock along the way.

"I'm going as slow as I can," I yelled back.

"Well, don't go too slow."

"But you said to slow down. Now you don't want me to go too slow?"

Below me, I could see Brenwar looking below him. It was a long way down to where we started, and a simple slip would be the beginning of a long, painful tumble.

"Just keep moving," he grumbled.

Like I said, it wasn't the worst climb for me, but I had Brenwar tethered to me by rope just in case. He didn't like that—I could tell—but he didn't protest, either.

"Just tug if you want me—"

"Keep moving!"

Up I went.

Two days. That seemed like plenty of time to make it up the mountain and back. It would only take half a day to make it to the top and less than that to make it back down. I couldn't imagine retrieving a Thunderstone would take much longer. Except for the issue with the guardian, whatever that might be. And why Corzan couldn't handle it but could handle me, I didn't understand. Magic items, for the most part, could be used by good or evil. There was something he wasn't telling me. So it must be something I could do that he could not. Good for me.

I clutched the ledge with my dragon-clawed hand and pulled myself up to the next ridge. Brenwar's stubby fingers made it to the lip, and I pulled him up by the back of his armor.

He rolled up to one knee, wiped the rainwater from his eyes, and combed out his beard with his fingers. He shook his head at me before turning away. That pixie had gotten to him.

The valley below us was a wondrous sight of black forest underneath the lantern of the moonlight. Even with all the rain, it was still something to behold. So peaceful. One wouldn't expect any danger up here.

"Look," Brenwar said, untying the rope around his waist.

The ledge we were on was moss covered, with tracks that looked like an old road.

"Better than climbing," I said as I readied my bow.

Something caught my eye. In the distant moonlight, I saw something sail across the sky, flapping its wings like a bird of prey before disappearing into the night. It could have been a dragon, but all I could think of was the winged ape. Still, it was hard to tell in all the darkness and rain, even with my keen eyes. For all I knew, it was just a really big bat.

The trail we took was steep, winding around the mountain like a giant snake. I wondered what had carved it from the mountain and why it didn't go all the way to the bottom. Oddly, it had started at the top. Perhaps they, whoever they were, had started at the top but never made it to the bottom. I'd seen stranger things.

The cold rain pelted my face like tiny icicles, and the whipping wind made my bones feel brittle. It was at moments like this that I missed the city, so soft and warm and amenable. And the women, oh how I missed their soft lips and compliments. It had been a while since I'd seen one, but fortunately many had burned a lasting impression in my memory. It was funny how my thoughts drifted to women at times like this.

The more I walked, the more my leg ached, until I finally had to stop and take a seat. The moonlight faded as it passed to the other side of the mountain, leaving us alone in the pitch black. The atmosphere was like a cold, windy tomb, alone on the mountain, biting and unforgiving. I longed for the sun already, but that was hours away, and we still had miles to go at least. I dipped my head and closed my eyes, trying to think of sunnier times.

"You should rest, Dragon." Brenwar said. "It's been a long time, and your limp is getting worse."

"Is it that noticeable?"

"It is to me. How about I take a look at it?"

I could hear the sound of concern in Brenwar's voice, and the truth was my leg should have healed up by now. But every so often you got a stubborn wound, one that festered and throbbed like a pulsating cyst. Still, pain was a steady reminder of what the blue razor was going through. I could live with a little pain; I felt guilty for even stopping. I closed my eyes again. I just needed a little rest. I brushed my mane of hair away from my face.

"Just give me a few minutes, Brenwar. I'll be fine."

A minute couldn't have passed before everything fell quiet. The wind stopped. The rain as well. I felt the hairs on my neck standing.

"That's odd." Wiping my soaked hair from my face again, I opened my eyes. "We've been on top of many mountains, but I've never known the wind to stop before."

"Me neither," Brenwar said, extending his arm.

I groaned all the way back up to my feet. So far as I knew, nothing could stop the wind. Sure, controlling the wind was one thing, but stopping it was another. Of course, the wind could stop itself, I suppose. Father always said the Earth, Wind, Water, and Fire all had minds of their own.

"Follow me," I said.

I churned up the trail, every step as heavy as the last, determined to make it to the top by dawn. As suddenly as the wind had stopped, it returned, more brisk than before. It gave me little relief, as my gut told me something was wrong. After all, we were heading to a graveyard, and there was no telling what kind of spirits and forces resided there. Cold rain splattering my face, I pushed on.

At last, we crested the top, and the rays of the rising sun caught my eyes. The warmth on my face invigorated me.

"Glad that's over," I said, putting my hands on my hips. "It should be easier going down than coming up." I slapped Brenwar on the shoulder. "Let's take a look around, shall we?"

The mountaintop was a grassy plain that stretched as far as I could see. In the distance, I saw the greater mountain ranges of Nalzambor and their snowcapped peaks. The grass and weeds were tall, the ground barren in some places, and I had to walk awhile until the first tombstone appeared. It was tall and marked in a language I could not read—and I could read a lot of languages, but I'd never seen anything like this before.

"Can you make anything of this?" I said.

Brenwar snarled when he squinted at the headstone.

"Giants!"

I took a closer look.

"No, it's not giants. Too small. And just because you can't read it doesn't mean it's giants."

As we walked, the tombstones appeared in more clusters. Some cracked, others broken, many almost completely covered in moss and roots. One stone marker in particular was three stories tall and half as wide. I couldn't imagine how such a large stone had made its way to the top of the mountain, but giants could account for that.

"Told you, giants," Brenwar said.

I shrugged. If there were any giants, they'd have to have died long ago. But I didn't care about that. I just wanted to find the tomb that held the Thunderstone. I rubbed the back of my head. I didn't see why it should be so difficult for Corzan to come up here and get it himself.

"Find anything?"

"No!" Brenwar said.

"Well, you should be able to find a tomb anywhere beneath this cemetery."

For an hour, Brenwar had stomped over the grass, the ground, the stone sarcophagi... and I would have thought he'd have found something by now, but he hadn't. So many graves, hundreds of them at least. Some small enough for a halfling, others big enough for ogres. He glared at me, hoisted his hammer over his head, and brought it down.

"NO!" I yelled.

Too late. Brenwar's hammer smashed into the shell of a stone sarcophagus.

CRACK!

It sounded like the earth split open.

"Are you trying to wake the dead? Have you gone mad?"

"There's a giant in there!" he yelled back.

"A dead giant, maybe! Brenwar, why did you do that?"

Chest out, war hammer hanging in his grip, he laughed at me.

"Take a look for yourself."

There it was: a staircase leading down.

"Well done," I said.

"Never doubt a dwarf."

I pinched my nose. "Ew... that's bad." I looked at him and said, "You first, then." He looked at me.

I said, "Well it's your discovery."

"Certain—"

A cloud of dark smoke crept out from within. A grey fog fell over us. Both of us coughed as we stepped back. That eerie feeling returned as the wind died again. Death. Something was shuffling up the stairs, and it wasn't alone.

CHAPTER 18

THERE'S NOTHING WORSE THAN THE smell of rotting flesh in the morning. Nose pinched, stomach knotted, I backed from the dark mist as I slid Fang from his sheath. I retched. And that's when the first ghoul appeared.

Ghouls. Creepy, long-fingered fiends with yellow skin and bright-green eyes. They spilled out from the hole in all shapes and sizes, arms outstretched, mouths frothing, each making its own ghastly sigh. They were men once, now turned to something darker, lingering between life and death by cursed threads of magic. My first impulse was to run, let them spill out, scatter—and then take them one by one—but it was too late for that. Like a hive of bees, they swarmed and struck fast.

"Fiends!" Brenwar roared. "I'll stomp you back into your dark hole. Come on!"

Brenwar smashed one in the face and another in the chest, knocking it to the ground. It was a good start, but where there had been ten, now there were twenty. We were in danger, grave danger. Forgive the pun.

"Let's get out of this, Brenwar! Quit swinging and start running!"

I toppled one over with a cut to its knee. The best thing I could do was slow them down. They weren't so easy to kill. Ghouls are terrors, ghastly things that crawl in and out of dark places in the night. The truth is, I'd never seen one in daylight before, and never so many all at once. The daylight gave us a little bit of an edge, but the fog didn't help. Where that had come from, I'd never know.

Two closed in on either side of me, as fast as well-trained soldiers. Ghouls, unlike most undead things, are pretty fast, and just as ugly, too. I leapt backward in time to see them crash into each other. Another pair of hands seized hold of me, a horrible face opening up to take a bite of my dragon arm. I ripped my arm from its grasp and punched it the jaw, drawing forth an eerie howl. They could still feel something, it seemed. Oh, and their bites. They can be quite deadly, so don't ever let them sink their teeth into you.

Brenwar slugged another one with his war hammer, sending it careening into a tombstone.

"Quit holding back, Dragon! They're already dead!"

I'd become so accustomed to holding back in a fight, I'd forgotten what it was like to let loose. It had been a long time. And what Brenwar was suggesting sounded really good. But was he right, or was he wrong? I swiped another one in the leg. They were everywhere now. I ducked, dodged, and dove. Struck, swung, and stabbed. I crippled some, slowed most, but where one fell, another rose.

I huffed and panted. They were wearing me down, and my bum leg wasn't doing much good. A steady erosion, they came undeterred. A nick here, a cut there, and I was bleeding from just about everywhere.

"Nath!"

I couldn't even see Brenwar, just a mass of bodies where the voice came from.

"Nath! I've been bitten!"

NO! I had to get to Brenwar! Or else he might die. I shouldn't have been holding back. If I hadn't, my friend wouldn't be in dire straits right now. The next ghoul swarmed into my face and I swung, hard. The ghoul fell to the ground and moved no more. I started to fight my way toward Brenwar.

"Get off him, vermin!"

They were fast and many. I was faster and angry. I swung hard and harder, but my arm began to tire. I was going to lose Brenwar if I stopped now, but I could barely lift my arm anymore. If it had been made of lead, it would have felt lighter. I was surrounded; the ghouls came at me from all sides. One at a time, then two. I couldn't fight them off much longer.

"Hang on, Brenwar!" I yelled.

Desperate times call for drastic measures. I switched Fang to my dragon hand. *Oh my!*

Remember, I told you before that things happen when my dragon arm gets hold of Fang. Bad things for those who are not holding the blade.

Fang glowed with new life, throbbing red with power. I felt energy racing through my fingertips and toes. My entire body was becoming a new living thing. The ghouls stopped, shielding their eyes from my blade.

Three rushed.

Shing! Shing! Shing!

Three fell.

"YES!"

Fast. The word had a new meaning. I twisted around one ghoul and skewered another. Two fell at once from one mighty swing. I almost would have felt sorry for them if I didn't enjoy it so much. After all, the notion to run was not part of their being. Not when living blood was around.

Shing!

One came apart from the middle.

Shing!

Another clutched at its missing face.

Four came. Four died. Two came. Three died. The one behind me must have thought I didn't see it coming. Ah, the energy. I felt invincible. I could fight a hundred of these things.

Shing! Shing!

But there were no more. The fog lifted from the battlefield, and Fang's blade went dim. Only the picturesque morning in the Mountains of Nalzambor remained, with a litter of dead ghouls on the floor. I dropped to my knees. A wave of exhaustion assailed me. Blood and sweat dripped from my nose. My own blood, that is. I must have been cut to pieces, but I didn't care. I'd won.

Fang hummed one last time then quieted like a stone. Not a single notch, nick, or drop of blood was on its keen blade. My dragon arm, well, it seemed blacker than ever in the morning light, but in my heart I felt I'd done no wrong. I just hoped Brenwar was right about killing ghouls not making me evil.

"Brenwar!"

I rushed to him.

He lay on the ground, banged up and stiff as a stone. His dark eyes were like marbles gazing into the bright sky. I put my head to his chest and sighed. His heart was beating like a heavy mallet. I patted him on the chest. "You'll be all right." *I hope.*

He had a nasty bite mark on his leg. It was deep, red and purple, and swollen. You couldn't wear armor everywhere. It would slow you down too much.

"Ah, Brenwar, I apologize. I should have acted sooner. But you're still alive, and that's all that matters now." A thought struck me. "Huh … Did I just save your life?" I looked at my dragon arm. No changes. "Well, I'm sure even saving a dwarf counts for something. Don't worry; I'm sure the paralysis will wear off in a while. But if you don't snap out of it soon, I'm going in there without you."

He blinked. His lip almost curled.

"See, you're moving already. But it isn't much faster than before," I said, looking into his eyes, grinning.

The thought of me saving him would get him going, I hoped. I swore I heard a rumble in his throat.

I heard a rustle of feet. Something else began emerging from the tomb.

I grabbed my bow, Akron, and readied a special arrow, saying, "Not again."

CHAPTER 19

T HE ARROW I DREW FROM my quiver was special: magic, powerful, and explosive enough to rock the entire mountaintop. I was going to take care of business with it. I drew the bowstring along my cheek and waited for the next ghoul to scurry from the tomb. *What?* Nothing came. Instead, I could hear tiny footsteps all over the grass. That's when I saw the first one. It was pink. It was fluffy. Not a ghoul. Instead, I beheld a cat-sized dandelion with rows of tiny feet and a mouth as wide as its body. A carrion caterpillar. I lowered my bow.

"Whew!"

It wasn't coming after me. No, it was coming after the dead ghouls, and it wasn't alone, either. Where there was one, there were two. Where there were three, there were ten. They came from all directions, bright pink, pale blue, and canary yellow, marching over the ghoul bodies and coating them one by one with strands of a wispy white fiber. Sure, it was creepy: giant caterpillars with teeth and a coat of brilliant and fuzzy colors, but just you wait. Those caterpillars would become the most beautiful butterflies in the world one day. And not just any butterflies, either, but a very special sort.

"Fortune's found us, it seems."

Brenwar didn't respond as I dragged him over to a tombstone and propped him up.

"I know, I know," I said. "Nobody drags a dwarf without permission." I felt a hundred tiny feet on my back as a lime-green caterpillar climbed over my shoulder. Weird. "See that? A good sign, isn't it?"

He didn't respond, but his eyes were glaring at me.

"I'll take that as a yes."

It was a good sign. The carrion caterpillars, strange and dutiful, were often spotted on battlefields, coating the bodies of those who were not buried. The farmers said they made the best fertilizer in the world, though I found it hard to imagine anything good could grow from such evil things.

"I'm going in."

There was another thing about the caterpillars: they didn't come out until the danger was gone. I put my arrow back in the quiver and folded up the bow. Fang's light was a torch when I drew it, and down into the darkness I went, two steps at a time.

Musty and cold. Typical of all the dead spaces underground. But there were plenty of good things underground, too. Just go to any dwarven city. Still, a tomb full of ghouls was disturbing. Whatever was buried down here needed a great deal of protection, and I couldn't help but think that the ghouls were only the first wave. After all, guardians came in many shapes and forms, but at least the ghouls were out of the way. I'd have thought Corzan could have handled the ghouls, though, with the help of his goblin horde. But why risk it if you didn't have to?

The stairs stopped about thirty feet below ground. Above me, I could still see the dawn's light creeping in, but it was awfully distant. The room I stood in was part tomb, part temple. Rows of ancient stone pillars held the ground up, and behind them on either side of the wall were shelves for bodies, some vacant and some occupied.

I shoved one, a weathered husk wrapped in deteriorating cloth. Its head rolled off and cracked on the ground. It was a man. The body above it wasn't human, however. Its jaw had a row of canine teeth jutting out at the bottom, and the face was shaped like a dog's. A gnoll, perhaps. There were lizard men, halflings, orcs, and faces of many of the other races, all shriveled and shrunken.

I couldn't imagine why so many different people would be buried together, their bodies all at rest. Was it possible there was a time when all the races got along together? *Be wary of the dead,* my father always said. Perhaps all these people were evil, a common bond that served the same cause. I wondered if they all shared the language I couldn't read on the stones above.

I treaded lightly, making sure my feet didn't land on any strange patterns or layouts. Tombs that held something of value would have booby traps.

"Perhaps I should have waited on Brenwar," I muttered to myself, wiping the cobwebs from my face and eyes. So many cobwebs, but I didn't see any spiders anywhere. I looked up. Nothing. Thank goodness.

So many bodies. Two dozen by the looks of things. Twelve on one side, twelve on the other, but a couple of shelves were missing bodies.

"Oh, there you are."

A pair of tarantulas crawled past my toes. I wondered what the spiders fed on down here. I couldn't shake the feeling that one if not all those bodies would reanimate and attack at any moment. The undead often did that. *Find the stone. Find the stone. Find the stone.*

The sad thing was, the Thunderstone might not even be down here. It could be anywhere on the mountain. I thought of the dragon, the blue razor. *Hurry.* I had to find the stone, make the deal, and free the dragon. My heart started to race. I didn't have time to waste.

I rested Fang on my shoulder.

"What do you think? Is it in here or not?"

I often talked to Fang when no one else was around. He was a good listener, and when he wanted, he could help, too.

Thrum.

Fang pulsated with life, a single burst of energy. I held him out before my eyes and made my way around the room. There was only one way in and one way out. The wall adjacent to the entrance was nothing more than a slab cut from the stone. The last thing I wanted to do was search all the long-dead bodies. It was a great place to hide things, but disturbing the dead was never a good idea. Bad things could happen and often did.

I ran my dragon arm along the pillars. The shelves. The barren pieces of wall. My sense of touch was extraordinary. With my eyes shut, I could feel the imperfections as if I could see them. Still, nothing remarkable. Just an old tomb filled with corpses that had once housed a horde of ghouls.

"Fang, they must have been protecting something," I said, circling the room. "And they couldn't have survived down here in this small a room very long, could they? Perhaps I just need to wait for Brenwar."

Thrum!

Fang flared again, its tip a red-hot glow pointing down at the tiles in the floor. I scratched the back of my head. "Huh? I guess I should have looked there before." I cleared some of the dust and dirt away with my boot. A colorful mosaic was underneath. On my hands and knees, I set Fang down and brushed and blew more dust away until I could make out a face of sorts. Perhaps an animal. Maybe a lycanthrope.

I found fingerholds around the edges of the stone, and my heart started to race. The floor was always a good place to bury things. And the face on the floor, well, so far as I could tell, it was a guardian. Something very important must lie underneath. Like a Thunderstone.

"What do you think, Fang? Should I wait for Brenwar?"

My sword glowed softly but said nothing.

"I'll take your silence as a no."

It was always easy for me to justify my actions with Fang, especially when his silence could easily be construed at will between yes or no.

I placed my hands on either side of the mosaic face, squatted, and pulled. It didn't budge. I tried again, putting my legs into it, straining.

"*Hurk!*"

Nothing. I sat down, trying to catch my breath, shaking my aching fingers.

"I hope this isn't one of those wizard locks. I hate those."

Every so often, it was good to travel with a magic user. As crafty as they liked to be, they loved to be challenged by magically sealed things. All things magical, really. But I didn't have one with me. I didn't sense any magic in the cover stone, either. This time, it was going to have to be my flesh versus the stone. I stared down at the odd animal face in the mosaic and said, "You will not beat me."

I hunkered down over it, got my grip, and threw all of my legs, arms, and back into it. I'm a big man, and a strong one at that. I pulled. Nothing. I groaned. Nothing. I shouted out loud like an angry giant.

"HAARRR!"

Stone began to scrape against stone. My fingers ached and my back burned, but I kept on pulling. I could feel my veins thicken like cords in my neck, and my knees cracked, but I was pulling it upward. Inch by inch. How thick was this stone?!

"RRRRRRR-RAAAAAAAH!"

I slipped free, toppling the stone over to the side and falling to my knees, panting for breath. It must have been the biggest stone I had ever lifted, because I didn't make a habit of lifting anything heavy if I didn't have to. I had Brenwar for that. A gaping square hole greeted me now. A trophy of my achievement. A blue hue glowed from within.

"It better ... *gasp* ... be in there."

I sucked in a deep breath, exhaled, and peeked inside.

A Thunderstone! Well, it was a stone, big enough to barely fit in my hand, smooth as marble, with jagged, brilliant blue markings. I couldn't imagine it being anything else. The question was... Was it safe to grab that thing? I ran my tongue across my lips. I wanted to grab it. Feel the power and magic within it. Perhaps it could even help reverse the effects of my dragon arm. Or it could make it worse. Father told me long ago of such things in the world that could help, help with anything, but you had to be very careful.

Eyes wide as saucers, I stared. Tempted. Tried. A struggle boiling within. How much easier would it be to save more dragons if I had greater power? I could wipe out the Clerics of Barnabus. Maybe destroy an entire temple. What kind of power was within that stone? I had to know.

"What do you think, Fang? A little touch couldn't be too bad."

Silence.

I rubbed my dragon finger under my chin. "Hmmm ... I ought to see what kind of power Corzan would be dealing with."

My golden eyes glimmered in the blue light. I grabbed the Thunderstone in my dragon claws. It was cold, and its markings were dim. Nothing. Nothing happened at all, and it felt just the same as before. I could only assume a mage could unlock the magic within. Disappointed, I flipped it up in the air and let it fall into my pack.

"Well, I guess that's it," I said, picking up Fang. "It's time to go."

To the staircase I went, limping as fast as I could. I'd spent enough time beneath the ground in the past day.

Crack!

The floor groaned, rumbled, and shook.

"Oh no!"

The bodies fell from their beds on the shelves, and the pillars popped with ear-shattering splits. The entire tomb was caving in. I dashed up the staircase, five steps at a time. The dirt from the opening above was pouring all over me.

Crash!

The staircase busted beneath my feet, and I tumbled back to the bottom. As the earth spilled inside my grave, I realized I was seconds away from my death. I leapt back to my feet and bounded up what was left of the steps, fighting my way through the dirt and sand that were spilling all over me. The tomb was filling fast, and all the dust was choking me.

I stuffed Fang back in the sheath and renewed my climb. Stepping. Digging. Clawing for whatever foothold I could find. I couldn't see the top anymore. The falling dirt replaced the daylight with pitch black. I pushed upward, head down, fighting for every step, only to be knocked down again.

I couldn't believe I was going to die like this. Choking on a mouthful of dirt, of all things. I yelled out, "*BRENWAR!*" but he was paralyzed. I had to make it, though. I was going up, up, slowly. I could beat this catastrophe. I was Nath Dragon: I could be anything. I would not be buried alive! I would not die like this!

My fingers found another lip of the stair. *Ah, the top set, finally!* Freedom would be mine in a moment.

Crack!

Again, the earth shattered and rocked. I lost my grip and fell.

Down I went.

My final resting place, on a lonely mountain barely known to the rest of the world, of all places. A tomb of dirt and bones.

CHAPTER 20

F INNIUS STOOD INSIDE A LARGE, circular stone chamber filled with many strange devices: cutting tools, bottles, knives, tables laden with power jars, and odd glass contraptions. Shackles and chains lined the walls, but no person hung there now. He imagined men had not so long ago. It was just another strange place, one of the many secrets beneath the Temple of Barnabus.

"This is it, Finnius," Selene the High Priestess said. "My special chamber of horrors."

Finnius swallowed. Despite his evil nature, a wave of concern for his own personal safety settled in.

"It's all right, Finnius. I wouldn't have brought you down here if I didn't want you alive. If I wanted you dead or tormented, my guards would have done that." She smiled, creepy yet beautiful. "And as you can see, business has been slow for a while. Now come. I've something to share."

He followed, now more honored than scared. Selene stood before a vat, rectangular in shape, big enough for the frame of a man, a large one at that. Inside it, a thick, waxy liquid bubbled, a little red, a little orange, a little blue, and all swirling together. It looked like a boiling cauldron, but it did not burn hot.

"Blood. Dragon blood," she said.

Finnius the cleric had never seen so much before.

"Well, dragon blood, and many other ingredients, but years of magic worked in and something else."

Finnius's mouth was dry, but his fascination got the better of him.

"What else?"

"Dragon teeth, bones, scales, and talons infused with another body."

"A man?"

"In some cases. See for yourself." Selene pulled her sleeve up over her elbow and reached inside the bubbling cauldron. Her lips twitched and curled as an ancient arcane language came forth. All the strange waters stirred before draining into the husk within. She released a small lever on the inside of the tub.

A man, or something like a man with a dragon-like face, lay within, eyes closed. Finnius looked at her, then back at the figure in the vat.

She said, "A soldier. A creation of my own. I call it a draykis. Part dragon. Part dead. Part hunter. Do you like him?"

"Fascinating."

"Awaken!" Selene said.

The draykis's eyes snapped open. They were yellow and slit like a snake's. It rose up and stepped out of the vat. A variety of dragon scales glittered all over its body. Whoever it was, it had been human once but was now turned into a dragon abomination. A defiance of the laws of nature. A hulking man combined with the finer parts of a dragon. A work of arcane art come to life.

Finnius admired it, a lot.

"He's magnificent," he said, stepping forward and back. "Tell me more, High Priestess."

She stroked the arm of the draykis and said, "In the case of this one, it's a man fused with the parts and blood of a dragon. He has the unrelenting strength of a zombie, combined with the armor and weapons of a dragon. The mind of a man keeps it all working together, along with all the mystic spells."

Finnius held his finger up and asked, "You said, 'one'?"

She patted him on the cheek and said, "Clever, Finnius, very good."

She clapped her hands together.

Four figures leapt from a concealed ledge above and landed on the ground.

Oh my!

Finnius stepped closer to Selene as four more draykis approached. They were awesome things: cloaked, with hoods drawn back revealing the scales and sharp teeth on their faces. Each moved with ease, but their stout frames suggested power, like the lizard men but more agile and cunning. Finnius wondered how much they could think for themselves.

"They are at my command, but soon they will be yours to command, Finnius."

"It would be an honor, High Priestess." He was wringing his hands. Anything that gave him power felt good. "Are we to hunt more dragons?"

"No, you are to hunt Nath Dragon."

Finnius rubbed his hand over his skull. He'd tried taking the man down with lizard men before and hadn't fared too well. But these draykis, he was confident, would do better.

"I see a hint of worry in your eye, Finnius. If you are not up to this…"

"Nay, High Priestess. I'm honored. With this brood, I cannot fail."

"Don't be so sure, Finnius. But, the draykis will be well armed. And you'll be taking more than enough reinforcements. They'll be of great help. Questions?"

"Just one, High Priestess," he offered a smile. "Do you want him alive, or do you want him dead?"

CHAPTER 21

I WAS COVERED IN DARKNESS. SUFFOCATING. I could barely move my arms and legs under all the weight. I'd faced death before. Fought my enemies. Beat them with cunning and steel. But now I was in the fight of my life against the elements. My foe was vast and undeterred—the very earth itself. I tried to scream again, but the dirt choked off my words. I had undone myself.

I thought of my father. I wondered how long it would take him to realize that I was gone forever. Even worse, I had failed him altogether. I would die of shame. Without honor. Failing my charge.

NO!

I could not let that happen. I had to hang on. I just had to! I took one last gasp and counted.

One... Five... Eleven... Twenty... Thirty... Sixty... It seemed this was it. None could save me. My face must be turning purple now. *Good bye, Nalzambor.*

"WAKE UP!"

I wasn't sure if I heard that or not.

"WAKE UP!"

I felt myself being pulled from my grave.

"NATH! BREATHE!"

I could hear.

"BREATHE!"

It was Brenwar. Or someone who sounded very much like him.

"This ought to help," he said, putting the weight of the world on my chest.

"ULP!" *gasp* "URK!"

I felt that. Hunks of dirt flew from my mouth as I spat, rolling back and forth on the ground. I coughed and hacked until my face became numb.

I'm ALIVE!

I managed to wipe the dirt from my eyes. The sunlight was, well, like sunlight on my face, but it had never felt so good before. The next thing, I saw Brenwar, his bulging arm outstretched, helping me to my feet.

"I hope you found what you were looking for," he said. "And I think we're even. Well, I'm pretty sure I'm still ahead, that is."

I shook the dirt out of my hair. Fang was still in his sheath. Thank goodness I had not lost him. I slung my pack from my back and reached inside. The orb was still secure.

"Well, if I'd died, I would have expected you to use this to free the blue razor." I managed a smile. "Thank you, Brenwar."

"Ah, it's nothing."

He stepped back as I opened my arms wide. "Stop that, Dragon. I said stop—"

I picked Brenwar up off his feet, hugged him like a bear, and swung him around. I felt joy. The joy of being alive. The joy of being able to fight for the cause of good once more. Being an adventurer, a hero, someone that does right instead of wrong doesn't mean you won't be put in the thick of danger. If anything, you'll find yourself in the middle.

"PUT ME DOWN, NATH DRAGON!"

I dropped him.

"Sorry. I couldn't contain myself."

"You ever do that again," he shook his fist at me, "and I'll kill you myself."

"I know. But right now, I'm so happy to be alive I don't care. Here." I extended my arm.

We bumped forearms, inside then out. "Better?"

"Better."

I held out the stone, letting Brenwar take a closer look.

"What do you think?"

"Dwarven made. Definitely."

I shook my head. But I wasn't going to disagree with the person who just saved my life. I'd do that later.

"Seems we have plenty of time to make it back, but I still don't understand why Corzan didn't think he could handle that. A magic user, even one not so powerful, should have been able to outwit a horde of ghouls. And the trap? A well-prepared magic user could handle that as well. Not much of a guardian, if you ask me. At least not to protect a Thunderstone."

Brenwar stretched his short limbs and yawned.

"What? I was paralyzed, you know."

"How's the wound?" I said, looking at the ghoul's bite.

"Wound? That's not a wound," Brenwar scoffed. "Now let's get going down the mountain. I've had enough of these ghouls, tombs, and fluffy caterpillars."

I raked the dirt from my hair and dusted off my clothes. I must have looked terrible.

"Say, where'd all the caterpillars go? They usually stick around for hours."

"Who cares?" Brenwar said, stomping away.

Not a blotch of pink, blue, yellow, or purple remained. I actually enjoyed watching them walk around on their tiny little feet. But their job was far from over. The ghouls lay dead, some covered, some not. The caterpillars never left their work until it was finished unless there was danger.

"Brenwar ... something's wrong."

I could feel the hair on my chin tingling when a black shadow blotted out the entire sun. A heavy wind stirred about me.

"You got that right," Brenwar said, eyes up, jaw down.

WHUMP! WHUMP! WHUMP! WOMP!

Oh no! There it was. Big. Monster big. Perhaps this was the guardian Corzan had spoken about. Clearly it was not something he could deal with.

"That's one big dragon," Brenwar said.

The dragon blotted out the sun as it loomed over us like a gargantuan bird of prey. His steel scales were like hammered metal. His nostrils flared with open fire. His claws were bigger and sharper than the deadliest spears. His horns, one broken, were as long as me. His tail was like a great serpent, swishing back and forth, shattering tombstones like twigs. Perhaps this was what I'd seen in the moonlight the night before. It had been so distant then.

I backed away. He snorted. His hot breath was like a furnace. His eyes, ancient as the stones, bore down on me like I was an insect as he approached. My father was far bigger, but I was used to him. This dragon was bigger than most I encountered. Much bigger. Bigger than rhinos, elephants, or a team of horses.

I drew my blade and swung it in front of me.

The dragon didn't blink.

I was scared.

"Nath," Brenwar said, "what do we do?"

I didn't have an answer to that question. In most cases, I rescued dragons; I didn't confront them. Even in my youth, the dragons had avoided me, both inside and outside the Mountain of Doom, or Dragon Home. It was lonely. That much I easily remembered. Being born of dragons but still not one of them. Oh, I still had dragon friends, not many—and family, too many—but over time, we'd gone our separate ways. I'd even had dragon teachers, too, but none of them had prepared me for this. Not even my father, I think.

I raised my arm.

His teeth snapped together in a clashing chomp that could have taken my arm off.

I moved away, but he cut off my path with a massive head that swung from one side to the other. I wasn't going anywhere. Not if he didn't want me to, that is.

"Just stay back, Brenwar. I'm not sure if he's for or against us."

I usually was big, fast, and strong, but not with this one. Right now, I was little more than a meal, shiny toothpick included. I mustered my courage, or what was left, anyway. The truth was that I wanted to run for it, but instead I locked with his gaze.

Inside, I was trembling like a leaf. Before me, a steel dragon. A fighter. A warrior. A soldier. I could tell by the scars on his body and the tears in his wings. A remnant of the Great Dragon War, he had to be. Yet there was another remarkable thing. The markings. Bright spots, green, orange, and yellow mixed with blue, adorned his frame, aglow with what looked to be arcane symbols. I'd never seen a dragon marked in such a way before. Perhaps he was enslaved or cursed.

Arms up, sword pointed down, I displayed the sign of surrender, trying to back away. I wasn't about to strike if he didn't strike first. I felt his tongue whip past my cheek then back again.

"What do you want me to do, Dragon?" Brenwar said, tucked behind a tombstone.

"Be still!"

I stopped. I couldn't just back down. All I needed to do was get back off this mountain. He came closer, massive head inches from my face, his hot breath ruffling my auburn hair. I opened my mouth to speak. He bumped me with his snout, knocking to the ground like a toddler. I was in trouble now. He pinned me to the ground with his nose.

"Dragon!"

"Be still, Brenwar!"

Now, I could stab the dragon, maybe put out his eye or scar his nose. They didn't like to be hit in the nose or poked in the eye, for that matter. But that tends to make one mad. And I've told you before about dragon breath. Small dragons don't hold so much, but a big steel dragon like this? Well, it could turn the entire mountaintop to flame. I put my dragon hand on the top of his nose.

"Peace and Home," I said.

You may have been wondering whether or not I can speak Dragonese. After all, I am a dragon, and I should be able to speak Dragonese—and I can. But just because I can speak to them doesn't mean they will speak to me. I was a very talkative and lonely boy growing up, but sometimes a speaking dragon gave me more than I wanted. When they did talk, it might take hours or days. And right now I didn't have time for a long conversation. But I said it again, in Dragonese, anyway.

"Peace and Home."

He snorted hot smoke, keeping the pressure on my chest.

Now it was time to worry, not that I wasn't already. Dragons were like most people: sometimes it was very difficult to tell if they were good or evil. This dragon, so far, was not giving me the friendly vibes that I was hoping for. The more pressure and uncertainty rose within me, the more I wanted to strike. For all I knew, his mind was battle damaged. His connection to his own kind lost. His eyes were heavy upon me. Any wrong moves and he was going to incinerate me. I tried to keep perfectly still.

"Peace and Home."

Who are you?

He spoke. It was a jolt, rocking my mind. Not vocal ... mental. This was good.

"The Son of Dragon Home," I said.

You are a man, but you smell like a dragon. Another wizard come to deceive me!

It pushed me across the grass.

"No! Not a wizard, a dragon! Son of Halz—"

Whack! The dragon reared up on his legs with a roar so loud it shook the very mountaintop.

"Brenwar!" I yelled. "What did you hit him for!"

The dragon filled his lungs with a big gust of air, and all I could think was *RUN!*

CHAPTER 22

A DWARF, EITHER OVERPROTECTIVE OR OVEREAGER to fight, had started all this. I didn't have time to think about that, though. I ran. Fast. The sound of a roaring flame erupted in my ears. I dove behind the nearest tombstone. A bath of fire surrounded me, hotter than the hottest thing I'd ever known. I swear I could feel my blood beginning to boil beneath my skin.

Dragon breath didn't last long. It didn't need to, and I felt nothing but relief when it stopped. The air, once as hot as a stove, was now smoky and chilly. One extreme to the other. The green grass, once fertile, now was brown and smoking.

"Take that, steely beast!" Brenwar yelled.

The dragon's roar was like a thunderstorm. Brenwar swung another mighty blow into the dragon, who stomped the earth, huffed fire through brandished teeth, and turned on Brenwar.

SWHACK!

The steel-colored tail licked out, whipped across Brenwar's chest like a striking snake, and sent him spinning head over heels, over both my head and the mountaintop's edge. Brenwar wouldn't like that. It was the second time in two days he'd been flung through the air like a toy, but there wasn't much to be done about it now. And I had myself to worry about.

Brenwar's abrupt departure left me alone with the dragon. An angry one at that. I could fight or try to surrender, but my gut told me he wouldn't want any part of my surrender. I remained with my back pressed against the tombstone and got Fang ready. If he came after me, I'd only get one shot. A kill shot, possibly. But I wouldn't kill a dragon! I just had to stop him. But how could I do that before he killed me?

I could hear him crushing the stones beneath his heavy feet as he made his way toward me. His head, long neck, and horns emerged before me. I fought the urge to thrust Fang down on his nose. It would hurt, but it wouldn't kill or subdue. I tried the only thing I could think to do.

"Peace and Home!" I yelled. "I am one of you!"

He eyed me the way a cat eyes a mouse before dinner.

I could only feel his anger. His curiosity from earlier was long gone. Only the hardened soldier from the Dragon Wars remained. His final mission was to protect this mountain. Protect the Thunderstone from invaders like me.

If I could presume such a thing, but I couldn't think. I could only feel right now. Fear. It stiffened the joints between my bones. Real fear was not something I was accustomed to. *Move. Move. Move.* I was too late.

A geyser of flame spewed from his mouth.

I was coated from head to toe in blistering heat. Agony. Pain. Fear. I stabbed Fang through the flames and into the soft flesh in his mouth.

The flames stopped as he cried out, recoiling on his paws, eyeing me with great suspicion now.

I patted out the flames on my shoulder. What had happened? Why wasn't I burned alive? I should be dead now. I could sense his surprise as well as mine.

He snorted. Shook his massive head. Tore a mausoleum from the ground with his great horn and stepped back. Perhaps he was willing to listen now.

I stroked my hair. It was still thick and warm in my fingers. How had I survived those flames? "Will you listen now, mighty one?" I was trying Dragonese once again. "I'm not here for harm. For good."

You!

I could hear him in my mind. Ancient. Irritated. Potent. This dragon hadn't even gotten warmed up yet. But I'd earned some respect.

The Thunderstone is my charge. My ward. My duty. My fate. My curse. Give it to me. Or die, little dragon.

Dialogue is a good thing. And I certainly had a better advantage than fighting. I liked these odds. I lowered my sword, and I chose my next words with care.

"You are a great one. As big as I've ever seen. As powerful as they come. How has this stone entrapped you? Perhaps I can help—"

GIVE IT TO ME... OR DIE!

My head ached. This dragon was holding back something. I could sense it. As intimidating as he was, he was desperate. I'd learned a few things about curses, too. I had a feeling the Thunderstone was protecting me, warding me from him. He needed it, though. I tried bargaining.

"The Thunderstone is mine. But I'd be willing to show it to you if you tell me your story, mighty one with scales as strong as iron." Flattery always helps, no matter how big and bad a dragon might be.

SHOW ME FIRST... OR DIE!

I opened my mouth to speak—

OR DIE... AND REMEMBER, I'VE NOTHING TO LOSE. NOT LIFE. NOT TIME.

Now he was letting me know in a nice way that he was being patient. I saw no harm in it. If I wanted to get off this mountain alive and save the blue razor, I'd have to give a little. I removed the stone from my belt pouch and revealed its smoothness from the cloth. It emitted a warm glow from the blue marking on the stone.

AH... MY TORMENTER. MY JAILER! MY LIBERATOR! GIVE... IT... TO... ME!

Ah, now I understood the curse. The dragon could not take what was not freely given. A common curse, but a strong one. Bonding, in some cases, forever and ever.

"The story, mighty one. I'll have that."

A growl rumbled in his throat. He shook his neck and fluffed his wings, stirring the air.

So be it, little dragon. A wizard, vile and despicable, duped me into service. Powerful he was, the Thunderstone the greatest source of his power. So envious was he of other wizards, he refused to relent his power. Mortality. The shortcoming of man. They thirst for such power, only to acquire it quickly and see it fade just as fast. The wizard did not want to share his power when he passed. He bonded me. Cursed me. Tricked me. I'm to protect the stone upon his death. I have been for centuries, sometimes flying far from the mountain—only to be drawn back.

I pitied him. I pitied all dragons in danger or exile. And had I not sworn to save them? Save them one and all. Those who would let me, that is. Some didn't want to be saved. They just wanted to be left alone.

"How can I help, mighty one?"

Give me the stone.

"Why do you need the stone? I thought you only needed to protect it. Why didn't you just dig it out and take it yourself?" I couldn't assume the dragon was telling me everything.

I can only take what is freely given. The wizard promised to return and give it to me long after his death. A lich, he said he'd be. I must possess the stone to be free. I can take it with me wherever I go and protect it. Give it to me. My patience thins. He looked up into the sun. A sad look came to his hardened eyes. A longing for the sky and the freedom it offered.

"Perhaps we can break the curse."

He slammed his clawed fist into the ground. *NOT POSSIBLE! GIVE ME THE STONE!*

No. I needed the stone to free the blue razor. And in case you're wondering why I didn't just tell him so, this steel dragon, he couldn't have cared less about the blue razor. I just knew. But perhaps I could free them both.

"I'll make you a deal, mighty one!"

A DEAL? THERE WILL BE NO DEAL! DEATH YES! DEAL—NO!

"If I die, you remain cursed. Stuck on this mountain, staring at a stone that you cannot touch. I can help you."

He shook his head and neck. Bared his fangs and teeth and snapped in my face.

I cannot burn you, but I can eat you.

Apparently, the curse prevented him from eating me so long as I had the stone. His mouth stopped inches from my head, and he got a sad look in his eyes. I held my arms out.

"Just hear me out, great one. Give me one day. I must take the stone to free a friend. Once I've done that, I'll bring it back and give it to you. If I don't return, well, you can come after me and kill me. I am a man of my word."

HA! HA! HA!

Of all the fearful things the dragon possessed—his claws, his tail, his breath—it was his laughter that scared me most.

You take the stone to the wizard in the mountain, Corzan? You're a fool, little dragon. Did you think I did not know about all in the mountain? I know every creature and every tree. HA! HA! HA! Go then, fool. You will give it to me in a day. If not, I will destroy you, your friend the dragon, Corzan, and all of his rotten goblins. I know the secrets of the stone. You and he do not. Be wary, fool dragon. But you entertain me. I shall wait. Sit. Watch. Death comes quick to the fools who seek it.

CHAPTER
23

I CAUGHT UP WITH BRENWAR ANOTHER hundred feet down the mountain, and he wasn't in much of a talking mood. It didn't help that I had to help him out of the tree he'd been stuck in, either, and he made me swear I'd never tell. His cheeks were flushed red behind his beard, so I didn't bother to tell him that it was all his fault. He should have waited, and he was lucky he wasn't dead. His impulsiveness could have killed us both. But I bit my tongue, forgave him inwardly, and moved on.

Down the mountain we went, and for some reason, the Thunderstone seemed heavy, as heavy as ten. I had a feeling it didn't like being moved around, but I had to take care of my mission. My own thoughts were filled with worry. The steel dragon had mentioned that he knew the secrets of the stone and then hadn't offered any more information. He was desperate, though. I could feel it in his thoughts. If things didn't work out, I was certain he'd wipe out everything on the mountain.

Corzan was another problem. Just as the steel dragon had been tricked by a wizard before, another magic user was trying to trick me. I had to stay focused. All I needed to do was get the blue razor free and hope the rest would take care of itself. Even though my goals sounded simple, they would be much harder to accomplish than they looked.

"We're almost there," I said. The sun was setting, the mountain becoming a black face in the night. I could hear the waterfalls in the distance. I jumped from one ledge to the other, reached out, and helped my friend over. "Any advice, Brenwar?"

It was always good to have a backup plan, but at this time I had none. I would have to convince Corzan to free the dragon before I gave him the stone. If he would not relent, well, I had no idea what I would do.

"Just free the dragon. Don't worry about the stone," Brenwar huffed, crawling down a ledge.

"What about the steel dragon? I gave my word I'd help him."

"You gave him your word he could eat you, not me."

"Brenwar," I said, alarmed "he wouldn't eat you anyway. Dwarves are too chewy and sour, they say."

Brenwar shot me a look and said, "Lucky for me, not so lucky for you."

Well, it seemed my dearest friend didn't have a backup plan, either.

"Thanks," I muttered.

Down we went, my back beginning to ache from the load of the stone and my leg still agitated from days before. I should have been healed up by now.

Goblin guards, yellow eyed with pointed ears and stiff jaws, greeted us with spears at the entrance of the Burrow Goblin home.

"Leave your weapons," one said, lowering his spear toward Brenwar's nose.

He ripped the spear from its hands and whacked it in the head. I clocked the other one in the face, busting his nose. I was tired. I wouldn't be playing any more games today.

My feet were dragging by the time I got there. The stone as heavy as a small boulder now. The sight of Corzan the Necromancer irritated me. The devilish man sat with a smug look on his coarse face, hairy hands folded over his robed lap. Meanwhile, I felt like a mouse that had just stepped into a trap.

"Ah … the son of the Dragon King has returned. And an hour not too late. I'm impressed," Corzan said. "Do you have it?"

I stretched my arms and shoulders. I was all too ready to get rid of it now. I should have given it to Brenwar.

"I have it," I said, folding my arms across my chest. This was it. It was time for Corzan to play his final cards. "Let the dragon go, and it's all yours."

Corzan chuckled. The great hall full of goblins, over thirty of them, chuckled as well.

Leaning forward, Corzan said, "Show it to me first."

His eyes were like dark moons when I removed the Thunderstone from my pack, and a collective gasp filled the air. The orb's arcane markings shone a brilliant blue in the dimness of the cave. Corzan rose from his chair, hands outstretched as he approached.

"Give it to me," he hissed. "Now!"

This was it. The moment of truth. The moment we'd all been waiting for.

"Free the dragon first," I replied, cradling the Thunderstone at my side. He wasn't going to push me around.

Corzan flicked his fingers. A shower of sparks hit the dragon cage, drawing forth a painful hiss from the dragon.

"Give me the stone, Nath Dragon! Or my next spell will kill the dragon."

My anger started to rise. Brenwar bristled at my side, war hammer in his white-knuckled grip. It was time to be rid of Corzan, the goblins—all of them. But the necromancer had the edge. He held the dragon's life in the balance.

Holding the stone out in front of his eyes, I said, "It is my stone to give, and I give it to you freely, Corzan."

"What!" Brenwar started.

Corzan licked his lips. A smile as broad as a river formed on his hardened face as he reached for it.

I tossed it into the dragon cage.

"You'll just have to get it."

The stone rolled into the cage, and the blue razor coiled over it.

Corzan's hands burst into flames.

"You FOOL! You'll die for this! Kill them! Kill them both!"

CHAPTER

24

THE GOBLINS SURGED. CORZAN DISAPPEARED. Brenwar threw himself into the entire force, war hammer swinging, goblins flying. Me, I had another idea.

I ripped Fang from his sheath. "Don't fail me now," I said.

Bang!

I struck the sword tip on the stone floor.

Fang vibrated with life in my hand and began to sing a terrible song. Terrible if you were a goblin, that is.

The sound echoed in the chamber, shaking the debris from the rocky ledges and ceiling. The goblins in the path of the sword fell to their knees, fingers plugging their ears, crying out in anguish, pain, and uncertainty. Half of them fled. Others cried and begged.

Whop! Whop! Whop!

Brenwar took them out, one by one, rattling bones and cracking their ribs.

I was elated. When Fang sang, it sang a beautiful song that repelled evil like baths repel goblins. A tuning fork gone berserk. The great hall, once a fortress full of many enemies, was now under my full control. I muttered a quick thanks to my father for crafting such a fine and magical sword for me.

Fang sang for another few seconds or so, and we found ourselves surrounded by a heap of broken, passed-out, or cringing goblins and a lone dragon in the cage.

"Corzan!" I yelled, my words echoing from corner to corner. "Come out! Surrender the dragon before it's too late!"

"He won't come," Brenwar said, kicking a goblin in his path. "The cowards run. They always do." A goblin burst from the floor and dashed away from the pack. "See! I'm going after it!"

"No, Brenwar!"

Too late. He ran into the tunnels and out of my sight.

Beside me, the blue razor remained huddled in the cage, eyes open, unmoving.

She was unafraid. I kneeled alongside the cage and said, "I'll have you free soon, sister. Just don't let go of that stone." I reached my fingers inside the cage.

"I wouldn't do that if I were you!"

It was Corzan, but from where I didn't know.

"Oh, Nath Dragon, you have infuriated me! Do you think you've defeated me, Corzan the Necromancer? NEVER!"

I could sense the man. He was hidden but not invisible. "Corzan, free the dragon and the stone is yours."

An arc of light shot across the room and slammed into the cage. The blue razor roared.

"STOP IT!" I yelled.

The dragon's scales began to smolder. My temper did as well.

"Fetch the stone, Nath Dragon. Give it to me, or the dragon shall suffer more agony than you can imagine!"

I couldn't stand the thought of her suffering any more, but I couldn't give in right now. I had to try something else. The Throne. The arc of light had come from behind it, and I could see the edges of Corzan's robes at the bottom. I stepped between the throne and the cage and made my offer.

"Last chance, Corzan. Free the dragon now, or else I'm coming after you. Nothing can stop a dragon!"

Corzan stepped from behind the throne, arms raised over his head, hands burning with fire. "You and the dragon both shall die, fool!"

"Last chance, Corzan!"

Another arc of light erupted from his hands. I swung Fang right into it.

KRYSAA—AK!

A shower of flame lit up the chamber. Corzan howled in rage.

The blow knocked me from my feet, and Fang flew from my grip. My vision was spotted, the wind knocked from me as I fought to stay conscious. *Where is he?*

I could see his face now. His eyes narrowed. His mouth snarled. His fists balled up at his sides.

"NO!" I shouted.

Hands like burning torches, he rushed for the cage. I could see the murder in his eyes. He'd have to kill the dragon to get the stone.

I struggled to rise, but my aching muscles were like lead.

Corzan's flaming hands reached for the cage.

Move, Dragon!

I lunged for his legs.

Corzan sidestepped me. He kicked me in the face, and I saw spots again.

I caught his robes by the hem and jerked him down to the ground.

Whack! Whack!

Two flaming punches burned into my face. It was like getting hit with a hot frying pan, but I held on. I'd been in a scrap before. But I'd never brawled with a magic user before. This one had a lot of fight in him. Anger, too.

"Let the dragon go, Corzan! I'm warning you!"

We rolled over the floor, back and forth, my human arm wrapped around his forearms, fighting to keep his flaming hands from my face.

He kneed me in the groin.

"Oof!"

A mage fighter, a dirty fighter, too.

"That's it!"

Pow!

I punched him in the chest with my dragon arm.

It took the wind from him. He sagged within his robes as the fires extinguished from his hands. I put my forearm on his neck and pinned him to the ground.

"Let the dragon go, Corzan!"

"Heh-heh. You won't hurt me, Nath Dragon." Corzan coughed and gasped. "I know that much about you."

He was right. I'm not sure how I could convince him otherwise, not without Brenwar, anyway. Why'd that dwarf have to run off? Still, that didn't prevent me from roughing him up a little. I walloped him in the stomach.

"Oof!"

"Let her go!"

Corzan grunted, but he did nothing else.

I tried it again. *Whop!* Same result, a more painful expression. I drew my fist back one more time.

"All right!" Corzan finally said. "But you must promise me the stone."

"I already have." I dragged him over to the cage. "Do it already!"

Corzan pulled himself onto his knees, put his hands together, closed his eyes, and began to murmur. I kept the pressure on his neck with my dragon hand the entire time.

The metal cage warbled like a living thing, popped, cracked, and slowly fizzled from sight.

The blue razor reared up, stretched her long, metal-blue neck and black wings, and batted her lashes at me. I smiled.

Zing!

Like a streak of lightning, she was gone. Not much of a thank-you, either, but I'd come to expect that. A shame; I'd like to have gotten to know her, a little bit at least.

Relief assailed me. I'd accomplished at least one good deed today. Now it was just me, Corzan, a bunch of roughed-up goblins, and the Thunderstone in the chamber. That, and of course—my word.

Corzan went for the stone. I went for my sword. I know you are wondering why

I let him have the stone. I'm sure you think I'm crazy. But I gave him my word. If my word's not good, then I'm no good at all.

We squared off. Corzan held the stone as if he had all the wealth and power in Nalzambor in his own hand. I could feel the scales shift heavily in his favor.

"So, what's it going to be now, Corzan?"

He didn't say anything. He just stared at the orb, its blue markings radiant with life.

"I've got what I want, and you have what you want. Can we go in peace or not?"

Of course, I still had to get the stone back, but I needed to buy more time. I needed to know what he was thinking first.

"Well?"

Corzan stroked his fingers across the orb. "Such power," he hissed. "I can feel it in my very bones. It strengthens me." His voice rose. "Like ten necromancers in one."

I stepped back. Corzan's robes blustered behind a radiant swirl that circled him from head to toe. I could barely make out his face now, but it was changing, transforming, stretching unnaturally. The necromancer had been formidable enough before, but there was no telling what he had inside him now. I had a feeling that I only had a few seconds of life left—or possibly some arcane form of lifetime imprisonment. I didn't want either of those things to happen, so I did what any reasonable fighter would do. I raised Fang over my head and attacked.

CHAPTER
25

"DRAGON! DRAGON!" Shouting out my battle cry, I crossed the distance between me and Corzan as fast as I could. I was fast. Thought was faster. One second Fang's tip licked inches from his face, the next I was sailing from one side of the room to the other.

"OOF!"

I slammed hard into one of the support columns and crumpled breathless to the ground.

"HAH!" Corzan shouted from the other side of the room. "I'm invincible now!"

Somehow, I rose to my feet. I wasn't going to die on my back.

"No one is invincible," I managed, wiping the blood from my mouth and coughing.

Corzan's smile was broad as a river, his evil deep as a gorge. His expression was intelligent, cunning, omnipotent. He was the wolf; I was the sheep.

"Your time has come, Nath Dragon. Say your farewells."

That's when I noticed the change. His arms were no longer hairy, and his face was more man, less goblin. He noticed me eyeing him.

"What? What do you see?"

I little honesty wouldn't hurt at this point, and it would buy me more time as well.

"You look more like a man than a goblin now."

Corzan inspected his fingers. The long, jagged fingernails were gone, the coarse hair over his hands and wrists removed. "Finally," he gasped. "The curse is controlled, if not removed." He returned his focus on me. "Heh, I bet you think I'll thank you, don't you, Nath Dragon?" He laughed. "The truth is, I'd consider it if I weren't so evil and you weren't so good. Can't have troublemakers like you sticking around." He pointed his finger at me.

Whap!

I punched myself in the face with my dragon fist.

Whap!

I almost knocked myself out cold.

Corzan had his fingers on the necklace of dragon scales and claws. I'd forgotten all about that. I should have ripped it off of him when I had the chance.

"I've total control over you now, Dragon. As a matter of fact, I can make you do whatever I want."

He was right. Unlike the last time he controlled my arm, I was completely at a loss to fight back this time. If I couldn't use my muscles, I'd have to use my mind. *Buy time!*

"So, you couldn't control the guardian dragon before. He was too strong. But I'd say you have enough power to defeat the guardian dragon now, and all the other wonders he protects."

Corzan stopped.

"What other wonders?"

This was the tricky part. I wasn't going to lie. But I could bluff. Besides, I didn't really know there weren't any other treasures.

"I didn't see any, but where there are dragons so big, there are hoards as well. Just think, Corzan, everything in the mountain could be yours."

"Am I to understand that the guardian dragon still lives?"

"Yes."

"How did you get the stone, then?"

Now was another time when I could tell the truth or lie. I didn't need to lie, though. There was still another weapon in my arsenal. Silence.

"I'll never tell."

Whap! Whap! Whap!

I dropped to the floor. I could feel my eye swelling. Nothing could really describe what it was like to give yourself a black eye.

"Is that all you got?" I said, not sure if I was talking to myself or to Corzan.

Whap!

"You are a fool, Dragon, to think that you can trick me into a fight with the guardian. But I'd be lying if I said I wasn't curious as to what happened up there. I can only assume you struck a bargain of some kind with him. After all, you animals have a way of sticking together in the herd."

With a motion of his arms, Fang was ripped free of my grasp and into his.

"A fine sword. Magic. Dragon magic. Hmmm. I could make use of this."

I needed to move. Far and fast. He was strengthening, and I was weakening. I could feel it. And I hoped Brenwar wouldn't come back, either. He'd be killed if he did. I had to have another trick up my sleeve.

With the stone in one hand and my sword in the other, Corzan was frightening—tall, gaunt, and indestructible.

Well, at least I had saved one dragon, but now I was worried about the other as well. What if Corzan could control him, too? The ancient wizard had done so. It was up to the steel dragon to beat him in battle, but it didn't seem likely right now. Not with the necklace Corzan wore and his knowledge of the dragons.

"Now what, Corzan? You have me defeated. Should I expect an unpleasant death?" I had to keep talking, at least long enough to figure out something.

"Be still," he said, holding the Thunderstone toward me.

Three purplish rings of magic appeared around me and squeezed. It felt like I was in the grip of an iron giant. I struggled, but all I could do was breathe, and that was difficult.

"I think I have a better use for you alive." He tossed my sword aside, its hard metal echoing on the hard stone floor. "Remember, the Clerics of Barnabus will be here soon, and I am without the dragon they came for. But I think I have something much better to offer them: their greatest nemesis, Nath Dragon, alive and well."

I hadn't even entertained that notion. The truth was, the Clerics of Barnabus hadn't even entered my mind.

"I thought you said you would be able to handle them with the Thunderstone now. Why don't you just test your powers and take them out?" I suggested.

"Living alliances will serve me much better than dead ones. You know that."

"You realize that once they find out you have the stone, they'll try to take it from you."

Raising the stone over his head, he laughed when it began to crackle with white energy.

KA-CHOW!

A bolt of lightning shot from it. The balcony above exploded into shards of rock.

KA-CHOW!

A large wooden door across the way was no more. Only smoke and splinters remained.

"No, they won't be taking anything from me. I can do this all day if I like." He looked around. "I wonder where that dwarf is. I'd like to test it out on that armor of his."

My heart sank. I'd never seen a man wield such raw power before. I could barely speak, but I managed spit out in vain, "You'll never find him! He's long gone by now. But if you follow the trail of goblin corpses you might get close."

Corzan laughed as he resumed his place on the throne, dragging me in my bonds before him.

"He'll be dead by dawn. I assure you of that."

CHAPTER
26

I DIDN'T KNOW WHAT HAD HAPPENED to Brenwar, but the longer he was gone, the better. *Buy time.*

"So, tell me about this curse of yours."

It was an unpleasant look he gave me, but he still opened his mouth and spoke.

"A goblin bite. It doesn't happen very often, but it does happen. The bite turns one from man to goblin. You didn't know that, did you?"

I shook my head. I hoped orcs couldn't do the same. Imagine getting bit by an orc only to become one.

"I'll elaborate. A goblin witch bit me. A curse it was, turning me from man to minion. In most cases, the witch can remove the curse for a price, but I ran out of patience and killed her. I set her horrid face on fire and watched her burn until she was dead." He shook his head. "I had a bad temper back then. Looking back, I could have been more gentle." He held the stone out and admired it. "But that's where this came in. Ancient, powerful magic such as this can cure most things, with a little help, that is."

I looked at my arm. Was it possible it could cure me? Remove the evil from my scales and lead me back to home? Father had told me that there were many secrets in Nalzambor that could heal anything.

"So how will you truly know if you are cured unless the stone isn't in your possession? I could hold it for you." Planting some doubt in his mind wouldn't hurt anything. There was a rustle behind me. The goblins I'd stunned with Fang's humming had started to stir. "Will they still follow?"

"My, so clever you think you are," Corzan said. "A dragon above, doubt below. Do you think I'm so easily fooled?"

"Either way, you'll still have to deal with them both," I said, smiling. "Just trying to help out."

"I'm getting the feeling the longer I keep you around, the more trouble you will be." He got up from his seat and thrust the stone at my chest, sending me skipping across the floor. There I lay, in the middle, where the dragon cage had earlier been, alone and unable to defend myself.

"The Clerics of Barnabus will have to settle for your corpse instead."

Defiant, I struggled back to my feet. If I was going to die, I would die on my feet. I'd had enough of him.

"Give it your best then, goblin!"

His lip curled over his white teeth as he held the Thunderstone over his head. It became a whirling white sun of energy.

"Let him alone, goblin!"

Brenwar rushed into the room, war hammer high over his head. The awoken goblins rushed him, and a few more were on his heels. He slammed the hammer into the floor.

KRANG!

The stone floor erupted. Some goblins fell between the busted stone, and others lost their footing.

Corzan laughed. Lightning sailed. Brenwar was lit up as he went spinning across the floor in a smoking heap and lay still.

"NOOOOOOOOO!" I screamed, stumbling forward.

Corzan was laughing again.

"Now that I've seen what I can do to dwarves, let's see what I can do to half-dragons."

The Thunderstone charged up again, its blue light brilliant in my eyes. I was so angry, I couldn't even think. Let him hit me with all he had. I deserved nothing less. After all, I'd just gotten my best friend killed.

Wild with power, Thunderstone in hand, Corzan charged. Hungry. Angry. Unrelenting.

I could see it consume him. I didn't think he was going to leave anything of me for the Clerics of Barnabus now. I clenched my jaw and braced myself.

Snatch!

The bright light faded. The stone was gone from Corzan's grip.

"What?!" he cried.

My bonds disappeared.

Above, the blue razor darted through the chambers, the Thunderstone in her back talons.

I couldn't believe my eyes. She came back. *She came back!*

She hovered over me, winked her beautiful eye, and dropped the stone into my hands. And with a crack of thunder, she was gone.

Corzan's faced contorted with rage as he said, "Give it to me! You cannot handle its power, animal!"

The stone was still heavy, even in my dragon hand, bewitched somehow. That didn't matter. What mattered was my friend lying still in the corner. Corzan would pay for that. He'd pay for it now.

His eyes widened as I rushed forward. My dragon arm popped me in the head with the rock.

"Ouch!" I cried, stumbling to the floor.

"Fool!" Corzan cried, grasping his necklace. "I control your arm."

Blood dripped into my eyes. I wasn't going to be controlled by anyone anymore, certainly not him. My dragon hand struck again, but I stopped it with my other hand. I wasn't going to be responsible for beating my own self to death. *Dig deep, Dragon! Fight it with all you can!*

"Give it up, Dragon! You have given the stone to me; it's mine, not yours. You cannot control its powers."

I could feel my dragon fingers peeling away from the stone. I fought it for a moment and let it go. The stone slipped free of my hand and into my other. It weighed like an anvil on my arm.

Whack!

The dragon arm hit me once, then tried again. I stopped it. The black scales on my arm trembled. My heart thundered in my chest. I would not surrender to Corzan anymore. It was my will against his. Shaking with every movement, I forged up the steps. Every fiber of my being was tested.

Corzan gasped as I took the first step. "NO! It's not possible!"

Sweat cascaded down his face and dripped onto the floor as he clutched the necklace of dragon scales and bones in his hand. He transformed as well. The coarse hairs on his hands returned, and his ears grew to points on the back. He reverted to more goblin than man. "The curse, it's back! You must give me the stone, Nath Dragon!"

I fought my way up two more steps.

"I'm going to give you something, all right," I said through clenched teeth. My heart was bursting in my chest. But it was my life or his. Fighting my own arm and carrying the stone was like dragging two anchors over the harbor.

"You cannot beat me!" he screamed.

I fought against belting myself again. Gritted my teeth and jumped up the last few steps. I could barely move. I gasped for my breath.

Corzan's hands burst into flames and reached for my throat.

"It's too late, fool! You shall burn alive this day!"

I looked at him and then at my dragon hand, eyed him again, and said, "No I won't!"

All of my muscles fought against me, but they were my muscles, after all. They served my will, not his.

Whack!

I punched him in the face with my dragon arm.

BOOM!

I popped him in the belly with the Thunderstone. Corzan's body slammed into his throne. He sagged into his chair and moved no more.

"Yes!"

I ripped the dragon necklace from Corzan's limp fingers and put it around my neck. The only thing controlling me was going to be me from now on. The Thunderstone had lightened now, the glowing runes now dim, its energy spent. Why it had been so heavy before and was light now, I didn't know, but I could try to understand that later. I jumped at the sound of a rustle behind me. *Brenwar!*

I turned in time to see him sitting up, holding his head. I rushed over and helped him to his feet. He smelled like a saddle that had sat in the sun too long.

"Are you well?"

He blinked, cocked his head, and said, "Ale."

The goblins, what was left of them, gathered around me.

Brenwar growled at my side.

I held the stone up. "Who wants to be the first to die?"

They gawped, shuffled back, and disappeared from sight. Without their leader, they didn't have much fight left in them.

But what was I going to do about Corzan the Necromancer? Groggy and defeated, he didn't put up much of a fight, but I still had a problem: he was still alive. And that was one of the tough things about being good. Sometimes you had to let your enemies live, and I figured Corzan would hold a grudge against me for a long time. So what could I do to keep him out of my hair in the meantime?

"This ought to hold you until your guests arrive," I said.

From his throne, Corzan looked up at me with blurry red eyes.

"What have you done to me?" he said, struggling in his bonds.

I continued to wrap the spool of copper twine around his wrists and legs. It was elven made twine, called *Elotween*, inescapable when applied, but temporary. In a few days, it would disappear, but nothing could untie it or cut it, not without magic, anyway. It would have to do for now.

"Now, don't struggle too much; it'll constrict and might cut your hands off," I warned.

"Fool, I can escape these—*mrph!*"

I stuffed a rag in his mouth. I'd had enough of his talk.

I waggled the stone in front of his face and said, "Have fun explaining to the Clerics of Barnabus why you don't have a dragon for them."

Corzan's eyes were as big as saucers.

"I'm sure they will be very eager to hear your tale."

If you can't dispel evil yourself, let evil do it for you. Leave evil to its own.

CHAPTER 27

TRAVELING BACK UP THE MOUNTAIN was even worse than the first time. The heavy rains splattered all over my armor, and rivulets of water slicked all the footholds. This trip seemed twice as long as the last. It wouldn't have been so bad if Brenwar had stayed back, but he insisted.

"Brenwar, there's a cave near," I pointed to the mouth of a jagged edge. "Why don't you wait there until I come back?"

"No," he grumbled, shaking his head and beard like a black sheepdog. "You go; I go."

You'd think the lightning jolt he took would have eased him, but all it did was make him tougher. The more punishment dwarves survived, the more stubborn they'd become. Brenwar had already survived enough battles to convince him he could handle anything, but often enough I'd seen otherwise. At least three times on this trip, anyway.

I pulled him up by rope, bringing him to the ledge along my side. Thirsty, I caught some rainwater in my mouth from off the edge of the rocks and drank until it filled me. I felt like I'd been beaten up by an ogre. My face and lips were swollen. The gash in my head ached, and my leg was as bad as it'd ever been. For all of my dragon's constitution, I was tired. And now I had to go and face a steel dragon, or at least catch up with him before he came after me. I had a feeling all of his patience had run out. It was time someone paid for all of his suffering.

I patted the Thunderstone tucked beneath my chest plate. It was warmer and heavier than when we had started. If it got any heavier, I'd have to stop climbing. What was with this thing?

"Bloody dragon can have the thing," I said, rubbing my hands together. "Getting cold again, too."

"What?" Brenwar said in the pouring rain.

I pointed at the cave.

"No!"

We weren't so far from the top, but I was still pressed for time. I couldn't leave Brenwar alone, on second thought. He always stuck by my side, so I'd stick by his. I just hoped he wouldn't attack the dragon again.

I tugged at the rope around his waist and almost jerked him from his boots, saying, "Let's go, then."

"Listen, Dragon," he wagged his finger at me, "nobody—"

"Tugs a dwarf!" I finished. "I know!"

We practically crawled up the mountain over the next few hours. If Brenwar wasn't slipping, he was falling, all the time blaming the giants for the rain. He wasn't a horrible climber, not by your typical standard, but by mine, he was pretty slow.

"Come on, you legless goat!" I said, pointing. "We're almost there."

"Legless what?"

We reached the top an hour later, and the rain was a steady downpour. And it wasn't your typical rain, but high-in-the-mountain rain, ice-cold rain, one step from ice and snow. The clouds above were dark, full of thunder and flashing light. It was the perfect weather for a funeral. Mine.

The graveyard hadn't changed since we left, which was no surprise, but all the ghoul bodies were gone.

"You know," Brenwar started, "if you give him that stone, he might still kill you."

"I know."

Of course, if I didn't give him the stone, he was going to try and kill me anyway. And I'd been thinking that exact same thing for the entire trip. At least we made it back in time. I withdrew Fang. Brenwar clutched his war hammer in his meaty hands.

"A great morning for a battle," he said.

Do you have it?

The dragon's voice startled my mind. If he was near, I couldn't see him.

"I wouldn't be here if I didn't," I replied.

Brenwar cocked his head at me and said, "What?"

Let me see it!

The dragon's voice was demanding, unpleasant.

I removed the Thunderstone from beneath my chest plate and extended it in my clawed hand. The radiant blue runes illuminated my hand like a torch. I hated to give up so valuable an item. For all I knew, it could cure the evil in my dragon arm as well as many other things. But it was almost too heavy to hold.

"Here it is," I said.

A great shadow dropped from the sky and landed, shaking the ground beneath me. He seemed bigger, more sinister, and as powerful as ever. The heavy drops of rain on his scaled frame looked like nothing but drizzle compared to him. The bright markings on his body grew brighter at every flash of lightening.

Have you come to kill me? he said in my mind, eyeing my sword.

"Just a precaution," I said, twirling it in my hand.

The dragon snorted a puff of smoke from his nose and flashed a row of his teeth.

A fine blade it is. I've seen it before; you should know.

I looked at the blade and back and him.

"How'd you—"

THE STONE, PLEASE. MY PATIENCE IS AT AN END.

He extended his clawed hand that was big enough for me to have a seat in.

"From me to you, this Thunderstone I give."

I dropped it into his hand. It looked like little more than a tiny egg. I swore the dragon smiled when he had it.

I started to ask, "What are you going to do with it now?"

The dragon tossed it into his mouth.

"What did you do that for?"

The dragon showed his teeth.

"Get back," Brenwar said, tugging on my arm.

The dragon's luminous spots pulsated with life, swirling over his body, a living thing of its own free will. I'd never seen markings move on a creature before.

The dragon roared. I covered my ears as it went on and on. His head was filled with many colors now: blue, purple, yellow, green, and orange, wrapping around his teeth and horns. The dragon shook and growled like an attacking dog. I retreated farther. He roared again and stretched his neck up high. Fire in all the colors of a rainbow shot from his mouth. A hundred feet high it went, creating a cloud of many colors.

"Let's go!" Brenwar said.

I kept my ground, looking skyward. A creature formed above, part man, part bird, an apparition of many colors. Its eyes were black, evil, beauty twisted into a terrible thing. It hissed, spat, and cursed something ancient and foul, its form dissipating and blowing away.

Brenwar's jaw was hanging when I asked, "What was that?"

He just shook his head.

A Weevilin. A spirit of evil that lives within. My tormentor, the lich, left me with that.

The dragon was face to face with me now. He was no longer dark or dreary, but his scales shone brightly like a new coat of armor. Polished armor, like the ones the Knights of Quintuklen wore. I had had the steel dragon all wrong. He was one of the most beautiful things I had ever seen.

"What happened to the wizard who cursed you?" I asked. "I did not see any sign of him in the tomb below. Is he dead, or does he live in some other shape or form?"

So nice of you to ask, Nath Dragon. And for your service, I shall tell you. The wizard died and returned a lich, yet he refused to free me. So I refused him the stone. We fought long hours for many days, but I won out. He is no more, but the evil spirit I was cursed with remained. Only the Thunderstone, freely given, could send it away.

"So," I eyed his great belly, "is the stone destroyed?"

It's safe.

As the rain stopped and the clouds parted, all I could do was gawp at the wonderful beast beating his wings and flying off. And just like that he was gone. I stood there, numb, as if I'd lost.

That sword you have, little dragon ... you should get to know it better ... that day your father forged it, I was there ... tell him hello ... and thank you.

CHAPTER 28

I T WAS A QUIET TRIP down the mountain, through the forest, and across where the small river went into the Shale Hills. I was frustrated. My arm was still as black as coal, and saving the dragons had given me little comfort at all. I felt empty, left out, and as confused as ever. Even Brenwar seemed perplexed.

Dragons! I'd saved a steel dragon, and all the thanks he'd given me was advice to talk to Fang. The fact that he knew my father—well, I presumed, seeing how they shared a forge—bothered me most. Certainly, he could give me a little more advice now that the curse was lifted. And what did he need the Thunderstone for, anyway? It had helped him. Maybe it could have helped me, too. I punched a tree.

"What's the matter with you?" Brenwar said.

I took a seat on a fallen log.

"All this work, and for what? My arm's no different than when I started." I held it out. "See!"

Brenwar took a step closer, squinting.

"What are you doing?"

"Looking," he said, "I haven't really taken a good look at it." He rubbed his chin. "I thought you said it was all black."

"It is," I said, eyeing my forearm and wrist. "What other color do you see?"

"White."

I fanned out my clawed fingers and turned my hand in the sunlight, saying, "Where?"

"In the middle of your palm."

"It's just the sun's reflection off the scales, I don't see a th—"

My lips froze. My heart stopped. A small group of scales in the middle of my palm had turned white. A thrill went through me, like the first time I flew on my father's great back as a child.

"Brenwar!" I exclaimed. "Can it be I'm on the higher road of doing good things?"

He didn't say anything, but he was smiling, in a dwarven way, a broad smirk, if anything.

I pumped my dragon fist in the air, jumped high, and shouted with joy! I couldn't remember the last time I'd felt so good in my life. I was finally getting somewhere.

"Maybe it's spreading, Brenwar?" I gave my hand a closer look. "My hand might be completely white by tomorrow, you think?"

He shrugged and said, "I hope so." He slapped me on the back. "You've done well, Dragon. But I still think you've got many good deeds to go."

I felt in my heart that saving the blue razor and helping the steel dragon had gotten me over the hump. I'd saved many dragons of late, but those two were different, the circumstances more tough. Perhaps I wasn't challenging myself enough. I needed to investigate further the whereabouts of more dragons. I knew there were more out there.

"I'm coming home soon, Father!"

I had a spring in my step, and my wounded leg was less bothersome as we traversed the black shale. I had two things on my mind: my dragon arm and the Roaming Rangers, Shum and Hoven. It had only been a few days, but I wondered if they'd had any luck finding the winged ape. I wanted to track it. Fight it. Defeat it. I couldn't explain why, but I did. It was just another menace that needed to die before someone else did.

"Where are you going?" Brenwar asked, wiping his sweating head on his forearm.

I pointed with my dragon arm toward the hill where we'd last seen the elves. I felt more comfortable using it now. A bad thing had turned good in my eyes, and I loved it all the more.

"Just checking on those—"

"No! You need to focus on the dragons. The elves can solve their own problems, and the men can as well. Come now, I thirst for dwarven ale."

"But—"

"Come!" Brenwar said, marching off with determination.

I didn't have to follow him, and he didn't have to follow me—unless my father had told him to, but Brenwar never said. I eyed the hill where the elves were holed up and some of their traps were set. I was dying to see them again. I had never seen elves like that. Potbellies on elves. Hah! Who'd have imagined such a thing?

"All right," I said, heading after Brenwar. We walked on mile after mile until the sun began to set in our sight. "You hungry? I could use some good meat about now."

"I'll find a spot and start a fire."

I unslung Akron.

Snap. Clatch. Snap.

It was ready

"I'll fetch the meat."

I hadn't made it a mile from camp when I heard a muffled cry. A struggle was ahead, and without thinking, I rushed for the danger. Darting in and out of the trees like the swiftest of deer, I emerged in a clearing. Shum and Hoven, the Wilder Elves, were interlocked in battle with the winged ape. It was hairy and blue-black with a slight blue sheen, roaring into the face of Shum, its mighty, long fingers wrapped around the neck of another ranger I'd not seen before.

Twang!

My first arrow hit it square in the back, and it let out a roar.

It turned.

I reloaded.

Brawny muscles, black claws, and dripping fangs charged me, faster than the fastest bull I'd ever seen.

Twang!

It ducked.

But my aim was low, intentionally, and the arrow exploded into its shoulder.

The winged ape crashed to the ground.

I ripped out Fang and charged.

"Dragon! Dragon!"

I couldn't let the evil beast hurt or kill another thing. I chopped at its stomach.

It rolled away, bounced up, and swatted me in the face. It was fast. Like a striking cobra.

I stabbed.

It turned.

I slashed, grazing its arm.

It swung its big paw at me, nails nicking my face.

I countered and clipped its legs, drawing blood.

It backed away.

"Come on," I said, taunting it with Fang's glowing blade. I was ready for it. I was ready for anything.

It eyed me, two red coals gleaming under its heavy brow. It was smart, thinking about its next move. But I was ready.

"You heard me! Come on, monster!"

It pounded its chest, lowered its shoulders, stretched out its mighty, thewed arms, ready to scoop me up, and charged.

It came.

I swung.

It leapt high in the air and left me gawping before dropping on me like a load of stones. The eight-hundred-pound ape drove me hard into the ground.

Fang fell from my grasp.

It pinned my neck to the ground and roared in my face. It was strong, like oxen. I kicked its stomach, twisted my wrist free, then clawed at its eyes.

It punched and punched me like a boxer. I found this odd, even in the midst of my face being punched in. It was bigger, stronger, but it was a beast; I was a dragon.

I drew back and punched it in the nose with my fist. I swore I heard it laughing as it shrugged the blow off and hit me back. Stars exploded in my eyes. I was getting beaten like a dusty rug.

A Wilder Elf jumped on its back, which one I couldn't tell.

With one arm, the winged ape flung him away.

I pulled my knees to my chest and kicked it in the stomach with all I had. To my surprise, it tumbled to the ground. Gasping, I rolled left and grabbed my sword.

Two more elves dove at the winged ape. They both fought hard before it slung them off like water. Another pair, from where they came I don't know, threw a large net at the beast. The net sailed beneath its feet as it jumped high in the air. How many of these elves were there, anyway?

I saw my chance. The ape had the elves in sight, not me. I lowered my sword, rushed in, and stabbed at its belly. It twisted a split second before I got there, but I struck a blow. The beast let out an odd cry, almost elvish, as its massive shoulders dipped to the ground. I had it where I wanted it now. Fang gleamed as I raised it above my head for the final strike.

"No!" someone screamed.

A Roaming Ranger slammed into me, knocking me to the ground. Another jumped on top of me, followed by another.

"What are you doing?" I screamed at them.

The winged ape groaned, holding its wounded side as it lifted its chin to the sky. Its black wings fanned out, flapped a few times, lifting it into the air, above the tree lines, and out of sight.

"Get off of me!" I said, kicking one of the elves in the gut. I was mad now. Why did the elves mess things up?

"Nath Dragon!" one of the rangers said, extending his hand to me. It was Shum. "We do not want him dead! We want him alive, and you've fouled things up."

"Fouled things up? Are you jesting? It was beating the tar out of all of you. Why wouldn't you want that beast dead, anyway? It's a killer!" I shoved his hand away.

"It's our king," Shum said, glumly.

"Your what?" I said, eyeing the others.

There were five of them now. One just as tall and heavy as the other.

"Our king, Sansla Lybor."

"Let me guess..." I hated to say it, but I did, "...he's cursed."

Not long after that, Brenwar arrived, huffing and puffing. Shum and Hoven had finished the tale of their cursed king. I felt for them. For more than a decade, they'd tried to trap him, and this was as close as they'd been in a while. I wasn't sure if I'd messed things up or not, but I only meant well. But as they left, I sensed their disappointment.

Shum said to me as he left, "You stick to your own, Nath Dragon. We'll stick to ours. And remember, Sansla Lybor is little more than a shadow of his glorious self now, but the curse within him is vengeful. He'll not forget that wound you gave him, but perhaps we'll find him before he finds you. Watch the skies. Farewell."

One thing was for certain: there were too many curses in this world! I had enough of my own problems to worry about. I eyed the white spot on my hand. It was a start. A dozen dragons freed, dozens more to go. *One dragon at a time, Nath Dragon, one at a time.*

"Come on, Brenwar. I think I'm ready for the dwarven home, Morgdon, for now."

Terror at the Temple

-Book 3-

CRAIG HALLORAN

PROLOGUE

THE DRAYKIS. BIG. SILENT. DEADLY. Finnius the acolyte of Barnabus had never seen or imagined anything like them. Men, with dragon parts grafted onto their bodies by magi: scales, talons, and another one with wings. Not just any men, but fighting men, men of skill and cunning. And they had something cornered, a dragon of all things.

They'd trapped a yellow streak dragon inside the mouth of a large cave. It was bigger than any one man, slender and about fifteen feet in length. Its spiked tail whipped out like the head of a snake, taking out one draykis's legs. In an instant, the draykis was back on its feet, charging. The dragon breathed a plume of white ash, engulfing the dragon man. The draykis turned stiff as stone where he stood.

Whack!

A draykis caught the dragon across the nose with his club as another draykis jumped onto its neck. Only a fool would wrestle a dragon, but the draykis were unrelenting, fearless. The yellow streak dragon bit one on the arm, clawed another on the face, but he was young and confined to a tight space. The fourth draykis appeared, the one with dark wings and a red-scaled face, swinging a club. As the dragon men held the yellow dragon down, the winged draykis beat it until it fought no more. Finnius had never seen men take a dragon so quickly before. Nor with such brutality, either.

"What would you have us do now, Acolyte Finnius?" the winged draykis said.

Finnius watched as the other two bound the defenseless dragon's mouth and wings. He could see the look in the dragon's eyes, drained, defeated. That look thrilled him as he walked over and stroked the dragon's dark-yellow belly. *Quite the catch. Quite the catch, indeed. High Priestess Selene will be pleased with this one.*

"Fetch a cart while this one thaws," he said, pointing his finger at a draykis that was coated in white and perfectly stiff. "And don't touch him—"

At that moment, a draykis touched the coated draykis and started to freeze.

"Either!" Finnius grunted as he turned back toward the draykis leader. "Fetch the cart while we wait for them both to thaw out." He shook his head. "Did I tell any of you to touch one another? Hmm? Did I? No! You follow orders. Explicit orders. Now fetch that cart and the rest of the acolytes, dragon man."

"As you command," the draykis said, ruffling his wings before heading outside the cave.

"You," he pointed at the last one, "stay with the dragon. We cannot afford to lose our bait for capturing Nath Dragon."

CHAPTER 1

MORGDON. HOME OF THE DWARVES. I was a captive here.

"Come on, Brenwar," I pleaded. "I'm ready to go. It's been three weeks already."

"Ah, but the Festival of Iron has just started. We can't leave now: you haven't even seen the best part yet," he replied, marching down a crowded street.

The opening parade had begun a week ago, and it hadn't finished yet. The dwarves only celebrated the Festival of Iron once in a decade, and they put a lot of effort into it. I stopped to watch as a regiment of dwarves marched by in full plate armor, with only their beards and weapons hanging out. They were in perfect cadence, every booted foot in step, not one out of a thousand dwarves out of line.

"How many soldiers are there, anyway?" I asked, looking over Brenwar's head. I was the tallest person in the entire city, at the moment, anyway.

"Oh, I can't tell you that, but I might entertain a guess."

I'd been asking questions every day for weeks. It helped pass the time. A certain question in particular always came to mind: "When are we leaving?" Still, I had to respect my host.

"One hundred thousand?" I said.

"No."

"Fifty thousand?"

"No."

"Can you give me a hint?"

A tiny dwarven boy was standing on the shoulders of his father, smiling at me and holding nine fingers up.

"Ninety…" I said.

The dwarven boy, whose beard had not started yet, showed six fingers.

"—Six thousand?"

Brenwar turned. I could see the surprise in his stony face. His eyes flitted from me to the boy and back to me when he said, "Humph… close enough." He eyed the boy again, stroking his beard, and said, "Ye should mind your own business."

I put my arm over Brenwar and walked him away, saying, "Ah. It's no wonder you all look so grumpy all the time. You don't encourage fun when you're young."

"Fun is for the foolish. A dwarf's work is never done. We don't run around looking for things to smile about all the time."

"You would if you could smile like me," I grinned.

He shook his head, saying, "That smile would be much prettier accompanied by a nice long beard."

I rubbed my clean-shaven face. I was the only beardless man in Morgdon, aside from the women and children. Of course, many of the women did have beards, and I never got used to that. It just didn't seem natural, a fuzzy-faced woman, but they could all cook a delicious feast. I'd give them that.

"Brenwar, honestly, when can we leave?"

I was restless. Now that I had a white spot on my dragon hand, I wanted to save the dragons more than ever. I felt like a piece of me was back, like my honor had returned. I hadn't been motivated before, but now I was more motivated than ever. And I couldn't help but wonder: *What do the white scales mean?*

"Soon, Dragon. Come now," he said, reaching over and grabbing a tankard of ale from the booth of a dwarven ale master. He quaffed it in one gulp and belched like a man-sized bullfrog. He patted his belly and grabbed another round and thrust it in my face. "Drink and be merry. Be merry and drink."

"I'm fine, thanks. Now, Brenwar, let's go," I groaned. "You know I have dragons to fetch."

"Wait until the song's over," he said with a wink.

"What song?" I said. "There's no one singing."

That's when I saw a smile from behind his beard as he raised his booming voice to the clouds and sang:

"HOOOOOOOOOOOOOOOOOOOOOOOOOOOO…"

Instantly, thousands of dwarves joined in.

"Home of the dwarves! Morgdon! Home of the dwarves! Morgdon!

We make the finest steel and ale. Morgdon! In battle, we never fail! Morgdon!

Home of the dwarves! Morgdon! Home of the dwarves! Morgdon…"

The singing went on and on, and I'd be lying if I said I didn't enjoy it. As much as I didn't want to sing, I couldn't help but do just that. The robust dwarves put everything they had into the moment. They jumped, swung, tapped, drank, and sang all at the same time. I'd never seen so many happy dwarves before, and it made me happy, too. There was no better army in all Nalzambor than an army of dwarves. They'd fight until their hearts were black and blue.

"Home of the dwarves! Morgdon! Home of the dwarves! Morgdon!

We make the toughest armor and ale. Morgdon! In battle, we never turn tail! Morgdon!

Home of the dwarves! Morgdon! Home of the dwarves! Morgdon…"

When it ended, I was fulfilled. The dwarves were ready for anything. I was ready for anything.

Brenwar slapped me on the back and said, "What did you think of that?"

"I liked it!"

I decided I should make the most of it. You just couldn't let every day of your life be filled with worry. "Trust in the greater good instead," my Father would say. So I did. After all, Morgdon was a fantastic city with the boldest architecture I had ever seen. A suspension bridge crossed from one side of Morgdon to another. The buildings and towers were all square-cut stone, but not just any stone: many stones of many colors, not bright, but not all dull, either. Where you didn't see stone, you saw metal. Burnished, hammered, polished, or riveted, it adorned their bodies, faces, buildings, and all places.

"Look at this, Dragon! Ho! You are in for a treat!" Brenwar pointed.

The parade was still going strong. The regiment of dwarves had marched on, but I could still hear their heavy boots pounding the ground like a steady heartbeat. I followed Brenwar's arm that pointed upward. A group of dwarven men was sitting in the sky.

"How are they doing that?"

They each sat in a tiny seat at the top of a pole that was ten stories tall, four of them in all. Beneath them, big dwarves with broad chests held them up on shafts of iron, eyes straight forward as they marched along. Every eye was filled with wild wonder as the dwarves stood high atop their perches and bowed.

"Are they crazy! What are they going to do?"

"Just watch, Dragon!"

A wild dragon couldn't tear my eyes away as one dwarf saluted, teetered backward, and fell.

CHAPTER 2

THE CROWD GASPED AS ONE dwarf fell, followed by another and another until the fourth one fell. My heart jumped in my chest as they plummeted to the ground amid the frightened screams. Certainly, there was a net, a magic spell, or something to save them from breaking their necks? As much as I wanted to be, even I wasn't fast enough or close enough to catch any of them.

"Brenwar, they're going to—"

The first dwarf was caught by two others.

The second was caught by two more, and so on, and so on. Cheers erupted as the falling dwarves bowed and raced back up the poles to the delight of the crowd.

Brenwar elbowed me in the gut, saying, "Had you fooled, didn't they? Wouldn't you say?"

I didn't know what to say, actually. It didn't seem possible for a dwarf to be caught from a ten-story fall, and it seemed even less likely for one to shinny like a spider monkey up an iron beanpole. *Maybe I should take a dwarven acrobat with me on my next adventure. Such agility would move things quicker.*

"That was incredible, Brenwar! I'd like to meet—"

"Hah!" He waggled his finger at me. "I know what you're thinking about them dwarves. They might be acrobatic, but they can't fight worth a hoot. Humph."

"Is that so?" I said, surprised. "I thought all dwarves could fight."

"They can," Brenwar grabbed a loaf of bread stuffed with pepperoni and took a bite, "better than men, orcs, and elves that is. But they're not dwarven soldiers. Dwarven acrobats is all, the best acrobats in all of Nalzambor!"

"Certainly."

The next few hours, I allowed myself to unwind and take in more of the city of Morgdon and all its rugged exteriors. They could hammer iron so thin that you could see right through it. An entire building was windowed with it. "No rock or arrow could shatter that iron glass," Brenwar boasted. There were so many objects and artifices of iron that it was just incredible, but as the sun began to set and the fervor of the festival renewed its rise, I realized it was time to go.

"Brenwar, I think I'm going to head back to your place and take a break," I said, walking away.

"What? But the festival has just begun!" he said, not looking at me but chewing his pepperoni loaf and watching the acrobats instead. "Just stay and watch a few hours more."

I could see he was enjoying himself, but frankly, I'd had my fill. And the white spot inside my dragon palm looked a tad smaller. I had to save more dragons; I just had to.

"I'll see you later, Brenwar," I said, waving.

"Wait a moment, Dragon!" he said, stopping me in my tracks. "Remember, you cannot leave Morgdon without me, and every dwarf in the city knows that. So you go rest and stay put. I've a few ceremonies to attend to."

I nodded.

He eyed me.

"What?" I said. I could see he wanted confirmation from me, a promise that I would not leave, but I wasn't going to give him that. Never make a promise you can't keep. Just let them think it's a promise.

"Give me your word, Dragon."

I shook my head, saying, "Why bother? I can't leave anyway. A thousand eyes are on me. My, Brenwar, I'm as much a prisoner as a guest."

"Prisoner?" he stroked his beard. "That's not polite, and you know it!" He combed his fingers through his beard and muttered under his breath. "Better be no pixies in there." Then he looked at me. "As for you, a prisoner? Pah! I'm looking out for you. That's all. Don't be hasty, Dragon."

"Every day we stay, the graver the danger gets for the dragons."

"You can't save them all, try as you might."

I glared at him.

"What if it were dwarves we were going to rescue? Would you wait then?"

"Ho! A dwarf needing rescued!" Brenwar laughed. "I've never seen such a thing. Nobody poaches dwarves. Not if they know what's good for them."

"Well, nobody poaches orcs, either!" I said, storming away.

"What!" Brenwar yelled at me. "You take that back, Dragon!"

I kept going.

He kept yelling.

"And don't you dare try to leave without me!"

Brenwar's home was small and quiet. His children were grown, and his wife was working at the festival. Such a fine cook she was, one of the finest I'd ever known.

Still, it was good to be alone with my thoughts. If I wanted to pout, I'd pout alone. I pulled up a stool on the balcony overlooking the vast and colorful city. It seemed like every torch and pyre was alive with yellow, green, red, orange, and even pink fires. The air smelled of roasted everything good, too, and I hungered.

"I can't wait any longer," I mumbled. I wanted to pass over the great wall that held Morgdon, dash over the plains below, and save the dragons. Holding my dragon hand before me, I studied it with intent. Was I getting close? Could I remove the evil curse on my own? But part of me wondered what would happen without my dragon arm. Making two fists, I punched one into the other. I could feel that extra power within me. Something great. It was part of me—the strongest part—and I didn't want to do without it.

Rubbing the white scales of my hand, I said to myself, "I wonder if the white are as strong as the black?" Standing up, I leaned over the balcony and looked as far out as I could see. There were dragons out there who needed me. And I needed them as well. But how could I get out of Morgdon without anyone finding out?

As the bats darted in and out of the night sky snatching the fireflies in their mouths, I snapped my fingers.

"That's a great idea, Dragon! A great one!"

I dashed inside Brenwar's place, found my pack and his, and tossed them both onto my bed along with my longsword Fang and my bow Akron. I wouldn't be going anywhere without them. I counted the arrows in my quiver. I had hunting arrows, warviin-tipped arrows, and magic arrows for extraneous circumstances, plus one that I wasn't certain at all what it would do, but supposedly it would do what I told it to do. "Can't wait to use you," I said, taking it out and stroking its bright-red feathers before sticking it back in. "Now what?"

I dug into Brenwar's pack. He'd kill me if he knew I was doing that, especially because he liked to keep things tidy, and I was not tidy, not by a dwarf's standards, not even close. I found a jeweled case trimmed in gold with a dragon-faced hasp. It was just what I was looking for. Opening it, I found two dozen vials filled with colorful liquids. Potions. And not just any potions, magic potions. I plucked three of them out. One of them was light blue, a healer. If I was leaving without Brenwar, I'd need to be more careful. The second, dark blue, a concealer. The third I shook in front of my face. The yellow colors swirled with white. "I hope this is it," I said as I closed the lid and put the jeweled case back in his pack as neatly as I could.

"I'd take the whole thing with me if I could," I said to myself.

It was heavy, though, like a hundred stones. I could barely carry it, but Brenwar had little trouble at all with his pack. It was my father's design, no doubt about that, filled with all kinds of magic from my father's trove. I was blessed, that much was certain, that my father allowed Brenwar to take the pack and be its guardian.

I slipped into my chest-plate armor, strapped my sword on my waist then snapped my bow in place. Slinging my pack over my shoulder, I was ready to go now.

I pulled the cork out of the yellow vial, stepped out onto the balcony, and started to drink.

"Oh wait," I said.

I left Brenwar a note.

Dear Brenwar,

The dragons can't wait, and I can't either.

Forgive me,

Nath Dragon

He would be furious, but I couldn't wait a moment longer. I yearned for freedom, not just mine, but for the dragons. They needed me. I put the vial to my lips and took the first sip. It tasted like berries and honey.

"Mmmmm," I said, smacking my lips.

A moment later, I pitched forward and fell to my knees as my mind turned to mud.

CHAPTER 3

EVERYTHING TURNED BLACK. SOMETHING WAS wrong. Terribly wrong. I couldn't see a thing, but my ears were just fine. I could hear everything in the street below but much louder this time.

What do I do?! What have I done?! That potion has me undone!

My plan was simple: take the potion of polymorph and turn myself into something else. I stretched out and fluttered on the floor. This shouldn't have been so hard; I'd done it before. But I'd never turned myself into a bat.

"Eek!" I screamed, but it came out a high-pitched shriek.

Bats are blind, you idiot!

What was I thinking? Oh, now I remember. I was going to blend in with the bats and fly away. None of the keen-eyed dwarves would pay attention to such a thing.

Think! Take a breath, Dragon. You can figure this out.

I flapped my wings. Nothing. I rose on my tiny, clawed feet and flapped once more. I lifted from the ground. *Yes!* I banged into a wall and plummeted back to the floor. *Ow!*

At least, I thought it was a wall; I couldn't see it. Head aching, I made my next attempt.

Up, Dragon!

Whop!

I hit something else and dove nose first into the floor. *Think, Dragon. Think!*

Morphing into a new body took some getting used to, and it didn't help that I was blind to boot, and—fair enough—I was stupid, too. I should have just turned into a bird. I rubbed my nose with the tiny fingers at the end of my wing and sniffed the air. Not only could I hear everything, I could smell everything as well. Pretty amazing. What I lacked in sight, I made up with everything else.

What else could bats do that I didn't know about? I had to think on that. Then I remembered they had a sonic power that helped them out.

"Eek!"

That wasn't it. I tried something else. A whisper of sorts. Soon after I let it out, an echo came back. *Ah! I get it now!*

I lifted my head up and sounded out toward the smells and sounds below. In my mind, I saw the shape of the balcony now. Gathering myself, I fluttered to the ledge. *Made it!* Then I took a deep breath. Well, as big a breath as I could, that is. I certainly felt like I was in a very small body. I sent out a signal. The bats and bugs were still there, but the rest of my path from Morgdon was all clear. *Here we go… Bat Dragon!*

I slipped from the ledge, spread my wings, and *whoosh*—I was flying! Everything in my body was tingling, making me all the more eager to become a dragon one day. Then a thought struck me: Not all dragons can fly. What if I was one of those? No, I must perish such thoughts; it shouldn't matter either way. Right now, I needed to enjoy that I was free!

I let out a signal. Moths and fireflies fluttered in the air, and a strange hunger came over me. I signaled again, and like a beacon, I knew where the firefly was. I zoomed in and snatched it in my mouth. That was fast! I liked that. *Yech!* It left an odd taste in my mouth, but I crunched it up anyway.

Time to move on, Dragon! The sooner you go the better. No telling when the potion's magic would wear off, and I didn't want to be in the air when that happened, either. I let out a new signal. The mountain was behind, but the open plains of Nalzambor were below. That's where I went, where the goat herders go.

Flap! Flap! Flap!

Something soared past me. What was that? I ducked and dove before I got a good look around. The other bats were attacking me. One after the other they came, nipping and clawing at me. What were they attacking me for? All I ate was one lousy firefly. It wasn't like there weren't plenty of them left out there, you know. But in full assault they came. I was in trouble now.

I shrieked. It didn't help. I dodged.

They struck.

I dove.

They bit. They were going to drive me from the sky.

I wanted to say something, but I don't think bats talked; they shrieked. *What would happen if they got me on the ground?* I was certain they'd tear me to shreds. *Ouch!*

One of them got a piece of my leathery wing, sending me spiraling downward. I wanted to swing my sword, but it was part of me now, as were all those other things. I regained my balance and dove into an alley of the city. Perhaps I could shake them from my trail; I understood things about the city that they did not. Maybe that would help. I flapped hard and fast, weaving into alleys and underneath bridges, drawing some cries from the crowds. I don't think the dwarves had ever seen bats chasing bats before. This might not be such a good idea, after all.

Clack. Clack. Clack.

Too late. Stones were clattering off the walls. The children were throwing stones now. Accurate ones, too. I flew under one and over another, one stone clipping the wing of a pursuer. It bought me time. Up I went. Down I came to find the bats in front of me. I was chasing them now. I sent out a signal. The one in the back, bigger than the rest, was driving the colony of bats. I knew what I had to do. I had to stop him, else they'd wear me down. I let out an awful screech. A challenge was my intent. Up, up, up! The big bat came after me.

Bat or man, I knew how to fight, and I'd fight anything anywhere. I wasn't sure how bat fights went, but I think the leader got the message. I circled him and he circled me, then in rush he came right at me.

Whop!

We clocked heads. Blind, I saw stars, and I realized his head was much bigger and harder than mine. *I swear; with one gulp, he could eat me. What kind of bat did I turn myself into, anyway?* The more I flapped, the more my wings began to tire. Flying all the time could be very exhausting.

I sucked it up, flying straight upward as he barreled straight downward. At the last second, I dodged, and the others were upon me, clipping and biting at me. It seemed either I fought one of them head on or I fought them all at once. The leader and I darted up and down in a wide circle. This was it: him and me, head to head for all the glory of the nighttime bug eating. I let out my final signal. He let out his. He charged. I charged and let out my "Dragon! Dragon!" screech. There was no need to close my eyes, but I think I did.

CHAPTER 4

I FELT SOMETHING BURNING IN MY stomach and projecting from my mouth. The big bat screeched in the sky. I let out a sonic signal. The big bat was engulfed in flames and plummeting toward the ground. I could smell it burning—its hair, its wings—as I dove after it. *Where did that flame come from? Did it come from me?*

My mouth was hot, and I could taste the bitterness of sulfur on my tongue. Below me, the burning bat crashed into a rooftop. *Yes! What kind of bat am I, anyway?* I'd never seen a fire-breathing bat before. I swooped up into the sky where the other bats waited and let out a screech of triumph. I felt another streak of flames shoot from my mouth into the sky. I sent out another sonic signal, and all the bats were gone. I'd won.

I could hear shouts and cries from below and had visions of stubby fingers pointing into the sky. I flapped my way past the walls of Morgdon, over and beyond where the green grass grows, and flew through the night, exhausted, until I could fly no more.

I awoke to find myself in a very cramped cave with the new day's light creeping in.

"Sunken Sulfur! Where am I? Where are my arms and legs?"

I could see again, but I couldn't move a thing. It was as if I'd been nailed inside a coffin. I struggled and strained, wiggling my shoulder loose then my arm and leg.

"Ah… I'm whole again," I said, crawling out of the cramped cave. "Whoa!" I tumbled down a rocky hillside and went crashing into the hard ground below. "Stupid!" *What was I thinking, turning into a bat? I almost got myself killed. And being blind wasn't any fun at all.* Next time I changed, it would be into something else, but I had to admit: all the flying was incredible.

I dusted myself off, and to my relief, everything was intact: my sword, my bow, and even my pack. You have to like magic like that, which transforms not only you but everything you carry as well. "Thank goodness."

Above me, the sun was rising, and Morgdon was nowhere in sight. The last thing I remembered was flying as far and fast as I could, putting the Festival of Iron far behind. Guilt crept into me, however, about leaving Brenwar behind. I knew he'd be mad, but I also knew that he didn't understand. He was a dwarf; I was part dragon, part man. He'd just have to understand.

I coughed. The inside of my stomach churned like a pot of boiling lava, and the taste of sulfur was still inside my mouth.

Smacking my lips, I said, "That tastes horrible." I stuck a finger in my mouth, feeling around, certain I'd find a piece of charred wood inside there. What had happened, anyway? Could bats breathe fire? Impossible.

I coughed again. No smoke. No fire. Doing my best impression of a dragon, I forced out a roar of air. Nothing came out.

"Hmmm… perhaps it was a side of effect of the potion," I said to myself. That happens, you know. I shrugged it off. It was time to go, but where to? I stretched my arms and legs and raked my fingers through my hair.

"Freedom!" I yelled, stirring the birds in the trees. "Ha-Ha-Ha-Ha!"

I ran! Long legs cutting through the woodland like a wild stag's, I ran hard and long, with nowhere in mind to go. I was free. Not that I'd been a slave, but without Brenwar tagging along, I was liberated. Too often, he'd slow me down and nag.

"Quit looking at your arm."

"Focus, Dragon. Focus."

"Slow down."

"I need ale."

"Did I ever tell you about the time I killed an ettin?"

It wasn't all that bad, most of the time, but there was nothing like being alone without anyone to answer to. I could do what I wanted now, and I was going to. This time, I was going to rescue many dragons on my own. *I think that might better help my cause.*

I ran several leagues before I came to a stop beneath a shady tree and took a seat. Wind in my hair, civilization long from sight, I had all the peace and quiet I had ever wanted.

"Ah, now this is the life!"

Finger on the white-scaled spot in the middle of my dragon hand, I found relief.

"I guess it's all right to kill bats, then." And why wouldn't it be? After all, that bat had been picking on me. I tapped my fist on my chest as another fit of coughing began, but the taste of sulfur in my mouth was gone. "Finally! That's much better." I took a pull from the canteen in my pack.

It was midday now, and I had a lot on my mind. Where was I going to go to find the dragons? And I didn't want to find just one. I wanted to find several at a time.

I knew they were out there and that the most likely spot was one of the Clerics of Barnabus temples that were scattered and hidden throughout the world.

"Not a good idea," I said, rubbing my scales on my dragon arm. Such a fascinating thing it was. I tried to imagine what it would look like in white. "If I were a careless dragon, where would I go? Hmmmm." I also wanted to get as much distance between me and Morgdon as possible, and I had to think about that as well. *If Brenwar came after me, where would he think I'd go?* Nalzambor is a very large place, with each major city several hundred leagues from the others.

The Free City of Narnum was the closest and filled with the most trouble, the kind I like, that is. Pretty faces from all the other places gather there in celebration.

The Home of the Elves, Elomehorrahahn, or Elome for short, is a fantastic place hidden in the mist and trees. Their surrounding forests are well guarded as they like their privacy, and as far as I knew, they didn't meddle with dragons. They were jealous is what I always figured.

Thraag, or Thraagramoor, the home of the orcs, is simply too smelly to go near. I'd had my fill for a while in Orcen Hold.

That left Morgdon, which I had to avoid, and Quintuklen, where I hadn't been for a while. The humans lived there, and I'd had some friends there. Perhaps it was time I checked with some. I missed their colorful ways and wonderful things. The humans had the most zeal for life compared to all the others—simply put, because they didn't live so long. They gave "living life to the fullest" new meaning, and I could relate to them better than to the rest. Especially now, when I had a sense of urgency within me.

But Quintuklen was a long way off, and I could probably rescue a dozen dragons by the time I got there. But there were many men and women in that city that knew an awful lot about dragons. Humans had poachers as well. Wizards, clerics, sages—many of them with questionable character—wanted the dragons, our magic, and the secrets that we held.

I could hear Brenwar's voice in my head as if he was here saying, "There's nothing but troubles and temptation for you in the cities." I sighed. I was focused. I could handle those distractions now if need be.

And of course, there were still all the small cities, towns, and villages spread out and in between. I would just head that way first.

"Perhaps I should buy a horse."

I had a long, long way to go.

By nightfall, I'd made it to a small town called Quinley, a thriving farming community. The buildings were well constructed, the people amiable but wary. I respected their hard-working kind, but I was certain they didn't care for a stranger like me. I fit in like a shiny button on a potato-sack shirt. Not that they were dirty, but grubby from all their hard work. I almost opted to remain outside to avoid the stares, but the steady rain convinced me otherwise, so I entered. My coins were as good as any, and I was certain they wouldn't mind my business, so inside the nearest establishment I went.

My stomach growled as the scent of hot food aroused my senses. I could taste the roasted lamb and baked rolls in my mouth already. One thing about the well-fed people in the countryside: nobody made better buttered bread—and the vegetables were always fresh and delicious. Patting my tummy, I smiled as I walked in, keeping my dragon arm concealed under my cloak.

"Can I help you, er, sir?" the innkeeper asked. He was tall and lean with a nice head of brown hair, for a man. He wore overalls underneath his apron and had a white scar on his clean-shaven chin. It was probably from some sort of farming accident as a child. He seemed all right, but his eyes were busy.

"I need food and a room for the night," I said.

"Eh," he started, wiping his greasy fingers on his apron, "we don't have any more rooms."

He was lying. There was no one else on the floor except me, him, and a table where a young couple sat. A pair of passersby like me, judging by their traveling cloaks and boots. They eyed me. I eyed them back until they turned away. I looked the innkeeper square in the eyes.

"Are you sure you don't have any rooms? I'd hate to think I came all this way, to the wonderful town of Quinley, home of the finest carrots and heifers, only to find they don't have any rooms. Perish the thought!"

The innkeeper showed me a toothy smile as he leaned back and I leaned forward.

"Er... it's true."

The innkeeper jumped as I rapped my knuckles on the bar.

"Well that's just horrible!" I said. And it really was, for him, because I was starting to get mad. I didn't like it when people lied, and it was even worse when they did it without batting an eye. Something strange, very strange was going on in Quinley. But that wasn't any of my business. Getting some hot food and a dry room was. I continued.

"And I suppose you are out of *food,* too?"

The innkeeper nodded his head.

A comely older woman emerged from the kitchen with two plates full of hot food. She stumbled as she saw me, eyes blinking, as she plopped the meals onto the couple's table. The woman turned toward me, pushed her hair back, straightened her shoulders, and smiled before casually making her way back to the kitchen. I smiled back and waved. Then I turned my attention back to the innkeeper.

"I suppose that was your last meal... eh, innkeeper?"

Palms up, he shrugged, smiled, and said, "Y-Yes."

LIAR!

Now, I was hungry. Really, really hungry. And tired. I wanted food and a room, and they were going to give them to me. *Liar, liar, britches on fire!* And all those years, I'd thought the country folk were nice.

"What are you eating over here?" I said, walking over to the other travelers. "Smells good!" Something was wrong here. Why would they serve this ordinary man and woman but not me? Sure, I had beautiful gold eyes and a wonderful mane of auburn hair, on the frame of an extraordinary man, but that's no reason to exempt me. Is it?

"Go away," the man said, hand falling to a small dagger at his side. "Just passing through, and we don't want any trouble."

"I don't want any trouble either, my friends. But I really don't want to sleep in the rain." I turned back to the Innkeeper. "Or on an empty stomach!"

A silence fell over the room. I could sense the innkeeper didn't want any trouble, but I was certain he'd seen stranger men than me before. There were many other races that had come into this place. I could tell by all the unique objects that decorated the walls: elven shoes, a dwarven shovel, and even the two-pronged forks of the orcs.

The waitress returned, a swagger in her hips, a smile on her lips, and a bowl of soup with a biscuit in her hands.

"Jane, no," the innkeeper warned, reaching for her.

Dipping her shoulder and shuffling over to me, she nodded and said, "Take this quick, and go."

I took the bowl from her and said, "Thank you, but why?"

She stared up at me and said nothing as she licked her lips.

That happens sometimes.

"Jane is it?" I said. "That's a pretty blouse you're wearing, and your eyes and ears, so pretty. Are you part elven?"

She blushed.

"No, none at all."

"Jane! Get back in the kitchen! You're causing trou—"

Two large men pushed through the door, each soaked from head to toe. One cursed the rain, the other shouted out loud.

"Ale! Food! Now, innkeeper. It's a lousy night, so it better be good. And none of that watered-down brew you have, either."

"You should have gone," Jane whispered. "It's not safe here." She scurried back to the kitchen.

Behind me, the couple were taut as bowstrings, heads down, chewing quietly.

I had the feeling they weren't expecting these men's company.

"As you wish, enforcers," the innkeeper said, fixing two tankards. "Right away!"

The men tossed their cloaks on a rack in the corner. Thick shouldered and heavy, each wore steel on his hip: sword and dagger. Strong chinned, beady eyed, and rugged, they had the look of enforcers. It seemed the friendly farm city of Quinley was under control of an unfriendly element. They were the kind that riled me.

Sluuuu-urp!

"Mmmm… that's good soup," I said. "You should try some, fellas."

Both men perked up, big hands falling to their swords. I don't think they were accustomed to anyone else's voice in the room, especially one as deep and rich as mine. They looked at each other and then at the innkeeper, and one said, "I told you not to welcome any strangers."

The innkeeper set the tankards down and said, "I d-didn't, sir. I told him we had no food and no rooms, but he's persistent."

One enforcer slid back out the door. The taller one's eyes drifted to my sword Fang that hung in its scabbard. He swallowed before he said, "This inn is closed, traveler. Set your soup down and be gone." He nodded at the door.

"But it's raining," I said, "And I'm really tired and hungry. So I don't think I'll be leaving right away. But maybe tomorrow."

"Don't be a fool, traveler. You don't know who you're tangling with."

I wanted to laugh, but I slurped another spoonful instead. The big man's eyes started to twitch. I don't think he was accustomed to anyone standing up to him. *I should be worried about who I'm tangling with? He's the one who should be worried.*

"Tell you what," I said, digging my spoon deeper into my bowl. "How about you leave, ugly face and all, and come back tomorrow when I'm well rested and gone?"

"What?!"

The innkeeper ducked behind the counter. The couple behind me got up from their table, heads down, and darted up the stairs.

"I'm sorry," I said much louder this time, "I didn't realize you had trouble hearing. I SAID—"

A half dozen well-armed men burst through the entrance—and one of them was bigger than two put together.

CHAPTER 5

INSIDE THE PILLARS OF AN old temple ruin, Finnius the Cleric of Barnabus was brewing something. Trouble.

"In order to catch a dragon, you have to have a dragon," he muttered, adding some ingredients to a mystic pot of stew. "Shaved scales and ogre nails. Blood from a vorpal snail." He sniffed the bubbling cauldron. "Yech. I never really did like this part." He covered his nose with the sleeve of his robes, saying, "Anything for High Priestess Selene." On he went, adding one more defiling component after another as the smell and activity of the cauldron became stronger and stronger.

"One more thing is all," he said, wiping the sweat from his head then wringing his hands. He produced a tiny vial of blood Selene had given him. She had told him it was the key ingredient of the spell. He dumped it in, and the entire cauldron lurched, smoked, sparked with gold fire then bubbled and dimmed.

"Acolytes, bring me the prisoner." He smiled. "It's ready."

Yes, catching the bait, the yellow streak dragon, was one step. Luring Nath Dragon was the next, and it would be awfully hard to lure someone with bait when you didn't know where he was. The last he had heard, Nath Dragon had been in the Shale Hills. Many of the clerics had reported this, but that was weeks ago, and Nath Dragon hadn't been heard from since.

"Must find him. Must find him soon," he said.

The High Priestess was very clear about that. She wanted results. She had expectations, or she'd have his head. The fact that she'd taken a shine to him was odd, but he knew he had skills that others did not. He figured at some point she must have noticed.

"Ah, here you come," he said, taking a seat on a stone bench.

Two acolytes approached, robed from head to toe in dark purple with silver trim. Their heads were bald, and the tattoos on them were very little, expendable at this point. Each man carried what looked to be a large, covered bird cage. Bowing, they set the cages down.

Finnius crossed his legs and draped his locked fingers over his knee. "Hmmmm."

The truth was that he wasn't so certain if this would work or not, but he didn't have any other ideas, either. Typically, when Nath Dragon entered one of the larger cities, he knew about it immediately. The Clerics of Barnabus were thick in those places, and the man was about as discreet in his activities as a weasel in a hen house. But of late, Nath Dragon had been lying low, and that complicated things. Selene's expectations must be met. He wasn't about to disappoint *her*.

He lifted the cloth cover from the first cage. A man, standing about one foot tall, stood inside, tiny arms crossed over his little chest. He had two wings. Like a hummingbird's, they buzzed on and off behind him. He was a pixlyn: rare, and almost impossible to catch unless you had honey from the trees where the stump giants sat.

"The time has come to earn your freedom, little pixlyn."

It turned away.

"Oh, come now. It won't be so bad," Finnius said, digging a large spoon into the bubbling cauldron. "Besides, failure to carry out my order will result in certain death."

The pixlyn shrugged. He was a handsome and obstinate little thing whose eyes glowed with a faint blue fire.

Finnius snorted as he approached, holding the spoon of bubbling goo up to the bars.

The pixlyn held his nose.

"Oh, I suggest you reconsider," Finnius said, nodding to the other acolyte. "Especially since it's not you I'm threatening."

The man removed the cloth from the other cage.

"It's her."

The pixlyn man let out a tiny cry of alarm. A beautiful pixlyn woman with radiant pink eyes and bee's wings shivered inside her cage. The pixlyn man's hummingbird wings made an angry buzz as he zipped back and forth in his cage, slamming into one barred side and then the other.

Finnius laughed. He loved seeing good creatures suffer, and it was especially delectable when it was the suffering of one loved one for another.

"Settle down now, pixlyn. All you have to do is seek, find, and report. Of course, what you'll be searching for could be anywhere in all of Nalzambor. Now, take a sip, a big one that will fill your little gut, and on your way you shall go."

The tiny woman rose up in her cage, her squeaky little voice objecting in a language only the pixie-kind could speak. Both their tiny little hands grabbed the bars as they faced each other. Tears went down the little woman's cheeks.

"How adorable," Finnius said. "Now drink!" He banged the cage with his hand. "Or I'll kill you both right now!"

Dejected, the little pixlyn man grabbed the spoon, gulped its contents down, and wiped his mouth.

"Good… Good-good-good. That will make you strong and help you find Nath Dragon's trail." He opened the birdcage door. "Go now, go! The longer it takes, the less likely she lives."

The pixlyn grabbed the woman's tiny hands on the bars, kissed them each, and with the speed of an arrow, he disappeared.

As the tiny woman sobbed in her prison, Finnius tossed one of his men an empty vial and said, "Get me those tears."

CHAPTER
6

Now there were six of them and one of me. They had leather armor and swords and even helmets on, too. Not the kind of odds I expected in a small town like this. And to think, all I wanted was a room for the night and some food.

"Sorry, fellas, but I think I just finished the last bit of food," I said, setting the bowl on the table. I patted my belly and burped. "Pretty tasty, though, worth the wait until tomorrow. Say, any of you ugly men happen to have a toothpick on you?"

"Shut your mouth," the one who'd hung back in the room said. He came closer, the rest of the enforcers at his sides and spreading out except one, the big one, abnormally large, who looked like he had part giant in him. He was almost eight feet tall, and his big and meaty arms were crossed over his barrel chest as he blocked the exit.

I backed up until I bumped into the table. What was I going to do now? I couldn't fight them all—or could I? They came closer, wary, weathered, and scarred, one just as mean looking as the other. A well-trained bunch of goons, mercenary and ex-soldier types, men for hire judging by the steel jangling on their hips. They were the kind of men who wouldn't hesitate to hurt or kill.

I put my hands out in front of me.

"Perhaps I should be going. I don't think a little bit of rain ever hurt anyone, eh?"

When facing a conflict of superior enemies, play nice before the first dagger strikes.

"Oh, ho-ho," the leader said, swinging his sword up on his shoulder. "So you want to play nice now, do you, smart fella? What's the matter? Are we too ugly for you?"

"As a matter of fact, yes, but that's not the reason I'm willing to leave."

The enforcers snickered as they drew their daggers.

"It's nothing personal," I said, "I mean, yes you are ugly, not like an orc—well, except you," I pointed at one with the turned-up nose, "and you."

"Be silent, you fool! You've crossed the line, big mouth. And to think, all you had to do was walk out when I said, but now you'll have to pay. Possibly with your life, you golden-eyed freak!"

A heavy thumping pounded inside my chest. They meant business. I slid between the table and the wall. They came closer. I didn't need this kind of trouble.

"Tell you what, uh, what do you call yourselves?"

"Enforcers, fool!"

"So it is, Enforcers Fool. Very catchy. Now here is what I offer. Leave me be, and I'll see to it that you can walk out of here, not crawl… or die."

They snickered.

"You've got a death wish, do you? So be it! Enforcers, take him!"

I stuck out my dragon arm.

They hesitated, eyes going back and forth between each other.

"What's the matter? Never seen a dragon's arm on a man before?"

Even the big one gawped and scratched his balding head.

I had them now. I had them right where I wanted them. I shoved the table aside, stepped forward, and towered over them, except the one in the back, of course.

"Men! What are you waiting for? We've taken down plenty of stranger things before, but never one with a mouth so big. And do I have to remind you who your lord is? The Jackal will not be pleased if you fail him in this. Now, don't make me tell you again, enforcers. Attack!"

They surged forward, striking high and low.

I leapt into the rafters. This isn't what I wanted. Not at all. These men were killers, and they wanted me dead. I couldn't stay up here forever. There was only one rafter and nowhere to go.

"Brock! Get over there and jerk that bird out of those rafters!"

The oversized man made it across the room in three strides, reaching up my way. His big fingers reached at my feet as I kicked them away.

"Go away, Brock!"

He was big and ugly but not stupid. He laughed.

"Get him, Brock!"

"Snap his neck like a chicken's!"

"I've got dibs on his pretty hair!"

I kicked Brock in the nose, drawing a painful howl. That last comment lit a fire in me. My problem was they could kill and seemed perfectly willing to, but I could not. Problem.

Brock threw his shoulder into the post. The entire building shook.

The innkeeper was screaming, "Stop it! Stop it!"

The leader shoved him to the ground.

It seemed these enforcers had a point to make. Something weird was going on here, and the Jackal, whoever that was, was behind it all. It was time for me to move.

Brock hit the post again, cracking it and shaking the room.

I dropped onto his shoulders and blinded him with my hands.

"Easy, Brock," I said. "What you can't see, you can't hit!"

"Get off of me, rodent!"

He reached for my hands.

I slapped him on his bald head.

"That will leave a mark. Woo! My, it's hot up here."

The leader shouted out, "Brock, kneel down so we can get a lick at him!"

The fun was over. Brock dropped to a knee.

I jumped from his shoulders to one table and then another. I had to get as far away from Brock as possible. He could crush me. Jumping, ducking, diving, and dodging, I got a few punches in as they chased me around the room.

"Blast it! You fools!" the leader said. "Do I have to do everything myself? Brock, guard the door! We can't let him get away."

They seemed pretty persistent about not letting me go for some reason. Perhaps they didn't want word getting out about their indiscretions. I jumped left, right, then found myself cornered, two daggers and a sword at my throat.

"Now we've got you!"

CHAPTER 7

"GIVE IT UP, OR I'LL cut your throat!"

I wouldn't yield. Not to them. Not to men lacking character. And my pride wouldn't let me give in to an inferior but skilled and well-armed force, despite the numbers.

I started to speak.

The leader cut me off. "Save it! Your tongue's caused you enough trouble. Keep your peace and get ready to die, freak!"

I was tired and no longer hungry but agitated now. I didn't like that word, "freak." I would not yield. Not to this scum. Not now. Not no-how. Especially when I was fast. Faster than them all. I could draw Fang faster than they could swing. I told myself to do it. I willed myself to do it. But I did not. I couldn't risk killing, evil men or not. There had to be a better way; there always was, my father said.

I locked my eyes on his and summoned my magic within. Dragon magic, ancient, wonderful, accessible. I could see my reflection in the man's eyes. His hardened features slackened at the sound of my thoughts.

Lower your sword, I suggested.

"Huh," he said, shaking his head, "what did you say?"

It wasn't working. I summoned all I had within, my gold eyes glowing.

"What is that?" one said.

"A demon!" cried another.

I made my suggestion again, putting all my mental strength behind it this time.

Drop your sword!

The leader's blade clattered to the ground.

"What did you do that for?" the enforcers said.

"He's a demon, I tell you!"

Whack!

I punched the man in the jaw, dropping him like a stone.

"I'm..."

Whack!

I knocked another's helmet off.

"Not!"

Twist! Crack! Boom! Twist!

I disarmed and disabled the leader.

"A demon!"

One rushed.

I had room to move now. I dipped and struck. My dragon arm's jabs were like black lightning.

The leader struggled back to his feet.

I booted him in the ribs, lifting him from the ground. Evil men calling me a demon, such gall!

One dove on my back; another climbed on my legs.

I slung one crashing into a table and drove the other's head into the hard floor.

I was dusting my hands off and saying "That should do it" when a large shadow fell over me. Big Brock was back.

Whop!

I crashed into the nearest wall, wondering, *How did I forget about him?*

Have you ever been hit by a log before? Me either, but I was pretty sure I knew what that felt like now. Brock was quick for a big man, not as quick as me, but as quick as an eight-foot-tall man could be. And when he punched, you could feel it from one side to the other.

Bam!

My head!

Bam!

My gut!

I struggled back to my feet and raised my fist, saying, "You want some more of this?"

Bam!

He knocked me off my feet and onto my butt.

Gasping for air, I held my hands out, saying, "You don't hit very hard for a big fellow."

"What did you say?" Brock said, his voice as loud as distant thunder.

I held my nose. It was all I could do. I felt like the only thing holding my body together was my armor. "What did you say?" I mocked back. I don't know why I did that. I guess it was a character flaw that exposed itself in moments of desperation.

Brock grabbed me by my collar, and with two hands, threw me across the room and into the bar. He was strong, very strong, and he hit as hard as an ogre. He came back.

I snatched Dragon Claw from Fang's hilt and stabbed him in the leg.

"Ouch."

That's all he said, "Ouch," as if I'd pricked him with a pin.

He swatted the small dagger from my hand, sending it spinning across the floor.

I was defenseless now. I was rattled. I couldn't understand why I couldn't handle this big man. I reached for the sword along my belt.

He stopped me.

"No! No! No! Demon!"

I'm not a demon!

He wrapped his arms around me as he lifted me from the ground. My feet dangled from the floor as he squeezed the life out of me.

"How's that feel?"

I managed to say, "Great! I haven't had my back cracked in forever."

He squeezed harder. I flexed my muscles. The harder he squeezed, the more I flexed. I just hoped my bones didn't crack. The pressure was becoming unbearable.

"Give up, demon! I've cracked bones thicker than yours before. Dwarves, orcs, elves, I've broke them all."

Who was this man, and what was he doing in this farm village?

I snapped my head back into his chin and saw stars as he laughed.

"Any moment, you will die," he said in my ear.

He might be right. I couldn't move. I couldn't breathe. And I didn't have an ounce of magic left inside me. Maybe venturing without Brenwar was a bad idea after all. One thing was for certain: if it wasn't for the dwarven armor I wore, I'd have been cracked like an egg already. I had to do something. Anything.

"You ate it, didn't you?" I said.

"Ate what?"

"All the food."

Wham!

He slammed me to the floor as hard as he could.

Breathless, I tried to speak but couldn't form the words.

Brock grabbed me by the hair, jerked my head back, and wrapped his arms round my neck and throat and squeezed.

Oh no! This was bad. Very bad. Brock the giant man had me in a sleeper hold. My fingers clutched for the door, the only way of escape. I expected Brenwar to burst through at any moment, but darkness came instead.

CHAPTER 8

I WOKE UP TO THE SOUND of rattling chains. When I opened my eyes, I noticed they were mine.

"What is this? Ow!"

I clutched at my chest. My ribs were broken. The big man had gotten the best of me. It got even worse. I was inside a metal cage, very much like the ones that held dragons.

"No!" I cried.

But no one answered. Groggy and dizzy, I rubbed a strange bump on my neck. I'd been injected with something. Possibly stabbed with a tainted stick, like the savages like to use.

Two lanterns illuminated the exterior walls of what looked to be an old barn. I could hear the heavy rain pounding on the ceiling above me. Large drops of water splashed on my face and back. The chains rattled as I wiped the water from my face and scooted into the corner.

"I can't believe this," I muttered to myself.

I was caged like an animal in a barn that smelled like livestock, manure, and hay. I pounded my head on the bars. It hurt. But I deserved it. I'd been stupid and careless, I guess. But it wasn't as if I had been looking for any trouble, either. If anything, I'd tried to avoid it. I sighed. I should have been happy that I was still alive. After all, the enforcers had made it clear that they wanted me dead. And Brock, that giant of a man, could have killed me easily with his own bare hands.

Cold, tired, and still hungry, I collected my thoughts. It seemed I'd have to think my way out of this. And who was my captor? Was it some sinister bunch of village folk or the character the lead enforcer mentioned, the Jackal? How could I get into this much trouble at some silly little farm? That was when a river of ice raced down my spine.

"Fang! Akron!"

I grabbed my head and tugged at my hair. I'd lost them. And not just them but my pack with all my supplies. No not only did my chest and neck ache but my head did as well. And how long had I been knocked out cold? That'd only happened one time before.

I grabbed the bars and tugged.

"Hurk!"

They didn't budge. I dug my heels in.

"HURK!"

A bubble of snot formed in my nose and burst. The bars bent a little but didn't budge from my disgusting effort. I labored for breath as I said, "Ew."

I kicked the bars. I hit the bars. I raked my dragon claws against the bars, but nothing happened. I was helpless in my cage.

And there I sat: friendless, weaponless, and helpless while the water from the roof dripped, dripped, dripped. I moved from one spot to the other, only to catch a new drip from another hole in the roof. The barn creaked and groaned from the weight of the wind, but little stirred. No animals, no rats, no cats, no birds, which seemed strange for a place meant to keep animals. But there was something else different and unique: the smell of decay and death. On one wall were more chains and some digging tools: spades, shovels, and picks. A few work tables were spread out with hammers, anvils, and saws. My eyes were good, even in the poor light, but I swore there were bloodstains.

"Not good," I said, cradling my dragon arm. What if they were going to cut it off? Perhaps they really thought I was a demon. I wasn't a demon. What an insult! I was a dragon! Well, I was part dragon—and any fool could see that. Perhaps it was my gold-flecked eyes that freaked them out.

"I've got to get out of here."

Grabbing the nearest bar with my dragon arm, I tugged. The iron of the cage was at least a half inch thick. The metal groaned. I could feel my black arm growing with strength. What it would not do before it was doing now.

"Come, Dragon," I said through gritted teeth. "You can do it!"

It moved no more.

"Sultans of Sulfur!"

I collapsed against the bars.

Now my head was pounding, and my body was sore all over. I felt like a bruised apple from head to toe, and I could feel my face was swollen as well. On the bright side, I guess whoever it was wanted me alive. On the dark side of things, I had no idea how long it would be until I found out who that was. Cold, sore, hungry, and held against my will, I waited.

CHAPTER
9

"How could I be so careless?!" Brenwar yelled.

A dozen well-armed dwarves stood nearby, awaiting orders.

Nath Dragon had escaped. How he escaped, Brenwar could not figure. Every dwarf in all of Morgdon knew who he was. Every dwarf in Morgdon knew that he was not supposed to leave. Every dwarf was to keep an eye on him when another wasn't. But like a ghost, he'd vanished.

Brenwar rammed his head into a stone wall.

"I can't believe it!"

He rammed it again.

"Knock some sense into yourself!" he said.

The other dwarves did the same.

Clonk. Clonk. Clonk...

"Stop it, dwarves! We don't all need our melons damaged. We'll be needing all of our wits to track him down." He tugged at two fistfuls of beard.

Brenwar had thought he had it all under control, but he'd miscalculated. Nath had gotten into his sack and taken some potion. What they did, Brenwar didn't know, but one of them had to be the cause of all this. His investigation revealed a few other things. A small fire-breathing bat was said to have been seen. Another one, as big as a large cat, was found burnt to a crisp. It had to have been Nath, because no one had ever seen a fire-breathing bat before. But with the Festival of Iron, anything could happen. But that wasn't what haunted him most. It was what Nath's father, the grandest creature he'd ever seen, had said the last time he saw him.

"I'll keep him alive, your majesty," Brenwar had promised.

Nath's father had replied, "I'm not worried about him dying. I'm worried he'll turn evil."

Nath turning evil? It didn't seem possible, but the Dragon King's words had shaken his very core.

"Get your horses, dwarves! Get your horns as well. He's got a three-day start and could be anywhere in the world. The one that finds him gets a trunk full of gold!"

Brenwar was the last one through the gate as they all exited with dwarven song and cheer. Brenwar took a deep breath as he watched them go, remembering another thing Nath's father had said. "If we lose him, it will begin another Dragon War."

CHAPTER 10

THE SOUND OF A BARN door opening jostled me from my sleep.

I wiped the water from my eyes and watched three figures stroll in. One was Brock, the big man, lumbering my way with the leader of the enforcers at his side. The other man I didn't recognize. He was lean, blond haired, and blue eyed, with my sword, Fang, hanging at his side. I would have stood up, but the cage wouldn't allow it. I sat up, and I crossed my legs as they approached.

"That's my sword," I said, glowering.

The man, light eyes intent on my arm, didn't even acknowledge me.

Rubbing his hairless chin, he said, "Peculiar, Barlow, but I don't think he's a demon. No, looks like a curse of some sort."

Barlow, an enforcer, looked at my eyes and then said to the other man, "But his eyes glowed. All my thoughts left me, and I dropped my sword. He doesn't even have a spellbook, Jackal."

The Jackal made his way around the cage and stopped alongside the bar I'd bent.

"Too strong to be a wizard. Hmmmm. Brock, get over here and fix this. Hm, he must have done this. It's practically a new cage."

Brock lumbered over and grabbed the bar. The metal groaned as he pulled it back into position. He grunted at me as he returned to his friend.

The Jackal said, "Well, you are pretty strong. I'll give you that. Probably a good thing Renny doped you."

The leader, Renny, nodded as he folded his arms across his chest and smiled.

"Care to tell me what this is all about, Jackal?" I asked.

The Jackal wasn't a bad-looking man, but there was darkness behind his beady eyes. There was something primitive about him. The way he moved was dangerous. He withdrew my sword and cut it through the air a few times.

"This," the Jackal said, fingering the blade, "is amazing! Tell me where you got it. Who made it?"

Good. He wants something from me. I can use that.

"The Mountain of Doom," I said.

Fingering the dragon-head pommels on the hilt, he said, "You jest! Am I to believe you stole it from there? No one goes into the mountain and lives."

"That's where it's from, and that's all I know."

"So you were told," he shot back.

I shrugged. *Let him think what he wants.*

He stuffed Fang back inside the scabbard and said to his men, "You two would be dead if he had drawn this sword." Then he turned his attention back to be. "Why didn't you draw and cut them down? I would have."

"I didn't need it."

"It seems you did."

"The big fellow was fortunate, is all. Next time, I won't go so easy."

Brock and Renny laughed.

"I wish I could have been there, but perhaps I can set up another encounter."

"Why don't you set it up now?" I demanded.

Brock smacked his fist into his hand. It sounded like a clap of thunder.

"Fine by me," Brock growled.

The Jackal's eyes lit up. He liked the idea.

Good. All I have to do is get out of this cage.

"No, there will be plenty of time for that later. I need him still breathing tonight."

I don't like how he said that.

"What's the matter?" I said. "Are you afraid of Brock getting hurt?"

Brock's fist slammed into the cage.

"I'll break your neck!"

"Hah! You couldn't break a chicken leg, you oaf!"

"I'll show you!" he roared, reaching through the bars for my leg.

"BROCK, STOP IT!" Renny yelled, trying to pull the big man away.

I jammed the nail of my dragon thumb into his forearm.

Brock's howl shook the roof.

I laughed at him as Renny pulled him back.

"You're going to pay for that!" he said, shaking his fist at me.

The Jackal applauded, saying, "Perfect. Just perfect... eh, sorry, I didn't get your name?"

"I didn't give it."

He waved me off, saying, "No matter. We'll think of something by tonight. Come on, men."

"What's tonight?" I said, pulling on the bars to my cage.

Renny and Brock both flashed sinister grins as they slid the barn door shut behind them.

I stomped my feet and punched the roof of the cage.

"DRAT! DRAT! DOUBLE DRAT!"

Again I was alone. To make matters worse, it seemed they had a short-term plan for me: death.

I yawned. Whatever poison they'd stuck me with wasn't wearing off. I spit a gummy, salty substance from my mouth, leaned back, and sat down. Now was not the time to panic. It was time to think.

"Excellent, Dragon. Look what you've gotten yourself into," I said, tossing my hair over my shoulder. At least the rain had stopped. But now I was thirsty.

An hour passed.

My stomach growled. My head swam. And I was seeing black spots from time to time.

Another hour passed.

Nausea set in and cold sweat as well, and I began to shake with chills.

What did they stick me with?

I wrapped my arms around my knees and huddled in the cage. And there I lay, spinning and spinning and spinning.

CHAPTER 11

BAD PEOPLE DO BAD THINGS.

A ray of sunlight warmed my face, but it didn't stop the shivers. Time was lost to me, the minutes agony, but from the fading light coming through the cracks in the barn door, it seemed the sun was setting. I remembered the Jackal saying something about the night. Something bad was going to happen. As if it hadn't happened already.

I heard wood rubbing against metal, a horrible sound in my distorted ears. Light flooded the barn as the door was slid open. Enforcers. I couldn't see how many. The squeak of older wagon wheels felt like jamming nails in my ears.

"Hurry up and get them in there," one enforcer said. "And double check those locks. We can't have any escaping. Remember the last time. Jorkan's dead. The Jackal saw to that. And I'll not be losing my head over some busted locks!"

"You check them, then!" one said.

"What? Who said that? Osclar, did you say that?"

"Yes!"

"Why, you little toad eater! Get over there and check those locks, those bars, that door—or it's going to be the stockade for you! Understand?"

"Certainly, Harvey. Certainly!"

I heard the one I believed to be Harvey grunt, and I started my wait. I closed my eyes and let the shivers take over.

"What have we got here?" Harvey said. "Not feeling so spry now, are you, demon?"

"He's not a demon," I heard one say.

"What?"

"He's not a demon; that's was the Jackal said. He's cursed."

I heard Harvey chuckle.

"Oh, he's cursed all right. He probably just didn't know it till now. That Uken poison Renny stuck him with'll have him feeling and seeing all kinds of crazy things."

Harvey checked the lock on the cage. "Tonight's going to really be something. You got those cages secured, Osclar?"

"Nope!" Osclar said, giggling.

Harvey grunted again.

"Shaddap and let's go; I'm hungry."

"Say, Harvey, how long do you think he'll last?"

"Shut your mouth, Osclar. The boss says no talking."

Oh, talk. Please talk.

"I don't see why not. It's not like it matters if they know what's coming or not."

"He likes the looks of surprise on their faces."

"Me too," the third enforcer said.

"Let's go, chatter mouths."

My tongue clove to the roof of my mouth. *Say something, Dragon!* My quivering lips stayed sealed.

"Huh," Harvey said, "looks like this man is done already."

"He got some good licks on Big Brock, though. Never seen anyone hurt Brock before."

"Me neither."

"Shaddap, you two! LET'S GO!"

Harvey's loud voice sounded like an explosion in my ears. I couldn't even open my eyes to see as I heard them walk out and slide the barn door closed.

Idiot. All I had learned was that things were not only as bad as before but worse.

I shivered and shivered. I needed the Uken poison to wear off. *Fight it, Dragon! Fight!* The darkness came, leaving me alone in the barn with two torches and two new cages. I managed to open my eyes to see. Two forms huddled, one in each cage. Perhaps they could tell me something. I opened my mouth, but no words came.

"Father?"

It was the voice of a young man speaking to the other.

"Sssssh, be silent, Son. Else they'll whip us."

Silence came. A little rustling around followed.

"Are they going to kill us, Father?" the young man asked.

"No, now be silent!" the father said, forcefully but quietly.

I heard the fear in both their voices. Innocent men. I could tell.

"Why did they pick us, Father?"

The father sighed, shaking his head as he said, "I don't know; they just did."

"But we were good farmers, Father. Good miners, too. I didn't steal any of the Golden Ore; I swear," the young man sobbed.

His father's silence told it all. The father had stolen; the boy had not.

My heart swelled. These men needed my help. Things came together.

Golden Ore!

It explained all the secrets in the small town. Someone, a farmer most likely, had found a vein of it. The Jackal and his enforcers got word of it and took over the town. It wasn't the first time such a thing had happened, and it wouldn't be the last, either. Golden Ore, however, wasn't gold, and it wasn't ore. It was a vein of mystic dirt that had a goldish hue to it.

"I'm hungry, Father. Do you think we'll eat again?"

Pitiful. I could make out the young man's face pressed against the bars. He was rawboned and lanky. Looked like he'd missed one too many meals already. It infuriated me, but the thought of action just made me sicker.

"Sure, Son. Sure we will," the father lied.

Don't think about it. Think of a way out. I allowed my thoughts to drift to the Golden Ore.

Farming was a big deal in Nalzambor. The land was rich, full, lustrous in many places. But working the land was still hard. It took time and a lot of work. And, in the case of hard work, many peoples and races were lacking. That's where the Golden Ore came in. Or, more simply called, Magic Dirt. A few pounds of it would turn a square mile of desert into a garden of vegetables. It was a pricey commodity, and it seemed the enforcers had happened upon it.

But what did they want with me and these two men?

My voice was dry and raspy, but I managed to say, "I can get you out of here."

Both men stiffened and huddled down.

"I said, I can get you out of here."

The young man started to speak.

"Don't talk to him, Son. He might be that demon the innkeeper spoke of."

"I'm not a demon; I'm a man, same as the two of you," I said. *Sort of...* "Now, do you want help or not? Ugh!" I slunk onto the cage floor. My stomach was killing me. I needed healing.

"What happened?" the young man asked, pressing his face against the bars.

"Son, be quiet!"

"No." The young man was adamant. "I won't be. Sorry, Father. That man over there is offering help, and we need it!"

"But, I just—"

"I'm a man as well as you, Father. I'll live with the consequences of my actions."

I made it back to my knees and said, "Good for you. Now, tell me, how many of these enforcers are there?"

"I'm not sure, but there's a lot of them."

"Thirty-seven," the father said.

He'd turned to face me now. Unlike his son, he was a barrel-chested man. The torchlight reflected dimly from the top of his head.

"How many of you in the village?"

"Almost a thousand," the father said.

Accounting for women and children, that didn't leave enough men to fight off a group of well-armed men. Fear doesn't wait long to rule.

"How long have they been here?"

"A few months. They showed up two days after we found the vein of Golden Ore. All the celebrating would have woke the dragons up. It's no wonder they showed up so fast with all the blabbermouths in this village."

I'd seen it happen before. If you didn't hire a well-armed force, the goons would quickly take over. Greed and treachery grew like weeds in Nalzambor. Better act quickly, before the roots got deep.

"And the Jackal? Where does he stay?"

I needed to find out where my gear was. It was the only way.

"He lords it over everyone in the day and diminishes in the night. He's wicked."

"He's crafty," the father added. "Dangerous. Something very strange about that fellow."

I'd sensed it, too. Something behind the man's eyes was raw, primeval.

The men jerked in their cages as the barn door slid open. Renny and Brock stepped inside, along with some of the other enforcers.

"Cover them cages," Renny said.

"What if they scream?" Harvey said.

"Oh yes, we can't have that, can we? All right, gag these two, but the demon over there, he'll need more of the poison. Shoot him up, Brock!"

I could barely move already when Brock came, a sharp stick in one hand, a vial of Uken poison in the other. He dipped the stick in the ointment, laughing.

"Be still, freak! Else I'll poke it in your eye."

I remained still. He stabbed through the bars. I tried to dodge but caught the full force in my dragon arm.

"Did you stick him good?" Renny said.

"Real good."

I didn't hear anything else after that as my prison world faded away.

CHAPTER 12

THE WAGON LURCHED TO A stop, and I awoke. It was still dark, but I knew I was outside because the breeze rustled the cover over my cage. Depressed and sick, I had a good idea how my brethren dragons felt. I had to escape, but I needed help.

"Almost time."

It was Renny, the leader of the enforcers. Footsteps were all around, and I could also hear footsteps going up and down.

"Take the covers off. The Jackal will be here any moment, with company. Look sharp! Especially you, Osclar!"

Where was I? I felt the bump on my arm where Brock had jabbed me. It wasn't as bad as the one on my neck. I think the dragon scales had something to do with that. It had been more of a reflex than anything else when I made him hit my dragon arm. I hadn't meant for that to happen, but maybe my arm had. And my head was a little more clear than before.

"Get over here, Harvey! Let's take this cover off and get started. Heh-heh! Won't be long now before the fun starts."

Fun for him, maybe. Fun for me? I didn't think so.

"Sure thing, Boss. Sure thing."

The first thing I saw was the moon peeking through the clouds. Then I could smell the enforcers' rancid breath.

"Huh, he's awake," Renny said, rubbing his chin. "Not sure the Jackal will like that. Harvey, let him know."

"All right," Harvey said, strolling off.

I was inside a wooden fort, but I had a feeling it was designed to keep people in rather than out. Catwalks ran twelve feet high from one corner to the other. Enforcers with spears and swords guarded every corner and the space in between.

"Welcome to our arena, demon," Renny said. "The final resting place for you and many others on Nalzambor."

I locked my eyes on Renny and said, "And possibly yours as well."

He stiffened, said, "We'll see about that," and walked away, casting one glance back.

Entertainment! That's what I was. I remembered the blazed ruffie battling the trolls. It turned my stomach, the cruelty of men.

"Go ahead and take those other two out," Renny ordered his men.

The farmers were pulled from their cages and the cages pulled away.

"All right, everyone. Get up on the wall. It's time for the battle to begin."

The father and son shook at each other's side.

"Please! Mercy, enforcers! At least spare my son. I'm the guilty one!" the father begged.

The son looked at his father, a sad look in his eyes as he said, "You stole, Father?"

The father shook his head and replied, "Son, they stole from us. It's our land and our Golden Ore. These vultures have no right to take what is ours."

The enforcers tossed down two shields and two clubs.

"I don't know how to fight, Father."

"Neither do I, Son." He hugged his boy. "I guess we'll have our first and last one together," the father said, picking the weapons up.

"Together then."

Renny shouted from above.

"That's the spirit!"

"Here he comes, Renny," Harvey said, looking over the backside of the wall.

The Jackal emerged from behind a wall and stepped onto the catwalk. My sword Fang hung at his hip. My breast-plate armor adorned his chest. My bow. My quiver and my pack. Infuriated, my heart thundered in my chest.

But he was different. His face was no longer that of a man but of an animal. A jackal.

"I see everything is in order," the Jackal said, yellow eyes glowering at me. "I see our guest is bright eyed and bushy tailed. No matter." He fingered his claws over my sword. "Nothing I can't handle if need be."

A were-jackal. Another cursed man, like myself, but more like Corzan: corrupted by the evil. I felt a sliver of fear inside as I wondered if they'd both been good men once. I wondered what was in store for me. I rubbed the white spot of scales on my hand and vowed to do more good, given the chance.

"Farmers!" the Jackal yelled, the moonlight shining brightly on his face, "the time has come that you paid for your deceit. I told you when I came: what's yours is mine and mine alone, yet you stole. You sought to warn my enemies. And now you must pay."

The father and son trembled. Nalzambor was full of wonders, but I was certain they'd never seen a were-jackal before. Lycanthropes were evil. And there were plenty of stories and legends about them tearing people limb from limb. I could only imagine what was going through their minds at this moment.

"It's not much sport, is it?" I managed to say.

All eyes were on me. *Good.*

"But I guess this is how cowards play," I added.

The Jackal leaned on the rail and smiled, his sharp teeth dripping in the moonlight.

"Oh, the do-gooder speaks. Interesting. And I can only assume you are going to talk and talk until it's over. Well then, I'll let the games begin. Enforcers, have at them."

Renny, Harvey, and Osclar climbed down the ladders while two more posted themselves at the top. The farmers readied themselves as more clubs and shields were tossed down from above.

Renny picked up his club and twirled it in the air.

"This won't take long. Watch my back, fellas."

The farmers shuffled back.

"Come on; take a swing," Renny said, sticking his chin out. "I'll give you a free shot."

The father's swing sailed over Renny's head.

Renny walloped him in the stomach, doubling him over.

The son caught Renny in the shoulder.

"Ow! You two idiots! I said to watch my back!"

Harvey and Osclar attacked, swinging hard and fast at that young man. The son gathered himself behind his shield, but they beat it down.

Wham! Wham! Wham!

The son folded like a tent.

Rushing to his son's aid, the father screamed, "NOOOOOO!" He huddled over his son, but the blows kept coming. I felt sick in my stomach when the men stopped, laughed, and walked off. There was nothing worse than seeing the work of evil firsthand.

"Excellent, men!" the Jackal said. "Now that the warm-up is over, it's time for the real fight to begin. It's time to see how tough our visitor truly is. Let him out!"

CHAPTER 13

RUN! THAT'S WHAT I NEEDED to do. But not without my gear. And I couldn't abandon these people. I had to do what I had to do: stand up and fight for what's right.

I took my time getting out of the cage. My limbs were sluggish, and my head was full of mud. But I could move at last, and maybe I had my dragon heart to thank for that. Father had said it could do wonderful things.

Above, the Jackal stood, arms folded over his chest, all of my gear in place. It made me wonder if I was looking in a mirror. If that was what I would become if I didn't get my act together, then I had better try, and fast. Dark, primal, animal. That's what Corzan had called me, an animal. The enforcers had said I was a freak and a demon. Sorrow and anger mixed in my stomach as I reflected on all I'd done wrong over the years. Holding my stomach, I shuffled forward and glowered up at him.

"I'll be needing my gear back, lycan!" I said.

He sneered at me. They didn't like that word, "lycan." But I didn't like the words "demon," "freak," or "animal."

"I didn't come here to entertain your talk," he barked. "I came to watch you die. Take him!"

Clubs raised, Renny, Harvey, and Osclar came at me.

Stomach in knots, weaponless, and with a dizzy head, I forged into battle.

I jumped over the three of them and darted for the farmers. They breathed, barely. I wrapped my fingers around both of their clubs, banged them together, and said, "Come and get me!"

They stopped, eyes wary.

"Fools! Take him!"

They screamed as they charged.

I cracked Renny in the jaw. Osclar in the head. Harvey in the knee.

Three down. Ten to go.

I smacked the clubs together and said, "Who's next?"

A wave of nausea assailed me, and I sank to my knee. The more active I was, the more the poison attacked my system. *Drat!* I had to fight it. I had to make my body do what it did not want to, or I was going to die.

I rose to my feet.

"Get the swords!" the Jackal yelled. "And get in there. You. You. You and you!" All the enforcers eyed the Jackal.

I smiled. All I needed was a blade. I could cut them to ribbons. They knew it.

"No! Just use clubs. And more men. You! You! You!"

They scrambled down, clubs and bucklers ready. That battle with the first three had taken a lot out of me. *Suck it up, Dragon!*

They came.

I swung.

They swung.

Back and forth we went, them chasing me from one side of the fort to another. I dodged, poked, and parried. Where one fell, another popped up. A hard shot on my back knocked me to my knees. I ducked under the next swing, clubbed one in the chest, another in the knee.

Hard wood cracked. Shields smacked. Alarm and pain cried out.

I took a shot in the back of my head and pitched forward.

Whop! Whop! Whop! Whop! Whop!

They beat me like a drum.

I roared out.

"His eyes!" one said, backing off.

"He's a demon!"

A spark. A fire. An inferno came. My head cleared. My muscles loosened. I could see my reflection in the nearest man's eyes. My own eyes flared briefly with life. The effects of the poison fizzled out.

I cracked the clubs together.

"Let's try this again."

They ran. I pummeled.

I caught one in the chin. One in the nose. One in the jaw.

I laughed. It felt good to laugh and swing. Torment those crueler things. A minute later, not one man stood except me.

I looked up at the Jackal and said, "So, what happens when you run out of men?"

"I'm not concerned about that. Get in there, Brock!"

Brock, all eight feet of him, hopped down into the arena like a big ape. Well armored, he carried a spiked mace with a round head in one hand and a heavy chain in the other. When he stretched his arms out, it looked like they stretched from one side of the fort to the other.

"I see you've grown since we last talked," I said.

His lip curled over his teeth as he came forward.

"My, what an awfully long stride you have. Have you been eating Golden Ore? It's dirt, you know. Is that why you grew so big?"

Swack!

I ducked as the chain licked out over my head.

His mace rose up.

His mace came down.

I dove away.

"I'm going to turn you into a mud hole," Brock said.

The mace and chain were like toys that he wielded like a child. A vicious child. The kind who plucks the wings off fairies.

He charged. I ran. He swung. I dodged. I ducked. I dove.

I could hear the Jackal's high-pitched laugh. Evil, condescending. I cast him a quick glance. He was twirling one of my moorite arrows in his clawed fingers.

Brock's chain whipped around my legs and jerked me from my feet. I rolled as his spiked mace came down, clipping my arm.

"You're as big as you are inaccurate—goon!" I said, whacking him in the hand.

He roared, releasing the chain. His mace came down, and rolling over the ground I went, kicking the chain from my feet.

"You are going to die!"

Brock swung.

I blocked. The impact of his hit jolted my elbows and ripped one club from my hand. The next blow was fast. I ducked. Brock knocked a small hole in the wall.

"What?!" he cried out. The mace was stuck in the wall.

I swung the club full force into his elbow.

Brock howled like a banshee. I cracked one of his knees, then the other. Down on his knees he went. Tears filled his eyes as he screamed.

"Stop! Please stop it!"

I did not. Evil never showed me any mercy, so why should I show it?

I struck fast.

Whack!

Hard.

Whack!

On the final blow, I used both arms.

CRACK!

Brock fell face first into the ground. A red lump on his bald spot quickly formed.

Chest heavy, I said, "How's that treat you, knothead?"

Above, the remaining enforcers gawked.

"Who's next?" I said, twirling my club around my back and front.

Every hair on my body lurched. *Move, Dragon!*

I felt my back catch fire as I spun to the ground, wounded, bleeding.

The Jackal loomed above me. Fang glimmered in his hand.

"You fight well against mortals. But you'll die against the power of the supernatural!"

CHAPTER 14

A PREDATOR. A TORMENTOR. THE JACKAL was a towering figure. Broad shouldered, strong, and supple. An animal with the cunning of a man, the killer instinct of an animal. And Fang dangled in his evil grip. I never would have imagined I'd die on my own sword's blade. Backpedaling, I danced, and the lycan's swift strokes licked at my skin.

"You are fast for a big man," the Jackal said. "But not as fast as me. I have supernatural speed. Skill. I'm your superior in battle!"

I laughed.

"You call this a battle? You wield a fine sword, and I use a club. Ha! You're letting my weapon and my armor do all of your dirty work, you oversized rodent!"

"There is no honor among jackals!" he said, talking a swipe at my gut.

I jumped away.

"Or lycans, for that matter."

The walls of the fort were closing in, and the Jackal was quite a sight as four feet of razor-sharp steel hung in his fist. My steel, that is.

"It's sad to see your men are so much braver than you. At least they had the courage to fight with what they had, not with what the enemy had given them.

Fang sliced the top off my club. *Drat!*

I snatched a shield from the ground.

Wang!

The Jackal struck, jarring my bones. Again and again he tore at my shield, making pieces of metal and wood scatter all over.

"Coward!" I yelled. "Fight fair! What are you scared of?"

Krang!

"Your men are watching you. When the day comes, what will they think of you?"

Chop!

Only the straps and a small strip of wood remained. "Will they respect you? Will they follow?"

The Jackal stopped. I fought for my breath. He was little winded.

"I tire of your mouth. Perhaps it's best that I tear your throat out."

With a flick of his wrist, he tossed Fang to the other side of the fort. He stretched out his arms and extended the long nails on his fingers. I'd never fought a lycan, but I once saw one break the neck of a dwarf with his bare hands. And there wasn't much that would kill a lycan except the pierce of silver or magic. I'd bought some time, but I was still a dead man without Fang.

"You'll wish I used the sword soon enough, fool," he growled at me. "Now I'm going to tear you to pieces!"

Claws and teeth bared, he sprang. I dropped on my back, jammed my boots in his gut, and launched him head over heel. He crashed to the ground and howled. Not like I would, but with the strange high-pitched howl of a jackal.

He gathered himself, eyes filled with rage, and came again. Legs and arms ripping up the ground like an animal. I braced myself.

Slam!

I gave it all I had. I punched, kicked, and clawed.

He bit, ripped, and howled.

Blood was in my face. My blood, not his; I was sure of it. I walloped him in the jaw with my dragon fist, snapping his head back. I drove the heel of my other palm into his gut.

He backed off, smiled, and spit a tooth from his mouth.

"That's a first. But you bleed. I do not. I cannot."

I'd hit him with all I had with that punch. A dragon punch, at that—to no effect. That was the problem with the supernatural. Only the supernatural could stop it or kill it.

"You sure you just don't want to talk about this, perhaps?"

He jumped again, his full weight landing on me. He rammed my face into the dirt and jammed a claw into my leg.

I thrashed. Drove an elbow into his ribs and rammed my head under his chin, crawling out from under him.

He shook it off like water and punched me in the face. My nose started to bleed. It might have been broken.

"I can do this all day," I said.

"Do what? Bleed? WHHHHHHEEEEEEEEEEOOOOOO!" he howled like a tormented banshee. "We'll see about that!"

I had to fight smarter. Fight harder. Or else I'd be dead in the next minute. I gasped for breath. *Think, Dragon! Think! How do you beat something that is indestructible?*

I balled up my dragon fist and said, "Come on. What are you waiting for?"

He came after me, claws striking like snakes.

Jab! Jab!

I hit him in the nose.

Jab! Jab!

I hit him in the face.

He was fast, but my jabs were much faster. I was the dragon. He was the animal, not me.

He broke it off.

"What are you doing, fool? You can't hurt me!"

"Stings, don't it?" I shook my fist. "You might as well surrender. I can do this all night, remember."

I was exhausted, and my knuckles ached. Hitting the Jackal was like hitting a statue, but at least I had him aggravated.

Balling up his fists, he circled me.

"So it's a fistfight you want?" He smacked his together. "Then it's a fistfight you'll have."

He lunged.

I jabbed.

He snared my wrist in his hands.

"Gotcha!"

He jerked me to the ground and drove his elbow into my gut.

All my wind left me. The Jackal had outsmarted me. Pinned to the ground, I couldn't move. I couldn't breathe.

He opened his jaws.

I could see a tunnel of fangs in his mouth. I tucked my chin down as he went for my neck. *NO!* My mind screamed, but I knew it was over.

An inch from my face, the Jackal stiffened. His grip loosened. His jaw fell open. I noticed the tip of a sword sticking out of his chest as I crawled out from underneath him. His eyes rolled up in his head as he fell over.

Fang hung in the farmer's son's grip.

I scurried to my feet and watched the Jackal transform from lycan to man, dead.

The farmer's son stood there, trembling, with blood on his hands. I didn't know what to say, but the remaining enforcers did.

"Kill them!"

CHAPTER 15

"**L**ET ME HAVE THAT," I said, holding out my hand.

"Oh," the son said, handing Fang over.

The metal was warm, welcoming, an old friend returned from a long trip.

The enforcers, five of them in all, surrounded us. A few others I'd knocked down before began to stir.

"I'll handle this," I said, twirling Fang around my body. Fang's radiant blade flared with light, a mix of many hues.

All the enforcers gaped, eyes filled with wonder and fear.

"The Jackal is dead. Your leader's defeated. Do you want to be the first to taste my steel?" I said, pointing Fang at the nearest one. He cringed. "Would you rather die or surrender?"

All the enforcers looked at one another and dropped their arms.

"Excellent. You soft bellies are not as stupid as you look. Now get in those cages."

They hesitated.

"Now!"

"We're going. We're going. We just weren't sure which one," one said, with shifty eyes and a black bandana on his head.

I gathered my pack, grabbed a healing vial, and applied a few drops to the young man's father's lips. He was barely breathing, but he coughed and sputtered.

"He's going to be all right," I said, extending my hand to the young man. "And I thank you. I owe you my life. That was a brave thing you did, you know?"

His chest swelled, and he couldn't help but smile as he grabbed my hand and squeezed it. He had a strong grip for a skinny fellow.

"I don't know what came over me. I didn't even think. I saw the Jackal tearing into you. The sword caught my eye, and I was moving." There was a watery twinkle in his eyes. "I've never wanted to kill anything before. Except food that is. But, I-I killed a man." He cast a look where the Jackal lay.

I squeezed his shoulder and said, "No, you killed a monster. You saved me. Your father. Yourself—and freed your village. One single act of bravery can yield great things."

Tears streamed down his cheeks as he helped his father to his feet.

"S-Son, what happened here?" the father said, looking around, a bewildered look in his weary eyes.

"Come on, Father. I'll tell you all about it on the way home." He stopped and looked at me, saying, "What is your name?"

"Call me Nath. Nath Dragon."

"Odd name, but memorable."

I smiled and asked, "What's yours?"

"Ben."

"A fine name, Ben. A warrior's name."

"I'll be back with help."

I gathered my armor from the Jackal's corpse. All the stitching and buckles were fine, but Fang's tip had gone straight through the armor. A normal blade couldn't have done such a thing. It would be a little something for Brenwar to stitch up. *I bet he's ready to kill me.*

Gathering all my gear, I made my way up the ladders and onto the catwalk. I had no idea where I was. Horses nickered along the wall, a good sign. The fort was erected on fertile land, between the rolling hills that stretched out mile after mile. Ben and his father traveled on horseback on a faint road that wound out of sight. I had a feeling it would be hours before I saw anyone else again, which left me and my prisoners, the enforcers.

I looked at the men crammed into the cages. They were rotten. Every last one of them. How many people had they terrorized? How many had they killed? If I could have killed them in battle, I would have.

"And to think, all I wanted was a good meal and a warm night's sleep. Now what?"

I would be hours before anyone else came around, and I wasn't going to wait. I had dragons to save.

I said to Fang, "I guess it's me, you, and the outdoors from now on." I slid him back into the sheath and hopped off the catwalk onto the ground.

"Let us go, demon."

It was the leader, Renny, who spoke.

"We'll ride out of here and never look back. I promise."

Ignoring him, I grabbed the cloth and threw it over the cage.

"We can't see! You can't do that! It'll get too hot in here."

"And you will all begin to stink really bad, too. You better hope the gnolls and orcs don't get wind of you."

I covered the other two cages as well, laughing at all their colorful complaints.

"It smells like an orcen bathhouse in here!"

"Please don't leave us!"

"We're sorry! We won't raid any villages no more!"

"Oh no!" one moaned, "Brock just farted."

I was bound for Quintuklen. And I wasn't alone this time, either. I took the finest horse the enforcers had, a big brown beauty. I rubbed his neck.

"No hurry, boy. No hurry."

I found horses the most fascinating and noble of all the animals. Noble, strong, and reliable. If you ever get a chance to know one or ride one, I suggest you do.

North I rode. Past the trees, through the ferns, over the streams from sunup until almost sundown.

"Wait!"

I heard someone crying out in the distance. Behind me, a man galloped, waving a rag shirt or something in the air. It was Ben. Something must be wrong.

He came alongside me, panting for breath.

"Your horse should be panting, not you," I said. "What's going on? Did the enforcers escape?"

"No, no!" he managed. "That's fine. The legionnaires are coming to haul them off."

"And you rode all this way to tell me that?"

He looked at me funny.

"No. I'm here because I'm coming with you!"

CHAPTER 16

"**N**O, YOU AREN'T COMING WITH me!" I said.

"Why not?" he said, grinning ear to ear.

Now it was my turn to gape. The young man was bruised from head to toe with a big knot on his head. He'd almost died hours ago, and now he wanted to follow me to a certain death.

"Because you'll die."

There, I'd said it. He'd just have to get over it.

He frowned.

"Ben, be realistic. You stabbed a monster in the back. It died. And you have my sword to thank for that, else you'd never have scratched his hide."

He brushed his black hair behind his ear and said, "I never really thought about it."

"What you did was as I said. Brave. 'Bravery is for the foolish', some say. But fortunate as well. Why don't you just go home and enjoy your days being the hero of the village? The man that saved the town. I'm sure the milkmaids would love for you to stick around."

A pleasant smile formed on his face.

"I hadn't thought about that, either. Do you really think they'll like me?"

"A handsome young hero like you? Hah! They'll swoon as soon as you enter the room."

He was eyeing the sky and rubbing his chin. I knew I had him thinking now. With excitement in his voice, he said, "No! I want to go with you, Nath Dragon."

I shook my head. *What has possessed this young man?*

"No, and I don't have a shovel with me, either."

"A shovel? What do you need a shovel for?"

I turned my steed and trotted away, saying, "To dig your grave. Goodbye, Ben. And tell the milkmaids hello."

The clopping of hooves was catching up. I turned.

"Ben, go home. I mean it!"

"But you owe me!"

"Owe you? For what?"

"You said, 'I owe you my life'. You can pay me back now."

Great! Ben had a point. I owed him my life.

Irritated, I said, "What do you want?"

"Uh, well, er... I just want to go with you. See the world. Travel Nalzambor."

Ben looked about as fit for travel as a one-legged horse. His trousers were held up by a rope belt, and the leather armor that he must have taken from an enforcer was too big. His arms jutted out from under the shoulder plates like sticks, and the sword strapped to his waist looked like it would pull him from the saddle. He would have been the most pathetic enforcer I ever saw.

"Are you certain you want to do this, Ben?" I smiled.

Reason with him. Talk him out of it.

"Absolutely. More than anything. I don't want to work on the farm anymore. It's boring. I want to see the world."

"And you want to face all the dangers therein?"

"Well, I guess."

"You ever seen an ogre pull a man's arms off?"

"No."

"Have you seen a chimera swallow a gnoll?"

"What's a chimera?"

I rolled my eyes.

"Do you know there are goblins that eat people?"

"No."

"Orcs that enslave people?"

He shook his head.

"Fierce dragons that burn the living to a crisp?"

His eyes fluttered in his head. Then he said, "Oh... I'd love to see that!"

"Really?"

"Well, not good people. Just ones like the enforcers and all."

I could see a dangerous look in his eyes. A fire. A twinkle. A zeal. Ben wasn't going home. He was coming with me, on an adventure.

I sighed.

"Come on, then. But I'll not feed you, clothe you, or baby you. So you better keep up."

His long face lit up like a halfling parade. "Really? You'll let me come?"

"It's your life to throw away, not mine."

"So it is," he said, grinning ear to ear. "Let's go!"

I led. He followed. Over the faintest of trails we went.

As the minutes passed and the sun set, Ben finally asked, "Er... Nath?"

"Call me Dragon," I scowled.

"Er... Dragon, where are we going?"

CHAPTER 17

"QUINTUKLEN, WHERE THE BUILDINGS ARE as tall as the Red Oak trees," I said. "But it's a long, long ride."

"I'm in no hurry," Ben replied, yawning.

Skinny as the young man might be, but he had some grit to him. Underneath all the bruises, he probably wasn't a half-bad-looking lad, either. He just needed to eat more. Dark-complexioned and tall, he was at ease in the saddle. His light eyes followed all the sights and sounds. And unlike Brenwar, he smiled and talked a good bit.

"Tired, Ben?"

"A good bit, actually. I haven't rested since being hauled off in that cage. Shouldn't we be making camp already? I can make a fire."

"What do you need a fire for? Didn't you bring a blanket?"

"No."

I shook my head.

"But I meant I could do some cooking. I'm a good hunter and trapper."

"I thought you were a farmer."

"Well, you can't survive in the country if you can't hunt or fish. You'll starve eventually."

As soon as the white owls began to hoot, I stopped in a grove and made camp, which consisted of little more than two horses and two men with a rough patch of ground to lie on. Ben yawned the whole time as he gathered twigs and started a fire. He did well. After a few minutes, the orange glow burst to life and the warmth came.

"Outstanding, Ben. You are pretty handy, are you not?"

Covering his yawn, he said, "I told you."

"Good, now you can take the first watch. Wake me up when the moon dips."

Ben had a blank look in his eyes.

"And keep your ears open. They'll serve you better than your eyes at night," I said, closing my eyes. I could feel Ben's eyes on my back as he rubbed his hands over the fire.

"I'll stay awake, Dragon. All night if I have to."

I lay and listened. Chirps of critters and crickets filled my ears. All those little things that crept and crawled in the night had come to life. A burning fire offered sanctuary, but it could attract the unwanted. Good thing I was a light sleeper. And I had a sixth sense for danger. The Dragon's Gut, I called it. An awareness I had when I slept, though I didn't sleep much. As I drifted off to sleep, the soft snoring of Ben drifted into my ears.

"Oh, great," I said, sitting up.

He lay alongside the fire, curled up in his armor.

"Looks like I have the first and the second watch."

The pixlyn flew as fast as he could fly, covering a mile a minute, hummingbird wings buzzing as fast as they had ever buzzed before. Over the treetops he went, scattering insects and small birds. Little noticed him. Little could see him.

In a day, he'd covered the northern part of Nalzambor. He'd seen many faces in that day: dwarves, elves, orcs, giants, and dragons, some hard at work or mischief, others at play. But there was yet to be a sign of the man he sought. Nath Dragon. He rubbed his belly, panting. The potion Finnius had given him was a nasty thing, like rotten stew boiling. It gave him strength somehow. A sense of direction, too. The man must be close. He could feel it.

He thought of his companion, the pink-eyed pixlyn he'd been with all his life. Find the man, save her. He couldn't bear the thought of horrible things happening to her. He took a deep breath in his tiny mouth, stuck out his chest, and buzzed into the sky.

A streak of red came at him. He rolled away, hovering in the sky. There were three of them. Each was as big as him, red scaled and black winged, tiny dragons called firebites. They circled, snorted puffs of fire, and dove.

The pixlyn shot through the sky, three dangerous dragons nipping at his toes. Firebites didn't play with pixies and fairies. They roasted them and ate them whole.

The pouring rain didn't bother him. Nor the stubborn horse between his legs. No, as Brenwar trotted along the road, he was consumed with something else. Guilt.

"I should have listened to him," he growled, wringing the water from his beard.

He had known Nath wanted to leave Morgdon, and Brenwar should have gone.

Instead, being stubborn, persistent, and consumed with the Festival of Iron, he might end up losing his best friend. And it might end up starting another war. Not that Brenwar would mind that. But he had to catch him. And catching Nath wouldn't be easy. Not if he didn't want to be found.

Another Dragon War, Nath's father had warned. That's what evil wanted. Another shot at the throne of Nalzambor. Nath's father, the Dragon King, wasn't the same as he had been of old. Not after the last war. He was ancient but not immortal. Brenwar sensed that the Dragon King's time on Nalzambor was coming to an end. And who would keep the peace without him there? It was either Nath Dragon or no one.

The horse nickered and stopped.

"What is it now?" Brenwar said, rubbing its neck.

A group of figures approached, cloaked from head to toe. Men, by the looks of them.

"Hail and well met," one said, fingers itching at the sword on his hip.

"Agreed," said another who stepped behind Brenwar's back.

As easily as a fish swims in water, they had him surrounded.

Brenwar stiffened as the next one said, "That's a fine horse you have there, little dwarf."

Whop!

Brenwar knocked him out of his boots with his war hammer.

"Little! I'll show you brigands little!"

Brenwar slid from his horse to the ground.

"Take him down!" one ordered, drawing his sword.

Two rushed forward. Brenwar busted one in the chest, dropping him in the mud. The other stabbed a dagger into his armored chest, snapping it at the hilt.

"Fool! This armor's dwarven made!"

"Drag him into the mud!" one of the brigands said.

Brenwar took in a loud draw through his nose.

"Ah, I smell an orc, a part of one at least."

Brenwar knocked a curved sword from one's hand. Kicked in the knee of another. He was a machine, a black-bearded typhoon in the rain.

A man screamed as he busted his hand. Another fell as his knee gave out. One caught Brenwar in the back of his leg with a knife.

"You should not have done that!" he said, swinging his war hammer.

Pow!

He lifted the man's feet from the ground.

The rain poured. The brigands tumbled down. No group of brigands stood a chance against a dwarven soldier with centuries of fighting under his belt.

Brenwar grabbed the fallen half orc by its head of hair and said, "Happen to see a man with long auburn hair and golden eyes pass through here, wart face?"

"I wouldn't say if I did, halfling. Heh-heh!"

"Why is it the ugly ones always have the smartest mouths!"

"Because—"

Brenwar clonked his head into the orc's, knocking him out.

"That was a statement, not a question. Now, what about the rest of you?"

"Mercy, sir," one said, clutching his broken arm. "Never seen such a man. If I did, I'd tell you. I swear."

"Sure you would," Brenwar said, hoisting himself back onto his horse. "If I ever see any of you again, I'll break every bone in ya!" He snapped the reins. "Yah!"

Aggravated, Brenwar felt he wasn't any closer to finding Nath Dragon than when he started. But he was certain time was running out.

CHAPTER 18

"SLEEP WELL?" I SAID.

Ben stretched out his arms and yawned.

"What happened?" he said, covering his eyes. "Where'd all this daylight come from?"

"I'm pretty sure it's from the sun," I said, roasting a rodent on a spit. "It does that most days, you know."

"I'm sorry. I didn't mean to fall asleep. I felt just fine, then I was out." Ben's stomach growled. "What's that you're cooking? Smells good."

"Just a little white-eared rabbit."

"Really? How'd you snare it? We can never keep them out of the garden. Too smart for snares, too fast to shoot."

I held out another rabbit on the end of my arrow.

"I shot this one, too," I said.

"Nobody's that good a shot," Ben objected. "Not even my uncle. He's a Legionnaire bowman, you know. He told me they could hear me pulling the string back before I shot." He tore a hunk of meat off the stick. "Hmmm... this is good. Really good!"

"Well, I'm sure your uncle is a fine shot. And the white-ears are impossible targets. You just have to know where to shoot before they go. It's called 'anticipation.' And, I had a little help, too."

I held Akron out.

"What is that?"

Snap-Clatch-Snap!

"Whoa," he said when the bowstring coiled along the bow and into place. "Is that magic?"

"No, all bows do that."

"Really?"

"Of course not. This is Akron. A gift from my father. Elven made. Elven magic. Can you shoot?"

"Can I shoot? You bet I can shoot. My uncle started teaching me when I was just a boy. I once shot a sparrow in the sky. I feathered a boar, too. Right between the eyes. It was him or me, that time." He licked the rabbit meat from his fingers. "Can I try?"

Ben rose, twisted, and cracked his back. His eyes were alert, and the rangy muscles throughout his body were supple, not stiff. If he had some armor that fit, he'd actually look like a soldier, and the fact that his uncle was a Legionnaire archer left me a little more comfortable. I handed over the bow and an arrow.

"*If*," I emphasized, "you can pull the string back, let it fly." I pointed. "That oak tree will do."

Ben took the grip in his hand, loaded the shaft on the shelf, and nocked it back like a seasoned soldier. Arms quivering, he pulled the fletching to his cheek.

"Hold it steady, Ben."

He took a small breath, held it, steadied his aim, and released.

Twang!

The arrow sailed with speed and accuracy.

Thunk!

"Yes!" Ben pumped his arm. "This bow is amazing!"

"That's a great shot, Ben. You're pretty strong for a scrawny man," I said, taking my bow back. "You were a little low, however."

The tree was thirty yards off, but I couldn't have him getting cocky.

"I don't think many men could do much better."

I loaded Akron, pulled the string back, and let one arrow fly after the other.

Twang! Thunk!

Twang! Thunk!

Twang! Crack!

The first hit above Ben's, the second below. The third went right through his shaft.

"Uh, that was amazing!"

"Of course it was," I said handing him my bow.

"Can you teach me to do that?"

"Probably not, but..." I eyed the heavy sword on his belt, thinking. "Ever swing a sword before?"

"Just the once. My mother didn't like weapons, and my father didn't care for them much, either."

"Well, if you have to use it, better try it two handed. I'll show you a few things later. Now run down there and fetch those arrows."

Ben started walking toward the tree.

"I said *Run!*"

He sprinted for the tree. *At least he's fleet.*

Looking backward, the pixlyn wiped the sweat from his brow. The skies were empty, his pursuers gone. The firebites, who in comparison to him, for all intents and purposes, might as well have been full-sized dragons, had chased him until it felt like his wings would fall off. He zipped down into the trees and took a seat on a branch behind the leaves. He'd never flown so much in one day before.

Chest heaving, he frowned as he thought of his companion: her beautiful pink eyes and sweet smile. Even if he returned with what the evil man wanted, he knew they were both still dead. But it was better they died together rather than separately. They'd lived for one another. They'd die for one another. That's what love is.

He shuddered as he thought of the firebites. He could only guess they had tired out or found the scent of easier prey. As for the rest of the journey, he'd have to be more careful. No doubt they would pursue if they found the scent again. He shivered, mumbling in Pixlyn to himself. He rubbed his belly. The strange aching had grown stronger. He could sense the man he'd been sent to track was getting closer. His toes lifted off the branch as his wings hummed to life, and he darted off. His neck whipped around at the sound of tiny dragons roaring.

Zip!

Into the night, he was gone.

CHAPTER 19

T HE NEXT COUPLE OF DAYS occurred without incident, and I was relieved. Ben had a strong core, and after a few lessons, he could swing his sword like a weapon. He was pretty adept for a long-leg with skinny arms, but working on the farm will do that to you. The problem with most farmers being soldiers was the only weapons they wielded were pitchforks, hoes, and buckets of slop.

"Slash, Ben!" I said, banging his sword away. "Don't poke. Don't stab. That sword's not made for that. You need a light, smaller sword if you want to stab. And a quick opponent will roll right past you and slash your arm off. Have you ever seen a man hack a man's arm off before?"

Ben shook his head.

"If you poke them, they might bleed, but slash a part off, and they'll run."

Ben's face tightened.

"Hard to imagine such a thing, but when you fight, these things happen. They can happen to you just the same." I slapped him on the shoulder. "But this *is* what *you* wanted, isn't it?"

He looked a little green as he nodded his head yes.

"But stabbing's how I killed the Jackal," he said, thumbing notches on his blade's edge.

"True, but the Jackal wasn't looking—and you had a magic sword to boot." I twirled Fang with my wrist. "He's a fine thing, isn't he?" I rubbed the dragon heads on the pommel then jerked Dragon Claw out for display. "Now, if you want to poke somebody, you need one of these."

"Whoa! I never would have imagined such a thing," he said, eyeing it with fascination.

"This is Dragon Claw, and he's helped me out of more than one jam or two. When we get closer to town, we'll find you a dagger for your boot." I tugged at his girdle. "Hmmm, probably can fit a nice one in there, as well. You can never be too careful."

As Ben rubbed the back of his neck, I could see the uncertainty build in his eyes. *Good. A young man like that needs to know what he's in for.* But I was going easy on him, for now.

"I'm hungry."

"I'll check the fish traps," Ben said, sliding the broadsword into his belt.

"And I'll start the fire," I said.

I liked Ben. He was good company, and other than a few glances, he hadn't even asked about my arm, which I found extraordinary. But country folk always did have the best manners.

After gathering a few twigs and skinning down some branches, I had a fire going in no time. It wasn't long after when Ben returned with a string of fish.

"Pretty nice catch you have there," I said.

He grinned from ear to ear.

"That stream is full of them. I could fish here all week."

He skinned, I cooked, and not long after I lay on my back and watched the wind blowing the black silhouettes of the leaves.

"Think you can stay up this time?" I said.

Ben covered his mouth, yawning.

"Oh, I'm feeling spry tonight." He grabbed a stone and ran it along the edge of his sword. "Dragon, I was wondering. What do you do, exactly? Do you hunt treasure? Where are you from? I've never seen a man like you before. And when I left, all the people were talking about you."

I sat up.

"Really, what did they say?"

"My cousin said you were one of those dragon poachers."

"Really," I held up my hand, "with an arm like this?"

He scratched his neck and said, "It is peculiar, but I've seen strange travelers before." He perked up. "I even saw some elves once. They didn't talk, but they had the most beautiful armor."

"Listen, Ben. If you're going to ride with me, and you might just die with me, you might as well know."

He leaned forward.

"Know what?"

"I'm looking for dragons."

His eyes brightened.

"You're a hunter?"

I shook my head.

He snapped his fingers.

"A poacher then? I've heard about them. Uh..." He shrank back. "...but aren't they... evil?"

"Yes, but I am neither. I don't hunt dragons. I don't kill them. I rescue them."

He scratched his head and asked, "Why would a dragon need rescued?"

"What do you know about the dragons, Ben?"

He shrugged.

"They have fiery breath and scales as hard as steel. Some are as big as horses and others as small as a goat." His face drew up. "Will you take me with you? To rescue one? Oh, they have treasure, too. Wagonloads of it, I hear. And… and there are thousands of them in the Mountain of Doom. They say there's one so large there he can swallow an elephant whole."

There was only one who could, that I knew of.

"Where'd you hear that?"

"A troubadour who was passing through one day sang about it. She was a pretty young thing. Half elven she said she was, with honey-brown hair and lips the color of wine."

"And she sang no songs of auburn-haired fellows with eyes as gold as the sun?"

'No."

"Are you certain?"

"I'd have remembered for sure. We don't get many bards where I come from."

I rose to a knee, hand instinctively falling to my hilt.

"What is it?" Ben said.

I put my finger to my lips.

He cupped his ear.

What I heard was flapping. And not the common kind of the night air. Not birds, not owls, nor any other common thing but something vastly rare.

The horses nickered. Their hooves stomped and stamped.

"Stay with the horses!" I said, pulling my bow out. "Something bad is coming."

CHAPTER
20

IT WAS BAD, ALL RIGHT. Three times as bad as I thought it would be.

"Firebites! What in Narnum are they doing here?"

Yes, they're dragons. No, they aren't good. Not evil, but not good. They're also known in the Dragon Home as firebrats.

I ducked.

A small creature zinged over my head. A pixlyn. A small, fairy-like man with wings. A firebite was on his tail, chasing him into the sky, darting in and out of the trees. I could see two more waiting above as their brother flushed the pixlyn out.

"Ben! Don't leave those horses, do you hear?"

Firebites are small, little bigger than my foot, but they're all dragon. Nasty dragons, red scaled, black winged, more than capable of handling their own in the big, big world.

"What did you say?" Ben shouted back. "What are those things, anyway?"

"Stay with the horses, Ben!"

I nocked an arrow. Not wiirvin. Not magic. Just one I used for hunting. The pixlyn came again. I shot. He dove. The arrow splintered off the pursuing firebite's nose. It howled a split second before it crashed into a tree.

"Excellent shot, Dragon!"

"Get to the horses, Ben!"

In a blink, I reloaded, eyeing the sky. Down the next two came.

"Always have to do it the hard way, don't you, fellas?" I said, aiming.

Twang!

The arrow split on its face. A normal arrow wouldn't harm it, but it would sting. I stepped out of the way as it crashed to the ground.

A stream of flame shot from the third one's mouth.

"What are you doing, firebrat?" I said, jumping away. The tree behind me burst into flame. If I didn't calm them down, they'd set the entire forest on fire. The next thing I knew, they had me surrounded. Vicious little lizards, tongues licking around their red-hot mouths, snorting smoke and flames from their nostrils.

"Why are you attacking me?"

I felt something brush against my hair.

"Sultans of Sulfur!" I had a pixlyn on my head. "Get off me!"

The dragons' razor-sharp teeth nipped at my boots as they circled.

I could feel the white-hot heat coming out of their mouths. They could fry me in an instant if they wanted. I could see the fury in their eyes. They wanted that pixlyn.

I tried some Dragonese, saying, "Go away. The hunt is over."

They stopped and cocked their heads like little red dogs.

"Peace and Home," I said, and repeated.

Firebites are rebels. They come and go as they please. And they're harder to catch than most dragons. They don't have the weakness for gems or gold. It's the hunt and torment of all creatures inferior that they live for.

Sitting back on their haunches, they growled a little. Behind me, the burning tree was beginning to crackle.

"That's more like it," I said, reaching my dragon arm out to the nearest. It growled, bloodstone eyes fixed on my shoulder. There, the pixlyn sat, huffing for breath, a worried expression on his tiny face. The poor creature was exhausted. "You better stay back," I said. I felt it conceal itself in my locks.

"I'll help you, Dragon!"

From out of nowhere, Ben came swinging his sword.

"No, Ben! Stop!"

It was too late.

"EEE-YAH!"

Ben swung hard, hitting a firebite, sending it skipping across the ground.

"Fool! I told you to stay with the horses! Now we'll—"

A stream of flames shot from two dragons' mouths.

I leaped, knocking Ben out of the way.

"Stay behind me!" I said, locking my bow on my back. *Shing!* Fang was secure in my grip.

"Are those dragons?" Ben said, behind my ears.

"No, fool! Those are angry dragons! Very angry!"

"You sound angry," Ben said, worried. "Are you?"

I didn't say anything. Ben only meant well, but good intentions were often a brave man's undoing.

Puff! Puff! Puff!

Three balls of fire shot my way. I swatted them away with my sword, the splatter burning my fingertips and arms.

"Ow! That burns!" Ben said behind me.

Whatever connection I'd had with the firebites was gone now. Not only did they want the pixlyn, they now wanted Ben and me as well. And these firebites were fully grown; their fire, though small, would last much longer than others'.

"What do we do?" Ben said. "I don't want to be burned alive."

I could feel Ben sliding away from me.

"Don't you dare run," I growled. "They'll turn you into char before you get within a dozen yards of a horse. Stand your ground and live. Give ground and die."

Nervous, Ben said, "That's what my uncle the Legionnaire says."

I didn't see any way out of this. They were going to hurt us, fry us, burn us. The intent was there as their tails snapped back and forth. They'd burn the entire forest down if they wanted to. I'd have to use Fang. I'd have to be quicker than them.

"Fang, if you have any advice, I could use it now."

"What?" Ben said.

"Nothing," I said. "Prepare yourself."

As Ben and I stood side by side, I saw the firebites' tiny chests swell. A torrent of flame shot out.

CHAPTER
21

INSTANTLY, A WALL OF ICE formed before me. Fang's blade radiated an icy blue color, the like of which I'd never seen on the metal before.

"Whoa!"

On the other side, the dragon flames crackled against the ice, causing the sheet to melt. With Fang glowing like a blue star in my hand, I seized the moment.

"Stay behind this wall," I ordered Ben.

Fang was pulsating with power. It was intoxicating. I stepped around the wall and faced the tiny dragons. In Dragonese, I spoke.

"That's enough! Be gone, firebites!" I said, pointing at them with my sword.

Fireballs shot from each mouth, pelting me with fire.

"Argh!" I screamed. It hurt, but just like when the steel dragon breathed fire on me, it didn't destroy me.

Fang moaned, angry, and blasted shards of ice into all of them.

Defiant, they let out tiny roars, mouths shooting with fire.

Fang hit them again, coating them with frost from head to toe.

Growling, shivering, they backed away.

I willed Fang to shoot them again. The firebrats deserved it.

"Get out of here while you can!"

Wings pinned to their sides, one by one, they scampered away. The last one, looking back, shot another blast of fire my way. I ducked, and when I looked back, it was gone.

Still filled with power, I shot another blast into the burning tree. The ice smothered the flames. Admiring Fang, I said, "That was incredible."

Fang flared and moaned, then returned to his shiny coat of steel.

"Well done, Fang. And thank you," I said, sliding him back into his sheath.

I remembered what the steel dragon had said. *That sword you have, little dragon… you should get to know it better… that day your father forged it, I was there… tell him hello… and thank you.*

There was certainly much more to that than I expected.

"You talk to your sword," Ben said, stepping from behind the wall of ice, "And it makes snow?"

I fought the urge to slap him.

"Ben! You almost got us killed. Do you understand that?"

He stood there, blinking.

"Do you want to continue this journey with me?" I said, patting out a patch of flame on my armor. I had burn marks all over me, and a nasty boil popped up on my arm.

He nodded.

"Then follow my orders from now on!" I punched him in the arm. "Got it?"

He grimaced, holding his shoulder.

I shrugged. That's what Brenwar would have done if I'd acted so foolish. I felt Ben eyeing my back.

"Were those dragons? They were so small."

"Yes, those were dragons. And as you can see, just because something is small doesn't mean it's not dangerous. Take a moment to think: what would have happened if they came after you without me? You'd be a human roast, right? And they have our scent now. They might come back, you know. Burn us in our sleep."

Eyes like saucers, tone somber, he nodded and said, "I'm sorry, Dragon. I guess we're even, huh?"

"I guess—say what?" Something rustled in my hair. I'd forgotten about the pixlyn.

Snatch!

I had him in my dragon claws.

"What is that?" exclaimed Ben.

The pixlyn struggled in my grip, but I wasn't hurting him. I wasn't letting him go, either.

"A pixlyn, part of the fairy race."

Ben came closer, gaping, and said, "I heard they granted wishes."

I laughed but not out loud. *This should be good.*

"Go ahead, make a wish then," I suggested.

"Well, why don't you make a wish, then?"

I closed my eyes, thinking, and said, "Hmmm… well, I didn't really have one in mind, but if you're not interested, I could think of one; I guess. I'm hungry: maybe some food."

"No! Do something bigger than that."

"What would you wish for, Ben?"

This should be interesting. You could learn a lot about a person if you knew what they wished for.

Scratching the side of his cheek, looking between me and the fairy, Ben said, "I'd wish for peace in all Nalzambor."

Well, that was touching. Naïve, but at least his heart was in the right spot. *He'll make a fine hero yet.*

"Impressive, but pretty big, Ben. Their magic is limited, so you might as well ask for something smaller."

"Can I save it?"

"Sure, you can do whatever you want."

He glanced at me and said, "He can't really grant wishes, can he?"

"I can neither confirm nor deny that.

The pixlyn chattered at me, but I had no idea what he said. I imagine it was "Let me go!"

"What are you going to do with him?"

The pixlyn was an exotic and handsome little thing. His skin was the color of pollen, his eyes like tiny gems. A perfect figurine of a man. Still, it was strange to find a pixlyn so far from the high mountains. And I found it hard to believe the firebites rousted him out from there. And the creature, though defiant in my grasp, seemed sad, almost worried.

"What is wrong—"

A puff of blue smoke shot from his mouth and into my face, my mouth, my eyes.

Oh no! The lights went out, and my memories began to fade.

CHAPTER
22

AWOKE WITH THE SUN IN my eyes and an ache in my head.

"Ugh... what hit me?"

"Nothing," Ben said. "That fairy or pixie thing just spat on you."

I rolled over. There was Ben, glum faced and dark eyed. He looked like he hadn't slept in a week.

"You been up all night?"

He rubbed his eyes, yawning.

"Yep. I couldn't sleep if I had to. I swore I heard those little dragons prowling around all night." He huffed out a breath. "I'm really glad you're awake, because I couldn't wake you, and I tried. Oy, did I try."

I sat up, looking around, rubbing my head. There was a lump on it.

"Sultans of Sulfur, Ben! Couldn't you catch me when I fell? What did I land on, a stone?"

"Sorry, but I was watching that pix... er—"

"Pixlyn!" I growled. "So I guess it's long gone by now. Hope you got your wish in. Now get the gear and the horses; let's go!"

I was agitated. It wasn't all Ben's fault, but having him around didn't help. It just slowed me down. I had dragons to save, and the only thing I was saving was myself and him. It was time to get him to the city and settle him in. I had things to do.

I saddled up as soon as Ben led the horses over.

"You get everything?" I asked.

"Certainly. Eh, Dragon?"

"What?"

"That blister on your arm, it looks painful. I could lance it for you. I saw my mother lance one on my father once. He burned himself really bad at the forge. A hot horse caught him."

The blister was as big as an egg and throbbed with a life of its own. A chronic reminder of my carelessness.

"Do I look like someone who's worried about a little blister on my arm?" I said, scowling. I didn't smile all the time, unless ladies were around.

"No."

I slit it open with my dragon thumb.

Ben looked like he'd swallowed a scorpion as the puss drained out.

"There, Ben. You don't have to worry about me anymore." I snapped the reins. "Yah!"

Quintuklen. A monolithic marvel against the northern skies.

"What do you think?" I said.

Ben stared, saying, "I never imagined it was so big."

It was big. The biggest city in Nalzambor, which I always found odd, because humans didn't stick around as long as the rest of us. But they were an ambitious lot.

"How tall are those... those things?" Ben pointed.

"Those are called *buildings,* and they're the tallest structures in the world. Excluding the mountains, of course. Naturally."

Even I admired them. It was a fascinating view from the top of one to the streets below. The people seemed so tiny. It made me long for flying once more.

We trotted along a road heading toward the city, which was still miles in the distance.

"Uh, Dragon?"

"Yes."

"I'm, well, I'm..."

I saw the lump in his throat roll up and down.

"Scared, I'd imagine."

He nodded.

"Don't worry, Ben. It's normal. And once we get in there and see all the people, those fears will trickle away. Just don't buy anything or talk to the painted ladies. The merchants have a name for newcomers like you."

"A name? What kind of name?"

"Lily pad. People will be nice, but too nice can be deadly."

He blanched.

"And if you have any money, keep it in your boots. There are pickpockets all over. Are you listening?"

"Oh... sorry, it's just those buildings. So big. I never could have imagined it."

"You'll get used to it. Now, stay close to me and don't smile. That only invites unwanted attention."

"All right, Dragon."

The city, like all the rest aside from the Free City of Narnum, was fortified. A stone wall just over six feet tall was the first line of defense, but there were no gates or guards, just gaps spaced out every half mile or so. A hundred yards farther in, we came to the second wall: about twelve feet high with soldiers marching back and forth on the catwalks.

Looking around, I said, "Hold on." Reaching into my pack, I grabbed the vial of concealment potion and dripped two drops on my dragon arm.

"What's that?" Ben said.

"Watch."

I thought of what I wanted. My black scales faded, and only my skin and fingers remained. I wasn't so sure I liked it, but I didn't want any attention, either.

"Whoa!" Ben said. "Can that make me look different, too?"

Does he think potions grow on trees? "No," I lied, "It just conceals my scales. That's all I wanted. Come on, now."

Two massive wooden doors remained open, and we passed through with a throng of merchants and travelers, maybe an adventurer or two.

"Follow me," I said, "And don't stare at anybody."

Through a gap in the wall we went; into the city we came. Ben gasped from behind me. There were people everywhere. Women draped the windows of tiny apartments: whistling, smiling, and carrying on. Pushy merchants shoved sticks of cooked meat in our faces.

"Try some. The best. Make you strong warriors!" an elder one said, flashing his gums.

"Stop that!" Ben cried.

A half dozen little children were pulling at his boots. He shoved one down and into the ground. All the children screamed and cried, "Soldiers! Soldiers!"

"Stick your boots in the stirrups and ride on, Ben," I said through my teeth. "Let's go."

"Halt!"

A group of well-armed soldiers was coming our way.

CHAPTER 23

EVIL GLEE ON HIS FACE, Finnius the Cleric slapped his hands together.

"Headed toward Quintuklen! My, that's perfect, maybe too perfect, but I'll take my chances. You've done well, pixlyn, very well indeed."

The pixlyn stood back inside his cage, tiny hands wrapped around the bars, speaking shrill words of fairy kind. Along his side in her own cage, the female pixlyn sat, knees folded up in her arms.

"Certainly, I'll let you go," Finnius said, leering down at the cage. "I'll let you both go, just as soon as I'm… FINISHED WITH YOU!" He motioned for one of the acolytes. "Cover them both. I've no need of them at this moment."

The acolytes each dropped a heavy dark cloth over a cage and bowed their bald heads at Finnius. He nodded. It wasn't so long ago that he had been one of them. A lowly cleric, given a simple task of confronting Nath Dragon. He had a limp to show for it, but that was all it had taken. Selene was pleased with his success. He'd earned her trust, which was no small matter. Now he had the tattoos and greater power to show for it.

"Follow me," he said, leaving one chamber for another.

The temple rooms were an excellent sanctuary for evil. Tucked in the rocky folds of the hills east of Quintuklen, they didn't get many trespassers in the long-abandoned temple. It was easy to keep secrets that way. And the constant howl of the winds kept the staunchest adventurers away.

"Nath Dragon," he said, laughing a little, "falling right into our hands. The High Priestess will be pleased, pleased indeed."

Down a short set of stone steps he went, torches bristling in the stiff wind, leading them into a chamber of worship. The draykis hissed as he entered. The accompanying lizard men stood at attention, spears crossed over their chests.

"At ease; I've news to share," he said, walking over to the cage of the yellow dragon they'd caught days earlier and squatting. Eyes closed, it didn't budge an inch.

"It seems our game is close. Close indeed, and if we plan and stay prepared, we can lead our prey right here."

"Just tell us where he is, Finnius," the winged draykis said. "We shall go and kill him."

The draykis towered over him, fists clenched at its sides, fiery eyes boring down on him.

Finnius's hand fell to the symbol of Barnabus that hung from his neck.

"Back up," he said, "and mind your distance, creature."

"Hah, mortal, don't be so certain that amulet will protect you. It's you who should show respect," it said, clutching the long claws on its fingers.

Unruly. The dead are so unruly. Finnius squeezed the amulet tight.

"Barnabus!"

A wave of dark and eerie light burst forth, knocking the draykis from their feet. The amulet shimmered, ebbed, then returned to form: two bronze dragon heads facing outward. Each different; both evil.

"I've been dying to do that," he said. "Now, as you can see, we have many prisoners that need protection."

Scowling, the draykis rose back to their feet, looking around.

Four cages were lined up along the walls of the worship chamber. The yellow streak, as big as a man, and three small dragons, each in a cage of his own. One white, the size of a cat, and two greens as big as dogs. The draykis made catching the dragons easy, and Finnius was astounded by their success.

"Finnius," one of the acolytes spoke up, a younger man in oversized robes, "the cages' enchantment ebbs. Shall I fetch the elements?"

"Certainly," Finnius said. "And you may handle it yourself. I can't have the dragons getting out, and a little more deterrent will help."

One dragon, a purple tail, had chewed through the bars and escaped. It had been an error on Finnius's part, and a costly one. Two lizard men and one acolyte were dead. High Priestess Selene would have been furious if she knew. Now the draykis remained on guard as well. They could handle the dragons, but some cleric magic was needed as well.

One acolyte sprinkled the cages with a mix of colorful powder. The dragons snorted and scooted away as he dusted. The elements adhered to the bars, glowing at the sound of the acolytes' words of power and spreading with a dark blue glow up and down the bars. From one cage to the other they went, one sprinkling and the others chanting, until all were finished.

"Very well executed," Finnius said, "and now I have another mission for you."

They bowed.

"Anything, Finnius."

"You, get word to our brethren in Quintuklen. See to it rumor of this temple finds the ears of Nath Dragon. And you, send word to the High Priestess Selene. Tell her that the trap is set. Go!"

Finnius took a seat on the stone bench and wiped his sweaty palms on his robes. Capturing Nath Dragon wouldn't be easy. He'd seen the man in action before. He eyed the draykis.

"He's faster than you. That sword of his can split an anvil in two."

The lead draykis folded his arms over his chest and said, "Do not underestimate us. We are many; he is one. He may be fast," the draykis flexed the thick scaled cords in his arm, "but we are strong."

"Certainly," Finnius dabbed the sweat from his head with a satin cloth. *They are a cocky lot. But they'll have to do.*

CHAPTER 24

"**B**EN, HAVE YOU EVER SLEPT in a dungeon before?"

"No," Ben said, confused.

"It's the worst food you'll ever eat and the worst company you'll ever keep. But, as they say, 'What doesn't kill you makes you wish you'd died anyway.'"

Ben gulped as the soldiers, each brandishing a long spear, approached.

"What's going on here? Are you harassing our citizens?" one said, helping the fallen child up.

Trouble with the local authorities was the last thing I wanted in Quintuklen. They kept things in order, and they had more dungeons here than in all the rest of Nalzambor. I'd been in their dungeons, and they were the last place in the world you'd ever want to go.

"The funny-looking one kicked me," the boy said, pointing. "Said he'd kill me if I didn't move."

"Liar!" Ben exclaimed. "I did no such thing. He tried to steal my boots. They all did."

The soldiers weren't much better than children in some cases. They'd rob you blind as well. I could see it in their eyes; they knew Ben was new to the city.

"Where'd you get that armor? It's not a very good fit," one soldier spoke up. "It looks stolen to me."

Ah great. I could see the dungeon doors closing on me now. I hadn't been back in the city five minutes, and I was about to be arrested. I had to do something, fast.

"Soldiers of Quintuklen, may I address?"

They turned and stared.

I leaned forward on my saddle horn and said, "We're just passing through. Supplies for us, food for the horses, one night's rest, and maybe a trip to Dragon Pond out west. My friend's never been to the city, either. He's from the country; can't you tell? But, his uncle…" I eyed Ben.

"Louis of Quinley," he sputtered out.

"Yes, Louis told us to stop in at the Garrison and say hello." I crossed my arms over my chest and shot each man a discerning look.

They glanced at one another, and a moment later the leader said, "Move on!"

"But what about my justice, soldier?" one of the children said.

"Shaddap, you lazy little rodent, before I whip you." He swatted at one. They scattered. "Troublemakers, the lot of you!"

"Are we really going to the Garrison *and* Dragon Pond?"

"Maybe," I said. Well, now I'd possibly told a lie. I didn't have any plans to take Ben anywhere else with me; I just wanted to get him settled in and go. And with any luck, his Uncle Louis could take him in for a spell.

The farther into the city we went, the less commotion occurred. Quintuklen was well laid out and organized. Gardens, fountains, colorful storefronts, and banners could be seen all along the way. The streets were cobbled, and lanterns were lit by magic at every turn of a corner. In the good parts of town, at least.

"Dragon, can I stay with you one last night? I know you're wanting to get rid of me, and I can only guess you're going to set me up with my uncle," he said atop his horse, dejected.

I felt bad now. I liked having Ben around. He was like a younger brother, and none of my dragon family ever hung around much. Ben had saved my life... and he'd almost gotten me killed. I had things to do.

"Tell you what, Ben. I've got a few things to do around town, and I guess you can follow if you like. But, I've got business. Serious business. Dangerous, sometimes. You follow my lead. Any more foul-ups, I'm leaving you lost in this city."

He shot up in his saddle, showing all of his teeth.

"Thank you!"

"Don't foul up. I mean it!"

He frowned again.

"Come on; let's get inside some walls and have a tasty meal. I guess I'm feeling a little cranky."

Horses clopping over the cobblestones, we made our way down the street. It was dark, but the lanterns made for ample light, but I didn't like that. I liked places that were more discreet. Not where the merchants went, but where the adventurers, soldiers, and troublemakers went. They always had the most interesting stories to tell. We stopped in front of a stable.

"This is good," I said.

A young girl came out. She had a button nose and her hair was pulled back in a ponytail. Her eyes lit up when she saw me.

I smiled and flipped her two coins.

"One night, pretty thing. A meal bag for each as well."

I slid off my horse, and Ben followed suit.

"Anything you wish, traveler." She grabbed the reins and said, "I'll brush them both and check their shoes. Just let me know anything else I can do."

"Thank you," I said, rubbing her head. "That will be fine."

"Yes, thank you, little miss," Ben added, reaching out.

She ducked under his hand and moved on, taking a glance or two back at me before she was gone.

"You don't have to do that, Ben."

"Do what?"

"What I do. Just stay close. Look. Learn. Listen, lily pad."

His face scrunched up as he said, "Look. Learn. And listen."

He'll figure it out.

A tavern sign hung nearby, and Ben squinted as he read the words above and said, "Hogfarts?" He grabbed his nose and shook his head.

"They have the worst ale in town, Ben. Let's keep going."

The next sign, another block down, seemed more appealing: the Ettin's Toe. A small crowd of men and women, a hard-looking bunch, were full of life on the balcony above.

"This will do," I said, stepping up onto the porch.

Two figures came crashing through the door. A very large, bearded man was entangled with a half orc: soldiers by the looks of their armor. The man bashed the half orc in the gut. The half orc walloped the man in the jaw. As the crowd came out jeering, we went in. Ben was pale when we sat down.

"Relax, Ben. It's best you see the best and worst of what the city offers. And, believe it or not, places like this have the best food to eat." I winked. "Trust me."

Wide eyed, Ben couldn't help but look around. And I couldn't blame him. There were all sorts of people, which was a big part of what I liked about this town. Small torches lit up all the walls but not the corners. Two men as big as ogres sat at the bar with shoulders bulging up to their necks. A squad of bowmen sat in the middle of the room, joking and jesting of high times. Robed women with dark eyes and painted hands read the palms and heads of others in the room. One woman squealed as she sat on the lap of a man in full plate armor, who was tickling her knee. I smiled. There was nothing more entertaining than people. Especially the human ones.

"What can I get you, handsome?" the barmaid asked. She was a short, buxom woman with blonde curls all over her head. "I recommend the roast and biscuits. We have some chicken and egg soup, too."

"Is it hot?"

She fanned her sweaty neck and winked, saying, "Everything is hot in here."

"Then that will do. Oh, and a small bottle of wine as well, pretty thing."

"And a glass of milk as well, pretty thing," Ben said.

The barmaid cackled like a hyena as she walked away.

"Ben, I don't think they have milk in here."

"But that's all I've ever drunk. Well, that and water."

I rolled my eyes. The two big goons at the bar were eyeing us now, and word was spreading.

"Did somebody order a cow over there?" one of the bowmen shouted our way.

The guffaws followed.

"What, what's he mean by that?"

"Next time, just ask for Honey Brown," I said. Honey Brown was ale, but it wasn't fermented. "It won't get you drunk, and your tongue won't take over your mouth, either."

The barmaid returned with two plates full of steaming food in one hand, a bottle of wine and a pitcher in the other. Setting them down, she said, "Sorry, young fella, we're all out of milk, but this should hold you over." She tousled his hair.

"Thank you," I said, placing coins in her hand. "And a room is needed as well."

"I'll fluff your pillows myself, handsome. My, where did you get eyes like that?" she said.

"From my father."

"Mmmm. Mmmm. Mmmmm. He must be something special as well."

"He is." I looked at our hands. "You can let go now."

"Oh," she blushed, walking away with a swing in her hips.

Ben was stuffing his face full of food.

"I'm starving," he raised the tankard to his lips.

I stopped him.

"Let me see that." I sniffed it. "Honey Brown. You're in good shape. Enjoy."

You couldn't be too careful in a place like this. I'd seen more than one man the night before his first adventure who'd never made it out of the tavern. People would do all sorts of rotten things to one another when you weren't careful.

I sawed up a bite of food and stuffed the meat in my mouth. *Tender and greasy, just how I like it.* And the biscuits, almost more butter than bread, were delicious. I never got to eat things like this in Dragon Home.

"Honey Brown, is it?" Ben said, gulping it down. "Tasty like a thousand honeysuckles." He looked over his shoulder. "What are we in a place like this for? What are you looking for?"

"Dragons."

"In here?"

The tavern door slammed open, causing Ben to jump in his chair.

"TORMAC WINS!"

The large man who'd been fighting outside moments earlier sauntered in, dusting off his hands. His beefy forearms were scraped up, and his beard reminded me of an oversized dwarf.

"Does anyone else want to tangle with Tormac?" he said, walking over and slapping the two goons sitting at the bar on the shoulder. "Anyone?"

Heads down, they shook their heads. They were big men, hardy, but not as big as Tormac.

Ben, chewing a mouthful of food, was all eyes as he gawped at Tormac.

"Ben," I said, snapping my finger, "eyes over here!"

He didn't budge.

The crowd fell silent when the leering Tormac said, "What are you looking at, bug eyes?"

CHAPTER
25

TURNING PALE, BEN CHEWED ONCE and stopped.

Tormac was a warrior. He had the scars to show for it. The steel on his wide hips was heavy, and the dark eyes over his big, flat nose made him all the more menacing. This was not what I needed.

"Well, bug eyes?" Tormac said in a grizzly voice, smashing his fist into his hands. "What are you staring at?"

"Don't hurt him, Tormac! He hasn't had his milk yet!" someone shouted.

The tavern erupted in laughter. Ben's cheeks turned red.

Tormac chuckled as he pawed at his beard.

"What's the matter, bug eyes? Did you leave your cow at the farm?"

More laughter.

Ben looked at me. Tormac looked at me. All eyes were on me.

I hitched my arm over the back of my chair, leaned back, tossed my hair over my shoulder, and said, "What are you looking at... ogre nose?"

It got so quiet I could hear Tormac blink. I continued.

"The last time I saw nostrils that big, dwarves were mining copper out of them."

Somebody laughed, somewhere. I think it was the barmaid.

"What?" Tormac said, hand falling to his blade.

"Ah, good idea. Get your nose picker out. I think I see a boulder... er... I mean a booger in there."

Chuckling ensued. Tormac leered around, bringing the chuckles to an abrupt stop.

"Or is that a toothpick? You could use it; I can see a halfling wedged in that gap between your teeth."

The entire room erupted.

"BRAHHHH—HA-HA-HA-HA!"

My chair clacked on the floor as I teetered forward and stood up, smiling.

Tormac's face was as red as his beard.

"You're going to die," he said through clenched teeth.

I fanned my hand in front of my face and said, "What happened with you and that half orc out there? Did you eat him?"

Food fell from Ben's mouth. The entire tavern was doubled over now, except Tormac.

He swung.

I ducked.

"Let's settle this at the table," I said, dodging another swing. "My arm against yours."

Tormac stopped. An ugly smile started on his face. He was taller than me and as thick as an anvil, an oversized man with the girth of a dwarf. I was strong. As strong as any man, but Tormac was more than that. He was a mountain. He pulled out a chair and sat down.

To cheers, I joined him. I looked at my right arm, my dragon arm. It was still well concealed. And Tormac, I'd known he was right handed when he reached for his sword. Of course, you could always tell by which hip it rested on.

We locked hands.

"I win, you leave. You win, I leave." I scanned the crowd. Hope filled the eyes of some. "For good."

"Hah!" He nodded. "You'll be leaving, all right," he growled, "in pieces. Your friend, too."

The barkeep raised his arms, hushing the crowd, then wrapped both hands around our knuckles. "That's odd," the barkeep said, looking at me, "you have very rugged skin."

"Get on with it," Tormac said, sneering. "I broke that last man's arm at the elbow, and I'm going to do worse to yours." He spat juice on the floor.

I winked.

His knuckles turned white as he began squeezing my hand. I'd never arm wrestled such a big, big man.

"Ready," the barkeeper started, "Set... wrestle."

Tormac put his shoulder into it, shoving my arm down. The crowd roared as my arm bent toward the table. He was strong. Every bit as strong as he looked. A real brute who knew what he was doing.

"Come on, Dragon!" Ben shouted.

I stopped the descent inches from the table and heaved back. Tormac's eyes widened as I began pushing his arm back.

The lively crowd found new life.

"He's pushing Tormac back!"

"Impossible!" someone said.

I loved the attention. I put more dragon muscle into it.

"Hurk!"

I forced Tormac's arm past the starting point and back.

"Golden eyes is winning!"

Sweat dripped from Tormac's forehead and down his nose. The salty taste of my own sweat stung my eyes. I pushed his arm downward little by little.

"NO!" Tormac yelled. "No one beats me!"

The big man snorted in fury, shoving me back, up, up, to the starting point and backward. The entire tavern exploded with shouts of cheers and triumph.

I felt my own ears redden now. My dragon arm was aching. It was fast, but how strong was it, actually?

"Hang on, Dragon!" Ben shouted.

I was, barely. I fought back with everything I had, shoving the brute's arm back. We teetered from the starting point, back and forth. Part of the crowd was chanting...

"Tormac! Tormac! Tormac!"

The other part chanted...

"Dragon! Dragon! Dragon!"

I liked that, but it wasn't helping. Tormac shoved my arm back down, my knuckles barely an inch from the table.

Tormac was huffing and puffing. I held on. Arm throbbing, head aching, I fought on. I didn't care who you were or what you did, I wasn't going to lose to anyone. Not while I lived. I shoved back with everything I had.

Tormac's eyes were full of triumph as he said, "You're finished!"

Something in the man's face angered me. An evil menace lurked there. A bully. A man of violence. A troublemaker. A thug for hire. A kidnapper. Maybe a murderer. I could see the truth. This man had preyed on the weak all his life. Used his gifts for evil, not good. My inner furnace was stoked.

"No, Tormac," I growled, "You're finished, not I!"

I shoved his arm upward. My dragon arm may not have been stronger, but it hadn't tired.

"No!" Tormac snarled.

Our wrists reached the starting point, and Tormac's arm went down.

The roaring crowd were jumping to their feet!

"Dragon! Dragon! Dragon!"

Tormac was shaking his head. Desperation filled his eyes. I took a quick deep breath and shoved everything into it.

"Nooooooo!" Tormac pleaded.

Wham!

I slammed his knuckles onto the table.

Chest heaving, I managed to say, "Time to go, Tormac!"

The crowd was all smiles as they helped the exhausted man out of his chair. His eyes were weak as he held his arm and was shoved toward the door, the crowd turning on him.

"Get out of here, Tormac! You stink the place up."

"Be a stranger!"

"Your mother's a bugbear!"

Raising my arm in the air and waving, I said, "That's enough, everyone. It's time to celebrate that he's gone."

The room fell silent.

I had a very bad feeling.

Someone gasped.

Others pointed.

Ben was pointing to his arm.

I looked at mine. My dragon arm had returned. Black as the night. Strong as steel. Beautiful as a black pearl. "Welcome back," I said.

"What manner of trickery is this?"

"He's a changeling!"

"A demon!"

"Fiend!"

I shot Ben a look and mouthed the words, "Get to the horses!"

Something as big as a ham and hard as a rock smacked into my face.

CHAPTER 26

TORMAC LEERED OVER ME WITH a face filled with fury. The man, I hated to admit, punched like an ogre. I could only imagine his booted heel descending toward my head would be twice as bad. Seeing spots, I rolled, gathered my feet, and sprang away. All the people who'd cheered me on moments before now screamed for my head.

"Cheater!"

"Changeling!"

"Kill him!"

"Bash his face in, Tormac!"

My, the tides change fast here.

A wooden tankard zinged past my head.

"Hold on!" I shouted, holding my arms up. "No one stated any rules! I've deceived no one. All I did was make a challenge to arm wrestle. Tormac agreed! He lost. I won. Now back away!" I said, shaking my fist.

No one moved. I had a way of capturing people's attention like that.

One woman in the back, dressed in a black vest of leather armor, spoke up.

"Men in disguises can't be trusted! Get him!"

"But—"

The two big goons who sat at the bar seized my arms, locking them behind my back. By the look and smell of them, they were ugly brothers. And not just any type of brothers, but wrestlers, judging by their tattoos and scars and how they locked up my arms.

"Them's scales on his arms," one said.

"Never seen anything like that," said the other. "He's a monster of some sort!"

"A changeling! They're evil; burn him!" a woman shouted.

"He's a demon! No one has gold eyes like that!"

"Hold him still!" Tormac said, rolling the sleeves up on his bulging arms.

"Tormac," I said, "you don't want to do—*oof!*"

The belly blow lifted me off my feet. I groaned.

"That…"

"Hit him once for me, Tormac!"

This can't be happening.

Whop!

I couldn't speak or breathe, and I swore my stomach was screaming from the other side of my back.

"Let's see if we can't take care of that smart mouth of yours."

He swung at me.

I jerked back, letting Tormac's fist hit one of the goons in the face.

"Watch it!" the goon said.

"Don't hit him in the face; he's too handsome!" one lady said, standing on a table wearing a helmet of lit candles on her head.

"Thank you!"

"No, hit him in the face!" one of the bowmen said.

"What is wrong with you people!"

Whop!

Tormac belted me in the stomach again, draining my strength from my head to my toes. I tried to fight, but the goons held me tight. They were like two pythons around my arms.

Whop! Whop!

Tormac laughed. "I told you you'd leave in pieces." *Pow!*

My teeth clattered in my face. *I have no business being here without Brenwar.* I'd settled for Ben the lily pad instead.

"Get him out of here!"

My body was moving, but not by a will of its own. I could hear the jeers as my knees were dragged across the floor.

"One!"

I felt the wind rushing past my ears.

"Two!"

My stomach was teetering inside my belly.

"Three!"

I was flying.

Crash!

Through a window I went, skipping over the cobblestone road. Struggling, I rolled onto my elbows, groaning when I touched my bleeding lip.

Everyone else spilled out the doors or gawped out the broken window.

I waved, saying, "Never let it be said the Ettin's Toe isn't full of charming hospitality."

Someone grabbed me by my shoulders and began pulling me up to my feet.

"Come on, Dragon."

Thankfully, it was Ben.

"Ah look, bug eyes has come to help his demon friend."

"I'm not a demon!" I said, grabbing my saddle. My leg wobbled in the stirrup as Ben shoved me up into the saddle.

It sounded like the entire city burst into laughter.

"Soldiers!" someone said, pointing.

"Tell them we've found a demon!"

I'd had enough already. I wasn't about to spend the night in jail. Even worse, I didn't need to be accused of being a demon by soldiers.

"Follow me, Ben!" I said, snapping my reins.

Tormac waved and laughed as we galloped away.

From one side of the city to the other we'd gone when I came to a stop. Aching and weary, I slid from my saddle and took a seat on a stone bench in a long-forgotten park. It was the Garrows. An old part of the city: quiet, discreet, creepy.

"I don't like this place," Ben said, eyes flitting around.

"It's not so bad in the daytime. See," I pointed.

Statues, fountains, and gardens were everywhere, but shaded in grey and black, leaving an eerie feeling in the air.

"Come on, I've a friend I was going to check on anyway. Now's as good a time as any," I said, clutching my side.

"You all right?"

"Just a couple of broken ribs," I said through my teeth. They hurt. How many more beatings was I going to take over Ben? Everywhere he was came trouble.

"Sorry, Dragon. I know it's my fault. I should have stayed in the country."

Yes! Yes, you should have!

I didn't say it, however. It was his life. He had the right to do what he wanted. *But I think he'd start to think first more often if his ribs got busted, not mine.*

"This is it," I said, wrapping my reins around a lantern post.

A single building, no wider than ten feet, stood in stark contrast to the larger buildings at its sides. There were no windows, only an open doorway with stairs leading up.

"You first," I said.

"What about the horses? We can't leave them here."

"Do you see any people?"

He looked around and shook his head.

"No."

"They'll be fine then. Trust me."

Standing at the bottom and looking up, we saw a stairwell lit with small gemstone lights leading to a doorway at the top.

"Is that," Ben squinted, leaning forward, "a door?"

"Yes."

"It looks like it's a hundred yards away, more maybe."

"Then we better get started."

"But?"

I grabbed him by the collar and shoved him forward, saying, "Trust your feet, not your eyes this time."

Up the steps we went. One flight. Two flights. Three flights. Ten flights. My body ached with every step. Ben was huffing in front of me, eyes wide as saucers as he kept staring back.

"Keep going."

Twenty flights. Thirty flights. Ben stopped, hands on his knees, scrawny chest heaving, looking back.

"Dragon, what is going on? We aren't going anywhere!"

I cast a look over my shoulder. We were only one flight up from where we started, and I could see the tail of one horse swaying at the bottom.

I smiled. "We're almost there, Ben. Keep going."

Forty flights.

"You did good back there, Ben."

"I did? How?" he said, wheezing.

I took a breath.

"You got the horses as you were told. You got out of harm's way like I said. If you hadn't, you might be dead, but you'd have been beaten up pretty bad still."

"But you got hurt."

"True, but I'm used to it." I squeezed his shoulder. "Up. We're almost there."

Fifty flights.

Sweating like orcs, we both let out sighs of relief as we placed our feet on the landing at the top. It was marble, checkered in red and green, with the pattern of a mage on the bottom.

Both of us looked back. We still weren't any farther than when we started.

"I don't understand," Ben said, blinking.

"And you probably never will."

I reached past him and grabbed the ring of a gargoyle-faced knocker.

Bang! Bang! Bang!

It echoed like thunder.

Ben stuck his fingers inside his ears.

"Who lives here?" he asked.

"Bay—*ulp!*"

The marble floor disappeared beneath our feet, and into the black we went.

CHAPTER 27

BRENWAR INSPECTED THE HORN HE had strapped around his shoulders. It was a horn carved from bone and gilded with brass and iron. It had two purposes. One was to make noise that was privy to dwarven ears. The other was to listen.

He took the small end and held it in his ear.

From a hilltop, he looked down on a small village. A few hundred residents lived there, and he knew that they, like most small-town residents, weren't welcoming to dwarves. He could hear voices, talking, and laughter, all of it as clear as a bell. After an hour of listening, he huffed. There were not sounds nor any talk of Nath Dragon. He slung the Dwarven Horn back over his shoulder.

"Two hundred years old and he still acts like a boy." He huffed. "And to think: he might live another thousand years."

Steady through the night he went, down the hill, through the trees. The sun and the rain and the days without sleep did not slow him. His brethren had been scattered toward all of the major cities, seeking for signs, yet none of them had sent word. The Dwarven Horn could send a sound over the air that only the dwarves with other horns could hear. It was dwarven magic, rare and ancient, more pertaining to their craft. One horn linked to another, forming a network of dwarven logic and mystic bounds. Normally they were used in times of war.

"We should have found him by now," he muttered under his beard.

He knew Nath would be looking for dragons. His friend could be anywhere in the world. But it would be easier to find a needle in a haystack if that's what Nath wanted.

He combed his stubby fingers through his black beard, eyeing it.

"There better not be any pixies in there," he warned. "Hmmm… perhaps my thinking is wrong. Should I be searching for Nath, or searching for dragons?" One would certainly lead to the other. "Perhaps the Clerics of Barnabus?"

What if the clerics had already trapped the man? Nath's father had said, "Keep him from the hands of Barnabus."

Many of the people in Nalzambor thought the clerics protected people from the dragons, unaware it was the other way around. But the clerics were a devious lot, doing good deeds in the day and dark things in the night. Many were fooled by that, and many were not. Barnabus had been a great warrior who fought alongside the dragons long ago, but now his memory had been turned into something else. No longer a dragon warrior, as the seers said, but a dragon hunter.

Just thinking about it made Brenwar want to pull his beard out.

"If men were as honest as dwarves, we'd never have all these problems."

Miles from the next settlement, he put the horn to his ear and listened hour after hour in the pouring rain.

"Nothing," he grumbled, then traveled on.

CHAPTER
28

"**B**AAAAAAAAAAAAAAY-ZOG!" I SCREAMED AS I fell. I couldn't even see Ben, but I could hear him in the darkness.

"HEEEEELP MEEEEEEEE!"

There was light.

Thud!

Pain.

Thud!

And Ben landing on top of me. Whatever hadn't hurt before hurt now, and everything else was worse. I pushed Ben's groaning body off of me and rose to my feet.

The room was filled with brilliant lights, colorful cushions, and silk drapes. The incense was so strong I could almost taste it.

"Whew! What is that?" Ben said, fanning his face.

I jerked him up to his feet.

"Just relax, Ben. He'll be offended if you don't."

"Who?" he said, pinching his nose.

Shuffling toward the center of the room, I said, "Bayzog, I know you wish to greet, else I would have landed on a harder floor."

"How big is this place?" Ben said, spinning around. "It was just a tiny building."

It was a huge room, like the ballrooms in the castles. A large sphere of square-cut crystals twinkled above. The floor was hardwood, the room a rectangle, with a fireplace of burning logs in every corner. Huge cushions were scattered all over the room, and in the middle was a large, square table, waist high with no chairs. Bayzog stood there, staring down into a book the size of ten. He turned and spoke in a strong, dark voice.

"If I'd known you were coming, I'd have left a pillow out... maybe." He bowed. "Unwelcome, Nath Dragon."

"Not glad to be here," I replied.

Bayzog was black haired, small framed, but sturdy. He wore a red wizard's tunic embroidered with arcane signs and symbols. Everything was impeccable about his character, and his violet eyes were bright, deep, probing. He was part elven, rich, and full of mystery.

I extended my dragon hand.

"My, how eerie are those? He grabbed my arm and started needling it with his fingers. "Nath, I've never seen black dragon scales before. But I've heard about them."

"You have?"

He grabbed a clear glass lens the size of a fist off his table and took a closer look. "Certainly."

"Sorry, of course you have." I said. "What can you tell me about them?"

"Hold on," he said, glancing over Ben. "Hmmm... I see you've replaced Brenwar... obviously a good choice." He grabbed Ben's hand, blinking.

"Nath," Ben said, pulling away, but Bayzog held him fast, "what is he doing?"

"Just be still, Ben. If he wanted to harm you, you'd know already."

Studying Ben, Bayzog said, "My, this one's nothing but trouble, isn't he?"

"Er... what do you mean? I'm not trouble." Ben looked at me. "Am I?"

I shrugged.

Ben tried to pull away again, but Bayzog closed his eyes and held him fast.

"Hmmm... could be good... could be bad." He released Ben. "He needs more time, Dragon." Opening his eyes, Bayzog said, "And some polishing up will do. Sasha!"

A lovely woman, all human, appeared in white robes.

"Sasha," I said, unable to contain my smile, "it's been too long."

She brushed her auburn locks from her blue eyes and said, "It's good to see you, too, Dragon." She took Ben by the hand and said, "Come along."

Ben, stupefied, said nothing as she led him, smiling, out of the room. I felt like a boulder had rolled off my chest.

"Unthank you, Bayzog."

"Unwelcome, and don't worry; she'll find suitable stitchings, but you'll have to do the rest," Bayzog said.

"I'm not doing anything. I agreed to bring him to the city. Promised him a meal and good rest. He's off to the Legionnaires after this."

"No he isn't," Bayzog said, thumbing through the book's huge pages.

"Yes he is," I objected. "And if you like him so much, he can stay with you."

"Did you come here to argue with me, or did you come for my help?"

I came to get answers. When it came to dragons, Bayzog could deliver. He knew almost as much about dragons as I did.

"All right, what's in that big book of yours?"

Somehow, Bayzog had everything he ever learned in one book. The Book of

Many Pages. It was one big book, or tome rather, on one big table, accompanied with magic ink and quill.

"You know, I have many things in this book. Stories, legends, maps, spells, histories. Everything I've ever learned or heard is right here."

"How do you add more pages?"

His cheerless face brightened a little.

"It can add as many as I need. That's why I made the book."

Looking at it, I said, "That's a lot of pages. How do you know where to look for something? Where do you start?"

"Book, black dragon scales."

The pages came to life, stirring the air, ruffling my hair before they came to a stop.

"Impressive." I squinted. The words would shift and move as I read. I leaned away, pinching the bridge of my nose, and stepped back. "How do you read that? It hurts my eyes."

He showed a wry smile.

"Right. I understand, wizard. So, what does it say?"

"The color of scales on black dragons," he said, running his finger down the page. "Rare. No black dragons seen since the last dragon war."

He closed the book and stepped away.

"What did you do that for?"

"Nath, tell me what happened. How did you get that arm? You're supposed to get scales, but black ones?"

I'd been friends with Bayzog for more than a hundred years, and he knew my story and who my father was. He was fascinated by dragons, but in a good way. So I told him about the people I had killed in Orcen Hold and the last conversation I had had with my father.

"But," I showed him the white spot on my hand, "I think I'm turning things around. I even saved a steel dragon and found a Thunderstone."

Bayzog's eyes lit up.

"Do you still have it?"

"No, the steel dragon swallowed it."

Pacing back and forth, Bayzog said, "That's a shame."

"Losing the Thunderstone?"

"Yes to that. No," Bayzog frowned, "to never going home again. I know how that feels."

The brief moment of emptiness in his eyes left me feeling empty again as well.

"So, Dragon, what is your plan?"

"I want to rescue dragons. Many of them at once. That will do it! I know the more I free, the more I can be cured. I know you can help me find them. I need to find a flock of dragons!" I grabbed his shoulder. "You have to help me, Bayzog."

"Ahem."

Sasha, now wearing loose-fitting robes, reentered the room with a pleasant smile on her face.

"Where's Ben?" I asked.

"He's taking a nap," she said, drifting to Bayzog's side.

"A nap?"

"The young man is tired, Dragon." Her blue eyes flared at me. "And *you* should do the same."

Suddenly, my lids became heavy, and I couldn't fight the yawn.

"Ah, Sasha," Bayzog wrapped his arm around her waist and smiled, "always trying to comfort her guests."

Covering my yawn, I fought back and said, "No, not this time, Sasha. Last time, you put me down for two days. I appreciate your concern, but your efforts won't work on me this time. I'm ready."

"Ah, Dragon, you know she can't help herself. She knows what's best for you, you know. And you look tired. I've never seen a tired dragon before."

I felt tired. My jaw ached, and my face felt swollen. And with every little movement, I felt my cracked ribs inside. *And I remember the last time I took a long nap and what happened when I woke up.*

"Come on, Dragon," Sasha pleaded.

A chair slid across the room and stopped beside me.

Magi didn't get guests very often, so when you came, they expected you to stay awhile.

"I'll sit, but you, Bayzog, need to tell me what you know. I saw that look in your eyes before your book closed."

Sasha looked at him and said, "What is it, Bayzog? You can't keep secrets from our friend."

"Please, dear," he said. "It's a delicate matter. "

She pulled away, fists dropping to her hips.

"Too delicate for my ears?"

Bayzog's hand recoiled to his chest as he pleaded.

"Certainly not, my love."

I liked Sasha. She was all about the truth, which was uncommon for a wizard. And as I've said, wizards, magic users, and necromancers could not be trusted. Not even an old friend like Bayzog. When it came to power, they had their weaknesses. Sasha, however, wasn't like that. What she lacked in Bayzog's power, she made up for with integrity.

"Well?" she said, tapping her bare foot on the floor.

Bayzog flittered his fingers and muttered the strangest words.

Where one fireplace blazed in the corner, cushioned chairs and a sofa accompanied it now.

"Shall we?" he said, arm extended to the corner.

I limped over and slumped into the furniture.

"It would have been nice if I'd landed on this sofa rather than your hard floor."

Sasha readied me a drink from the serving station.

"Coffee, tea or—"

"Wizard's Water would be fine."

She smiled, saying, "Excellent choice."

She poured a red melon-colored drink in a crystal glass and served us all.

Bayzog hoisted up his glass and said, "To old friends."

"And dead enemies," I added.

I drank. Smooth, bitter, and invigorating. I felt my mind and body begin to rest. Tea, coffee, wine, ale did little for me, but the wizard's magic elixir did much. It filled me, refreshed me, and cleared my senses.

"Ah... I needed that." I clopped my glass on the table and leaned toward Bayzog. "So, tell me what you saw, wizard."

Sasha leaned his way as well, her beautiful eyes intent on his face.

"Dragon, listen, it's not something that I think is worth mentioning. I can't confirm any of it."

"Bayzog, tell him!"

Bayzog, the epitome of poise, slumped back in his chair, face drawn up with worry.

Sasha gasped, "Bayzog, where are your manners?"

He sighed, one eye open, one on my arm.

"Dragon, your arm, its curse is much worse than suspected."

CHAPTER 29

"**H**OW MUCH WORSE CAN IT be?" I said. "And besides," I showed him the white scales in the palm of my hand, "I think it's getting better."

Sasha took my hand in hers and traced her fingers over it.

"I've never felt live dragon scales before, at least not on a man," she said. "They're beautiful."

That made me feel good. After all, how could something beautiful be bad? I knew I was good.

"Sasha, please, can't you tell he's enough in love with himself already?" He paused, looking at me. "You like it, Dragon. Don't you? The raw power it contains."

I reached over, refilling my glass of Wizard's Water.

"Wouldn't you, Bayzog?"

"Power, yes. Cursed power... no. Listen, have you ever seen a black dragon before?"

I shook my head.

"There's a reason for that," he said, sitting back up in his chair. "They're all dead. They all died in the last dragon war."

"So?" I shrugged. "I'm sure many dragons died off in the last dragon war."

Rising to his feet, Bayzog walked over to the fire, rubbing his hands.

"How much did your father tell you about the Great Dragon War?"

I had to think about that. My father had told me many things, but he never spoke about the dragon wars, and I'd never really given them much thought until now.

"I see," Bayzog continued. "Just so you know, legends say that it was the black dragons that started the Great Dragon War."

I fell back in the sofa, glancing at Sasha's eyes. I could see she was worried.

"And my father killed them?" I asked.

Bayzog shook his head slightly, saying, "We don't know that *he* killed them.

Any of the dragons could have killed them. But they were the cause. They were the solution."

I pulled my arm from Sasha. It was no wonder my father was so furious with me. Black dragon's scales. A reminder of the war. But why did I have them? I was good, after all.

"Bayzog, how come I've never heard of this: the black dragons, the war? You'd think I would have crossed paths with it by now."

"There are legends and histories, some true, some not, in some cases neither, others both."

"That's not really an answer."

"Well, the Great Dragon War might be over, but the evil remains. Much of it is hidden from our eyes, but some of it is right in front of us, mixing the truth with lies."

I took another drink because I was feeling weary again.

"Like the Clerics of Barnabus?" I sighed.

"Do you know the legend of Barnabus, Dragon?" Sasha said.

"Well enough, I suppose."

"Oh, show him, Bayzog. Show him how the story unfolded." She batted her eyes at him. "Please."

He frowned at first and then smiled, saying, "You know I can never tell you no."

She huffed. "You tell me no all the time."

"Only when I study."

She whispered in my ear.

"That's all the time."

He brushed his black hair past the point of his elven ear and said, "I heard that."

Then with a twitch of his fingers, the flames swirled into a sea of color. In the flames, the image of a mighty man appeared, fully armored, carrying a great sword over his shoulder.

"Barnabus," Bayzog said. "One of the few Legionnaires who aided the good dragons in battle."

The image of Barnabus was doused in flames as a dragon appeared from behind.

"I love this part," Sasha said, hugging my arm.

Barnabus turned and ran his sword right through its heart. The flames roared out, and only Barnabus remained. You could see nothing of the man, only his armored metal shell.

"Barnabus, the histories say, killed the last black dragon. It was his bravery and his sword, Stryker, that ended the war. But the Clerics of Barnabus would have Nalzambor believe differently. Under his name, they claim to protect us from all kinds of dragons, claiming they are evil, dangerous. We know better, but most people don't. They fear the dragons. They loathe them. They capture them and sell them from the temples of Barnabus."

"Oh, I hate those clerics!" Sasha said, reddening. "I'd kill them all if you'd let me."

"It's not our fight, dearest."

I eyed Bayzog, saying, "What's that supposed to mean?"

Holding his hands up, he added, "At least not yet. Dragon, I'm fascinated by you and your kind, but it's the people I protect, not dragons. That's your charge. But," he bowed, "I'll help you with whatever you can do."

I felt that Bayzog was holding back. Wizards always did.

"Tell me where the dragons are?"

"I can't help much there, Dragon. They're hiding. The Clerics have their ears, and they have been as thick as wolves' fur out there. And then you, you of all people, come strolling into this city, knowing full well they've a bounty on you."

I jumped to my feet.

"How did you know that?"

He rolled his eyes.

I threw my arms up.

"Of course! Of course you knew! All right, Bayzog, if you don't want to help, just say so."

I slammed my glass down on the table.

Sasha grabbed me, saying, "Dragon, behave yourself. You know Bayzog means well."

"Does he? Sorry Sasha, but I don't have time for games. I took the risk coming here certain you would help me out. But all you offer is fairy tales and water." I glared at Bayzog. "Let me out of this crazy place." I scoured the room but saw no door.

"Calm yourself, Dragon," Bayzog demanded. "You need rest, and your fresh wounds need to be healed. Have a few hours of peace. I'll see if I can find something, and you can leave when I do."

"Let me out now, wizard!"

"You're a guest; you can leave whenever you wish. But what about your friend, Ben? Will you abandon him as well?"

I'd forgotten about Ben, but I didn't care. I just wanted out of there.

"Yes. Goodbye, Sasha. I hope you stay well."

She kissed me on the cheek and said, "Be careful."

I shot Bayzog another look, and then I closed my eyes. Remembering how this went, I thought of the front door. I opened my eyes and saw the gargoyle knocker. Behind me, the stairs. Maybe I'd been hasty. Maybe I'd been rude, but I had things to do.

I stomped down the stairs.

"I don't need your help anyway."

"Bayzog! What is wrong with you?" Sasha said. "Dragon is our friend, and he needs us."

He sighed as he took her by the hands and said, "Yes, he does need us, but we cannot help him. Only he can help himself. If he can't ... we'll all need help."

"What do you mean?"

Bayzog strolled over to his massive table and opened his book.

"I read something that I can only assume is true."

Sasha came to stand beside him, eyes intent on the pages.

"What does it say? You know I can't read it yet."

He said nothing.

"Bayzog, what does it say?" she demanded.

He cleared his throat.

"The ancient scribes say...

And the black dragons were vanquished, and peace was on Nalzambor until the black dragons returned. So it was. So it has been. A Circle. And the last black dragon shall envelop the world forever.

He closed the book and finished, "... this is much bigger than us. I feel for his father. I feel for the world."

CHAPTER
30

"**B**LASTED WIZARDS!"

I wasn't happy. I wasn't mad, but I wasn't happy. Bayzog hadn't really done anything wrong other than disappoint me. He was holding something back, something big, something bad—about me; I could feel it in my bones. So I wandered, alone on horseback, through the streets from one side of the city to the other.

"What to do?" I mumbled, drawing a few stares from passersby.

The night wasn't much different than the day in Quintuklen, just darker and quieter. I didn't care for it. I liked watching the people, but tonight, I wanted to be alone. I wanted to sulk. But I knew better. Instead, I headed for the wall, near where we came in.

"Should I go or not?" I said. I hated to leave empty-handed. I had come here to find out about the dragons, and I couldn't leave without something.

Above, the moon was full like a brilliant pearl, casting dark shadows in every corner. I had an idea. I just needed to find the Clerics of Barnabus. Like Brenwar would say, "Face the problem axe up and head on!"

The Clerics of Barnabus were the problem. Find them; find the dragons. They'd been looking; I'd been hiding. I decided to take my problem straight to them.

"If I were a cleric, where would I be?" I was gazing up at the moon when it hit me. "The Sanctuary." There were always clerics there.

It was early morning when I arrived at the bubbling fountains just outside The Sanctuary's gates. Within, monuments and statues were covered with dew, and clerics in a colorful variety of robes were milling about. The Clerics of Barnabus were easy to spot, and within seconds I spotted a few tattooed foreheads. My first urge was to gallop over there, snatch one, ride off, and beat the information out of him. But, I donned my cloak and pulled my hood over my head. Leaving my horse, I moved in.

About twenty feet away from them, I took a seat on a bench, head down and listening. There was no loud talking in The Sanctuary, but there was a lot of whispering. And much of it was in a language you couldn't understand. The Clerics had their ancient dialects in which they spoke, but I'd picked up on Barnabus words over the years, sort of. But it was Common I heard.

"We've many to sell. Small ones. Dead or alive, as you will," one Cleric of Barnabus said, speaking to a Cleric in stone-colored robes. I could feel my blood run hot. The Stone Clerics drew their power from the rock, and they weren't noble. According to them, the stone was neither good nor bad, only the one who threw it.

"I've no need of such things."

"Any word on dragons?" the Cleric of Barnabus asked. "We aim to keep the world safe from the menace. Keep them under control we must."

"You can tell those tales to the regular folk, but I know better. Most dragons are as good as you are evil. Be gone with you, I say."

"Pardons and blessings, stone wielder." The Cleric bowed and slowly backed away.

Good for him. I'd have to remember that. The Clerics of Stone were neutral, but they weren't fools. It was good to know.

The Clerics of Barnabus split up, spreading the word about dragons from one group to the other. One of them had the attention of a small group in gold lace with heads hidden under their purple hoods. I didn't recognize the order, but there must have been a hundred different ones in Quintuklen. I got up, stooped down, and picked my way through the people. It was getting crowded.

Ten feet away, back turned, I was leaning on a monument when an odd feeling overcame me. Peering around, I caught the eyes of another cleric of Barnabus who quickly glanced away. They couldn't have seen me, could they? I didn't exactly fit in, but there were all sorts of robed figures and cloaked characters in the Sanctuary. I turned away, took a moment, and glanced back. He was gone.

"We have a yellow belly, with pollen breath that turns one to stone," I overheard one cleric say. "Some of the dragon tykes that don't have breath yet, they make fine pets, when broken."

I bunched up my fist and fought the urge to walk over there and punch him in the face. I could barely stand it. *Patience. Look. Listen. Learn.* I might explode first.

"Where do we meet?" the cleric in the purple said.

"Five leagues west, in the Crane's Neck. After the sun sets tomorrow. Gold only."

"Agreed."

That's all I needed to hear. As I turned to head back to my horse, it felt like a bucket of ice water hit me when someone said, "Dragon!"

CHAPTER
31

"**D**ELICIOUS, SIMPLY DIVINE," FINNIUS SAID, wiping his mouth with a cloth napkin.

Good food was hard to come by in the Temple ruins, but the lizard men were excellent hunters, and the acolytes, when prompted, were decent cooks.

Thumping his fist on his chest, he burped as an acolyte refilled his goblet with wine.

"At least the cellar kept the bottles in order all these centuries, and it would be a shame for it all to go to waste, wouldn't it?" he said, eyeing the cage that sat on the small table.

The pixlyn woman was there: tiny, pink, knees drawn up, head down.

"Oh, you can speak to me, little faerie. As a matter of fact, I'd like to hear you sing. They say the song of the faeries is a beautiful and magical thing, but I've never heard it."

Finnius pulled the cage closer and peered in.

"What do you say?"

She didn't budge.

He slammed his fist on the table.

"SING!"

She flinched, then rubbed her tiny fists in her eyes, sniffling.

"Oh, how adorable." He tapped the cage. "Little pixlyn, sing for me, else I'll pluck your husband's wings off when he arrives."

Her bee wings buzzed as she hovered up, nodding her head.

"Oh, I have your attention now, don't I? Sing, little one. I want to feel the mystic words you hold. Sing to me," he beckoned, "share your powers… or die."

Her tiny little mouth opened up, and beautiful words flowed out. Not words men could recognize, but a beautiful, ancient language. Harmonious and delightful.

Finnius sat back and sighed, letting the music fill him from head to toe.

"Wonderful," he muttered. He'd been weary, but no more. His once-spent energies from his mission now recharged. His mind refreshed and cleared.

"Excellent," he muttered, slumping back, tears forming in his eyes. *So pure, so good, so amazing.* It was nothing like he'd felt before.

Something banged into the pixlyn cage.

Finnius lurched up, rubbing his watery eyes.

"What?"

The male pixlyn was back.

Finnius shook his head, saying, "What is the meaning of this, pixlyn?"

The little man's tiny mouth was a buzz of words.

"I see. Hmm... Excellent, I see. Nath Dragon is on his way already." He clapped his hands together. "My, won't the High Priestess be pleased. Tell me. Tell me about it all."

Finnius muttered a spell and sprinkled powder over the pixlyn.

The words of the pixlyn were high and garbled momentarily, and then a sound of man came forth.

"It took me no time to find the man. I told your men who he was and where to go. Your men spread word as I watched. The man overheard the conversation about the dragons. Your men spoke to your men in disguise. The man you want believed it. He and they travel this way now."

"Hah!" He slapped his knee. "Keep me posted then, pixlyn! Go! Spy!"

The tiny winged man flew into his face and said, "My mate?"

"Yes, well, she'll be quite all right," Finnius flashed a wicked smile, "assuming she keeps her wings, assuming you do as you are told and I don't have to clip her wings. Now go!"

CHAPTER
32

BRENWAR'S STOMACH GROWLED. HE COULDN'T remember the last time he was so hungry. His horse bent its neck toward the stream and began to drink. His stomach growled again.

"Ah, be quiet, will you?" he said, reaching into his pack and withdrawing peppers and bread. He took a bite. "That might hold you, until we find Dragon, that is."

He hadn't eaten since he left, or slept either. He rubbed his mount's neck, watching the trout swimming upstream. He'd like to fish, but he didn't have time.

"It's a shame you horses don't eat fish," he said. "You don't know what you're missing."

The horse nickered, raising its neck. Brenwar got a sour apple from his saddlebag and fed the horse. At some point, the horse would need rest, he knew. And stopping in the next village might be in order.

"I hate stopping," he grumbled.

"Me too," a deep voice responded from the nearby trees.

Brenwar jumped from his horse and rolled over the ground, rising with his war hammer ready.

"Who said that?"

The woods were tall, green, and quiet. Only the wind and rippling waters hit his ears.

"Easy, dwarf," a tall figure said, stepping from behind the trees. "Remember me?"

Brenwar squinted his eyes beneath his bushy black brows.

"Bah! You're one of those fat-bellied elves."

"And you're one of those short-legged orcs," the Wilder Elf replied.

"I see you've got a death wish, don't ya?" Brenwar said, pointing his weapon. "Come, then, I'll make a fine grave for you!"

Eyes twinkling in the light, Shum laughed like a man laughs at a child. With the grace of the elves and girth of a large man, he approached, swords silent on his hips. He clasped his hands over his belly and said, "I mean you no harm, dwarf."

"That may well be, but I can't say the same."

Brenwar moved in, taking a chop at Shum of the Roaming Rangers' legs.

The elf sprang away.

"Stop!" Shum held out his arms. "I'm not here to fight, as much as I'd like to teach you a lesson."

"A lesson!" Brenwar rushed.

Shum jumped back, Brenwar's axe clipping his cloak.

Brenwar would fight anyone, anyplace, anytime. Especially an elf. They bothered him. Not so much as orcs and giants, but still, they were elves. Dwarves and elves: both on the side of good, but unable to get along since the days their races were young.

"You would strike me down when I'm not even defending myself," Shum said, aghast.

Brenwar swung.

Shum dove.

"I would."

He chopped.

Shum rolled.

Brenwar kept coming, swinging, chopping.

Shum was off balance as he waded into the waters.

"Stop it, dwarf! I apologize," he said, holding his arms out.

Brenwar swung his war axe into water-laden log where Shum's toe had been.

"For what?"

"Calling you a short-legged orc."

Brenwar stopped and pointed at him.

"No one calls a dwarf an orc and lives."

"Well, you shouldn't call me a fat-bellied elf."

Brenwar's black eyebrows cocked over his eyes.

"But you *are* a fat-bellied elf."

Shum huffed, dragging himself out of the water, towering over Brenwar, and replied, "And proud of it." He extended his arm. "Can you talk, Brenwar?"

They bumped forearms, outside, then inside.

"Aye," Brenwar said, "what is it you want?"

"Nath Dragon."

Brenwar walked over to his horse and fed it another apple.

"Why?"

Shum's jaw tightened.

"I think we need his help finding our king again."

Brenwar pulled himself up onto his horse.

"I don't know where he is."

"But you're looking for him; I know. I've been following you since you left Morgdon. I was waiting for him, but he never came, only you. I've been trying to figure out what was going on, but I didn't realize you'd lost him until now."

Brenwar stiffened in his saddle, saying, "What do you mean, days? I got attacked by brigands, and you didn't help!"

"And you handled them quite well. I respect your skills, Brenwar, and I'd have aided if needed."

"Humph! What makes you think Dragon can help you find your king? You're the best trackers in the land, aren't you? Why would you need Nath?"

Shum ran his long finger back and forth on his chin and said, "It's just a theory, really, but we think they are linked. They have the same needs."

"Pah," Brenwar started leading his horse away. "They aren't linked. He's an elf or an ape, and Dragon is a man, or a dragon. He shall tend to his affairs, the dragons; you attend to yours, the elves or... er the apes."

"We're all linked whether we admit it or not. Dragon has a curse. My king is cursed. It's a common evil they share."

"It's your king, not mine, not his. And, Nath is not evil, and I can't say the same for your king." Brenwar waved as he galloped off. "Goodbye, fat-bellied elf!"

Shum shook his head, watching him go as he said, "I can walk faster than that little horse can run." He took off at a trot. "You're getting my help whether you want it or not, dwarf. Too many lives depend on it."

CHAPTER
33

"**D**RAGON!"

I whirled, knocking a man over. It was Ben. Despite the bewildered look on his face, I could have killed him.

"What are you doing here?" I exclaimed under my breath, lifting him up and with haste guiding him away.

"Bayzog—"

"Keep it down, you idiot," I hissed through my teeth.

Every eye in the sanctuary was looking.

"Sorry, Drag—"

I squeezed his arm.

"Quiet, will you?"

"Ow," he whined as I dragged him to where my horse was as discreetly as I could.

His horse was next to mine.

"How did you do that?" I said, grabbing the reins and getting out of The Sanctuary.

"Bayzog did it, how I don't know. I was talking to him, and he said you'd be here, and I said, 'Where?' and poof, here I was. He said you needed to come back, that he had some information for you that could help." He rubbed the back of his head. "Sorry, Dragon, did I do wrong again?"

"Get on your horse," I ordered.

I was angry. If Ben had shown up seconds earlier, it could have ruined everything, and I wasn't so sure it hadn't. When I glanced back, all the bald heads and purple robes were gone.

"Great."

I led; Ben followed.

"Are we going back to Bayzog's?"

"No."

"He said you'd say that, but he also said, um…" he looked up into the sky, "It's your burial, not mine."

"Figures." *Lousy wizard!* "Listen, Ben, you didn't do wrong, but you aren't coming along, either. I'm taking you to the Legionnaires to be with your uncle."

Ben shook his head.

"No! I don't want to go. Please, I want to stay with you! I'm ready, see?" He pulled his cloak open, revealing a well-fitted tunic of leather armor. A nice sword and dagger were belted at his sides. I could tell by the pommels they were elven made. He even had boots to go with it.

"So, you think if you get some armor that fits and sharp and shiny blades, that makes you a soldier? You haven't even had any training, Ben. You almost died once on the way up here, and now I'm heading into the mouth of danger. You think you're ready for that? Do you?"

Biting his lip, he fingered the pommel on his sword.

"We'll just go back and see what Bayzog says. It was important."

"No, Ben. I'm on my own from here. Now don't follow me anymore."

Good luck or bad luck Ben was, according to Bayzog. The part-elven wizard had a way of reading people.

"Bayzog said I should come, no matter what."

I stopped my mount.

"Really, Ben, how well do you know Bayzog? You barely spent a minute with him in there."

"Well, it's not him so much as," he smiled, "Sasha. Ooh … She is so beautiful."

"And troublesome, Ben." I got closer and checked his blades. "Fine steel for a wizard to keep. What else did they give you?" I reached into his belt pouch. Two potion vials were within. "What do these do?"

"He said I'd know when to take them."

I slapped Ben upside the head.

"Ow!"

"You don't know when to do anything!"

I'd had enough and headed for the wall. It was time to make way for the Crane's Neck, and I didn't care whether or not Ben followed.

"So be it, Ben. It's only your life."

The trip was long. Not because it was far, but because my tongue was tired from trying to convince Ben not to go. He wouldn't have any part of it, however.

"It's my life; I'll do what I want with it," he'd decided, saying it over and over, with his chin up.

Oddly, he was starting to remind me of Brenwar—aside from his shivering in the rain.

The Crane's Neck wasn't hard to find. It was a valley of enormous rocks, some of which looked to be left over from a battle between the giants. I followed a faint trail over the brush and climbed up a rocky cleft that overlooked the Crane's Neck. It was a rock, stretching fifty feet in height, shaped like a long, flowing neck. The setting sun peeked from behind the dark clouds, shining on the beak-like peak at the top.

"Lie down. Be quiet. Don't move." I said to Ben, lying down myself.

Ben did. I actually wanted to thank him. It wasn't very often that he did what I said.

"It'll be a few hours before dusk, so we'll just lie low for now. Got anything to eat?"

Ben shook his head.

"Great. I'm surprised Bayzog didn't prepare you better. Are you sure one of those vials isn't a bottle of Tasty Wonders?"

He scrunched up his face, shook his head and said, "I don't think so."

"Well, that's too bad. Those are pretty good, and they can hold you over for days. Stupid wizard. You'd think he'd have better prepared you." I looked at him. "Right?"

He nodded, his eyes focused on the Crane's Neck, lying on his belly sopping wet. The rain would start and stop, between drizzle and heavy drops. He shivered even though it wasn't that cold. At least he was quiet. At least he had obeyed for once, and that was a comforting thought.

Rain pelting my face, I lay alongside him thinking. How many dragons did the clerics have? They'd spoken of at least three, but there could be more. I rubbed my dragon arm, imagining if my scales might turn white after I freed them. I could go home then. I wanted to see my father more now than ever, and I couldn't remember ever wanting to see his giant dragon's head so much before. I pulled my hood over my head, hunkered down, and waited.

A few paths led past the Crane's Neck, some narrow and some wide, between the rocks and ridges. There wasn't much else in the valley, either, just a small variety of trees and bushes, enough to be hospitable to the critters. Another hour had passed when I heard Ben's stomach growl.

"Still glad you came?"

He didn't say anything.

It was getting annoying.

"All right, Ben, you've made your point: you can be quiet."

He rolled over and smiled, saying, "See, I told you I could be a good soldier."

"Indeed," I said, rolling my eyes. "Well, there's no sense in having your ravenous stomach give us away. It could wake up a drunk bugbear. Run down to the horses and fetch the rations hanging from my saddle."

He quickly ambled over the rocks, down and out of sight. I had to admit: I was hungry, too. I rubbed my ribs. Tormac had given me a good walloping, and my jaw still felt loose. It was a shame; he'd be a good ally if he wasn't such a bad man. The world was full of men like him, but there was always something worse. The orcs. The ogres. The goblins. The bugbears and gnolls. You'd think men would act better than them, but often—too many times—they disappointed me. Their short lives made them particularly greedy.

Ben shuffled back over the rocks and fell to his knees.

"Here you go, Dragon," he said, holding out a small sack.

"Eat, Ben."

He reached into the bag and dug in. I grabbed a bite as well.

Ben shook a canteen in my face.

I took it and drank, handed it back, and said, "Drink, that dwarven bread is hard to get down sometimes."

"Kind of bitter," he said, talking a swallow. "But I feel full already."

"Brenwar would kill me if he knew what I was doing."

"Who?" Ben said, looking up at me.

"Oh, sorry, Ben, just a friend of mine, a dwarf. He's usually with me on days like this, telling me what I can and cannot do. Or what I should or should not do."

"Kind of like you do me, huh?"

I felt like I'd swallowed a bug. I was nothing like Brenwar.

"Just eat."

Down in the valley, about an hour later, I noticed a small group of figures coming from behind the Crane's Nest.

"Get down, Ben!"

From our bellies, we could see the Clerics of Barnabus, five of them in all, and a small cage. I had a pretty good idea what was in that cage, too. A dragon. Two broader figures emerged with spears and armor. Lizard men. I could feel Ben tense up at my side.

"It'll be all right. Don't move, Ben. Don't make a sound."

The five Clerics faced the path leading from the east. The lizard men began searching the nooks and crevices in the area. The rain became a steady pour, and I lost sight of the lizard men.

"Not good, Ben. Not good."

CHAPTER 34

INSTINCT. SOMETIMES IT WAS THE only explanation for why some men lived while others died. My own had bailed me out many times, but I wasn't sure about Ben as he kept looking over at me. It takes time to develop instincts in some; in others it's quite natural. Some don't get it at all.

Keeping my voice low, I said, "What are you thinking?"

"There's probably more of them, isn't there?"

"Good." I was reassured. He wasn't stupid; he had some savvy to him. "Maybe a couple. Just keep an eye out."

I rose up to my knee and readied Akron.

Snap. Clatch. Snap.

"You going to shoot them?" Ben asked.

"Hopefully at some point in time, but right now I'm just being prepared."

"Oh."

I wasn't really sure why I readied my bow. I just did. Something bothered me. Tired, swollen, and stubborn, I felt a little off, and there was a nagging warning bell behind my eyes. Peering through the rain, I looked for any sign, anything odd.

"Can they smell us?" Ben asked.

It was a good question. *Good for him.*

"They're pretty good trackers, but not like most hunters, and their snouts are so-so. It's the orcs you have to watch out for. But this rain keeps our scent down, plus we're downwind. So I'd say we're safe for now."

The farther the sun dipped, the colder it seemed as we waited. The lizard men reappeared about an hour later and gathered near the clerics.

"Dragon, I see something coming," Ben pointed.

I could barely make out the purple through all the rain, but it was the clerics from Quintuklen, riding on horseback.

My heart raced as they greeted one another and revealed the covered cage.

"What is it?" Ben asked.

Despite the heavy rain, I could make out a small, white dragon inside. Not just any white dragon, but a long-tailed white. They weren't very big dragons, either, but one of the smaller breeds.

"A dragon. A powerful one at that."

Below, I could see no coins were exchanged, and the talk had stopped. The Clerics of Barnabus led, and the Clerics from Quintuklen followed.

"Are we going to rescue it?"

"Don't you worry about that," I said, grabbing his shoulders. "Now listen to me, Ben, and listen good."

He was all ears.

"Stay with the horses. There's plenty of food with them. If I'm not back in two days, go back to Quintuklen and see Bayzog and Sasha. Just tell them what you know, not that it will matter."

"But I want to go."

I squeezed his shoulders until he grimaced.

"I'm counting on you. We can't follow those men on the horses. They'll catch us. We can't leave the horses, now, either, can we?"

He shook his head, eyes down, saying, "No."

"What you are doing might not seem important, Ben, but it is. It is to me and to the horses. This is what a good soldier does."

He frowned, saying, "But Bayzog gave me these weapons, and potions too." He unsheathed his dagger and stuck it in my face. "See?"

In a single motion, I twisted it away and jammed it back in his sheath.

"Yes, Ben. Perfect weapons and potions to protect yourself and the horses with." I slapped him on the shoulder. "Remember what I said, and take care, Ben."

As he started to object, I turned and leapt off the ridge, hopping down from one boulder to the other like a mountain cat. When I made it to the bottom, I looked up and waved.

He was gaping.

"Sorry Ben, I can't have you following me, now can I?"

Off into the rain I went. I had monsters to stop and dragons to save.

The sun had set by the time I traveled the first league, and the trail was already faint. Ahead, I could see one lizard man had drifted back, waiting. It was a common tactic.

The lizard men made good guards and soldiers, ferocious soldiers, but not as loyal as hounds. They were known to take bribes now and again. No, the lizard men were the orcs of reptiles, a blasphemous creation and insult to dragonkind in my opinion.

I crouched into the bushes, waiting. "Come on," I said to myself, "get going, will you?"

He stood like a statue alongside the path, a dark statue. Five minutes passed, then ten, then twenty.

I heard him chew on something, swallow, spit, then begin to tread up the path. *Finally!*

I had followed him another league when he stopped and waited again. Ahead, I could see a series of hills forming into the perfect place to hide in. "There are always secrets in the hills," the seers said. I hunkered down. *What to do?*

The lizard man was making sure no one followed. But how did I know he was following them and not leading me somewhere else? With the time all his breaks took, they could have gone anywhere by now. The heavy rain would easily wash away their tracks.

"Drat!" I cursed under my breath.

Maybe they knew I was onto them already.

Frustrated, I ambled down the path.

Twenty paces away, the lizard man stepped full into the path, spear lowered.

I unleashed Akron's arrow into his scaly green thigh.

Thwack!

The lizard man pitched forward, hitting the ground with a painful hiss.

Lizard men don't scream, but they hiss something awful when you shoot them in the leg.

It took a stab at me as I walked over. I sidestepped, then ripped the spear from its hand and broke that over its head.

"I can't have you following me, now, can I?"

I slugged it in the jaw, and its eyes rolled up in its head.

"I hope they weren't expecting you. You'll be awfully late with that arrow in your leg," I said. *Got to move, Dragon.* I didn't have much patience left, and the disturbing thought of caged dragons infuriated me. I hooked Akron on my back and jogged up the path. *It shouldn't be that hard to catch up with a bunch of clerics, even if they do know the terrain better than I do.* An hour later, I stopped and kneeled down. I ran my fingers over some muddy footprints in the path. *Excellent!* Through the slop, I forged ahead.

Two more leagues I had followed the trail when the rain let up. The bright stars peeked over the trees, and the waters rushed over the hillside while I heard the sound of people shuffling up ahead. I crept up until I could see them. It was them, a small band of clerics accompanied by one lizard man that guarded the rear.

The path wound up the hill, through the trees, and alongside a gulch. That's when I got my first look at it. A temple jutted out in stark contrast to the woods. The exterior wall was overgrown in vines and withered with decay, and many of the stone columns behind it had fallen. The party of men filed through a gap in the wall and disappeared from sight. The lizard man hung back at the gate. I remained behind the trees.

Great.

The temple wall, or what was left of it, was a hundred feet long and fifteen feet high. It ran from hillside to hillside. On the wall, a few lizard men stood watch, and for all I knew, the place was full of them. Now, I could handle a few lizard men, but ten or twenty? That would be something.

What to do, Dragon? What to do? Sneak inside, or bust them all in the face?

I unhitched Akron.

Snap. Clatch. Snap.

The string coiled into place.

Clerics. Lizard men, whoever else. No one was going anywhere until I freed those dragons. I had them trapped.

I whipped out an arrow and rubbed spit on its tip. It twinkled with life. My dragon heart began to thunder inside my chest. I knew the dragons were in there, but not for long. The time to fight had come.

"Show evil no mercy," I said through gritted teeth.

I took a deep breath, nocked the arrow, pulled back, aimed, and let it fly.

CHAPTER
35

THE ARROW SAILED TRUE TO its mark, smacking into the temple.

KA-BOOM!

My blood coursed through my veins with new energy. Explosive action. That's what I liked. The lizard men on top went flying into the air with a shower of rock before crashing to the ground. I don't know if that killed them, but it wouldn't hurt my feelings if it did.

The lizard man at the gate stood gaping at the hole in the temple wall, waiting, uncertain.

Still hidden from sight, I nocked another arrow, waiting. *One. Two. Three...*

Lizard men poured from the gate, and even more of the reptilian heads popped up over the wall again. *I knew it!* I let another arrow fly. It juttered at the feet of the lizard man at the gate, drawing grunts and cries. I stepped into the clear and waved at them as they raised their weapons at me.

"Wait for it, snake face!" I yelled.

KA-BOOM!

A half dozen lizard men filled the sky with green.

A crossbow bolt zinged past my head. Nocking another arrow, I charged the gate. Three reptilian faces peeked over the wall, crossbows pointed at my chest. The crossbows rocked into action as I tried to dodge. A bolt skipped off my chest plate as I let the other arrow fly.

KA-BOOM!

Shards of rock flew everywhere. The top of the wall where the lizard men stood was a smoking ruin as I scrambled over the rubble and through the smoky hole. I heard the lizard men hissing and moaning nearby. I put a normal arrow in my teeth and loaded another in my bow. I aimed through the dust and smoke.

Twang!

I caught one in the thigh.

Twang!

Another in the shoulder.

Their loud hisses caused another alarm. I let my other senses guide me through the ruins and dust as another throng of lizard men came on. I didn't care.

Twang! Twang! Twang! Twang! Twang!

I had plenty of arrows.

Twang! Twang! Twang!

Hisses and smoke were all I heard, and the lizard men weren't going anywhere without severe limps.

Locating one, I kicked the crossbow out of its hands, wrapped my dragon arm around its neck, and squeezed.

"Where are the dragons?"

Lizard men could speak; they just didn't speak much.

It shook its head, hissing.

I cranked up the pressure.

"Where are the dragons?"

It pointed its scaly finger as it choked out the word, "There."

Two columns led the way from the courtyard into a narrow tunnel.

"How many more?" I demanded.

"Many clerics. No more lizard—" it started as a shadow fell over me.

I jerked away.

Clonk!

Something clipped the back of my head, drawing spots in my eyes. It was a lizard man, a big one with brawny arms and shoulders. It reminded me of Tormac, but with scales and not as ugly.

It swung its club into my shoulder, almost breaking my arm, as I dove to the ground.

I rolled onto my back, pushed off, and landed on my feet, ripping Fang from his sheath.

Shing!

The bullish lizard man charged, club high, swinging down.

Fang sheared its club in two.

The slits inside the lizard man's skull widened as it stared at what was left of its club. Shielding its eyes from Fang's glow, it backed away.

"Run," I said. "Or die," I warned. "It matters not to me."

Tongue flicking from its mouth, it eyed me and my sword.

Poised to strike, I took another step forward.

It turned, ran toward the gate, and was gone, leaving me alone with a bunch of groaning lizards.

It took everything I had not to kill that big lizard man, and if he had attacked, I'm not so sure I could have held back. I'd had enough of clerics, lizard men, dragon poachers, orcs … the whole lot of them.

"You should follow your comrade if you know what's good for you," I said as I headed for the entrance, waggling my sword under the nose of one lizard man as I passed. "You better not be here when I come back, or I'll slice every bit of lizard from your skin."

Hissing and crawling, they slowly made their way toward what was left of the entrance.

"Good."

Still, my anger rose as I made my way inside the tunnel. I told myself it was the heat of battle, but I loved to battle. I just had to exercise control.

"Just free the dragons, Nath," I said to myself. 'Knock all the clerics out if you have to."

Into the darkness I went, following a stone corridor in which no torches were lit. My keen eyes could barely make out the faint lines of the corridor I traveled, but I could smell them. The men, the sweat, the evil, and something else.

"Hmmm... Be ready, Fang," I whispered.

His razor-sharp edge hummed in reply, flaring once then winking out.

The air was still: quiet, like a tomb of the dead. Using caution, I planted one foot after the other until I found myself at a crossroads. Three tunnels opened like mouths. There was no telling how far this temple went back into the mountain.

"What do you think, Fang?"

The cold steel didn't sing.

"Thanks." Peering down the middle tunnel, I inhaled. Decay, men, incense, and dragons. If I got close enough, I could smell their blood. "A little light would be nice. Besides, I'm sure they know I'm coming—unless of course they are deaf acolytes."

Fang's hum added a soft white light.

"Thanks," I said, making my way down the middle tunnel. That's what Brenwar would have done, I figured. "Take the direct approach," I said in my best Brenwar voice.

Ancient markings—carvings and paintings long worn and faded—lined the walls. It was hard to tell what race of people had lived here so long ago because it was another ancient language I did not recognize. A door greeted me at the end, or at least what was left of one. I heard something on the other side and pressed my ear along the door. Beautiful humming or singing grabbed me by the ears and pulled me through.

It was wonderful, sweet, and melodious as a waterfall of honey, removing all the anger and pain from my body. Fearless and carefree, I went forward, a smile stretching across my face, ignoring Fang throbbing in my hand.

"It's all right, friend," I said, sliding him into his sheath.

Drunk with elation, I hummed and twirled my way down the ancient corridor, its pictures and traces now colorful, vibrant, and real. I hadn't felt this way in years. I laughed, a hundred laughs in one, following the music.

"Oh, dragons," I half sang, half said, "Where are you, little dragons? Come and play with your brother. You cannot hide from me."

The warm glow of a fire was in the distance and my compulsion drove me onward. Up there must be the most wonderful place in all of Nalzambor. *The dragons,* I thought as I drifted forward, *they aren't prisoners at all, but instead the luckiest dragons in the world.* And somewhere they were being sung to by the most beautiful woman in the world. I couldn't wait to see her as I passed from one room to the other. There she was, simply captivating.

"My, you are so beautiful."

CHAPTER
36

SHE WAS EVERYTHING I IMAGINED. The kind of woman so magnificent that the entire room lights up in her glory. And it did. Fires burned with vibrant life, and many robed men sang praises to her along the walls. Every face was happy, joyous, elated, and my heart cried out in my chest as I longed to be with her. To hold her. To kiss her. To love her like no other.

"Who are you?" I said, stretching out my hands.

Her face was gorgeous: part human, part elf, part dragon, a combination of all the most beautiful faces I'd ever seen.

"Relax, Nath Dragon. Sing." She poured me a goblet of wine. "Drink. You look thirsty."

I took it as her hands caressed my face, and she unbuckled my sword belt and tossed it aside. I didn't even notice the singing acolyte lifting my quiver and bow from my shoulder. No, I was too infatuated with her dark gossamer robes blended in with her lustrous hair and how her toes did not show as she floated over.

"We've been expecting you," she said, draping her long, sensuous arm over my shoulder. "Come, sit, rest." She led me toward a magnificent chair and sat me down. "Comfortable?"

My tongue clove to the roof of my mouth, and my mind swirled. I wanted to be with her so bad. I'd do anything she said. But why, the recesses of my mind asked, did she smell so bad? I had to ask.

"You are so amazing, but why do you smell... er... smell so funny?"

Her beautiful face suddenly turned dark as the music stopped.

I shook my head saying, "What's happening?"

Whop!

A fist made of dragon scales lashed out, striking me in the chest. She howled in triumph, her face contorting with rage as she struck again.

Whop!

My neck snapped back, slamming me into the chair.

"What in Nalzambor are you?" I said, holding my busted face.

She growled. Part animal. Part something else.

All the colorful images began to fade, the beauty of the ancient sanctuary melting away, leaving only the fires (which were just torches) and the clerics (some bald as eagles, the others draped like purple curtains).

Behind me, the chair came to life, arms as strong as iron wrapping around me, crushing me.

My dream had become a nightmare, and it was just beginning.

The woman changed as well, her lustrous face and figure drifting like smoke and forming something else. A horrible, hulking abomination loomed over me, almost seven feet of meat, muscles, and bone. It was built like a man and armored, with a face like a dragon and scales, too.

It curled up its clawed hand as big as my face, drew back, and punched me again.

I groaned in pain. I'd thought it was over with the lizard men.

A human voice cackled as whatever it was that held me slammed me into the ground. I couldn't move. I couldn't breathe. I could feel, though. I felt like a pane of glass catching a giant stone.

"Ugh..."

"Welcome to your party, Nath Dragon. I hope you like your surprise," said a robed man with a slight limp in his step.

I looked up, face bleeding, getting a glimpse of the source of the familiar voice through my swelling eye.

"You, I know you," I managed. It was the Cleric from Narnum, the one who had ratted out the Orcen Hold, where the blazed ruffie was freed. The one I saw the day before my arm turned black. I tried to smile. "Tell you what: if you let the dragons free, I'll go easy on you. It won't be nearly as easy walking with two limps instead of one."

Finnius nodded at his dragonian goons.

One kicked me in the ribs, then the other wrapped his monstrous arm around my neck.

"Easy, draykis, we need something left of him before dinner." Finnius squatted down beside me. "Tsk. Tsk. Catching you was so much easier than I'd thought it would be, Nath Dragon. Look around. The best plan is a well-executed one. See?" He motioned to the clerics in purple behind him. They pulled back their hoods, revealing the same bald heads with tattooed signs that I had seen in the garden.

I felt like a fool. They'd known I was coming all along. *Ben!*

"Oh, what is wrong, Nath?"

"It's Lord Dragon to you," I said, shifting his focus. Maybe he didn't know about Ben.

He shoved my face into the dirty floor, saying, "Fool!"

"Don't touch my hair, you little worm," I warned. "Ow!" I felt a dragon claw poking into my leg. "What are these things... uh... what is your lowly name anyway? Ow!"

He rose, wrapping his hands behind his back, and said, "Finnius. Hah. And even you should know that it only takes a little worm to catch a big fish. A big bald fish once this day is over." Some of the acolytes chuckled as he paced the sanctuary. "Perhaps some of the draykis would be more appealing with some of your locks attached. Or maybe I can fetch a fine price for your hair in the cities."

"It would certainly do wonders for that bald head of yours, but these," I stared over my shoulder, "draykis are well past ugly. I don't think hair would help. What in Nalzambor are they?"

"Men fused with dragon skin, dragon blood, and magic," he said, stepping on my dragon hand. "A glimpse into your future." Looking at my hand under his boot, he went on. "My, what have we here? It seems there is part draykis in you. This is a fortunate day for you indeed, the day you get to see what you are about to become. Dragon? Draykis? Or one and the same."

My stomach knotted. What he said didn't so much anger me as worry me. But there was a ring of truth to it. I was a man with dragon blood and magic, and there was no telling what I might become.

"So, Finnius the Worm, now that you have me, what is in store for me? Death? Collect a bounty? Sell me off with the other dragons?"

"Oh, Nath, as much as the Clerics of Barnabus despise you and your heroic doings, we have no intention of killing you. You see, I follow orders whether I like them or not. It's why I have this limp." He tapped his thigh. "These signs." He fingered the patterns on his head. "And more to command. More power. Why, I even control these powerful draykis." He grabbed a torch off the wall and held it to the standing draykis's mouth. "Eat."

The draykis snatched the torch from his hand and stuffed it inside its mouth, chomping it to splinters and swallowing it whole. It burped a puff of smoke.

"Charming." I struggled to get out. "Show me some more tricks. Can it eat worms, too?"

Finnius bent over, picked up my sword belt and scabbard, and handed it to one of the acolytes. He tossed another one my bow and quiver.

"Take these away," he said.

The bald men disappeared through the door that I had come in.

Finnius clapped his hands together. "Now the festivities shall begin."

"You mean ole torch eater has more tricks?"

A wry smile formed on Finnius's face, sending a chill down through my bones.

"I'm not supposed to kill you, Nath Dragon, but the High Priestess didn't tell me how alive she needed you, either."

Finnius almost pinched his fingers together when he said, "Almost dead will do." He waved his arms over his head. "Algorzalahn!"

Finnius disappeared in a puff of smoke, leaving me sealed in the room with the draykis.

"This is going to hurt, Nath Dragon," one said, tugging on my hair.

CHAPTER
37

T HE ONE DRAYKIS, OR WHATEVER type of evil it was called, released me as the
other watched me rise to my feet.

"So, are you monsters going to teach me a lesson?" I said, woozy.

Both were taller than me, framed like big men, coated in assorted dragon scales.
One smiled, showing an extra row of teeth, as it continued to smack its man's fist
into its hand. The other wasn't much different, aside from two horns, and both wore
a mishmash of metal armor. I couldn't imagine what they needed that for. Their eyes
were bright yellow dots of evil that glowered at me as if I was their last meal.

"Aren't you going to introduce yourselves?"

Circling me, both creatures howled and gnashed their teeth, their bare arms
grasping the air.

One said, "Pain."

The other said, "Destruction."

"You," one said in a growl as it waved me forward, "come fight. Come."

"So many words you know; good for you. I imagine that's no small chore with
all those rotten teeth in your mouth." I stepped up, squared up, and raised my fists
as it approached.

It chuckled.

"Have it your way, then," I said, jabbing my hand into its rock-hard chin.

I danced back, shaking my human hand. Now my hand would be as swollen as
my face.

Use your other arm, idiot! Sultans of Sulfur!

I ducked under one blow and sidestepped another. It was fast, but I was faster. I
launched my dragon fist into its face, rocking its head back with a smack.

It staggered back, hissing and shaking its head, eyes narrowing.

"Rooooar!"

The other came, hard and fast, almost bowling me over as I leapt over the top
of it.

"You're fast for such a big and ugly thing. I'm impressed, but I can do this all day."

No, I couldn't do it all day. My body felt like it had been shot out of a catapult, and my strength was fading.

Roaring, they both charged again. I swept the legs out from under one and kicked the other in the gut, doubling it over. Shrugging off my blows, they snarled.

Great! Every monster, no matter how big or strong, has a weak spot. I just had to find it before they found mine—which was probably any place on my body right then.

I caught the charging draykis by its horn, swung onto its back, and slugged it in the ear. It shook its head like an angry bull. Like a gorilla, the other one pounced on my back and dragged me to the ground. I rammed my knee into its ribs. I drove my boot heel into its crotch. Nothing. And that move almost always worked.

"Sultans of Sulfur! What are you things made of?!"

The draykis tore into me, claws tearing into my legs and arms, shredding my clothes until I could see my blood dripping on the stone floor. Quicker, I wrestled out from underneath it and made a dash for the wall. Chest heaving, I stuck my arm out and said, "A moment... *gasp*... Please."

Dragons are fast, and these dragon abominations were fast as well. I could outsmart them or out-quick them, but I didn't have anywhere to go. It was like two big cats chasing a bird in a cage. Scanning the room, I saw no other doors or windows. Just columns, stone benches, and ancient symbols. *Drat!* I needed another plan. Fast.

Find a weakness. Save the dragons!

Catching my breath, I stepped out from behind the column. The two monsters stood tall, mouths snapping, claws bared, dripping my blood. They were fiends. Men turned into monsters against their wills. Like me. My arm, I saw, wasn't so much different than theirs. But mine was perfect: black and shiny, a glorious work of art. Their scales were drab. They, unlike me, were monsters. Stone-cold killers. Heartless and cruel. I hated evil! A cauldron erupted inside me. A flood of energy came as I charged.

I struck like a viper—*pow!*—driving my fist into the nearest draykis's jaw. It wobbled on its knees.

"I AM!"

I ducked under the other's fist and shoved my elbow into its ribs. *Crack!*

"NOT!"

Like a tornado, I hit them with everything I could.

Whap! Whap! Whap! Pow! Pow! Pow! Boom!

"A DEMON!"

One fell face first to the mosaic floor.

"A FIEND!"

I hoisted the other one over my head and slammed it through a stone bench.

"OR A MONSTER LIKE YOU!"

Neither draykis moved while I fell to my knees, clutching my sides, shaking. *I did it. I defeated them, but now what?* I was still trapped.

"Impossible!" Somewhere, Finnius raged, his voice echoing throughout the chamber.

I brushed my hair from my eyes and spit the taste of blood and dirt from my mouth.

"Where are you, worm?"

Stone scraped against stone somewhere as a secret passage opened.

"Come, Nath Dragon. You've earned the right to live," Finnius said from somewhere beyond, "but I'm not sure about your friend."

I dashed into the tunnel as I heard the voice of a man, screaming.

"Ben!"

CHAPTER
38

INSIDE HIS CAGE, THE MALE pixlyn fought against the bars. His mate sang encouraging words that filled him with power. With his straining, the bars began to bend. Exhausted, the pixlyn squeezed free. He flew over and grabbed a ring of keys that hung from a peg on the wall. Seconds later, he unlocked his mate's cage, and they were free. Tossing the keys on the floor, neither looked back, and they were gone. From a lone cage in the corner, a little white dragon saw it all.

The temple was a series of catacombs that wound from one room or corridor to the next. I passed shelves, tombs, and altars but nothing undead. In pain, I trudged forward as fast as I could, worried, exhausted.

"Nath!" a voice cried from out of nowhere. Stopping, I turned and saw a familiar face in an ancient mirror bigger than me. It was Ben, bleeding and beaten. "Help me, Nath!"

All my hairs stood up on end as the haunting voice faded and the image disappeared.

I stood staring at the mirror and gawped at myself. I'd never looked so bad before. My face was swollen, my nose broken, and my ribs felt like scattered pieces from a dwarven puzzle. "Ben," I muttered, touching the glass. I had to save him. I had to find him fast.

I turned my back to the mirror and yelled.

"Enough, Finnius Worm, show yourself!"

Nothing.

I decided to renew my search, and I was heading toward another tunnel when I heard Finnius say, "So close yet so far, fool."

Now Finnius's image was inside the large oval mirror, taunting me, mocking me.

"You'll never find your friend in time, but I thank you. He'll make a fine meal for the draykis. Even monsters get hungry."

Finnius's words went straight through me.

"Noooooo!"

I charged across the chamber in two leaps, lowering my shoulder as I crashed through the mirror.

Glass shattered as I passed from one side to the other and kept going. Fear assailed me. I spiraled downward, free falling through the darkness before hitting the hard ground with a thud. I could have sworn I had broken every bone in my body when I tried to rise to my feet.

"Welcome, Nath Dragon. How fine of you it was to join us."

Finnius stood on the other side of thick metal bars, gloating.

"My, I never imagined you would have fallen for that one. You actually ran through the mirror and fell into the pit. It's one of the stupidest things I've ever seen. And coming from you, Nath Dragon, one of the greatest warriors of all. Tsk. Tsk. I can't begin to express how disappointed and elated I am." He drummed his chin with his fingers. "Then again, maybe I'm just, oh, I almost hate to say it... Brilliant!"

My prison was solid steel, corroded, but solid nonetheless. High above me, a trap door was being pulled up and into place. I wasn't going anywhere, not without help.

"Where's Ben?"

"Oh, the young man whom you have doomed? Why, he's over there, dying," Finnius said, pointing.

I felt my heart stop in my chest. Ben spun in midair, surrounded by acolytes muttering a spell. Ben's eyes were watery with terror as his unmoving lips seemed to cry out for me. We locked eyes, but he couldn't even blink.

"What are you doing to him, Finnius?" I shouted through the bars.

Finnius lifted his finger and said, "Ah, well, you are going to like this, really. You see, when the High Priestess arrives, she is going to teach me how to create a draykis. You see, Nath, all we have to do is add dragon parts." He pointed farther back in the room. "And dragon blood."

I could see several cages with coiled dragons inside. One was a yellow streak, the other two evergreens inside eerily glowing cages.

"That's not going to happen, worm. I'll see to that."

Finnius let out a creepy, bubbly laugh as he walked over and grabbed my sword from one of his acolytes.

"I wouldn't draw that blade if I were you."

"What is the matter, Dragon? Are you afraid I'll kill you with it?"

"It doesn't like evil," I said, pulling myself up by the bars. "You'd best let go of that."

"Hah. Nice try, Dragon. But I believe I'll be all right. Oh, and don't worry: as

I said, I'm not going to kill you. The High Priestess will do that. But, I will at some point, have to kill your young friend, Ben. And won't it be agonizing to watch him die by your own blade? Hmmmm?"

"He dies, you die, worm."

Holding Fang by the scabbard, Finnius eyed me then the sword and said, "Acolyte, withdraw this blade."

"Again, Finnius, I wouldn't do that unless you want another man dead," I warned.

The acolyte's fingers stopped inches from Fang's hilt. He widened his eyes on me.

"Withdraw it, servant, or die anyway! Draykis!"

Several hulking figures stepped out of the shadows, two of which limped and had busted faces. It seemed all of my valiant efforts from earlier had been deflated. One stepped over the acolyte and wrapped its clawed fingers around his neck.

Sweating profusely, the acolyte wrapped his trembling hands around the hilt. Taking a sharp breath, he slid Fang from the sheath, holding my sword out in his robed arms. Fang's steel flickered with life in the lantern light but was otherwise dim. I sagged. I hadn't really expected Fang to do anything, but you never know with him.

"Huh, I see your bluff has failed you, Dragon. Perhaps you should have stayed in bed. You look awfully tired. Maybe you should just sit down and rest." Finnius jerked the sword away from the acolyte and pointed it in the acolyte's face. He clipped one cheek, then the other. "Next time, it will be your neck with a large hole in it." Finnius whirled toward the others and said, "Lower him."

Ben's body slowly drifted over next to a large stone altar, where he sat upright, listless and catatonic. They had done something to him. His eyes flickered between me, the draykis, and the ceiling.

"Don't give up, Ben. I'll save you!"

"No, Dragon, no you won't," Finnius said, stepping over toward Ben and stabbing him in the chest.

"NOOOOOOOOOOOOO!"

CHAPTER
39

I DIDN'T FEEL A THING WHEN my buttocks landed on the cold stone floor. I was dead inside. Worse, Ben was dead! The only thought racing through my head was, "It's your life to throw away, not mine." I'd tried to warn him, yet guilt overwhelmed me. It mixed with something else: anger. It was all my fault. I had failed.

"Good, Dragon," Finnius started, "you should rest, as you look absolutely horrible. I hope the High Priestess doesn't mind when she arrives any minute now." He clapped his hands. "Acolytes, begin the summons."

Listless, I watched the Clerics of Barnabus gather around an archway off center in the chamber and begin their moans and mumbles. I felt my heart explode in my chest when the draykis hoisted Ben's body onto the slab altar.

"I'll kill you, Finnius," I muttered.

Finnius cupped his ear, saying, "What's that?" He jabbed Fang into the stone floor by the altar. "A fine weapon, a fine-fine piece of steel. Is it made of jaxite? I didn't even feel it go in or slide out." He turned his attention to the archway and looked back at me. "Won't be long now, Dragon. And I can't wait to see what the High Priestess has in store for you."

Smoke of many colors swirled inside the archway, pulsating with life and energy. The sound of the acolytes chanting increased in volume and tempo. I didn't care. Whoever the High Priestess was and whatever they wanted to do with me didn't matter. I'd failed. I'd abandoned one friend, only to see another one dead. Huffing for air, I rose to my feet. I wrapped my hands around the metal.

"I'm going to kill you, Finnius!"

I wasn't supposed to kill anybody unless it was life or death. *What about Finnius's death for Ben's life?* It was more than fair.

Finnius leered at me, wringing his dirty hands together and saying, "Not even in your wildest nightmares. It's over for you, Nath Dragon."

The draykis, no longer two but ten, sprang into action as something small and white skittered across the floor.

"What is it?" Finnius cried out as a small, white dragon leaped past his face and into the corner. "Who let it out? I'll kill one of you! Acolyte, get me those pixlyn!" One broke from the group and dashed off. "Draykis, capture that dragon!"

It was a long-tailed white, the same one I'd seen in the cage on my way in here. It was quick and fierce, and the draykis were no match for it. One sealed off the other way out as the other three chased it around the room. It scurried, hissed, snapped, and slipped through the claws of one then the other.

"Get it, draykis! Kill it!" Finnius screamed. "It doesn't matter how!"

I jumped to my feet, pulling at the bars, fuming.

"I'll not see any more of your murders, Finnius."

"You'll see many more before this day is over, I assure you."

The acolyte rushed back into the room.

"Well?" Finnius snapped.

"Gone, Cleric Finnius."

Finnius wrung his hands and tugged at his robes, screaming at the draykis, "You idiots! Why did you abandon those cages?"

The draykis at the door replied, "We did as you requested."

The long-tailed white flew from one side of the room to the other.

Finnius stomped his feet.

"Catch it! NOW!"

The long-tailed white locked eyes with me, and I felt a connection. It wanted the dragons free, and so did I.

Finnius howled. He saw us.

The dragon darted across the room toward me.

"Stop it!" Finnius yelled.

Lunging, two draykis collided with each other, but a third caught the end of the dragon's long tail and jerked it to the ground. The dragon screeched, tiny claws digging into the stone floor, straining toward me. I reached through the bars, my arm inches away.

"NO!" I screamed as another draykis, wielding a sword, rushed over, swinging it.

"Kill it!" Finnius shouted. "Kill it!"

CHAPTER 40

T HE WHITE DRAGON'S EYES GLOWED with green fire as the draykis swung the sword. A jet of white smoke shot out of its mouth, filling the room in an instant. I couldn't see a thing, but I heard a blade chopping into flesh and stone. Something let out a nasty grunt, and I could hear Finnius hack and cough while I tried to fan the smoke away. As the smoke dissipated, I could hear him scream.

"Did you kill it? Where is it? Find it!"

Through the thinning smoke, a draykis rose from the floor, staring at the stump of his arm. The other with the sword was looking around, and that's when I felt it. The tiny dragon had squeezed through the bars and was crawling up my back and onto my shoulder. His extra-long tail coiled along my waist and arm.

"Ahem," I said.

Finnius turned my way. His face reddened and his chin quivered when he said, "Give me that long-tailed white, Dragon. Or I'll kill the rest of them."

"If you want this dragon, worm, why don't you come and get it?"

The dragon's tail tightened around my arm and waist. A surge of power raced through me like never before. Every muscle in my being pulsated as the purring dragon filled me with awesome power. I wasn't a man any more. I felt the strength of a full-grown dragon. I grabbed the bars, and the metal groaned as I pulled them apart like noodles. Finnius's jaw dropped to the floor when I stepped through the gap I'd just made.

"Unless you can bring my friend back to life, it's time to die, Finnius!"

I knocked the first draykis that came at me from one side of the room to the other. I ducked under another blade that almost took my head from my shoulders. I was fast. Faster than ever before. Stronger than ever before. The power the little dragon was giving me was unbelievable!

"You're dead!" I said, rushing Finnius.

He had turned to run before I closed in when two armed draykis jumped into my path. A sharp blade tore past my stomach, and a large hammer ripped an inch away from my head. I was faster and stronger, but I wasn't impervious to metal. I did a backflip toward the altar and landed in front of Fang. I ripped him free.

"Now it's even, uglies," I said. I could feel the dragon's power flowing from my shins to my neck. Fang's blade hummed with life. "Who's the first to pay for the life of my friend?"

"You cannot kill us," said one draykis, holding a sword. "We are already dead."

"We'll see about that," I boasted, knowing full well the odds were against me. I'd never faced such a formidable force of warriors before. So be it. I felt like I could fight an entire army now. I felt even better than when the crowd had cheered me on, "Dragon! Dragon!"

Faster than sight, I drove Fang into the nearest one's chest, drawing forth a groan as it fell. I chopped another one in the arm and kicked another one in the face. Another parried my strike and countered with a deep cut across my leg. On they came at me with the skill and precision of hardened soldiers, forcing me backward to parry again and again.

"NO!"

I knocked a blade free from one and stabbed another in the shoulder. Another fell as I hacked through its knee. Fang sizzled through the air like a living thing, cutting, blocking, and chopping. But all my strength and speed didn't stop them from coming. Limping, snarling, and slashing, they pressed.

"Gah!"

One ripped its claws through my arm. Little dragon or not, I couldn't keep this up much longer, and if I died, the dragons would all die as well.

Without thinking, I said, "Fang! Do something!"

Fang flared with brilliant icy light.

Striking like a snake, I jabbed a draykis that wielded a sword.

It stopped in its tracks, its scaled body turned to ice. I struck another draykis and one more. Instant statues of ice they'd become. I cut one in the arm and another in the leg with the same effect. Weapons poised high over their heads, the last two charged.

Slice! Slice!

They crystalized into pure ice.

There I stood among seven frozen horrors, feeling almost as astounded as they looked. Fang throbbed in my hand.

"What's that, Fang?" I saw the tip flare up. "Ah, I see."

I struck Fang's tip on the stone floor.

KRAAAAAAAAAAANG!

The vibrations of the perfect metal resonated through the chamber like a giant tuning fork.

One by one, the icy figures of the draykis exploded into a thousand shards of ice.

"NOOOOOOOOOOOOOO!" Finnius screamed from right behind me.

I whirled just in time to catch a long dagger plunging at my chest. I twisted it free from his wrist, punched him in the face, and sent him sprawling to the floor.

"You're going to pay, worm!"

Crawling backward, he shouted back, "It's too late, Dragon. She comes."

The mystic smoke in the archway was filling the room, but all the clerics but Finnius were gone. Eeriness covered me like a blanket. I shook it off.

"Great, then she'll be here just in time to make arrangements for your funeral." I raised my sword and closed in. I didn't ever want to see this man alive again. "But there might not be much left to bury once I'm done with you."

"Go ahead! Kill me! My High Priestess will just bring me back," Finnius said, chuckling. "But that's much more than I can say for your friend." His eyes twinkled with darkness as his lips curled in a smile. "Come, Dragon, avenge your friend."

"I'll do more than that!"

The dragon on my shoulder hissed out a warning.

Crack!

It felt like a large mallet collided with my skull, knocking me to my knees. Finnius seized my wrists and shouted.

"AZZRHEEM-KAH!

It felt like lightning exploded inside me as I lay on the ground, hair smoking, every fiber of my being throbbing in pain. My eyelids hurt as I opened my eyes to witness a winged draykis reaching for me. Bigger than the rest, it scooped me off the floor like a doll and crushed me in its arms.

"Break his back!" Finnius yelled from somewhere. "I want to hear it snap, draykis!"

It didn't have lips, but it smiled.

"Certainly, my lord."

CHAPTER
41

ALL MY STRENGTH FLED WHEN I gazed at the small, white dragon lying still on the floor. Completely drained, I fought on, legs kicking, but the monster had its mighty paws locked behind my back.

"That's it!" Finnius said with glee. "Ooh! Your face is awfully red, Dragon, but I think it will look even better in a nice dark shade of purple." Finnius limped over, leering up at me, triumphant.

I felt it. I was defeated. I'd failed. Any moment, the winged draykis would crush all my bones, leaving me living but an invalid.

"Worm!" I managed to spit out.

My spit sizzled through his robes.

"Eh… What is this?" Finnius asked, fingering the hole in his robes. My stomach churned with fire, and the taste of brimstone charged inside my mouth.

The draykis licked its lips, said, "I'm hungry," and squeezed me with all its might.

I felt something snap as hot smoke burst from my nose.

Eyes filled with horror, Finnius backed away. "NO! What are you doing, Dragon? Stop that! Make him stop, draykis. NOW!"

The draykis, jaws filled with long sharp teeth, opened wide.

I tried to scream, but a jet of flaming liquid erupted instead.

One second the draykis's horrible face was about to eat me, in the next it was a ball of fire. There was nothing left of its face but bone as it released me and fell to the ground.

I jumped up from the floor to chase Finnius down.

He slipped on the shards of ice and fell hard to the ground on his knees, saying, "Mercy, Dragon! Mercy!"

Evil shows no mercy. No mercy shall it receive.

"Where was your mercy when you killed my friend, worm?"

"Mercy! I'll do anything! Please!"

I wanted to stop it, but I couldn't. A geyser of flame shot from my mouth, coating Finnius from head to toe. In an instant, he was burnt to a crisp.

A new rush of power assailed me as I chased the other acolytes down. Some burned, some escaped, and some died before it was over.

The only ones left were me and the dragons. One by one, I freed them from their cages, and one by one they were gone, the long-tailed white as well. Exhausted, I fell to my knees and fought the tears coming from my eyes.

"Ben," I moaned as I crawled over to the altar.

There he lay on the granite slab altar, pale as a ghost. His energetic face, once full of life, now as stiff as stone. I'd saved the dragons but at what cost?

I brushed the hair from his eyes and said, "Ben. I'm so sorry, Ben."

"For what?" he said, blinking.

I stiffened.

"Huh? Ben?"

He yawned, stretched out his arms, and asked again, "For what?"

I stumbled backward, clutching my heart.

"BEN! You're alive!"

"That seems to be the case," he said, fanning the eerie smoke from his face. "Is that your breath that I smell? It's awful."

"I guess that's why they call it dragon breath."

Sitting on the altar, Ben said, "Is this place shaking?"

Shards of rock and debris fell on my head and his. The High Priestess. Was she still coming? I rushed over and grabbed Fang. But where was Akron—and the rest of my things?

"We need to get out of here, Ben."

Something was coming through the portal, something big.

"Ben, do you see my bow?"

I swung Fang into the archway, splintering rock, but it held. I felt the urge to hew the thing down. I felt evil as great as I'd ever felt before.

"Found it!" Ben said, hoisting it over his head.

"Bring it over here."

I snatched Akron from his hands and nocked it with a powerful arrow. I rubbed my spit into the tip and watched it glow.

Holding his ears, Ben shouted, "What are you doing?"

"I don't know," I said as I let the arrow fly. It disappeared into the smoky archway. A split second later, a roar came out that shook the entire temple. I grabbed Ben by the arm and led us dashing through the corridors. The floors wobbled and the walls warbled as we rushed past the dust and debris through one winding corridor and another until we arrived outside in the courtyard. The night air was like ice in my lungs.

"We made it," I said, leaning over and grabbing my knees.

Ben was lying on the courtyard grass, wheezing.

From inside the ruins of the temple came a mighty thud like someone closing the lid on a giant sarcophagus. I fell to my knees, rain pelting my face, and scanned the area. No acolytes, lizard men, or draykis. It was over.

For a moment, I took it all in. I was alive, but more importantly, so was Ben.

"Look," Ben said pointing.

A group of small dragons flew across the moonlit clouds in the sky.

I wanted to hug Ben but didn't. Smiling, I squeezed his shoulder instead and said, "Ben, why aren't you dead?"

He shrugged.

"I think Bayzog's potion did it."

"How so?"

"Well, he said that I would know when it was time to take it, so I did."

"And when was that?"

"Well, I was with the horses, like you said, guarding them like you told me. After you'd been gone a little while, the horses started whining."

"Whining?"

"Yes, I've never seen such nervous horses before. And that's when I noticed it." He stopped, thinking.

"Noticed what?"

"A giant shadow circling in the sky." He shivered. "I'd never been so scared in all of my life. And I knew, instantly, that it was coming for me. That thing, those eyes, locked on mine, and I knew I was dead. I grabbed that vial and swallowed the entire bottleful. The horses galloped off, and the next thing I knew I was face to face with it. I'm embarrassed, but I think I fainted in its arms. I awoke, and I was sailing across the sky like a bird. That monster was carrying me. That's when I blacked out again. Next time I awoke, I was spinning in that room, surrounded by those clerics and beastly things. Then that man took your sword and stabbed me."

He pulled off his leather armor, which was cut clean through. He ran his finger along the white scar on his chest. He shook his head. "It was cold, the blade going in. As if someone shoved ice in my chest. But I didn't die; I felt strange, outside of myself. I just closed my eyes and played possum." He put his armor back on. "What was in that vial, Dragon?"

"Let's get out of here," I said, grimacing.

I headed for the forest—limping, bleeding, and aching all over. I'd had enough of these temples.

"Well, what was it?"

"I can't say for sure, because you can never tell with Bayzog, or any other wizard, for that matter, but I'd say what he gave you was Moments of Immortality. And that's very potent magic."

"Whoa... How many moments do you think I have?"

I socked him in the arm.

"Ow! Why'd you do that?"

"Do you feel Immortal?"

"No," he said, rubbing his arm.

"Then I'd say your moments ran out. Now come on: maybe we can track down the horses by dawn if we run."

"Run?"

I took off, but not as fast as I would have liked. My joints ached. My body was swollen like a watered-down log. I'd taken a pretty heavy beating those last couple of days. But Ben, despite his huffing, tried to keep up. I had to let him catch up.

"There should be a potion to make this running easier," he wheezed.

"There is. Come on."

We arrived back at the Crane's Neck as dawn broke and began the search for the horses. Starting from where Ben had left them, I spotted the hoofprints in the dirt.

Kneeling and pointing, I said, "See these horseshoe prints, Ben? They left deep impressions after the rain, so they shouldn't be hard to follow—unless another storm hits. And they won't take off more than a mile. With any luck, they're grazing somewhere. Why don't you see if you can track them?"

His face lit up.

"Really, me?"

"Now's as good a time to practice as any."

"All right, then," he replied, giving me a funny look. "Well, uh, Dragon, do you feel all right?"

"I'm fine. I've been in plenty of bad scrapes before. Why do you aaaaa—?"

I forgot what I was saying. My lids became heavy as Ben's eyes filled with alarm. His mouth twisted like a pinwheel as he yelled, and his fingers stretched out like worms. *What's happening?* The light of the dawn faded to black.

Inside the temple ruins, a magnificent woman surveyed the chamber where the battle had taken place. It was High Priestess Selena.

"Interesting."

Hours earlier, she had been attempting to enter the portal when a magic arrow sailed through the smoke, struck a draykis, and blew it and another to pieces. Her chamber was half destroyed, and her roar wiped out most of what wasn't already rubble. She'd gotten over it. Not all plans were perfectly executed, but the execution still had its rewards.

She stepped through a puddle of water, kneeled alongside the charred corpse of Finnius, and said, "The best pawns end up being dead pawns." She grabbed the magic amulet from around his neck and pulled it free of his ashy remains. "Here," she said, tossing it to a man among the draykis. He was big and armored, with many colorful tattoos on his head. A cruel-looking warrior's mace hung from his belt.

"Clearly, this was a job for a High Cleric, but..." She waded past the other burnt and broken bodies in the room. "I still think it will bear the results that I was hoping for. Humph. Nath Dragon evades traps with the cunning of a snake, but he'll never escape the biggest trap of all."

"And that is?" the deep-voiced warrior cleric asked.

"Himself."

Before she stepped through the smoke in the archway, she commanded one more thing.

"And bring along all the corpses of the acolytes. The dead tell the most accurate tales."

Clutch of the Cleric

-Book 4-

Craig Halloran

PRELUDE

A FLUTELIKE SOUND DRIFTED INTO MY ears.

My head started spinning. My fingers turned numb. Limp.

Brenwar's eyelids fluttered. His meaty hands clamped over his ears. "No!" he growled.

I couldn't say anything. My tongue felt like water. But I could see. Both of them. Shadows in the forest coming out of the darkness. One was male, the other female. Each pressed a set of small pipes to their lips. Tiny horns protruded from their heads. They stood on stout legs with the hooves of mountain goats.

Satyrs. Crafty and merciless.

The music tore at my mind.

I screamed, but I couldn't hear myself. I had to move. Had to escape. Run. Flee. I knew the stories. I knew the tales. Whatever the satyrs captured they kept, never to be seen again.

CHAPTER 1

I FELT LIKE I'D GONE DAYS without water when I opened my eyes. A soft, soothing light shone into them, but I still felt weary.

"Uh… where am I? Ben?"

The smell of sweet ginger filled my nostrils, and someone placed a cold, damp cloth on my head.

"Sssssh. Rest, Dragon."

The warm face of Sasha greeted me with a smile as she reached over and touched my face.

"Bayzog, he awakens again."

Again? I didn't remember waking the last time.

"It's not time yet, Sasha," Bayzog said. A faint image of him in his red wizard tunic caught my eye.

Her perfect lips started singing; the gentle, mystic words of an ancient lullaby churned in my ears.

"No, don't do thaaaaaa—"

The soft lights turned dark again.

"Wake him up!"

Slowly, I opened my eyes, the thirst I remembered now gone. Then I saw Brenwar, as angry as I had ever seen him before.

"What are you yelling for?" I said, shielding my eyes, squinting.

He whirled on me, so angry I could see the red behind his beard.

"WHAT AM I YELLING FOR?"

A large figure stepped between us. It was one of those Roaming Rangers.

"Shum?"

"Get out of my way, elf," Brenwar growled.

"Brenwar," Bayzog intervened, "now is not the time."

"Oh, it's the time, all right!"

Brenwar shoved past Shum, stuck his stubby finger in my face, and said, "Why did you leave me, Nath Dragon?" His voice cracked. "Why did you do that?"

I didn't know what to say. I was feeling great, but I had the feeling I shouldn't be.

"Why is everyone looking at me like that? Where's Ben? Is he all right? And how did I get here?"

Brenwar stood frowning and tapping his foot, Shum unmoving, Bayzog muttering, and Sasha twitching her nose.

"What?" I said.

Bayzog took a seat beside me and said, "I'll catch you up. Ben led you back here on the horses after you fainted."

"Ah good, I knew Ben had it in him. I guess my wounds were much worse than I thought. So, where is he?"

"He's with the Legionnaires, on a mission."

"Huh, a mission. He couldn't be on a mission already. Could he? Don't they have to go through training?"

Brenwar stormed forward.

"Fool! He could have been on twenty missions already. He's been gone for weeks. You've been asleep for weeks. I've been looking for you; my men have been looking for you, and we might never have found you if we hadn't come across that temple. And we might not have even known you were there if we hadn't found this!" He held out a black dragon scale. "And this led us here."

I grabbed the scale with my left hand and pinched it in my fingers. My black dragon fingers. I jumped off the couch.

"SULTANS OF SULFUR! I have two dragon arms!"

"You can say that again!" Brenwar shot back. "You foolish dragon!"

I touched my toes, my shins, my thighs, chest, and face.

"Am I—?"

"Just the arms, Dragon," Sasha said. "You'll be all right."

"No, he won't! He'd have been all right if he'd done as he was told. Dragon! What have you done?" Brenwar exclaimed.

"I saved dragons!" I yelled back. "And if I'd waited on you, they'd probably be dead!"

I gazed at my scales, my hands, my claws. A thrill went through me. I felt unstoppable! But there was something else. The white spot of scales was on both palms in the middle.

Brenwar poked me in the chest, saying, "I was at the temple. I saw what you did. And your new friend, Ben, confirmed it. You killed again! Now look at you!"

"You started it!" I said, pointing at Brenwar.

"You did this, not I, Dragon! You ran off on your own, like a fool, and now you have twice the problem!"

"Don't call me a fool again, Brenwar," I said, glowering down at him. I was ready to rip his beard off.

He rose up on his toes and said, "What are you going to do, breathe on me? Fool!"

I took a deep breath.

He laughed at me.

Sasha's vibrant form stepped between us. "Please, everyone, stop yelling. You aren't children; you're men," Sasha said, gentle hands pushing me into the sofa.

Calmness fell over me. "We have to work together on this," she said, eyeing all of us. "It's that important. Bayzog, tell him."

I slumped into the sofa, feeling incredibly angry and guilty, but I let Sasha's charm calm me.

"Yes, Bayzog, Ben mentioned there was something you wanted to tell me. What is it?" I said, noticing my beard. "Ugh! Really?"

Bayzog gave me a funny look.

I shook my head, which was beginning to ache, saying, "Go on then."

"Dragon, I can't say that I, or anyone in the world, for that matter, can understand your unique constitution—well, excluding your father, of course."

My headache intensified. What would my father think?"

"I don't think things are as bad as they look, however. I would venture that it was inevitable that you would start turning into a dragon eventually, and your scales, well, they aren't a true reflection of your nature. Nath, we all know that you are good, as good a man as we all know, but there is darkness in all of us. No one person is perfect or without blemish; most just hide it better on the outside. That's why it is difficult to tell the good people from the evil sometimes."

"This isn't helping, Bayzog," I said, holding my head in my hands, irritated.

"Our deeds are what define us. Our actions. Our words. Not our garments, not our looks. What is inside a man, in his heart—his dragon heart—is what counts. Keep doing what you are doing."

"But I want to get rid of it." *Sort of.*

"And what if you can't? Will you stop being good altogether, then? Will you join the Clerics of Barnabus?"

"NO!"

"So stop whining, then," Bayzog said.

"I'm not whining."

"You are whining," Brenwar added, folding his arms across his chest. "Like a baby orc."

"Fine, I'm whining, but I'm sure all of you would do the same if you had these."

I lifted my arms. "I'm not going to be wooing the ladies like I used to; that's for sure. But I imagine I could be used in a carnival to frighten children."

Brenwar harrumphed.

"I like them," Sasha said, rubbing my scales, smiling. "I think they are marvelous."

Her sweet words made me feel better; they really did. I guess I was just going to have to get used to it, but I really needed to fix it.

"Bayzog, my father says there are many things in this world that can heal. Perhaps you can help me find some of those things. Maybe I just need a different Thunderstone or something."

Bayzog walked over to his large table, opened his tome, thumbed through the pages, and threw his hands out. When he twitched his fingers, an image of a mystic amulet formed and hung in the air, gold and silver with a bright-green gemstone in the middle.

"The Ocular of Orray. The legend says that it can bring health, peace, and prosperity. Its powers have been known to cure lycanthropes and liches and to restore the undead. Perhaps it can help."

"So, where is it?"

Bayzog flicked his fingers. The amulet broke into several pieces.

"It was stolen from the elves in Elome a century after the last Dragon War, never to be seen again. According to the lore, the thieves broke it up into many pieces and spread them all over Nalzambor, for the Ocular cannot be destroyed."

"So, who stole it? Who can go into Elome and steal anything?" I sighed. "It's a fortress."

"We'd have to ask the elves that," he said, closing the book.

"So, I'm supposed to search the entire world for this Ocular? I'd rather just save the dragons." I looked at Shum. "And what are you doing here?"

"I have an interest in the power of the Ocular as well. Remember my king? He needs the healing, too."

"I see. And what about the dragons? I'm not going to abandon them for this quest."

Brenwar shoved my sword and scabbard into my chest.

"We won't!"

Bayzog and Sasha donned their traveling cloaks.

"Where are you going?"

"With you," Sasha said, tying the neck with the magic of her fingers. "I've been needing to stretch my legs. Bayzog has kept me cooped up in here too long."

It seemed everybody was ready for a trip but me as I shook my head and rose to my feet.

"So now I need supervision everywhere I go?"

"And then some," Brenwar huffed. "Let's go!"

"Fine," I said, buckling my sword around my waist as Sasha draped my quiver over my shoulder and handed me Akron. I was ready for anything. But before I closed my eyes, I said one last thing. "But I'm going to save whoever and whatever I want to. Agreed?"

Everyone shook their heads except Brenwar, who laughed.

"Well, let it never be said I didn't consort with highly unreasonable people."

As soon as I closed my eyes, the adventure began.

CHAPTER 2

H IGH PRIESTESS SELENE SAT ON her throne. Dark. Cold. Cunning. She was
beautiful, dark eyed and raven headed. Her hair was pulled back behind her
shoulders as she shifted in her chair, eyes intent and focused on the great doors
on the other side of the room.

Nath Dragon. She looked forward to the day he was dragged to her on hands
and knees, bound and broken. *I shall have him. I shall have him and all the world of
Nalzambor.*

Something fluttered above. A dark birdlike creature landed on her shoulder. It
had a mix of dark-green and red feathers, but it was not a bird. It had the face and
mouth of a dragon. Its tongue licked her ear and its feathers shuddered when it
roared with little sound.

She patted its head. "Ah, my little drulture. Such a caring and endearing pet,"
she said. "Are you worried about me?"

It stretched its neck, feathers ruffling on its wings, and let out another tiny roar.

Her black lips pecked its cat-sized head. The drulture was her companion when
no one else was about. So she sat alone in her thoughts in the grand room. She liked
the open space. The quiet. She needed time to plan. Nath Dragon had escaped her
clutches again.

"Are you hungry?" she said.

The drulture bobbed its head.

"I see," she said. "Just give me another moment." She snapped her fingers. *Pop!*

The great doors across from her opened and a pair of lizard men stepped inside
and kneeled.

"It's feeding time," she said.

The pair departed and returned less than a minute later carrying a barred cage
between them. A spotted bobcat, every bit of thirty pounds, was inside, its eyes and
ears alert.

"Leave us," Selene said, "and seal the door behind you."

The lizard men departed, leaving her, the drulture, and the bobcat all alone.

"He's a big one," she said, "bigger than the last. I hope you won't have any trouble."

The drulture let out a tiny roar and hopped to the ground. The dragon-bird was less than half the size of the bobcat. It strutted around on two legs, making a chirping sound. The bobcat licked its lips. Its cat eyes narrowed.

Selene tapped her fingers together. She liked games like this. Who is the hunter and who is the hunted? She'd tried to trap Nath Dragon in a similar way before, letting him think he was freeing a dragon when in all reality the dragon bait was trapping him. It had almost worked a couple of times, but Nath had come out on top again. It had been costly, too. She'd lost many of her draykis, and one of her temples had been wrecked. She clenched her fists.

"I'm going to break him," she said. "Soon." With a wave of her hand, the metal cage opened.

The bobcat jumped out and gave chase after the drulture. The bobcat pounced. The drulture flapped and soared into the air and began circling the bobcat. Once. Twice. Three times. Then it dove.

Swish!

It snatched the bobcat by the back and lifted it high in the air. The bobcat hung by the scruff of its neck, clawing, scratching, and growling. Higher they went, toward the domed ceiling. The drulture dropped the bobcat. The big cat plummeted fifty feet toward the ground.

The drulture dove, snatching it inches from the ground. Then swooped up to the rafters once more.

Drop. Dive. Catch. Drop. Dive. Catch.

Three times it happened. The bobcat fought and clawed until its strength was out. The fourth time, it hung limp in the talons of the dragon-bird and fought no more. Circling thirty feet high in the air, the drulture swung the bobcat up into the air and opened its jaws wide. They became wider and wider.

Gulp!

It swallowed the bobcat whole and landed softly on the floor. Its belly bulged. It waddled around like an overstuffed chicken for about a minute, burped an awful sound, and returned to normal.

"Now there's an idea," Selene said. She patted the drulture when it returned to her shoulder. It purred. She snapped her fingers. The grand doors opened and the lizard men came forward and bowed.

"I need the High Cleric," she said, "and take the cage and fill it with something bigger. A halfling or gnome perhaps."

The dragon-bird purred and batted its eyelashes.

Selene smiled. "You've given me an idea. If it works, my master will be pleased. If I can't beat Nath Dragon as he is, then perhaps I should wear him down first."

CHAPTER 3

"ARE YOU POUTING?" BRENWAR SAID.

"No," I said.

"Don't lie, Dragon. I can see your brows buckling. Straighten up."

The ride from Quintuklen wasn't so bad the first day. It was good being in the company of Bayzog the part elf, Sasha his apprentice and mate, and Shum, one of the Elven Roaming Rangers. It had been a long time since I'd spent time with so many people. Usually it was just me and Brenwar.

I kicked my steed and rode ahead of the party, leaving Brenwar in the rear. The day was dreary, a little chilly, and nothing but rolling green hills and wildflowers lay ahead.

"Don't leave my sight!" Brenwar said.

I didn't even look back. Instead, I rode farther out. Far enough until I got the feeling I was alone. As I said, it was nice catching up with everyone, but their chronic presence was disturbing. Every eye seemed to watch everything I was doing, and Brenwar kept commenting on what he thought I was thinking.

"Don't think you're gonna sneak off!"

"Stay on this side of the river."

"Shum, go with him."

"Bayzog, can you cast a spell that can track him?"

It got old. It was aggravating. I was a man. I was becoming a dragon, and I didn't need anyone's protection. Especially now. Now I had two dragon arms, not just one, and I was itching to see what I could do with both of them. I massaged my arms. I loved the slickness and toughness of my scales. And my claws—mostly yellow, but a little gold—came in handy when I gutted fish for dinner. I clicked them together. I loved the sound they made.

Burp.

A white puff of smoke came out of my mouth. My nostrils steamed. I tapped my fist into my chest.

I guessed I'd had too many fish earlier, but I was still hungry. Hungrier than ever. Nowadays I was even eating more than Brenwar, and he always ate a week's worth.

I fanned the smoke. I didn't want Brenwar to see. He'd say "Smoking's bad" or something silly like that.

I had been able to burp smoke a few times when no one was looking, but I hadn't summoned any more fire yet. I wasn't certain how I'd done it the last time, but I knew it was in me, brewing. A volcano ready to burst. Remembering the cleric Finnius whom I'd turned into a human roast bothered me, but not as much as it should have probably.

Well, remembering the smell did make me grimace. A little.

I heard horse hooves trotting up behind me. *Oh great.* I hadn't even been alone for a few minutes and already—still well within eyeshot—I had company.

I turned and yelled, "Will you leave me alone!" *Gulp.*

It was Sasha. She sat tall and splendid in the saddle. Her blue eyes were bright and her auburn hair was lustrous. Her apprentice robes hung loosely over her elegant form. She was one of the prettiest women I'd ever seen. And she was smiling.

"No," she said, smiling bigger.

"What?" I said. "Oh. Well, I'm glad you aren't Brenwar and I'm sorry that I yelled, Sasha. I'm just not used to having all of this bossing around."

She rode alongside me, giggling.

"I understand, Nath," she said. "Even Bayzog is demanding from time to time."

She called me Nath, and that was fine by me, but I didn't like it so much when others called me that. Nath was just the beginning of my long name. Longer than a hundred men's strung together, and whenever I heard Nath, my mind would start running through it.

"I believe you do know what I'm talking about. Bayzog's rigid as a dwarf sometimes." I winked at her. "But don't tell him I said that."

"I won't," she said. "So, Nath, tell me. What's it like having two dragon arms?"

She caught me off guard with that one. I figured she was going to ask how I was feeling or in her own polite way offer some advice. And I'd hate to tell her I'd had all the advice I could swallow. My father was bad enough, but Brenwar was worse.

"Uh …," I said, glancing over my shoulder, then back at her, "can you keep a secret, Sasha?"

"So long as it doesn't place me in conflict with the others," she said, nodding.

I hesitated. I could see her point, but I didn't think what I was about to tell her would create a conflict.

"All right … It's wonderful, Sasha. I feel like I can do things I could never do before. I feel faster. Stronger." I held my hands out in front of me and gazed at the black scales that shone like black sheets of ice in the sun. "I feel like I could fight anyone, anywhere, and win." I flexed them. "I was strong before, but now, well, I just want to test them out."

"Whoa," she said, "you really are infatuated with yourself, aren't you?"

"Well, no, it's not like that. I'm just amazed."

She giggled. "I'm just teasing you, Nath. I really like them too…"

She trailed off, her light eyes glancing away.

"But?" I said.

She reached over and rubbed my arm. Her eyes brightened when she did it.

"Oh, but nothing, Nath. I trust you and I'm thrilled for you. Who wouldn't want to be a dragon anyway? And Nath, you know I think the world of you. I always have. You're a hero. You've done great things and you'll do more…"

She did it again. Trailed off and glanced away.

"But?" I said.

"As long as you stay on the right path. Let us help with that, Nath. Why do you rebel?"

"Because I'm a rebel," I said, laughing a little. But it wasn't very convincing. Not to me or her.

"Oh Nath," she said, "you just have to be careful. This world, Nalzambor, it has a way of changing people who aren't careful. I lost some family because of that. I don't want to lose you too." Her eyes watered up and she was looking right at me.

It got me right in the heart, the dragon heart. And I felt guilty. Unlike the others, Sasha had a way of saying things in a manner that I would listen to.

I think it helped that she was pretty and her soft voice gave me chills.

I cleared my throat. There was a lump in it still. I did it again.

"Sasha," I said, touching her hand, "you don't really think anything will happen to me, do you? I'm a good dragon, remember. I'll never turn evil." I said it as if I was trying to convince myself. That bothered me. "Look, I know I have to be careful and that I can't run off on my own like I did before. But, what if it happens anyway? Didn't you say something about it mattering more what's on the inside that on the out?"

She nodded.

I went on. "And we don't know that black dragons were all evil. Maybe just some of them. Aw… I don't know, Sasha." I shook my head and ran my fingers through my mane of hair.

I blew a puff of smoke.

"Wow!" she said, "I'm impressed. When did you learn to do that?"

"I've been practicing when no one is looking—what now?"

I glanced back. Brenwar, Shum, and Bayzog were galloping toward me. "Aw, here comes another lecture." I started to fan the smoke away but thought better of it. "All right, there's nothing I can do about … what's going on?"

They galloped right past us and Brenwar was yelling.

"Are you coming or not, Dragon?"

Sasha and I looked at each other and then our eyes followed them.

Up ahead, miles distant, was a giant, black plume of smoke.

I might get to test my arms out after all. Whatever it is, I hope it's big. Dangerous. Because if it is, I've got a surprise for it.

"Let's ride, Sasha! Yah!"

CHAPTER 4

ELENE SAT WITH HER SCALED black tail coiled around her, petting her drulture, as the great doors opened. The lizard men led a large man inside. He wore dark crimson and purple robes and was accompanied by two dragon-like men. The draykis.

The man stopped at the edge of her throne's dais, kneeled, and bowed his big shoulders. The draykis kneeled at his side.

"I come as you wish, High Priestess," the man said. His voice was dark and cheerless. "My life is yours."

It warmed her cold heart whenever he said that.

"Arise, High Cleric," she said, "and tell me what you know."

He nodded, rose, and pulled back his hood. The High Cleric's bald head was covered in colorful tattoos. They moved, shifted, and changed. Different shades. Different hues. The man's face was hard. Not old. Eyes dark and mean. His hands were thick and calloused. A heavy war mace hung by a strap over his broad shoulders. He looked more like a warrior than a cleric. A destroyer, not a healer.

"The draykis are excellent soldiers. Hunters as well." He ran his hand over the amulet that controlled them. "Nine dragons have been captured in the last month. Our poachers are in good order."

"Any unusual run-ins, Kryzak?" she said.

"No, Selene," he said, "not as I'd hoped to report, I'm afraid."

"Selene?" she said, leaning forward.

Kryzak shrugged. "You know how deep my love is for you, Selene." His eyes sparkled and flared. "I've died once for you. I'll do it again."

She eased back into her chair. Kryzak was the only man who spoke to her so informally. He'd earned it. He used it. She liked that about him. Cold. Confident. Fearless.

"Of course, Kryzak, but mind your tongue. You might lose a soldier if he followed your insubordination."

"Certainly," he said, nodding, "And if he did, I'd kill him myself."

He stood still, chin up, arms folded behind his back, waiting.

She sat, quiet, thinking. Nath Dragon had disappeared once more. But he would show up. He always did. Even Finnius the acolyte had tracked him down, but the High Cleric Kryzak could do better. He never failed any charge. Not once. Not ever. The man was on a mission. Her mission. The mission of Barnabus. Capture the dragons. Sell the ones that could be sold. Kill or turn them. But most importantly, stop Nath Dragon. Run the world.

"Find him, Kryzak," she said. "Grind him down. Torment his friends. His allies. No mercy. I want him weak. His purpose meaningless. His focus frayed."

Kryzak caressed the long wooden handle of his war mace. The wood was weathered, the flanges of the head a dark metal. He nodded. "Our spies are everywhere. As soon as he shows, I'll know. Track him. Trip him. Snare him. Bust him up. Break him. It will be a pleasure."

"Don't get too carried away, Kryzak," she said, "I want him alive, but his friends, his allies—do with them what you wish."

He patted the head of his mace.

"Then his friends and allies," he said, glowering, "will be dead. Or horribly mutilated."

Her black tail uncoiled from her body, stretched out, and brushed his rugged face.

"My resources are yours," she said. "I have many. Be sure you keep me informed."

"As you wish, Selene," he said, closing his eyes. "Your touch inspires me." He smiled and stroked her scales.

Her tail coiled around his neck and squeezed.

"Do not fail me, Kryzak."

"Ah," he moaned, "Your touch is divine, and I won't fail. When Nath Dragon is in my clutches," he said, "you'll be the first to know."

Her tail slid away and draped over her shoulder.

"You're dismissed, Kryzak," she said.

Kryzak bowed, turned, and walked away. The draykis followed. The great doors closed behind them, leaving her and the drulture all alone once more.

Selene let out a sigh and patted the creature's head.

"I don't know who to feel worse for: Nath Dragon or his friends."

The drulture flicked out its tongue and let out a tiny roar.

Selene chuckled.

"No, of course I don't feel for them. It's just an expression." She got up from her throne and walked down the steps. Her tail swished left and right from behind. "Stay, my pet. I have a grave meeting to attend."

It chirped and growled.

"No, you can't come," she said, headed for a concealed exit in the back. "I fear my master might eat you. He's eaten too many of my pets in the past."

CHAPTER
5

W̶E RODE HARD THE NEXT few miles. Ahead, a small village was smoking and in tatters. Men labored. Children scurried back and forth and some cried. It must have happened days ago. Beyond the village, the smoke was coming from somewhere else.

"By Guzan," Brenwar said, "who'd do such a thing?"

"Who, or what?" Bayzog said, pulling a spyglass from his robes.

I hopped off my horse.

Sasha followed me down into the disaster-struck village.

The charred remains of houses and storefronts still smoldered. The farmers, tanners, bakers, herders, and blacksmiths were dirty and drained, milling about and scraping up what was left of their homes. Their memories. Heirlooms and such things. It tugged at my heart. Their peaceful lives had been destroyed.

A farmer, covered in dirt and soot, picked up pieces of a fence and stacked them nearby. A little boy, maybe twelve with tawny hair, wiped his eyes and stared.

"Sir," I said, "what happened? Who did this?"

The man didn't even turn. He kept working and told his son to look away.

"Sir," I said again. I didn't like to be ignored. I was only trying to help.

Sasha put her hand on my arm and led me away. "They are still grieving," she said. "And I don't see the mother. Seeing how they've lost a home, you'd think the mother would be near."

Scanning the village of broken wood and busted storehouses, I noticed something else. I didn't see a single woman. Dread filled my chest.

"Sasha," I said, "I don't see any women at all."

She pinched her lips with her fingers. "Oh dear." A crease deepened in her brow. "Perhaps one of them can help," she said, gesturing toward an organized-looking group of men.

The Legionnaires were a welcome sight. Two soldiers approached on foot, the

City of Quintuklen colors and insignia emblazoned over their breast plates matching a small plume on their open-faced helmets.

"Dragon! Is that you? Draaagon!" a man yelled at the top of his lungs.

It was Ben. He ran up to me and gave me a firm embrace.

"Easy, Ben."

"Oh," he said, patting my arms, "I'm sorry, I'm just so glad to see you. I was worried." He gasped, eyes widening. "You've got two dragon arms now. That's incredible!"

"Ahem," Sasha said.

Ben lost his breath. "Up … er …" He swallowed a lump, took off his helmet, and bowed a little. "So nice to see you again, Sasha. You are even more beautiful than I recall."

Sasha giggled. "Thank you. It's good to see you too."

"Why Ben," I said, "you really are a soldier, aren't you?" I patted his armored shoulder. "Complimenting a lady and everything. I'm impressed."

Ben stuck his chin out and grinned. He'd changed. His armor fit well. He'd thickened up in his chest and shoulders. He looked good. Like a soldier. He was no longer a lanky son of a farmer but a strapping young man with some grizzle on his chin.

"Nice bow you have there," I said.

Ben had a full quiver of black-feathered arrows and a short bow. He beamed at me. "It's not Akron," he said, "but it's a good one. I strung it myself. Dragon, I'm actually one of the top marksmen on account of my training and all. The commander says I'll get to train new recruits in the future."

"That's great, Ben." I tuned my gaze to the soldier beside him. He was stout and short bearded, with a heavy axe on his belt. "And who's your friend?"

"Oh, forgive me," Ben said. "This is Garrison. He's my comrade."

I nodded and said, "Nice to meet you, Garrison."

"Aye," Garrison said. Head down.

"Don't worry about him, Dragon," Ben said. "He's not the talker that I am. But he's a fine fighter and wrestler. I've seen him pin a goblin and an orc. One right after the other."

"Impressive."

Sasha nudged me.

"Huh? Oh," I said. "Ben, what is—"

"No, Dragon, you owe him something else," she said.

"I do?" I said, looking at her. I didn't take her meaning right away, but then it hit me. "Oh, I do. I, uh, certainly do."

But what I owed him didn't come easy. It was Ben who had dragged me back to the city of Quintuklen after I blacked out. He'd secured the horses as I ordered.

Ridden me back to safety. He'd done everything by himself. Done it right. But saying thanks didn't come easy.

He wasn't supposed save me. I was supposed to save him.

I rubbed the back of my neck and said to Ben's friend Garrison, "Did Ben tell you how he saved my life?"

Garrison nodded.

Ben was beaming.

"Ben," I said, extending my hand, "thanks for taking care of me."

He accepted my hand. "Well, you taught me. Told me all about adventuring and responsibility. It was easy."

"Oh, is that so?" Sasha said. "My, you sound like someone I know."

"Don't say it," I said.

"I won't," she said.

Ben tried to hug me again but I stopped him. "That's enough of that. Now tell us, what is going on?"

"Ettins, Dragon! Ettins are doing this!" he said.

Sasha looked at me with a funny look on her face. "Ettins are awfully rare. It doesn't seem likely that ettins are about."

I had only seen one once before, and I'd gotten little more than a glimpse. "Really, Ben? How can you be sure? Did you see them?"

He nodded his head with vigor. "I swear it, Dragon! I even shot at one with my bow. My arrow skipped right off it, like its eyelid was made of stone."

"I don't know. Ettins are pretty big and slow," I said. "You only got one shot off? Not at least three or four?"

"Oh, it's big, all right. At least thirty feet tall." Ben stretched his arms up and held them wide. "And I only got one shot off because I had to run for my life."

"Why?"

"They're like rolling boulders when they run! They would have crushed us," he said, "so Garrison and I ran. We hid!"

It seemed a stretch. The ettin I'd seen was only twenty feet in height, if that. Maybe just fifteen. "Thirty feet tall?" I said.

Both Ben and Garrison nodded their heads vigorously.

Ben went on in a high-pitched rush. "And it has two heads! Ugly as an orc. Well, kinda. Scary, though. Really scary. It ate a man whole!"

"And they kidnapped the women?"

Again, they nodded.

Ben said, "You believe me, don't you, Dragon?"

"Sure he does," Sasha said, "and I believe you too."

"So," I said, "where is the ettin you shot at now?"

Ben pointed toward the smoke over the next hill.

"The Legionnaires followed him that way. The commander ordered us to stay put at this village and help out. This isn't the only village to fall. Another burns. They like setting things on fire. Why do they do that?"

I exchanged another odd look with Sasha. "Have you ever heard of an ettin raiding a village or stealing women?"

"No," she said. "That makes no sense. Not one bit."

"What does it look like, Ben?"

"Well, like I said, it's really tall. Has two heads… "

"We've established that, Ben. Can you tell me a little more? Does it have skin, scales, or fur? A tail? We can't be sure it's an ettin."

"Uh … uh …" Ben's eyes were growing.

Garrison stepped behind me.

"Dragon!" Brenwar yelled from out of nowhere.

The ground shook under my feet.

Thoom! Thoom!

I whipped my head around. Lumbering downhill it came. Two heads. Thirty feet tall. It had a squirming Legionnaire in one hand and a club the size of a whole tree in the other. It skipped the soldier over the ground like a stone.

"There be an ettin!" Brenwar said. He hoisted his war hammer over his head. "Battle ho!"

CHAPTER 6

I T WAS AN ETTIN. Two heads of matted brown hair. Thick skin covering hard packs of muscle. It towered even more than thirty feet in height. Its massive legs shook the ground.

Sasha wrapped her arms around my waist. She was trembling.

"Dragon!" she said. "Can you stop that ... that monster?"

"I told you he was big," Ben said, nocking an arrow.

I jumped on my horse.

"Stay here!" I said. "Ben. Garrison. Keep an eye on Sasha!"

Thoom!

Thoom!

Thoom!

The ettin's club went up and down, pulverizing everything in sight. A host of Legionnaires scrambled. Others fell. Horses bucked and whinnied.

Brenwar, Bayzog, and Shum had galloped toward the monster, obstructing its path. I sped after them.

"Yah!"

Brenwar was the giant expert. Not me. But he'd told me stories about how the dwarves fought the giants. And as best I could recall, and I recalled plenty, it took many, many dwarves. Today we only had one. I could hear Brenwar's thunderous bellows. He was fighting mad. But he was happy.

A blue ball of fire erupted from Bayzog's fingers, shooting across the sky and into the ettin's face.

It roared and shook its thick neck. Face smoking, it turned on its attacker, roared again, and charged.

"Bayzog!" I yelled.

He couldn't hear me. There was too much noise. The Legionaries galloped by, hurling spears into its legs. Arrows ricocheted off its faces. Just like Ben said.

"Bayzog!" I said. "Get out of the way!"

The ettin loomed over them and raised its crude club.

Brenwar attacked its ankles with his war hammer.

Its great club came down. Bayzog was right underneath it.

Boom!

"Noooooo!" I screamed.

Bayzog was down.

I snapped the reins. "Monster!" I galloped up the hill at full speed.

A man was standing in my path. Waving.

"Huh?"

It was Bayzog. I'd almost run over him.

I jerked back the reins and stopped.

"Pretty fine sorcery, eh, Dragon?" he said, lifting his black brows.

"You trickster you!" I said. "Get on, will you?"

Bayzog shook his head. "I do my best work from a distance. That illusion was just a test. He's strong, Dragon. Resistant to normal weapons—and to some magic too. That ball I sent was no illusion. It should have knocked one head out."

"What do you suggest, Bayzog?"

He lifted one brow. Everyone else was fighting, and he was thinking.

I didn't have time to wait. I pulled Fang from his sheath and charged onward. Behind me I heard Bayzog shout something, but the wind carried it away.

"Dragon! Dragon!"

Fang flared with blue life.

Chaos surrounded the ettin. A score of soldiers attacked from all directions. Shum was nowhere to be seen. I searched for Brenwar. *Where are you, dwarf?* The heavy head of his war hammer flashing in the air caught the corner of my eye.

KaRoom!

Brenwar smashed the bones in the ettin's ankle.

The ettin screamed like the world was going to end. *Good!*

Thoom!

Thoom!

Thoom!

It hopped up and down on one foot. The club swiped over the ground. Brenwar ducked beneath it. Soldiers and horses skipped over the ground.

I dug my heels into my steed. I had to stop this monster before it killed or hurt anyone else.

KaRoom!

Brenwar hit it again.

The ettin toppled forward.

"Nooooo!" I yelled.

It landed on top of Brenwar.

"Great Guzan!"

I was almost there. The Legionnaires piled onto the monster. They pinned it down with weighted nets and ropes. Bound its arms and legs.

Shum appeared on the ettin's great chest. Agile. Graceful. The Elven Ranger flung a sparkling dust into the eyes of one of its heads.

The ettin thrashed and rolled. The soldiers holding the ropes were flung into one another and scattered. Its huge fists came down, crushing one soldier, crippling another. Its powerful legs snapped the ropes that bound it. It ripped them from its body like threads.

It was going to take a lot more than plain ol' manpower to take this monster down. I readied my sword.

"Fang," I said, "don't let me down."

I held onto Fang with both my dragon hands and swung into its knee like I was chopping into a tree. I got halfway through in one swing.

Both heads cried out.

White-blue energy erupted from the blade. Ice formed. Spread above and below the knee.

"Brenwar!"

The dwarf lay smashed face-first into the ground.

I jumped off my horse and pulled him up. His full-body impression remained in the grass.

"Are you all right?"

He was moving. His voice was muffled. "Blecht!" He spit out grass, wildflowers, and dirt. "Bloody ettin sat on me," he said. "Don't you dare tell anyone, Dragon. No one sits on a dwarf and lives to tell about it." He picked up his hammer. "Where is it?"

I pointed.

The ettin was standing again, right behind us. Its legs were stuck together. The ice had frozen everything between its knees and ankles. Its ugly heads bickered at each other, speaking in Ettish. One hand rubbed at the dust in one of its head's eyes. Arrows and spears zinged off its bare chest. Spears dangled in its other arm, which swung wildly, pounding at the ice.

Brenwar huffed. "It's a tough one, it is!"

"I agree. So, you're the giant killer. What do we do now, Brenwar?"

He shrugged. "Keep fighting. We'll wear it down!"

"That's it? Five hundred years of dwarven wisdom and it narrows down to 'Keep fighting. We'll wear it down'?" I said.

"Don't have time for a longer answer," Brenwar said. He slammed his war hammer into one toe, then another.

The giant's club swept over the grass, with Brenwar right in its path.

I jumped and knocked Brenwar out of the way.

Wok!

The club hit me square in the chest. Head over heels I crashed. I saw spots. I was dizzy. My chest felt like busted glass. I couldn't catch my breath. I made it back to my feet and fell again.

Ahead, the ettin whacked at the ice, but it held.

Somehow, Shum managed to lasso the ettin's necks.

The Legionnaires tied the ropes off with a team of horses. They snorted. Dug their hooves in. Tried to pull it down.

The ettin wasn't going down. Not for anyone. It fought. It yelled. Then one head yawned. The one Shum had dumped the dust on. The monstrous body quavered. One head looked with dreamy eyes at the other. The wakeful head shouted at itself. It clonked itself on the sleepy head with its club, but the head dipped into its chest. One side of its body went slack. The horses heaved one more time.

Down it went.

Boom!

So did I.

CHAPTER 7

"WAKE UP, DRAGON! WAKE UP!" I heard Brenwar say.

Oh no! I thought. *Not again.* I opened my eyes.

Brenwar held a hard stare on me. Shum, Bayzog, and Sasha looked concerned. Even Ben was there, kneeling at my side, fanning me with a shield.

"How long have I been out?" I said, looking at my hands.

"Ho! How long! What do you ask that for?" Brenwar said, fists on hips. "Afraid ye might wake up with a tail?" He held out his arm and pulled me up. Checked my behind. "All clear."

The others laughed.

"Are you all right, Dragon?" Sasha said. "You've only been down a few minutes. Were you worried that you might have changed again?"

"No," I said, clutching my chest. It ached, and yes, I had been worried. But now I was relieved. Same day. Same me. A good thing. I rubbed my chest. "Great Guzan, that was quite a walloping. I don't think I've ever blacked out before from a hit. Ugh. Still hurts."

"Good thing you had dwarven breastplate on," Brenwar said. "Else yer stomach be on the other side of the village. Hah."

A good thing indeed. But something troubled me.

"I took that blow for you, Brenwar. If you weren't so slow—"

"Slow!" His beard bristled. He shook his hammer in my face. "I'll show you slow, Dragon. On yer feet! I'll put another bump on yer head."

Shum stepped between us. "Let's focus on the wounded. We're all fine. For now, that is."

"What do you mean by that?" I said.

"Can you walk?" Shum said.

"Of course I can." I started to stand. "Oof!" Sweat beaded on my head.

"Let me help you, Dragon," Ben said, offering his hand.

"No, I'm all right." I eyed Brenwar. "I'll just be more careful who I decide to save next time."

"Pah!" Brenwar said, walking away.

Shum stood and waited, fingers locked over his pot belly. Bayzog was beside him.

My eyes rested on them a moment, thinking how both were elves, but different. Shum, dressed in worn leathers, was tall, broad, relaxed, and thick wristed. Bayzog's dark robes were elegant, his features stern, his movements purposeful, even for a part elf. They were the kind of people I liked to be around. Different. Like me.

"Where we going?" I said, following.

Shum pointed.

The ettin. It was right where they had left it: sitting up, coiled in ropes, chains, and mystic banding that sparkled. One head snored. The other was silent. Searching. It locked eyes on me. I felt a chill. Most giants were ornery and stupid. This one was pure evil.

"What are the Legionnaires doing?" I said.

"Building a fire," Shum said. His brows pinched. "A big one."

"For what?" I said.

"Burn it!" a farmer yelled. He brandished a hoe in his hands, and tears fell from is eyes. "It took my wife. It killed my friends! Burn it!"

A crowd of villagers gathered around. Several threw rocks and stones at the ettin. It laughed.

"Garrison," I said. "Who is in charge here?"

"Commander Wuzlin. Why?"

"Make sure he realizes that ettins don't burn. And if we kill the ettin, how are we supposed to find the women?"

"But—" Ben said.

"Just go! Make haste, Garrison, before they burn down everything."

Garrison scurried away. Ben frowned and watched his friend go.

Sasha patted Ben's back, and he smiled, just a little.

I shook my head and spoke kindly to Ben. "These villagers are angry. Scared. Being unreasonable will follow. They want justice. They want blood. But I want answers." I turned to the rest of my friends. "Come on. Any of you speak Ettish?"

"Perhaps he speaks Common," Ben said.

"I can speak a little giant," Shum said, "and ogre. He might understand that."

Bayzog stepped between Ben and Sasha and took Sasha's hand. "Even if the ettin understands what we say, why would he acknowledge it? Ettins, like all giants, are as stubborn as they are big."

I thought that unfortunately, Bayzog was probably right.

And this ettin, he was massive. A thick slab of hair and skin slapped over solid muscle. One head had a nose ring, the other two hooped earrings.

I couldn't help but wonder who had made them such things. Did ettins have blacksmiths?

I hopped up onto its ice-coated knee, walked over its leg, and poked Fang into one of its noses.

"OW!" it said, shaking its awake head, looking away. "Don't do that again."

I understood it. It was a rugged language but not ancient. Clear enough to make out.

"Ettin. Where are the women?"

One head snored. Drooled. The other turned back to face me and breathed.

"Ew!" I covered my face with my arm. It was foul beyond words.

"Heh-heh-heh!" it said. "Like that, do you? The smell of many men I ate."

I poked its nose again.

"Ow!"

"I'm not playing games, ettin. Where are the women?"

It shook its shaggy head. "Hah! You'll never know!"

A rock pelted me in the head.

"What are you doing?" I turned and locked eyes with a villager who stood there wide eyed.

A moment later Ben tackled him. "I got him, Dragon. What shall I do with him?"

Knock some sense into him. I wanted to say that. I really did. "Take his rocks and send him home!"

"Burn it!" someone said.

"Burn it! Burn it! Burn it!" They started to chant.

The bonfire was getting bigger and bigger. Flames went up and black smoke rolled over the hills. If I was going to get an answer, I would have to get it quick.

"All right, ettin," I said, "Tell me this. Why did you take the women? Why did you attack the village?" I tapped the flat blade of Fang on its nose. "Hmmm?"

Its voice was gruff. Harsh. A deep tunnel when it spoke. "Why not!" it said. Quick. Angry.

"I see. So, you just like picking on little things. Perhaps where you're from they pick on you? You are a bit small for an ettin."

"Ggggrrrrrrrlll!" Its brows buckled. The other head started to wake up.

"Dragon!" Brenwar said. Shum was helping him up onto the ettin's leg. "Let me at him! I'll make him tell us where the women are!" He raised his hammer over the ettin's icy knee. "Answer up, ettin!" Brenwar yelled.

"Hold up, Brenwar! Give me a few minutes at least," I said.

"Hah! Stupid dwarf can't hurt me!" The ettin laughed. "Little bearded hogs. That's what we call them."

Brenwar brought that hammer down.

Whack!

Both of the ettin's heads let out ear-splitting howls.

Ears covered, the villagers fled, screaming.

I yelled at Brenwar. "Did you have to do that?"

"Aye!" Brenwar said, raising his hammer again.

"Stop it, will you!" I said.

I watched the villagers. They sprinted. Panicked. It didn't make sense to me. The ettin, loud as it might be, wasn't going anywhere. But I'd had enough of their lousy rock throwing already. How could you miss an ettin at close range?

"Nath!"

"What?" I said, looking around.

Shum and Bayzog, standing on the ground, were waving their hands at me.

I shrugged. "Really, what is it?"

The sound of a Legionnaire's War Horn blasted through the air. Briefly, I thought, *What is taking Garrison so long?*

Then the elves pointed toward the smoke over the horizon.

I turned.

Thoom!

Another ettin cleared the hill.

"HA! HA! HA!" My ettin prisoner laughed. "My brother is here!"

CHAPTER
8

ONE ETTIN ENCOUNTER IN A day was enough to last you a lifetime, but two? That seemed impossible. I shook my head and looked at Brenwar.

He had an expression I'd never seen before. His brows were lifted. His mouth was open. The grumbler was puzzled.

"Nath," Bayzog said, "suggestions?"

Thoom! Thoom! Thoom!

The second ettin strode past the tall trees, head higher than the branches. A heavy chain was draped over his neck with a massive anchor on the end of it. He uprooted trees from the ground like pulling carrots, and he slung them across the land. He was bigger than his brother. Dark bearded. Terrible. Mean. Cruel expression. Heavy muscles over a solid round belly.

"You die now, dragon man," the first ettin said.

The other head shook. Blinked its blurry eyes. Snorted. "What happened?"

"Quiet! I'm in charge of this."

The other head snorted. "No, I'm the oldest." It whipped around. "Say, who tied me up?"

Thoom! Thoom! Thoom!

"Dragon!" Bayzog said. "Time to act!"

"Hold yer ground, Dragon," Brenwar said. He raised his hammer. "We've got a prisoner."

I nodded. Watched.

The Legionnaires lined in rank, making a wall between our prisoner and the brother ettin. The bright plumes on their helmets billowed in the wind. They lowered their lances. The ettin heads stopped and bickered. The War Horn sounded again. The Knights of Quintuklen charged. They were brave men. Some of the bravest men I ever saw.

The first ettin laughed in my face. Low. Wicked.

Hooves thundered up the hillside. Shiny armor gleamed in the sunlight. It was a glorious sight. Brave men riding into battle. Doing what was right. Fighting evil.

The second ettin lifted the chain from his neck and roared. The anchor circled like a lasso over its heads. A fierce grin crossed its faces.

SWOOSH!

The ettin struck, scattering horses and riders all over the ground.

I yelled, "Nooooo!"

The bound-up ettin laughed.

More people would die if I didn't stop this.

A white streak of power slammed into the second ettin's face. It howled and dropped the anchor on its toe. One face was smoking. Angry.

The Legionnaires struck again. Their volley of arrows skipped off its face. Lances shattered on its limbs.

It swatted them away, knocking men into men, toppling horses and riders.

"Retreat!" I yelled.

It picked up its anchor and came right at us. Angry eyes locked on Bayzog.

I could see Bayzog's eyes were drained. Weary.

"Shum!" I said, "Get Bayzog and Sasha to safety. I'll handle this."

Shum scooped his hands behind them and scurried them away.

Thoom! Thoom! Thoom!

"YOU GONNA GET IT NOW, DRAGON MAN!"

"Be quiet," Brenwar said, shaking his war hammer in the first ettin's face.

I reached over my back and grabbed Akron.

Snap. Clatch. Snap.

The ettin brother would overtake us in two more steps.

I loaded a moorite arrow and pulled the bow with my two dragon arms.

Twang!

The arrow buried in its knee.

The second ettin roared and turned on me.

I reloaded. A different arrow this time. I rubbed some spit on the tip and it glowed white hot. I pointed it at one face of the ettin prisoner, whose chest I stood upon.

Towering over me and the others, the ettin brother swung his anchor and chain.

"LET MY BROTHER GO!" it said.

I pulled back on the arrow and pointed right at one of the ettin prisoner's eyes. They all widened. The tip of my arrow was still white hot. I took my aim back and forth from face to face, eye to eye.

"You better tell your big brother to back off," I said. "You don't you want any part of an exploding arrow, do you?"

"No!" one head said.

"No! No! No!" said the other head.

I touched the tip of the arrow on one of the ettin's noses. It sizzled.

"Tell your brother to back away, then," I said.

Tears formed in the eyes of one. A grunt came for the other.

"Don't do it," one said.

"No! I don't want my head exploded," said the other.

"Oh, don't worry," I said. "I have plenty of arrows for the both of you."

Lumps rolled up and down their throats. They shouted.

"Brother! Back off!"

The ettin swinging the chain did no such thing. He stomped his foot, shaking the ground. He growled.

The Legionnaires continued their attacks. Some spears and arrows stuck in the ettin's hide. Others broke. The ettin didn't seem to notice.

A spear zinged by my head.

An arrow splintered on Brenwar's chest. "Who shot that?" he said.

"Ben!" I said. "Find the commander. Tell them to back off!"

"All right, Dragon!" Ben dashed away.

I stood on the ettin's chest, thinking. *Why the sudden attack on a small village? I have to find the women. Get them released.* But the Legionnaires would want to avenge their casualties. The villagers would want payment for the lost.

"Dragon," Brenwar said, "you can't trust what they say."

Crack!

Another arrow shattered on his armored chest.

"That's enough of that, I say!"

The ettin turned. Swung his anchor into the ranks, scattered the soldiers like leaves.

"Ettin!" I yelled. "Don't do that again! Else your brother's going to have one head, not two!"

It turned and lowered its big eyes. Its hairy brows buckled like giant caterpillars, and one head licked its lips. It stopped swinging and draped the chain and anchor around its neck like jewelry. What was taking place was just not normal.

"Let me hit him in the knee again," Brenwar said.

"No, just give it a moment."

The War Horn sounded. The Legionnaires, on horse and foot, made another formation and trotted back up the hill, leaving me, Brenwar, and two ettins all by ourselves.

"Can we talk now?" I yelled up to him.

His words were loud. Slow. Deep.

"FREE MY BROTHER. OR DIE!" Its ugly faces smiled. "I CAN KILL ALL OF YOU. I WILL KILL ALL OF YOU IF YOU HARM MY BROTHER!"

Great Guzan! I hadn't thought of that. Supposing I did kill the ettin—which even though it was evil, I shouldn't—what was to stop its brother from going on a rampage and killing more people?

"You won't be killing me," Brenwar said, "you smelly animal. I've taken down giants bigger than you!"

"GO BACK TO MORGON," one head said.

"YOU BEARDED HALFLING," said the other.

"Bearded what?" Brenwar started to bring his hammer down.

"Don't!" I said. "Brenwar, let me handle this."

Delay him, Nath, a voice said in my mind. It was Bayzog. *We search for the women as you speak.*

"You better make it fast," I said.

"Make what fast?" Brenwar said. "Hitting the ettin?"

"No," I said, "I was ... never mind. Just be still."

I didn't want to tip the ettins off. They weren't the smartest of the giants, but they weren't stupid as orcs either. Well, maybe.

"Listen, ettin," I said, "No one has to die. Not me. Not you. Not your brother. Let's just trade. Your brother for the women. Even is even."

"It's a good idea, Brother," the ettin prisoner said.

"THERE CAN BE NO DEAL." Both of the free ettin's heads shook as they said it.

Something about the way it said that ran a chill right through me.

"Of course there can be," I said. I didn't want to say the next thought I had in my mind, but I did. "Unless something has happened to the women."

"HA, HA, HA," it laughed. "THEY ARE ALL DEAD."

CHAPTER
9

"**T**HIS IS PERFECT. DELICIOUS. SALIVATING.**" Kryzak wiped the sweat from his colorful head.

Before him, a small image of a man shimmered inside his grand tent, speaking on a bright carpet.

"It's going well, High Cleric," the man said in Common. "Nath Dragon battles the ettins as we speak. Others have split up. I must go now." The gray image bowed.

He snapped his fingers. The image faded away.

"I wish I could see it," Kryzak said, wringing his hands. He walked over and sat in a plush chair.

Two draykis were on each side. Four acolytes in grey robes and with single tattooed rings on their bald heads stood inside the tent as well.

He snapped his fingers.

One acolyte readied a goblet. The other poured.

Kryzak took the goblet and drank.

For years he'd been hunting dragons. Now he was hunting the most valuable one of all. Nath Dragon. He had longed for this day. Longed for the day he could prove himself to be the one, the only one for High Priestess Selene.

"I want to be alone now," he said.

The acolytes departed, ducking through the tent flap one by one. Behind him, the draykis, nearly seven feet of brawn and scales, stiff as statues, remained. He liked them. Commanding things so big and powerful gave him a thrill.

He patted the bright tattoos on his head with a satin cloth.

"Nath Dragon," he muttered. "So far, so easy... "

The Clerics of Barnabus were a crafty lot. Their eyes and ears were everywhere. In cities, large and small. In villages, but not all.

He slumped back in his chair and closed his eyes. He smiled.

"No one can evade Barnabus."

Nath Dragon and his party had been caught leaving Quintuklen. It was the last place he'd been seen since they trapped him at the temple. That's where the drultures came in, flying notes back and forth faster than eagles. They tracked his every move southeast, toward Narnum.

Kryzak's guess at Nath Dragon's destination was the elven city of Elome, judging by the direction of his travel and the company he kept. An elven wizard. A Roaming Ranger. Why there he didn't know, so he kept his distance. He had to work fast, though. Find any help he could get.

That's how he'd found Ettin Cove. The giant brutes had taken some convincing, but in the end, they had agreed. Kryzak had his ways. Now the ettins laid into one small village after the other. There was no way Nath Dragon and his party would miss them. No way the cries and despair of the voices wouldn't lure him.

Especially when Kryzak had spies within the ranks of the Legionnaires.

"I wish I could see it." He mumbled some words, and smoke billowed from his mouth and nose, filling the tent in thick layer of gloom. "But we'll see how it goes."

CHAPTER
10

O N HORSEBACK, SHUM AND BAYZOG made their way from the village.
Shum the Roaming Ranger was leading the way, following the trail of the
ettins, when he pulled his horse to a stop. The big-boned elf slid off his
horse, stepped into one of the giant foot impressions in the tall grass, and kneeled.

Bayzog, a bit weary, prepared a spell on his lips. He didn't feel comfortable.
He wasn't ready. Over the decades, he'd spent most of his time indoors. Studying.
Crafting. And it had been a decade since he'd last ventured into the wilderness. He
was a little unsettled. He sneezed.

Shum looked up at him with a funny expression on his face.

"What?" Bayzog said, "Nothing to worry about. Probably from the excitement."

Shum shook his head and sniffed the air. The smoke in the distance was dying
down.

"I could smell them before," Shum said, pushing his long hair from his face, "but
the wind has changed. The tracks, however, hmmm, well, they come from separate
directions."

Bayzog coughed a little. Tapped his chest with his fist. He'd been uncomfortable
since they had left. Not so much about the woodland but about heading back home.
To Elome. He was an outsider. Part elf. Part human. His human side didn't fight
off the elements like the elven blood did. It bothered him. It always had. Shum was
different, too, but a pure elf. One born in the harsh outdoors, living among the
beasts and the monsters. A part of nature itself. The big elf stood in the footprint
as tall as himself, staring over the horizon. Bayzog wondered if Shum felt the same.

"I say we follow the bigger one. Away from the smoke." Shum swung himself
into his saddle. "Their lair can't be too far." Shum looked at him. Waiting.

"After you," Bayzog said.

They rode until the hills became steep and the terrain rugged, moss over rock-
covered ground. This was the part Bayzog didn't like. The sudden changes. The air.
The wind. The setting sun. No roof over his head. He wasn't sure if it was the man

or the elf that preferred the indoors over the out. Elves, by nature, liked open spaces, the comfort of greenery blended with stone and tree trunks.

Shum slowed. Hooves splashed over a creek bed into a denser patch of woods. He looked over his shoulder at Bayzog with narrow eyes.

Bayzog felt it too. A shift. A darkness. The fine hairs on his arms tingled. That was the elf in him. He was certain. He still had the instincts, just a little dormant. He thought of Sasha. He hated not having her by his side. She gave him comfort. Security. She understood his nervousness and the edginess he fought so hard to hide. He made a sound in Elvish. A hoot of sorts.

Shum let him catch up.

"I should check in with Dragon. It's been awhile," he said. "And if we go too far, I can't connect."

"Do as you will, wizard. I'll scout ahead."

"No," Bayzog said.

"Beg pardon?"

"Oh, nothing," he said, scanning the area. "Don't let me hold you up. I'll be fine."

Shum and his horse blended into the brush and out of sight.

Bayzog took a deep breath. It was still day but dark under the heavier foliage. The trees seemed foreboding. The sounds of nature—the trickle of the creek, the buzzing wings—did little to soothe him. He was alone and anything could happen. Like running into an ettin. He shuddered. They were some of the most fearsome things he'd ever seen. So big. Strong. Unpleasant.

"Ease yourself, Bayzog," he said to himself. "Check in with Dragon and Sasha."

He started the incantation for the communication spell, and magic filled his body. His mind became a spring of energy.

Thoom.

The ground shook. He lost his concentration.

Thoom.

His horse stamped and snorted. He clutched at the reins, heart pounding.

"All right, Shum, where are you?"

CHAPTER 11

THE VILLAGERS. THE LEGIONNAIRES. SASHA and Brenwar. They all fell silent. The ettin had said, in words all could understand, "The women are all dead."

Children sobbed. Tears watered in men's eyes. The hardened soldiers' faces were creased in worry. And there stood the second ettin, arms folded over its chest, gloating.

"NO WOMEN TO TRADE." All four of its brows lifted. "BUT, LET MY BROTHER GO, NO MORE HARM. NO MORE DEATH ... SCALY ONE."

"You lie!" I said.

I've said it before. I'm good at telling the truth from a lie. And Brenwar had already told me a thousand times that giants are liars.

But the villagers didn't know that. The soldiers didn't either.

I searched for Sasha. She was tending to the wounded in the field. I hoped maybe she could contact Bayzog. Tell him to hurry. At the moment, we were at a standstill. I had to buy time. I had to calm the villagers.

"Ben!"

He ran over to me. Marveled at the ettins, then turned to me.

"Yes, Dragon?"

"He's lying. The women aren't dead. Spread the word around."

He started to run off.

"And be convincing!"

The villagers wouldn't stand for this much longer. They'd attack. So would the soldiers, and more of them would die. I couldn't let that happen.

"I'm losing my patience, ettin." I turned my bow on the second ettin. "Perhaps it's you that would be better off without one head. Perhaps one doesn't agree so much with the other."

The ettins scratched their heads. Turned to one another and whispered in Ettish.

I could understand it.

I whispered to Brenwar. "Get your chest."

"Why?" he said.

"Just do it."

"And what?"

"I don't know. Think of something. Ask Sasha."

Brenwar looked at me and the ettin's knee.

"Just one more lick, ay?" He lifted his bushy black brows.

"Go!"

"All right, then." He hopped down and marched off.

The ettins turned back to me. The second one scratched one of its heads. The first one looked worried. At least I had them thinking.

"YOU WON'T SHOOT. YOU SHOOT, WE SMASH PEOPLE."

"I shoot, one of you won't be smashing anything. And need I remind you I have plenty of arrows?"

I knew one of my arrows would hurt them. But kill them? Maybe. And I wasn't so sure it was all right to kill an ettin. Even if it had killed many innocent people. It was all confusing. But I should be able to outsmart an ettin.

Twang!

The ettin ducked. My arrow sailed high over its head.

"HA! YOU MISSED!"

"No, no I didn't. Take a look behind you," I said.

The ettin's heads turned.

KABOOM!

The ettin flinched and covered its eyes.

Everyone screamed.

Less than a hundred yards past the second ettin, a hundred-foot-tall oak cracked and groaned. Its trunk was bigger than the ettin's hairy legs. It wavered. Teetered and toppled and crashed to the ground.

The second ettin turned to me, grunting. Scratching its heads. A worried look grew on its faces.

I had another arrow aimed right at it.

"HMRPH," it said. "We think about this."

"You do that, ettin. In the meantime," I said, pointing my bow at its brother, "I'll keep a close eye, a very close one, on your brother."

"No shoot!" it said. "No shoot!"

Its chest rose up and down under my feet. I could feel its heart beating in my toes. Heavy rapid thumps. It was worried. The more worried the better. It gave me control.

For some reason, I was thirsty. I felt really hot and uncomfortable, not to mention the ettin's hot breath was so foul and nasty. It took away my appetite. Still, something else was gnawing at my stomach.

Earlier, I'd felt great. I had two dragon arms. I was bigger, faster, and stronger. Now I felt so small and ineffective. I wasn't sure how to fight a monster more than thirty feet tall. Its hands were so big that it could squeeze my head off. Snap me like a twig. Perhaps I wasn't such a big deal in Nalzambor after all.

The second ettin turned and took a knee, facing me and its brother. It spoke more quietly.

"Let my brother go and we'll bring back your women," the head on the left said.

"I thought you said they were all dead."

"I didn't say they were alive," he head on the right said, "but at least you could bury them." It chuckled and showed a toothy grin.

Now I had to wonder, did one head lie? Did the other head tell the truth? It was best to assume they both lied. But it angered me. It was a horrible thought, them killing innocent women. I adjusted my bow. Drew it tight. Aimed at the last head that had spoken.

"I've had enough! Take us to the women or your brother will suffer."

"All right! All right!" it said. "We'll take you. Just, please, put down your bow. We don't want to lose a head. We don't want to have a hole in us." It leaned back. "You win, dragon man."

"That's better." I unnocked my arrow. "Now, tell me where—"

"*ACHOO!*"

The first ettin sneezed. My footing shifted, and I dropped to my seat. The disgusting spray was all over me.

"Yuck!" I said, slinging my hands and wiping my face.

Snap! Snap! Snap!

The first ettin's bindings were breaking. A howl of villagers and soldiers filled the air.

"What is going—"

Whap!

The recumbent ettin's big hand swatted me from its chest. I tumbled to the ground and Akron fell from my grasp. Above me, the second ettin was cutting the cords with a stone knife I hadn't noticed earlier. I dove for my bow. The first ettin slapped its hand over it.

"No 'Boom Boom' for you, dragon man!"

They had me surrounded. A pair of great hands clutched after me. I ducked under a swinging fist and hopped over a clutching hand. They were quick for being so big. Their size negated my speed.

Wham! Wham! Wham!

Fists bigger than barrels shook the ground. Big fingers grasped for me. I went for my sword.

Swat!

The second ettin backhanded me and flattened me to the ground. The first ettin scooped me up in both hands, pinning my arms to my sides.

I flexed my dragon arms. I tried to kick. But I could only move my toes.

The ettins chuckled.

"Look what we have here, Big Brother," the first ettin said. "We got us a dragon man. Let's take him, throw him in a pot, and turn him to stew like the others."

CHAPTER 12

THE GROUND SHOOK. BAYZOG SHUDDERED. Pictures of angry ettins danced in his head. He had to run. Hide. Do something. He muttered a protection spell. A mystic surge coursed through his blood. Calmness and security followed. He sighed.

"That's better."

Thoom.

The footsteps were distant, and he didn't have to be an elven ranger to know that. But how close was too close?

Something else caught his ears, and he hunkered down in his saddle, eyes searching. The rustling foliage. Darting. Jumping. It was fast and coming right at him. He dove to the ground and covered his head. A herd of gazelles burst across the path, leapt over him, and disappeared. His spooked horse trotted out of sight.

"Oh, great," he said, rising and dusting off his robes. "Shum would laugh, maybe, if he saw that. Every elf in Nalzambor would. Shameful."

He ambled down the path—tripping over his robes before pulling them up—and went after the horse. The beast was well trained and wouldn't run far unless it was really spooked. He figured on the worst-case scenario for Shum. *Probably being eaten by an ettin by now.* He forged ahead, pushing branch after branch from his face. He caught his robes on one, jerked the material free, and tore it.

"Drat it all," he said, under his breath. He wiped the sweat from his forehead.

Thoom.

His heart skipped and beat faster.

"Thank goodness for protection spells. Otherwise I'd be on the other side of the creek by now."

He moved on.

Thoom.

He stopped.

Breathe, Bayzog. Breathe.

The points on his ears bent a little. Something else was running toward him.

He grabbed a stick and waited. *I'm not getting my robes dirty this time.*

A woman's voice cried out.

"Aiiyee!"

He ran toward the sound of her voice.

She screamed again.

He jumped over a log, smashed through the branches, and ran right into her. They both tumbled to the ground. The woman was distraught and her clothes were in tatters. She had to be one of the villagers.

"Woman," he said, "it's all right. You are safe now."

Her eyes were wide, darting, and glossy. Her entire body trembled. Bayzog brushed her dark hair from her scraped-up face. She just blinked at him like he wasn't there.

"Did the ettins have you?"

She nodded.

Thoom!

She grabbed his robes and said, "Please! Please! Take me home! Get me away from here!"

"Easy," he said. "We'll get you home—"

Thoom!

She tore away from him and dashed into the woods.

"Wait!" he said, jumping after her.

"Aiiyee!" she said.

Bayzog ran after her, darted behind the trees, and stopped. Someone had a hold of the woman, and she beat and clawed at his chest. It was Shum. The big elf grabbed her by the back of the neck and squeezed. The woman collapsed in his arms.

"Is she all right?" Bayzog said.

"She'll be fine."

"What happened? Is she hurt?"

Shum showed a few teeth and said, "No, just a little Roaming Ranger trick."

Thoom!

"That thing's getting closer," Bayzog said. "Is it an ettin?"

"I suppose. And looking for her, no doubt. Come on."

They wove in and out of the trees. Shum carried the woman in his arms like a baby. Seconds later they found both horses.

"Ah, good," Bayzog said, "I thought he was lost."

"No worries," Shum said, "can you ride with her?"

"Me? Why not you?"

"I'm not going back," Shum said, "you are."

"What are you going to do?"

"What I always do," Shum said, "find the missing."

Bayzog swung himself up on the horse. Shum handed up the woman and draped her over the saddle. Then Shum whispered in the horse's ear.

"Can you speak Horse?"

Shum nodded.

"What did you tell it?"

"To carry you right back to where we came from," Shum said, guiding the horse away.

Thoom!

The trees shook and birds scattered. Several critters dashed under the horses' bellies.

Bayzog was saying, "I'll come back with the others—"

When Shum whacked the horse on the rear, and it leapt forward.

Bayzog surged ahead, glancing back over his shoulder.

Shum leapt onto his horse and disappeared.

A tree crashed down right behind Shum, followed by a loud yell.

"WHERE ARE YOU?"

An ettin emerged. It stood as tall as the trees. Its dark eyes found Bayzog.

"Oh no!" he said, snapping the reins.

Thoom! Thoom! Thoom! Thoom!

The ettin ran right after him.

Shum realized his error. He had assumed the ettin would come for him, not Bayzog. That had been his plan, but plans change. He turned his horse and galloped after the ettin.

Ahead, two big heads bobbed up and down. Massive arms swung at its sides like hammers. The ettin's giant strides covered the ground as fast as a horse. He dug his heels into his steed.

"Yah!"

The horse thundered ahead. Shum's horse wasn't just any horse but a special one bred by the Roaming Rangers. Big and sleek, the Roamer Stallions were the rarest breed in the land. This was one of the fastest creatures on four hooves. In seconds, the chestnut horse was on the heels of the ettin, but Shum rode right by with the wind whistling in his long, pointed ears.

Ahead, Bayzog was doing little to distance himself from the ettin despite his mare's efforts.

Shum ran out in front of the ettin and angled the other way. The ettin didn't follow. It kept after Bayzog. It wanted the woman. *Time for plan two.*

Shum's long fingers wrapped around the shaft of a short spear that was hooked to the saddle. Its tip was intricate. Elven crafted. Only two feet long. He charged after the ettin. Its big steps would close in on Bayzog at any moment. Shum caught the worried look in Bayzog's eyes.

He pressed the spear to his lips and spoke in Ancient Elvish.

The spear extended. *Snap.* Three feet. *Snap.* Four feet. *Snap.* Six feet. The spearhead grew, widened, and brightened. Shum hopped up in the saddle and stood tall. He readied his spear over his head. He closed in. Five horse lengths. Three lengths. He dove at the ettin.

Ettins aren't as slow and stupid as they look!

Bayzog's protective spell did little to calm the fear in his belly now. Instead, he was riding for his life. A monstrosity of hair, heads, and yellow eyes followed him. Feet almost as big as his horse were ready to crush him. *I'll never leave home again.*

Shum appeared, riding hard, eyes narrowed, right on the giant's heels.

Yes! Follow him, ettin!

He glanced forward. The open plains to freedom waited. He glanced back over his shoulder.

No!

The ettin was still coming. Closer. One world-shaking foot after the other. He tried to think of a spell. Anything. *I can't ride and cast.*

The ettin's long arms stretched toward him and touched the horse's tail.

"Shum!" he yelled. *Where did he go?*

The ettin roared, "I HAVE YOU NOW!"

Bayzog cracked the reins.

"No!"

Shum reappeared, standing on the saddle, a spear as tall as a man glimmering in his hands. He was heading right for the ettin. One ettin head turned his way. The ettin stopped, whirled, and braced itself for impact. Shum leapt off his horse with his spear high over his head.

The ettin swung both fists at the same time. They came together like a clap of thunder. The elf and ettin tumbled to the ground. Shum disappeared under its bulk.

"No!" Bayzog yelled, pulling on the reins. The horse kept galloping. He pulled harder, but the horse kept going. The ettin's form disappeared behind the dale and out of sight.

"What do I do?"

CHAPTER 13

Pain. I was familiar with it. I'd been in pain before. But not like this. The first ettin was squeezing me to death with both hands.

I tried to yell, but I couldn't get enough air. It came out like a frog's croak. "Brenwar …"

All four ettin heads laughed.

"Dragon man hard to squish," the first ettin's one head said. Then its other head said, "I likes a challenge."

"Let's just eat him," the second ettin's one head said. His other head said, "My belly groans." Both of its heads smacked their lips.

The first ettin's mouths both watered, dripping spit all over me. "Wonder if he tastes like fish, with those scales."

Eaten! I can't let this happen.

I flexed my dragon arms as hard as I could, pushing out with my elbows.

My dragon arms pushed back the first ettin's grip on me just enough that I could gulp in some air.

I yelled, "Brenwar!"

The second ettin came closer. Its one head said, "He's loud." Its other head said, "I don't like that!"

"SILENCE!" all four ettin heads yelled.

My ears were ringing. It made me dizzy, they yelled so loud.

"You!" Brenwar yelled from somewhere.

I gazed all around. The ettins did as well.

"What do you want?" the second ettin said.

I spotted Brenwar, a vial of bright liquid in his hands. He tipped it up and drank it down. Eyed the ettin and yelled back up.

"I bet your rotten teeth can't gnaw through dwarven hide," Brenwar said. "I bet my beard you can't even catch me." He teetered back and forth on his feet. "Stupid giants!"

I had no idea which potion Brenwar had drunk. Perhaps it made him fast, like me. Well, maybe not that fast. Or hard as stone. Invisible, maybe.

But nothing happened.

The second ettin reached for Brenwar.

"Move, you stubborn dwarf!" I yelled.

My dragon arms weren't even getting tired. I could breathe just fine now. I wriggled, but I still couldn't get out of the first ettin's hands. If I stopped pushing out with my elbows, I would suffocate. I was stuck.

Brenwar just stood there. Shaking his first. Screaming at the giant. He was going to die. I was going to die. I could feel it.

The second ettin reached down and snatched Brenwar up from the ground.

"TIME TO SQUISH DWARF!" its one head said. It started to squeeze, and both of its heads groaned, "*HURK!*"

I almost turned my head. I yelled instead. "Put him down!"

The first ettin, the one who held me, the one whose spit was all over me, was laughing now with both heads. Low. Loud. Evil. "Hum, hum, hum, hum, HUM!"

Brenwar didn't even flinch. Instead, his beard got bigger. So did his head.

"WHAT?!" both the second ettin's heads said together.

Brenwar was laughing. Growing. Six feet. Ten feet tall.

The second ettin dropped him on the ground.

Brenwar kept growing. Fifteen feet. Twenty. He was the biggest dwarf in Nalzambor. A bearded mountain.

The second ettin stepped back, gaping.

Brenwar closed in on him. Socked him in the gut with a fist as big as a boulder. *WHOP!*

The ettin doubled over. A chorus of cheers went up from villagers and soldiers.

Brenwar grabbed the second ettin by the shaggy hair on its two heads and clonked them together. The ettin staggered back. Fell.

"Make him stop!" the first head of the ettin holding me said. Its other head said, "Stop him, or I'll crush you like a bug!"

"Crush me," I said, "and you'll make him mad. And you don't want to see him mad."

All four eyes blinked, drifting among me, Brenwar, and its brother.

"Maybe you should help your brother," I suggested.

"Quiet, dragon man!" it said with both mouths, narrowing all four eyes at me. It was getting mad. Thinking.

I struggled.

Its grip was like iron bars around me.

Brenwar and the ettin thrashed over the ground. Rolling. Punching. Cursing at each other. I didn't know how long the potion would last, but I didn't think it would last long.

POW!

Brenwar took a solid shot in the jaw. Shrugged it off. Punched into the ettin's ribs. Quick. Powerful blows. One right after the other.

BAP! BAP! BAP! BAP! BAP!

"Stop it, dwarf!" the first ettin's one head cried. His other head said, "Or I'll kill your friend."

Brenwar paused. Looked over. Giant drops of sweat beaded on his head. His broad chest heaved.

"NO!" he said. Then he socked the ettin again.

"What?" I said.

The angry first ettin squeezed harder.

My dragon arms gave in. My eyes bulged out of my head.

Zzzzzap!

The hairs stood up on both of the first ettin's heads. Its grip fell open. I dropped to the ground. Sasha was there, delicate hands glowing with flecks of energy.

Withdrawing Fang, I croaked in my frog voice, "Thanks, Sasha, but you better get out of here."

I blushed at how funny I sounded and gulped in some air. Whew!

The first ettin roared, "RRRRRAAAAHHHH!" It looked down and boomed, "WHO DARES?"

"Fast!" I said.

Sasha ran.

"You better help me," I said to Fang.

I banged the blade on the ground. Nothing!

"Drat it, Fang! I need you!"

The blade shimmered with blue light, almost mocking me. I shook my red mane. I was getting frustrated. But I had a bigger problem to deal with: the first ettin.

Both its fists came down.

I jumped out of the way.

"Fine, then," I said to Fang. "I'll do it the hard way!"

I darted between the ettin's legs. Chopped halfway through the back of its foot with Fang and my dragon arms.

It howled and hopped after me, fingers stretching for my neck.

But I was fast. Angry. Stronger now than ever. My blood was up, too. And I could breathe. I'd had enough of this. I poked its hand. It howled again. I ducked under a fist. Hopped back from a kicking toe. Stabbed Fang into its other big toe.

"Stop it! Stop it!" both of its heads yelled. It was hopping up and down on the foot with the bleeding big toe.

I did no such thing. I struck out at its legs. Hit one. Then the other. I wanted to punish it.

It wailed. It begged. Finally it fell.

"No more, dragon man!" "Stop now!" It waved its bleeding hand in my face.

I cut off a finger.

It howled and rolled.

"Dragon!" Brenwar yelled. He towered over me. Hands on hips. "Get ahold of yourself."

"Would it show mercy to me?" I said, raising the sword over my head. "To the people it's hurt? Killed?"

"No," Brenwar said, "but it's evil. You're good." He nodded to the ettin that was out cold behind him. "Besides, I think they'll tell us what we want to know now."

I took a deep breath. I was shaking.

The ettin was bleeding. Badly.

I didn't feel bad. I felt frustrated.

"This is your fault, Fang." I slammed him into the sheath. "Well, start the interrogation then, giant beard!"

"Don't you dare call me a giant ever again!" Brenwar poked me in the chest with his oversized finger. "And settle yourself down, Dragon."

I walked away, clutching my ribs that ached from the first ettin's grip.

"Dragon."

It was Sasha, coming after me.

"Just go away," I said.

She stopped, a sad look on her face, and turned away.

I just wanted to be alone. *How can I fight evil when I can't kill it?*

CHAPTER 14

"**U**RK!"

All four eyes of the ettin widened. Shum had gotten it right in the heart. The great elven spear jutted from its chest.

"Ugh," he said, removing his spear.

Shum had been fighting for hundreds of years. He'd killed and hunted many beasts, some mystical, some natural. Killing didn't bother him. It was survival. Him or them. Such was the Roaming Rangers' way.

He closed the ettin's eyes and muttered in Roamer, "May Nalzambor make good soil from your wicked bones."

He called for his horse.

It trotted over.

Shum hopped on, muttered a word.

The spear collapsed to little more than a pointed rod that he tethered to the saddle.

He looked for Bayzog.

The wizard was gone. Safe now, he hoped.

"Good," he said. He patted his horse on the neck. "Let's go."

Over the plains, across the creek, and into the forest he went, picking up the trail where he had left off. The ettin had made it easy. Branches were broken or crushed on the forest floor. It had been sloppy, trying to find the woman.

Even an ettin can be cautious. It must have been in a hurry.

His horse nickered.

Shum stopped. Cupped his ears and closed his eyes. His nose crinkled.

The sweat of ettins caught his nose. Pungent. Like a rotting rain.

"Ah," he said, "more mystery, it seems."

The scent and trail led him to a crater. Not one of the small ones that littered the hot lands in the south, but a huge crater a mile across, filled with rocks and greens. It was the biggest crater he'd ever seen. An inverted mountain. Its sides were lined with caves, clefts, and other openings.

"You better wait here," he said to his horse.

This crater was different. Ancient. Mysterious and out of place. Maybe it had been carved out by the giants or dwarves at one time. Maybe it led to the mines. His keen eyes scanned it from one rim to the other.

"Ah," he said. He hopped over the lip and—nimble as a spider—climbed down the wall.

It was deep. A hundred feet down, maybe two in some places. The farther down he went, the more he heard. He pulled his cloak up to cover his head. The fine hairs on his arms stood on end. His hand fell to his sword. He sniffed. Shook his head.

Not good.

The bottom of the grade was a forest of rocks and trees. Birds, dark and black with yellow eyes, darted in and out of the treetops. The sunlight was blocked by the rim, bringing darkness early. Shum could see the warm patterns of the creatures that scurried.

The smell became stronger the farther toward the middle he went. On cat's feet he moved. Swift and quiet. He could hear them better now.

Voices. Harsh. Unfriendly. Threats were made. Whips were cracking.

Women sobbed and cried.

He climbed a tree, fingers digging into the thick wood and knotted branches. Up he went. Across a branch toward the sounds. He hunched down and narrowed his eyes.

Goblins.

Wolf faced, hairy, and ugly.

Gnolls.

Thick-skinned, yellow-eyed minions.

Village women.

Dozens of them sat in a barren clearing. A camp. Sewing nets similar to what he used for fishing, hunting, and trapping.

It was a surprise. Why would poachers be aligned with giants? Shum made a quick head count. Five gnolls. Nine goblins that he could see. It would take hours of scouting to cover the rest of the crater. He watched. Waited. The goblins stood guard, hand axes on their belts or in their hands. The gnolls ate slabs of meat and barked out orders. Every so often, a gnoll would come and go out of sight, but no others returned. *Manageable.*

The women's fingers worked hard at the nets. He could see they were frightened, hungry, and thirsty.

"Water, please," one said. She held her hands out.

A goblin walked over, held out a jug, tipped it to its lips, and gulped it down. It wiped its mouth and shook the jug in her face, the water swishing around.

She clutched for it. The goblin jerked it away. Swatted her in the face with its other hand. The goblins laughed, holding their little pot bellies, mocking the cries and tears of the women.

Shum had seen enough of that. His blood stirred. The muscles in his jaw tightened. Roaming Rangers weren't the aloof clan the other races made them out to be. They believed in doing right wherever there was wrong. Slavery was wrong. Goblins were wrong. Gnolls were wrong. He slid his sword from his scabbard. It was time to make it right.

He hopped out of the tree. Strode right into the camp, sword resting on his shoulder.

The goblins froze. The women stopped working. Silence fell among them. The gnolls didn't even notice.

"Let the women go," Shum said, looking down at the goblins.

"Huh?" a goblin said, turning his way.

"What?" a gnoll dropped its bowl on the ground and snatched up its flail.

The others jumped to its side, reaching for weapons. "You dare!"

The gnolls were big. Bigger than orcs. Bigger than Shum. He wasn't much of a threat to them at first glance.

"Kill him, the trespassing elf, goblins!" the tallest of the goblins ordered.

No hesitation. No fear. The goblins raised their axes and charged.

Swish! Swish!

The women screamed.

Two goblins fell dead at Shum's feet. The other goblins stopped, blinking.

The lead gnoll's lip curled over its long canine teeth. Fear was in its eyes. It looked like it might consider talking.

Shum decided to give it another try.

"Let the women go," Shum said, "and no harm will come to you."

The goblins, the remaining seven, had him surrounded now. Axes poised to attack him from all directions.

"Come any closer, little minions," Shum said, "and I'll finish the rest of you."

They backed off a step, maybe two, eyes darting between him and the gnolls.

"I know what you are," the gnoll leader said. "You're one of those rangers. A Roamer. Is that so?"

The gnolls' eyes were all intent on him. Reputation alone could win battles, stop wars.

"I am."

The lead gnoll started laughing. The others followed suit, weapons jangling with their armor.

"Does something amuse you?" Shum said.

"Hah!" The gnoll hitched its foot up on a log and slapped its knee. "You really do have a big belly. Kinda like an orc."

"Your insults won't earn you any mercy," Shum said, "and my patience thins. Let the women go. I won't ask again."

It coughed a laugh.

"There's more of us in this crater than you know, Ranger. I think you better surrender." It picked its slab of meat back up and tore off a chunk with its teeth. "Might even have you for dinner."

If there were more, he hadn't seen or heard them. But the tactic was sound. Even for a gnoll.

"Well," Shum said, "I hope you have enough for all of us."

The gnoll stopped chewing. Looked around.

"All of who?"

"Surely you didn't think I came alone. A half dozen arrows are pointed right at you." Shum held his hand straight up. "Awaiting my signal."

Every pair of eyes shifted from tree to tree. But Shum's gaze was steady. Right on the gnoll. Not blinking.

It raised its arm and smiled.

"I've got a dozen in the trees," the gnoll said, "and they're all pointed at you. Your bluff has been called, Ranger."

"I don't think so," Shum said.

"I do," the gnoll grinned. The leader dropped its arm.

Clatch-zip!

Clatch-zip!

Shum spun away from the first bolt that found a home in a gnoll. The next bolt ripped into his thigh, sticking through one side to the other. He dropped to a knee.

"Argh!" he said.

The village women cried out.

"Didn't see that coming, did you, Ranger?" the gnoll said. "Kill him!"

CHAPTER 15

W E HAD THEM. TWO ETTINS slugged along over the grassy knolls with their
four chins down. Arms shackled behind their backs, they led the way, one
heavy footstep after the other. A host of Legionnaire riders accompanied us
along with Ben and Garrison, who ran along on foot.

"Dragon," Ben said. "Can I ride with you? My legs are tired."

"No, Ben," I said. "Commander's orders."

"But—"

"None of that now. Why don't you scout ahead or something?"

"Aw," Ben said, drifting back with a frown.

Sasha rode alongside me.

"Are you feeling better now?" she said.

I felt ashamed. The way I'd shunned her earlier was wrong. Even worse, I'd have
to admit it. I couldn't treat her like Brenwar treated me and hold a grudge for days,
weeks, or months.

"I'm sorry, Sasha." I didn't look at her. "I really am. It's just—"

"Don't explain yourself," she said. "I understand. After all, you had just come
out of a battle. Men are different when their blood runs hot. I wish Bayzog would get
upset every once in a while. I don't think I've ever seen his cheeks flush."

I looked at her, smiling a little.

"Well, maybe he doesn't have any blood."

"Dragon!"

"Sorry," I said.

She giggled.

"No, that was funny. I think we needed it, but I am a bit worried. Do you think
he's all right with Shum? I don't know anything about him."

I reached over and patted her arm.

She didn't flinch or pull away, which surprised me.

I said, "I'm sure he's all right. The Roamers are the greatest Rangers in Nalzambor. He couldn't be any safer if he was with me." I squeezed her arm. "And thank you."

"For what?" she said, staring at my arm, stroking it with gentle fingers.

"Er … well, saving me, Sasha. That ettin nearly popped my head off."

"Oh, ho ho, don't sound so surprised, Nath. Did you think I was just going to stand there and let you get all the glory?"

"Well, uh…" I rubbed the back of my head. "It's just, I wouldn't want you to endanger yourself on my account."

She rolled her eyes. "You men wouldn't make it through the day without us women," she said. "How old are you?"

"Old enough to know that."

She didn't say anything for a moment. "Nath," she said, still rubbing my arm. She was trembling inside. I could feel it.

"Truth is…" She swallowed, looked me in the eyes. "I was terrified. I don't know how I did it. I just did." She squeezed my arm. "My heart starts beating like a rabbit just thinking about that. Did I really do that, Dragon?" She looked forward at the ettins. "Those things are huge."

Now I was laughing.

"What are you laughing about?"

"Nothing," I said.

"Tell me, Dragon."

"All right, it's just an old saying, is all."

"And the saying is?"

I took a breath. "Little women make big men stumble."

"That's it?" she said. "That's not so bad."

"Well, that's not all of it, but that's all that applies in this case," I said, trying to pull my dragon arm away.

She held firm. "I want to hear the rest of it."

"Loud women make a boastful man grumble. Pretty women make all men bumble. Wise women make a proud man humble."

"Hmmm," she started, "I think I like the last part best. Is that a song?"

I nodded.

Her eyes brightened. "Can you sing, Dragon?"

I shrugged.

"Really," she said, "please sing for me. I love singing. I sing all the time, but sometimes Bayzog has to quiet me down."

"Why don't you sing, then?" I suggested.

"You first," she said.

"Well, it's been a while, but I think I can remember a few verses."

Yes, I could sing. Dragon music was the oldest in Nalzambor, and I knew many songs. Long as rivers. Ancient as the oldest forest. Songs men and women had never heard and never would hear. It had been so long I wasn't sure I could do it anymore. I could try something in Common at least. I cleared my throat.

Sasha's eyes brightened.

"In the meadow, the dragons play, their scales sparkle—huh?"

"Why'd you stop, it sounded so—"

"Sssssh," I said. I could hear something. Horse hooves coming our way.

"What is it?"

"Not what, but who. Yah!" I galloped off.

"Where do you think you're going, Dragon?" Brenwar said. He had resumed his normal size.

I kept going, racing up the hill, leaving the Legionnaires and ettins far behind.

A lone figure on a horse rode over the crest. It was Bayzog, with a woman draped over his horse, sleeping, I hoped. "Dragon! Thank goodness I've found you!"

Brenwar had come, too. We rode right up to one another. Formed a triangle of horses.

"Are you all right, elf?" Brenwar said. "Where's the big belly?"

Bayzog took a breath. "He's a couple leagues back. Dragon, I'm sorry. He was fighting with an ettin."

"Who is she?" Brenwar said.

"One of the villagers, I assume. We were close. She escaped and the ettin came after her."

"Bayzog!" Sasha said, riding right up to him. "Are you all right?"

"I'm fine, dear. It's Shum I'm worried about." Bayzog's stern face was wracked with grief. "I left him. The horse wouldn't stop and I, I couldn't leave the woman."

"Shum can handle himself, I'm sure, Bayzog. Come on, Brenwar," I said.

"Come on? Hah, I'm already going, Yah!"

"Bayzog. Sasha. Stay with the Legionnaires. Help them keep an eye on those ettins." I snapped my reins and off I went.

There'd been a battle, all right. An ettin was face first in the ground, dead as a stone. There was no sign of Shum.

"Took an ettin all by himself," I said, looking at Brenwar. "Pretty impressive, you have to admit.

Brenwar kept his arms folded across his chest. "Humph. It probably died laughing at his belly."

"Brenwar," I said, "would it kill you to give an elf some credit?"

"Don't know. I've never done it before. But it just might, so I'll not chance it. Ever! Humph. Luck. Elves have lots of it. Even the big-bellied ones."

"Let's go," I said. "It's getting dark."

"So?" Brenwar said. "Monsters die in the night as easy as in the day."

We followed the hoofprints.

I couldn't get the image of the dead ettin out of my mind. It was now a lifeless clump of hard bone and muscle, soon to be sweet soil for the world. But it ate at me.

Shum was good. Very good. And he'd killed it.

Why couldn't I do that? If it came down to me and an ettin, what was I supposed to do, knock it out? It wasn't possible.

"Outsmart it," Brenwar said.

"What?" I said. "What're you talking about?"

"I can see the look in your eyes, Dragon," he said. "You want to know why Shum can kill an ettin and you can't. How you fight evil without killing."

"I wasn't thinking that."

"Yes you were."

I hated it when Brenwar was right. Crusty old dwarf.

"No I wasn't!"

"If you say so," he said, "but I can answer you this. You can outsmart an ettin. That's how you beat it. But can you outwit evil? That's the question."

"Put a sword through it," I said, riding off up ahead.

Dwarves don't know everything anyway. They just think they do.

But the question gnawed at me.

Outwit evil. My father had said that. Many times. In hours-long form. And it had never sunk in until now. How do you outwit something that kills and destroys? Shows no mercy or compassion?

We navigated into the forest. It was dark, but my eyes didn't have a problem with that. The horses had little trouble navigating, either. They were well trained, accustomed to hard travel and treacherous terrain.

"Whoa," I said.

"What is it?"

I motioned up ahead. Something was moving. And it wasn't a small creature that scurried but something much bigger.

"Wait here."

Brenwar started to object but I was already gone, a shadow slipping through the foliage. Not bad for a dragon. My ears caught more rustling. I hunched down. Something was coming right at me.

Clop. Clop. Clop.

Shum's horse emerged. It stopped, dark eyes looking right at me. I made my way over. Grabbed the reins. Felt the saddle.

"Where's Shum?" I said.

The horse pulled away as if saying, "Follow me."

A rustle caught my ears. I whirled around. It was Brenwar fighting through the pine branches.

"Stay with the horses," I said.

"The horses can stay with themselves," he said, "besides, I smell something as well." He snorted. "Ettins and something else."

"Just come on," I said.

Shum's horse led. I followed, Brenwar huffing right behind. I wasn't sure what Brenwar smelled, but there was something in the air. It didn't blend with the smells of the forest.

The horse stopped. Nickered a little.

"What have we here?" I said. It was a crater. Strange to see. Like a gargantuan spoon had dug it all out. The rising moonlight lit up the trees of the thick forest below. "What do you make of it, Brenwar?"

He peered over the side, glancing back and forth, squinting. He shrugged.

"Let's go."

"That's pretty steep, Brenwar," I said.

"It's just a hole in the ground," he said, shuffling over the edge. "It's not a cli—*ulp!*"

"Brenwar!" I jumped out, reaching for him.

He disappeared over the rim. I heard him tumble and complain. I followed his dark, sharp rolling. Heard his grumbling. Then nothing. My keen eyes searched for a sign. Anything. He was gone. This crater was deeper than I thought. I started after him.

"Should have tied a rope to him," I said, climbing.

"Dragon!"

I heard a voice. It was faint, but it was Brenwar.

"What?" I yelled back down.

"Watch out for—"

There was a rustle. Then nothing.

Brenwar!

CHAPTER 16

ELVEN STEEL SANG. GOBLINS DIED. One. Then two. Shum, hobbled, a bolt in his leg, was all over them.

The third goblin chopped its crude axe at his midsection, glancing off his leather armor.

Shum popped it between the eyes with his sword hilt.

It cried out and flailed.

Clatch-zip!

Shum dove onto the ground.

The bolt sank into the dirt by his face.

He rolled. The bolt in his leg snagged, drawing tears from his eyes.

The goblin swung wild after him.

Clatch-zip!

The goblin stopped. Fell face first to the ground, a bolt stuck in its back.

Shum scrambled for cover. He pressed his back to a boulder and took a breath. The Roaming Ranger was calm. Collected. He'd been in plenty of fights before. He slid his dagger from his belt. Both hands were filled with sharp elven steel.

Clatch-zip!

The bolt whizzed high over his head. It was a good thing. The shooter wasn't the best shot, but he had Shum pinned down. Crossbows took more time to reload than bows, too. He could take advantage of that. He was fast, but not as fast as he'd been. Not with a bolt stuck in his leg. He grabbed the shaft and yanked it out.

The women screamed. Running every which way.

One of the gnolls barked and chased after them.

The others, the leader particularly, he'd lost sight of.

"Ranger!" the gnoll leader growled. "Come out!"

Shum tied a bandage over his thigh. Lifted his hand over his head. Waited.

"Are you surrendering, then?" the gnoll said.

He didn't reply.

Clatch-zip!

Another bolt shot high and to the left of his fingers. Gritting his teeth, blocking the pain in his leg, he charged from behind the boulder.

The gnolls were waiting. Three of them. One lowered its spear at his chest.

Shum swept it away with the flat of his sword and plunged his elven dagger into its chest.

The gnoll leader roared. Its spiked flail whirled like the wind. Lashed out like a snake's tongue, catching Shum in the chest.

He doubled over. Tumbled to the ground.

Clatch-zip!

The bolt whizzed past his head and stuck in the ground between the gnoll's legs. Its eyes widened. "Stop shooting, fools!" The gnoll twirled the spiked ball of steel over its head and brought it down again.

Shum rolled left.

Up it went. Down it came.

He rolled right.

Bang!

The flail got him in the thigh.

"Hah!" the gnoll said. "Not so tough for a Ranger, are you?"

Shum pushed himself back over the dirt, chopping back and forth with his longsword, keeping the gnoll at bay. His sword was a superior weapon to the crude flail, but the gnoll swung with fury. Power. Juttering his arms with every blow. It didn't help that his leg was banged up and bleeding. Shum was concerned. Was he overconfident? Foolish? He'd just killed an ettin, after all. Couldn't he handle a handful of gnolls and goblins?

An elven proverb danced is his head. *Death comes from any corner.*

The gnoll kept swinging. Harder and harder. Every blow fast and heavy.

Shum dropped his dagger. Wrapped both hands around his sword.

Clang!

The flail chain wrapped around his blade. Locked the weapon up. The gnoll heaved, ripping Shum's sword from his hand. The gnoll's dog face let out a howl. It tossed its weapons aside, bared its claws, and pounced on Shum.

My dragon claws dug into the rocky dirt of the crater wall, making it easy to climb down. I caught myself wondering if I could scale city walls with them, and then I forced myself to concentrate on finding my friend.

"Brenwar!"

Still, I heard nothing. I hopped from one foothold to another. Traversed gaps and ledges like a critter. I had to admit, I was getting used to this climbing. Having two clawed hands made it much easier.

A hundred feet I descended. It was dark above and below me now. All I could make out were the outlines of the crater rim and the treetops below it.

"Brenwar!"

Great Guzan! I couldn't believe I'd lost him. The climb wasn't so risky, but Brenwar wasn't the best climber. The last time we'd climbed, I'd tied a rope around him.

He must be getting old or something.

Straight down I went, sliding on the steepness of the crater the final fifty feet. There was no sign of Brenwar. I sniffed the air.

There was that smell again. The one from earlier. The one Brenwar mentioned. What was it? Not as bad as orcs, but bad. *Ew!* I felt as if I should know, but I'd forgotten somehow.

I scanned the ground and the trees, looking for heat. Anything. I could see small creatures nesting. Some scurrying through the night, but not much of anything else. I ran my hands over the ground. My touch was sensitive. So sensitive I felt like I could almost taste the ground with it.

"Come now," I said, "a crusty old dwarf couldn't have gotten too far."

On hands and knees, I searched. I sniffed. I was an excellent tracker. But it took a while when I was dealing with new terrain. The out-of-the-ordinary wouldn't be as plain.

"Ah, there it is. There it is, indeed."

Whatever it was had tossed a net over Brenwar and dragged him away. But what? That was the question. I looked for prints. I found them, and they weren't at all what I expected.

"Oh no," I said. I readied my bow. *Snap. Clatch. Snap.* And darted along the trail. Brenwar was in trouble.

CHAPTER 17

"**A**RE YOU ALL RIGHT?" SASHA said.

Bayzog nodded, but his face was drawn up tight. His dark eyes looked through her, up ahead, past the ettins. He was worried. Sasha could feel it. It left her unsettled. Her stomach fluttered. She'd never seen Bayzog out of sorts before.

She brushed his hair out if his eyes and held out a canteen of Wizard's Water.

He pushed it aside, gently. "No," he said, "It doesn't seem right. Not with them out there at risk. And here I am, doing nothing." He looked at her, then looked away, fists balled up at his sides.

Anyone who didn't know Bayzog would see nothing but a part man, part elf who oozed confidence. Chin high. Speech polished. Impeccable in character. But he was rattled.

"You saved the woman, Bayzog. You've battled ettins. We guard them as we speak. We march them over the plains, our prisoners." She tried to sound reassuring. "You've done well. The others, they can take care of themselves."

He kept riding. Focused.

Up ahead, the ettins lumbered over the ground. Their four heads glanced back, then muttered to themselves.

They were up to something. Sasha could feel it. But surely they could not break the bonds that Bayzog had cast on them. Bright-green shackles bound their wrists behind their backs.

Sasha didn't know if she felt good or bad. She didn't know how to feel, actually. It was thrilling and dangerous all at the same time. What was to be a simple trek south toward the elven lands had become a full-blown adventure. And it had all happened in moments. She didn't know whether she should feel proud or scared to death.

"Sasha," Bayzog said, looking back at her, "come."

She caught up. "Yes?"

"I'm sorry." He caressed her cheek with the back of his hand. "I didn't even take the time to ask you how you were. Are you all right?"

"Just a little edgy." He eyes drifted to the ettins. "Do you think they can get free?"

"No, no, my dear. Ten ettins couldn't break those bonds. And if they try," he said, offering a grin, "they'll be in for a shock."

"I hope they struggle then," she said, glowering.

"Sasha!"

"Well, it's true. They're evil. I can feel it. I get chills looking at them. And those eyes. So big and dark." She tore her stare away and looked at him. "I hate them."

"Strong words, my dear." He cleared his throat, lifted his brow. "Try to ignore them. They're ignorant of their actions. Born that way. It's a shame. I used to think there was good in everyone, but over the centuries, I've come to know better." He squeezed her hand. "But what I have learned is even worse."

"What's that, Bayzog?"

"I've learned about the evil that resides in all of us. The evil that lurks beneath the surface of love and hate. The good roots without the strength to grow out. How it's so much easier to do the wrong thing instead of the right. I worry, Sasha." He looked up to the clouds, a frown forming on his face.

"About me?" she said, following his gaze.

Night was almost upon them. The clouds that drifted were black and the stars behind them gone. A strange fog rolled over the grass. What had earlier been a blustering day in the sun had become a land more sinister. A distant flash of lightning caught her eye.

"Yes, of course I worry about you," he said. "I sometimes wish you hadn't come. I want you safe. I fear I can't always protect you."

"I don't expect you to. I have to learn how to protect myself."

"And you've done well with that," he said, "but I wanted you here with me, Sasha. I needed you here with me."

A chill went through her. Bayzog never needed anything from anybody.

"Why?"

He looked her straight in the eye.

"In case none of us make it back."

Her heart stopped. Then started again. At least it felt like it did. What was he saying? What did he mean?

"Bayzog, I'm certain we'll make it through this. We'll find the Ocular of Orray, heal Dragon, and then things will be as they were."

He shook his head.

"The climate changes. Even though my elven instincts aren't as sharp as they used to be, I know. That's why I wanted to have you with me. I wanted you by my side, selfishly, just in case."

"Just in case what?"

She could see her reflection in his violet eyes when he said it.

"Just in case we're near the end of this world."

CHAPTER 18

SHUM PULLED HIS KNEES UP and caught the full force of the gnoll's greater weight on his chest. He locked his hands around the creature's wrists and hung on. Shum was centuries hardened by training and battle, his muscles as taut as steel. But he was no match for the raw strength of the gnoll. Its thews were thick. Savage. More animal than man. Its dog face snapped at his neck. He turned his face away. Hung on with all the strength he had in him.

"Time to die, Ranger!" Saliva dripped from its mouth. "I've never tasted a Roamer before." It snapped at him.

Shum shoved it back. Still lithe, he got one foot underneath the gnoll's hard belly. "Not today, gnoll!" He thrust. Lifted the gnoll up and over the top of his head.

It let out a howl, crashing into the dirt.

Shum dove for his sword.

The gnoll regained its feet and pounced right onto his back. Its claws tore into him.

His elven leather kept him from being torn to shreds.

They thrashed back and forth over the dirt.

Whop!

The gnoll punched him in the face, drawing bright spots in his eyes.

Jab! Jab! Crack!

The gnoll howled. Jumped off, holding its nose.

The creature might be bigger, meaner, stronger, but Shum was smarter, faster, and tougher. And he knew the weak spots of all the races. He spotted his sword. Limped over and snatched it up. "One more step, gnoll, and it will be the end of you," he said, shuffling forward.

The gnoll backed away, eyes darting from side to side.

The women and other gnolls were gone. Hiding. Leaving the two of them in the darkness. The only light came the small campfires' glows.

"Surrender, gnoll, or meet your—"

Clatch-zip!

Shum's sword fell from his grip.

The gnoll let out a triumphant howl and charged.

I was on alert. Eyes peeled. Ears sharp.

That smell. That smell in the air. I knew what it was. The prints on the ground gave me a good idea. Trouble. The kind of trouble wise people sought to avoid. The kind of trouble that was hard to get out of.

I hurried along. They could move fast, even with Brenwar. Possibly faster than me. One mistake on the trail and I myself could be in jeopardy.

I stopped. Looked. Listened.

Something rustled over the ground yards ahead. I could've sworn I heard Brenwar grumbling under his beard.

I nocked an arrow, a normal one, and sped after him. I jumped along, winding through the trees, my footfalls light as feathers.

There he was. A clumped dwarf fighting in a net surrounded by pines and a floor of pine needles. I didn't see anyone else. Still, I remained hidden.

"Dragon!" Brenwar said. His voice a loud hush. "They're gone. Get me out of this net!"

I peeked at him.

His dark eyes were right on me.

I wasn't sure how Brenwar could see me, but he could always find me when I was close. I never knew for sure if it was my scent or his vision, but the only way to escape him was to outdistance him.

I crept over, withdrew a dagger, and quickly cut at the net.

"Hurry, will you!" he said.

"Stop struggling, will you!"

"You're not the one in the net."

I laughed.

"Stop laughing and hurry. You spooked them, but they'll be back. They always come back."

I cut at the cords. It wasn't easy.

"Use your claws, Dragon!"

"Oh, good idea." I cut. One. Two. Three at a time. "Nice."

"How many of them?" I asked.

"Two."

"Two that we know of." I sawed away. Brenwar was almost free.

Clop. Clop.

Clop. Clop.

I wanted to stop, but I didn't. I ignored the sound. Kept cutting.

"Hurry!" Brenwar said.

A flutelike sound drifted into my ears.

My head started spinning. My fingers turned numb. Limp.

Brenwar's eyelids fluttered. His meaty hands clamped over his ears. "No!" he growled.

I couldn't say anything. My tongue felt like water. But I could see. Both of them. Shadows in the forest coming out of the darkness. One was male, the other female. Each pressed a set of small pipes to their lips. Tiny horns protruded from their heads. They stood on stout legs with the hooves of mountain goats.

Satyrs. Crafty and merciless.

The music tore at my mind.

I screamed, but I couldn't hear myself. I had to move. Had to escape. Run. Flee. I knew the stories. I knew the tales. Whatever the satyrs captured they kept. Never to be seen again.

Shum lay still, eyes closed, his mouth full of pine needles, a crossbow bolt sticking through his back. Bleeding. Over him, the gnoll leader gloated.

"Great shot!" it said. "Now get down here. It's time to skin him."

Shum remained still. Ears picking up his surroundings. The gnoll leader kicked him hard in the ribs. He didn't move. Didn't flinch. The gnoll walked away, footsteps crunching over the ground, and picked up its flail. The air whistled as it twirled around. Another pair of footsteps approached. Followed by another. There were three of them.

"Get those bows ready. If he moves so much as a hair, shoot him."

"Isn't he dead?" one said, cranking back its string.

"If he's dead, he won't feel it," the leader said. "Of course, he's a Ranger, so you can't be too cautious. Humph. Go ahead. Put another in him. Right in the heart. Maybe between the ears. That'd be a funny trophy now, wouldn't it?"

They snickered a howling sort of sound and stretched their strings.

Shum had been in tight spots before, but this was ridiculous. *Death comes from any corner. The darkness sings.* Hands under his belly, he scratched at the dirt. Tapped the world's power. He was an elf, attuned to nature and magic. Using it when needed to save others. To save himself. He focused. Concentrated. Stretched out the powers he summoned.

"What is this?" one of the gnolls said. Its crossbow trembled in its hand. The wood creaked and groaned.

"It's cursed!" said the other. The crossbow in its hand warped too. It let out a cry.

Both crossbows were now twisted like roots. The strings snapped. The gnoll leader let out an angry cry.

"It's the Ranger, you fools!" It jumped forward, swinging its mace. "Draw your blades! Have at him before he escapes."

Shum felt the flail coming down. In a blink he dove into the gnoll's legs, toppling it over. He kept on going, blocking out the blinding pain in his legs and his back. He had to free himself.

The gnoll snatched his leg.

He kicked it in the face. He was free.

The other two were coming. Drawing their weapons. Still gawking at the twisted crossbow and bolts that writhed on the ground.

Shum went for his sword, snatching it from the ground. He wished he could keep running. Into the forest. Lose them. Survive. Fight later. He was bleeding too badly, though. It was fight now or never. He stopped. Turned.

They swarmed him.

The first one was big, clumsy.

Slash!

It died.

The next lunged. A big axe in its hands. Shum sidestepped.

Crack!

Drove the pommel of his sword into the back of its head. It was out.

"You're good, Ranger," the leader said. "But yer bleedin' to death, too. I think I'll watch. Wait for the reinforcements to arrive."

"Trust me, gnoll, you'll be dead cold before they get here."

"Is that so?" it said. "How you figure?"

Shum swayed. A wave of nausea hit him. His chin dipped. His knees buckled.

The gnoll barked at him. "You've got nothing left. I'm taking you out." It came at him. Savage. Powerful. Flail spinning like stars in the air. Its eyes widened. It caught the steely eyes in the elf. It tried to stop, but couldn't.

Shum struck like a cobra. His blade went in one side and out the other.

The gnoll leader died, mouth wide open.

"They always fall for that," Shum said, removing his blade and fetching his dagger. Still ailing, he hobbled after the women.

CHAPTER 19

IT WAS STRANGE. THE MUSIC the satyrs summoned bent my knees, my ears, even the trees right before my eyes.

The little beady-eyed horn-heads were full of surprises. Deceivers. Stealers. Enslavers. And dragon poachers. They loved dragon charms, bones, teeth, and scales more than gold itself.

I fought for my focus. Locking my eyes on their twisting and distorted faces, I yelled. At least I think I did.

I could see my bow, Akron, in my hand that I could not feel. An arrow was stuck between my numb fingers. I fought against the music. The horror. The carnival erupting in my mind.

Come on, Dragon! Do it! Do it or you're done for!

Muscles straining, I forced my dragon hands to respond. Shaking, I nocked the arrow. I rolled onto my back. I think I did, anyway. I couldn't feel anything. It was as if I was watching someone else's hands draw back the string. An out-of-body experience of sorts. I took aim at the nearest obscured image before me and let the arrow fly.

The snapping string cracked in my ear. Not tight, but slow. The arrow drifted away from me at an agonizing pace. Even an ettin could have dodged that slow arrow.

I felt my breath thinning. Drops of sweat fell in front of my eyes. All I wanted to do was escape the madness. Sleep. Find my legs and run. But at the moment, I could do nothing. Just suffer the insufferable sound of the pipe-playing satyrs.

"Uh!"

The music shifted. Stopped.

My head pounded like a drum, but my vision began to clear.

The male satyr clutched at its belly. Its pipes were no longer pressed to its lips but lay on the ground.

The woman dashed over on her hooves, distraught and full of worry. She leaned her mate back in her arms. Tears swelled in her eyes.

The male gasped for breath. Clutched its side. Looked right at me. Then at my dragon arms. Its eyes widened, and it whispered to the female satyr.

I gathered my feet under me and stumbled over. I didn't want to see him die. Brenwar beat me there.

Crack!

He walloped the female in the back of the head with a leaden bag called a Dwarven Sap.

She pitched forward, knocked out cold in her mate's lap.

"Brenwar," I said, "did you have to be so gruff? She's a—"

"She's no she. It's a satyr. A monster. About to kill us both."

Crack!

He stomped her set of pipes under his boot. Crushed them into the ground.

The male satyr let out a whine. Like a goat.

Pop!

Brenwar slugged it in the jaw. It fell over. He snatched its pipes off the ground and crushed them in his hands.

"What about his wounds?" I said.

"It will live."

We grabbed the net and bound them up. Satyrs—little taller than dwarves, not as wide—weren't very formidable without their pipes.

Still, I was a little surprised Brenwar hadn't killed them.

"So, you think they won't come after us again?" I said. "There could be more, you know. Maybe an entire herd of them lurks in this crater."

"Then I suggest we get out of here before they get out of this," he said, storming off.

I guessed it was my turn to follow. I gave the satyrs one last look. They never looked as bad as they seemed. They looked almost peaceful with their faces calm and expressionless. I just hoped I'd never hear those pipes playing again. After Brenwar I went.

We found a camp.

"Look at this," Brenwar said. He was kneeling beside some dead goblins. "Look at how clean that cut is. That's elven steel. Shum must be close by."

I inspected the gnolls. Three of them were dead. Big ones, too. All bigger than Shum. I could tell by the dirt it had been a hard-fought battle. A nasty one, judging by the blood.

"Looks like he went this way," I said, "but I don't think he was followed."

"Hmmm," Brenwar said, "look at this." He held out what looked like a crossbow, but the wood was twisted.

I picked up a bent bolt. "Now this is something. Pretty impressive." I waggled it in Brenwar's face. "Wouldn't you say?"

"Pretty sad if you ask me. Pot Belly must not be much of a fighter if he can't get the upper hand on the likes of these. Using magic. Pah!"

"Of course," I said, rolling my eyes behind his back. "What was I thinking? Let's go."

I took the lead this time. My keen eye picked up drops of blood on the ground, the needles, and the stones. There were footprints now. Many. I could smell the women, some of them still touched by the natural fragrances of the flower and vegetable gardens of the village.

"Brenwar," I stopped. Hunched down. Something was coming.

Brenwar leaned over my shoulder. Farther down the crater, a large group of people was coming. We waited. Closer and closer they came. The silhouettes became familiar. One, taller than the rest, was limping. Wheezing a little.

"Shum!" I said, dashing up to him.

Two women were holding him up, his long arms draped over their shoulders.

"He saved us," one woman said. "Saved us all. Killed all those nasty dogs and goblins!"

Indeed, he had saved them all. Every last one by the looks of it. The women all chattered among themselves. Excited. Free.

"Shum," I said, bracing him over my shoulder. "Are you all right? Can you make it?"

"Just," he said, wheezing. "Just get me out of here, Dragon. Take me to my horse."

"Pah!" Brenwar said, rolling his eyes at me. "I bet he wants us to carry him, too."

The brisk wind picked up, chilling Bayzog's bones. The warmth from the Legionnaire fire looked good right now, but he remained back in the dark, peering toward the crater.

"Come, Bayzog," Sasha said, taking his arm. "You need some food. The soldiers have plenty, and their tales are very exciting."

He turned his eyes toward the ettins that now sat on the edge of the camp. They kept looking into the sky. What they were looking for, he couldn't imagine.

"I appreciate it,' he said. "I really do. Perhaps you can bring me something."

"As you wish, Bayzog." She pecked him on the cheek. "I'll be right back."

Being around men left Bayzog a little uncomfortable. He was more elf than man and never felt his human part was well received. And he didn't have the color of the humans, either, at least not in terms of personality. He was resolved. They were vibrant. Most of them, anyway.

Staring into the sky, he noticed the dark clouds seemed to lower like a fog that fell rather than lifted.

"That's odd."

It wasn't uncommon for the night air to become misty, but not so early in the night. Over by the campfires, a haze was dropping over the men's heads. But they kept talking and eating, and many of them were smoking pipes. His nose crinkled.

He looked at the ettins. They were fifteen feet high sitting. But he could see their heads no more.

"Bayzog," a man said, approaching from the camp. "Have you have seen such a fog before?" It was Ben, trying to fan the haze from his face.

"No, have you?"

"Great Guzan!" a soldier said. "I can't even see my roll-up. Stop smoking, will you!"

"That's not my smoke," another soldier exclaimed. "It's this infernal fog. It's thicker than a mud hole!"

"Get out of my way!"

A chill went right through Bayzog. Suddenly he couldn't see a hand in front of his face.

"Sasha! Sasha! Where are you?"

It didn't do him any good. Everyone was yelling. Shouting. Ordering.

"Ben! Ben!" he said. "Can you hear me?"

"I'm right here," Ben said. "I think I am, anyway. What do you want me to do?"

"Be still. Don't move!"

Bayzog muttered. Incanted. The magic within him came to life. Raising his arms over his head, he summoned the wind.

At first nothing happened.

He focused. Concentrated.

Then it came. Up the hill, flattening the grasses, it pushed through the camp to the astonishment of many voices. It was a strong wind. Not a storm. Not a gale. Strong and steady like right before a storm. It whisked the fog away and scattered it into the sky. Carried it far away and beyond.

When he opened his eyes, Ben was standing there fixing his hair, gaping at him. Sasha toward him and wrapped her arms around him. He was relieved.

"Great Guzan!" another soldier shouted.

"What now?" someone said.

"The ettins are gone!"

CHAPTER
20

I T WAS EARLY MORNING WHEN we ran into Bayzog, Sasha, Ben, and the Legionnaires. Bayzog explained everything that occurred the night before. I listened intently while Sasha tended to Shum's wounds.

"What do you make of it, Bayzog?" I asked.

Bayzog's face was calm but his voice was intense.

"I never figured the ettins to wield magic," he said, "and the fog. It came from nowhere. Unnatural. Dragon, it takes a lot to summon the weather and make such big monsters disappear. Someone powerful had to have done it."

"Or several someones," I said.

There was no sign of anything. No tracks. No scent. Nothing. Even Brenwar and Shum seemed astounded.

"What do we do now, Dragon?" Ben said. "What if the ettins come back? And why did they take the women?"

I hated to admit it, but it was perplexing. Why did they take the women, indeed? And why were they aligned with dragon poachers? Even though it was night, I'd still gotten a close enough look at things at the camp in the crater. The goblins and gnolls were poachers, no doubt about it. They had the tools, traps, and snares. And the women had been working on nets. Dragon nets. The kind that pinned dragons' wings together or to their backs. The mere sight of such tools infuriated me. There'd been no sign of dragons, which was good. But Shum said there were caves. That was bad. There had been no time to search them. What was important was getting the women to safety.

"Easier to control," Shum said. "Easier to scare. Men are rebellious and children can be difficult to keep track of. Plus, the women from these villages are good menders. Quick hands. Hard workers." Shum rose up to his full height, put some weight on his leg, and grimaced.

"Take it easy," Sasha said. "It'll take some time for those wounds to mend."

Shum looked down at her and showed his dashing elven teeth.

"You've done well." He helped her up and kissed her hand. "You've got excellent hands. A soothing touch."

Sasha's pale cheeks turned pink and she tossed her hair.

"You've found a special partner, Bayzog. An honor for any elf."

"I know," Bayzog said. He walked over, grabbed Sasha's other hand, and led her away.

"Hmmm," I said, looking at Shum. He was watching them go. "So," I said, "maybe we should check on that ettin you killed. Perhaps it's gone as well."

Shum pulled himself into his saddle. "Makes you wonder if any of it happened at all, doesn't it?"

I got on my horse and spent the next couple of hours leading the women back to their village. The men and children were overjoyed, and for the first time in a long while, I felt like I'd done something positive, right.

"Does the heart good, doesn't it?" Sasha said.

"Indeed it does," I replied. "Seeing such joy come from tragedy is an amazing thing."

"Do you think they'll be all right?" she asked.

I looked at her seriously. "Sometimes people just have to fend for themselves. If they felt the need to leave, they'd leave. This is their home. I wouldn't leave if I didn't want to, either."

She gave me a weak smile.

Ben and Garrison rode up to us.

"Well," I said, "what did the commander say, Ben?"

"They're going to stay. Help the villagers settle themselves and send for more help from Quintuklen." He was grinning from ear to ear.

"Well, you seem pretty excited about that. Are you looking forward to helping out or maybe getting a quick trip back to the city?"

"No-no-no," he said, waving his hands. "I've got even better news than that."

"Really, and what might that be?"

"The commander. He says Garrison and I can go with you!"

I looked at Sasha.

She shrugged.

"Go with me where?" I said.

"To Elome the Elven City, of course. The commander says we can go!" He hoisted his helmet up in the air. "YEEHEE!"

I didn't have any reason to bring Ben. There were plenty of us already. But a part of me liked his enthusiasm. People liked Ben, liked having him around. And he'd proven he could take care of himself. He was a Legionnaire, after all. Even looked formidable in his well-fitted armor.

Still.

"Come on, Dragon," he said, voice excited. "Don't tell me no. You know I want to see the world, and this is my chance. Just another journey. After this trip, I'll do whatever you say. I'll head right back to Quintuklen. Plus, I have to be back in a month anyway."

"A month!" I said. "We won't be there a month, Ben. Did you plan on starting a family while we were there?"

"Uh," he said, scratching his head, "no."

Sasha was laughing. Bayzog sat in is saddle, silent, distant.

"Garrison, do you want to do this?" I asked. The man wasn't much of a talker. Hard to read.

He shrugged and said, "I wouldn't mind seeing the home of the elves. Sounds interesting."

"Interesting, indeed," I said. "All right, gather your things. Let's go." I scanned the hills and what was left of the village.

The people were hard at it already. Hammers and saws were working, and the women—some of them and the children were singing.

"Say," I said, "shouldn't Brenwar and Shum be here by now?"

They'd gone to check on the third ettin, to see if it was still there or not. My scales tingled at the thought of it. The thought of all of it. Everything was out of place. Unordinary. Villagers. Ettins. Dragon poachers and craters, not to mention the satyrs. I hadn't even mentioned them to Sasha and Bayzog yet. But something was amiss. I wanted to go back to the crater. Take a closer look. For all I knew, there were dragons there. It bothered me.

"Here they come," Sasha said, waving.

The pair bounced in their saddles at a trot and came to a stop.

Brenwar propped his hands on his hips. "Seems the elf didn't kill that ettin after all. It's gone." He slapped his knee. "Ha!"

"Any signs?" I said.

"None," Shum replied.

Something was wrong. I could feel it in the tips of my claws. It ate at my stomach. I was missing something. We were all missing something.

"Let's go, Dragon," Bayzog said. "We've done all we can do here. We should ride to Elome, before things get any more weird."

CHAPTER
21

K RYZAK STOOD IN THE CENTER of the dragon poacher camp, inspecting the carnage. The gnolls were dead. The goblins were dead. But that was not all. One ettin out of three was dead, another's hand maimed. The two that lived now roamed the woods in the crater, awaiting his call. He picked up the flail of the gnoll leader. Eyed it.

"Interesting," he said, running his finger over the blood on the metal. "I can make use of that." He motioned for one of the draykis. Its hulking frame made its way over, silently as a cat. He handed the draykis the flail. "Keep this. It may have more uses."

Making his way around the camp, Kryzak reenacted the battle in his mind. A Roaming Ranger. That made him curious. Why would a Roaming Ranger be with Nath Dragon? It bothered him. Ranger Elves he'd just as soon avoid. They were a formidable bunch. Strange and deadly. And he didn't like to take on things he didn't understand.

He picked up one of the gnarled crossbows, grunted, and tossed it aside.

He took a seat on a log near the extinguished campfire, pulled his hood down, and let the sunlight warm his head. His tattoos sparkled in the bright light. He rubbed the sweat that glistened on his head away with a dark cloth and tucked it back inside his robes.

"It's a great day."

He grabbed his canteen, took a drink, and closed his eyes. Bounced his war mace on his heavy shoulders. Ground his teeth a little.

Kryzak liked to fight. He was a warrior just as much as a cleric. He hated missing the melee and combat that had occurred over the past couple of days.

But he was a planner, too. Strategic. Cunning. He'd set a trap. A test. He had to get some idea of what he was dealing with in Nath Dragon and his companions.

The encounter with the ettins told a lot. Nath and his companions were strong.

Powerful. An efficient team. They trusted one another. It surprised him. He'd figured the ettins a match for them.

But he'd been wrong.

He smashed his mace into the ground. Again and again. It was a big thing. Heavy. Meant to be wielded by a big man such as himself. He could cave plate armor in with it. Bash the locks on heavy doors. He'd killed a giant with a single blow to the head once. And he was itching to use it again.

"Barnabus!" Kryzak cursed. "I need a fight."

He would get it, too. But not before he was ready. He needed to know more.

His spy would have to fill in the details. His spy had earlier filled him in on everything that had happened. The giant-sized dwarf. The magic the part-elven wizard used. The female wizard as well. Not to mention the arrows and sword that Nath Dragon could wield.

Even with the help of ettins and draykis, Kryzak would be hard pressed to defeat Nath's party. He'd have to separate them. Maybe kill them off in pieces. He grinned.

"I like the way I think."

He clapped his calloused hands and muttered a mystic word.

The blackened logs in the pit burst into flames.

He liked the fire. It had magic, warmth, and power. It could do good or bad. Destroy life or save it.

He poured out his canteen into a pool of water on the ground. Muttered some mystic words and watched the water take form. Then the fire.

Two tiny elementals, each less than a foot tall, started to battle. Like gladiators that hated each other.

He laughed, watching them fling tiny balls of fire and water at each other.

Ssssz. Ssssz. Sssssz.

They locked up. Wrestled like minotaurs until they extinguished one another. It made him wonder if evil could truly defeat good. Where would all the excitement be?

He rubbed the amulet around his neck.

A draykis came forward, towering over him. "Do we hunt?"

"No, not yet. We'll wait until they depart the elven lands," he said.

"And then what? Care to let me in?"

Kryzak scoffed. The draykis weren't mindless things. They were the best dragon hunters he'd ever used. They made typical poachers—gnolls, goblins, and orcs—look like halflings and gnomes. They were fearless. Never rattled. And if it weren't for his amulet, he was pretty sure they'd rip him to pieces.

Kryzak respected them. He had to make sure they respected him.

"You heard what the spy said. Now we wait until he reports more," he said, rising to his feet. The pair were almost eye to eye now. He dangled the amulet between his fingers and slung his mace over his shoulder. "I want to know what they are after. And I don't want to fool with the elves. Come."

The crater made for an interesting hideout. Filled with dangerous predators and excellent places for monsters such as giants to conceal themselves. Even dragons. For years poachers had roamed this location, and now Kryzak had taken it over.

And no one had challenged him.

There was no need now that word was getting out.

Another war was coming.

Maneuvering through the woods, he came across a hole more than a dozen feet wide that led into the ground and formed a tunnel. It was pitch black, but the eyes of the draykis and the tattoos on his head both gave off a soft glow. Damp and cold, a hundred steps down the steep incline he came to a stop.

He muttered, "*Shompin.*"

Torches lit up a large cavern. Inside were many cages. Some big enough for an ettin, others for something as small as a cat. Many of them were filled with dragons.

Two more draykis emerged from the dark corners, followed by something else. A dragon, dark scaled, bigger than a horse, wingless, with bright-yellow, catlike eyes. The feline fury. Its long whiskers touched the floor. He stroked its face. Its purr was like thunder.

"Ah, my favorite," Kryzak said.

The feline fury had been instrumental in capturing other dragons. It was an excellent hunter. It and the draykis had become the most effective poachers of all. The captured dragons lay curled up in their cages, eyes closed, unmoving. The biggest was a red-belly dragon. It was male, dark-yellow scales on top, dark red on the bottom. A fire breather and hot land dweller. Smelled like sulfur all the time. Not much of a flyer. It would fetch a great price in the market. Its parts, that is. It was too big to keep alive. Too dangerous.

The others—most as big as tigers—would make pets or catalysts to magic. The wizards preferred them. They were all fantastic creatures. Beautiful in some cases. Metallic in color, some pastel, others with chameleonlike powers. All in all, the dragons were worth a fortune.

"Almost a shame to put an end to them," he said, stroking the whiskers of the fury. "Of course, like you, maybe some of them can be turned to our service."

CHAPTER
22

WE MADE IT TO THE Elven Lands without any more trouble. Shum and the rest of us were in good shape. Even Brenwar had loosened up. I spent most of my time hunting and fishing with Ben and Garrison when we weren't riding. They were good company, especially Ben. I was amazed at how much he had changed in a matter of months. A boy to a man.

It almost made me feel ashamed of myself, for some reason.

But my sense of guilt and worry started to subside in the Elven Lands. They were well protected and monitored. Filled with wild animals of incredibly rare sorts. People said unicorns were seen from time to time. But the elves kept a close watch on such things—assuming of course they could find them.

One thing was for sure: there wasn't much to do with evil. At least not that they knew of.

The Elven Lands weren't so different, just more lush and colorful. The water sparkled in the streams and ponds. There were roads, farms, and villages—and so long as you traveled with elves or weren't suspicious, they didn't seem to notice you.

Slighter in build than men, the elves didn't care to answer questions and would just wave and offer smiles. Elves were pleasant, laid back, easygoing, at least in the country. It was the serious ones that kept things in order. And they were in the main city, Elome, which was right where we were going.

"What's that?" Ben said, pointing ahead.

"That's Elome, Ben," I said.

He squinted. Held his hand over his eyes.

"Are those trees? Or buildings? They're touching the clouds, whatever they are."

"You'll see," I said. "You'll see."

We were miles away, but the object in Ben's eyes, all our eyes, was miles long. Everyone was solemn. Bayzog's face was tight. Sasha's eyes were saucers. Shum and Brenwar didn't look any different than they normally would, but I was sure Brenwar would have something contrary to say about it.

We took our time, too, the horses clopping over the road at a normal pace. Things seemed to go much slower in the Elven Woods. There wasn't a great deal of business about them. It was different. Calm. Serene.

"I don't think we're getting any closer, Dragon," Ben said.

"We'll get there when we get there, Ben," I said, raking my hair out of my face. "Enjoy it. It's not the same going as it is coming."

Onward we went, one mile, then two, three, and four. As we got closer, the city widened, impossibly so. The trees that reached for the clouds weren't all trees but a network of stonework, cut blocks and polished stones that looked as natural as nature itself. There were no city walls, not like Quintuklen, nor steep mountain ridges like Morgdon. It was the imagination and cultivation of elven kind and nature working as one. Fantastic. Almost magical.

"By the Sultans," Sasha said, "it's absolutely beautiful."

"To you, maybe," I heard Brenwar mutter under his beard.

We made our way through one of the massive arches that led into the city. Elven soldiers were spaced throughout the structures but hardly noticeable. The elves went about their business—trading, selling, buying—the same as other people, just talking in Elvish. The men were slender and purposeful, the women elegant, pretty, even exotic in some cases. But not a one batted an eyelash at me, which was disappointing. But on the other side of things, they didn't gawk at my arms, either.

"Dragon," Ben said, trying to look everywhere at once, "this place is fantastic. Not anything I ever imagined."

It was true. The buildings were of all sorts and sizes. Some carved from stone, others wood. Soft mosses—blue, green, even yellow—coated many places like paint, and the roads were laid out in pale red stone. Children ran through the streets, darting in and out of wicker hoops. Others chased after one another, filling the air with laughter and giggles here and there.

"Smells good," Ben said, rubbing his stomach. "I've never had elven food before."

"Pah," Brenwar said, "you won't like the taste."

"I won't? Why not?" Ben said.

"Well, do you like meat?"

"Sure, everyone does," Ben said. "Don't they?"

"Well, their meat tastes like fruit and gardens, farm boy. And their ale tastes like honey. Do you like honey, boy?"

"Uh," Ben said, scratching his head.

"Well?"

Ben rode up to me and said, "Brenwar scares me."

"Ho! Ho! Ho!" Brenwar said from behind.

"Take it easy, Ben. Brenwar's set in his ways, you know."

"Does their meat really taste like vegetables?"

"Don't worry, you'll like it," I said. "I always do."

Well, I mostly did. The elves didn't eat much meat. Not much of any at all. As a matter of fact, they ate very little.

That was one of things that was different about Elome. There weren't taverns like the other cities. Whatever they needed they just plucked from the vines that cropped up everywhere.

The elves nurtured.

The plant life fed.

I plucked some fruits from a vine we passed and tossed one to Ben and another to Garrison.

"Eat," I said. "There's plenty."

Brenwar was scoffing in the back. I tossed him a fruit. He snatched it from the air, eyes filled with venom.

"What's this for?" Brenwar said.

"To eat," I said. "It won't kill you."

"Dwarves don't eat fruit! We eat beast. We eat stew!" He chucked it at one of the children.

The light-headed boy snatched it with his hand, nodded, and took a bite out of it.

"Next time I'll toss him a rock to eat."

"Come," Bayzog said, taking the lead. "I'll take us to the Place of Meets."

The Place of Meets was marvelous: a gathering space a mile long and a mile high. We weren't so unique there. Men and elves consulted. Halflings and gnomes appeared, shuffling by with smiles and intense conversations. Brenwar, arms folded over his breast plate, made it a point to scowl at each and every one of them. He took pride in being part of the tallest of the short races and didn't hesitate to make it known.

"Sit, everyone." Bayzog took his place on a sofa carved in a tree with violet-covered moss cushions.

Sasha sat close beside him.

"Sit, everyone," he said again. "Relax. They won't be with us anytime soon."

"You can say that again," Brenwar said.

Ben hopped from spot to spot. Sampling the foods. Tasting the drinks the elven servants laid out. Finally he stretched out on a padded lounge and stuffed fruits and cheeses in his mouth.

"Sit!" he said. "How about live? This room is the most wondrous thing I've ever seen. I could live here!" He thumped his arms on his furniture. "Right here. This spot! Never move again."

An elven maiden with pale-violet hair and green eyes sauntered in with another tray. She was petite, pretty, eyes engaging.

Ben choked. Thumped his chest with his fist. Took a drink. "Hello," he managed to spit out. "My name's Ben."

She nodded and walked away.

"Ah!" Ben said. "Did you see that, Dragon? The way she looked at me? I think she likes me!"

"I think you need to ease up on the elven fruit juice, Ben. It's pretty potent."

Sasha and Garrison chuckled along with me.

Everyone else was quite serious.

"What?" Ben said. "I swear she liked me. She really did."

After an hour, everyone had settled in, chatting openly with one another. The elven juice often did that to you.

Brenwar groaned when he took a seat. "I'm sitting, but I swear I won't be comfortable." He combed his beard with his fingers. Grumbled. "Better not be no pixies."

Now came the wait.

The waits weren't so bad for the likes of me, Brenwar, Shum, or Bayzog. But to humans like Sasha, Ben, and Garrison, it could be agonizing. It was one of the reasons men didn't mingle with the elves so much. Elven things took a long time. A simple meeting might not start for days, maybe weeks, unless you planned it out well in advance. In the case of us, our business was unexpected. There was no telling when they'd officially greet us.

I took a chair near Bayzog and Sasha. Tried to enjoy the tunes of the elven bards who strummed and strolled along. I was uncomfortable, though.

Waiting, which really wasn't much of an issue with dragons, made me think of my father. He always made me wait. Well, maybe not wait as much as dragon things just taking a long time. But right now, I wouldn't mind *waiting* to see him again as opposed to maybe never seeing him again at all.

I set down my goblet of elven juice. I needed to focus.

"Thanks for bringing me here," Sasha said to Bayzog. "I've always wanted to come."

Bayzog sat with his arm on her knee, poised but not relaxed.

I could feel the tension in him. I understood it. I could relate. But I had to wonder what he was thinking. I didn't know much about Bayzog and his family.

Sasha gently turned Bayzog's chin with her fingers, to face her.

"Why don't you go see them while we wait? I'm sure they miss you."

I saw a little fire ignite in Bayzog's violet eyes. But that fire was met with Sasha's sweet determination.

Good for her, I thought.

"Perhaps," Bayzog said.

The night came. The leaves on some of the trees glowed, and all the humans in our party fell asleep. The rest of us sat in the quiet. Alone in our thoughts.

Contemplating the next step in the journey. Would the elves help? Or would they shun our efforts?

There was only one way to find out.

Wait.

CHAPTER 23

HIGH PRIESTESS SELENE, ACCOMPANIED BY a dozen acolytes and lizard men, had finished her journey west toward the Ruins of Barnabus. It was there her lord lived, hidden from prying eyes deep inside the belly of the mountainous terrain. They rode on horseback, traversing the narrow trails until they stopped at a cave mouth. It resembled a maw, dragonlike, more than forty feet tall. Standing just outside the entrance, she rubbed her shoulder. It was cold in there. Dark. Vast. She could feel eyes all over her.

"Stay here," she said. "And make no sudden moves." She pointed at the ledges of the cave's entrance.

Several carved dragons blended in with the stones and vegetation. As big as men, some bigger. They were breathing. Their eyes sparkled like gems.

"You don't want those guardians to greet you. One bite and it's over."

Inside she went, heavy, dark robes dragging over the ground, tail swishing back and forth. She felt cold. Nervous. She was the High Priestess of Barnabus, so she shouldn't fear anything. Yet she did. Her breath showed. Her heart beat faster. The cavern smelled of death. Decay. A tomb of sorts.

Straight she went. Down a gentle grade until a distant light shone. Torches, the fires green and blue ignited by magic.

A massive stone archway adorned in gargoyle heads and dragons looked down at her.

She kneeled. Bowed. "High Priestess Selene comes to see the master of all masters. The priest of all priests. The one true Lord of Nalzambor."

On the other side of the archway, two stone urns flared with icy, burning light. In between them, a throne made for someone ten times her size waited. Empty.

"COME."

The voice was deep as a canyon. Powerful as a stormy wind.

Selene made her way inside. Stopped at the marble step as high as her head and bowed.

She felt small. Insignificant. Her hands went cold. She waited what seemed to her a long time.

"YOU TREMBLE. WHY, SELENE?"

She swallowed. Words were stuck in her throat. She trembled.

"HAVE YOU NO GOOD NEWS TO BRING?"

"I-I do."

"LOOK AT ME!"

She snapped her chin up. A presence sat. Huge. Ominous. A dragon-like being of shadows and scales. His eyes were black pits with burning stars in the middle. A crown of thorns adorned his head. He sat like a man. Shoulders like a Titan's. But all dragon.

"THAT'S BETTER ... DAUGHTER. WHAT NEWS DO YOU HAVE FOR ME?"

She yelled, even though she didn't have to, her voice echoing.

"Nath Dragon has black scales, Father."

"HEH ... HEH. SOON NALZAMBOR WILL BE OURS. BUT I GROW IMPATIENT." He reached down his hand. "COME."

She stepped onto the center of his hand.

He lifted her like a doll and set her on the arm of the chair.

Still looking up at him, she waited. The dragon was her father so far as she knew. She'd never known any other parents other than the family of Barnabus.

Unknown to her, this was a lie. Barnabus had been a hero in the first dragon wars. His legend had been twisted into something else. His good name used to spread evil. It had all been the idea of Gorn Grattak, the Dragon Lord on the throne. King of the evil dragons. One of a few survivors of the last Dragon War.

"TELL ME MORE, CHILD."

The tightness in her chest eased. Her confidence returned. She'd made it this far. She'd live.

She said, "We capture dragons by the dozens now. We've turned the world against them. For every one Nath Dragon saves, we take ten. Extinguish them. Sell them. Or bring the willing ones here. As you wish, Father.

"We watch Nath Dragon. Wear him down. Hunt and destroy his friends. His allies. He's still attached to this world. Banished from the Dragon Home. A wayward one, trying to redeem himself."

Again, Selene waited what seemed to her a long time.

"HIS REDEMPTION MUST NEVER HAPPEN," Gorm Grattak said. "SEE TO THAT PERSONALLY, IF YOU MUST."

"Yes, Father."

"I CANNOT LEAVE, DAUGHTER. ELSE I BE DISCOVERED. I FEEL MY STRENGTH GROWING. MY ARMY BUILDS."

He waved his arm across the air. The entire chamber lit up. Bones, treasures, and tributes covered the edges of the room. A mural filled with dragons battling in a storm spanned the entire back wall. There were hundreds of them. No two alike. They moved. They hissed. Trying to escape one world for the other.

"THEY ARE READY TO FIGHT. THEIR BANISHMENT ALMOST OVER. SOON WE WILL RUN THIS WORLD OVER." He lifted her chin with his clawed finger. "THE TURNING OR DEATH OF NATH DRAGON WILL MAKE IT CERTAIN. I PREFER HIM TURNED." He snorted. Smoke billowed from his nose like icy air. "GO NOW, DAUGHTER. RETURN ONLY WHEN YOU HAVE SUCCEEDED." He set her down.

The room went black.

She didn't turn. Just walked away. Though she had no aversion to darkness, she welcomed the light of the sun that greeted her at the end. She would do things right or else she would be dead.

As she cleared the mouth of the cave, her heart stopped.

She gasped.

All of the lizard men and acolytes were dead. Devoured in most cases. Even all the horses but one. She got into the saddle and eyed the guardians above the mouth of the cave. The statues didn't move or blink, but their bellies bulged where'd they'd been flat before.

Her eyes narrowed.

Her jaw set.

Nath Dragon will be mine one way or the other. "Yah!"

CHAPTER
24

THREE DAYS LATER THE ELVES came. It was a good thing, too. Ben and Garrison were getting antsy. Pestering the elves. Almost stalking them.

I didn't have the patience to explain elven etiquette to them. Don't touch. Don't stare. Eat and sleep until they get here.

Brenwar grumbled every half day or so. Hadn't eaten a thing.

Sasha lay on the sofa, legs over Bayzog's lap. She slept most of the time.

Shum sat by himself. Eyes closed the entire time. But I could tell he saw everything through his ears. He was the first one to rise moments before the elven delegation appeared.

There were eight of them in all. Light and dark headed. Fair skinned and tanned. Adorned in soft and intricate robes. The tallest was half a foot shorter than me, the shortest half a head taller than Brenwar. Their expressions were stern but friendly.

I knew two of them and nodded.

They led us to another open room with a large oval table. It looked more like it was grown than carved.

"Dragon Son, it's good to have you among us again," one said. "I see Akron is still honored in your possession."

"Yes, Laedorn," I said. "Your excellent gift has never failed. Put a lot of new holes in orcs, I'll say."

He chuckled. "Those were the days," he said. "So, Nath, I see you've changed since last we met. Is that what brings you here? I understand you seek the Ocular of Orray."

I wanted to shrug. I only did this by the prompting of my friends and for the benefit of Shum and his king. I felt great.

"Yes," I said, "my friend Bayzog believes it might heal me."

Laedorn's eyes drifted between Shum and Bayzog. The other elves' eyes did as well. I could feel the tension among them. Something old. Unsettled.

Laedorn rested his eyes on Bayzog. Smiled briefly at Sasha.

"Bayzog, you should visit with your family. They miss you. But they respect your privacy. They don't anticipate your arrival, but that's up to you."

"Tell them I'll return when the time is right," Bayzog said, "but that time is not now. Certainly the elves are aware that damp winds have begun to prevail. The seasons change. Rapidly."

"We know this. The evil races are emboldened. Their skirmishes increase. They've crossed our lands and hunted our game. Testing us day in and day out." Laedorn's brow furrowed. "Tell me what you have learned of the Ocular of Orray."

Bayzog furrowed his own brow. "It can heal anything. Curses. Lycanthropy. Disease. I've even read it can take you from one time to another. Perhaps it can return Dragon to form. Take him back to before the trouble started."

"Possibly."

"But," Bayzog said, "it's been taken. Stolen. Scattered in six pieces all over this world. Taken from right underneath the elves' noses. A hundred years after the last war."

"You suppose," Laedorn said. "But you do not know for certain."

"And you do, Laedorn? Are the histories wrong? My sources polluted?"

The elves at the table muttered in Elvish among themselves. There weren't speaking thoughts so much as grumbling at one another. I spoke Elvish and many other things, but they muttered with uncertainty.

"Enough," Laedorn said. He turned his focus to Shum. "And what is your interest in all of this, Roamer Shum?"

"I'm doing it for my king, Sansla Libor," Shum said.

The elves stirred.

"There is no king but the one Elven King," Laedorn said. His eyes narrowed. "Mind your manners."

"Your king is here, in these lands. The Roamers have one king and one alone. Sansla Libor is the king of the Roamers." Shum said it matter of factly with a bow. "Always has been; always will be."

"Your *king*," Laedorn said, voice hardening, "is wanted for murder, Shum. Over a dozen elves died by his hands. There's blood on that winged monster's claws. You know this. All of the elves know this."

"He's cursed!" Shum said, slamming his fist on the table.

All the humans jumped in their seats.

Shum went on. "He cannot be blamed."

Laedorn said, "Curse or no curse, the blood is on his hands, not someone else's, Roamer. We hunt him, yet you protect him."

"You don't seek to cure him," Shum said. "You seek to destroy him."

"He needs to stand trial. He must answer. He must be stopped. He kills, Shum. You've seen it. He'll kill today. Kill tomorrow." Laedorn tapped his fingers together. "So I presume you want the Ocular to cure your king?"

"You would do the same thing for your king, wouldn't you?" Shum leaned forward on the table. "Isn't that what this Occular is for—healing?"

"Healing the sick. Not murderers!"

"All right, everyone," I cut in. "Let's back up. About the Ocular, Laedorn. We want to help find it. Will you let us do that at least?"

The elves went stone cold silent. Expressionless. One and all. They had secrets deeper than the world. They guarded them well.

All eyes were on Laedorn. Except Brenwar's. His eyes were closed. Head back. Snoring softly.

Laedorn sighed. "Dragon, I need you to come with us. As well as Bayzog and Shum."

"Why?"

"It has been required of me. You see, Dragon, as soon as you showed up, we met. Our full council, not just these elves. Even the king. The decision has been made."

"What decision?" I said, easing my way out of my chair.

"I need you to leave your weapons and come with us," Laedorn said, "Now."

Elven Guard sealed the room. Leaf-shaped helmets on their heads. Elven steel on hips and spearheads. There must have been thirty of them.

Sasha clutched at Bayzog's arm. "What is going on? Laedorn, is this how you treat your guests?"

"I'm sorry, lovely lady, but you'll just have to trust me. Dragon, must I ask again?"

I unhitched Akron, unbuckled Fang, and dropped them on the table. "Lead the way."

After all, I still had my claws.

Not to mention my breath.

CHAPTER 25

T HE ELVEN GUARD LED US on a casual march through the city. Not a single eye batted. It was as if strangers and armed guards strolled through the city all the time. The three of us were side by side, Bayzog in the middle, the elven greeters in front and behind us, with Laedorn close by.

"I wasn't expecting this, Laedorn," I said, not hiding the irritation in my voice. "Didn't you forget to shackle us?"

He said nothing.

We kept going, following a planked roadway that led up and around the trunk of a tree. We came to a tunnel concealed behind the woodland. I'd never heard of an elven dungeon before, but this had to be one.

The hair on my neck stood up.

"Where is this?" I whispered over to Bayzog.

"I don't know," he whispered back.

We stopped. Dark hoods were placed over our heads.

I said, "You can't be serious, Laedorn."

He said nothing.

We were prodded along. Prisoners. Our footsteps silent through every twist and turn.

I couldn't keep track of where we were going. I was disoriented. And I had to wonder if it was the structure or the hood.

It tingled on my head. Muffled sounds. At times it seemed to guide me.

I lost track of time. Seconds. Minutes. Or hours. But my legs didn't tire.

KaRoom!

It was the first notable sound I heard. A large metal door closing. The stuffiness of an enclosed room. Like a tomb.

My hood was lifted. Laedorn and many others stood before me.

"We're here," he said.

"Where?" I said. "Our prison?"

"Sort of," he said. "It's a place more secure than a prison, Dragon. It's a vault."

My eyes adjusted quickly. The room was ornate, metal, completely sealed with one door going in and out. Lit by mystic lapis lazuli that hung from chains on the ceiling. Behind Laedorn, the other elves stood on a dais the color of pearl. The elven guards were gone.

"A vault for what?"

"Ha! For centuries we've been searching. Redeeming ourselves for what we lost. We scoured Nalzambor from one corner to the other. Sailed the waters. Crossed the lava. Tunneled where no elf had been before." He smiled at me. "And now we have it." He stepped aside. The other elves parted in the middle. "Dragon, behold the Ocular of Orray."

A cluster of diamonds in the middle shone brilliant like stars. Encased in the purest gold and platinum, the Ocular was spectacular.

Bayzog's violet eyes were wider than I'd ever seen.

Shum's narrow eyes were circles.

I found myself swallowing a lump in my throat. It was as great a treasure as any in my father's throne room.

"How long," I said, squinting my gold eyes a little, "have you had it?"

"Not long. Little over a decade," Laedorn said.

"Have you used it?" Bayzog asked.

"Once," Laedorn replied.

Bayzog stepped forward, eyes on the pendant.

"Did it work?"

"Of course."

"And what did you heal?" Bayzog said. "Or let me guess, you won't reveal?"

"You are wise, Bayzog," Laedorn said, shifting his feet a little, "but it's not anything you should concern yourselves with. It is Dragon and Sansla Libor that you are concerned with." He looked at me, my dragon arms. Waiting. Studying. "Well, Dragon. Is this what you want? Are you ready?"

All eyes were on me.

I wasn't ready. Not at all. If anything, I'd just gotten used to my dragon arms. My stomach quivered. Knotted a little. What if the Ocular did cure me? I looked at my scaly hands and sharp golden-yellow claws. I would miss them. I could do more good with them. Could I do as much good without them?

"Dragon," Bayzog said.

"Huh?" I replied, shaking the fog from my head. "Oh, well, will it heal me, or send me back in time before the trouble started?" I was buying time now. But I had to be smooth. Make certain no one suspected it.

"The Ocular heals, that much is certain. But the other effects of the artifact are unpredictable," Laedorn said.

The tightness in my chest began to unravel.

"Well now, that's the trick, isn't it? You can't really guarantee what will happen, good or bad." I folded my arms over my chest, held my chin in my hand. "I've a great deal of thinking to do. Weighing the consequences of this action."

"Dragon!" Bayzog stomped his foot. "This is a great honor and opportunity the elves are offering you! This is what we came for. We don't even have to risk our necks. The gift is there. Your only thought should be to take it!"

I'd never seen Bayzog angry before. There was fury under his creaseless brown skin that was now crinkled. Fists balled at his sides. His human part had come out. If I hadn't known him better, I'd have supposed he'd strike me.

"Easy, Bayzog," I said. "I'm a dragon. I don't rush into things."

"You rush into everything! That's what got you here in the first place!" Bayzog said, getting right in my face. "Don't be a fool, Dragon!"

My belly caught fire. My eyes narrowed on Bayzog.

"What did you—"

"I said what Brenwar would say. What your father would say!"

"It's not your decision, elf." I poked him in the chest. "It's mine and mine alone." I stepped away from Bayzog's glare. Faced Laedorn. "What about Sansla Libor?"

"We've discussed this already," Laedorn said, "and we agree to the following." He faced Shum and looked up into his eyes.

Shum stood still, hands crossed over his belly.

Laedorn said to Shum, "Capture Sansla Libor and bring him to us, and we promise we'll use the Ocular on him before he stands trial and judgment is delivered."

"How can he stand trial for something he'll have no recollection of?" Shum said, leaning forward.

"You don't know that, Shum," Laedorn said.

"And if he's not healed, how do you try him then?"

"The same as we try any other murderer and monster in our lands," Laedorn said. "I'm sorry, Shum, but the elves won't budge on this. I won't either. Justice must be delivered."

Shum's face drew tight. Conflicted. His loyalty to his king was unquestionable. He'd give his life for Sansla Libor.

I felt for him. I really did. "Shum," I said, "what would Sansla Libor do if he were in your boots?"

"Well said, Dragon," Laedorn said.

Shum's steely eyes drifted onto me. There was sadness mixed with determination. "Are you going to help me find him, Dragon?"

"I give you my pledge."

"I too," Bayzog said.

Shum extended his crossed arms to Laedorn and stretched out his hands.

Laedorn took them in his and nodded. "Agreed, then."

"Now, Dragon," Laedorn said, "what is your decision? Sometimes opportunity such as this only comes once in a lifetime.

"Give me a moment," I said, stepping away. I pinched the bridge of my nose. Rubbed my eyes. Raked my claws through my hair. A hundred thoughts simultaneously raced through my head. I felt the greatest decision in my life pressing upon me. At times like this, I would make a mental list. The good side and the bad side of my consequences.

"Dragon," Bayzog said, "the elves are offering you a gift. Don't test their patience."

"Another moment, please," I said, spite in my voice. "What seems so easy to you might not be so easy to me. There are consequences to everything. And Laedorn clearly noted there could be side effects. Did your pointed ears not note that? Because I'm pretty sure everyone else heard."

I moved farther toward the corner. I thought of Brenwar.

If he were here, he'd shove the Ocular down my throat.

And what would Brenwar say once I left and told him I received an offer of healing and didn't take it? I'd never hear the end of it.

And my father. Should I not do it for him? I could be healed and go back to Dragon Home again. I could clean my slate. Start all over again.

But I wouldn't be as powerful.

I flexed my arms. Felt the tough but pliable scales over layers of hardened muscles. It felt amazing. I snorted a puff of smoke from my nose. I would lose that. The fire in my belly that could melt metal bars. I was twice as powerful now as I'd ever been before.

It was my choice.

Mine alone.

I could save more dragons with my black scales than without them.

I turned. Faced them. Shook my head.

"I'm not doing this."

CHAPTER
26

Thomas HE ELVES IN THE ROOM had resolve. They weren't easily rattled or surprised. They weren't without passion or personality, either, but they were quick minded. Brows lifted. Mouths sighed. The expressions on their faces were unforgettable.

Bayzog sat on the dais, holding his head.

Shum was the only one who didn't change at all.

"Are you certain about this?" Laedorn said, frowning.

It bothered me. Laedorn always featured a pleasant smile. Nothing ever bothered him. Not a hundred charging orcs. Not a thousand. But this did.

I stared at the Ocular of Orray.

It was brilliant. Beautiful. Pure as the face of an elven maiden. It hummed. Twinkled. Stirred the bones under my scales.

My dragon heart thumped in my chest. "No," I said. "I'm not."

I stepped onto the dais alongside Bayzog and patted his shoulder.

His eyes looked up at me. Pleading. *Do it, Dragon. Do it.*

I could feel the warmth of the Ocular.

Its glow caressed my scales. Warm. Inviting. A mother. An old friend.

My eyes began to water. The closer I went, the more my stomach turned. A struggle brewed within me. Pride. Vanity. Arrogance. Power. They clashed with all that was right within me. What was left?

An image of my father formed in my mind. Patient. Powerful. Kind.

"Do it," I said.

The elves encircled me. One twitched his slender fingers. The pendant floated from its station and dropped over my neck. Someone was holding my hands. My arms. Others muttered incantations. Soft. Strong. Melodious chanting.

I closed my eyes. Exhaled. Let go.

Warmth coated me from head to toe. Every hair tingled on my head. My legs.

My arms. My chest. The mystic power soaked in, washing me from the inside out. I squeezed my eyes shut.

The light was blinding through my lids.

I heard voices. Ancient. Wise. In languages no man had ever heard.

Cleansing energy raced between my feet and my heart. My heart thundered in my chest. Something deep inside me was being dug out. Strong. Dark. Like a tick made of moorite.

I started to shake.

"What's happening?" Bayzog cried out.

I slung one elf from my arm. Then another. I let out an ear-splitting roar.

Zzzzzzt!

The light of the Ocular died. It floated from my neck, back onto the pedestal.

I fell to my knees. A shaking leaf. A snake's rattle. My mind a cloud in the air. Time passed. Faces drifted in and out.

"Dragon, Dragon," Laedorn said, jostling my shoulder. "Can you hear me?"

"Huh?" I had a funny taste in my mouth. Unpleasant was more like it. "Yes, yes, Laedorn. I can hear just fine."

They were tending the elves I'd slung into the wall.

Bayzog stood alongside Shum, staring.

I stood up, gently pushed Laedorn aside and extended my arms. My black dragon arms were as beautiful as ever. Claws still as sharp as knives. I felt my face.

"Anything happen?" I asked.

Laedorn eyed me from head to toe. "Nothing at all that I can see. It seems either you're still cursed or you were never cursed at all. I believe it's the latter, Nath Dragon."

I hid my smile. I was elated. But what should I say?

"I felt something, though. Old wounds being mended." I feigned a sigh. "I am disappointed. I really thought this would work. Even though—and don't tell Brenwar this—I was scared at first." I patted Laedorn on the shoulder. "I don't think I'm cursed. I think I am the cure. Thank you for trying, Laedorn."

With a thoughtful expression on his face, he squeezed my hand that rested on his shoulder.

"It was our pleasure, Dragon. And I wouldn't speak of this to the others," Laedorn said to everyone. "We prefer that the rumors of the Ocular of Orray being lost remain so. It is a closely guarded secret. Come, they'll show you out."

I shuffled by Shum and Bayzog, head down, hiding the golden glimmer in my eyes.

Back at the Place of Meet, Bayzog separated himself from the others in his mind.

The others talked, partially explaining where they'd been. But it was clear enough. They planned their trek to find Sansla Libor the Roamer King.

The Ocular of Orray wasn't mentioned. It bothered him that he couldn't speak of it to Sasha. What if she asked? What would he say? Wizards were masters of the partly true story. But he couldn't deceive the one he loved.

"Bayzog." Laedorn approached, alone. A solemn look in his eyes. "What do you think?"

Bayzog said, "I think Dragon is glad he isn't cured. I think he wanted it that way."

Laedorn looked over his shoulder where the others gathered. Dragon was laughing. Joking. All eyes were upon him. Even those of the elven troubadours and maidens.

"I share your thoughts, Bayzog. And I wonder if the Ocular could cure him and he didn't let it. The council certainly hoped that it would. This news that it didn't will be dreadful." Laedorn shook his head. "Dreadful, indeed."

"Why do you say so? What do they know? What do they suspect?"

"Some of us were still around for the last dragon war. I was younger then. But many saw the black dragons. Nath makes them uneasy. Nalzambor is in unrest. We were hoping to prevent something that might not be preventable."

"Are you saying war is inevitable?" Bayzog said.

"You are as much a great historian as you are a wizard. What do you think?"

"I think I'd better keep a close eye on him."

Laedorn looked hard into his eyes. "I think we all better do that." Laedorn slipped a bracelet over Bayzog's wrist.

"What this for?"

"Keep me posted, Bayzog." Laedorn turned to walk away. "I wish you all the fortune in Nalzambor."

CHAPTER 27

T HE RIDE OUT OF THE Elven Lands was quiet. Steady. A soft rain accompanied us after the Elven Guard departed. For some reason I felt happy, but the others' expressions weren't so bright.

Shum was determined to find Sansla Libor.

Bayzog, I could clearly see, was disappointed. He hardly even spoke to me.

Up ahead, Brenwar slowed. Allowed me to catch up. Wrung the water out of his beard.

"What's the plan?" Brenwar asked. "We taking the boys back north or do we follow Shum, after Sansla Libor?" Brenwar's brown eyes narrowed as he gazed after the big-boned elf. "What happened with those elves, anyway? Back in Elome. No one's talking. And I'm not stupid, Dragon. You're holding back something."

He looked me in the eye. His stare hard. Penetrating.

I couldn't lie to Brenwar. But I could keep a secret. I could tell part of the truth. Not all.

"I've agreed to help Shum find his king for now. Bring him back to the elves for trial." I looked away and rode on. "My problems will just have to wait until later."

Brenwar came right after me. "Am I to understand we no longer search for this Ocular? That's all we talked about on the way here!"

"Plans change," I said. "It can't be all about me, you know. Now keep your voice down."

Brenwar harrumphed. "What do ye mean, keep my voice down?"

"Just do. I don't want to have a group discussion about it, if you don't mind. I just want to ride. Find Sansla. Save some dragons along the way. It's bound to be a long journey."

"Most journeys are—pah—when you don't know where you're going," he said. "And you, Dragon, don't know where you're going. And I know yer hiding something. I can feel it in my bones." He rode off toward Shum. Far enough ahead where I could barely see him in the fog and rolling mist.

Ben and Garrison rode up alongside me, excited looks on their faces.

"Look at this, Dragon," Ben said. He had a horned rabbit skewered on a stick. "Snared the both of them we did. Just like you taught me. Like I taught Garrison."

Garrison had another one.

"Somebody's going to eat well tonight," I said, "and those pelts are worth a week's pay, I bet. Each, I'd say."

"Told you," Garrison said. "Say, what's wrong with Brenwar? Does he always get mad at everything you say?"

I laughed. "That's a good observation, Garrison, but you'll get used to it."

"Are all dwarves like that?" Garrison asked.

"Some more so," I said, "but most not nearly so bad."

Garrison shifted in his saddle. Eyeing me. Catching my eyes, then looking away.

"Is there something else you wanted to ask?"

The young Legionnaire brushed his bangs from his forehead. Wiped the water from his face.

"Who's Sansla Libor?"

"Yes, Dragon," Ben said. "Tell us about that?"

I didn't see the harm in telling Ben and Garrison about it. They'd need to be prepared for such things in case he showed up again. But I wasn't going to tell them the part about him being the Roamer King.

"He's a monster."

"What kind of monster?" Ben said.

"Give me a moment. I just started."

Garrison hit Ben in the shoulder. Motioned for me to continue.

"Ahem. A winged ape. Bigger than me. Fast as a cat and powerful as an ogre," I said. "It drops out of the sky as quiet as rain. Snatches its prey up like an eagle does. Sweeps them away, never to be seen again. I faced it twice. Took my lumps, I did. But the next time I face it," I held out my claws, "I'll break it."

We rode on. The rain was a drizzle now. Silent until someone spoke again. It was Garrison.

"What do the elves want it for?"

"Murder," I said.

"It killed elves?" Ben said.

"That and other things. And we have to stop it before it kills again."

"Well, I'm ready," Ben said, sticking out his chest.

"You're going home," I said, bothered. "It's back to the Legionnaires where you belong, Ben. This mission's dangerous enough already."

"What? Really?" Ben said. "It's only been a week. I have a month and I can handle myself just fine already. Think about it, Dragon. I've survived fights with both draykis and ettins."

"And horned rabbits," I said, laughing.

"Draykis," Garrison said. "What's a draykis?"

"Sort of like a lizard man, but more like a dragon," Ben said. "Right, Dragon?"

"Close enough," I said. Ben and Garrison were starting to bother me. I didn't want them around, but it was going to take some convincing. "But honestly, Ben, this journey might take months, years maybe. You might be an old man before we even find him. If we find him."

"But I want to stay with you, Dragon. I want to travel. Adventure. I'm ready. You know I am."

He was ready. But he still wasn't coming.

"Oh," Garrison said, turning his horse around.

"Where you going?" Ben asked.

"There's another snare I forgot to check back there. I'll be right back," he said, riding off.

"Want me to come along?" Ben yelled after his friend.

I grabbed his shoulder. "He'll be fine. Let him go. Besides, I need to work on that hard head of yours. You're going back, Ben. No choice."

"But what about Sasha?" he said. "She's human too."

He made a good point, but Sasha wasn't my problem. Not that she was a problem, but that was up to Bayzog. I did find it strange that he let her travel with him at all. Especially as protective as he was.

"She a sorceress, Ben. She can live longer. You can't do that, can you?"

He frowned. "No."

"And she's not a Legionnaire either, is she?"

Still frowning, head down, he rode away.

I felt bad for him. I really did. But it was the right thing.

Garrison drifted back, out of sight, taking a spot in a sparse grove of turning trees and falling leaves. He hopped out of his saddle, checked his surroundings, and procured a small figurine from one of his pouches.

It was a robed, bald man carved out of wood. An evil look in its eyes.

He rubbed it between his hands, faster and faster. His hands glowed. Became hot. He dropped it to the ground.

"Sheesh!" He rubbed his smoking hands in the dirt. Gritted his teeth. "Hate doing this."

An image formed over the figurine. A man-sized shadow. Almost as real as his nose. Dark eyes encircled pupils that burned like fire.

Garrison kneeled down. Bowed. Rose up a hair.

"High Cleric Kryzak," he said, "I have news."

The image wavered in the wind, then stiffened. The voice was strong. He could feel it.

"Share, soldier, share," Kryzak said, "What business had they in the Elven Lands? We could not communicate with you there."

"My lord, they sought aid to find Sansla Libor. He's cursed and seeks a cure. Nath Dragon does too."

"Are you certain of what you report?" Kryzak said, his image coming closer.

Garrison broke into a cold sweat. He'd seen what the war cleric did to those who failed.

"I'm certain," he said. "I've picked up on what they've tried to keep hidden. My ears," he said, rubbing a small metal earring on his lobe, "are picking up lots of things thanks to this enchanted jewel."

"Tell me more," the dark voice said.

"They sought an item. The Ocular of Orray. It heals. Removes curses and disease, they say. The elves search for a winged ape. White. Powerful. He is the Roamer King, Sansla Libor. Nath Dragon sought to remove his black scales but does not talk of it now." He caught his breath. "He seems content."

"I see," the shadow said, rubbing his chin. "And what of you, soldier?"

"He sends us back toward Quintuklen."

"Hmmm," Kryzak said, "journey back to where you started. Convince Nath Dragon to follow. If needed, I will assist you. Worry naught about the others. I'll take care of them when the time comes."

Garrison bowed again. "As you wish, my lord. I'll not let the Clerics of Barnabus down."

The image faded. The glow of the figurine went out.

He picked it up and stuffed it into his pouch. Stuck his boot in the stirrup and boosted himself up. "This will be interesting."

He wondered what Kryzak had in mind for Dragon. *Death. Torture. Mutilation.* He'd heard about Nath Dragon much in his life. His parents were servants of Barnabus. It was all he'd ever known. He had been raised to hate the dragons. But he hid it well. Unlike his parents, he wasn't deft in magic, but he had a clever tongue. A simplistic, nonthreatening demeanor. It made him an excellent spy, and he liked it. *How I enjoy messing with people. Pulling rugs and dragons out from underneath them.*

He rode with a sly smile under his nose until he got there. This was the greatest mission ever.

CHAPTER
28

"**D**RAGON, COME," SHUM SAID.

I followed him on horseback, leaving the others behind.

We were another day into our journey. Garrison had pleaded that we escort them back to the village the ettins attacked to see that everything was all right. Shum and Brenwar saw no problem with it, seeing how the last time we saw Sansla Libor, it was in the north, and it was the most likely place to head anyway. Personally, I didn't mind. I wanted to get a look at that crater again anyway. Something ate at me about it.

Shum hopped off his horse, and I followed suit. The big elf had been scouting ahead the whole time, keeping out of sight until night sometimes. His movements were purposeful, his gestures quick.

I followed along up a faded path, past the naked branches, and stopped behind the bushes that overlooked a cliff.

"Smell that," he said.

My nose crinkled. It was offended. "Orcs!" I whispered, my blood charged.

Shum nodded, battle awakening in his eyes.

If there was one time when dwarves, elves, and men got along, it was against orcs. We all hated them and they hated all of us.

Shum stuck his long finger out. There must have been two dozen of them camping, that I could see.

"Pretty close to the Elven Lands," I said. "They are getting braver, just like Laedorn said."

"We can go around," Shum said, "but I figured you'd want to get a look. You've tangled more with them than I have recently."

I flexed my arms. Clenched my claws. What an opportunity! Turn loose both my arms and my breath on the orcs. Sure, I couldn't kill them. But I could hurt them. Maim them. Frighten the hair off their backs.

We hunched down. Watched. Waited. Shum was right. No sense in endangering ourselves or the rest of the party on account of orcs.

The breed below were wild ones. Some had small tusks under their noses. Some hard, flat bellies, while others' bulged over their belts.

I just wanted to punch them out. Break some bones. Leave some with a limp for life maybe.

They tussled, grunted, and poked fun at one another, making coarse sounds and jokes.

"I suppose we should go," I said, "but do you think it necessary to send word to the elves?"

"No," Shum replied, "they've doubled patrols already on the borderland. Perhaps these are some of the ones that have been hunting game on their land."

"I wonder what kind of game they're after," I said, watching one of the orcs.

It was stirring up a commotion, beating its chest about something. It waved another orc over with a face filled with metal and rings. It had a leash.

It has a dragon on that leash!

My blood turned white hot.

Shum grabbed my shoulder. "Don't react, Dragon. Plan, then attack," he said in my ear.

I took a sharp breath.

They had two dragons, not one, each the size of a large goat. They were golden flowers. Canary-yellow scales sparkled with pale bellies. My keen eyes picked up the long lashes on their eyes. Two girls. Sisters, probably. Beautiful and sleek. Hissing and slashing their tails while the orcs stood by laughing. Jerking the collars on their necks.

I tore out of Shum's grasp.

"Dragon!" he half yelled. "Let's get the others!"

As I dashed down the hill, the wind whistled through my ears. My auburn hair flowed around me.

An orc pointed my way. Sounded the alarm.

I kept on going.

They formed a row at the bottom. Weapons ready to greet me. Axes, hammers, and flails, wielded in handfuls of ugly.

I leapt over the tops of their heads—leaving them to their cries of astonishment—and made a bee line for the dragons.

A big orc, rock solid and black haired, charged after me.

I struck. Snapped its head back. Knocked it out.

One dove at my legs.

Another swung a cleaver at my head. The blade skipped off my scaled arm as I jumped up.

I tore a hunk of its chest armor out. Twisted the blade from its grasp and hoisted the orc over my head.

Three orcs with wet pig noses closed in.

I gave them a gift. Hurled their pig-faced brother right into them.

Wham!

They rocked and reeled.

I kept moving.

The orcs were dragging the golden flowers away. Jerking at the ropes.

I yelled something. I don't know what, maybe "Stop!"

They didn't listen. They should have.

My black arm flashed into the nearest orc's chin.

Crack!

It wobbled to the ground.

Slit!

I cut the leash from the first dragon's neck with my claws and went after the rest of the orcs.

The metal-faced orc greeted me with long, sharp steel in hand.

I chopped. I blocked.

Its blade skipped off my scales.

I didn't feel a thing. But the orc did.

Crunch!

I drove my knee into its crotch.

Its eyes exploded in their sockets. At least I could slow the orc breeding process.

Whop!

I knocked it out with another punch. Grabbed the second leash and sliced if off with my claws.

Two yellow dragons scurried over the ground, squawking like birds.

Orcs dove after them from all directions.

They spread their wings and darted into the air like shooting stars.

Crack!

Someone clubbed me in the back of the head. Stars circled. The orcs piled on.

Shum hesitated. Didn't move. Watched Dragon dash down the hill. There were too many orcs, way too many to take on at once. They'd need help. At least Brenwar to even things out.

"Probably dead if I do, dead if I don't," he said, pulling out his sword.

He kept his eyes fixed on Dragon. The man was fast. Fluid. Strong. He cleared the first wave of orcs in a single bound. Assaulted the others with the fury of a storm.

Dragon disappeared under a wave of orcs when he hit the bottom of the hill. He stabbed the nearest orc.

Krang!

He clocked the helmet off another. The orcs responded. Their forces divided. Coming after him and Dragon.

"Har! It's an elf," one yelled. It was a big orc. Heavy and gusty. A heavy sword in both hands. "A big one at that. I'll have his head."

Swish!

Shum ducked under the orc's swing and countered. *Slice!* The orc fell to the ground with its head missing.

"No, I'll have yours."

A fervor rose among the orcs. A cry of alarm.

Dragon rose from the pile with two orcs by the necks. He slammed their heads together and let out an inhuman growl.

The orcs stabbed and chopped.

Dragon brushed them away. Dragon's eyes were wild. Golden flares.

Shum sliced, dodged, and parried. Kept the orcs at bay with the sword and dagger both quicker than snakes. "Dragon!" Shum yelled, "Make a run for it. The dragons are free. We've no quarrel left with them."

Whop!

Dragon uppercut one in the belly, lifting it off its feet.

Shum had seen Dragon fight before. Against the winged ape, Sansla Libor. Dragon had been strong then, but he was stronger now. Quicker. Dragon's claws were cutting the orcs to ribbons.

"Don't lose control, Dragon!" he said. "Run! I'll hold them off!"

If only the orcs were wiser, they'd run from the danger. But they were stubborn. Stupid.

For a moment, Shum wasn't sure if he was saving Dragon from the orcs or the orcs from Dragon.

And there were still twenty of them. Slow. Angry. Strong. Coming at him three, four, five at a time. Shum killed some, wounded others, but they kept coming. Their crude weapons nicked him up. Drew his blood.

I've got to get us out of this.

Shum was yelling, "Run!"

I wasn't running anywhere. I laid into the orcs with no mercy. Left them alive, but bleeding. Limping. Crawling. I was Dragon. And I hated orcs!

An orc took a wild chop at my head.

I caught the blade in my hand and yelled. My scales were as tough as steel. I laid that orc out. Tore into the others. I was faster. Stronger. Tougher than they were.

And the thought of them capturing dragons! I would make them pay. Punish them. Hurt them.

Whop! Crack! Bang! Slice! Slam!

They cried out.

I laughed.

Someone was saying something. Yelling again. Perhaps Shum was in danger, but I didn't see him.

BOOOOORANNNNG!!!

The ground beneath me burst open. Rocks and dirt flew everywhere. The orcs fell and tumbled all over. I stumbled but didn't fall. My ears rang. Orcs snorted and started to flee. I was going after the nearest when someone pounced on my legs. I took a swing. Landed a hard shot, cracking its ribs. Drew back again.

"Dragon!" a voice bellowed. "STOP!"

I hesitated. Looked down at my victim. It was Ben. My hot blood turned cold.

CHAPTER 29

"**I** CAN'T BELIEVE IT," BRENWAR SAID, grumbling from his saddle. "Fighting orcs without me. Bloody elf. You could have gotten yerself killed. Would've if I hadn't come along and dropped down my war hammer!"

The orcs had fled, and that had been more than a day ago. I'd apologized to Ben several times since. I'd busted his ribs. Put a dent in his armor. I'll never forget the look in his eyes when I realized it was him.

Fear. Pain.

I couldn't believe I'd done that to him. I just wanted to crawl into a pit. Bury myself. I'd lost control again.

"And you, Dragon!" Brenwar said, "Like a fool you run off. No plan. No backup. Not only did you hurt yourself, you hurt your friend. I saw that look in your eyes." He shook his head and stroked his beard. "You could've killed him."

My mane dangled over my eyes. I couldn't even look at Brenwar. He was right. He could chew me out all he wanted. All the way back to the village. Back to Quintuklen. I deserved it.

Brenwar rode along my side, the others much farther ahead. No one was saying much of anything, at least not to me. Shum had spoken to Bayzog and Sasha separately, and I saw worried expressions whenever they turned to me.

I'd freed two dragons, but I felt like I'd let everyone down somehow.

"You can't be running off on your own, Dragon. We've got to stay together." Brenwar poked his stubby finger at me. I hated that. He continued. "And don't you ever, and I mean ever, fight orcs without me. Ol' Pot Belly ended up taking more of them down than me." He growled. "Never again."

He went on and on. A thorn in my side. A nagging companion I wouldn't shed. A burr in my saddle.

I kept my eyes open and my mouth closed. I paid no attention to the wonderful terrain and babbling brooks we passed. I didn't fish in the streams. I didn't eat a thing. Mile after mile. League after league. I just wanted to get Ben back to safety.

He told me he was all right and there was nothing to forgive.

But I couldn't forgive myself. I'd hurt a friend. *Never again*, I recounted in my head, *never again*.

Garrison kept busy tending to Ben and the others. He helped hunt, cook, and gather the wood. All the time he listened to their whispers. Their worries. He rubbed the mystic earring. It was perfect.

"How are you feeling, friend?" he said, helping Ben off his horse.

The wiry country boy held his ribs and groaned. "I'm getting better. That potion Sasha fed me really mended me, but I'm still sore." Ben looked around. "Say, where're Dragon and Brenwar?"

"They're coming," Garrison said. "I think Brenwar's still lecturing him. I didn't think dwarves talked so much, but when they start, they get on a roll." He helped Ben sit down. "I'll fetch you some fresh water."

"No need," Ben said, looking around. "I wish Brenwar wouldn't do that. I'm all right. Dragon is all right, too. He seems sad. I don't like seeing him so sad."

"Well, I'm sorry too, Ben," Garrison said, shaking his head.

"For what?"

"I never should have told you to grab him. But I thought that's what they wanted. Everyone was yelling at him." Garrison sighed. "It should have been me, not you."

"Oh," Ben said, "you know I'm faster than you." He turned away, eyes searching for Dragon.

"I know you are," Garrison said, a sneaky smile parting his lips.

I was counting on it. Kryzak will be pleased.

"What is it, darling?" Sasha said. "Are you still worried?"

Bayzog *was* worried. He was worried about Sasha, Dragon, all of Nalzambor. The encounter with the orcs filled him with fear. Dragon's eyes had been wild. Filled with lust and power. Dragon had almost killed Ben—and there was something else that he and the rest of the party had allowed to escape Dragon's attention. He'd killed some orcs.

Bayzog shifted in his saddle. Long rides he'd never gotten used to, but it was better than walking. He replaced his long face with a smile. "That obvious, is it?"

"You can't fool me," she said, smiling back at him. "Dragon will be all right, Bayzog. He's good."

"He's lucky," he replied, glancing over his shoulder. The party was spread out but closing in on the village border. "And dangerous."

"Bayzog, they were orcs. Since when are you so compassionate about orcs? You've told me countless horrors about them. Why can't Dragon take them out? The best way to stop evil is to kill it." Her jaw tightened. "I hate evil and so do you. It causes all the terrible things. Good for him, I say."

"Sasha!" he said, neat brows lifted. "Watch what you say!"

"Well," she said, flipping her hair. "Shum and Brenwar killed some of them, and you would have too if you were there. Why can't Dragon?"

"He's not like us," Bayzog said with a sigh. "He's different. He's a dragon. The son of the King Dragon, and his standards are not ours. It's complicated. But as I understand it, the more Dragon kills, the more danger for the world."

"Well, I think it's ridiculous. He's so young, and that's too much responsibility."

"He's over two hundred years old, Sasha. He has to do what dragons do."

Sasha's eyes got big at hearing how old Nath was, but she tried to cover up her surprise. "Dragons kill, don't they?" she said. "I really want to see them. Those two yellow ones were so magnificent. I only got a glimpse of them. What were they called?"

Bayzog wasn't fooled, but he let it go. "Golden flowers," he said, "and, yes, dragons kill, I suppose. But Nath is not like other dragons. He's a dragon born a man. He's special. We have to guide him. You understand that, don't you?"

"Uh," she said, mouth open, her smile gone, "of course I do. I'm just talking to you, Bayzog. I'm not a fool."

"Sasha, you know that's not what I—"

She rode way, auburn hair bouncing on her head.

"—meant. Great Guzan."

His Sasha was miffed. It happened, just not often, but when she was angry, she stayed that way awhile. He let her go. She'd be back to give him an earful. But if she didn't come back within a reasonable time, then he'd better go after her or she might get even madder.

The drizzle turned into rain and splashed off his robes.

He sighed. "If I ever understand women, I'll be the world's most powerful wizard."

Everyone needed to be on the same page. Everyone had to keep an eye on Dragon. He was changing. For all Bayzog knew, Dragon might be transcending into another age. From a young dragon into a mature one.

And Bayzog had already shared the secret about the Ocular. He'd told Sasha and Brenwar. If they were going to work together, they'd have to trust each other.

But they didn't tell Dragon they were working together to keep an eye on him. They didn't tell Ben and Garrison, either. What they didn't know wouldn't hurt them. They'd be leaving the company soon anyway.

He'd ridden onward alone for another hour and Sasha hadn't returned.

A strange feeling overcame him. The plains were open, but no one was in sight.

Lost in his thoughts, he must have fallen behind. "I better go after her," he said to himself. He snapped the reins.

Another mile into his ride, the rain came down so hard it stung his face. Horse hooves splashed through the water. He couldn't see a thing.

CHAPTER
30

Sasha's horse nickered and they came to a stop. A heavy rain was coming and the distant trees were bending.

"Oh, great." She tugged on the reins to turn around. Those cool raindrops might extinguish her temper. She rubbed her horse's neck and spoke to it. "It's not like me to get so upset. I'm sorry, but I'm glad you're here. We women need to stick together."

Her horse snorted and wriggled its long neck.

Sasha laughed a little. "Good to know someone understands."

She felt a bit guilty. After all, Bayzog wasn't the best communicator. She knew that. What he'd said wasn't that bad. She'd just overreacted.

"He must think I'm a witch."

Bayzog was normally calm, in control, intent on his studies. But now he was worried. And that worried her. It scared her.

She sniffed. Took out a handkerchief and blew her nose. "Dratted weather, always does this."

Two riders approached, side by side. She smiled. It was Ben and Garrison. Ben was waving, hand high in the air.

"Sasha! Sasha! Storm's coming!"

"I know," she said, "Did Bayzog send you for me?"

Ben and Garrison looked at each other, then back at her.

"No," Ben said, "we just saw you riding alone and thought you might want some company. Besides, we humans need to stick together. We don't live forever like the others."

Sasha giggled. Ben had a strange charm in how he said things. And he was right. The others tended to take their time about things.

She brushed her hair from her eyes and yawned. "I don't guess there's any way around this storm," she said. "Do you think we can make a ride to town? Where are the others?"

"I hate storms. I hate being wet," Ben said. "You'd think you'd get used to it, but the Legionnaires insist on sleeping out in the rain. They say it makes you tougher. I say it's stupid. Why would you be wet or cold if you didn't have to be?"

"I agree, Ben," she said. "And what's your opinion on all this, Garrison?"

He shrugged. "It's not so bad, I guess. Ben just complains too much."

"I do not!"

"Do too!"

"All right," Sasha said, "let's find the others. Maybe they have a plan. They couldn't be too far, right?"

"Shum said to just whistle and he'll find us," Ben said, putting his fingers between his lips.

Garrison pushed his hands down.

"We're almost to the village. Let's just ride through the rain and find shelter. They'll catch up with us there. Come on, it's less than a league away."

"What do you think, Sasha?" Ben said.

She squinted her eyes and looked around. There was no sign of Bayzog. It riled her anger up again. *He should have come after me by now.*

Ben looked at her kindly. "I think there's no chance of avoiding the rain either way." He patted his stomach. "And I have a feeling there'll be some warm food cooking. And I'm ready to eat. The elven bread's tasteless. Needs some salt and pepper. I'm sick of it."

"Come on," Garrison said, waving after them. "Let's ride right through it. We'll be safe together. After all, we're Legionnaires."

Ben lifted his eyebrows at Sasha. "He's right, you know. I say we go."

"And I say," Sasha said, "last one to the village is buying our meals!" She dug her boots in. Snapped the reins. "Yah!"

They'd raced the first mile when the hard rain hit. It soaked Sasha to the bone, but she liked it. She'd been indoors so much she'd forgotten how much fun the outside could be.

"You all right, Sasha?" Ben called out.

"I'm fine, just stay close. How about you, Garrison?"

The young man motioned with his hand from up ahead.

She squinted to see him. "Lead the way, Garrison."

They moved at a trot. The rain was heavy to ride through, and they didn't want to slip on the rugged spots. Besides, there was no hurry. They'd see the warm torchlight of the village at any moment.

"Well, we'll make it before dark, anyway," Ben said.

"It's pretty dark now," Sasha said. "I wonder how long this rain will last. Seems like it's been raining forever."

"Like I said, you never get used to it."

"If you were a rock maybe," she said.

"Or a river?"

"A pond," she said.

"A fish."

"A kraken."

"A dwarf," Ben said. "I bet Brenwar is just fine with it." He cupped his ear. "I think I can hear him singing a cheerful song right now." He started to work his elbow and sing:

"Dwarves smell bad—Hoy! Dwarves smell bad— Hoy!

We like to stay mad—Hoy! We like to stay mad—Hoy!

Being sad makes us glad—Hoy! Being sad makes us glad—Hoy!"

"Hahaha," Sasha said, holding her belly. "Ben, only you could find humor in this rain."

"Well, it's just part of soldiering, is all. Making up silly songs to lighten the mundane," he said, beaming. "But I thought of that one myself."

"Well, you have a gift for it," she said. "Whoa!" Her horse nickered and stopped. "What is it, girl?" Both horses stomped their hooves and nickered again. "Ben, do you see Garrison?"

"No," he said.

The heavy rain started to feel like ice, and Sasha's nose tingled.

"Stay close to me, Ben. I'm going to cast a little spell," she said. "I think we need some more light in the darkness."

Ben's horse reared up and neighed. A dark, hulking form emerged from the rain. It was bigger than a man. Black wings spread over its back.

"Sasha, get behind me," Ben said, whipping out his sword.

Sasha's words froze in her mouth.

Ben struck. The creature was faster and ripped Ben out of the saddle. It tossed him through the rain and out of sight.

Sasha fumbled with the locket on her neck and tried to speak, but her tongue was tied.

Thunder cracked.

The monster spread out its thick arms and snatched her up. Smothering her in its powerful arms, it leaped from the ground and flew up, up, up.

Helpless and tongue-tied, she couldn't even scream. Arms pinned at her sides, she couldn't do a thing.

CHAPTER
31

THE VILLAGE HALL WAS REBUILT but not finished. Water dripped through the cracks in the incomplete roof and soaked the rafters of the wooden structure. Several lanterns gave them all the illumination they needed, but it was still dim.

Inside, Bayzog paced back and forth. A dozen villagers dwelled there for now, riding out the storm, still eager to finish their own homes. Their offers of food brought him no comfort. Ben, Garrison and—most importantly—Sasha, were missing, or perhaps lost. Back and forth he went, hands locked together, thumbs circling one another. *This is my fault.*

Dragon, Shum, and Brenwar had been with him when they entered the village just before dark. They'd waited almost an hour for the others to arrive. Every minute of that hour had become more miserable than the previous.

"I must go look for her," Bayzog had said. "Something is wrong, I know it."

Dragon's voice had been so reassuring. "They're fine, Bayzog. I'm certain they're just waiting out the storm. Probably found shelter somewhere close. They might be here in one of the homes. I'll send one of the villagers out."

"Do as you wish," Bayzog had said, "but I'm heading back out."

"Tell you what," Dragon had suggested, "let the three of us go. We'll find them."

"No, I insist. I wouldn't feel right not searching for Sasha myself," Bayzog had said, "and my magic can be of assistance."

Dragon had put his hand on Bayzog's shoulder and smiled. Nath had a soothing way about him when he wanted to. He voice was convincing. Smooth. "You need to be here when she shows up and we're still out searching, getting our boots full of mud. Things like this always work out that way. Trust me."

Bayzog had reluctantly agreed. More than two hours ago. He'd been in torment ever since.

I should've gone. I should've gone. I should've gone.

"Please, Elven One," a village man said. He was older, with salt-and-pepper hair and big brown eyes, "have some honey tea. It will soothe your worries. I promise." The man held a mug out to him, his hand shaking a little.

"Why do you tremble?"

"Er, well ... you're a wizard and an elf. We're not so used to that. We fear that if you get too upset, things will explode."

Bayzog sighed and took the mug in hand. "Is it that obvious?"

The man nodded.

Bayzog took a sip. It was good, soothing like the man said. He had a seat on a bench and leaned back. "Perhaps I am overreacting," he said.

The man sat at his side. Another man pulled out a small set of pipes and played. It was upbeat, but not fast. The children clapped. The women and men swung arm in arm and danced.

"I must admit," Bayzog said, "you people certainly have a way to overcome dreariness. Such a great spirit among you." He drank the rest of the cup. "Refreshing actually."

"We're used to hard times," the older man said. "Life's filled with the good and the bad. You just have to deal with it. The rainbows will come again. The crops will grow. They always do."

The front door banged open. The room jumped and gasped. A large, cloaked figure filled the doorway and stepped inside. A man was in his arms. It was Ben. Bayzog jumped to his feet when the figure removed his hood. It was Dragon.

"Is he—" Bayzog started, but he didn't want to say.

"He's wounded, but he lives," Dragon said, laying him down on a table. "Find something for him to drink."

Ben's face bore a nasty gash, and there was a large purple knot on his head.

"What happened?" Bayzog said. "What about Sasha? Did you find her?"

Dragon shook his head and held out something in his hand. It was her locket. The chain was snapped.

"Nooooo!" Bayzog slumped to his knees. He punched Dragon in the arm. "What happened?"

Two more figures made it inside and shook off the rain. Brenwar and Garrison. Garrison's arm dangled at his side. His face was pale, and he shivered.

"Get him something to drink," Brenwar ordered.

The villagers did so. Someone threw a blanket over the young soldier.

"Thank you," Garrison said, taking the first hot sip, wincing. "My arm hurts."

"Dragon," Bayzog said, "what is going on? What happened out there? Where is Shum?"

"I'm here," Shum said, stepped through the door and closing it behind him.

"Anything?" Dragon asked.

Shum shook his head. "All the tracks are washed away. Assuming there were any."

"What do you mean by that?" Bayzog demanded, rising to his feet.

"Tell him what you told us, Garrison," Dragon said. "Recount it all again."

Bayzog's mind raced. *Maybe the ettins came back. Or the orcs followed. What in the world could it be?*

Shivering, Garrison said, "We decided to make for the village. Slog through the rain. I was leading when the horses stamped and screamed." He winced. Adjusted his arm. "Something knocked me from my horse and I landed hard on my shoulder. I couldn't see much in the rain, but I heard Ben scream, 'Sasha, get behind me!' That's when I saw it. It grabbed Ben and flung him like a doll out of sight. It grabbed Sasha ..." He swallowed and his eyes watered.

"Go ahead, Garrison," Dragon said. "You're doing well."

He sniffled. "It was horrible. Fanged. The wings spread out and it just scooped Sasha up and leapt into the night. I-I-I was terrified." He looked right at Bayzog. "I'm sorry. I wanted to help, but I was too slow. And I was scared. That thing's eyes were pure evil."

"Sansla Libor did this!" Bayzog said, pointing at Shum. "You know it!"

"We don't know that," Shum said.

"Don't you dare defend him!" Bayzog shouted. "He's a murderer. And knowing you and your Roamer kin, you probably had some idea he was near. Well, I'm going after her." He bumped past Shum and slammed open the door. "No thanks to you!"

Brenwar wrung out his beard and said, "Now that's my kind of elf. Humph."

I'd never seen such emotion from the elf, but I reminded myself that Bayzog was part human. And even though my friend was angry, it was good to see a little color in his cheeks. I checked the wound on Ben's head. It was ghastly but not fatal.

I sighed. Ben had been through much since coming to know me. The young man had fought a jackal-were, even killed it. Almost been sacrificed by the Clerics of Barnabus. Battled ettins. Been punched out by me, and now this. Flung over the rocks by the winged ape.

"Sometimes, Ben, I wish we'd never met," I whispered, handing a vial to one of the village women. "Rub a couple drops in his wounds every hour or so." I put my clawed hand on Garrison's head. "You, take care of that shoulder."

"Wait, where are you going?"

"After Bayzog and after Sasha."

"But I want to go. I can help. I've seen the monster."

"And lived to tell about it," I said, walking away. "Live storytellers are better than dead ones. Share this adventure with your fellow soldiers."

Garrison watched the dragon, elf, and dwarf depart and hissed in relief. He'd fooled them. There'd been a moment when he doubted himself. When Dragon looked at him. His eyes. Those golden eyes he swore saw right through him. But as he'd been taught, it's easy to hide a lie with a layer of truth.

He drank his honey tea and closed his eyes.

Garrison hadn't lied about one thing. The winged monster *had* terrified him. He'd rather face the ettins than face it again. It was evil. And even though he'd known it was coming and had led them right into the trap, he still hadn't been ready for what he'd seen.

It wasn't Sansla Libor.

It was a winged draykis.

What they don't know might kill them. Heh. Heh.

He dabbed a damp cloth on Ben's head. He felt bad for him. For the second time, he'd almost gotten the young man killed—once by Dragon, again by the monster—yet Ben still lived.

"You're different," Garrison said. "Lucky and unlucky. But it'll catch up with you sooner or later."

He thought about Bayzog. The look on the elven wizard's face when had heard about the winged ape. *Almost made that elf cry. Now that was a performance.* He checked the figurine in his pocket. It was time he sent word to his master. The last trap was about to be sprung. He just wished he would be there to see it.

CHAPTER
32

THERE WAS NO STOPPING BAYZOG. He insisted we take him to where Sasha was abducted, which we did. He scoured the spot where the necklace had been found, holding a small rod in his hand. It glowed like a lantern but was fueled by something else. Magic. It formed a wide beam of light, illuminating the ground.

"That's not going to help," Shum said. "Even with a full day of light, the water washed all signs and tracks out. I can't make out one single hoofprint."

Bayzog kept going about his business. On his knees, he rubbed his hands in the dirt where the locket had been found.

The rest of us did our best to assist him. Even Brenwar dug around.

After we'd been stumbling around for hours, the rain came to a stop and dawn began to break. Birds chirped, and the distant sound of a rooster's crow caught my ears.

"We can broaden the search now," Shum suggested.

"Oh, can we now, Ranger?" Bayzog said. "Perhaps you can lead us right to him, unless you're protecting him."

"You know better," Shum said.

"Shum, I hardly know you at all, or your kind. You're practically shunned by the rest of elven kind, and now I'm supposed to trust you?" Bayzog extinguished his rod with a word and stuffed it into his robes. "Your king snatches women and children. Is accused of murder. Is cursed. A monster. And now he has Sasha!"

"We don't know that for certain," I said, stepping between them.

Bayzog turned on me with his fists bunched up. "What?"

"We only know what Garrison said he saw," I said, "and I don't fully trust Garrison. Maybe Ben saw something else. It was dark."

"I don't follow," Brenwar said. "What is it you sense with Garrison, Dragon?"

I smiled grimly at Brenwar. He knew the sense I had. A detection. I could tell the truth from a lie most of the time. "I'm certain Garrison is holding something back from us. Maybe from fear or maybe from embarrassment."

Bayzog swung himself up into his saddle.

"Where are you going?" I said.

"Wherever I have to go to find Sasha."

He trotted off, leaving the three of us looking at each other.

"Let's just follow him," I said. "I'm certain he has his own way of tracking her."

We spent the next few hours scouring the plains. Bayzog cast detection spells here and there and kept his eyes up often.

Shum rode along my side, talking. "It's possible it is indeed Sansla Libor, Dragon," he said.

"Why do you say that?"

"As I've said before, I think you two were connected when the both of you met. He searched you out, remember?"

"Of course," I said, "but why would he take Sasha? Why not come right after me? Besides, we were far north the last time."

"Anything can happen," Shum said, riding his horse away.

"Look!" Bayzog cried out from afar, pointing into the sky.

There are many things that fly, particularly birds and dragons. But this was neither. Whatever it was, it was shaped more like a man. A big man.

Bayzog was already at a full gallop. Everyone else was riding behind.

The creature was high in the air and seemed to hover at times, but I couldn't tell. It wasn't getting any farther away, and we weren't getting any closer. Bayzog wasn't going to stop, and we weren't either.

All my doubts about Sansla Libor faded away. *It must be him. What else could it be?* And I'd expected a lengthy search, weeks if not months, to find the Elf King turned monster. And now there he was, flying high above us.

It seemed Garrison had been right after all.

We'd kept pace for a few more miles when it finally dipped and dove into the mouth of the crater. Bayzog stopped and looked back at me. He wasn't the only one. Shum and Brenwar's eyes were intent on me as well. In a world full of monsters, I shouldn't have been surprised. Perhaps all along the winged ape had been hiding in the crater. Back in the caves that I had wanted to search through earlier. Now it must have sniffed me out. Been waiting. Perhaps luring me within. It wanted me for some reason. Perhaps another fight like the last time, but this time I'd be ready.

"I suggest we leave the horses," I said. "They'll be all right."

Shum swung his long leg out of his saddle and hopped to the ground. He whispered in his great stallion's ear and turned to face us.

"Aaryn will keep them safe," the ranger said, slipping his small spear from the saddle and hooking it behind his back. "He'll lead them out of danger if need be."

Brenwar unhitched his small chest from his horse and dropped it to the ground.

"Brenwar," I said, "careful, there are potions in there."

"So?" he said, unhitching the catches and opening it up. Rows of color-filled vials popped up. "See anything you need, Dragon? Wizard?"

Bayzog came and leaned over.

The bottom of the chest was filled with trinkets and other items I hadn't noticed before.

Bayzog slipped his fingers around two of the vials.

Brenwar grabbed a strange metal horn and stuffed it into one of his pouches.

The chest made me think of my father and his throne. When he banished me, he didn't let me take a thing. But he let Brenwar take what he thought would be needed. I reached inside and wrapped my fingers around a large, bright marble. It was a Dragon Eye. Not a real one, of course, but it might aid us on our search.

"Got everything ye need?" Brenwar said. We nodded. He grabbed the Cloth of Concealment, sealed the chest shut, carried it to the edge of the woods, and covered it up.

"You sure that's safe?" Shum asked.

"You sure you're an elf?" Brenwar grunted and headed into the woods.

But it was Shum who led us to the lip of the crater. "There's a path up ahead," he said, "that took us out of here before. I don't advise that we take it back down again."

"I say we go in right here," Bayzog said, twisting a ring on his finger. "Stay close." He jumped off the edge and floated down. "Hurry!"

"Dwarves don't float," Brenwar said.

Shum and I grabbed him by the arms and jumped after the wizard.

"You dare!" Brenwar said. That, and a few other things, all the way down.

We landed soft as feathers and trekked into the woods on quiet feet before stopping briefly to speak.

"I say we search the caves first," I suggested.

Bayzog disagreed. "We should split up. Cover more ground."

I looked him in the eye and said, "This needs to be a united effort. We stay together."

Bayzog glared at me. It was a new look. I'd never even seen the elf rattled, for that matter, but now he was.

I didn't blame him. I put my hand on his shoulder. "We will find Sasha."

Bayzog nodded, kept his chin down and said, "Agreed."

The leaves on the trees started to shake.

Thoom. Thoom.

CHAPTER
33

B RENWAR'S BROWS BUCKLED. "GOOD, ANOTHER giant."

"No," I said, keeping my voice down. "We aren't taking this one head on."

"Why not?" he said.

"We're here for Sasha," I said. "We won't be fighting anything if we can avoid it."

"Says you," Brenwar said, smacking his war hammer into his hand.

Thoom.

"I'll take us around," Shum said, "and let's hope there aren't many more around."

"It might not be a giant anyway," I said.

"Oh, it's a giant, all right," Brenwar added, following along after Shum and Bayzog.

I took up the rear. I didn't want any of us to get separated.

Ahead, Shum led us away from the heavy steps of the ettin, giant, or whatever it was. Fighting that would let the entire crater know we were there. We just needed to get in and out. Be quick about it.

Navigating the forest wasn't difficult. The dwarf and the elf both had keen vision, as did I. But satyrs did, too, so we had to be careful. They were dangerous and known to be vengeful.

Shum stopped and held up his hand.

The heavy giant steps had faded away, but something howled. A predator. Wolves, I believed. The crickets and bugs still chirped, however. That was a good thing. If danger or evil were near, they'd fall silent.

Shum signaled back to me with his fingers flashing in the air.

I'll be right back.

I signaled a reply.

Wait!

He was gone as if he'd never been there at all.

Brenwar slung his hammer over his shoulder, shaking his head.

Bayzog stood with a frown.

I trusted Shum, but in truth I didn't know him that well. Not like Brenwar and Bayzog, both of whom I trusted with my life. I brushed my hair out of my eyes and sat down. Shum didn't have any business running off like that. Not at a time like this.

I could feel Brenwar's eyes on me. He was saying something. Nodding a little.

I looked away from him. I got it. I just didn't want to admit it. The feeling you get when someone runs off without your permission. It makes you worry a little.

Minutes later, Shum emerged and we gathered around.

"The gnolls and goblins are gone. Disappeared. No tracks," he said.

That was odd. There had to be tracks of something.

"Did you notice anything else?" I asked.

"Just the entrance to the tunnels. Wide open."

"Tunnels, you say?" Brenwar said. "Guess I'll be leading, then."

"Hold still, will you?" I said. I pulled out the marble. The Dragon Eye.

The tunnels were many. Some were goblin sized, others large enough to ride a horse inside. We needed to choose one out of the many.

Brenwar kneeled at the mouth of one, tasted a handful of dirt, and spit it out.

"What do you think, Brenwar?"

"It's dirty."

"Well, yes," I said, "I think that's obvious."

"No," he said raising to full height. "Evil dirty. Bad something in there. Real bad."

"Shum," I said, "don't you find it odd that Sansla would live in a cave?"

"No," he said, "we use caves for shelter and hideouts all the time. It's not uncommon, not for us, anyway."

"I'm going in," Bayzog said. "Brenwar, will you lead the way?"

"Certainly," Brenwar said, marching inside.

"A little caution, please," I said, holding out the Dragon Eye. "Let this be our guide. No offense, Brenwar."

He turned his cheek and harrumphed.

I flicked the marble into the tunnel. It glowed a pale green like a lantern bug and hovered forward into the darkness until it disappeared.

"Lead the way," I said, gesturing to Brenwar.

"I thought we were following your little bauble," he said, marching along with Bayzog right in step behind him. "What's that thing do, anyway?"

"Sees what we cannot. Warns us of any danger," I said.

"Good, then I guess we don't have anything to worry about now, do we?" Brenwar said, marching off.

The tunnels led from one to another. It only made sense to head through the openings big enough for a large ape to manage.

"Look," Brenwar said.

In a cave nook were some gnawed-up bones and other remains. Cloth, ashes, and embers from a fire. We kept going, seeing traces of life here and there. It made me think of the goblin hideout we had ventured through before.

"Hmmm," Brenwar said, stopping and pulling at his beard. He eyed a cave wall and ran his hands over the rock. "Seems there have been some civilized settlements here after all. Sloppy work. Probably from orcs or some other beast that's not smarter than the pick it swings."

I checked with Shum behind me. "Anything?"

"No," he said. "But these tunnels probably go for miles."

Bayzog was silent at my side, a faint glow on his fingertips.

"We're going to find her," I said.

"I know we are," Bayzog said. "We have to."

We spent the next hour following Brenwar, and I only assumed the Dragon Eye was still ahead. I grew more and more puzzled. We saw fewer and fewer signs of life.

Finally, Brenwar put his hand out and gestured, touching his nose. *Something ahead.*

I could smell it myself. Life. Blood. We kept moving.

From the way the air moved, I knew the tunnel had opened into a large cave. But it was pitch black, and I couldn't see from one side to the other. There were no outlines. No nothing. We crept inside, keeping close to one another.

Something shuffled in the dark. Its breath was heavy, and it grunted a little.

My fingertips tingled beneath my claws, and my heat-sensitive eyes adjusted a little to the darkness.

A warm figure was huddled on the floor, trembling.

Sasha! That was my first thought. I wondered if Bayzog saw her as well. Her fragrance filled my nostrils. It was her! I reached for Bayzog. We had to be careful. Take it easy. Slow. I touched his shoulder and pointed toward her.

Bayzog's body stiffened.

I waved my finger in front of his face. *Hold.*

The Dragon Eye hadn't alerted me, so perhaps there wasn't any danger. Maybe the winged ape had left her and taken off.

But I heard something else breathing in here. Something big.

I picked up a stone and chucked it over the room. Something bounded after it. Heavy and powerful.

Bayzog dashed toward the figure of Sasha.

Brenwar and I stood guard, waiting for the creature to return. It was coming back.

"Why can't I see it?" I said.

"Perhaps you need more light," an unfamiliar voice replied.

Pop!

Fire pits erupted throughout the cavern in orange-green flames.

"Is that better, Nath Dragon?" the dark voice said.

I tore Fang out and faced the sound of the voice.

Shing.

"Who are you?" Brenwar came along my side, with Shum right behind us. Bayzog held Sasha in his arms. "What is this?"

"Well," the voice said, emerging from a darkened cove. It was a large, hooded man in deep-purple robes. In his hand he tossed my Dragon Eye up and down. "It's called a trap. Certainly you know that." He tossed the marble to the floor, and it rolled to a stop between my feet. "This might have worked if I weren't expecting you."

"Told you, can't always count on magic," Brenwar said, crossing his arms.

"Your little friend is right, Nath Dragon," the man said. "You can't always trust what you see or hear, either."

A large winged figure came forward.

"What in Nalzambor is that?" Brenwar said.

"A draykis," I replied.

"You didn't tell me they were that ugly."

"You didn't ask," I said.

"Dragon," Shum's voice warned.

The walls and rocky floor started to move. More draykis popped up all over. More than a dozen of them.

"Bayzog, get Sasha out of here," I said. "We can hold them off."

"No, we stay together."

"Don't be a fool," I said.

The tunnel we had come through began to fill with goblins and gnolls.

"Ah, too late now," the robed man said.

"So, this is another ploy of the Clerics of Barnabus? An effort to what, capture and kill me? And just who might you be?"

"Kryzak," he said, swinging a war mace over his shoulder, "and I think my effort to capture you has succeeded. I even have your friends. Now the question is, do I kill you all or let some of you live?"

CHAPTER
34

W E WERE TRAPPED. FLATFOOTED. DOOMED maybe. My head was racing.
Kryzak had been ten steps ahead of us the entire time, and that meant only
one thing: Garrison was a spy. Which led to another problem. Ben was in
danger. Perhaps the entire village was.

Brenwar set his war hammer down, spit in his hands, rubbed them together, and
let out a gusty laugh before picking it up again. "It is you who are mistaken. I'm no
man's prisoner, but you are mine."

Brenwar hurled his hammer into the winged draykis. *Crack!* Sent it reeling, head
over heels.

I banged Fang's tip on the ground. Nothing. "Fang!" I launched myself toward
the Cleric Kryzak.

Three draykis cut off my path, swinging heavy swords and axes at me.

I ducked.

Swish.

Rolled.

Clang.

Kicked one in the chin.

The brutes were fast and strong, raining down one pulverizing blow after the
other.

I parried and swatted.

Slice!

Caught one in the leg.

Stab!

Hit another in the shoulder. "Blast, Fang!" I said. "Freeze them or something."

They'd beaten the snot out me the first time I encountered them, but I hadn't
had my sword that time, either. Now the fight was a little more even. I was still
quicker. And now two of them were slower, but I lost sight of one of them.

"Ulf!"

It bear hugged me from behind.

Not this again! I wheezed for breath.

The other two came at me.

I kicked one in the nose, drawing a roar.

The other one slugged me in the face. Walloped me in the belly.

The stars I saw made my aching stomach queasy.

"No!" I tried to yell, but I couldn't breathe. Again.

Snatching up his war hammer, Brenwar slammed into the toe of the reeling winged draykis. "That'll teach you." He didn't stop there.

Wham! Wham!

The monster's howl was desperate. Angry. It ripped at Brenwar with its claws.

Wham!

Brenwar broke its hand, drawing forth a howl. He raised his hammer for a final blow. "Yer one of the ugliest things I ever … eh?"

Swack!

A tail licked out, sending him tumbling over the cavern floor. A second later, something pounced on top of him, pinning Brenwar under its greater weight. A round dragon face with long whiskers peered down at him with bright-yellow cat eyes. Its purr was a rumble.

"Get off me, you scaly cat!"

It dug its claws into his shoulder.

"Ow!" Brenwar said. "Ya poked a hole in my armor. Yer gonna pay for that!"

Streams of smoke drifted out of the cat's nose.

Brenwar's eyes became heavy. "Ye better not eat me," he said, dozing off, "Dwarves make lousy mealzzzz …"

Shum, short spear ready, braced himself.

A draykis with a large iron club charged.

Shum muttered a word in Elvish.

Shtikt! Shtikt! Shtikt!

The spear grew from two feet to six, piercing the draykis in the middle of the chest.

Its club clanged off the cave floor. It was dead.

Shum went after the next one.

Bullish and scaled, it wore a helmet with metal horns.

Shum jabbed at it.

It backed away, swinging a pole axe from side to side with the skill of a veteran soldier but more power.

Make it quick!

The cavern had erupted in chaos. Bright flashes and bursts of energy brightened the room. Howls and screams followed. It all happened fast. Sometimes fast is good. Sometimes fast is bad.

Shum swatted his spear into the pole axe of the draykis, jarring his arms.

The part-man, part-dragon monster was formidable. Fast. Strong. Vicious. A lethal blow ripped over Shum's head.

He bounded back.

The draykis kept coming. Swinging hard. Chipping the stone from the ground. Making sparks.

Shum ran his spear through its side.

It roared and twisted away, ripping the spear from Shum's grip.

He went for his sword and dagger.

Two goblins dove into him. Drove him into the ground. One stuck a dagger in his leg. The other punched him in the face.

Pinned down, he somehow wriggled free. Bounced to his feet and freed his elven steel, leg throbbing.

Goblin after goblin fell. The gnolls barked and howled, swords and axes ready. The draykis pulled the spear from its side and came back after him. They had him surrounded.

Bayzog sent an arc of blue energy into the oncoming goblins and gnolls, throwing them back into the tunnel. He'd had it. They'd taken Sasha, and she wouldn't wake up. But she was breathing.

Around him, everything happened at once. Brenwar threw his hammer and everyone burst into action. Including him. The gnolls and goblins scrambled back to their feet and scurried into the room, breaking off in all directions.

Bayzog tipped a vial full of pale-red liquid to his lips and drank. His mind became sharp. Focused. Everyone in the cavern slowed down. Either that or his mind sped up. *I like it.* He pulled out a small wand and let them have it.

Bwing! Bwing! Bwing!

Purple hornets of energy showered the horde. Small explosions erupted all over them. They hopped and screamed, danced around, swatting at the balls that danced off their heads.

A gnoll broke through and came at him. But it was slow.

Bayzog muttered a quick word and sent the creature hurtling through the air into the others.

They kept coming at half speed. But there we so many. He and his party were outnumbered greatly.

Perhaps I should get Sasha out of here while I have the time and energy.

Bwing! Bwing! Bwing!

He sent the purple hornets back into the horde then gathered Sasha in his arms.

"Wake up," he said, shaking her.

She remained still, in a deep sleep.

That cleric, Kryzak, must have done something to her. He searched the room for the man. He'd take out the leader and put an end to this. "Where are you?"

"Right behind you," a dark voice said.

Bayzog whirled around and faced the tormenter.

Impossible!

Kryzak towered over him with his arms over his chest. "You have no power over me here, elf. I was expecting you."

Bayzog cast the wand right at the man.

It sizzled out.

"Seems you're empty," Kryzak said.

"My wand, maybe, but not the rest of me."

He raised his arms over his head and summoned sunbursts of energy forth, blasting Kryzak full in the chest and skipping him over the floor.

The cleric rose in his smoky robes, laughing over the chaos.

Bayzog sent another blast.

Kryzak swatted it away with one hand. "You have no power over me, elf, but I have power over you."

Bayzog felt the hairs rise on his neck. The shadows of the gnolls and goblins took on a life of their own and slithered toward him.

He summoned his words, but no sound came out. The cleric had silenced him.

The shadows slithered around his ankles, his waist, his chest, his neck—and dragged him to the ground.

CHAPTER
35

M**Y SWORD CLATTERED ON THE** stone floor. Pinned in the bear hug of one draykis, I took a shot in the stomach from another. Smoke erupted from my nose, and that wasn't all. My blood boiled. My temper flared.

The draykis drew back to punch me again.

I opened my mouth.

A geyser of flames shot out, coating the monster from head to toe.

It shrieked. Engulfed in flames, it sputtered around, igniting others in its path.

I wasn't finished, either. I kept on breathing.

The gnolls and goblins ran from the flames. Still the draykis held me tight. But nothing could hold me now. No draykis. No ettin.

I flexed. I heaved. I roared.

The bats above scattered. The draykis lost its grip.

"Now you've had it!" I spun away and slugged it in the face. We exchanged blows.

Whop! Crack! Jab! Jab!

I was faster. Madder. Furious. I was Dragon! I pounced on its chest. Drove it to the ground and beat it into submission. Chest heaving, I looked for my friends. Flames were scattered everywhere. Thick smoke was rolling.

"Dragon," a voice shot out.

I found Shum. Goblins and gnolls had dragged the elf to the ground. I dove into the fray. Grabbed hair, arms, and legs and slung them away.

Shum clutched at his side and bled from many wounds.

I helped him to his feet. "Can you still fight?" I said.

"Certainly," he said.

Back to back, we faced the horde, surrounded by barking faces and cautious eyes. Then I caught sight of something else: a dragon almost as big as a horse. Below it, an unmoving Brenwar.

"No!" I cried out. I didn't think. I reacted. Grabbed Akron from my back.

Snap. Clatch. Snap.

I whipped out an explosive arrow from my quiver and nocked it.

"Better duck if you want to live, vermin!"

They dove.

I loosed the arrow.

Kaboom!

The dragon, the likes of which I'd never seen, leapt screeching like a cat jumping out of water. Wingless, catlike, and serpentine, it landed on all fours facing me, whiskers dragging on the floor. Part of its back was smoking.

I nocked another. "Great Guzan!"

The arrow should have slowed it, maybe even killed it.

But it was a dragon. A powerful one.

I spoke at it in Dragonese. "Better back away, feline fury." Normally, I wouldn't attack another dragon for anything.

But this wasn't an ordinary dragon. It was a mean one. And it had done something to Brenwar. It flashed its razor-like claws and narrowed its eyes.

I fired.

It jumped.

The arrow zinged by it. *That was fast!*

Kaboom! The cavern shook.

The feline fury pounced right at me.

I jumped over its head and onto its back.

It twisted beneath me.

I fell to the ground but jumped right to my feet.

Its claws slashed, clipped my chest armor, and spun me around.

I struck back, clipping its nose.

It bounced back.

Dragons hated that. Still, I had to find its weakness before it tore me to pieces.

The feline fury was much bigger and far stronger than me. It was a beast. It'd take more than my claws and speed to stop it.

I dashed for my sword, Fang. Dove and wrapped my hands around the pommel.

The feline fury crashed on top of my back.

Fang skittered from my grip.

"No!" I elbowed it in the nose.

It slammed my face into the dirt with its paw. A cat toying with a mouse.

I wriggled and squirmed. Found myself on my back, pinned down. I struggled and strained.

The foul beast had me. Smoke billowed from its nostrils.

I opened my mouth and breathed, bathing its face in fire.

It sprang away, shaking its flaming head. Mewling, it roared and disappeared into the caves.

Fang's shiny blade caught my eye.

I crawled over, picked it up, and rose.

Goblins, gnolls, and draykis were all around me. Some living, some smoking, some dead. Where were my friends, though?

Clap! Clap! Clap! Clap!

"Well done, Dragon," the cleric said. "But I suggest you put your weapon down. It's time to surrender now."

That's when I saw. A chill went through me, dousing the flame in my veins within. Shum was in a gnoll's stranglehold with two blades on his belly. Brenwar's arms were bound behind his back. A draykis tossed his snoring form over its shoulder. Bayzog and Sasha's limp forms lay at Kryzak's feet, unmoving.

"They better not be dead," I said, pointing with my sword.

"They all still live at the moment," Kryzak said. His voice was deep and rough. Merciless. "But my word can be the death of them all."

The draykis dropped Brenwar to the floor. The goblins bound and gagged all of them.

"Drop your weapons," Kryzak said.

"What is it you want?" I said. *Keep him talking. Think of something.*

Kryzak reached down, grabbed Sasha by the hair, and pulled her to his chest. "Such a pretty lady," he said, "I'd hate to hurt her. Of course, I could leave her with the goblins and gnolls maybe. They appreciate a pretty face more than I do."

The goblins howled and panted. Beat their chests. Danced back and forth on their feet.

"Enough!" Kryzak shouted.

They fell silent.

"What will it be, Dragon?"

"Are you exchanging their freedom for me?" I said.

Kryzak nodded. "Certainly."

I stuck Fang's tip in the floor. Nothing.

CHAPTER
36

SURRENDERED. IT ATE AT ME.

Above was an opening, and rain was pouring down from on high. I'd been moved, shackled with mystic bonds to some sort of sacrificial rock marked in bright colors. My friends, every last one, were gone.

Kryzak stood before me. Hooded. Shaded face gloating.

Testing my bonds, I said, "How do I know my friends are free?" The harder I tugged, the more they bit into me. "Argh!"

"You're a strong one, Dragon. I can feel it," he said. Purple energy raced around his hands and wrists. "Such raw power. Incredible." He removed his hood. His face was big and scarred, his bald head tattooed with many bright colors. Shoulders broad and thick. Not the typical cleric but a warrior. Seasoned. Formidable. "They are almost free," he said. "For now."

"What?!"

He tapped his war mace on his shoulder. It was crude and ugly with a twinkle to its dark metal. "You'll see in a moment." He came closer, eyeing me up and down.

Smoke steamed from my mouth. "What game are you playing, Kryzak?"

A twisted smile formed on his lips. He said, "Game? I thought you liked games, Dragon. Games where you show off your speed, skill, and underwhelming intellect." He didn't get any closer. "And that breath of yours, really something. A surprise I wasn't expecting. But don't use it on me. You might need it for later, Dragon."

He's a strange man.

He was cold. Familiar. He acted like I should know him. And he liked to play games, it seemed.

So I played along. "Hmmm ... So, you have me. And I guess you went to all this trouble so I could play a game with you. What did you have in mind? Unhitch me—fiend—and we can play all the games you like. You look like you might be really good at painting eggs or something."

"Heh. Heh. Also a fast tongue, haven't you Dragon," he said. "Generally fast. You'll find out how fast you really are soon."

He seemed to know me, and I wasn't without my enemies. After all, I'd been roaming Nalzambor for more than 100 years. I'd crossed paths with many men once or twice. But the Clerics of Barnabus? I had no friends among them. I was getting antsy, though. Where were Brenwar, Shum, Bayzog, and Sasha? Had I surrendered for nothing? Should I have fought to the end?

"You seem bitter," I said. "Perhaps it's that ugly face of—*umph!*"

He slugged a mallet-like fist into my belly.

I grimaced and groaned.

"You always talked too much. Never shut up. And all the women seemed to love your meaningless words," he said through clenched teeth.

"And don't forget my hair," I said. "They love the hair just as mu—*oomph!*

My eyes watered. I had that coming. Well, from evil, anyway. I knew the Clerics of Barnabus hated me. Hunted me. But what grudge did this man have with me?

Smoke steamed out of my nose.

Kryzak stepped aside.

Two gnolls walked over and set down two man-sized mirrors in iron frames in front of me.

I finally caught my breath. "I appreciate it, but I can't reach my comb at the moment," I said. "And why two? I don't need to remind myself I look twice as good as any of you."

Kryzak stood off to the side with his thick forearms crossed over his chest. "Just keep watching," he said. He made a cup with his hands that quickly filled with rainwater. "During the long rainfalls, the deepest tunnels quickly fill with water. If one's not careful, one might drown. Lots of bones down there to be found when it dries out."

My heart skipped a beat.

Colors shimmered in the mirrors, and images formed.

Shum and Brenwar were in one mirror, Bayzog and Sasha in the other. Water was pouring around them. Rising over their waists. They were chained to something. Soaked. Eyes darting up and down. Sasha was yelling or screaming, but I couldn't hear a thing.

"What are you doing?" I yelled. "You said you would free them!"

"And I will. Free them from life, that is," he said. "But, Dragon, there is hope. You're fast, remember? You can do things most men can't do. Can't you?"

I fought my restraints.

Kryzak laughed. "Save your energy. I'm going to allow you to save one a pair of them, assuming you can find them inside these caves. But who do you save? Who is closer? I am confident you'll find one pair, but I'm not so sure about the other. Then again, they all might just die if you're not careful."

"I'll make you pay for this!" I yelled. "I'll kill you if anything happens to them!"

I was coming unglued, my temper unhitched. I didn't know what to do. I needed to think. Concentrate. Settle down.

"No doubt you'll try, hothead," he said, moving away. "But you better save your efforts for what awaits. Plenty of obstacles will be in your path. It will be interesting to see how you handle them, Dragon."

"Why? Why are you doing this? Why take my friends?"

"Good for evil, evil for good. That's the way it is in this world." He turned and started walking away. "Your bonds will fade soon. When they do, I'll be long gone. See you around, Nath Dragon." He stopped and turned. "Next time I see you, I'm sure you'll have more wonderful stories to tell. It's always fun to talk about the dead."

Hunt for the Hero

-Book 5-

CRAIG HALLORAN

CHAPTER 1

H EAVY RAINDROPS SPLATTERED OFF ME, the ground, and the mirrors, distorting the images. I was alone. The water rose faster. Up to Brenwar's chin and Shum's belly.

I couldn't hear Sasha's screams, but I could feel them. Through my scales. Into my bones. The panic in her face surrounded by the cold surface of the iron mirror's frame made my spine chill. I fought my bonds. The purple bands pinched into my wrists, but not as much as they had before. Either I was getting stronger or the magic was fading, just as Kryzak had said it would.

"Brenwar!" I yelled. The thought of him perishing had never occurred to me before. But he'd be the first to drown. He was the shortest. "I'll have you, Kryzak!"

The rain overpowered my voice. I was alone in another room of the cavern where a pair of ember-filled urns burned dimly. Kryzak and his brood had long since departed. I still heard the chuckles of the goblins and gnolls in my ears. Helplessly, I watched my friends struggle for life, dying in some cruel game because of me. What were the Clerics of Barnabus trying to do to me? Why not just kill me and be done with it? Why did my friends have to suffer as well?

Scaly arms bulging, I tore at my bonds. The cuffs bit deep, like burning razors. I screamed. My mind was racing. What if Kryzak had lied? What if the bonds weren't going to fade? Maybe it was just another part of his twisted game. Watching my friends die. Drown slowly. He must have lied. Why wouldn't he? He was evil.

"I can't let this happen!" I pulled. It felt like my wrists would snap off. "I won't let this happen!" I braced my feet against the stone behind me. I had to break free and break free now! I needed to buy all the time I could.

"*Hurk!*"

The bonds crackled. Bit. Burned. I put everything into it and roared.

Snap!

I pitched forward and crashed into the mirrors. They toppled and the glass shattered.

"No!"

On my knees I picked up one of the large pieces and thought I saw Sasha's pretty eyes before the image faded. I was alone. Worried. Stomach turning. I dashed into the nearest tunnel with my heart thundering inside my chest. My dragon eyes could make out the faint outlines of the tunnels. The entire time I was shackled, I'd been thinking about what I was going to do. I'd have to figure out how I would find them.

I rubbed my wrists. They were warm and wet. I'd bled. I was seeing red when I came to the first fork in the tunnels. I stopped.

Settle down, Nath. Think. What's the plan?

I'd had a plan a minute ago. A sound one, but it was lost at the moment. What was it? Assuming what Kryzak had said was true, I could save one pair, not the other. And if I had my choice, who would I save? In my mind it would be Sasha. That's what the others would do. It was an unspoken code among men: save the women and children. Then the men can save themselves. But Brenwar. The thought of not hearing his voice again haunted me already. I couldn't imagine it. Couldn't think it.

I tore a hunk of rock out of the wall.

"Guzan! What do I do?"

The only reply was my echoing voice. I didn't have a choice, it seemed. Whoever I found first would live. Whoever I didn't find would die. Unless I was fast enough.

Quit wasting time or they'll all die.

CHAPTER
2

I DASHED INTO THE TUNNEL ON the right. Right always seemed to be the better path. My natural inclination at crossroads time and again.

The tunnel twisted and turned and branched off again.

I stopped. Fury built inside me. I needed to clear my head and my mind. Use my wits and instincts. I closed my eyes and sniffed the air. I wasn't a bloodhound, but my dragon nose was pretty good. I could smell gnoll and goblin sweat. Their stink. The dirt from their matted hair. I just needed to find some of them and wring the location of my friends from their greasy necks.

I trotted right again, following the stench. My eye caught water flowing downward in the sloped tunnel. A good sign.

If Brenwar were here, he'd know exactly where to go.

I followed the cave wall and stopped at the edge of an alcove naturally concealed off the path. Heavy breathing caught my ears. Several pairs of feet shifted on the ground and weapons and armor creaked a little.

"Be still, will you?" a gnoll whispered. His voice was gruff and throaty.

Another good sign. They expected me. My clawed fingers drifted to my waist. Fang was gone. What was I thinking? I had no armor or weapons aside from my scales and claws.

I might not see Fang or Akron ever again!

I didn't have time to worry about that, though. I needed to act!

Gnolls and goblins saw well in the dark, but their vision wasn't better than mine. So they waited to ambush me, but it was I who would ambush them.

I peered around the corner.

Clatch-zip!

I jerked back. A crossbow bolt zinged past my eye and clattered off the stone.

"He's here! Kill him!" a gnoll ordered.

A mass of warm bodies swarmed me. I launched myself into them. Reckless. Wild. I'd had enough of evil.

Whap! Whap! Whap!

I hit a gnoll so hard its teeth shattered. Two goblins wheezed from broken ribs.

Crack! Crack! Crack!

They cried out. Cursed.

I poured it on. My speed and power were unmatched. Relentless. I punched and kicked until none of them moved anymore … except one. I clenched a goblin in the crook of my arm, suffocating.

"Where are they?" I said in its hairy ear.

It said nothing and opted to try and dig its thick nails into the scales of my arm. Stupid goblin.

I shook the goblin, rattling the bones on its necklace.

"I'll ask one more time … WHERE ARE THEY?"

Its fingers no longer clutched at me. They tapped my arm a little. I released it.

It fell on all fours, coughing and sputtering.

I kicked it in the ribs.

"Oof!" it said.

"*Oof* better be a place," I said, squatting down, "and my friends better be there when you take me there."

It shook its ugly head. "No, don't know. Don't know. Don't—*ulp!*"

I slung it into the wall.

A sad thing. I needed Brenwar to find Brenwar. He had no difficulty beating information out of these things. My higher standards prohibited me, but what was I supposed to do in this kind of an emergency? I had to convince this goblin. Now!

I tore a spear from a gnoll's grasp and poked the tip into the goblin's leg, drawing blood.

"Ack!" it said, pushing itself against the wall.

Goblins could inflict pain, but they couldn't take it. They were weak like that.

I rested the spear tip on its nose. "I might not kill you, but I have no issues poking tiny holes in you," I said, watching the yellows of its eyes darting back and forth.

"Come," it said. "Come. I show. Just poke no more holes."

I backed off. "Lead the way."

Limping, the goblin traversed the tunnels with my spear at its back.

We were going deeper. I noticed something else. I was limping a little as well. My side and legs were wounded. Seems the goblins and gnolls had gotten a piece of me after all. The scary thing was I hadn't felt it before. Burning. Throbbing. *Blast!*

Ahead, the sound of rushing water became louder.

I jabbed the spear into its back.

It screeched.

"Move faster!"

Its short figure half scurried, half limped along. I could see the hoop earrings dangling from its ears. The bones and armor rattled when it moved. Noisy.

I didn't have time to worry about another trap, however. I just had to hope this was the right direction. Hope that the goblin was more scared of me than of its master.

It slowed again.

I pressed the spear into its back, lifting it up to its tiptoes.

It whispered and pointed. "Up ahead. Up ahead."

There was light wavering from a lantern or torch. Water was splashing.

"You go first," I said.

The goblin looked back at me with its bottom lip drooping.

"But… "

I glared at it.

Forward it limped with its hands up a little.

I stayed a few feet back, and I could feel the hairs rising on my neck.

The goblin glanced back over its shoulder, flashed a toothy grin, and bustled around the corner.

I started after and stopped. Something was wrong.

"No! No!" I heard the goblin say. It stepped back into my sight with its arms up and pleading.

A sword flashed.

Slice!

The goblin's head fell from its shoulders.

The brawny body of a draykis blocked the exit of the tunnel. Its big, scaly hands were holding a dripping sword.

"Fang!"

The monster had my sword.

I flung the spear at its face.

It batted the spear away, bringing Fang down in a flash.

I jumped aside.

Swish!

"Fang!"

Death by Fang was never a thought that had occurred to me. In most cases, Fang wouldn't even let another creature pick it up. The hilt would burn hot as fire. But maybe that was a dragon thing and the draykis's scales confused it.

Of course, I didn't know what Fang thought about anything.

I ducked. Twisted. Turned.

Swish. Clang. Swish.

"Nath!"

"Huh?" I said, looking around.

It was Bayzog. Far away. The water was over his neck and almost to Sasha's lips.

Water poured in from above, filling the pool. Sasha's chin was covered in water. Her lips fought for gulps of air.

"Hurry!

I ducked under the next swing and dove into the pool of rising water. Something powerful jumped on top of me and dragged me into the depths.

CHAPTER 3

THE DRAYKIS LOCKED ITS ARM around my neck and dragged me down. Now I was drowning. Maybe. I could hold my breath for a long time compared to others. But in this case I was choking, and I didn't have a good breath from the start.

I drove my elbow into its ribs. Jammed my head under its chin.

Its grip slacked.

I twisted away, swam to the surface, burst from the water, and sucked in more air.

"Urp!"

The draykis dragged me back under. Its huge arms were wrapped around my legs, and its great weight was pulling me down into the black depths.

I grabbed its face and pushed my thumbs into its eyes.

It let go.

I kicked it in the face. Then I slipped behind it and locked my arms behind its neck and squeezed with all my might.

It rocked and reeled in the water. I held on. I wasn't sure if these things needed to breathe. They were strange—living but dead somehow. Life reincarnated in an evil form. I squeezed harder.

Crack!

Its body went limp. I released it and was watching it float toward the bottom when I noticed something twitching in the water above.

Sasha! Bayzog!

I could see their feet chained at the deep pool's edge to a ring hooked at the bottom. Bones were layered on the bottom. Skulls and whole skeletons. I cut through the water and popped up right beside them. Sasha's eyes were widened and her mouth was filling with water.

"Hang on!" I said.

"Nath, there is no key," Bayzog said. "You'll have to break them."

I dipped below the surface, wrapped my hands around the chains, and braced my feet on the bottom.

I put every ounce of energy I had into it.

The metal groaned. My bones popped and cracked in the water. *Come on, Nath! Do it!*

The chains held fast. Sasha swam down beside me and Bayzog did as well. I could see their eyes. They weren't pleading. They weren't helpful. They were forgiving. They placed their arms on my shoulders and grabbed each other's hands. Sasha smiled a little as if saying, "It's all right. You tried your best."

Noooooooo! Pull, Nath, pull!

My dragon heart pumped. My energy surged. I put everything I had left into it.

The chain snapped.

I pushed them up out of the water and onto the ledge, where we all lay coughing and gasping. I was the first to gather my breath.

"Brenwar and Shum!"

"Let us help, Nath," Bayzog said, coughing and trying to stand.

"Do you have any idea where they are?"

There was a blank look in his violet eyes. He shook his head.

I dove back into the pool and swam across.

Fang lay on the ground, and I snatched him up.

"Wait!" Sasha said. She pushed her soaked hair out of her face. "I have a spell that might help."

"You can't cast through those iron shackles," Bayzog said, showing the heavy cuffs on his wrists.

But good wizards always have something up their sleeves.

"Hurry!" I said.

Bayzog led Sasha along the rim of the pool and stopped in front of me.

"What do you have in mind?" Bayzog said.

"I created a spell that I've kept on my tongue since I was a girl who feared getting lost." She kneeled down. "And if I ever got lost, I'd summon a pathfinder to lead toward something good. There's nothing good in these caves, I figure, save us."

"Do as you will," Bayzog said, taking a place at her side. He placed his hand on her shoulder and nodded.

Sasha closed her eyes. Her lips didn't move, but sound came out. Sweet. Peaceful. A humming from her throat.

I was tapping my foot.

Wizards take a long time to cast spells in many cases. I just hoped this wasn't one of them.

Her body quivered. Her teardrop face tightened.

Ping!

A spark of light appeared from nowhere and hovered before her. It grew and glowed into a sphere of light a little smaller than my hand, pink and yellow and pulsating. Sasha opened her eyes and held out her hand. It dropped onto her palm like a colorful dandelion.

"Find anything good but us," Sasha whispered to it, "quickly, Pathfinder."

It rose and darted away back through the tunnel I'd come through and disappeared.

I was looking at Sasha and she said, "What are you waiting for? Get after it! We're right behind you."

Pathfinder moved fast. My legs churned, winding in and out of the slick corridors.

Behind me, Bayzog and Sasha puffed for air.

"Can you keep up?" I said.

"Just go, Nath," Bayzog said. He was holding his side, and Sasha was too. "We'll catch up. Save the others."

It tugged at me. I didn't want to leave them again. They were practically defenseless.

"Protect yourselves," I said. "There are draykis about."

Either Pathfinder was getting faster or I was getting slower, because it was hard to keep up along the caves that sloped up and down. Water rushed over my toes in some places. It was bone dry in others. With every step, I expected something to pop up—a draykis, goblin, gnoll, or something else.

The seconds became minutes, the tunnels endless catacombs. The small orb of bright color might as well have been lost for all I knew.

"Where are you going?"

My voice only echoed.

My heart thundered in my ears. My friends were dying, drowning somewhere.

Pathfinder slowed.

I found myself trudging through ankle-deep water and into another cavern where torches hung on the walls. A large pool of water greeted me, and more water cascaded from above. Pathfinder dipped into the water and burned with bright light.

Two figures stood, heads below the water, chained to the bottom—and not moving.

My heart stopped. My jaw dropped open.

"Brenwar!"

CHAPTER 4

BEN SAUNTERED IN AND OUT among the hard-working men and women of the village with a long face. Hammers and saws pounded and ground the wood. Men shouted back and forth to one another. Ropes hoisted up walls. Logs were brought in by horse-drawn carts, and the Legionnaires stood guard. Everyone was working but him this morning, it seemed.

His head ached and his face was swollen. Every step was difficult. He had bruises and scrapes all over him like he'd been skipped over a gravel road. Whatever had slammed him into the ground had been a nasty thing. Strong. Powerful. Familiar. And there had been a smell. It bothered him.

A pair of boys dashed back and forth, rattling their sticks like swords with one another. They stopped and stared at him, blocking his path. One's hair hung over his eyes and the other's was closely trimmed.

"We're going to be Legionnaires," one said.

"Can you teach us how to kill ettins?" said the other, blowing the hair from his eyes.

Ben rubbed their heads and smiled.

"Not now, but maybe later."

One kicked at the dirt.

"Ah! I want to learn now."

Ben squatted down.

"A Legionnaire has to be patient and able to follow orders." He looked into their eyes. "Can you do that?"

One nodded, but the long-haired one said, "My mother's always giving me orders. 'Fill the bucket.' 'Shear the sheep.' 'Pluck the chickens.' 'Skin the rabbits.' 'String the beans.' Blah! I want to get out of this place."

Ben stuck his chin out a little and bobbed his head. He understood. He'd done all those things hundreds of times if not thousands. His home village of Quinley was a little bigger than this one, but the work was still the same. He didn't hate being a farmer, but he didn't love it, either. If anything, it had prepared him for the Legionnaires. The training was tough, but his body and mind were already used to the work. He'd succeeded where many failed.

"I used to love plucking chickens," he said to them.

The boy's eyes widened.

"You plucked chickens?" the long-hair said.

The other teetered on his toes.

Ben smiled.

"I was the fastest feather-plucker in the village, and I just loved stringing those beans. You want to know a secret?"

They nodded their heads.

Ben looked around and lowered is voice. "Farm boys make the best Legionnaires. My commander told me so." He winked. "And I'm a pretty good one, you know."

"I'm going to be the fastest feather-plucker in my village!"

"No, I am!"

They took off running, tackling and bumping each other all the way back home.

Ben stood up, stretched his back, and smiled. Then he frowned. Giving advice to children made him feel old. And he'd never worried before, but now he was worried about Sasha. He felt responsible, and it left his stomach a little sick. He shuffled along, rubbing the knot on his head.

"I should have gone with them," he said to himself. "I should be the one to find her. Dragon's probably mad." He adjusted his sword belt on his hips. "I can't fail again."

He rubbed the bump on his head. It felt like a tomato was growing under his skin. Garrison said it had been the winged ape that grabbed him and tossed him like a fish. But Ben wasn't so sure. There was something about Garrison that didn't seem right. Ben had asked his friend several times what he'd seen and what had happened, but the story seemed to go back and forth.

"I'm not sure."

"It was an ape, like they said."

Ben knew Garrison wasn't telling him everything. Dragon had taught him a bit about liars. "Just watch their eyes," Dragon had said. "Their hands. Sometimes they fidget a little. And sometimes, if you're wise, you can just tell. Your gut will tell you."

Garrison's story, though a bit inconsistent, did seem sincere. His eyes and hands were steady. Maybe too steady. But what would Garrison have to hide?

Ben's stomach rumbled. He decided to head back to the lodge room and dig up a biscuit. He could smell them better in the air the closer he came. Hot. Buttery. Village or no village, these people were gonna make their biscuits. He patted his tummy. "Well, not all of my body has to be unhappy."

Walking along, he noticed a man making his way through the tall grasses in the distance. It was Garrison.

"Say, where's he going?" He rubbed his chin. He was hungry, but he was more curious. Something about the way Garrison moved bothered him. His friend checked over his shoulder a couple times and disappeared over the dale. "I've a feeling I'd better find out."

CHAPTER
5

I DOVE INTO THE POOL, CUT through the water, and grabbed the chains. I didn't look at either of them. I couldn't. Brenwar and Shum's chains ran through a metal ring in heavy stone, and the pool was littered with bones at the bottom. I pulled at the chains. They were thicker. The stone bigger. I don't think Kryzak had any plans for them to survive at all. I dug my feet in and pulled again. The metal didn't groan or twist. The ring in the stone didn't loosen.

Nooooooo!

I felt a hand tapping me on the shoulder. I jerked in the water and faced Brenwar. He was still alive. He slid Dragon Claw out of Fang's hilt, stuck it between the links, and twisted. I slid Fang between the links as well. Its steel was unbreakable. I was turning the blade, twisting the links in the metal, when something else happened. The chains crystalized like ice, stretching from one link to the other. *Yes!* I kept twisting. So did Brenwar.

Snap. Snap. Snap.

The metal links busted away. I grabbed Shum, pushed him to the surface, and swam for the edge. Brenwar crawled out of the water, gasping for air.

"Dwarves can hold their breath longer than any other mortal race, but that was pushing it."

The Ranger was limp in my arms, his lips pale blue. His eyes were closed and his body was cold.

"Shum," I said, slapping his face. "Shum, wake up!" I pushed on his chest.

Brenwar stood over me as I sat on the pool edge and squeezed my shoulder.

"He's gone, Nath. He's gone."

"No," I said, looking up, "he can't be."

I'd seen Brenwar's mad face plenty of times in my life, but never his sad one. Beard dripping, his expression was long, eyes wet. He rubbed his nose and sniffed.

"I tried everything to save him," he said. "But those chains would not give. I've never seen anyone die like that before. Such evil, Nath. Such evil."

I hit the wall.

"Noooooo!"

Bayzog and Sasha appeared on the other side of the pool, mouths gaping. I could hear what they were saying without the words. "Is he?"

I just shook my head and wiped the hair from his face. Our friend, Shum, had died.

I lifted him in my arms and headed back for the tunnel. Everyone stepped aside with long faces and followed.

"Let's get out of here," I said with determination.

Tears streamed down Sasha's face. "Pathfinder will lead us out."

I followed the light. Numb. Angry. This was my fault. My friends were pawns set up to torture me, and now one was dead. It could have been all of them. They insisted on protecting me, but I couldn't protect them. I sniffed and my eyes watered. I wanted to cry. I wanted to kill. I felt cold.

There was evil here. Death and decay, but there was something else. Something I'd missed before.

Dragons.

Somewhere. Caged. I could feel them. Smoke rolled from my nostrils. This wasn't over yet.

Unmolested, we made it out of the tunnels and into the pouring rain. An evil echo of laughter followed us out. We all looked back, then at one another. I kept peering down the tunnel.

"We stay together, Nath," Brenwar said, "We can go back in later. We should head back to the village and give a proper burial." Brenwar sniffed. "He'd want that."

Jaw clenched, tears in my eyes, I whirled.

"I'll do what I have to do!"

"One of us is dead," he barked back. "Do you want to see another? We came for Sasha. Our lives for hers. Shum knew that. He died with honor. Now don't dishonor him and get more of us killed. That fiend has you rattled, Nath." He tossed Dragon Claw into the dirt at my feet. "We can get him later. We need a plan."

He was right, but I didn't care. I plucked Dragon Claw out of the ground and stuffed him back in Fang's hilt.

"Then you can stay here," I said, stepping toward the tunnel.

Thoom! Thoom! Crack!

An ettin pushed through the trees, uprooting them. Both heads showed ugly sneers. It wore an anchor and chain around its neck.

"Time to eat," one head said, looking at the other, patting its belly.

"Ah," the other head said, "it seems they've prepared an elf for us. Mmmm-mmmm-mmm. They're the most delicious."

It stepped closer.

Brenwar, Bayzog, and Sasha were still shackled and weaponless. I moved in front of them.

"One step closer, ettin, and you're dead," I said, holding out Fang.

The ettin towered over us, hands on hips, laughing.

"HA! HA! HA!"

Smoke rolled from my mouth. I bent over and took a swing, sinking Fang into its wrist.

The ettin howled.

I struck again, dodged, and sprinted through its legs and chopped into the back of its heel.

It roared, teetered, screamed, and brought down the anchor.

I dove out of the way.

Smash!

It tore out a clump of boulders and scattered them like ninepins.

I dashed under its thigh and stabbed it behind the knee. *Come on, Fang!*

Glitch!

I hoped it would freeze or something.

But the ettin only screamed and brought the anchor down again.

Crash!

It missed.

"YOU'RE FAST! BUT YOUR FRIENDS ARE NOT!"

It stomped after them.

Brenwar, Bayzog, and Sasha scattered.

"THEY RUN LIKE CHICKENS! SLOW ONES!"

"Over here, ugly!" Brenwar yelled, waving his hands over his head.

It went after Sasha. She'd disappeared behind a large rock. The ettin picked it up like an egg.

She screamed.

It laughed, looked over its shoulder, and hurled the boulder at Brenwar, hitting the stone he hid behind. The ettin reached down for Sasha, fingers clutching at her tiny frame.

Something exploded inside me.

Slice! Slash! Slash! Stab!

I ripped into the back of its leg.

It arched its back, arms wide, and started howling in fury.

Slash! Slash! Stab!

Bayzog appeared. He swept Sasha up in his arms and scurried her away.

The ettin's arms flailed for balance, and it toppled to the ground like a great tree.

I jumped on its chest and raised Fang over my head with two hands.

"Nath, no!" Brenwar yelled, rushing toward me.

I drove Fang into its heart.

All four eyes popped open, and the beating under my feet came to a sudden stop. Its anguished stare was frozen, and its arms fell limp at its sides.

Silence and rain filled the crater.

I sheathed my sword and hopped down.

"Ye didn't have to do that," Brenwar said, limping over, "I could've, you know."

I headed for the tunnel.

"Where do you think yer goin'?"

I didn't reply. I didn't stop, either.

CHAPTER
6

"**B**RENWAR," BAYZOG SAID, "SHOULDN'T WE go after him?"

The dwarf stood like a tree stump, thick fingers clutching at his sides, brows buckled.

"No," he said under his beard. "We've lost enough already. Nath should know better." He turned back toward them. "I'm afraid we can't help him any right now. He's temperamental."

Bayzog's hand wrapped around Sasha's. It was cold, and she was shivering.

He looked up, hand over his eyes, and said, "Let's get shelter. Perhaps under those trees."

"What about Shum?" she said.

The elf lay on the ground with a layer of wet dirt and rain muddying his armor.

Brenwar tended to him. Picked him up, moved him, and set him down somewhere more suitable. He crossed Shum's arms over his chest, took a knee, closed his eyes, and bowed his head. Placing his hand over Shum, he began to sing in Dwarven. A throaty melody. Pleasant and strong.

Bayzog held Sasha tight, but her sobs shook both their bodies.

Brenwar finished.

"That was beautiful," Sasha said.

Brenwar nodded.

The rain splashed on Shum's face, bringing life to it a little. Everyone stood and stared, but Sasha was still crying. Bayzog's stomach twisted and turned.

"I-I feel so guilty," Sasha said. "He shouldn't have died over me."

"He'd have died a hundred times for all of us," Bayzog said, "That's what good does. Gives its life so others may live."

"The Roamers say 'Act or evil takes the reins.' He told me that once in our travels," Brenwar said.

The rain slowed, and the clouds began to part. The sun was warm, but Sasha felt cold. Nath was gone, buried in a well of darkness. They'd barely made it out the last time, and now he had to make it out alone. It didn't seem right. She felt helpless.

"Sasha," Bayzog said, "Your spell. It saved us, too, you know. And Brenwar. You did well." He kissed her on the head. "Shum would be proud."

"Aye," Brenwar said, stepping over and patting her hands. "I'm grateful to you, Lady Sasha. I'm pretty sure I only had a few more seconds at most in me."

His kind words did little to lighten her spirits. But she was glad she lived. Just miserable.

"I think I need to sit down," she said. She sat where she stood, folded her arms over her chest, and watched the tunnel. It was dark. Foreboding. She never wanted to go in there again.

"If I can find some metal," Brenwar said, "I can get these cuffs off. Maybe you can then cast a spell to warm yerselves." He sauntered away.

Bayzog sat down and draped his arm over her shoulder.

"Did you see Nath's eyes?" she said. "When he killed that thing?" She nodded back toward the ettin. "And when he left into the tunnel?"

"Yes, dear."

"I think I was more scared of him at that moment than I was of the ettin. His eyes were like fire. I almost felt bad for the ettin," she said. "Is that wrong?"

"I don't think it's wrong at all. There's light in all creatures, Sasha, but many prefer the darkness."

"Why?" she said, scratching her head. "Why do they do such things?"

"Doing right is never as easy as doing wrong," he said. "And I fear our friend Nath is doing wrong now."

She rested her head on Bayzog's chest and stared down into the tunnel. "Me too," she whispered.

CHAPTER 7

DIDN'T NEED THE LIGHT. FANG provided that. A pale blue light adorned the
blade. I didn't need an orb to follow, either. Now that I knew where the dragons
were, dark or light, I'd never forget. No twist or turn would fool me.

I didn't run. I didn't trot. I dared anything to cross me.

Two gnolls did.

Two gnolls died.

No one would harm any of my friends again. No one from this tunnel, anyway.
Not ever again!

I wasn't far from the large cavern with the urns of light where I'd met Kryzak the
first time when another draykis greeted me in the large tunnel.

It held Brenwar's war hammer in its hands and smiled.

"Put that down," I said.

"Take it," it hissed.

I didn't realize they could talk so well. It surprised me.

We charged. Our weapons clashed.

Krang!

It sounded like the world exploded.

Fang kept humming.

The draykis kept swinging, hammering away at the sword in my grip.

Fang's humming got louder and louder. The ringing rose.

The draykis dropped to its knees. The war hammer fell from its fingers.

I struck it down with a single blow.

Its head rolled away.

Fang's humming stopped and the blade's light went cold.

Laughter echoed in the chamber. I picked up Brenwar's war hammer, stepped
over the draykis, and strode into the light of the cavern.

Twang! Zip!

An arrow buried itself in my scaled shoulder.

"Welcome back, Nath Dragon," Kryzak said. He was holding Akron and nocking another arrow. "I sure like these moorite arrows. They'll put a hole through anything. Extra light and fast, too."

"Shoot all the arrows you want," I said, yanking the bolt from my arm and tossing it. "They won't prevent your imminent death. I'll avenge my friend."

"Friend?" Kryzak said, cocking his head. "Are you certain about that, Nath Dragon? Perhaps I did you a favor."

The words struck me funny. Cooled my inferno. My stance softened. What was he talking about?

Kryzak lowered the arrow tip toward my chest. He was alone. I sensed no more draykis, gnolls, or goblins. But certainly the feline fury was near, ready to pounce from anywhere. I scanned the nooks and crannies. But it was only the two of us and the flames. Where was everyone else? What game was he playing?

Shoulder aching, I switched Fang to my good arm and stepped forward.

"I think it's time to close that mouth of yours, permanently."

"Ah, yes, you never were one to let others do the talking, now were you?"

Again, what was he talking about? How did he know me?

"No," I said, "I always found the conversation of others quite boring, just like the one we're having now." I continued forward.

Kryzak closed one eye and took a half breath.

Twang!

Cling!

The arrow ricocheted off Fang's blade. I bolted toward Kryzak and swung.

Swish!

Like a phantom, he faded and was gone.

"Ah-ah-ah-ah," he laughed, his voice echoing. "Awfully hard to hit what you can't touch." He was distant now, on the other side of the cavern, standing by one of the urns. He lowered Akron to the ground and held up a finger. "A moment, Nath Dragon. Then you may have at me with all your fury."

My blood raced. His tone and demeanor irked me. He slid his deep-purple robes from his big frame, revealing a thick leather chest plate. His long arms bulged with hard muscle and tattoos. He wiped the sweat from his tattooed head, rubbed it into his hands, and slid one mailed gauntlet on over the other. He reached down and wrapped his meaty hand around his crude-looking war mace and nodded, closing his eyes and murmuring.

I didn't attack until he was ready. This was a challenge fight. All of me against all of him. So be it, then. No one ever stood against me one on one. I didn't care what weapon he had. I had two dragon arms.

He opened his eyes. "I'm ready now." He banged his mace on the floor. It started to glow. "Prepare to feel my power."

"No, prepare to feel mine!"

I raced across the cavern floor, Fang high over my head in one dragon hand and Brenwar's war hammer in the other. I leapt.

He swung. His mace exploded into my chest like a crack of thunder. It hurled me backward and slammed me across the floor.

That was fast. That was powerful. Like a giant.

"I've been dying to do that," he said.

I could barely breathe. *Not again!* I gasped and coughed and rose to my feet. "Why is that?" I said, walking back over.

He didn't say. He swung instead.

Krang!

Bang!

Clang!

I blocked and shuffled.

Kryzak hammered at me, each strike getting faster than the last. Every blow juttered my arms at the elbows and buckled my knees.

Magic!

He was using magic, and a great deal of it at that. Speed. Strength. You name it, he had it. No mortal was that strong or that fast. His head glowed with bright colors and his eyes like fire.

"What's the matter, Nath Dragon?" he said, "Nothing smart to say?"

I drove my fist into his mouth. It felt like hitting a rock.

He drove a mailed fist into my belly.

"Woomph!"

Steel clashed against steel.

I struck.

He parried.

He struck.

I countered.

We banged back and forth for another minute.

"Tell me how you know me," I said, shoving him back. I backed up and rubbed my aching shoulder. My chest burned and heaved.

"Ah," he said, "so now it matters what I think, does it? Well, after I've beaten you into submission, perhaps I'll tell. Assuming you survive."

"Oh, I'll live, all right," I said, "I just wanted to give you a chance to talk before you die. You see, Kryzak, I'm not holding back anymore."

"Is that so?" he said.

"Absolutely."

I sheathed Fang and pulled Dragon Claw out. Its blade shimmered and shone.

Kryzak narrowed his eyes. "Have at it then, Nath Dragon."

I puffed smoke and let the dragon out.

Kryzak was a skilled soldier, but his technique was flawed. It was all strength and no finesse.

I ducked under the war mace ripping over my head and drove Dragon Claw into his shoulder.

"Argh!"

I busted his iron chin with Dragon Claw's hilt.

Kryzak's knees wobbled. He was fast, but not the fastest thing I'd ever seen. Dragons were faster. He wasn't a dragon. I was.

Bang! Bang! Bang!

I busted his wrist with one blow after the other.

"What are you doing?" he said, wrapping two hands around his weapon.

"Picking you apart," I said, laughing.

Stab!

Dragon Claw dug into his leg.

Kryzak busted me in the arm and Dragon Claw slipped from my grasp. He punched me in the face and rocked my head back. I punched him back. We locked up.

"Drop yours and I'll drop mine," he said, staring into my eyes.

"Gladly," I said.

I broke the clinch and tossed Brenwar's war hammer and Fang to the ground.

He dropped his mace.

Kryzak was bleeding badly and limping. He didn't stand a chance. He wiped the blood from his mouth and spat. My shoulder burned, but I could still take him. One dragon arm was better than two man arms, magic or not. I would make him pay for what he'd done to Shum. But I wanted answers to my questions. Why was he doing this? Who was behind it all? I was going to pin him down and squeeze his neck until I found out. I balled up my fists and took a step forward.

He raised his mailed fists, said, "Next time, Nath Dragon," and bumped them together.

Boom.

The cavern shook and started to cave in. I jumped out from under a falling boulder. When I looked up, Kryzak was gone. His war mace as well.

"Guzan!" I swore. But I wasn't alone. Goblins and gnolls spilled into the room, weapons raised and mouths crying for my blood. I snatched up Fang and the war hammer and faced the horde that came at me. A furnace erupted inside me.

I yelled out my new battle cry.

"Dragon! Dragon!"

CHAPTER 8

THE RAIN HAD STOPPED. A foggy mist remained over the grasses, but Ben kept Garrison in his sights. He stayed back far enough, looking like little more than a squirrel in the distance, and trudged after him.

"What is he up to?" Ben asked himself, wiping the rain from his face. "Ah, I've had enough of this already."

Garrison had been wandering off plenty over the past few days. He'd had a zeal for snaring and trapping lately, and he'd wanted to hone his skill. He'd sell the pelts for extra coin, but his business wasn't very good. Rabbit pelts didn't go for much unless you caught a bunch of them. Garrison hadn't.

Ben stopped and squatted in the grasses. Garrison's head was over his shoulder, and he spun around. Ben's heart pounded in his chest. *Oh great, he must have seen me.* He kept down and waited. When he peered up again, Garrison was gone.

"By Guzan! How'd he do that?"

Following the path in the tall grasses, Ben trotted after him, heading in a direction he'd never been before.

Trees were ahead, tall pines, oaks, and birch that stretched over a mile in each direction. It would've been as good a place to set snares as any, but plenty of dangers lurked in the woods. It was safer in the open plains. Easier to spot people or things. Easier to spot anything. At worst, a herd of deer or gazelle might pass, or you might spook a flock of birds.

He stopped a dozen feet from the woodland's edge and fingered the pommel of his sword.

"What are you up to now, Garrison?" he whispered. His heart pounded behind his ears.

Maybe I should go back? No, maybe he's in danger.

He looked over his shoulder. The rolling hills offered safety. The forest offered another element: danger. Chill bumps rose on his arms.

"Better be no ettins in there," Ben said, moving on.

He pressed through the branches. The ground was covered in needles and leaves. He kneeled down and picked Garrison's trail back up. Garrison hadn't bothered to cover his tracks, and Ben had a keen eye for them. Dragon had taught him that.

Taking his time, he picked his way through the forest and stopped. Garrison's voice caught his ears. Ben crept toward the sound and pressed his body against a tree, then peered around.

Garrison kneeled in a clearing, rocking back and forth, rubbing something in his hands. He wasn't alone. Ben froze, and his chill bumps got more bumps.

Who is he talking to?

Garrison was talking to someone or something. A shadow or a shade.

And it was talking back.

"Well done, Garrison," it said. Its voice was deep and creepy. "Keep me informed."

"As you wish," Garrison said, bowing. "All hail Barnabus."

What did he say?

"All hail indeed," said the shade. The image shimmered and faded away.

Ben remained hooked to the tree. *What was that? Who was that? Barnabus?*

Here was the itch that Ben had needed scratched. Ben could feel it in his gut now.

Garrison's a spy! A traitor.

He stepped out from behind the tree and drew his sword.

Garrison jumped.

"A ... Ben, what are you doing here?" Garrison said.

"No, Garrison, what are *you* doing here?" He took a step closer. "Traitor!"

Garrison stepped back and lifted his hands, palms up.

"I'm just checking the snares, Ben. You know that." He eyed the lump on Ben's head. "Say, you aren't feeling so well, are you? And that bump's looking worse. Let's get you back to the camp."

"Checking snares my behind, Garrison," Ben said. "You work for Barnabus. You know about Sasha, don't you! Where is she?"

Garrison's smile was like a fox's. Ben had never seen that look before. All these months his friend had been quiet and agreeable, even dull, but now he was different.

"Ben, really, whatever it is you think you saw, I can explain," Garrison said. "Listen, let's get out of this rain. There's a spot nearby where we can talk."

"Here is just fine," Ben said. "I'm all ears."

"You're trembling, Ben. Are you afraid of something?"

Ben swallowed. He'd never been in this sort of confrontation before. He was alone. No backup. His eyes slid through the trees. *Maybe he's not alone.*

"Out with it, Garrison!" Ben said. "I want to know everything."

Garrison shrugged his broad shoulders. He had about thirty pounds over Ben and was strong as a black bear. He took a step forward.

"You going to kill me, Ben? With your little sword?" Garrison rubbed his chin.

"I don't think you have it in you. Killing a man. Your friend. A fellow soldier? How are you going to explain that, Ben? Murdering a Legionnaire. Over what? They'll hang you for certain."

"I'm sure they'll figure it out," Ben said. "I'm an honest man."

"You aren't going to stab a man whose sword is snug in the scabbard, are you, Ben? Tsk, tsk. No, I don't think so." He kept his hands up and offered a smile. "Listen, Ben, no one else has to get hurt. Not me, and not you. And do you really think I'd be doing this if I didn't have to? I don't have a choice, Ben. The Clerics of Barnabus ... they have my family."

"Say again."

Garrison's eyes drifted left.

"They have my family."

"Liar," Ben said. "I know it, and you know it. Now, you're coming with me. Keep those hands up."

"What?"

"Clasp your fingers together on your head," Ben said. "You know that drill. Don't play stupid with me, Garrison."

"Oh, with you, never, Ben." Garrison rolled his eyes. "Never at all." He locked his fingers over his head. "All right, then, is this better?"

Ben stepped around behind him and poked his sword into the other man's back. "Go!"

"Do you want to march me back, or can I walk normal? Ow!"

"Waddle like a duck for all I care, Garrison. Just get moving."

Garrison waddled forward and started making quacking sounds.

"Stop it!"

Garrison kept at it.

All these months I never suspected a thing!

Garrison had been quiet, but not too quiet. He'd worked hard, trained hard, and fought hard. He'd always had a steely quality about him, but Ben had put that down to his being a soldier. Now Garrison was a different person. Sly and confident. Speaking with another level of intelligence.

Ben wiped his sweaty palm on his trousers and swallowed.

"So Ben," Garrison spoke up as they cleared the forest. "What are you going to tell the Legionnaires? There's only a few of them. And the sergeant in charge isn't so bright. The villagers won't know who to believe. Are you going to tell them I'm a spy? Where's your proof?"

"I'll figure it out when we get there," Ben said. "Just keep quiet."

"Certainly, Ben. I wouldn't want to interrupt your thoughts. After all, you've much thinking to do. Very much indeed." Garrison shrugged and barked a laugh. "Let me know if you need any help with that."

Ben didn't know what do to. He knew that Garrison had information that would help him find Sasha. But his gut told him something else. Garrison was dangerous. Evil.

Maybe now is the best time to stop him.

He poked Garrison in the back again.

"Ow!" Garrison whirled. "There's no need for that, Ben!"

Ben clipped his thigh, drawing blood.

"Ben! Cut that out!"

"You want me to stop, Garrison? Draw your sword!"

"You can't be serious. Ow! Stop doing that!"

Ben was seething. "Stop me."

Garrison backed up and withdrew his sword. "I'm much better than you." Garrison smiled. "You know that."

Rain splattered off steel.

Ben said, "Prove it."

CHAPTER
9

Gashed from head to toe, I trudged back to the mouth of the cave and out into the rain.

Sasha was the first person I saw, huddled down out of the rain under a dead tree. Her blue eyes widened, and she gasped. Froze.

"N-Nath," she said, slowly rising to her feet.

"Aye," I said. "What's left of me."

"What-what happened to you?" she said, running up to me. She hooked my arm over her shoulder and helped me along.

"Nothing I care to talk about," I said, "but this is over, for now." I tossed the bundle under my arm to the ground.

That's when Bayzog and Brenwar appeared.

"You're all bloody," Brenwar said. "What did you do?"

"It's good to see you too, Brenwar." I kicked the bundle open. "I brought you gifts."

Brenwar's war hammer lay there along with Shum's sword and Bayzog's baubles. I'd even put my armor back on.

Brenwar crossed his thick arms over his barrel chest. "Did you kill him?"

Kryzak. I wished he was dead, more than anything. He'd killed Shum. And now he'd escaped. It really burned me. I shook my head.

"Give him a moment, Brenwar," Sasha said, "he can barely walk, and he's wheezing."

"So?" Brenwar said.

I eyed him. "Kryzak escaped," I said.

"What about the rest?" Brenwar said.

I shrugged. "Maybe dead," I said, "except them."

"Them, who?" Bayzog said, his violet eyes like saucers. He looked at me like I'd turned into an ogre or something. It made wonder. *Have I changed again?* I swung myself and Sasha back toward the mouth of the cave.

"Them," I said, pointing.

Sasha let out a sharp gasp. The first dragon appeared. She was bigger than a dog, with bright-yellow scales and white stripes. Dark eyed and winged, she batted her long lashes at me and brushed past my leg.

Sasha started saying, "He's so—"

"She," Bayzog said, kneeling down and holding out the back of his hand.

The yellow dragon, a golden flower, lifted her nose and snorted past. She then spread her wings and rose into the sky.

Another came, big as a man and long necked.

"A purple tail," Bayzog said.

Its clawed feet splashed into the mud, and the rain splattered off its dark-violet scales. It showed a row of sharp teeth six inches long, dragged its belly over the stones, and disappeared into the woods. Good thing, too. The wingless ones were ill tempered and harsh. Their heavy tails could shatter bones and rock.

The others came out, some on two legs, most on four. All splashed with vibrant colors. Most of them were little taller than my knee. They were rubies, diamonds and emeralds in the muddy rain.

"I want to hold one," Sasha said, kneeling down.

"No you don't," I replied, pulling her up. "And don't ever try it. If they want to be held, they'll come to you."

"They're just so," she clasped her hands, "magnificent."

One by one they darted into the sky. Only one out of the many thanked me. Barely.

"That," Sasha said, gawping as they went, "was incredible." She looked me in the eye. "You saved them all, Nath. You did something good."

I groaned and shuffled to a log and sat. Sure, I'd done some good, but I'd also done an awful lot of killing.

Was that bad?

I watched the rain wash my blood off into a puddle between my feet. My blood and theirs. It would take more than the rain to cleanse me of what I had done. Those goblins and gnolls, they were dead. But it had been them or me.

Brenwar picked up his war hammer and slung it onto his shoulder.

"Let's go," he snorted. "We've got a friend to bury."

Brenwar had a stretcher made, but despite my wounds, I carried Shum's body out of the crater. Unlike most elves that were lither in frame and lighter in weight than men, the Elven Ranger was heavy. I didn't complain. His death was my burden and mine alone. I'd walk him all the way back to Elome if I had to.

Silently, we picked our way through the woods and back to the plains. It had stopped raining, and the sun began to set. The horses awaited us there. Shum's Roamer Stallion stood taller than the rest, and I lay Shum down before him. The horse nickered, stamped his hooves, and snorted. I grabbed the reins and patted his nose.

"I'm sorry, boy. I'm sorry."

I probably knew more about the Roamers than anyone except the Roamers themselves, but that was still very little. They were a discreet bunch, always moving through the lands and keeping to themselves.

"What do we do?" Sasha said. "Do we bury him here or do we take him somewhere else?"

I looked to Bayzog.

He shrugged with his eyes. "It's not good to keep the dead above the ground for more than a day." He shook his beard. "Not good at all."

"They're a private people," I said. "I suppose a modest burial will do."

"I think he'd like that," Sasha said, picking at her lips. "I'll pick some flowers."

"I'll help."

Shum's stallion nudged me, almost knocking me over.

"What is it?"

It dug its hoof by Shum and slung its head over its shoulder.

"Huh?"

It did it again.

"I think Shum's horse wants to take him," Sasha said.

"Is that what you want?" I said in its ear. "You want to take Shum?"

It nodded its head and neighed.

I looked at the others. "I suppose we can follow him. What do you—"

A black shadow crossed the sun and dropped into the grass.

Sasha screamed.

It was Sansla Libor.

CHAPTER
10

SANSLA LIBOR STOOD WITH HIS black wings spread and his knuckles on the ground. He was a towering figure, the breadth of two men, and the muscles of a savage beast rippled under his fur. He beat his chest with one mighty fist and bared his fangs. He grunted.

"Get behind us," Brenwar said to Sasha and Bayzog.

He brought his war hammer to the ready. I went for Fang.

Sansla's wings collapsed behind his back, and his arms spread wide. His eyes grazed over all of us and rested on Shum's body. He barked and shuffled back and forth.

"You think he wants Shum?" Sasha said.

"Well, he ain't getting him," Brenwar said, storming forward. "Get out of here, you ape! I'll put a dent in your head as big as that crater. Do ye think I forgot what you did to me?"

My blood charged. I remembered the last scrape I'd been in with the ape. I could barely handle him then, but now, with my two dragon arms, his timing couldn't have been better. I limped after Brenwar. I couldn't hide my limp, and I didn't care.

"Let's do this for Shum," I said.

We flanked the ape. Brenwar was left and I was right.

The ape didn't glance at either of us but headed toward the others.

Brenwar charged. "No you don't!"

I followed suit.

Sansla sprang over the top of Brenwar and swatted him in the back. Brenwar's boots flew over his head, like a child had flung a doll.

"Now you've done it," I said. I brought Fang down.

Sansla snatched my wrist and twisted.

"Argh!"

Fang fell from my fingers. I punched Sansla in the face. Then the gut.

The winged ape winced and slammed me into the ground. It was bigger and stronger. Just as fast. It twisted me around and stuffed my face into the grass, putting its full weight upon me.

I don't remember it being so big or powerful!

Whop!

Its body shook, and it let out a howl.

"Get off him, you hairy beast!" Brenwar yelled.

It pounced off my back and onto Brenwar.

The dwarf disappeared under its girth, only to reappear hanging in Sansla's grip by his beard.

Sansla slung Brenwar right at me.

I caught Brenwar in my chest, and we tumbled head over heels before we pushed off one another.

"Not a word about this," Brenwar said.

"I think I've had enough of this myself," I said, rising to my feet. I stuck Fang in the ground and clicked my claws.

I narrowed my eyes at Sansla. "I'm going to rip your wings off."

Brenwar was already moving.

I passed him in a blink.

Sansla met me halfway, and we tore into one another.

I pounded into his ribs.

He socked me in the belly and slung me to the ground.

I jumped up and busted him in the face. The chin. The belly.

His hairy arms flailed me with savage fury.

I got my fingers around his neck.

He wrapped his big paws around mine.

I squeezed with all my might, feeling my eyes bulge from my head.

"You've met your match, Sansla," I managed to say.

Sansla dropped a knee into my chest, kicked me off him, and grabbed his bleeding neck.

I grabbed mine and rose to my feet again.

Brenwar stepped in between.

"You've met double your match, beast!"

Sansla Libor held out his oversized palm and said, "Stop."

I froze.

Brenwar huffed and looked back at me. "Did it speak?"

I nodded, cocked my head—chest heaving—and cupped my ear. "Say again?"

"Stop," Sansla said. "I can speak, but not for long. The curse. The curse will take over."

Sansla Libor kneeled alongside Shum's body with a sad look in his eyes. It was the first time I got a close look at him. His eyes, a rich brown, were flecked with blue and distinctly elven. There was a sleekness to his face, and his expressions were elven. There was even a notable point to his ears, and his husky and powerful body moved with an agile quality about it.

He leaned over Shum, brushed his face with his paw, and closed his eyes. A savage beast turned inside out. He opened his eyes and studied the four of us. I couldn't tell if he was angry or not, but something bothered him.

"How did you know?" I said.

"I'm the king." His voice was throaty but still elven. "I know of such things." He shook his head. "Who is responsible for this?"

"I am," I said.

Sansla rose to his full height. His face twitched, and he squinted. His paws clutched into fists. He shook it off and sighed. "No, it was not you that killed him. Who was it?"

I explained.

When it was over, he said, "I see." He scratched his chin. "Times are dangerous. Beware. Anything can happen." He pointed at me. "Especially to you. Your curse can mislead you. It gives you power but takes control."

My breath left me. Coldness filled my belly.

Sansla twitched again. His face contorted and turned. Mean and ugly. He gasped.

Brenwar's knuckles were white on his war hammer.

My hand fell to my hilt.

"I've not much time," Sansla said, forcing the words out. "I must take him."

"Hold on, Sansla," I said, "Where did you have in mind?"

"Home," he said. His voice thickened.

"Come with us," Sasha blurted out. "The Ocular of Orray can heal you, the elves say. That's what Shum was here for. He was trying to find you. He wanted to help you."

Sansla shook his great head. Pain filled his eyes. "Do they have the Ocular?"

Bayzog and I locked eyes for a moment.

Brenwar's brows buckled as he looked at me. "Why, you liar!" He stormed away.

I hadn't told Brenwar that the elves had the Ocular of Orray because I simply didn't think we'd find Sansla so quickly. Plus, I didn't want him to know that it had failed on me.

But I had lied to my best friend, and that was as bad as it got. I'd have to try and settle up with Brenwar later.

"Did you try the Ocular?" Sansla said to me.

"It failed," I said. "But I might not be cursed. This might just be me." I showed my arms. "I am a dragon, after all. You're an elf. You're not supposed to be a monster."

"Nath!" Sasha said, eyeing me. "He's not a monster."

"Sorry," I said, "but I'm not cursed and he is. Sansla, you need to come with us and take your chances with the Ocular. I'm certain it will heal you."

He stepped forward and looked down on my snorting face.

"We are cursed, Nath. Evil grows within the two of us. I can sense it in you. I could smell the blood on your hands from miles away. Death and decay surround you now. A cloak you cannot shed." His thick neck twitched and strained. "You should mind your friends better."

I balled up my fists. "I'm not cursed! I'm a dragon!"

"I can't stop what is happening to me," Sansla said, "But you can." He turned his back on me and picked up Shum. "The Elome elves would kill me," he said. "They won't trust me. I must control the darkness that consumes me. There are other ways. Shum's death awakened the good within me, but the curse takes hold again."

"Let us try," I said.

Sansla placed Shum on his horse. "Secure him." He rubbed the Roamer Stallion between the eyes. "He knows where to go."

"But—" I said.

Sansla stepped back and spread his wings. "We'll meet again, Nath Dragon," he said. "Next time, I might have to kill you or you kill me." Sansla jumped into the air, batted his wings, and soared into the sun and out of sight.

CHAPTER
11

BACK IN THE SADDLE, HORSES walking through the grass, we headed for the village. We'd talked, all of us except Brenwar, about what had happened. I wasn't so sure what Sansla Libor meant about meeting me again and fighting to the death. Did he mean he should die because he was cursed or that I should die because I was?

Am I cursed?

I didn't know. All I knew was that I was beaten and angry and had unanswered questions. But something else ate at me. There'd been more unneeded deaths.

Bayzog and Sasha rode up along either side of me. Sasha was smiling. Bayzog showed a bit of a smile over his slender chin.

"What?" I said.

"Are you wanting to pursue Kryzak?" Bayzog asked. "We're with you."

It irritated me. They'd almost died because of some twisted test and now they wanted to tag along again. I couldn't have it. I might not be able to shake Brenwar, but I could at least shake them.

"Come now, Bayzog. You know I can't have that." I shifted in my saddle. "I think you'd be safer in Quintuklen. After all, we found the Ocular of Orray like we set out to. Sansla Libor found us, and he seems to be faring better than me." I shook my head. "I'm going to the village to make my goodbyes to Ben and move on."

Both of them frowned.

I frowned, too. Our quest was over, and now all I wanted to do was get back to saving dragons. I'd hunt down Kryzak later if I had to.

"So," Sasha said, "you don't want to track down the fiend that almost killed all of us? You're just going to ride the opposite way?"

"Sasha," Bayzog intervened, "vengeance isn't always the answer. I think Nath is wise with what he speaks. There's been enough death already, hasn't there? And what was gained for it?"

"I'll tell you what was gained," she said. "We took down more of them than they took down of us." Her knuckles were white on the reins and her cheeks reddened. "I say we hunt them down and take it to them."

Bayzog and I locked eyes.

I wanted to smile.

He continued his frown. "Let's reassess when we get back to the village."

Sasha huffed and trotted up ahead.

Bayzog followed right after.

My eyes drifted onto Brenwar. Rigid in the saddle, he kept his eyes forward. *I should be glad.* He might not have meant to speak to me ever again, but I was certain he couldn't contain himself. I was confident that he'd yell at me at some point. Something tugged inside my chest. A notion. A feeling.

Sorry. I should just ride up there and say, Sorry.

I didn't.

Ben could feel his heart pounding inside his chest and the blood rushing behind his ears. Garrison stood, stout and formidable, with cold steel ready. Ben swallowed. He knew he had to stop the man. Put him down before more people died. Wait, the ettins. Had Garrison been in on the ettins, too? A dozen thoughts rushed through Ben's head. He locked his eyes, readied his stance, and lifted his chin.

Garrison charged.

Ben's knees locked.

Garrison chopped right at him.

In an instant, Ben dove away. He scrambled back up to his feet and regained his stance. Shaking. Heart beating like a rabbit's.

"Hah!" Garrison said, chopping his sword into the grass. "This will be over in seconds. Sorry, Ben. I hate to kill you."

Fight, Ben. Fight!

Garrison closed the gap between them and swung hard.

Ben's lanky sword arm snapped up.

Clang!

He winced.

"Yes, Ben. We aren't practicing anymore." Garrison chopped.

Ben parried.

"Rattles the joints doesn't it, farm boy?"

Clang. Clang. Clang.

Ben's hands ached and fear blossomed inside his chest.

Slit!

Garrison cut his thigh open.

Stab!

Poked the other.

"Hurts, doesn't it, Ben? Now we're even, though. I just wanted to see you bleed before you died. I might even poke extra holes in you after you die."

Garrison struck harder and faster.

Bang. Bang. Bang.

Ben blocked and parried every strike.

"Stop doing that and die, will you!" Garrison said, spitting blood from his mouth.

Ben saved his breath. *He can't hit me. Just hit him!*

Garrison was stronger, but his technique was routine. They'd sparred dozens of times.

Ben knew every move, but did Garrison know his? Did he even have a move?

Think of something, Ben!

Garrison backed away, chest heaving.

"I'm not—*gasp*—going to hold back any longer."

Ben took a deep draw in through his nose. He wasn't tired. He was loose. A spring of energy was inside him.

"I'm not holding back either," Ben said. He darted in and struck with all his speed.

Bang! Bang! Bang!

"Stop it, Ben!

Bang! Bang! Bang!

Garrison fought him off with two hands on his sword. Desperation crept onto his face.

"Stop, Ben!" Garrison said, sucking for breath.

Bang!

Garrison's sword flew from his hands. He collapsed to his knees with his head down.

"You win," Garrison said, still huffing for breath. "Go ahead—*gasp*—kill me."

Ben inched closer and raised his sword over his head.

Garrison slowly shook his head back and forth.

"Go—*gasp*—ahead, Ben. I deserve it."

"Yes you do," Ben yelled. "You're evil. You hurt people and you'll hurt more people."

Garrison's head rose. Laboring for breath, the man offered a sheepish smile behind his short beard. "I know," he said. "Might as well continue the trend with you."

"Huh?"

A small dagger appeared in Garrison's hand. "For Barnabus!" In a flash, he struck Ben in the belly.

Ben's eyes widened, and then narrowed.

"NO!"

He brought his blade down on Garrison's head.

We'd made our return back to the village only to find both Garrison and Ben missing. Garrison worried me. When Sasha was abducted, Garrison's eyes had drifted and his voice had trembled a little. He was either a good liar or really confused, but I'd given him the benefit of the doubt.

None of the villagers or Legionnaires had seen them coming or going, either. It made me wonder if Ben had come after us or if maybe something bad had happened to them.

"Look!" a villager yelled, pointing.

A man staggered down the path of a grassy gnoll. It was Ben, and he was clutching his belly. I ran to him and caught him in my arms when he collapsed. His eyes were weak and his hands were bloody.

"Ben," I said. "What happened? Who did this?"

"G-Garrison," he sputtered out.

He pushed his hand into mine and handed me something. It was a small totem. A figurine.

"Barnabus," Ben said. "He spied for Barnabus. Set us all ..." his body shook, "u-up." His eyes rolled into his head.

I screamed.

CHAPTER 12

L EAGUES AWAY, KRYZAK WAITED IN a strange grove in the woods. The trees stood, but they had no leaves. Reptiles and bugs crawled over the dirt. A draykis carried stones as big as skulls and placed them on the ground, completing a full circle. It was big enough for a man to lie down in.

"That will do," Kryzak said.

He reached inside a pouch and tossed a colorful powder inside the ring, adding some small dragon bones and dragon claws. He clutched a large dragon tooth inside his hand and squeezed.

The time to report to Selene had come.

He took a deep breath.

Selene. As much as he adored her, he feared her. Perhaps that was what drew him to her. He'd never seen anyone so beautiful and evil before.

She didn't tolerate failure, however. She'd kill him at the slightest sign of weakness.

The draykis concerned him. They weren't pawns the likes of lizard men, gnolls, goblins, and acolytes. They were powerful weapons, and many of them had died. He wasn't happy with that. So why should she be?

He stretched his fist over the circle and squeezed the tooth, breaking his own skin. Blood dripped through his fingers and to the ground. Then he chanted an incantation, stepped back, and watched.

The dust inside the circle stirred, and a tiny vortex of mystic colors formed. A woman's figure took shape. It was Selene, standing with her arms folded across her chest. The image twinkled with tiny sparks, filling it with color.

Kryzak's fingers stretched out.

"Don't you dare, Kryzak," she said.

He withdrew his hand.

"My," she said, "so eager to see me again, are we?"

He bowed.

"As always, but now more than ever."

"Your flattery is charming, but it won't compensate for your failure," she said, her colorful image darkening. "What is the situation of Nath Dragon?"

"He lives, but his company is smaller."

"Go on."

Kryzak told her everything. How he had incorporated the ettins and enlisted the aid of the dragon poachers. How he had trapped them in the tunnels and almost drowned them all. About his spies and Nath's search for the Ocular of Orray and about the cursed Wilder Elf, Sansla Libor.

Selene's tail brushed back and disappeared where it crossed the rocks. Her face was a mask of concentration.

Kryzak's hand fell to the wooden grip on his war mace. It gave him little comfort.

"How many did Nath Dragon kill when he came back?" she asked.

"The tunnels were filled with death."

"And Nath Dragon," she said, toying with her robes, "what was his condition?"

"He was distraught. Confused. A storm trying to hold back its anger."

"And you saw the Roamer die?"

He nodded.

"Interesting," she paced inside the circle and folded her arms behind her back. "And what of *my* draykis? Are they all dead as well?"

"Save one," Kryzak said, his head beading with sweat.

"And the dragons you mentioned," she said. "I assume you still have them captured?"

"It was me or them, but the fury still remains."

"What?" she screamed. The dust exploded around her feet. "How many?"

"Nine," he said. "I'll capture eighteen—"

"With what, you fool? You have one draykis!" Her eyes blazed like fire. "It will take months at least. "You have failed me, Kryzak! Perhaps you are helping Nath Dragon save the dragons now!"

"Never, High Priestess! I erred, that is all! I misjudged him!" He pleaded. "It was me or them!"

Selene's face was a mask of fury.

"Do you value your pathetic human life above that of dragons?"

"I-I—certainly not, High Priestess!"

"Close your eyes," she commanded.

"Er," Kryzak swallowed, "as you wish." He shut his eyes.

"Draykis," she said.

It stepped alongside Kryzak.

"Strike him."

Its long tongue licked out of its mouth and along its teeth. "With pleasure," it said, balling up its clawed fist.

Whop!

It flattened Kryzak to the ground.

Kryzak could feel his face swelling already.

"Find my dragons!" she yelled. "And don't lose Nath Dragon, either! And if you don't have better news to report soon, you'll be dead."

When Kryzak opened his eyes, she was gone. The one remaining draykis stood over him with a grin on its face. Kryzak dangled the purple amulet and said, "Looks like you're going to be the next one to face Nath Dragon."

Selene sat on her throne with a smile on her face, petting the drulture on her shoulder. Kryzak had done well. Even better than expected.

"I have to hand it to him: he's very creative."

The drulture let out a tiny roar, and its feathers ruffled.

"Oh, not as creative as you, my pet, but he's awfully good for a man."

Yes, Kryzak had exceeded expectations, but letting him know that wasn't a good motivator.

"I have to keep him on his toes."

And it seemed Nath Dragon was wearing down. The evil within was growing. He couldn't fight it forever. Not when his friends died or when dragons were captured. He'd meet with failure after failure. She almost felt sorry for him. He was naive. His head was filled with a standard that was impossible to live up to, set by his father.

"Not killing anyone. In this world. Hah!"

Gorn Grattack had told her about the high standards set by the Dragon King, Nath's father, and they'd both laughed. No, it was so much easier to do evil than good, and Nath would learn that. And why wouldn't he want to learn? Why wouldn't he want to rule Nalzambor and do whatever he wanted? He didn't need his father. His father needed him. She'd show him that.

"Are you hungry?" she said to the drulture.

It offered a growl.

She clapped her hands.

The great doors opened and the lizard man soldiers stepped inside and kneeled.

"Feeding time," she said.

Moments later they returned with a cage. Inside it, something wide eyed trembled.

"Think you can handle it?"

The drulture's eyes narrowed. It hopped onto the back of her throne, spread its wings, and growled.

CHAPTER 13

"**N**ath," a soft voice said. Someone shook my shoulder. "Nath, he's going to be fine."

I looked up and found Sasha's soft eyes. She sounded confident, but I wasn't so sure. Ben had looked gaunt and pasty when I left. I'd wanted to stay by his side, but Bayzog and Brenwar had insisted that I go. Said they had it under control. At least someone did.

"He's breathing well now, Nath."

"And the fever?" I said.

"It will break," she said, taking a seat on a stone bench beside me.

It was late in the night. The clouds covered the moon, and the villagers' lanterns twinkled from inside their homes. It was a peaceful setting.

"Sasha," I said, "I-I just couldn't forgive myself if Ben died. And I'm far from over Shum being gone."

The stiff wind blew her hair into her face, and she pushed it away and offered the sweetest smile.

"You can't control everything, Nath. You can only control yourself. You can't protect everyone. Not your friends or the dragons. You just have to do your best with what you have."

I shook my head.

"That's not helping, Sasha. Sorry."

"Oh, Nath …" She looked away up the hill and sighed.

I sat there pondering all that had taken place, searching for answers. The Clerics of Barnabus were trying either to kill me or to scare me. The question was why? Did they think I would give up? That I would quit trying to save the dragons?

"Why didn't they just kill me when they had me, Sasha? Why go after my friends instead?"

"Evil has a twisted way of doing things." She pulled her robes tighter and scooted closer. "They must know something we don't."

I stiffened.

"I don't like that."

"I don't either," she said, looking back at me. "I think we should go after them, Nath. Find answers to your questions. They hunt you. Perhaps you should start hunting them. We'll find that Kryzak and put an end to him."

"Sasha! I like the way you think."

Her eyes were bright sapphires. Her voice was excited.

"Well, I can't help it, Nath. I think it's too much that you can't kill those who try to kill you. If it's me or them, it's going to be them." A spark of energy burst from her hand into the ground. "Oops."

"Well, I can kill, but only as a last resort. I'm not supposed to seek it out. I'm supposed to find another way."

"It seems the other way will get you killed."

"It hasn't killed me yet, and plenty of dragons have been saved. Perhaps I should focus on that again." I sighed. "Maybe Brenwar and my father are right. Maybe I need to focus on saving the dragons and not dally with all the problems of the rest of the world. Sorry, Sasha, but I really need to be more careful."

I couldn't believe I'd said that.

"Perhaps you're right," she said.

I caught her trying to hide a smile.

"Hold on," I said. "Are you toying with me, Sasha?"

"I don't follow."

I stood up and glared at her.

"Yes you do," I said. "You're doing that thing."

"What thing?" she said, touching her chest.

"That thing. That thing Bayzog does. Whenever I want to do something he doesn't like, he'll go along with it and for some reason I talk myself out of it." I pointed at her. "It's deceitful."

"No, it's thoughtful," she said, standing up. "And you found the right path on your own. Vengeance is not the way. You need to do what your father told you to."

Now I was mad. Seething. It seemed everyone was against me.

"No Sasha, I like your suggestion. I think I should go after them and put an end to them. Who's to stop me?"

I turned to walk away. She grabbed my arm and pulled me back.

"Nath! When you came out of those tunnels ..." her voice trailed off.

"What?"

"I ..."

I could see more than worry in her eyes. There was fear, real fear. But for what?

"Just say it, I won't tell anyone."

"You scared me, Nath." Her voice trembled. "You weren't yourself, but something else. Savage and unpredictable. And when you killed that ettin?" She paused. "I didn't know you."

My heart dropped into my toes.

"I'd never hurt you, Sasha, or any of my friends." I touched her cheek and brushed her hair from her eyes. "That couldn't ever, ever happen. I swear it."

She grabbed my hand and held it to her face. She started crying.

"Don't do that, Nath. Don't swear anything. It's better that way."

I'd never felt smaller. How could this woman be scared of me? I was her protector. I slumped back down on the bench and buried my head in my claws. I couldn't believe what I was hearing.

"I'm going to go check on Ben," she said, wiping her eyes. "And then I'm going to get some sleep. Perhaps you should do the same."

I didn't wave or do anything, but I heard her walking away. Each step left me emptier inside until I was all alone.

CHAPTER
14

"I'M ALL RIGHT, DRAGON, REALLY," Ben said. He swung himself up onto his horse and groaned.

"You don't need to be riding, Ben," I said. "It'll shake your guts out. Just give it another day or so." I grabbed his horse by the reins. "Get off. Go rest. That's an order."

"I'll not do it," Ben said. "No offense, Dragon, but I know when I'm ready."

It had been almost a week, and in that time, Ben's fever had broken and his belly had mostly healed. I still hadn't spoken with Brenwar and had said very little to Bayzog or Sasha. But I'd made my intentions clear. I was going after Kryzak.

But now Ben wanted to come along.

Everyone gathered around. Bayzog, Sasha, Brenwar, and I sat on our horses watching Ben. He was tormented. Garrison was dead. A man who'd pretended to be our friend had betrayed us, and it had almost cost Ben his life.

Ben's face became long and downcast.

"I should have just let him be," he said. "I should have walked away, but he was just, so... "

"Evil," Sasha said.

Ben nodded.

I felt sorry for him. I think we all did. He'd killed a man whom he'd come to trust as a friend—only to be betrayed.

"You did the right thing," Sasha said. "His deception led to Shum's death. Ben, more people could have died if you hadn't stopped him." She rode over and patted his back. "I'm grateful."

Ben didn't even look at her.

"The Legionnaires were going to hang me!"

It was true. The Legionnaires were a brotherhood, sworn to give their lives to one another and never to harm one another.

Ben had known that, but he'd gone after Garrison anyway. It was a brave thing. Risky too.

Given Sasha's abduction and Garrison's evil magic totem, Ben had been spared. But humiliation followed. His helmet, sword, and armor were gone. His bow and arrows as well. He was an outcast like me now.

"Ben," I said, releasing his reins. "Let's go, shall we?"

He sat up in his saddle. "You're letting me go with you after Kryzak?"

"No, I'm letting you go as far as I let you."

Brenwar harrumphed and took the lead.

I knew I needed to talk with him, but there would be plenty of time along the way. Plus, I needed to find the right words to say. It would have to wait.

It was morning when we left, and Brenwar led us in a zigzag north of the village.

Bayzog made his way along my side for a chat. His violet eyes were tired for a change, and I knew the loss of Shum had shaken him.

"You look like you might yawn," I said.

"Me? Not ever," he said, offering a smile. "How are you feeling, Nath?"

"Well enough. And you?"

"I'm not sure what we're doing?" Bayzog said.

"We're looking for Kryzak," I said. "And the best way to find him is to find the poachers. At least now we have the advantage of knowing who is in charge of all this." I gave him a hard look. "You don't have to come along, Bayzog. I think you, Sasha, and Ben should go back to Quintuklen. Brenwar and I can handle this."

"You and Brenwar aren't even speaking."

I smiled.

"I don't miss the nagging. You don't plan to fill in for him, do you?"

"Come now, Nath," Bayzog said. "Do you know so little of me? We've all been through much the past few days. I think it's time we stopped and talked things out for a change. Right now I'm not so sure what we're doing—or rather, if what we're doing is best."

"It's best for me," I said. "That's all that matters. I need to save dragons. You need to save yourself from me."

"You need us, Nath."

"You mean what's left of us? Shum died, remember. Ben almost died and so did you and Sasha. Not to mention Brenwar. What would you have me do?"

He grabbed my arm, narrowed his eyes, and spoke through his teeth.

"Slow down and think, will you? Perhaps they set another trap. An ambush perhaps. We need more caution and less action. We need council."

Council. Elves loved councils and long meetings. So did dwarves, for that matter, but I wasn't going to bite on any of it. No, all he wanted to do was talk me out of doing what I wanted. I was going to save the dragons, and in order to do that, I was going to stop the poachers that captured them.

"Here is my counsel for you, Bayzog. Go home and leave my life to me."

Bayzog led his horse away, saying, "You're as stubborn as Brenwar."

I had to admit: that stung a little.

CHAPTER 15

W E SCOURED THE COUNTRYSIDE OVER the next few days, taking our time on the journey. No one was saying much of anything, and we hadn't sat down for council. They had offered, but I'd refused. For the most part, they were all just tagging along, and that was fine by me. Eventually we'd be close enough to Quintuklen and they'd head home. That was my plan, anyway.

"So, Dragon," Ben said. "How do we go about tracking down someone when the world's so big?"

It was a good question. I waded into a nearby river and acted like I didn't hear him. I was getting hungry, and I had an appetite for fish. The cold water rushed past my knees as I searched for signs of life. The sun was bright and the water was clear, and I could see my reflection shimmering in it. My mane of auburn hair looked fine. Of course, it always did.

A fish darted through my feet, followed by another. Moments later one of them settled.

I readied my claws and licked my lips. I could taste the meat already. I slipped my hands into the water.

Ben sloshed up behind me.

The fish squirted between my fingers.

"Ben!" I cried. "Quit scaring the fish. I've taught you better than that." I frowned and shook my head at him.

"Then you stop ignoring me," he said. "You've been ignoring everyone, and I'm getting tired of it."

"They you should go home," I said.

"To what?" he said. "I don't have anyone anymore. Just you, Dragon."

"I'm sure Quinley could use you in the cornfields," I said. "And you're a better bowman than you were. You'd be the best shot for miles around." I sloshed away, eyeing the water.

"What's wrong with you, Dragon?" he said. "You didn't used to be like this. You used to be nice. Now you're just—"

I turned and faced him with my hands on my hips.

"I'm just what, Ben? Mean?"

"I wasn't going to say that," he said.

His eyes drifted to the left.

"You were going to say that," I said. "And guess what, Ben. I don't care. I'm being mean because I don't want you here, and I've told you that. I've told all of you that, but none of you listen."

"You need us," he said.

I laughed.

"For what, Ben? You don't even have a sword or bow. What are you going to fight with, your hands?"

I took a jab at another fish and missed.

"Blast it!"

My stomach was growling. I was growling. Why wouldn't they leave me alone?

"UGH!" Ben said. He threw up his arms and sloshed away in the stream.

"Goodbye, Ben," I said.

He stopped and turned. His pleasant face was turning red and his fists were balled up at his sides.

"You know, Dragon, there's a saying in Quinley. *You can tell a lot about a man by the friends he keeps.*"

I shrugged and said, "So, I've heard that one before, and you didn't say it quite right."

"I don't care if it sounds right or not, because I've got a better saying. *You can tell a lot more about a man who doesn't have any friends.*" He pointed at me. "That's for you, Dragon!" He stormed through the water, fell, and completely soaked himself.

I started laughing and holding my belly.

Soaked, Ben shook his fist at me and stormed away. As he was leaving, Brenwar, Bayzog, and Sasha were coming up along the sandy riverbank. I rolled my eyes.

"What's the matter, Ben?" I heard Sasha say.

"Nothing!"

They all stood there gawping at me except Brenwar. He was glaring. I didn't care, though. I just wanted to eat some fish and be left alone. I made my way downriver a ways, and when I looked back, they were gone. Good.

I readied my hands, spread my feet in the river bed, and waited for the next fish to pass. A fat-bellied bass swam by. My hands splashed into the water and dug into its scales. I got him! A big one. He wriggled in my hands, tail flopping back and forth with his wide mouth gawping.

"You look like some people I know," I said.

My belly groaned again. I was hungry. I made my way out of the water, sat down and gutted the fish and scaled it with my claws. I could feel my fire in my belly.

"Hmmm," I said to myself, "I have an idea."

I tried to summon my fire. Just a little bit. Only enough to roast the fish whole. Who needs a fire when the fire's in you already? Gently, I exhaled. Nothing came forth. I put a little more wind and belly behind my next breath. A whoosh of flame rushed out.

The fish charred and crumbled in my hands.

"Sultans of Sulfur!"

I stormed back into the water. A minute later I found my next fish. It was bigger than the last, green scaled, and speckled. I licked my lips. The speckled bass were the best. I wasn't going to waste this one.

I plunged my hands in and snatched him up.

"Woohoo—*ulp!*"

Something wrapped around my neck and jerked me under the water. I couldn't breathe. I clutched at the creature that coiled itself around my neck. I didn't know what it was. I ripped at it with my claws. It dragged me to the middle of the river and down toward a dark hole.

"Brenwar! Ben! Help!" I said in my frog voice.

No one could hear me.

No one would even know.

CHAPTER 16

I WAS PULLED DEEPER INTO THE water, and the surface receded, way above my head. Below waited a darkness surrounded by wriggling things. Tentacles! They stretched out and grabbed me by the ankles and bound my hands. I jerked at my bonds, but I was helpless. It pulled me down toward a mouth big enough to eat a horse. The tentacles, like tongues and snakes, were pulling me inside. I wanted to scream! I wanted to breathe! That mouth full of teeth chomped at my feet.

All I could think of was how bad I'd been to my friends.

Those last few moments … I'd like to have them back again.

I stretched out my arms with all my strength. I could see the sun wavering in the water above me. I fought against my bonds, but nothing helped.

A splash of water erupted above me. Ben swam at me with a glowing dagger between his teeth. Dragon Claw. He cut the first tentacles and freed my arms. The creature jerked and made an eerie underwater whine. Ben sawed at another tentacle that was wrapped around my neck. The river monster reeled again. The tentacles released me. I swam for the surface and burst out of the water, gasping.

"Ah!" I gulped in mouthfuls of air. I wanted to kiss the riverbank. Wait.

"Ben?"

He'd disappeared.

I ducked back under the water.

The river monster had Ben wrapped up in its tentacles. He was snared by the wrists and being pulled down into the mouth.

I swam after him.

More tentacles burst out.

I saw Dragon Claw fall from Ben's fingers and sink toward the maw. I snatched it with my fingertips and started cutting. There were too many of them. Dozens of the sticky things. *Enough of this! I'm a dragon!*

I swam straight into the monster's mouth and started stabbing. I looked up and saw Ben free and heading for the surface. Then the massive jaws closed upon me.

Ben treaded water in the river, yelling, "Dragon! Dragon!"

He coughed, fought for his breath, and ducked his head into the water. He didn't see Dragon or the monster. Even the tentacles were gone. He swam deeper, eyes searching, but everything was blurry.

What happened to you, Dragon?

He dove deeper and found nothing. Chest burning, he swam back to the top and gasped for air.

"What is going on?" a voice said from the riverbank. It was Brenwar. Bayzog and Sasha were right beside the dwarf, and their faces were filled with worry.

Ben fought to tread water. His arms and legs were exhausted from fighting the current. His face dipped up and down in the water.

"It's…" He gasped. "It's Dragon. He's—*gasp*—gone under. A monster got him!"

Brenwar and Bayzog waded into the water and reached out for him.

"Swim back here, will you?" Brenwar said, gesturing with his arms.

Bayzog slid out of his robes and swam toward him. The wizard hooked his arms beneath Ben's chest and towed him back to the bank. Huffing for breath, they both sat waist deep in the bristling water.

"He went down over there," Ben said, pointing. "It had tentacles like snakes and was stronger than iron. I cut them and freed Dragon, then they got me. Dragon saved me, and when I swam up, I looked down and he was gone."

Bayzog patted Ben's back with his slender arm, and Brenwar studied him with a cocked eyebrow. The black-bearded dwarf pointed at him.

"You say he's in there?" Brenwar pointed in the water. "That way?"

Ben nodded.

Brenwar, in full armor, marched into the river, one step at a time, until his head disappeared.

"What's he doing?" Ben said, looking at Bayzog.

The wizard shrugged.

"Come on, Ben, let's get back out of this. The water might still be dangerous. And I need to think of a spell that I can cast." His face was filled with anguish. "I hate to admit it, but I'm not very prepared for dealing with water. I'm surprised I could still swim."

Ben, exhausted, remained in place.

"I've got to go after him," he said. "I'll just make one more dive."

Bayzog held his arm tight. "I've thought of a spell that might help. But I need to be on shore to cast it. Come, we must hurry."

Ben slowly backed toward the bank, frowning.

"Sasha!" Bayzog yelled. "Get my pack. I need my components. And fetch Brenwar's chest. That might help as well."

Ben stood ankle deep in the water, watching. Every second felt like a minute. It was torture. Bayzog and Sasha worked behind him, trying to get something ready that would help. He had a feeling that whatever it was they came up with would be too late.

"Is it ready?" he said, turning his head, but not taking his eyes from the water. "I need to get back in there!"

"A moment, Ben. A moment!" Bayzog said.

Life begins and ends in moments. His father had told him so. *The important thing is to make the moments you have count.*

Ben waded back into the water.

"Ben, hold on!" Sasha said. "Don't be foolish."

"I'll be fine," Ben said, waving his hand. "And if I don't make it back—"

Splash!

Nath's head burst out of the water.

"Dragon!"

A clawed hand waved at him.

Ben swam for him. He grabbed Dragon and guided him onto the bank.

Dragon was covered in river muck and severed tentacles, gasping for air. Dragon Claw glowed in his hand. He had cuts and scrapes all over him.

"You made it!" Ben said.

Dragon nodded.

"What about Brenwar?" Ben asked.

CHAPTER 17

DRAGON LOOKED AT BEN, THEN back into the water. There was no sign of Brenwar.

"He's coming, I think." Dragon started to wade back in. "He was right behind me."

At last Brenwar's head popped out of the water, and foot by foot he walked up the bank. He looked at Dragon and kept going.

"Did he save you?" Ben said.

"I was fine," Dragon said, coughing. He slung some purple tentacles off his shoulders. "He showed up right after I didn't need him."

"What happened? What was that thing?" Ben said.

"I've no idea what it was," Dragon said, "but it was nasty. It swallowed me whole. I couldn't see a thing." He dangled Dragon Claw in front of his face. "I jammed Dragon Claw into anything it could bite and finally the mouth opened up again. I swam out as fast as I could."

"Is it dead?" Ben said.

Dragon's golden eyes drifted over the water.

"I think so."

Growl.

"Was that you, Dragon?"

Dragon stood up, slinging his hair from his eyes and rubbing his belly.

"It's my stomach. I'm famished." He marched toward Bayzog and Sasha. "Say wizards, do you have any of that water? I need something to hold me over. I'm so hungry I could eat goat horns."

"Certainly," Sasha said. "We have other things we can procure as well, but it will take some time."

"It's got to be better than hunting," Dragon said, stretching out his great scaled arms and yawning. "I think I've done enough of that today. Tried to catch a fish and almost caught my death." He climbed up the bank, took a seat on the grass, and motioned for Ben to come over.

Ben took a seat beside him.

Dragon patted him on the back.

"How did you know, Ben?"

"Know what?"

"That I needed help?" Dragon's face was puzzled.

"Well, I don't know," he said. "I just knew. And Brenwar, well, he knew too, because he came over right at the same time I did."

Dragon shook his head and huffed a little laugh.

"You know, Ben, you're right. I need my friends. Without them, I would have died."

Ben patted Dragon's knee. "We need you too."

"Well, you deserve better than me," Nath said. "And I promise to do better. Honestly Ben, I just don't want to put anyone in danger." Nath's voice was solemn and humble. "Shum died because of me. Almost everyone did. That's not easy to live with. I just want those evildoers dead." He jammed Dragon Claw into the ground.

"Me too," Ben said, nodding. "Me too."

They didn't speak after that. Ben watched Bayzog and Sasha do their thing, and Dragon kept his eyes on the river. Ben glanced back at him from time to time, but Dragon didn't seem to notice. He sat there like a statue. A large muscular man with black scales that stretched across his arms to his shoulders. His features were chiseled and his face was like polished stone. The wind whipping through his red hair was the only thing that seemed real about him.

Dragon sniffed the air. "Mmmm, something smells good." He patted his stomach and headed toward Bayzog and Sasha.

Ben fell into step right behind him.

A sand bar lay along the riverbank, and Brenwar had stacked up some wood and begun a fire.

Bayzog and Sasha bowed when they arrived.

"I hope you like!" Sasha grabbed both of them by the arms and led them down the riverbank.

Ben's jaw dropped open. Dragon's eyes were golden plates.

"How did you …?" Ben started to say, but he had to swallow the water in his mouth. "And where did the …?"

Sasha giggled and Bayzog laughed.

A table and eight chairs sat in the sand, loaded with every dish he could imagine. A roasted hog stuffed with an apple, a turkey as big as a pig, steaming potatoes, vegetables, pies, and jugs of water and wine. Silverware sparkled in the setting sun with cloth napkins laid along the sides. It was a feast.

"I've, well, we've," Bayzog said, "never cast this spell before, and we didn't know what to expect. I assume it was meant for a larger gathering."

"Is it real?" Ben asked.

Brenwar ripped off a leg of turkey and tore a hunk off with his teeth.

"Mmmm," he grumbled, "It's as real as my beard."

Ben stuffed a handful of meat into his mouth, chewed it up, and washed it down with some sort of delicious wine. Sasha gently carved small bits of food on her plate, and Bayzog did the same. Brenwar bit into chunks of ham that were poised on his knife. He grunted, and his brows waggled up and down with a dwarven sort of praise. He did have one complaint.

"No ale?" he said, eyeing the bottom of a jug he had drained.

"Sorry," Bayzog said, "but I didn't know what to expect."

Nath stuffed the feast in his mouth with his claws and a heaping spoon. He smiled a lot and talked little and ate as fast as Brenwar. He was putting food down like he'd never eaten it before. The pair kept eating long after the others finished and most of the food was gone.

Ben stood up at the end of the table and cleared his throat.

"Ahem."

Sasha and Bayzog stopped, but Nath and Brenwar were still chewing.

"I just wanted to say something," Ben said, picking up his goblet.

"What is it, Ben?" Sasha said, "Please speak."

"Well, where I'm from, we always thank the preparers. To the both of you, Sasha and Bayzog, I want to express my thanks. This has been wonderful. And to all of you," he raised his goblet, "I'm honored to be among you. I'm honored to be your friend. Thank you all."

"Well said." Nath halted in tipping his goblet to his lips. "Well said."

"Agreed," said Brenwar. "Now pass that cheese."

"Brenwar!" Sasha said.

"Oh, sorry," Brenwar said. He straightened himself up in his chair. "Please pass the cheese."

"Hahahaha! That's not what I meant," Sasha said, holding her belly.

"What? I just want the cheese. What's the humor in it?"

Everyone started laughing. Everyone but Dragon.

"Dragon," Ben said, "Lighten up, will you? You're as stone faced as Brenwar."

Dragon didn't move. He sat stiff as a board with his eyes closed.

"Nath," Sasha said, worried. She rose from her seat and gasped.

Nath fell face first into his plate of food.

CHAPTER 18

"**W**HAT'S WRONG WITH HIM?**" BEN said. "Is he breathing?"

Dragon lay stretched out on the table with Bayzog's pointed ear on his chest.

"The heart beats," Bayzog said, "but slowly."

Brenwar punched Nath in the arm and said, "Wake up!"

"Easy," Bayzog said.

"Easy nothing," Brenwar said. He pinched Nath's thigh. Nothing happened.

"Why don't you tickle him or something?" Ben said.

Brenwar eyed him.

Ben shrugged.

Sasha dripped some water over Nath's lips.

Nothing moved. Nothing twitched.

"I think he's changing again," she said. She held her fingers over his lips. "He breathes, same as the last time. Barely."

"I agree," Bayzog said. "Brenwar, what do you think? You were with him the first time this happened, were you not?"

"Aye," Brenwar growled, "And I had to haul his carcass all over until he came to."

"So did I," said Ben. "And he was out months the last time. Do you think it will be months again?"

"What if it gets longer every time?" Sasha said.

Silence fell, and all eyes were on Nath. He was the reason they were gathered. He was the future, and now he lay still as a stone.

"What do we do, Bayzog?" Sasha said, brushing Nath's hair away from his stony face. "Do we take him back to Quintuklen?"

"I say Morgdon," Brenwar said. "Let the dwarves keep him safe."

Bayzog clasped his fingers behind his back and began walking around the table. They had all pledged to look after Nath, but he was their leader, and he was down. So the question was, who did they follow now?

"They are both good suggestions, but Quintuklen is closer," Bayzog said.

"And full of the Clerics of Barnabus," Brenwar said. "I say we take him to the hills. He'll be safe there. We don't have the foulness of the races up there."

"You don't have the security of my home there either," Bayzog said.

Brenwar bristled.

"Security! No one's ever penetrated Morgdon. Not once. Not ever." Brenwar rapped his fist on the table. "He's my charge by the Dragon King himself, not yours, elf. I'll decide what's best for him."

"This could go on for months again, maybe a year," Bayzog said. "I don't want to wait in Morgdon that long. Not when I can do research and seek other help. There are other things we need to prepare for, Brenwar. What happens when he wakes up? What if he changes even more? Will you be ready for that?"

"As much as you, elf!" Brenwar thumbed his bearded chest. "He comes with me."

Bayzog made his way back to Brenwar and looked right down at him.

"I disagree."

Brenwar poked him in the chest three times with his stubby fingers. "I—don't—care."

"Are you the only two that have a say in this?" Sasha said with her arms folded across her chest. "I think I can offer some direction."

Ben pulled back his shoulders and said, "Me too."

"Pah, this is ridiculous. I'll not be taking orders from the likes of you three. No! Nath comes with me."

"Who do you think you are?" Sasha said, approaching the dwarf.

"I'm under the charge of the Dragon King, lady. Who do you think you be?"

Bayzog stepped in front of her and held her back.

"All right, let's not feud with each other. We all want what's best," he said. He walked back over to Nath and put his hand on his chest. "I have an idea."

"I don't care," Brenwar said. He tapped his foot on the ground and combed his fingers through his beard.

"Just hear me out," Bayzog said. "We'll take a vote."

"No," Brenwar said, crossing his arms over his chest. "And with that we'll be leaving." He grabbed Nath by the ankle and dragged him off the table. Nath's head bounced off the ground with a thud. Brenwar kept going.

"Brenwar!" Sasha said, "What in Nalzambor are you doing? He's not hunted meat to be dragged. How disrespectful!" She grabbed Nath's arms and pulled back.

Brenwar pulled both of them forward without looking back.

"Will you stop it, you bearded child!"

Bayzog spread his arms wide, exasperated. "All right, Brenwar! You win!" He practically yelled. And Bayzog never yelled. "We'll head to Morgdon first."

Brenwar stopped and looked back over his shoulder.

"You don't need to come."

"Well, we're coming anyway," Bayzog said. "Just show a little more respect for our friend."

Brenwar dropped Nath's booted leg.

"Pah ... His head's harder than mine."

After dawn broke the next day, Brenwar, Ben, Bayzog, and Sasha rode the horses south toward the Mountains of Morgdon. Nath Dragon lay on a stretcher Brenwar and Ben had hewn from the woodland and was towed behind Brenwar's horse. Brenwar led and the others followed, all quiet and resolute.

"What about the table and all the food?" Ben had asked Bayzog.

"What you had, you have. All the rest will pass," the part-elf said. "I'm sure some creature will finish it off for us. Don't worry, Ben."

"Well, I just hate to see it go to waste."

"It won't. I'm sure of it."

Following the river south, the company disappeared from the view back toward the table. A small head popped up from the tall grasses before the trees and crept up to the table on the legs of a goat. Another one popped out from behind the trees and followed. The pair stomped around the table, sniffed the bouquet of food that was left, and took seats. They nodded at one another and stuffed food into their horned faces. One burped. The other guzzled. Then the satyrs began their conversation. Their voices were low and evil.

"We'll have them now, aye, my dear," the male said.

"Yes, all of them," the female said, "and to think they even left a fine meal for us. It won't be our last, but it just might be theirs." She sucked down a pitcher of wine and wiped her lips with her forearm. "And that dwarf who busted my pipes and clocked me in the head ... I can't wait to get back at him. I think I'm going to shave every hair from him and stand him before a mirror before I cook him."

The male laughed. His voice was loud, part goat and part man.

"And that elf," he said. "What would you do to him?"

"Oh, I'll shove the dwarf's beard into the spellcaster's mouth and then I'll nibble on his fingers and toes."

"And the man?" he asked.

"I'll make him chop the wood and start the fires." She pulled out her new set of pipes from under her vest. "And make him smile as he does it."

"And the woman?" he said, stuffing some leftover cherry pie in his mouth.

She grabbed a goblet and lifted it to the sun.

"I'll drink her tears and bring her greatest fears to life."

He swung his hairy legs up on the table and drummed his hooves on the wood.

"You are so terrible," he said. His teeth were covered in cherries. "We are only allowed to spy on them. We aren't supposed to eat them. Kryzak won't allow that."

She pulled her long dark hair over her head and tied it in a knot. She was pleasant looking. All woman from the waist up, fluid in her motions and stout in frame. Leathers and skins covered her chest and formed a short kind of dress. Her smile was pretty but wicked.

"He just wants the dragon man," she said. "He didn't say anything about the others. And now it seems the dragon man sleeps, and he'll be down for quite some time."

"What are you thinking?" he said. "We must tell Kryzak this news. There will be a great reward in it."

She pulled the apple from the pig's mouth, hitched one arm over the chair, and said, "I think the sooner he knows, the better." She bit into the apple, chewed it up, and spit the seeds out. "And the sooner he knows, the sooner we avenge ourselves. The only question is, who follows them and who tells Kryzak what we know?"

"I could use the run," he said. "Hiding in the woods has started to make my legs stiff as stone."

"Fare thee well," she said, winking. "You run, and I'll hunt."

He hopped on the table, and his hooves became a blur, shaking everything off. He pounced through the air and dashed up the river faster than the fleetest deer. He paused, waved, sped along, and disappeared into the woods.

"He makes a fine ally of evil ... *burp*," she said, tossing the core away, "but never as fine as me."

CHAPTER
19

K RYZAK STOOD ALONGSIDE A STONE-HEWN doorway in the midst of a temple
ruin. Columns and rubble scored the grounds of what had once been a fine
work of man. Such ruins were scattered over the land of Nalzambor. Many of
them served as hideouts for the Clerics of Barnabus, and many of them held secrets.
Catacombs and caves lay below the surface of some, and others were portals from one
to another. It was powerful and ancient magic the Clerics of Barnabus had harnessed
long ago to serve their will and spread their destructive ways.

"And there are only the four of them guarding Nath Dragon?" Kryzak said.

The young satyr nodded his head.

"That is all, High Cleric. Only a few leagues away and heading south toward
Morgdon," he said, raking his hoof over the ground. "I can take you straight to them.
We can stop them and capture them. But there is a price for our services."

Kryzak swung his war mace over his broad shoulder with one arm and took two
steps forward. The satyr looked up at the man twice the size of him and swallowed.

"What is your name?" Kryzak said.

"Finlin."

"And this price, little hooved one," he said. "What did you have in mind?"

The satyr's thumbs rolled between his clasped fingers, and his eyes bounced back
and forth.

"The dwarf, elf, woman, and a small dragon would suffice."

"Hah! You think too much of yourself, horned rodent. What would you do with
them?"

"We shall make a feast of them," it said. "A fine dining—"

Kryzak slung his mace into the dirt.

The satyr hopped back.

"Don't jest with me, satyr! Your legends only frighten children, not the likes of
me." Kryzak poked the satyr with his mace. "What will you do with them?"

The satyr cringed and said, "High Priest, do you really care what we do with them?"

Kryzak moved his head from side to side, and his thick neck cracked. He showed a toothy grin and jutted his chin out.

"Gutsy. Foolish, but shrewd. Fine, make a legendary pot of stew with them, but you aren't getting a dragon," Kryzak said. He then ran his mailed fist over the stone archway and muttered something.

The satyr looked around. There was only Kryzak, him, and the moss-coated ruins.

"Who are you talking to?" the satyr asked.

"Stand back and you will see."

Kryzak backed up from the stone doorway. Two huge slabs of stone jutted from the ground, standing twelve feet tall, and another stone cut in a semicircle was laid over the tops of them, perfectly aligned. Kryzak slipped his gauntlets from his hands and dropped them to the ground. He rubbed his fingers together, kneeled, and stretched his arms out wide. Chin up, eyes closed, an incantation spewed from his lips.

"*Oleenapaaaawwwwn... Oleenapaaaawwwwn... Oleenapaaaawwwwn...* "

The tattoos on his bald head pulsated with life.

The satyr stepped back, biting his nails.

A swirl of dark colors filled the archway, and a grey mist rolled out and covered the grasses and the ground.

The satyr couldn't see his hooves. His heart beat faster. His tiny horns tingled. He couldn't take his eyes from the archway. And time seemed to stop.

A woman stepped through. She was tall, dark, and raven haired. Her eyes were like black pearls.

Kryzak didn't move, but his eyes popped open. A crease formed on his brow.

The satyr fell to his knees. His gaze remained on the woman. Her eyes glossed over him, bringing a chill, before falling on Kryzak.

"Rise, Kryzak," she said. Her voice was polished and commanding.

Kryzak rose. His fingers twitched at his sides.

"High Priestess! I was not expecting your audience." His strong voice trembled a little, shaken. "It was not my desire to disturb you."

She sauntered through the mist, looking around with her arms folded over her robes. She was graceful and purposeful when she moved.

Finlin felt his heart flutter. He feared her yet was drawn to her.

"You've summoned much without my consultation, Kryzak. Did you think it would escape my notice?" she said. "You must have tracked down many dragons. And so soon?"

His feet didn't move, but he turned the best he could to face her.

"I have the greatest dragon of all in my grasp," he said.

"Oh," she said. She stepped in front of Finlin and rubbed the hair between the horns on his head. His hoof pounded the ground. "And how is that?"

"Nath Dragon," he said. "He sleeps."

Her fingers stopped and she turned.

"Tell me more," she said, stepping away.

Finlin felt his heart sink. His fingers stretched through the mist and after her. *Oh, my queen!*

"This satyr is my spy, and he's trailed them and heard their speech. Nath Dragon slept months the last time. They suspect he'll sleep just as long again. He'll change. They fear the change is bad for him. I suspect that is good for us."

A black tail rose out of the mist and struck Kryzak across the face. He was lifted from his feet and disappeared into the mist. The tail slithered under the fog and jerked Kryzak back to his feet by the neck. His face was red.

Finlin trembled, eyes searching the mist, backing away. *What is that thing?*

"Satyr," she said.

"Yes?" Finlin blurted.

"Are you certain of this?" Her eyes probed his. He could feel it in his bones. "Every bit of it?"

"As certain as I am of my hooved feet," he said, bowing. "I can take you right to him. Anything you please."

The black serpent tail lifted Kryzak farther from the ground. His feet dangled over the mist, and his fingers dug at the scales. He tried to speak but couldn't. He was choking.

"I feel you've done well, Kryzak," she said. "Possibly better than I hoped. Nath Dragon is changing even sooner than expected." She lowered him and faced him eye to eye. "Would you still die for me, Kryzak?"

His hard face dipped up and down.

"Good," she said, smiling a little. She gave his forehead a kiss.

The tail squeezed his neck until his big body went limp. She flipped the body through the air, and it disappeared through the swirling portal.

Finlin shook without control when she turned and faced him.

"What are you shaking for, fawnish man?"

"Why-why d-did you d-do that?" he said. "You said he'd d-done well."

Her tail petted the hair between his horns, and she showed him an icy smile.

"And he had done well, but his part is over." She coiled her tail around his waist and lifted him to face her. "No one is indispensable." She checked her colorful nails. "And I tired of him. Will you still help me?"

Finlin nodded vigorously. "What would you have me do?"

She set him down. The tail patted his horned head. "I want you to lead my servants. Do well and reap the rewards. Fail and suffer my disappointment."

"Will do. Will do. Will do," he nodded fast. "Will do."

She walked away and stepped into the portal, but before she disappeared she said, "Come."

A big creature, like a man but with scales and black wings, followed.

Finlin gasped. He hadn't seen it there before.

"Eep!"

Something scaly and big as a pony brushed by Finlin's feet. He jumped four feet off the ground. A big face with long whiskers turned toward him with bright cat eyes. It licked its lips and bared its fangs.

Finlin froze.

The feline fury followed Selene into the archway, and they disappeared from sight.

He couldn't tell if he was thrilled or scared. His heart pumped like a racing horse's. He waited, pacing back and forth before the swirling archway. What was going to come through there next?

What do I do? What do I do?

A large figure stepped out of the archway and waded into the mist.

Finlin stopped pacing.

The figure wore crimson cloth robes. Thick-thewed arms emerged from the sleeves. A great scepter of dark metal was clutched in one hand. A horned metal helmet in the image of an angry bull covered his face. His eyes were dark behind the eyelets.

Finlin looked up at him and stepped backward. "Who are you?"

Something snorted behind the mask.

Finlin stepped aside as the figure marched right past him.

More figures emerged. Lizard men with spears and swords led small, gray-scaled dragons on leashes. There were a dozen of them, sleek and black winged. Bald men with tattooed heads followed. Their robes were simple, their faces grim and hard. They carried clubs, maces, and flails. All in all, there were more than a score of lizard men and acolytes. They formed ranks on both sides of the arches.

The man in the bull mask stood at the end, leaving Finlin alone facing the archway.

"Awkward," he muttered. He turned in time to see a great shadow emerge and swirl off the arch and come forward. He darted to the man in the bull mask.

A dragon, bigger than him, appeared. Its long neck was dark copper, and streaks of black stretched all over its body. Its eyes were like fire and its breath smelled of acid. It lumbered forward on soft feet, bigger than two horses. A great terrifying beast. A lone figure sat saddled on its wingless back: a petite young woman with a curtain of long, white hair flowing from a mostly bald head. Jewels adorned her robes, which enhanced her figure. She sat perched high in the saddle with her arms folded on her waist.

My, she's pretty. He combed the hair between his horns with his fingers.

Her light eyes found his.

"I am Marlay, a priestess of Barnabus," she said. "And you are?"

"Finlin," he said, stepping from behind the warrior.

"Lead the way, Finlin," she said, chin up and eyes forward. "We have a sleeping dragon to catch."

CHAPTER
20

"I WAS SCARED," SASHA SAID TO Bayzog. "I, I'm so sorry."

"Darling, it is all right. I understand." His voice was soothing, and he reached out and held her hands. "Please let it go. It will pass. It happens to all of us."

"What if it doesn't pass?" she said, hugging him. Sobbing.

They were two days into their journey to Morgdon and still had days to go. Sasha had been very quiet, strangely so, and it had irritated Bayzog. So he had pressed. Slowly. Gradually. Politely. Until she broke. A flood of tears had come.

"If it doesn't, it doesn't," he said. "We'll just be cautious."

She looked right into his face. Her beautiful features were contorted with deep fear and worry. He'd never seen her so. Not ever.

"I was so scared. I just stood there, helpless and frozen. Watching and doing nothing. You have to be able to count on me, Bayzog, and you can't now. Not ever." She looked away and started to walk away. "Ever again."

They'd stopped traveling for the day, but Brenwar and Ben were gone gathering food and making camp. He hadn't left her side since.

"Sasha, come back," he said. "Let's talk about this."

"There's nothing to talk about!"

He let her go. The river. The river where Nath Dragon almost drowned had triggered it all. Sasha, after almost drowning herself deep in the tunnels of the crater, had become terrified of drowning again. Bayzog had wondered what happened in that moment he swam in and helped Nath and Ben in the water. Sasha wasn't there, and she'd loved water. She was even a better swimmer than him, though they didn't go swimming often. But they did travel the lands from time to time and had been to the Dragon Pond several times. She had loved it there.

He tossed a rough sack on the ground and snapped his fingers. Slowly a tent took form. He slipped inside and waited. It was best to leave her alone at times like this. He didn't like her being out there alone, not after he'd lost her once, but he'd take his chances.

He pulled a golden locket from his robes, opened it up, and muttered an incantation. A small image of Sasha formed. He could feel how close she was and feel her heart in his palm. He sighed. She was safe, and he could sense Ben and Brenwar were nearby as well.

The peaks of the mountain ranges of the dwarven city of Morgdon could be seen if Bayzog squinted his keen eyes. He felt uncomfortable with the unfamiliar, particularly with being an elf in a dwarven land. But Brenwar hadn't seemed bothered in Elome, so why should Morgdon bother Bayzog?

Don't overthink it. You've still got days to go.

He searched for Sasha. She rode in the front, not far from where Brenwar led, towing Nath on his stretcher. They had hardly spoken since last night.

Despite the dry weather, his elven bones felt cold. He wished Shum were still here. The Roaming Ranger had brought him a great comfort. Shum had been older, at least by a few hundred years or so, and his wisdom was needed. Perhaps Shum could have convinced Brenwar that Nath would be better off elsewhere.

His eyes drifted back over Nath, and he sighed.

He wasn't sure if Nath being out was a good thing. It certainly left them vulnerable. In all truth, he was excited to see what happened. What kind of change would Nath go through? Would it make him stronger? More savage? It seemed the more Nath changed, the less control he had, but dragons weren't impulsive creatures.

He should have more control than he had. If he gets any more powerful, he might not listen to any of us at all.

He looked up to the clouds. They were dark, and even though it hadn't rained, he hadn't seen much sunshine the past few days. Something didn't seem right with the world. Not at all.

Be as prepared as you can be. Wise as a dragon. Slick as a snake.

It wasn't an elven saying, but he liked it, wherever it came from.

"Bayzog," Ben said, riding up to him, "may I join you?"

Bayzog nodded.

"Why, certainly, Ben." Ben's typically loose and smiling face was drawn tight. "Is there something on your mind?"

Ben's eyes met Bayzog's and glanced away just before he said, "Evil."

Bayzog felt his tongue catch in his throat, but he didn't show surprise. There were very few things that rattled him, but this word coming from this young man did. He offered a simple smile.

"Do you want to discuss it, or were you making a confession of sorts?"

"Well, uh," Ben said. His long face turned a little red. "I just don't understand how…" He reached back and scratched his head. "Ah, never mind."

"No, no," Bayzog said, "It's a good topic, Ben. Well, in the sense that it's much better to talk about it than ignore it. You see, the way I understand it, evil doesn't want us to discuss how to deal with it."

Ben blinked his light-brown eyes, leaned forward in his saddle and said, "Go on, please."

"All right then." Bayzog cleared his throat and tapped his chest. It felt good to talk about something like this. "Ben, let me see if maybe I understand some of your thoughts, and remember I'm no sage, but I am part human, and at some point I was a young human like you. So it's possible … well, actually, I'm certain I've asked the same question. What is evil? What is good?" He eyed Ben. "Am I on the right track?"

"I think so."

"Maybe, just maybe, you are wondering how we know whether our actions are good or evil. Right?"

Ben nodded.

"And you want to be sure about that, don't you?"

"Absolutely."

"Ben, there is no easy way to explain it, but I offer this." Bayzog locked his violet eyes on Ben's. "There is evil in all of us."

Ben's eyes widened like saucers.

"Sounds really bad, doesn't it?" Bayzog said.

Ben blinked a few times. "Yes, but does that mean there is good in all of us as well?"

"Certainly." Bayzog grabbed his canteen, pulled off the top, and took a drink. He offered it to Ben.

The young man shook his head, and one of the horses nickered.

A stiff breeze came and blew hair into Bayzog's eyes. "But it's often buried deep beneath the surface, choking, you might say."

Ahead, he noticed large birds dipping in and out of the distant tree tops. The bright leaves on the trees started to bend, and lightning flashed behind them. The hairs on his arms rose.

There's that feeling again.

"It sounds more confusing than it should be," Ben said.

"There is a fine line between the two, but a good heart will warn you."

"How do you know which is which?" Ben asked. "There are so many things to consider. I mean, I'm good, aren't I?"

Bayzog chuckled.

"Of that I have no doubt. Don't let your mistakes confuse you, Ben. Or guilt either," Bayzog said. "Those are traps evil prepares for you. They can distract you or immobilize you. Doubt and worry are deadly."

"Oh," Ben said. "But …"

Bayzog interrupted.

"Listen, good wants you, all of us, to be free. Evil wants to enslave and control things. And when in doubt, ask yourself this: which is easier? Doing the right thing or the wrong thing?"

Ben looked up at his brows and rubbed his chin. A moment later he said, "I don't know."

"Well, you're a farmer, right?"

"I was a farmer. Now I'm a soldier." Ben's brows buckled. "Aw, I'm not even that anymore."

"Sorry, Ben, but let me continue. Is it easier to steal the food from the farmer or farm the food yourself?"

"Steal it, I guess, but nobody better steal my food." He shook his fist. "They'll get busted up for that."

"So stealing's evil, right?"

Ben sat up in his saddle and nodded his head.

"Right!"

"What about what happened with the Golden Ore in your village? Those brigands could have bought it or bartered for it, but instead they stole it. What do you call that?"

"Evil."

"Would you ever do that?"

"No," Ben said, shaking his head.

"Nor would I."

Ben cocked an eyebrow and said, "Huh, now that I think about it, it's always tougher to do the right thing than the wrong thing."

"Doing right builds character. That much is certain."

"But," Ben said, "do you think they know it's wrong?"

"At one time, maybe they did, but over time, evil debases the mind."

"Hmmm," Ben said, "are you worried that can happen to Dragon?"

Several horse lengths in front of them, Nath's big body was being towed through the tall grasses. His body was covered in cloth and his head was wrapped up in a cowl, still leaving his face and jaw exposed.

"I shudder to think such a thing, Ben. Nath's been nothing but good, but those scales … his moods … they seem to be gaining control of him. The catacombs of evil are deep, and it's easy to get lost if you go too far. Many never return. Guilt, worry, and power can consume you."

"This is bigger than just Dragon, isn't it?" Ben said. "But he has something to do with it."

The statement was a surprise, but Bayzog found relief in it. Ben had wisdom, and that could help them.

Still, Bayzog shrugged.

"What about wars and such things?" Ben asked. "How do we know when they are right or wrong?"

"We are allowed to defend ourselves, Ben. The important thing is that in the name of peace, we don't compromise with evil."

"Why?" Ben said. "What if it saves more people?"

Bayzog looked right at him.

"Evil always does bad things, Ben. It never moves closer to doing good. Trying to compromise with evil only moves you closer to doing bad."

"I guess so," Ben said.

They kept riding, and Ben finally drifted away. Bayzog figured he'd given him plenty to think about and even more for himself to consider.

What an interesting young man. The world could use more like him.

Still, Ben's questions plagued him more the farther they rode. Bayzog wasn't sure he'd made himself clear, but hopefully Ben had understood.

There were other examples he could have told, such as the stories of the elves and orcs. The Elvish strove to live by the highest standards, relishing peace, knowledge, art, and beauty. Orcish standards were deplorable: fighting and wallowing in filth for power. That was evil to see.

But what about the evil that wasn't so easy to see? Beautiful, cunning, and lethal. A beautiful flower whose leaves were poisoned. How did one prepare for that?

Ahead, Brenwar had stopped. Shifting in the saddle, the burly dwarf sniffed the air and combed his fingers through his beard.

Bayzog rode up to Brenwar's side, as did the others.

"Why are we stopping?" Sasha said. "Is that a bad storm ahead?"

"The storm isn't anything to worry about," Brenwar said in his gruff voice, "just water for the trees and the flowers. It's those birds." He pointed.

They were circling now, floating on their wings above the trees, but moving forward.

"Looks like vultures," Ben said. "Or other carrion eaters. I'd assume something's dead below. You aren't worried about birds, are you, Brenwar?"

Brenwar eyed Ben and then made a sound. His horse started forward.

"Are you ready for anything?" Brenwar unslung his war hammer from his shoulder. "Because anything is coming."

"What do you mean?" Sasha said.

Bayzog placed his hand over his brows and scanned the sky.

"Those aren't birds," he said, squinting. "Those are dragons."

CHAPTER
21

"Maybe they're good dragons," Ben said.

"Good dragons aren't so easily seen," Bayzog said. "Remember the last ones we saw at the crater? They scattered."

"Oh," Ben said.

Bayzog's heart pounded. Dragons were the most exciting things you'd ever see, but only because sighting them was a rare thing. Like watching a flower bloom. This was different. Dragons flying in plain sight and coming right at them. Reason for concern.

"Brenwar," he said, "Perhaps we should venture on another course. There's no rush, after all, is there?"

Brenwar grunted. "Perhaps." He tugged at the reins, taking a more westward direction. The dragons, less than a mile away, still headed right for them.

This is not good.

Sasha came along Bayzog's side. "I can't tell if they're dragons or birds. They're just specks to me. Are you certain they're dragons?"

"I am," Bayzog said, reaching over and grabbing her palm. "Stay close, Sasha, and have a spell prepared."

"What kind of spell? Don't I need to know what kind of dragons they are?"

Every dragon had a weakness. It might be an element such as water or fire. It could be a sound, loud or soft. Different metals and different magic. If you didn't have what you needed in a battle of mortal versus dragon, they'd rip you apart with their teeth and claws. In most cases, that was all they needed.

"I'm not sure. Not without a closer look. What do you think, Brenwar?"

"Yer eyes are better than mine, elf," Brenwar said, squinting, "Tell me what you see."

"Black wings and grey scales," he said, "and a smooth oval head. A little more color in the tail, a dark red."

"Oval head," Brenwar said, rubbing his beard. "Hmmm, what about the belly?"

"Dark grey, almost black, I'd say."

The dwarf made an ugly sound in his throat and pulled his horse to a stop. Brenwar had at least a few centuries on Bayzog, and he was certain the dwarf had had more dragon encounters than him by far. Bayzog also knew that Brenwar had been inside the Mountain of Doom, where he'd probably seen things an elf could only dream of.

"Those," Brenwar said, "if they are as you say, then they are grey scalers."

"Why do they call them that?" Ben said. "Because they have grey scales?"

"It doesn't matter why they call them that!" Brenwar huffed. "What matters is what happens if they come after us." Brenwar eyed their surroundings.

The mountains were still distant. The closest forest was miles away. For now, it was just them, the dragons, and the plains.

"Do you know how to handle grey scalers?" Sasha said to Bayzog.

He shook his head.

All this time with Nath, and I've never bothered to ask him about all the different dragons. You always think you have more time than you have. What a fool I've been.

"Whatever you've got, wizard, get it ready!" Brenwar hopped off his horse and slung his trunk on the ground. "Sorceress, see what you can find in there." He fumbled with Nath's wrappings and pulled out the bow and quiver. "You know how to use this?" he said to Ben.

Ben nodded his head.

Brenwar tossed it to him. "Load it up, then. And use the moorite." He started to walk away and stopped. "And aim for the belly when they ain't looking. And don't fire until I tell you."

"How powerful are those things?" Sasha said.

"Just pretend they're big scaly dogs with wings." He winked at her. "A few good licks and we might scare them off." He looked up at Ben. "Get off that horse, will you? And kneel down in the weeds. They come!"

CHAPTER
22

S NAP. CLATCH. SNAP.

A circle of dragons, wings beating, screeching a terror, was coming right at them.

Ben wanted to plug his ears. Instead he took aim, but his arms were shaking.

"Don't shoot, boy!" Brenwar growled from somewhere near.

Ben didn't take his eyes off the dragons.

They flew in a ring, stretching their long necks and screeching down. Their talons clutched in and out and clicked and clacked. Their jaws snapped in the air, and their tails rattled.

Ben swallowed hard, closed one eye, and took aim. "You can do this, Ben," he muttered to himself. "Be brave. Not foolish."

A grey scale swooped down and snapped at Brenwar.

The dwarf swung and missed.

Another dragon came, snapped, and darted back into the ring.

"Keep coming, you ugly birds," Brenwar said, waving his hammer. "I'll show you!"

A grey scaler dove straight at Ben.

He hunkered down.

It clipped his helmet with its claws, screeched, and flew away.

Ben rose back to his feet with his heart pounding in between his ears. He couldn't breathe.

One by one, the dragons dove, dipped, and snapped, like eagles snatching at fish in the river.

Ben heard Sasha scream. He whirled.

A dragon stood on its hind legs, facing her and snapping.

Brenwar charged it.

Twang!

When the first arrow embedded itself in the dragon's chest, the dragon screeched an awful sound and twisted in the grass.

"I got him!" Ben pumped his fist in the air and raised his knee.

"Quit talking and start reloading," Brenwar said. "Now they're all coming!"

Ben nocked another arrow and aimed at a diving dragon.

Twang!

It dipped under the arrow and barreled straight into his chest, driving him into the dirt.

"Get off me!" Ben yelled.

The dragon pinned him to the ground, biting and clawing at him. He felt his skin start to burn. It was like a big dog with a long neck. Strong and fierce. It bit Ben's leg.

He screamed.

"Let 'em have it," Brenwar yelled. "All of them!"

A missile of blue light blasted through the wings of the dragon on top of Ben.

It shrieked and darted away.

Nearby, Bayzog's hands were bright with energy, sending one missile after the next.

Ben slipped an arrow from his quiver and nocked it. Kneeled and searched the sky. His heart was racing. His breath was lost.

Dragons streaked through the sky from all directions, swooping, circling, and diving.

"They're too fast!"

Twang!

The arrow sailed. The dragon rolled from its path and darted straight for him.

"Ben, look out!"

Brenwar swung his war hammer. Bayzog fired his missiles.

Too late.

A dragon swooped behind Ben and knocked him to the ground, making Akron fall from his grasp.

He looked up in time to see a dragon wrap its talons around it. "No you don't!" Ben jumped on his bow.

The dragon's claws tore into his arm.

"Argh!"

The pain was blinding. Ben held on. He was bigger than the dragon by at least a hundred pounds, but the smaller creature was stronger than him.

Swap!

The dragon's tail cracked him across the face.

Akron fell from his fingers. He hit the ground. There was blood in his eyes. Dizzy, he stumbled forward, chasing after the dragon.

It hissed and took flight with Akron gripped in its talons.

"Dragon's going to kill me," Ben said, dropping to his knees.

A bolt of light flashed over his head.

Ssssram!

The dragon exploded in the sky and spiraled to the ground. Akron dropped to earth as well.

"Hurry, Ben!" Sasha said.

She was right behind him with her hands smoking.

He ran over, snatched up the bow, nocked an arrow, and pulled the string back.

"There!" Sasha pointed.

Two grey scalers flanked Bayzog. The wizard had a long mystic shield up that only protected one side.

Twang! Twack!

The arrow struck the pressing grey scaler on its back between the wings. It fell to the ground and died.

"Look!" Brenwar yelled. "They flee!"

Less than a dozen of them took to the air, screeching and roaring, and disappeared.

Bayzog's shield winked out, and he jogged over to Sasha, who was dusting off her smoking hands. "Are you all right?" Bayzog said.

She swallowed hard. "Just a little faint, but I think I'm all right."

"You made that dragon explode!" Ben said. "Into pieces! How did you do that?"

"Yes," Bayzog said, "how did you do that? It was certainly impressive."

"I drank from this," she said. She held a sparkling vial that looked like lighting lived in it. "It was in Brenwar's chest."

Bayzog leaned over and kissed her forehead.

"Excellent choice. I think you saved us."

Brenwar walked over with a dragon in his arms. An arrow jutted from its back. "It was a good shot," Brenwar said.

Ben reached over and touched it. The creature didn't seem so deadly anymore. He wondered if Dragon would be upset.

"Well, what are you waiting for?" Brenwar said.

"What do you mean?" Ben said.

"Take the arrow out of it, boy! Great Guzan! It's moorite. Do I have to do it for you?"

"Uh ..."

Brenwar set the dragon down at his feet. "Whenever yer ready."

Ben stroked his neck and said to Bayzog, "Do you think it's evil? Maybe this was one that Dragon would have saved?"

Bayzog furrowed his eyebrows at Ben. "Do you think it would have killed us?"

"Ah," Ben said. "I see." Ben pulled the arrow free, cleaned it on the grass, and slid it back into his quiver. "Do we just leave them? Won't the dragon skin be worth something?"

"Ben!" Sasha said. "What would Nath say if he heard you say that?"

"He wouldn't say anything," Ben said, grinning. "He'd just knock me out."

They laughed.

"Ben, chances are the dragons will come back for their own. I don't think any poachers will get them." Bayzog stretched out his fingers and ran them over the dragon scales and wings. "They are such magnificent creatures. It's hard to believe they can be evil."

"Get yer heads down!" Brenwar yelled.

Zip!

Something hit Bayzog and spun him to the ground.

"Bayzog!" Sasha yelled. A hail of arrows followed.

Zip! Zip! Zip! Zip! Zip!

Beads of energy showered everyone in a hail that came from the distance. Everyone was cut and scraped up already, but these magic missiles took things to another level.

"Get us some cover, wizards!" Brenwar yelled. "Return fire, boy!"

"Where?" Ben said.

Brenwar pointed toward the mountains where the light was flashing.

"That way!"

Ben unslung an exploding arrow, nocked it, and let it loose. It sailed through the sky in what seemed to take an age then disappeared into the ground.

Brenwar stormed back at Ben and said, "You got to be a dragon to fire those! Gimme that!" He spun Ben around, snatched another exploding arrow, stuck the tip in the grey scale's wet mouth, and handed it to Ben. The arrow tip glowed like fire.

"Stop staring and shoot it!"

Ben let the shaft fly.

A bright flash of light and the sound of an explosion followed.

Zip! Zip! Zip! Zip!

A green wave of missiles ripped into them. The sound of a thunderclap followed. A bolt streaked down from the sky and knocked Brenwar clear out of his boots.

Head ringing, bones aching, Ben crawled up on his knees.

"Brenwar! Bayzog!"

He couldn't hear himself yell. One of their horses darted by him, knocking him back down. Smoke was everywhere. When he looked up again, he was at the center of a circle of spears. They were held by lizard men.

CHAPTER
23

"**C**IRCLE NATH!**" BRENWAR ORDERED ABOVE** the commotion. He stood tall for a dwarf, waving his war hammer back and forth. "Wizards, what are you doing?"

"Can you move?" Sasha said to Bayzog.

"I'm all right," he said, taking her hand. "It's you I'm worried about. Just get us over to Brenwar." He got up, wincing and clutching his side. His robes had burning holes in them. Whatever had attacked them had rocked them, and he wasn't sure where he was. There was smoke everywhere, and it burned his eyes. "Brenwar?"

"Get over here, wizards," Brenwar said. "Hurry!"

They stumbled through the smoke and almost ran right into Brenwar.

"Where's Ben?" Sasha said. "Ben!"

Bayzog didn't know who had hit them, but he could feel their energy now. It was dark and powerful. It had hurt him. Rattled him. He fine-tuned his thoughts and found something.

"They're not after us," he said. "They're after Nath."

"Who's after Nath?" Brenwar said.

An unnatural breeze started, bowing the grass and pushing away the smoke. The horse Nath's stretcher was harnessed to nickered and whined. The smoke cleared, and Sasha gasped.

They were surrounded.

A group of lizard men had Ben pinned down.

"I'll be," Brenwar said.

There were men in robes with rings on their bald heads, well over a dozen lizard men, and some with grey scalers on leashes. Two satyrs—one male, one female—stood with their arms crossed over their chests in front of a really big man wearing a metal bull head.

Bayzog felt Sasha wrap her arm around him and squeeze him tight.

Their attackers weren't here to bargain. They were here to take.

"What do you want?" Brenwar said. "And make it quick. I've got things to do."

No one said a thing. Instead they all stood ready, glowering. Ben struggled in his bonds and tried to say something, but he was gagged. A lizard man held Akron. Something snorted behind them. They all jumped around.

"Where in Narnum did you come from?" Brenwar said with wide eyes.

The dwarf looked startled, and Sasha was distraught.

A tiny woman sat atop a wingless bronze dragon with a long, black tail. She was pretty, with a long strand of white hair flowing from her head. The rest of her head was tattooed like Kryzak's. Her dark robes were sleeveless, and she had a gentle demeanor about her, but her bright eyes were penetrating and evil.

She leaned forward on the horn of her saddle. "I'll make this simple for you, dwarf. I am here for Nath Dragon. Stay out of my way, you live. Get in my way, you die. Do you understand that, bearded one?"

Brenwar huffed. "So it's just me that dies and not the rest of us." He rubbed his bearded chin. "I'll have to think about that."

"A witty dwarf," she said as her pleasant voice turned to venom. "Or a stupid one. Any fool would know I'm referring to all of you."

"Ah," Brenwar said, "so if we fight, we die. Hmmm. But did you think to consider that when we fight, you will die?"

"Hahahahaha," she said. "I assure you there in no chance of that. But if you care to try, I'll see to it your young friend over there will be the first to die." Her eyes drifted to Ben.

Bayzog's mind raced to assess the situation while Brenwar delayed. The woman would be ready for anything thrown at her. He was certain of that. Just moments ago, she had appeared from nowhere, and he could only assume she'd just as easily disappear. He wondered if that was her power or the dragon's. That left all the rest of their aggressors.

What can I do that wouldn't endanger Ben?

He had some spells ready, but what help—if any—would they offer?

"Can I have a moment to think about it?" Brenwar said.

"I don't think there is much to think about, but why not?" the young woman said. "A moment, then, but not a dwarven one. When I say it's done, it's done."

I hope Sasha remembers this.

He squeezed a series of signals into Sasha's arm, which was still hooked to his. She squeezed back!

Good.

"My, you are a pretty lady," the young woman said. "What is your name?"

Sasha released his arm and stepped forward. "Sasha, and what is yours?"

"I am Marlay," she said, flipping her white hair back over her shoulder. "And I must admit I admire that hair of yours. It would be a shame to lose it, wouldn't it?"

"You seem to be doing well without it."

Bayzog grabbed her arm and pulled her back, whispering, "Sasha, please."

"You have a spirited woman, part-elf. It would be a shame to watch her die, wouldn't it?"

"Certainly," Bayzog said, locking eyes with Marlay. She seemed young but powerful. Harmless yet deadly.

Careful, Bayzog.

Marlay made a short smile. "Talk some sense into your friend the dwarf," she said, stroking her dragon mount's horns. "I've a feeling he's about to get all of you killed." She made a clicking sound, and the bronze dragon opened its mouth. Its breath was repulsive and sour.

Bayzog covered his nose.

Sasha's knees buckled.

Marlay's dragon mount raked a hunk of ground out with its claws.

"My dragon hungers, and I don't think you want to see this pretty woman devoured, do you?"

"A parlay, perhaps?" Bayzog said. *Delay. Delay. Delay.*

"There's nothing to parlay about," Brenwar said. "We don't parlay with this brood!"

Marlay leaned back in the saddle and folded her arms over her chest.

"Interesting, wizard, but my patience thins. I've no need to parlay." She pursed her dark lips before she spoke more. "Look around you. Dragons, acolytes, and lizard men—not to mention my finest warrior, Kang. And those satyrs are something. Now, I know you've survived Kryzak—well, most of you—but you won't survive me. Walk away and you live. Stay and we will destroy you one piece at a time."

It was a moment. One that splintered Bayzog in two. His elven side would never give in to evil, but his human side was unpredictable. Half of him wanted to run and the other half wanted to fight, but there was so much to consider. Sasha was in danger. Nath was too. His gut told him if they lost Nath, they'd lose everything. Sasha squeezed his arm again.

Bayzog stepped back and gestured toward the lizard men who held Ben.

"Show some good faith, Marlay," he said, "and let loose our friend. There is nowhere for him to go."

She nodded.

The lizard men cut Ben's bonds and shoved him forward. Ben fell to his knees, got up, and ripped out his gag.

"Akron," Ben said to Marlay, looking at the bow. "I need Akron."

"Oh," she said, smiling a little, "about that. I can't have you leaving with your weapons, or your horses, for that matter. I'll need just about everything you have on you. After all, I have to pay my henchmen and make offerings to the temple."

"What?" Ben said, stepping forward.

Bayzog grabbed his arm.

"What is your life worth, young man?" she said. Her voice became louder and her eyes flickered with lightning. "Now, drop everything. We'll start with you, dwarf."

Brenwar, stalwart as a tree stump, didn't blink. He just stood there with his hammer crossed behind his arms, eyeing her.

"It's a well-crafted war hammer, dwarf. Perhaps it has a name?" she said.

"Aye," Brenwar said, "it has a name."

"And what might that be? My warrior Kang is in need of a new scepter, and I think that one will do."

Brenwar tilted his head in the direction of Kang and snorted.

"I call my weapon war hammer." He held it out with his arm. "And if he wants it, let him come and get it."

"There's no need for that," Marlay said. "Just drop it."

"So be it, then." He lowered the war hammer down to the ground and set it down, head down, shaft up. His chin dipped into his chest.

Marlay cocked her head and narrowed her eyes. "I'm surprised. Now the rest of you."

"Bayzog? Brenwar? Are we really doing this?" Ben said, exasperated. "Is this a *compromise*?"

"What choice is there?" Bayzog said, loosening his robes. "It's this or death."

"What about Nath?" Ben said. His voice and eyes were filled with confusion.

"Mrrrruh...Muh...Muh...Mrruh...Muh...Muh," Brenwar muttered under his beard.

"What is that you say, dwarf?" Marlay said. She snapped her fingers. All her servants started forward. "I can't hear you."

"It's dwarven," Brenwar said, lifting his head, "for 'war hammer.' In Dwarven it's pronounced 'mrrrummaah.'"

"Interesting," Marlay said, "and does that mean something?"

"Aye," Brenwar almost smiled, "in Dwarven it means 'war hammer.' We covered that already."

"I don't believe you, but if you say so."

"Mrrummaah!" Brenwar said. He looked at Kang, who was coming closer. "Don't forget it. Mrrummaah!"

Kang walked over in front of Brenwar and set his scepter down. He bent over and picked up the war hammer and tested its heft. The thick muscles in his forearms rippled with effort. He turned and nodded his bull head at Marlay.

She nodded.

Then Kang looked at Brenwar and said, Mrrummaah."

In a flash, Kang twisted his hips, raised his huge arms, and brought the hammer down.

Marlay shouted, "No!"

CHAPTER 24

A FLINCH SAVED THE BRONZE DRAGON'S skull from cracking like an egg. Kang's blow landed right between its eyes. The beast let out a roar so awful, Bayzog's knees buckled.

It was Marlay that screamed. Heaved from atop the dragon's back, she crashed to the ground and disappeared in the confusion.

Where did she go?

Bayzog set his first spell loose.

A circle of bright white and yellow light launched from his arm into the air, where it hung high above them. Its glow was mighty and blinding.

The lizard men cringed, dropped everything, and fled.

The grey scalers ripped their leashes and flew away.

The satyrs disappeared in the grasses.

The acolytes fled, tripping over their robes.

The wounded dragon quickly backed off, snapping its maw.

Bang! Bang! Bang!

Kang kept hitting himself in the head with the hammer until Brenwar crawled up his body and ripped it free. The stunned man fell to his knees.

"Lay hands on my hammer, will you!"

Bang!

The bull helmet clanged off the man's face. Kang wavered on his knees, still taller than Brenwar, eyes blinking slowly.

"Huh…" Kang managed to say.

Brenwar brought a right cross through Kang's jaw, knocking him over. "That'll teach you!" Brenwar said. He shifted back and forth on his feet, eyeing his enemies. "Wizard, what is the plan?"

Bayzog held his arms up with outstretched hands, face straining. "I can ward off evil with this, but not for long. A few minutes at best." Sweat dripped into his eyes and over his face. "Sasha, see what you can find in Brenwar's chest. Find anything that can get us out of here."

Ben appeared at his side with Akron ready in his hands.

"Should I start shooting?" Ben said.

"Just hold," Bayzog said. "Save those arrows for when we really need them!"

All of their enemies had covered their eyes and scurried away to a certain point and then turned—hooting and gloating—little more than a couple dozen yards outside the circle. Once the spell faded, there would be an all-out battle.

"Again, what's the plan?" Brenwar said, guarding Nath.

"Perhaps you should come up with one," Bayzog said, irritated. "I thought dwarves were masterful planners."

"We are when it comes to everything else but this magic stuff. Whisk us out of here or something."

"Easier said than done. Sasha, have you come up with anything?"

Sasha rummaged through Brenwar's chest, shaking her head. "No!"

Bayzog ground his teeth. There were the four of them to move, plus Nath, not to mention the horses—and they had nowhere to go. He had his own spells, but that wouldn't be enough, not to hold the horde that surrounded them.

At least one enemy was down, thanks to Brenwar.

"Perhaps you and I should take on Marlay and the dragon," Bayzog said. "Ben and Sasha will have to handle the rest."

Marlay reappeared alongside the bronze dragon, laughing.

"Hahahahaha! Such fools you are," she said. Her voice was taunting and exaggerated. "Now you all will die, but perhaps I'll let that woman of yours live, wizard. Hah-ha. I might just convert her to an acolyte of Barnabus yet."

"No such thing will ever happen!" Bayzog said. "And lives will be lost on your end. Certainly yours!"

"Aye!" Brenwar said. "There be no mercy on the likes of you, woman!"

Bayzog wondered if Brenwar meant that. Protecting women was one thing, but fighting them was quite another. The situation was new to him. Marlay seemed young, but more than formidable. The tattoos on her head were many, more than Kryzak had had, which meant she wielded greater power. And that bothered him. Bayzog was far more than some adept of magic, but he wasn't a magic user of the highest levels, either. His powers were limited, but he couldn't let on about that.

Standing on the ground, Marlay patted the head of her dragon. The beast's tongue licked in and out of its mouth, and it chomped in the direction of Brenwar. It could easily swallow the dwarf in a single bite.

"My pet will make a fine meal of you," she said to Brenwar, "and all the rest of you as well."

The dragon's great tail swept back and forth, flattening the grass.

Bayzog didn't figure that even all four of them could take the beast if they tried.

He reached behind Ben and pulled an arrow from the quiver. The tip sparkled in the light. It was moorite.

"What do you want me to do?" Ben said. Despite his age, the young man seemed confident.

Above, the halo of the ward against evil wavered, its bright light winking in and out.

The hisses of the lizard men became louder.

Bayzog's concentration was strong, but his strength was fading. He motioned for Sasha. "Well?" he said.

"I cast a summons," she said, wiping his forehead. "But I've no idea what will come, if anything, or if it will offer assistance."

Bayzog wanted to roll his eyes. Summoning spells took time and weren't very effective. But Sasha liked them. The last time she'd cast one, a herd of deer had come, and some horned rabbits. "All right, then," he said with his voice quavering. He was sweating.

Sasha said, "You need assistance. Let me lend my strength to yours."

"No," he said. "Take Ben and do as I say." Bayzog whispered quickly in her ear.

Sasha said, "Come, Ben."

Marlay came closer, eyeing the halo of light. Her eyes and hands began to charge with a dark, mystic, purple power. An evil smile formed on her lips.

Beside her, the dragon's claws ripped up the dirt, and its tail swished back and forth faster.

"This is it," Brenwar said. "What is the plan?"

"You know the plan."

"Aye."

CHAPTER
25

"**W**HAT IS THIS?" BEN SAID, standing over the chest.

"Just hand me those arrows," Sasha said.

One by one, Sasha coated the arrow tips with dark green liquid from a potion vial. The metal sucked it up and turned a little green.

"What will that do?" Ben said.

She shrugged. "Maybe something, maybe nothing. It's an experiment." She whispered the plan in his ear, finishing with "Good luck, Ben."

Ben returned to Bayzog's side and faced the lizard men with his bow and arrows ready. Sasha came, too, and now they all stood in a half circle around Nath.

"On my signal," Bayzog said under his breath. "In only a few moments, the ward will go."

The halo of light winked in and out.

Bayzog wiped the sweat from his brow and eyes. *Here goes.* "Now," he whispered.

Brenwar charged at Marlay.

Sasha fanned out her fingers and shot forth streaks of light at the dragon, striking its eyes.

Bayzog held the halo of light a split second longer.

The lizard men and acolytes came at them from the back.

Ben turned toward the dragon and fired his first arrow.

Thwack!

The arrow struck the dragon in its hindquarters, drawing a roar.

Brenwar swung his war hammer into Marlay's shield, rocking her back.

A split second later, she blasted him full in the chest with a handful of energy. He fell to the ground.

The dragon lowered its horns and barreled toward them.

Ben fired another arrow.

Thwack!

A dozen yards away, the dragon levitated. Up and up it went, claws ripping at the air. It let out a confused and angry roar.

"Did I do that?" Ben said, incredulous.

"Yes!" Sasha said, "With a little help from a potion. But I don't think it will last long."

Bayzog gathered his thoughts and cast at Marlay.

The woman stood over Brenwar, slamming bolts of energy into him one at a time.

Bayzog's arc of light slammed into her, driving her back.

Brenwar popped up and charged again.

All over the field of battle, the rest of their enemies were coming. If there was ever a time they needed Nath, it was now, but Nath lay still as a corpse on the stretcher.

Ben fired another arrow at Marlay. It sailed high.

"Blast!" Ben said, whipping out another.

"Ben, watch out!"

Two lizard men slammed him into the ground.

The acolytes formed a ring around them, wielding their flails and maces.

Bayzog pulled Sasha to him, unable to hide the disappointment in his face. "I'm sorry," he said.

"It's all right," she said. "You tried."

Bayzog's plan had been simple: bring down Marlay in one swift strike. With the leader down, chances were the others would flee.

He looked up.

The bronze dragon still drifted, a lone speck high in the sky, floating like a cloud. Its distant roars could still be heard, and when the spell faded and the creature landed, no doubt it would come back to devour them. Perhaps it would be better if they were killed first.

I should have been better prepared.

The lizard men prodded them forward and pushed them all to their knees before Marlay. The small woman stood with her boot on Brenwar's chest. Mystic bindings corded the grizzled dwarf's arms and legs. There was even one around his mouth.

He still squirmed and struggled.

"Clever," Marlay said, "very clever, part-elf. You almost pulled something off here, but what it was I don't know." She checked her bright blue fingernails. "Ah, you at least managed to chip one of my nails. Of course, the penalty is death for that."

"What are you going to do with Nath Dragon?" Bayzog said. "I'd be curious to know before I die."

"Ah, well, if you must know, he'll come with us to the Great Temple of Barnabus. Selene, the High Priestess, will be the one to decide his fate."

Bayzog had a name at least and a location. If they survived somehow, they'd at least know who to look for, and where.

"I see," he said, head downcast.

Marlay turned, started to walk away, and said, "Grab Nath Dragon and," she looked back at Bayzog, "bring the woman along."

"No!" Bayzog said, holding onto Sasha.

A lizard man ripped her out of his arms, picked her up, and slung her over its shoulder.

"Let go of me!"

Something struck Bayzog hard in the head, and he fell onto his face, seeing spots and blood. He rolled over onto his back and stretched out for Sasha, who was being hauled off.

A dark blot dashed over the sky.

"What was that?" Ben said, looking over at him.

"Ayyyyieeeeee!" someone screamed.

"Great Guzan!" Ben said. "Is that what I think I'm seeing?"

A great winged ape swooped out of the sky and snatched Marlay off the ground. He was holding her by her long, white ponytail.

"Sansla Libor!" Bayzog exclaimed.

Everyone—man, elf, dwarf, and monster—stopped and watched.

High in the sky, energy crackled from Marlay's fingers. Tendrils of energy dug under the great winged ape's fur.

Sansla held on, his ape face in agony. Higher and higher he soared.

Marlay's face was filled with rage. Her screams shattered the air.

There was a bright light and an explosion. The two plummeted hard to the ground.

A long moment of silence followed.

Please be dead, Bayzog thought.

His heart stopped when the small, lithe form rose in the tall grass and staggered forward. There was a scowl on her lips, and her eyes locked on Bayzog. He could read her lips.

"I broke another nail. You'll pay for this."

The acolytes ran to her aid.

Sansla Libor's large form rose high above the grasses. He roared and beat his chest with his great fists.

Marlay whirled around, screaming, "Noooooo!"

A blast of energy slammed into Sansla's chest.

He snarled.

Marlay blasted him again.

He charged right through the next blast. A second later, he had the tiny woman in his great clutches.

"Let go of me, you beast!" she yelled. "Let go of me—"

Crack!

Marlay's life ended, and the acolytes froze until Sansla tossed her body aside like a doll.

Then they bolted away, afraid of him.

Sansla bounded right after them. He caught one in one hand and one in the other and smashed them together.

Bayzog cheered.

A lizard man shoved him into the ground.

"Ahem," another voice said, "lizard face."

Krang! Krang!

Brenwar knocked them down one right after the other. "Get off of my wizard!" The dwarf stretched out his hand and lifted Bayzog to his feet.

"Sasha!"

The lizard man whisked her away.

Sasha grabbed its back and yelled something.

Zzzzzrt!

The lizard man lurched, stiffened, and teetered to the ground.

Sasha dusted the energy from her fingertips.

Bayzog ran up to her and caught her hands in his. "Are you all right?" he said.

"I'm woozy, but I'm well enough. How are you?"

Bayzog looked around. Brenwar had the lizard men on the run, and Sansla Libor was tossing acolytes around like dolls. The winged ape was fearsome.

After all evil had fled or died, Sansla stopped in front of the pair of them, nostrils flared, chest heaving. Sounding more ape than elf, he spoke to Sasha.

"I heard your summons. Strange, but I could not ignore." His dark face jerked a little. "Such desperation. Such evil. Grrrr. You ... must ... go." He turned his big frame around and glanced at Nath. "He lives?"

"Yes," Bayzog said, "And we're taking him to a safer place until he wakes."

Sansla moved away from them and pointed. "The bronze dragon comes." He looked back at Bayzog. "Get on your horses. I'll slow him down."

There was a terrible roar far away from them. It seemed the Potion of Floating had worn off, and now the bronze dragon stormed their way.

"On the horses, everyone!"

"What about Nath? We can't gallop with him behind us," Brenwar said.

"I can help," Sasha said. She slipped a vial out of her robes and held it out. "This is what is left from the Potion of Floating." She dabbed some on Nath and the stretcher and rubbed it in. "This should last a bit."

"Ben!"

The tall country boy lumbered over, shoulder sagging. He grabbed the reins of his horse and stuffed his boot into the stirrup.

"Let's get out of here," he said, exhausted.

Everyone mounted up, and Brenwar eyed the stretcher behind him.

"Well?"

"It'll work! Just start moving," Sasha said.

They started at a trot, and gradually the stretcher lifted Nath from the ground. Bayzog looked back at Sansla Libor.

The big ape waved his huge arm. A second later, they were galloping away until the battlefield was long out of their sight.

"Sasha," Bayzog said with his hair whipping in his face. "You did well. Your summons spell, I believe—I know—saved us all."

She smiled. "I told you it was a great spell."

CHAPTER
26

THEY MADE IT AS FAR as the first run of forested hills and found shelter in the rocks. It was evening, and the rain had come in a downpour. Over the rocks, Brenwar and Ben stretched a canopy that kept them dry. It wasn't an ordinary canopy, either, but something Brenwar had kept rolled up on his saddle. Another treasure from Dragon Home.

"It'll keep you dry and warm, even cool during the hot seasons and such," Brenwar grumbled, wringing out his beard. "Made for man, not dwarf. The harsh elements are a dwarf's best friend. Well, that and ale."

"I'm thankful, Brenwar," Bayzog said. He cast a quick spell that made a small pile of rocks begin to glow red hot.

Sasha was dripping wet. She shivered and said, "Yes, many thanks."

"Me too," Ben said, nodding.

The ground dried out quickly, thanks to Bayzog's magic fire. As soon as it did, he sat down and leaned back against one of the warm rocks nearby.

Sasha sat next to Bayzog and leaned against his shoulder.

"That was a close one," Brenwar said. "You did well, all of you. I believe our friend Nath would be proud."

"It was close, all right," Bayzog said, "but my concerns are far from over, Brenwar."

Brenwar grunted.

"They knew Nath was down and they wanted him this time. They sent a small army after him." He shook his head. "They'll still be coming after him. Wherever he goes, war will follow."

"He'll be safe in Morgdon," Brenwar said.

"But will Morgdon be safe from him?"

No one said anything, but at least Brenwar was thinking.

At the moment, there was peace in Nalzambor. No major wars were stirring. According to Laedorn and the elves, the orcs had started to press, and the atmosphere of the world was getting prickly. And now it seemed that the evil forces at work wanted Nath Dragon—alive, not dead.

Bayzog could imagine why: to spark the next Great Dragon War. He feared that Nath would be the prize of that war.

"They want to turn him, I fear," Bayzog said. "We can't let them have him. We don't need to risk an all-out war, either, and you know as well as I do, Brenwar, that the dwarves require little provocation. Our enemies are counting on that."

Brenwar huffed. "The dwarves won't overreact, and I assure you that he…" he pointed at Nath "…and the rest of us will be plenty safe in Morgdon. We have plenty of places to hide him."

"Didn't you lose him the last time?" Bayzog said.

"No! Don't you worry. He's asleep now. He was plenty awake the last time." He pointed at Bayzog. "We'll keep a close eye on him."

Bayzog closed his eyes and rested his cheek on Sasha's head. She was sound asleep. Across from him, Ben was yawning and stretching out his long arms. Inside himself, Bayzog's human side felt a thousand years old.

Close calls with death will do that to you, I suppose.

Bayzog missed his home in the City of Quintuklen, the perfect sanctuary for study, rest, and quality time with Sasha. She'd turned his dull lab of magic into a home, and her good spirits kept him entertained. Now, for reasons he didn't entirely understand himself, he sat in the harsh elements where the word "relax" had no meaning.

He stroked Sasha's soft hair as her chest rose and fell gently on his. He felt guilty she was here, but she wouldn't want to be anywhere else in the world. She'd made that clear.

That's what people who love each other do. They stick together.

It was one of those things he'd learned to understand in his experience with the conflict between good and evil.

Love grows. Evil destroys.

His eyes drifted over to Nath, who lay still as a corpse. Without saying so, they'd all pledged to protect their friend from one end of Nalzambor to the other. And they probably weren't going to get much help, so they'd better take what they could get.

"To Morgdon on the morrow, then," he said to Brenwar and closed his eyes. A moment later he slept.

Brenwar, eyes alert, huddled over Nath's deep-sleeping form and brushed the hair from his face. "We're going to get you back to Dragon Home one day. I swear it."

Nearby, two horned forms huddled over the rocks with their necks craned: Finlin and

Faylan, the satyrs. She tugged on his shoulder and led him away, their hooved feet gently passing over the rocks.

"Morgdon, pah," she spat, "I hate the dwarves and their city. I wish a gargantuan sinkhole would swallow it up."

Finlin giggled.

She smacked him across the face.

Whap!

"Now is not the time for laughter. Now is the time to plan."

"Who do we tell?" he said. "Marlay is dead, and all of her followers have died or fled. Do you suppose that we can snatch the dragon man on our own? The reward would be great, would it not?"

She gored him in the head with her horns.

"Ow!" he said. "Stop that, will you?"

"Ow? Don't be such a fawnee boy, Finlin. You need to get tougher." She pushed past his shoulder and down the rocky slope. "I'll take the message to the clerics. You follow the dragon man. Be sure to leave a trail—and don't use your pipes unless you absolutely have to."

"As you say, as you say."

Whap!

"Ow!" Finlin said, rubbing his cheek. "Stop doing that."

She glowered at him.

Whap!

He started to speak but bit his tongue. He glowered back at her.

"That's better," she said.

CHAPTER 27

"**M**ORGDON!" SELENE SLAMMED HER FIST onto the arm of her throne. "Gorn Grattack will not be pleased!" She grabbed her golden goblet and slung it across the room. Not an acolyte or a lizard man moved. The draykis remained tall, still, and silent near her sides.

At the foot of the dais, the satyr woman, Faylan, kept her eyes and horns down.

Selene's tail slid over the marble floor, hooked around Faylan's leg, and dangled her upside down. "I am not pleased with this news, little fawn. How did this happen?"

Faylan crossed her arms over her chest and said, without trembling, "The winged ape showed up and ripped your servants apart. All the acolytes and lizard men dropped like bleeding stones after that. Your lone remaining dragon, the bronze one, was negated. That winged ape diverted its path, but me and Finlin followed them all the way to the rocky cliffs of Morgdon."

Selene looked into the steely eyes of the satyr, trying to decide whether or not she should rip them out. The evil goat-legged woman was brassy, borderline sassy, and maybe a bit too much to swallow. However, Selene needed her for now, which bothered her. And the fact that Faylan knew it bothered her even more. But the satyrs had at least survived, and they were excellent spies. She dropped Faylan on her horned head.

"Morgdon, Morgdon, Morgdon," Selene hissed more than said. "I hate dwarves, so stalwart and strong. It will take an army to pry him loose from there."

Faylan backed away.

Selene smote Faylan with her tail and sent her spinning across the floor.

The satyr woman didn't move. Still as a possum.

"What to do," Selene said under her breath. "What to do."

Nath Dragon was in a deep sleep. Gorn Grattack had talked to her about that. Her lord had told her to seize the opportunity. Nath might sleep for weeks, months, or even years. And it would be easier to turn him when he wasn't fighting against them. But even with Nath Dragon down and sleeping, his friends had foiled her plans and even killed her most precious servant, Marlay. That was what angered her most of all.

She resumed her seat on the throne, and her drulture landed on the arm. She stroked its head and long neck. "Have you ever eaten a satyr before?"

The colorful drulture flashed its teeth in the direction of Faylan, stretched its neck, and hissed.

"Too big?" Selene said. "I could always feed you a piece at a time."

Faylan clenched where she lay.

Selene sighed.

She wanted to avenge Marlay. She had adored the dedicated and adorably evil woman who now was gone. Killed by a cursed elf, of all things. An elven monster, Sansla Libor, the Roamer King. Someone was going to pay for that. Pay dearly.

"Hmmm," she said, twisting her hand in her robes, "every dwarf, elf and good human that gets in my way is going to pay. And those dwarves will wish they'd never taken Nath Dragon in at Morgdon. Every village and every town within leagues of their mountains will cry for mercy. Because I'm going to ruin them."

She stood up and stepped down from the dais with fists at her sides. "We'll burn their crops! Ransack their homes! Soil their fertile land with innocent blood! They'll have to turn him over to me. That will be my ransom for peace!"

She straightened her robes down over her excellent figure.

"Get up, goat woman. I'm not finished using you yet."

CHAPTER 28

"Ugh," Nath said. "My head's killing me."

Slowly he sat up, squinting his eyes. The light was dim, blurry, and wavering, but it felt like he was waking up to the dawn's bright light. Something covered his mouth and face. It was sticky. A thin layer of webbing. He peeled it away, swung his legs over the edge of the slab of stone he sat on, and rubbed his aching eyes.

"I have a bad feeling about this," he said. Opening his eyes for what seemed like the very first time, Nath Dragon took in a sharp breath. "Where am I?"

He sat on a slab of granite like an altar, big enough to hold three men. The room was an octagon, with a lone candelabrum flickering above. It was sparse, but the stonework was magnificent. Round columns were carved from the stone, and the floor was tiled in patterns he did not know. It made him think of the tomb in the Shale Hills where he and Brenwar had confronted the steel dragon with the Thunderstone.

He slid off the slab and began walking around. He wobbled and stumbled.

"Guzan," he said, grimacing, "my legs are leaden."

The chamber was big enough to hold a hundred people if not more, and a single iron door straight across from him was the only exit.

"Where in Nalzambor is this?" he said. "Brenwar?"

There was no answer.

He shook his head and rolled his neck. It cracked and felt funny. He stretched out his great arms and locked them behind his neck, yawning a long yawn.

"How long have I been sleeping this time? Feels like months." He swallowed hard. "Oh no."

He held out his arms. His clawed hands jutted out of the heavy green robes that covered him. His fingers seemed the same as they had before, but the nails seemed a little longer and thicker. He reached back and rubbed his neck.

"What?"

He felt a series of bumps on his neck.

They felt like hard, rigid, protruding *scales*.

"No!"

He grabbed the heavy robes that covered his chest and tore them off.

His chest was covered in black scales that reflected the candlelight.

"No!"

Gaping, he stared at the long nails on his scaly toes and fell back against the granite altar. "This can't be," he said, grabbing his head and shaking it in his hands.

"My face!"

He ran his scaly fingers all over it and found long locks of his auburn hair. His chin was covered in a beard. He stormed through the room, looking for anything that might give him a reflection of his face. But only the door was there, and it showed nothing.

Gently he traced his face with his fingers once more. "I think it's still the same." He gave himself a once-over. Everything he could see was covered in scales. And they weren't smooth like a snake's, either.

"What is this?" He ran his hand over the armor-like ridges on his arms. They were as hard as rock and metal. "I don't think I'll need Brenwar's breastplate anymore."

He combed his fingers though his long hair in front of his face and shook his head. "It's never been this long before. I wish I could see myself … I bet I look magnificent." He sauntered through the chamber. "But first things first. Where in Nalzambor am I?"

The last thing he remembered was eating enough food to feed an army, sitting at that magic table down by the river with Brenwar, Bayzog, Sasha, and Ben. Licking his lips, he could still taste the pie on his tongue…

His tummy rumbled. Worry crossed his features.

"I've got to get out of here," he said.

He walked over to the iron door, started to pound on it, and stopped. He'd been assuming Brenwar must be on the other side, or another of his friends, but what if that wasn't the case?

What if he was captured?

If his enemies had him?

And his friends were dead?

The Clerics of Barnabus could easily be behind it. He pressed his ear to the great metal door and closed his eyes.

A minute passed, then two. Nothing.

"Hmmmm," he said, rubbing his chin and eyeing the torches high above him.

The flames didn't flicker or waver, and no wispy smoke billowed from them.

"Magic is behind this."

He ran his hands over the great columns with ancient carvings in them. He tested the tiles on the floor. He knocked on all the walls high and low, but the chamber was as solid as a mountain of stone.

He punched his fist into his hand. Ground his teeth. Let out a puff of smoke. "I need out of this tomb." He took a deep breath and yelled at the top of his lungs, "BRENWAAAAAAAAAR!"

His voice fell flat. Not even an echo. Nath felt alone. Scared. Angry.

"No! Someone must know I'm in here!"

He punched the iron door over and over.

Bang! Bang! Bang! Bang! Bang…

He beat it until his knuckles ached and he couldn't hit it anymore. Chest heaving and sweat rolling down into his eyes, he glared at the door. He'd dented it, but the door was just as tight as ever in its ancient frame. Whatever was put in this room was never meant to get out. That much was clear.

He rubbed the sore knuckles on his hand.

"This is bad."

Nath's mind started racing. Had they put him in here to protect him or to keep him? How long could he live inside the chamber without starving to death? Without water? Why was he even alive? All of that food he'd eaten must have lasted him.

He began pacing back and forth, angry and muttering under his breath.

What is going on? I can't die like this. I'll starve.

He hit the columns. He kicked the slab altar. He let out a roar. Smoke billowed out.

Hmmmm.

He felt his great chest fill with heat. He wanted nothing more than to let it out. He eyed the door.

How hot is my breath, anyway?

He squared up on the door. Inhaled a deep breath.

WHOOOSH!

A geyser of hot flames roared out. Nath poured it on. The entire chamber lit up in the red-hot light. He breathed until he was out of breath.

Smoke was everywhere. The stink of charred metal filled his nose. He fanned the smoke from his eyes and saw a large hole of dripping iron greeting him like the mouth of a melting giant. He jumped right through it.

"Yes!"

It was dark on the other side, but the glowing metal gave him a little illumination. His keen sight came into focus. He stood at the bottom of a stone staircase that led up in a spiral. It wound along the inner sidewall that stretched into the fathomless darkness.

"Great Guzan!" he said, exasperated. "Where am I?"

He headed up the slowly winding steps, traversing what seemed to be the mouth of a volcano or geyser or something. It must have been a hundred feet from one side to the other. The rock walls were smooth, the steps wide as he traveled upward, minute after minute, hour after hour until he stopped and sat down.

He wasn't tired.

What madness is this?

He could see thirty feet up the steps and thirty feet back, but everything else was black as a moonless night. Below, the warm illumination of the torches gave him comfort. Above, uncertainty was wrinkling the thought of freedom.

"Perhaps I dream," he said to himself. "Perhaps I'm dead." He groaned. "On your feet, Nath Dragon. Even if you are dead, you can at least act like you're alive."

Running his hand along the wall, he ascended two steps at a time, sometimes three. Losing track of time, he moved onward, upward, higher and higher.

This is madness.

"Bayzog!"

CHAPTER
29

NATH'S VOICE ECHOED IN THE cavern and fell flat. A brisk draft of cold air hit him like a stone.

"Perhaps I'm alive after all," he said, resuming his trek up the stairs.

The sensation of the moving air tingled his senses, and up above, way in the distance, he swore he saw a wink of light.

That has to be a door. It has to be.

Minute after minute, he continued his ascent while the dot of light became bigger and bigger. He doubled his pace, taking five steps at the time, sometimes six. If he had to guess how far he had walked, it must have been miles, maybe leagues. Oddly, this didn't make him impatient, only more determined.

"If the Clerics of Barnabus are behind this, I might kill them all," he said when he reached the top, where a small portal of light gleamed like a white star.

A large wooden door—girded in straps of iron with a ring for a handle—greeted him.

He reached for it, then pulled his hand back. "Better at least take a look first." Holding his clawed hand out, he felt a cold breeze blasting through the cracks around the door. He took a peek, popped backward, and shook his head.

"What in the world? This can't be." He grabbed the ring in the door and pulled it open.

Icy wind and snow blasted into him.

Forcing his way through the stiff winds, covering his eyes with his arms, he trod into what looked like the icy mouth of a cave. Icicles dangled from above like great dragon teeth, and sunlight sparkled on the jagged tips. Drawn to the sunlight like to a hot bath on a cold day, Nath lumbered forward with his teeth chattering.

"Where in Nalzambor am I?" he said yet again, stepping through the cave and eyeing his unfamiliar surroundings. "Who brought me here and why?"

There he stood outside the mouth of the cave with icicles already forming on his eyebrows. He waded through knee-deep snow until he found himself peering from the overlook of a great mountain. Above him was more rock and mountain, and the bright sunlight was a ball of fire behind a misty and cloudy sky. Ahead and below him were more snow-covered peaks as far as the eye could see. The sight was both beautiful and terrifying. The bitter cold felt like a blanket of death. He had to get moving. But who had put him up here and why?

"Did I just crawl out of my own tomb?" He stretched out his arms and yelled, "Where am I?"

A snow-covered crop of boulders nearby shifted, and tiny balls of snow trickled off them.

Nath watched with a keen eye as a renewed sense of danger coursed through his freezing blood.

The boulders started to move.

Nath's hand fell to his waist.

Fang wasn't there.

Like cracking eggs, the snow split, and thick-thewed, hairy monsters emerged carrying razor-sharp battle axes.

Nath backed toward the edge of the overlook.

They flanked him. Closed in, trudging through the snow. They were grisly, inhuman, and bearded.

"Finally finish yer nap?" one spit out from a snow-covered beard.

Nath leaned forward, squinting. "Brenwar?"

The old dwarf shook the snow from his face and beard and nodded.

The rest of the dwarves dusted the snow from themselves and remained in their places.

"Of course it's me," Brenwar said, dusting off his shoulders. "Now come on, we have to get going."

"Wait a moment," Nath said, trudging through the snow toward him. "What are we doing up here to begin with?"

Brenwar looked Nath over, snorted, and started shaking his head.

"What?" Nath asked.

"What? I'll tell you *what*! Ye've changed again. It's even worse than I expected." Brenwar started to march away through the snow. "Now come on."

Nath grabbed Brenwar by the arm and stopped him. He looked him dead in the eye and said, "What am I doing up here?" He gestured toward the cave where the door was. "And what was I doing way down in there?"

Brenwar jerked his arm away. "We were hiding you."

"From who?"

"Who do you think?"

"Barnabus? All the way up here? That's crazy!"

"It's a crazy world," Brenwar said. "Why do you think we put you in there?"

Nath took a pause. He didn't like the way Brenwar had said that, not at all. There was something edgy about the dwarf's tone. Brenwar seemed to be in a hurry. *He's never in a hurry.*

"I'm just as ready to get off this mountain as you are," Nath said, starting after him, "but you could at least act like you're glad to see me."

Brenwar stopped, swung his war hammer over his shoulder, and glared.

"I'm hungry! Can't you tell?" Brenwar said. "Me and my dwarves didn't get much food up here guarding you, and in case you didn't notice, there ain't no ale. No taverns or toasty fires either."

"Well, how long have I been asleep?"

"Long enough," Brenwar said, moving down an icy path that only the keenest eyes could make out.

Nath fell in behind him, and the rest of the dwarven soldiers followed.

"Longer than the last time?"

"What do you think?"

"I think these icy peaks are warmer than you!"

"Good!"

Nath didn't have any trouble keeping up with Brenwar, but he was irritated. Once again he could tell that Brenwar was holding something back. Brenwar was normally very forthcoming with the truth.

And there was another thing that bothered him. If he'd been out for months like the last time, had Brenwar and the rest of the dwarves been guarding him all this time in this intolerable climate? Why hadn't they just kept him in Morgdon? No one could have gotten to him there.

Nath fought the urge to ask more questions, opting to keep his mouth shut until they returned to a more palatable climate. His cheeks were numb, but the rest of him didn't feel that bad. Even his clawed toes weren't cold. He puffed out a cloud of warm smoke, and Brenwar caught it out of the corner of his eye.

"Don't do that," Brenwar said. "They're looking for you."

"I doubt anyone is looking up here. I have to say, I wouldn't follow anyone up here."

Brenwar huffed along through the dusk and until dawn before he finally came to a stop. The snow had stopped, and there were green trees and tall grasses on level land that greeted the mountains.

Nath still didn't know where he was, but now that Brenwar had finally stopped, it was time to ask questions.

"How long was I asleep?"

"Long enough."

Nath grunted. He figured it couldn't have been much longer than the last time.

"Where are Bayzog, Ben, and Sasha?"

Brenwar shrugged.

"Why didn't you just take me to Morgdon?"

"You didn't like it much the last time," Brenwar said, "did you? You think I'd let you wake up and sneak out again? No, no, no."

"Where are we?"

"Between the Ruins and the Pool of the Dragon," Brenwar said. He combed some snow out of his beard and shook it.

"I think you missed some," Nath said, reaching out his taloned fingers. He stopped. "Is that white hair in your black beard?"

Brenwar pushed his hand away and turned his back.

Nath jerked him around. "Brenwar, how long did I sleep?"

Brenwar mumbled something that Nath heard just fine.

"Not long," he said, "for a dragon."

CHAPTER
30

NATH SAT SHAKING HIS HEAD with his eyes fixed on Brenwar. It seemed pretty clear he'd been asleep a couple of years, maybe more. The lines in Brenwar's face had gotten deeper and his scars more numerous.

"Come on," he urged. "Out with it."

Around him, mostly standing, were the rest of the dwarves. Though younger by maybe a century or two, they looked like they'd seen a lifetime of battle. Nath recognized some of them, but they'd changed. One was missing an arm, another a hand. One's face was badly acid burnt, and another one's hairless arms were scorched. In one way or another, it was clear they all had suffered a loss of some sort, even Brenwar. His wounds might be less visible, but they were deep. Nath could tell.

"We kept you in Morgdon the first year, but the Dwarven High Council voted you out," Brenwar said. "And I agreed. The Clerics of Barnabus raised an army, and the senseless slaughter began. They tore through every town and village they could, terrorizing women and children. There was only so much the dwarves could do to protect them, so they turned you over."

Nath popped forward. "You turned me over!"

Brenwar stuck out his hand. "Settle down. I'm not finished yet. We turned you over and rescued you. It was Bayzog's idea."

"Well that figures," Nath said. "Blasted wizards. So what happ—"

"I'm getting to that. Let me tell the story, will ya?"

Nath sat back, frowning, but motioned him to continue.

"It was you, and it wasn't you," Brenwar said. "It fooled them, anyway. It especially worked when we rescued it and you were taken away to be hidden. But a great many paid for it. A great many indeed. It was one of the bloodiest battles we'd ever been in. But it had to be convincing."

Nath's brows buckled. He hated to ask, but he did anyway.

"How many died, Brenwar?"

"It doesn't matter how many died. What matters is that you are safe."

"No," Nath said, crossing his arms over his knees, "I want to know how many, and I want to know their names. I can at least honor them. I'm grateful. I need to say thanks of some sort. It's hard to take that so many died on account of me. I have to do something. Just tell me."

"All the fallen are written on a wall in Morgdon, and their heroics have been noted. You can take a look at them the next time you're there."

Nath looked around at his surroundings and everyone else. Sadness mixed with anger in his belly.

"Just tell me now. We don't seem to be going anywhere at the moment. I don't even know where we are. Just give me some names."

Brenwar put his hand on Nath's shoulder. "Let it go. We've got other things to do."

"Like what?" Nath rose to his feet and towered over Brenwar. "Finding more ways to not tell me anything?"

"More than a thousand, you black-scaled, red-headed stepchild!"

Nath whirled. "What?"

It had come from the smallest dwarf. He came forward, walking with a limp. One eye was missing, and what was left of his brown beard was corded and braided. His remaining eye bright and fiery.

"I'm Pilpin, and since you want to know so much, I'll tell you. My brothers, six of them, Chilptin, Kiltpin, Lilpin, Farpin, Stigpin, and Zerpin are dead. My father Lanpinpin is dead from defending you too. You see all these dwarves?" he said, flailing his arm their way. "They've got dead kin too, and that's just the ones that were fighting. That's not counting the thousands that died in the towns and villages, and that's just the ones that we know of. So sit down and I'll give you all the names you want! Harrumph!"

Nath grabbed his own head and dug his nails in. His blood stopped. Guilt set in. Thousands had died because of him? Why? He stepped backward, shaking his head.

No. How can this be?

Pilpin started rattling off names.

"That's enough," Brenwar growled. "He's got plenty to chew on now."

Nath offered Brenwar a blank look and took a hard swallow.

"Tell me more, Brenwar," he said, "I must know. Everything!"

"All right, then," Brenwar nodded. "So we rescued this pseudo version of you. And it's still alive."

Nath groaned. More guilt was setting in.

"After that, we moved the real you from place to place, trying to hide you. We tried the Settlement, Borgash, and all the borders west and north. Morgdon would not have you. No, not after the losses. Every time we settled, we were found out." He cracked his thick neck. "Barnabus has spies everywhere. At every turn there was betrayal, but we did our best the first few years."

"Few years!" Nath said.

"Aye!" Brenwar shot back. "And dragging you around all those years wasn't no festival, either! Hah! Nath, you be fortunate I had these volunteers to protect you. And thank Bayzog, too. He did some mighty convincing that wasn't easy. That said, we finally found a safe place for you."

Brenwar peered up the mountain. "And you've been here ever since. We've been here ever since, fighting off anything that came and waiting for you to wake. We're about all you have left."

Nath shook his head. He wanted to hit something. He wanted to cry. Crawl back into that mountain and maybe die. He was supposed to saves lives, not lose them.

"How long was I in this mountain?" he said, patting a rock.

Brenwar just said, "Long enough for the entire world to change."

"Ah, blast it, Brenwar," Pilpin said, limping over. "I'll tell him." He stood in front of Nath and clapped his hands three times, saying. "Twen—tee—years!"

Nath blinked.

"Shall I say it again?" Pilpin said. "Twenty years! Twenty years! I've been freezing my fanny off for twenty years!"

Nath was numb. His mind scrambled.

How can this be?

"I … I don't know what to … Uh … How did you survive up there in all that snow with no food?"

"We're tough," Pilpin said, poking him in the chest. "Tougher than sleeping dragons."

"Twenty years!" Nath said. "How do you know it was that long?"

"Because we counted the sun rising and falling, stupid," Pilpin said.

"And I can tell by how much snow has fallen," said another who was missing an arm.

"Enough," Brenwar said. "We rotated. Are you satisfied now?"

"No," Nath said, rising to his feet. "I'm not satisfied. I'm not satisfied at all. And I won't be until all the Clerics of Barnabus are wiped out." He clenched his fists.

CHAPTER
31

"WE CAN'T JUST GO STORMING through the countryside," Brenwar growled. "Everyone is looking for you. Looking for us." He motioned to the others. "We're wanted dwarves, you know."

Ever since they had made it to the bottom of the mountains, Nath had been determined to see what was going on. How much had the world really changed while he'd been asleep? It couldn't be that bad.

"Certainly not everyone is looking for us," Nath said. "There must be allies, and I find it hard to believe the Clerics of Barnabus have taken over everything. There's always been plenty more of us than them."

Brenwar stormed ahead, cutting through the forest and into the valleys, veering clear of any noticeable paths.

Nath didn't notice much of a difference in anything. The air was chill and the sky was cloudy, but the day wasn't any different than the last he remembered.

Brenwar stopped his march in a small clearing near at the bottom of the valley where a gentle stream trickled. Nath's old friend turned and faced him with a serious look in his eye.

"Let me explain this once again, Nath. All that is evil in Nalzambor is looking for you. There is a bounty on your head higher than those mountains. They want you. Alive. Wars are going on everywhere. The good fight and the good die, all because the evil want you." He scooped some water out of the stream and drank. "According to Bayzog, you are the catalyst for the next Dragon War. Perhaps the last war of all time."

"That would be a good thing," Nath said.

"Not if the other side wins. Not if we lose you. Everyone needs you."

"Why?" Nath said. His stomach growled. "I'm starving." He sloshed into the stream, hunkered down, and spread his arms over the water that rushed past his legs. Fish, big and small, darted between his legs. "Ah, there's a meal."

Nath jabbed his hand into the water and pulled out a large, wriggling, black-spotted fish. He gutted it, scaled it, torched it with his breath, and swallowed the rest down whole. He tapped his fist with his chest.

Buurrp!

One of the dwarves applauded.

"Pah!" Brenwar said. "Let's go. As for why they want you, I can only assume it is to turn you."

"It won't happen," Nath said through a clenched jaw. "Ever."

"Don't say that. Come on."

Nath snatched another fish and gutted, scaled, torched, and ate in on the way.

Hours later, dusk had returned when they happened upon a broken and overgrown village. He stopped, looking down at hundreds of stone markers. They were simple stones with names carved in them, noting all who had fallen but not been recovered. The layout of the village was familiar, and Nath knew that he'd passed through here before, maybe a hundred years ago.

"It's like this all over," Pilpin said. "Some save themselves, some are saved by others, but we can't save all of them. The peace in the land is gone." He nudged Nath. "Come."

Pilpin led him to a half-sunken stone building that looked like it was being consumed by the ground. Nath ducked under a doorway that was tall enough for a dwarf and followed him down into a tunnel. All the dwarves funneled inside save for two, who remained outside with their battle axes crossed over their chests.

At the end of the tunnel, they emerged into a large room, like a barracks, lit by smokeless torches. In the middle, a table large enough to feed twenty was stacked with bread cakes and littered with jars of jam and honey and slabs of dried meat. The dwarves sat and dug in, while a pair emerged from another entrance with an oaken barrel between them and set it on the table.

"Welcome," a dwarf with a white curly beard said, teetering in. "I see we have a visitor."

"No," Brenwar said, "we have *the* visitor, Gorlee." Brenwar made his way out of the room.

"Ah," Gorlee said, stroking his beard. He pulled out a chair. "Then I imagine he is hungry. Come, have a seat. Eat."

Gorlee might have been the most pleasant dwarf Nath ever encountered. He was rugged, but robed in grey, without a stich of metal showing. The rest of the dwarves were coated in steel, sharp and dull, and armored in thick leather and dull metal. They all ate like they'd never eaten before and guzzled down tankard after tankard.

"Help yourself," Gorlee said. "It won't be there forever."

Nath tore off a hunk of beef and grabbed a roll of bread. He stuffed it in his mouth. The dwarves weren't known for their cooking, but what they made sustained you.

Gorlee eyed him intently. The dwarf seemed to be counting each and every scale.

"How many are in here?"

"Forty-eight," Gorlee said.

"And you've all been watching over me?" Nath said. "All these years?"

"It's what we're sworn to do."

"And now that I'm awake, what will you do?"

"I don't know," Gorlee said, scratching his beard. "But now that you're awake, things will be a lot more exciting around here." He clapped his hands, and a jar of honey slid down the table. "Put some honey on that bread. It doesn't taste so good without it."

Nath waggled his hunk of bread in Gorlee's wizened face. "I wish more dwarves were like you."

Gorlee laughed a little. "Me too, but then I wouldn't be so special. You see, I'm not really a dwarf."

"You look like a dwarf to me," Nath said. "Even with all those teeth in your smile."

Gorlee laughed. "Watch this." The old dwarf began to stretch and thin.

Nath felt the scales on his arms tingle. A few seconds later he found himself staring at—himself.

Gorlee showed a mouthful of bright white teeth. "I'm a Chameleon."

CHAPTER
32

"The hair's wrong," Nath said. "It's supposed to be parted in the middle, not the side." He rubbed his chin, staring the Gorlee version of himself in the face. "I've never seen myself bearded before. It's really handsome."

"Agreed," Gorlee said, helping himself to a tankard. "You might be the finest creature I've ever mimicked."

"But can you do this?" Nath said. He huffed out a ring of fire.

Gorlee's face bunched up and he shook his head. "No, but I can cast some wizard spells. Watch this," he said, pointing at a chair and twiddling his dragon claws. "Tweeedleee Ickle Steeeezzz!"

The chair turned into a goblin with wild and savage eyes, wielding a spear. Four dwarves pounced on it with their fists hammering and mouths yelling. One by one they popped up with a piece of wood in their hands or teeth.

"What's all the clamor?" Brenwar said, bursting back in the room. "Aw, cut it out, Gorlee, and quit looking like that, will you? One Nath is bad enough around here, let alone two. Blast my beard." He dropped onto a seat at the table.

Gorlee resumed his dwarven form and shrugged. "They don't much like my other visages, so for the past two decades I've been mostly stuck in this one."

"That must be frustrating," Nath said.

"Well, I do get out sometimes. I'm the supplier. I can travel the world without notice. The dwarves can't go much of anywhere as they aren't very popular right now. Unless they're in Morgdon, they aren't anywhere else. So I get the food and whatever other needs might be met. I also pick up any information that might be pertinent."

"Such as?"

Nath could sense that as friendly as the Chameleon seemed, he was nothing short of dangerous. Why Brenwar trusted him he'd have to ask later.

Gorlee said, "Dragons, Nath. The Clerics of Barnabus search for you and not the good dragons but the bad ones. The turned ones. They aid Barnabus. Their frustration grows, and they take it out on the weak." Gorlee dipped a piece of bread in the honey.

"Sure, the cities and towns are getting by, but the pressure is great. The people no longer smile. They frown instead, as if waiting for the entire world to explode."

"I can't run and hide forever," Nath said, "and I won't. Before I slept, the plan was to take the fight straight at them and end them. Destroy the snake before it got too big." He looked at Brenwar.

"We tried that," Brenwar said, "but it turns out the snake was too big already."

"And now it's bigger?" Nath said.

"Much," Gorlee said.

"I want to see this," Nath said, rising from his chair.

"Sit down," Brenwar said, slapping the table. "We've got to wait for the wizard."

Nath made for the tunnel, but three dwarves barred his path.

"See?" Brenwar said to Gorlee. "I told you he'd try to run off again. He always does. Thinks he can fix the world by himself. Hah."

Gorlee nodded.

"I'm just going outside to get some fresh air," Nath said, hunching down under the low ceiling. "My wardens can come along. I'm not going to sit here until Bayzog shows. I've been asleep long enough already. I need to fill my lungs and stretch my limbs. I need to run."

Brenwar huffed and left the room, but no one else moved.

"Give it some time, Nath," Gorlee said. "After all, we've been waiting a score of years. You can at least give us a few days."

Nath folded his arms over his chest and plopped down in a chair.

"Fine."

Over the next few days, Gorlee did his best to entertain Nath. He changed his appearance from one dwarf to another. He animated the food and made it dance while the dwarves sang merry songs.

But not too loud.

Brenwar wouldn't allow it. He swore eyes and ears were everywhere, and he went outside now and again.

Gorlee said most of his kind were good and that they'd chosen him to aid the dwarves and the elves when the world began to change. He said he was glad to do it, that he'd already known the stories about Nath Dragon as much as anyone. He said time wasn't a factor, either, that the lifetime of a Chameleon was as long as a dwarf's or an elf's, maybe longer, but that he was young, the same as Nath.

"The dragons are turned or killed," Gorlee said. "And they change. Many have black stripes and tails. Some even take riders now."

"Riders?" Nath said. He thought back to his time as a boy, riding on his father's back. He hadn't flown since. Thinking on that, a great emptiness filled him.

"Just like the paintings you've certainly seen. Some of the dragons even perch on the spires of the cities, watching every little thing. It's scary," Gorlee said. "The people practically dart from one street to the other, and the strange ones set up places of worship. The dragons that were once reviled are now being embraced."

"But the dragons were reviled for all the wrong reasons before," Nath said. "They were good and made out to be evil and now you're saying the evil ones are being made out to be good."

Gorlee shrugged. "I suppose."

Nath rapped his fist on the table. "That's sick." He clenched his teeth and rubbed his temples. "I have to stop this."

"*We* have to stop this."

"Huh?"

It wasn't Gorlee that spoke but someone else.

Nath turned.

There stood Bayzog. The part-elf wizard's black hair was streaked in white, and his violet eyes were hard. A white scar ran from his eye and over his lip to his chin, and his robes were in tatters. He held a gray staff of wood with a twisted metal tip at the end. He looked tired but strong.

Nath clasped Bayzog's hands. The grip was much firmer than before.

"Then *we* need to get moving," Nath said. "I'll do anything to get out of this mole hole, and I'm more than ready to stop all this madness."

Brenwar bustled forward and looked up at Bayzog. "Is it safe to go out?"

"Yes, but the hunters are close." Bayzog released Nath's hands. "We need to get the jump on them."

"Why's that?" Brenwar said.

"Come."

Nath was all too happy to be outside again.

It was dusk, and the dwarves that guarded the door were not alone. They had company much taller than them, but they were also looking down at something.

Bayzog made his way over, and they parted, revealing a small dragon, little bigger than a cat. It was white. On its wings were strange black streaks Nath had never seen before.

Nath pushed his way through and fell to his knees beside it. It wasn't breathing, and something had pierced its side.

"Who did this?" Nath said, angry and eyeing the others.

"Nath," Bayzog said. "This dragon was a spy for Barnabus. It had to be put down. We're fortunate we got it before it disclosed our location—"

Nath rose to his feet, towering over Bayzog, and pushed him in the chest. "Who did this? Was it you?"

"Does it look like something I did?" Bayzog said. He held his ground. "Do you want to push me again?"

"I did it," a deep voice replied. A big man stepped forward. His face was short bearded, and his eyes were hard as stone. He had a bow slung over his shoulder and dwarven leather plate that covered his chest but not his sinewy arms. "Do you want to shove me too, Dragon?"

Nath balled up his fist. "No, I think I'm just going to punch a hole in you."

Brenwar stepped between the two. "Not through dwarven plate, you won't. Now settle yourself down, Nath. Can't you see who this is?"

The man didn't seem familiar at all. His features were hard and his body was scarred like that of a veteran soldier. His brown beard was salted with grey. A fine longsword hung on the man's hips and a pair of daggers too. He had the look of a seasoned fighter.

The man shook his head and turned toward Bayzog. "We don't have time for all this. We need to move. The Pool of the Dragons can't wait. But I'm not so sure we need to bring him." He eyed Nath. "Seeing how he's the one they're after."

"I don't think it matters now," Bayzog said. "The next stage has begun. Sooner or later they will know that he has awakened. In the meantime, we need to properly bury this dragon. No offense, Nath."

"Ben?" Nath said, taking a closer look at the man. "Are you Ben?"

Ben turned to face him. "Yes, do I look so different to you?"

"Well, yes," Nath said. "You have a beard and muscles like an old warrior now. It's strange to see you. What have you been doing?"

Ben huffed. His expression was agitated.

"What have I been doing? I've been protecting you."

CHAPTER 33

THEY SPENT THE NEXT SEVERAL days traipsing with discretion through the small towns and villages, making their way to the Pool of the Dragons. It was there that Bayzog said they had allies and information. They traveled on foot, but the dwarves towed a couple of pack mules. Nath spent the time catching up on things with Bayzog and Ben. Even Brenwar began to warm up to him. Gorlee played a big part in that.

"Many of the wild dragons have been turned," Gorlee had said. "The rest, I'm certain, are back in Dragon Home. The poachers no longer hunt them for profit. They turn them into soldiers. Well, the clerics do that."

The news got worse and worse. It gave Nath a headache, and the guilt consumed him. He should have been awake all this time. He could have saved many of them. Most of them.

"Sometimes they have to save themselves," Bayzog said.

But Nath couldn't live with that. Not another day longer, now that he was awake again and feeling stronger than ever. He wanted to sink his claws—or a blade—into something.

"Say, Brenwar, what happened to Akron and Fang?"

Brenwar growled in his throat and signaled to the rear.

Pilpin rummaged through the mule packs, brought over a rugged-looking bag, and dropped it at Nath's clawed feet. The little dwarf eyed him with suspicion and strutted away.

Nath reached into the bag and found the quiver.

"Some of the arrows are missing," he said. "Exploding ones at that. How did that happen?"

"Are you really worried about a missing arrow?" Brenwar said. "It's not like you made the thing."

"Well, I was just surprised is all," he said, slinging it over his shoulder. He took out the compact form of Akron.

Snap. Clatch. Snap.

The string coiled right into place. Nath stuck his chin out and smiled. He reached over his shoulder to hook it when he realized he no longer had the armor to latch it onto.

Brenwar rolled his eyes and walked away. "That's a problem."

Nath did have clothes on, however. A jerkin covered his chest and most of his arms, and a pair of trousers covered his legs. Bayzog said that was best in case any distant eyes were spying. The wizard had tried to get Nath to cover his head, too, but he'd flat-out refused. "One should never hide something as beautiful as this," he'd argued.

The last remaining item was Fang. The beautiful weapon with twin dragons on the hilt sent a charge of energy through him.

"Have you missed me, old friend?" he said, wrapping his clawed fingers around the hilt. "Ow!" He jerked his hand away.

Every eye in the party fell on him. Bayzog's expression filled with worry.

But Nath didn't pay attention.

"Fang, what's wrong with you? Do you not know me? It's Nath." Slowly, he wrapped his hand around the hilt once more and gently pulled the blade from the sheath. "That's better, Fang. It's me."

The mystic blade throbbed in his palm and was hot in his hand. Nath made sure he didn't grimace. *Stop it, Fang! It's me!* The hilt got hotter and a bead of sweat dripped from his forehead. *Fang! It's me, your master!*

"Problem, Nath?" Bayzog said.

"No," he shot back. The sword began to cool in his palm. "I just think Fang was a little uncertain." He pulled the great blade out to its full length, smiled, then slid it back in. "We're fine now." He buckled the blade over his shoulders. "Shouldn't we get moving?"

Troghlin the Harbor Town. It was one of dozens that circled the Pool of the Dragons, and it was under siege.

"Is this where you were taking me?" Nath said to Bayzog. "It doesn't look to be as safe as I presumed."

Bayzog stood silent, peering through a spyglass that Pilpin had handed him, shaking his head.

"No, we've another hideout, but this town is full of friends. I fear the worst; there's no doubt someone in there is bound to give us up." He shut the spyglass and handed it over to Ben. "We're going to have to find another place to hide. Again."

Nath's eyes were sharper than they'd ever been. He couldn't say for sure, but he felt like he could see five times farther than he had been able to before, and that was pretty far. Troghlin was burning in some places, and the people that weren't fleeing were hiding in boarded-up stores and apartments. The enemy marched prisoners through the streets, and some were dead already. Nath's dragon heart pumped faster.

"I see that look in yer eye," Brenwar said. "Settle it down."

Nath ignored him. Troghlin was a wonderful little town that was more like an oversized fishing village with large piers connected by a series of storefronts and boardwalks. People from all over Nalzambor came to rest and enjoy food by the sea in hopes of observing the sea dragons that appeared now and again. Now it was in ruin.

Nath said to Bayzog, "Are those the hunters that you spoke of?"

"Indeed."

"Hmmm," Nath said. "Can I see that spyglass, Ben?"

"Sure," Ben said, handing it over.

There was a draykis leading the soldiers that consisted of robed clerics, gnolls, goblins, and lizard men. They pushed and shoved their way through the town, busting windows and bullying people. The lizard men had two dragons with them that were wingless and black tailed. Their scales were maroon, and their bellies were a darker color, almost black. They sniffed around more like dogs than dragons, with lizard tongues licking out of their snouts. They were burrowers and hunters called red rocks.

"Those dragons are awfully far from home," Nath said. "They like the lava in the south. It seems awfully strange to see them way up here. Hmmmm." *Snap. Clatch. Snap.* "I think they don't like it here."

"Oh no you don't," Brenwar said.

"Nath," Bayzog began, "Those hunters are looking for us. They're looking for you. We can't risk it."

"Risk what? Our hides, while those people's lives are on the line?" Nath whipped an arrow from his quiver and spit on the tip. "I'm not going to let anyone else suffer on account of me if I can help it. And I'd expect you to do the same."

"I'm with Dragon," Ben said, taking a place beside Nath. "We've been running too long. Sometimes you just have to stand and fight … for what's right."

"Agreed," said Pilpin. "I didn't stand years in the snow for nothing. I stood because I knew a big fight was coming. My beard's itching for it."

Brenwar looked at Bayzog and Bayzog back at him. They both nodded.

"We need to have a plan," Bayzog said.

"Don't worry," Nath said, "I've already got one. It's called…"

He drew the string back along his cheek and let the first arrow fly.

"… Surprise."

CHAPTER
34

T HE ARROW'S FLIGHT SEEMED TO take forever, with the tip winking at its zenith before descending.

"What are you doing?" Bayzog exclaimed. "Are you crazy?"

More than two hundred yards away, the arrow finished its flight and buried itself in the shoulder of a draykis.

"Did you see that?" Pilpin said, holding the spyglass to his eye. "He hit it. Egad, but it still lives."

Nath could see it just fine. It was a perfect shot, and the draykis's bewilderment was amusing.

"What happened?" Brenwar said, standing on his tiptoes. "Shouldn't something be exploding?"

As the hunters gathered around their ailing leader, the rest started to point right at Nath.

"You have to wait for it, Brenwar."

"Wait? I'm not waiting. Can't you see they're coming? A small army of them." He punched Nath in the arm. "All you did was waste an arrow and get our necks exposed."

Nath stood tall, eyeing the draykis in the distance. It wrapped its clawed hand around the arrow, barked a laugh, and started to tug.

Nath's keen eyes picked up a click and a mystic whine. All the surrounding hunters leaned in toward the sound.

KABOOM!

Bodies flew into the air and others were flung on the ground.

"Did you see that?" Pilpin said, jumping up and down. "I like that!"

The dwarves let out a gusty cheer and raised their weapons high in the air.

Troghlin was shaken. Its captors were rocked.

Nath raised Akron over his head. "Time to finish what I started!"

In the distance, the lizard men unleashed the pair of red rock dragons. They scurried over the ground. Fast for lizards. The red rocks covered the distance between them in seconds.

Nath blocked their advance, shouting in Dragonese, "Go home. Be free or suffer."

They exchanged glances among themselves before turning back to Nath and his party. They opened their mouths like tunnels, and a blast of hot air came out.

"Sultans of Sulfur!" Brenwar cried.

The intense heat dropped everyone to their knees. The dwarves backed away. Nath stood his ground. And someone else. A tall man he hadn't seen before stood at his side.

"Who?" Nath said.

"It's me, Gorlee," the Chameleon said. "I've thick skin." Gorlee dropped to a knee beside him and sucked the contents of a vial into his mouth. "Ah, perhaps this will help."

Nath nocked another arrow and spoke in Dragonese again. "I'll warn you no more. Go home or suffer."

The hot blast of breath kept pouring out.

Nath could barely keep his eyes open.

Twang!

The moorite arrow buried in a dragon's side.

It lurched. Its breath stopped.

Nath loaded another arrow, pulled the string back, and fired at the other dragon.

Twang!

The red rock roared back. Both dragons eyed him. Tongues licked from their mouths. Jaws snapped open and closed.

I'm going to have to kill them.

The pair of dragons slowly came forward.

The dwarves jumped into their path and formed a blockade.

"No," Nath said, "Your weapons won't hurt them. Leave them to me!"

The rest of the hunters were almost on top of them.

Gorlee grabbed Nath's shoulder. "I can handle these dragons." He pointed at the horde of draykis, goblins, gnolls, and lizard men. "You better take care of them."

"What can you do?" Nath said.

"You'll see," Gorlee said, pushing him onward. "What do dragons love more than anything?"

"Gold," Nath said.

"Aye," Gorlee said. But he had changed. His body was solid gold.

The red rocks drifted from Nath to Gorlee.

"I'll be fine," Gorlee said. He took off running. The dragons darted straight after the golden man.

Nath shook his head. *That was strange.*

"Nath!" Brenwar yelled. "Quit standing and start fighting."

He turned.

The hunters and dwarves clashed, metal on metal. He dropped Akron on the ground. His hand went to his hilt and stopped. He clenched his fists and smiled.

Let's see what you can do on your own.

A shadow dropped out of the sky and punched him in the face.

Pop!

It was a draykis.

Ben stood flanked by two gnolls, being beat on with flails.

Bang! Clang!

Ben kept his shield up and his sword moving.

Wait for it…

The gnolls pounded at him, heavy, furious blows that juttered his arms. They knocked down his sword and shield arm only to see them snap up again. Their strength was raw and relentless. Their jaws snapped and howled at him.

"Human meat," one said.

"Dead meat," said the other.

The gnolls stopped and backed away.

Ben lowered his guard.

"Tired," he said, huffing for breath.

"Fool!" one said.

Both gnolls struck at the same time.

Bang!

They tore his shield off his arm.

"Dead meat now, human," one said, closing in.

The gnolls twirled their flails at their sides. Snapped and growled.

"He's got some meat on him."

"Bet he tastes good."

They struck high and hard.

Ben ducked and rolled. The gnolls' weapons slammed into each other.

Ben's sword was a stroke of lightning.

Slash! Slash!

The gnolls howled and fell dead to the ground.

Stupid gnolls. That must be over fifty.

Bayzog stood behind the melee with anger in his eyes. All of his plans were unraveling, no thanks to Nath.

Why do we guard a man who refuses to play it safe?

For the past twenty-five years, they'd risked their lives to protect him and keep his whereabouts secret. Now, in a matter of seconds, all of Nalzambor would know where he was and that he lived.

Bayzog shook his head. His eyes glimmered with power.

The dwarves, led by Brenwar, were knotted up with the goblins, gnolls, and lizard men. Gorlee had distracted the dragons, and Nath was battling a draykis.

That left the Clerics of Barnabus that had not advanced. Some were dead from the explosion, and in the spyglass he counted only six remaining. He set it aside. Most of them stood their ground, watching from the edge of the lake town. Bayzog had no doubt they'd sent for reinforcements already, but how close were they?

Everyone is fighting but me, it seems. He rested his staff over his shoulder and muttered an Elvish incantation. The staff glowed with life, and Bayzog's feet lifted from the ground. He drifted over the fracas below and straight toward the town's edge, where with wide eyes the six robed acolytes waited. *All those bald-headed fiends. I'll take care of that.*

Goblins were fierce. Gnolls were strong. Lizard men were deadly. They all hated the dwarves.

And the dwarves hated them.

"A barrel of ale to whoever crushes the most!" Brenwar yelled.

Forming a wedge with Brenwar leading the way, the dwarves crashed right into the oncoming horde. Brenwar whopped the first lizard man he came across in the chest, dropping him dead. Pilpin rolled beneath the blades of goblins and cut into their legs with his axe. Another dwarf, the roundest and biggest of them all, bowled a gnoll over with his girth and cracked its head with a round mace.

"Powder their bones!" Brenwar yelled.

The horde of evil pressed, but the well-oiled dwarven squad hacked right back with centuries of skill and precision. The dwarves weren't as fast as their attackers, but they were stout as stumps and tough as kettles of iron in armor.

Brenwar's beard was clipped by a lizard man's sword.

"You dare, you lipless pair of boots!"

With both arms on the shaft of his war hammer, he brought it down with all his might on the lizard man's scaly foot.

Crunch!

It dropped its sword and started to hop and hiss.

Brenwar busted it in the knee.

It fell to the ground, raising its arms in defense a split second before Brenwar put an end to it.

Pow!

He checked his beard. A small portion was dangling off.

"Now I'm mad!"

He was surrounded by angry howls and cries of pain. His dwarves were busted and bleeding, but they didn't cry out. They cheered, snarled, and fought back. But they were in trouble. The enemy wasn't falling fast enough.

"Blast my beard!"

Pilpin slipped to the ground and fell underneath four goblins.

Brenwar rushed over and starting swinging his hammer like a sickle. He knocked two aside with one blow. Dented the helmet of the third, cracking its skull.

"Pilpin!" Brenwar said.

The dwarf lay on his back, eyes wide, bleeding. A goblin lay on top of him, unmoving.

Brenwar shoved it off. Pilpin's dagger was in its chest, but its dagger had found a home in Pilpin's stomach.

"You'll have to finish the rest, Brenwar," Pilpin said. "It's been an honor…"

CHAPTER
35

Nath's eyes went straight to the draykis. It towered near seven feet tall, and its eyes were dark and beady, with a glimmer of fire behind them. It pointed its clawed paw at Nath, flexed its brawny muscles under its scaly skin, and beckoned.

Nostrils flaring, Nath went right at it.

It took a swipe, and its claws tore across Nath's scaly chest.

He laughed and punched it in the face.

Whap!

The draykis spit out a tooth and narrowed its eyes.

"It's not like you needed that," Nath said.

It popped him in the nose. Blood dripped onto Nath's chest.

His gold eyes flashed. Fury swelled inside him.

Back and forth they went. Punch for punch.

Bap! Bap!

Crack! Pop!

Pow! Pow! Boom!

Nath beat into it with reckless fury.

It fought back with power and cunning.

Duck, you fool!

The draykis threw a haymaker.

Nath dodged, shifted his head left and right, tucked his chin back, bobbed his head.

"Enough of this!"

Nath jacked it in the jaw with an uppercut, snapping its head back and shattering more of its teeth.

It shook it off with a shiver and pounced.

Nath caught it in midair and slammed it into the ground, pinning its wings. In

Nath's mind, this triggered the memory of the winged ape and the kidnapping of Sasha. The image of Shum drowned and dead.

"You will die!"

Nath's fists were like metal gauntlets busting up rocks. They broke bones and busted teeth.

The draykis snapped up its forearms, protecting its face.

Nath pummeled its ribs and belly.

Whop! Whop! Whop!

The draykis gasped, flailed, and kicked. Desperate, it wrapped its claws around Nath's hair and pulled him off. It scrambled to its knees, spread its wings, and tried to jump away.

"No you don't!"

Nath jumped on its back. He wrapped his arms around its neck and squeezed.

The pair thrashed over the grass.

"You aren't going anywhere!"

Nath felt his strength growing. He squeezed harder and harder, hanging on with his dragon legs and choking it with his dragon arms.

The bulging muscles of the draykis started to slacken.

Crack!

Its neck broke.

Nath shoved it away, sucked for air, and wiped the blood off his face. "That's better."

Clonk!

His head exploded. Stars burst in his eyes. He took another shot to the chest and belly.

A gnoll loomed over him, raising a club high.

Nath caught it in his hands and ripped it loose. "You shouldn't have done that," he said, shaking the club.

The gnoll barked a warning.

Whack!

It barked no more.

A sea of lizard men swarmed Nath and dragged him to the ground.

The Clerics of Barnabus fanned out and pointed at Bayzog while he sailed over the grass on legs of air. There were six of them in all—bald, robed, and cunning.

He could see their lips moving and the air before them beginning to stir and the pendants on their chests beginning to glow. Bayzog readied his staff and touched the ground.

"I'm here to negotiate your surrender," he said.

The clerics huffed a laugh, but it was far from gusty.

Bayzog could see the air shimmering before them.

"I see," he said. He muttered quick words in Elvish. His fingertips glowed with life, and a streak of orange shot from his hand. It flicked over the grass and ricocheted off an invisible force, inches from the closest man's face.

The clerics flinched. Two began to mumble and mutter while the other four, wielding maces, flanked him, two on each side.

I need to put a quick end to this. He opened his mouth to summon another spell, but everything fell silent. His words were gone. The sounds of the battles behind him had disappeared. He was silenced. A chill went through him.

I should have seen this coming.

Bayzog started to back away.

The clerics had him surrounded now. Maces raised high, they closed in to deliver death blows.

Bayzog's heart raced. He had nowhere to go.

The lizard men, five of them in all, pinned Nath down. The biggest one had his arms wrapped around Nath's neck and was squeezing. Another took its spear and jabbed it into his ribs. The metal tip skipped off his black scales.

"Nice try. Now get off me!" Nath said. He kicked one in the face.

The lizard men kept poking at him. Their serpent eyes were wild, and their long tongues licked out of their mouths.

Nath felt like a pincushion.

They poked and poked and poked. One spear shaft broke. A lizard man slugged him in the jaw. Then the rest joined in and started to pummel him.

He didn't feel a thing until he caught a punch in the face again.

Saying, "That's enough of this! I am Dragon!" Nath gathered his knees under him, flung the lizard man off his neck, wiped his bloody nose, and laughed.

"You can't hurt me," Nath said. "But I can hurt you."

A lizard man hurled a spear at his chest.

In one smooth movement, Nath caught the spear in mid-air, snapped it in half, and then twirled both pieces in his hands, holding the lizard men at bay with one of their own spears.

Their eyes slid over one another. Lizard men were good soldiers, brave but not foolish like the orcs. They rushed him anyway.

Nath didn't hold back. He clawed and punched. Harder and faster. He slammed heads together. A dagger broke on his arm. Another spear snapped on his back.

"Is that all you have, reptiles?"

Whap! Whop! Whomp!

He kept slugging.

The lizard men piled up at his feet, busted or maimed.

"Dragon!" someone yelled.

Ben was hemmed in by three goblins, and four lay dead at his feet.

Nath dropped the lizard man he had in the crook of his arm.

"Hold on, Ben!" he said.

Ben's sword licked out.

Bang!

A goblin dropped its axe.

Slash!

Ben cut a streak across its chest.

Glitch!

The third died on the end of Ben's blade the moment Nath arrived.

"Ben," Nath said, wide eyed, "I thought you needed help."

Ben pushed the dead goblin off his sword with his boot. "No, I was seeing if you needed my help."

Bayzog's simmering anger was beginning to blossom. The man in him was no brawler, nor was the elf either, but fighting evil had a way of making you tougher and meaner, no matter how polished you tried to be. His violet eyes narrowed. He didn't like being muted.

How dare they!

He couldn't speak, and that limited him, but it did nothing to the staff he held in his hands. It was an elderwood staff that Bayzog had filled with wondrous powers. And it was time to let those powers loose. The metal on the top of the staff flared like a sunburst. Bayzog's entire self was soaked in its power. His feet again lifted from the ground.

The mystic smolder in his eyes stopped the clerics in their tracks. One of them started to turn.

A ball of light shot from the staff and socked the man in the back, knocking him face first into the dirt.

The others started to run.

Bayzog swept his staff over the ground, and they all stumbled. He turned his attention to the two chanting clerics and pointed the elderwood straight at them.

They raised their arms, and another shield of transparent energy formed.

A dark ray of light burst from the staff.

Their shields shattered.

The elderwood staff blasted the two Clerics of Barnabus out of their sandals. They moved no more.

Once more, sounds of life and battle filled his ears.

"That felt good," Bayzog said. He turned his attention to the three remaining clerics.

Two were kneeling and begging for mercy. The third ran as fast as his feet would take him.

Bayzog choked back his urge to destroy them entirely but then shrugged and let loose, blasting them apart. A ball of energy formed in his hand, and he tossed it at the cleric who ran.

"I don't take prisoners," Bayzog said.

The ball of energy glided over the grass and struck the man square in the back, lifting him from the ground. The man sailed through the air over the town where the people waited. He dropped the man in the middle of them. "But maybe they do."

Bayzog turned his attention back toward his friends, ready to unleash more of his fury on his enemies. He'd bottled up his frustrations long enough, and he had plenty more to let out. But by the time he got there, the battle had been won.

Nath, Brenwar, Ben, and the dwarves were all busted up and bleeding, but all the enemies looked to be dead, or at least almost dead.

"That was a fine show you put on, Bayzog," Nath said, holding a rag to his nose. "And not a scratch on you. Maybe you can teach me how to do— "

"If you didn't act like a child, you wouldn't have to!"

Nath shrugged. "Sorry."

CHAPTER
36

"**Y**OU COULD HAVE GRABBED SOME steel and start swinging, Gorlee," Brenwar said. "Fighting every once in a while wouldn't kill you."

Gorlee was still golden when he laughed and said, "Well, I suppose I could have, but how often do I get a chance to play with dragons?"

"We're not here to play. We're here to fight, and Pilpin's dead because of it."

"Well, more might have been dead if I'd not spared you from the dragons." Gorlee yawned and took the shape of Pilpin. "I think my strategy was sound."

"Are you mocking the dead?" Brenwar said, angry.

"Dead?" Gorlee said. "Who's dead?"

"Why you disrespectful…"

"Yes, who's dead?" someone behind Brenwar said. "Say, is that me?"

Brenwar turned and found himself facing Pilpin. He did a double take between Gorlee looking like Pilpin and Pilpin. There was a nasty wound in the real Pilpin's belly.

"Is this a trick?" Brenwar said, poking him.

"No," Pilpin said, "I'm quite alive. I couldn't let a mere goblin kill me. A dragon maybe, but a goblin? Never!" Pilpin teetered and clutched at Brenwar. "But its steel is a tad uncomfortable and my legs feel numb."

"Someone bring me a horn of dwarven ale!"

"We spent twenty-five years trying to hide you, and this is what you do? The whole world can hear you now! Is that what you want?" Bayzog said, tapping his staff on the ground.

Nath kept his back turned. He was busy with Gorlee, inspecting the red rock dragons. Both of the savage reptiles lay still and had burrowed half their bodies into the ground. Nath placed his fingers on one's back, where he could feel its breath and the warmth of its life.

"What did you do to them?" he said to Gorlee the Chameleon.

"Well," Gorlee said, resuming his golden form, "after they chased me for a few minutes, they started to slow. I'd forgotten you'd sent those arrows into their bellies. I think that took the wind from them, and they dropped and started hibernating."

"Hmmm," Nath said, rubbing his chin, "I can't believe I did that." He grabbed one of his arrows by its shaft and pulled it out.

"Are you certain you want to do that?" Bayzog said. "They'll come after us again."

"Agreed," Gorlee said.

"No," Nath said, "they'll burrow for days, if not longer." He put his ear on one's back. It was almost too hot to touch, but the thump-thump of its heart was strong. "If they were near the lava pools, they'd heal faster." He sighed. "They're usually much closer to Dragon Home. And these black stripes and the black tail … that's far from normal."

Nath pushed the dragon's eyelid open with his fingers. Its eye was almost black as coal.

"Those eyes should be orange as amber," Bayzog said, kneeling at his side, "shouldn't they?"

"Absolutely," Nath said. "They've been poisoned or majicked or something. I know some dragons are bad, but not the red rocks. They are being controlled."

Nath's nostrils flared, and his breath became hot. He stretched back up to his full height. "We're going to find who is doing this and put an end to them." He eyed Bayzog.

The part-elf wizard parted his lips, shook his head, turned, and walked away.

"Where are you going?" Nath said.

"Where I'm needed," Bayzog said.

"You're needed here."

"No, I'm needed where my counsel is considered. It can't penetrate that great stone between your ears."

The dwarves let out a gusty chuckle.

Brenwar even smiled, sauntering with the others behind Bayzog.

Gorlee resumed human form, a pleasant and mild-mannered man. "You might want to take some time to catch up on things," he said. "Bayzog's been an outstanding leader and has suffered many trials since you've been down. Much has changed. You need to become wise to the new season."

"Perhaps," Nath said, "but the Clerics of Barnabus are after me, not them."

"They're after all of us, Nath. And now you've led them right to us."

Wherever they'd been going before, they were going again. Nath chose to keep his mouth quiet and let Bayzog lead. He'd make his case later, after Bayzog's emotions settled. He'd never seen his friend so angry before, but the world had changed. His friends had changed.

A few strides ahead of him, Ben walked. The cheerful country boy was gone, replaced by a thick-thewed warrior with a steely gait.

Nath stretched his strides and caught up with him.

"You're a master of the steel, I see," Nath said. "I like how you turned those goblins into troll food. I envy you."

"Because I can kill?" Ben said.

"You could say that. Being able to fight without holding back must be exhilarating."

"I don't enjoy it, but it's me or them. I can't afford to think about it. If you think too much, you die."

Nath placed his scaly fingers on Ben's broad shoulders. "Ben, I'm glad you live."

Ben looked at him with his hard eyes and managed a smile.

"I'm glad you're back among us." He huffed a sigh. "I didn't think you'd ever wake up. I've never slept more than a day before, and that was only because I was wounded. As soon as the rooster crows, even if I don't hear it, I'm up and about."

The boyish charm started to return to Ben's voice. Nath felt the tautness in his jaw loosen.

Ben went on. "And traveling with dwarves and a moody Bayzog isn't the most fun, either. It's hard on a fella. I feel like I'm the only one getting older."

The hard lines and scars on Ben's face told it all. Nath felt guilty. Ben had dedicated his life to protecting him.

"Have you no wife or children, Ben?"

Ben's bright expression dimmed. "I did."

Nath's heart sank. "What happened?"

"They died. All of them."

Nath felt empty. All this time, he'd only been thinking about himself, not appreciating the sacrifices others had made for him, for the world, in the battle against the evil forces that wanted to enslave them.

"Ben, I'm so—"

"It's all right, Dragon. That was long ago. Besides, it helps me empathize with Bayzog."

"Is Sasha dead too?" Nath said, grabbing Ben. His heart burst inside his chest.

"No, she lives, but Bayzog hasn't seen her in fifteen years. Nor his children either. I think that's why he's so moody. I miss my family too, but at least I know they're in a better place."

Ahead, Nath watched Bayzog lead. The wizard's long, black hair whipped behind him, and the stiff winds billowed his robes. The part elf's shoulders seemed heavy, and he rested part of his lithe frame on his staff. If Nath were to guess, Bayzog was tired, and he was probably angry too.

Nath decided to show a little more caution, but he still had to do what he had to do.

He's just going to have to get used to me being awake. I needed guarding while I slept, but now that I'm awake I'm not holding back and watching this world get destroyed.

With the Clerics of Barnabus vanquished, the lake town of Troghlin welcomed the heroes. The finest food from the Northern Sea was unloaded from the docks on the gritty beaches, dumped onto the boardwalk planks, and fried, boiled, baked, and sautéed. The people were happy. They danced and sang arm in arm and drank with the dwarves on top of the tables.

Even Bayzog's dour mood had lightened. He stood by the railing staring out over the great lake and holding a pleasant memory on his face. He thought of Sasha and his children and hoped they were well. Perhaps now that Nath had awakened, it was time to return to see them before anything else terrible happened.

Sitting outside the boardwalk tavern, most of the once-grim faces smiled. Nath and Ben were stuffing their faces with fish meat and crab cakes while the town's women swooned over them. The dwarves, as hard as they were, seemed jolly as they showed their fresh wounds off to one another.

Perhaps Nath is right, Bayzog thought. *Perhaps now is the time to take it to them.*

He placed his palm over his mouth and yawned. Using magic always drained him, but using it felt so good. Blasting those acolytes had felt better than good. It had felt great. He finished off his goblet of wine, closed his eyes, and enjoyed the sun. Troghlin was a fine place, for a human settlement anyway, and he could stand where he was for hours watching the birds glide over the water in hopes of seeing a dragon snatch them in its jaws.

A wave crashed into the rocks and splashed heavy mist all over him.

Is that odd?

"That's odd," said a fisherman standing nearby. "We don't get tides so high." He looked at Bayzog and pointed. "You better move; here comes another."

A wave bigger than the last busted on the rocks and soaked him.

"Whoooweeee!" the fisherman said. "Never seen anything like that!" He squinted. "There's no storm over the sea, either. Huh."

"Sheesh," Bayzog said, wringing out his robes.

"Braw-haha," one of the dwarves pointed and laughed. "The pond is welcoming you! Say hello back!"

One wave rolled in and crashed after the other. It doused beards and soaked the bread on the table. Almost everyone was wet now. The boats on the docks were rocking and creaking in their slips.

"What's going on?" Nath said, wringing out his long hair and scanning the water. "There's no storm out there."

"Look!" the fisherman cried. "Something is floating in the water. It looks like a rock."

Bayzog's violet eyes locked on the object. Closer and closer it came, and a chill went through him.

"I've never seen a rock that could float," Brenwar said. "Nor a dwarf either."

"That's not a rock," Bayzog said.

A gargantuan spiked head emerged with bright-blue glowing eyes.

"That's a dragon!"

CHAPTER 37

"**G**ET EVERYONE OUT OF HERE!" Nath said.

The dragon rose from the lake and let out a terrifying sound.

Troghlin shook. The townsfolk fell. Covering their ears, they ran screaming.

Nath rallied his men and dwarves.

"What kind of dragon is that?' Bayzog said.

It towered more than thirty feet tall. Its body was armored in sharp horns and scales. Its footsteps were storms surging out of the water. It was terror. It was power. It was evil.

"It's a hull," Nath said. His heart pounded inside his chest. "Part of the Titan race. I've never seen one before. They lurk in the belly of the sea, only surfacing every few centuries." He shook his head. "This is not good!"

Nath loaded his first arrow onto Akron's string.

"We need to lead it away," he said. "Ben! Get those people to safety. The same for your dwarves, Brenwar! Get them all out of harm's way! Hurry!"

The hull sloshed through the water. Walked through a pier and crushed it into pieces. Busted boats up like twigs. Picked them up and smashed them together. In three strides, the hull was on the beach. It drew a deep breath into its lungs.

"Move!" Nath yelled.

The enormous dragon's horned head and tail ignited with brilliant blue energy. Nath fired.

Twang!

His arrow rocketed through the air into the dragon's face.

Ka-Boom!

Its blue breath shot out all over the sky. Bursts of blue lightning rained down, igniting everything they touched. The boardwalk was burning. The store roofs caught fire.

"Come on!" Nath yelled, waving his bow at the great beast. He fired again.

Boom!

The hull's head snapped back. Its nostrils flared. Its eyes narrowed on Nath.

"That's right. Here I am!" He backpedaled away. "Come and get me, you ugly beast!"

The hull let out another terrifying roar. Its great foot stomped the ground.

Nath's feet flew out from underneath him.

"Sultans of Sulfur!"

He licked and nocked a moorite arrow and let it fly.

It sank into the hull dragon's eyelid.

The hull reared up. The muscles in its neck bulged.

"KAAAAAAAAAAAABOOOOWWWWW!"

Nath fell to the ground, covering his ears. His legs turned to noodles.

A shadow covered him. The dragon's foot hung above him and started coming down.

Great Guzan!

Nath curled up into a ball and closed his eyes.

Stomp!

Nath didn't feel a thing.

That wasn't so painful.

He popped open his eyes.

The hull was twenty yards from him. He lay in the grasses on the bank.

"How'd I do that?"

You didn't, Bayzog's voice said in his head. *Now get moving. He sees you.*

The hull craned its neck from side to side. It checked under its foot and grunted.

"Ha-Ha! You missed me!" Nath yelled.

It roared and started running.

Nath ran away from the town, legs pumping.

The hull wasn't moving fast, but its long strides shook the ground and kept pace with him. Nath stretched his lead to a hundred yards. *He'll never catch me.*

A bright light caught the corner of his eye. He glanced over his shoulder. A blast of blue lightning was coming straight for him. He dove to the ground.

"Argh!" he screamed.

The fire danced over his arms and chest. It sizzled and danced on his scales. It was painful. Awful. He screamed again.

The hull stormed right toward him.

Nath scrambled up, grimacing, and ran.

Ahead, the great rocks promised shelter.

Faster, Nath! Faster!

He began to stretch his lead.

The hull was still coming.

The town became smaller. Safer with every stride.

Good!

He turned and started running backward while loading another exploding arrow. If he could shoot into its mouth the next time it took a breath, he just might be able to stop it. Otherwise, he had no idea what the hull's weakness was.

The hull dragon slowed its pace and stopped. Its scales and horns lit up. Crackled with blue energy.

Nath stopped and drew the arrow along his cheek.

"Perfect!" he said. "Open wide!"

Its scales and tail twinkled and its blue eyes narrowed. It was there, evil and enormous.

SSSZZZRAT!

There was a blinding blue flash.

"What?!"

Nath covered his eyes. Colorful spots exploded all over. He shook his head and rubbed his eyes. He felt dizzy. Finally, he reopened his eyes. The hull was gone entirely.

Bayzog kept his eyes fixed on Nath. The dragon man was moments from death, curled up in a ball on the beach. Bayzog summoned the power of the elderwood staff. He reached out with an invisible hand, grabbed Nath, and flung him from harm's path.

"That was close."

Smoke. Fire. Shouts and screams. The people of Troghlin formed a line on the beach and raced buckets up the shore. The fire was spreading fast. Brenwar had ordered his dwarves to assist, but their efforts so far were in vain. The dragon's fire spread too fast. Troghlin would perish.

"What is that fool doing?" Brenwar said, watching Nath run.

"Drawing the menace away," Bayzog said. "And it's working."

"He knows I can't keep up with him," Brenwar said, shaking his war hammer. "That's cheating. He wants to kill it all by himself! Well, I ain't going to let that happen!"

Bayzog would never get used to the dwarven spirit of fighting anything anywhere. The hull dragon's roar was the most terrifying thing he'd ever heard. Not to mention what he'd seen. This was a monster in every sense of the word. Terrifying. He wanted to run. Hide. He had to act.

"What are you waiting on, wizard?" Brenwar pointed. "Get us up there."

"What do you mean?" Bayzog said with a tremor in his voice.

"We've got to help Nath," Brenwar said. "Pilpin! Get the chest and make it quick!"

Bayzog's mind was scrambled. Fighting humanoids was one thing. A three-story dragon was another thing. It might be impossible to wound. He rubbed his smoke-stung eyes. The town was about to perish. He wasn't sure what to do. Save the town or his friend?

"I hope yer doing something, wizard!" Brenwar said. "Because standing here isn't helping anything."

Bayzog shook his head and pointed his staff at the lake. He started an Elvish chant, twirling the staff in tight circles. A funnel spouted out of the water.

"Get everyone clear," Bayzog yelled.

The tornado of water raced up the beach, over the boardwalk, and into the town, washing every burning building in sight. The flames started to sizzle and extinguish. Smoke began to roll like a heavy fog.

"Let's hope that does it," Bayzog said, watching the tornado attack any flame in its path. "Let's go after Nath."

Bayzog and Brenwar raced after the hull. Nath was leading it away, toward the rocks, a good thing, but they were too far away to help. The beast was distant, and Bayzog was already laboring for breath. Brenwar didn't move very fast on his short legs, either.

The hull had slowed to a stop. There was a bright-blue flash, and the great dragon disappeared.

"By my beard! Did you see that?" Brenwar said. "It's gone. Nath better not have killed it!"

Bayzog could see Nath standing all alone in the field with his bow ready when another blinding flash hit. While Bayzog was blinking the stars from his eyes, the hull appeared again. It was right behind Nath.

Bayzog and Brenwar started waving their arms and yelling and pointing.

"Move! It's behind you."

Nath was staring at an empty field. Where a moment earlier a hull dragon the size of a large building had stood was nothing. A strange smell of something burning tickled his nose. Something flashed like lightning behind him. That's when Bayzog and Brenwar appeared far away, waving frantically. He felt a giant shadow above him. He turned. The hull was right over the top of him, clutching at his head.

"No!"

He fired into the hull's great belly. Point-blank range.

Kaboom!

The blast blew him off his feet. He sailed head over heels. His limbs were numb. A lizard's foot the size of a horse rose and came down.

"Not again!"

Nath balled up like a rock.

Thoom!

Pain erupted all over. Things cracked and squished in his body. He couldn't move. He'd only been awake a few days, and now the thought of any more days was over.

Death lingered over Nath in the form of the ugliest dragon he'd ever seen. It leaned down and roared at him once more. He thought his ears would burst. He tried to cover them. His arms wouldn't move fast enough.

If I can move, I can fight.

He rolled up to one knee and reached for his bow. It lay in the grass a few feet away, but it might as well have been a mile. With every muscle in pain, he stretched out for it.

The hull sucked in another great breath and fixed its fiery blue eyes on him.

Shoot it, Nath! Shoot!

He was too late. Down came the fire. Down came the pain.

"Take hold of my staff, Brenwar!" Bayzog said.

"What fer?" the dwarf replied.

"Never mind then," Bayzog said. He started summoning his power. He needed to get to Nath and get there quick.

Brenwar wrapped one paw around the staff and said, "Oh no you don't. You won't be fighting that dragon without me. Now hurry up will youuuuuuuuu—"

Bayzog fixed his eyes on Nath. Power surged in his veins. He envisioned himself moving instantly from where he was to where he needed to be. A portal opened. He stepped through time and space. A split second later he was under the hull's gaping mouth.

"You trying to get us killed, wizard?" Brenwar yelled.

Bayzog jammed the elderwood staff into the ground and shouted.

"*Moooorentanglaheeen Looooores!*"

A geyser of blue fire erupted from the dragon's snout. Blue jags of lightning scattered everywhere.

Bayzog took a breath. His protective dome had formed.

It covered them all: Brenwar, himself, and Nath.

Nath fought his way back to his feet, shaking. He clutched his head and sides. He looked more dead than alive.

"Thanks," Nath managed to say.

The hull started pounding away at the mystic dome. It scratched, clawed, and kicked. Its blows were thunder, its eyes lightning.

"I can't hold it much longer!" Bayzog said, arms shaking. "We have to be ready to run!"

"Run?" Brenwar said. "There be no running. Take down that shield. Me and my war hammer be ready."

Bayzog's arms trembled and his knees started to bend. The hull was seconds away from overtaking them. All of them.

"Just give me a little more time, Bayzog!" Nath said.

The hull rammed his horns into the dome. It started cracking.

"I can't hold it any longer," Bayzog said. "If you're going to do something, do it now."

Nath had hunting arrows, moorite arrows, and exploding arrows, but he didn't think any of them could do the trick. Not alone. He laid his quiver down at his side and pulled his last three exploding arrows out and wet the tips. They glowed with red light. He nocked them all on Akron's string.

Taking a knee, he took aim. Stretching the bowstring tight, his chest and shoulders burned like fire. Something inside him had broken, but he held his aim.

"Give me your best, Akron," he said.

The hull drew back its great arm, punched, and shattered the dome.

Bayzog collapsed in a heap of robes, bleeding at the nose.

The enormous hull dragon reared up and exposed its great neck.

"Cover Bayzog, Brenwar!"

Nath let the arrows fly.

Twang!

KABOOM!

The hull stumbled backward and toppled like a stone.

Nath skipped across the burning grass.

Everything was hazing. Ringing. Quiet and smoking.

Somehow, Nath rolled to his knees.

Brenwar helped Bayzog to his feet, and they stood there gaping.

The hull was slowly struggling to rise. It shook its great neck. It was angry. Worse: it was still living.

Nath's clawed hand fell on Fang's hilt.

"I need you now more than ever, brother."

The hilt was hot, but not burning.

He unsheathed the blade. It was bright as the sun.

Nath raised it over his head and charged, yelling, "I am Dragon!"

Brenwar sped after him with his war hammer ready.

Bayzog rushed with his staff.

Nath jabbed Fang into the hull's chest. Ice formed over its scales. It spread fast.

Bayzog encircled its legs with mystic energy.

Brenwar busted it in the snout.

Ka-Raaaaang!

The great beast writhed over the ground. It squirmed and hissed.

"Get out of here, Bayzog!" Nath yelled. "And watch out for its tail!"

The tail flickered with blue fire and struck Nath like a jolt of lightning.

"Aargh!"

Pain erupted in every inch of his body. He held on. He drove Fang deeper.

The great hull dragon roared.

Brenwar popped it in the snout again.

The tail licked out. Cracked like thunder and struck Brenwar in the chest, skipping him over the stones.

"Nooo," Nath yelled, yanking Fang free.

He gritted his teeth.

"Try that again!"

The tail flicked his way again, flashing like lightning.

Nath swung Fang with all his might.

Slice!

He clipped the end of the tail off.

The hull twisted and howled. The blue lights in its eyes went black. The crackling energy on its horns disappeared. Its tail swished back and forth like a headless snake.

Brenwar rose up from the rocks and charged over. He brought war hammer down on the back of the hull dragon's skull.

The hull moved no more.

CHAPTER
38

THE BATTLE WAS WON. TROGHLIN was saved and everyone was celebrating. Everyone but Nath, Bayzog, Ben, Gorlee, Brenwar, and the dwarves. They'd moved on, leaving the remains of the hull to the townsfolk of Troghlin to deal with.

"I don't suppose there is any turning back now," Bayzog said. His eyelids seemed heavy. "I agree. Now that you're awake, we might as well take it to them. But let's pursue with wisdom."

Nath groaned. Everything ached. His head. His toes. And the air tasted funny. Awful actually. Everything felt awful. Still, he limped along, just like the others, glad to be alive.

"I don't think a little caution ever hurt anyone," he said. "I'll do my best to heed your advice."

"Sure you will," Brenwar said. "And the day that happens, I'll shave my beard. Har!"

They headed west along the lake for miles until they reached a series of huts stretched out over the water. They were connected by a series of catwalks and piers, and Bayzog took them inside one near the middle. It was larger on the inside than it looked on the outside and sparsely furnished.

"Remote enough to hide us for now," Bayzog said. "Let's rest our eyes and keep our ears peeled. Now that the hull is down, our enemies will hesitate before they come after us. We'll be long gone by then."

"Gone to where?" Nath said.

"Wherever you lead us," Bayzog said.

Nath eyed Bayzog. It was hard to believe that he really meant that.

"We're going after the head of the Clerics of Barnabus," Nath said, "And there will be no fuss about it."

"This is your decision, not mine," Bayzog said. The wizard set down his staff and leaned back against the wall. His violet eyes seemed to glow. "I'm just here to advise you. It's up to you to lead." He looked over the room. "To lead all of us."

Nath felt all the eyes on him. He felt sacrifice. Courage. All the good in their hearts. There were plenty of people in Nalzambor just like them, suffering something dreadful. All because of him, and he still didn't understand why. War was coming. He felt it in his busted bones. It was time to make things right.

They'd just defeated a hull. If they could handle that, they should be able to handle anything. He forced a smile. His golden eyes flashed.

"Then *our* hunt begins tomorrow."

This series continues in Series 1, Boxed Set #2, Books 6 thru 10

Check out www.craighalloran.com to find more great books and bargains.

ABOUT THE AUTHOR

Craig Halloran resides with his family outside his hometown of Charleston, West Virginia. When he isn't entertaining mankind, he is seeking adventure, working out, or watching sports. To learn more about him, go to: www.thedarkslayer.com.

Check out all of my great stories ...

CLASH OF HEROES: Nath Dragon meets The Darkslayer

THE CHRONICLES OF DRAGON SERIES

THE CHRONICLES OF DRAGON: SERIES 2, TAIL OF THE DRAGON

Scales of the Dragon
Trial of the Dragon
Teeth of the Dragon

The Darkslayer Series 1
Wrath of the Royals (Book 1) Free eBook
Blades in the Night (Book 2)
Underling Revenge (Book 3)
Danger and the Druid (Book 4)
Outrage in the Outlands (Book 5)
Chaos at the Castle (Book 6)

The Darkslayer: Bish and Bone, Series 2
Bish and Bone (Book 1) Free eBook
Black Blood (Book 2)
Red Death (Book 3)
Lethal Liaisons (Book 4)
Torment and Terror (Book 5)

The Supernatural Bounty Hunter Files
Smoke Rising (2015) Free ebook
I Smell Smoke (2015)
Where There's Smoke (2015)
Smoke on the Water (2015)
Smoke and Mirrors (2015)
Up in Smoke
Smoke Em'
Holy Smoke
Smoke Out

Zombie Impact Series
Zombie Day Care: Book 1 Free eBook
Zombie Rehab: Book 2
Zombie Warfare: Book 3

You can learn more about the Darkslayer and my other books deals and specials at:
Facebook – The Darkslayer Report by Craig
Twitter – Craig Halloran
www.craighalloran.com

Made in the USA
Middletown, DE
03 February 2019